All is Wild, All is Silent

A Novel

I0561667

JOE ARCHER

THE CHOIR PRESS

First published in the United Kingdom in 2023 by
The Choir Press

ISBN 978-1-78963-402-0

A born n' bread Notts Man.

Joe Archer is nearing the end of his training as a psychotherapist. He is the author of *Doubting Descartes' Elbow* and his next novels *Giant Hands* and *This Weirdish Wild Space* will be published by The Choir Press.

for Steve Woolley

'pals'

PART ONE

PART TWO

PART THREE

AFTER THE END

Part One

"*Youth is not a time of life; it is a state of mind; it is not a matter of rosy cheeks, red lips and supple knees; it is a matter of the will, quality of the imagination, a vigour of the emotions; it is the freshness of the deep springs of life.*"

Samuel Ullman

Before The Beginning

Markus

FUCK THIS WORLD. FUCK LIFE.

Little Markus Venner saw those words every day. They were spray-painted on the side of a house, which stood at the end of his terraced street. People on the estate said it was written in blood because the lettering was dark-red and dribbled down the bricks like a horror movie. He skidded up on his silver Mongoose and stared at it. He always stopped to look at it for some reason. He didn't quite know what it meant but he liked looking at it. He knew that *fuck* meant *sex* so he wondered if it was something to do with making babies.

Markus moved on, wobbling all over the road because the bike was far too big for him. Arms high above his head as he tried to guide the handlebars in a straight line. It took him awhile to build momentum and sit on the seat properly. Mongoose was a gift from his father. It was probably the only gift his dad had ever got him, although Markus had a feeling the bike was stolen. He came home with it one night after the pub with Uncle Nigel, out of breath, laughing his head off.

"Merry Christmas kiddie!"

It was July, and one o'clock in the morning.

Markus was moving at pace now, bombing it all the way down Priory Road, towards Fraser Square, over onto Edwards Lane where his mate T lived. Markus always had to call for T because T was lazy and didn't have a bike. Plus his house was bigger and he had a better TV and more food in the cupboards. T always had loads of yoghurts in the fridge and the two would eat them all and his mum didn't seem to mind. Markus pulled up at the gate, dismounted Mongoose and unhooked the latch with his thick fingers. He placed his bike in the hedge. He'd done this so many times now the hedge had a BMX-shaped hole in it. Walking down the path Markus felt a slow tightening of stress. It always got him mad when he couldn't see his little mate through the living room window, curled up on the couch like a cat, watching cartoons. This meant there was a good chance he wasn't in.

T did this a lot. Tell Markus to come over and then not be in. *Gets me so fucking mad.*

Markus was already hot and red-faced by the time he got to the front door. He pushed his thumb into the hard black circle of the doorbell and waited, waited for voices or footsteps or the sound of the stairs.

T!

He pressed again, harder, like the harder he pressed the louder the bell would be?? He watched his thumb shake and go white at the pressure. Rage was already starting to build, from the tips of his toes to the top of his skull. Now came the knock, knuckles wrapped across the door like the door had done something wrong. Markus knocked so hard and for so long the sound reverberated through the entire street. A neighbour came to his porch and watched on.

Nosey old bastard.

Markus lowered his head like a bull, before shooting a sideways stare at the neighbour. The old man got trapped under his scowl. His eyes weren't right, they were *off,* unsettling.

There was something not right with this boy. Something wrong.

The white-haired onlooker suddenly pretended to do something else; touched some flowers in his porch, looked at the sky, before quickly taking himself back inside.

Markus stood square and squat on the mat. His left foot on the *W* and his right on the *M* of the word WELCOME. He stared at the door and the glass made his reflection look blurred and bizarre, each triangular pane cut into his features, making him look like he had about ten different faces. T was not in and this made Markus want to kill him. *Literally*, kill him. He imagined ramming his fist through his rabbity teeth. T did look like a rabbit, or a rat, or some other kind of rodent. He was little and ginger and irritating. Markus only hung-out with him because there was no one else to hang-out with. All the other mums had stopped Markus from playing with their kids. They said he was a *bad-un, bad news.* They said he was a *bad apple.* Markus wasn't allowed to go to their houses. He wasn't even allowed to play with them at school. If there was ever any birthday parties Markus wasn't allowed to go. T's mum was the only one who let him play with her kid. She was fat and dumb and

Markus had a feeling that she didn't have a clue what *really* went off in the world. He rang the bell again and then knocked again. After a while he kicked the door full-pelt before going around the back to look through the windows. He made a tunnel with his hands and gazed inside. The emptiness was apocalyptic, darkly soothing. Markus wanted to be in there. He wanted to be sat on the sofa eating a large bag of crisps. He moved around to the kitchen and peered in. It seemed brighter than the rest of the house and for a moment Markus thought that the light was on and this gave him hope. It was loaded with sunshine even though there was no sun. It bounced off the lemony walls and radiated the whole room. The breakfast dishes sparkled in the drainer. Markus suddenly heard sounds in his head. The rustle of cornflakes in a box and the chime of them landing in a bowl. He heard the pop of a toaster and butter being scraped across its rough surface. He heard the plop of orange juice in a tall clear glass. Markus felt hungry and he craved to be in that kitchen.

More than anything else in the world.

He stepped back and tilted his head, gazing up at T's bedroom. He picked up a pebble and dashed it at the window. He threw it harder than he wanted and the window made a piercing crack. For a moment Markus wondered if the glass had split. He stood on the wall and saw that it hadn't so he picked up more pebbles and bits of mud and started a full assault on the window.

Bastard.

Markus began pacing, up and down, faster and faster. In the middle of it all he grabbed his hair and pulled it until his head hurt.

Why won't you be in?

When T wasn't in it meant Markus would have to spend all day on his own and he hated that. He couldn't stand the boredom. He couldn't bear the tedium of riding around for hours on his own.

Being on your own is stupid.

He felt determined in waiting for T, wherever he may be. He felt determined in *out*-waiting T, almost like it was a challenge, a competition.

Two can play that game.

Markus sat on his lawn and waited. He lay on the damp grass and waited, looking at his dirty fingernails and then at the dirty clouds that were stuck in the bruised sky. Twenty minutes passed, then an hour. Markus groaned and wanted to scream. In the end he went into T's dad's shed and waited for him there. He looked around at the small shed. There were lots rusty blades and hammers and sprays and bags of sand and stuff. There was an orange and black lawn mower with a cable dangling. In the corners of the shed were lots of white spider webs. Markus flicked them to see if a spider would come out but it didn't. He went back outside and began to collect dead insects and bits of leaves and dirt. Inside the shed he put them in a row and began to toss them into the web one by one, eventually a big spider ran out. He watched it, amazed. He loved spiders. He loved how they moved, all creepy and elegant. He thought spiders had a tremendous amount of power. For something so small they seemed to command a lot of respect. Spiders scared humans. Spiders didn't give a fuck. After a time Markus got bored so he took out his lighter and torched all the webs, until there was none. He went back out and started banging on the door again.

Nothing.

Little lying bastard, he said. I will never come back here *ever* again. Our friendship is over.

Markus jumped back on Mongoose and did five laps around the block. He then stole a bag of popcorn from the Polish shop. He didn't really like popcorn but it was near the door and easy to pinch. He sat on the curb and flicked most of the popcorn down the drain. Afterwards he stood and stretched and yawned.

One more chance then Tea Bag. I'll give you one more chance.

He rode back onto Edwards Lane. This time he felt the neighbours watch from their windows, *there's that kid again.* He threw Mongoose in the bush and stormed down the path, knocked, rang, knocked, rang, knocked, rang. He punctuated it all by booting the door so hard the glass rattled in its frame. A muddy footprint was tattooed into the wood. He went up to the window and put his mucky hands on it, peered through at the dark furniture and wondered how long it would take to burn the whole lot down.

Gone. Markus was gone. He took his feet off the pedals and let Mongoose freewheel all the way down Cromford Avenue. His head unlocked. He started to feel better. All of a sudden being alone felt like freedom. Why did I waste all that time at T's house, he thought. Being on my own isn't so bad. The day had cleared and Markus felt a blue sky on his back. A breeze pushed him all the way down the hill and by the bottom he had built-up a lot of speed. He kept on, feet pushing pedal and he couldn't remember ever going so fast. He had a flash, a thought, what would happen if I fell? He envisioned clipping a car or hitting a bump in the road. He imagined being vaulted over his handlebars and landing on his back in the middle of the road. Maybe a car would hit him, or a bus? Markus reached the flat road in one piece. His big hair was all blown back from the wind. He moved slower now, a gentle cruise to the underpass where Brown Bowl was.

Brown Bowl was a hidden place where the kids played. It was surrounded by trees and had a road running over it. There was the sound of traffic above. Sometimes it was busy and sometimes it was empty. Today was empty and Markus liked that because he got to do jumps without queuing. The bowl itself was a pit of hard mud that kids used as a BMX ramp. There was a root sticking out at the bottom and if they didn't know about it, if it was their first time, they'd often get it caught in their spokes and end up in A&E. Markus always found that bit so funny.

He himself had broken his little finger once. He only had one baby-tooth left.

Today Markus did about ten jumps before going on the rope-swing. Some kid had hung himself on the swing three years ago but that could not be true. Like the blood on the wall it could just be made-up. People in the town of Kimble Wells often got so bored they told stories to pass the time.

Mostly they don't know what is real, and what is not.

Markus did about ten swings and then saw a grey cat walk across the top opening. He jumped off quickly and found a rock. Threw it at her as hard as he could, but missed.

Bastard.

He got back on Mongoose and started to do more jumps when he heard a noise from the bushes. He leapt off and picked up another rock and aimed. Only it wasn't the cat this time, but three human figures. He dropped the rock and picked up Mongoose and waited. Murmurs grew into distinct voices and perhaps he recognised them. Then he heard the dull thud of a football being bounced. It was some older boys that went to the big school. The one in the middle was known as the toughest kid on the estate. Markus was no good at remembering names but he saw him a lot. He was always picking on people and kids had to hide whenever he was around. He was tall and skinny with a long nose. He was tanned like he'd just come back from holiday. He wore a denim cap with blonde hair sticking out the side. The thing Markus always noticed about him was his Adam's apple. It looked freaky, like he could put his hand around it like a tennis ball and pluck it from his neck. Next to him were the two mates he was always with. One was spotty and pale and always wore a Manchester United football shirt. Not the same one but different ones from different seasons. Today he wore a red retro with a collar, image of the club's stadium faded into the fabric. White lettering of the word SHARP stamped across his puny chest. Markus hated Manchester United because he supported Liverpool. He supported Liverpool because his dad did, and his dad said if you supported Liverpool then you *had* to hate Manchester United. Markus hated Manchester United. The other boy was fat and pink and bald like a baby. He was short for his age and really he wasn't much bigger than Markus.

The three shadows came together and made one big one.

"Alright?" Leader said.

Markus didn't say anything, just looked right at them. He knew there was going to be trouble. Markus was only little but he knew what trouble looked like, and felt like. He'd had experience and knew when it was coming. He had a nose for it. And this was trouble.

He regretted dropping that rock.

"What's your name?" Leader said.

"Why?"

Leader spluttered and laughed at the same time, eyes widening in disbelief, "*Why*?"

Manchester United screwed his face up and Baby looked away with a slight shake of the head.

"Hey is that a Mongoose?" Leader said, suddenly excited.

"Why?"

"Not much of a vocab on ya have you kid?"

Markus didn't know what that meant. But Leader wasn't smiling anymore, and he knew what *that* meant: trouble.

They were up close. Markus could see their faces clearly.

"Do you know who I am?" Leader said.

Markus nodded, but the nod didn't have compliance. It had irritation.

"Do you know my name?" Leader went on.

"I don't remember names."

Something about the boy mystified Leader and he began sizing him up. Markus stared right back. His eyes, a hot brown, locked onto his blue. Leader blinked first.

"Give us a go," Leader said, nodding at the bike, acknowledging his defeat.

Colour drained from Markus's face and he gripped onto the handlebars, drawing Mongoose closer into his chest.

"Oh go on," Leader sang cheerfully. "It's too big for you anyway."

"No."

"Just two laps round brown bowl?"

Markus held the rubber handlebars so tight his hands were beginning to burn.

Manchester United was sniggering. His spots looked raw and pussy and disgusting and Markus didn't want to be anywhere near him.

"I said, *no*." More force to his voice this time.

There must have been a line of trucks upon the overpass because it got really loud for about ten seconds. Leader was saying something but Markus couldn't hear what. His mouth was moving without sound, like the volume turned down on TV.

"Give me a go!"

"No!"

Leader put his hands on Mongoose. The first thing Markus saw on his face was shock, shock at the young boy's strength. People are always shocked at how strong he is. Dad is. Brother is. Cousin is. Teachers are.

Leader yanked hard and Markus fell forward, Mongoose still in grip.

"Fuck kid, let go," Leader yelped, half rage, half embarrassment.

"No!"

"Grab him Reg."

Markus didn't know if Reg was Baby or Manchester United but it didn't matter because both were on him, hands invading from either side. Still Mongoose was in his grip, as if the handlebars were welded into his palms.

Leader began to peel his fingers back, one by one.

"Let go you little shit."

"Fucker must be on steroids," one of them gasped.

Markus didn't know what that meant either. Mongoose was coming loose and he began to scream, a demented howl mangling with the traffic above. The three boys looked at each other, a little disturbed, each one hoping that one of them would stop so they all could. What have we got ourselves into? The kid was going insane. At last Leader came out with the bike. He jumped on it and was glad to get away from the kid. He bombed around Brown Bowl twice before dipping into its centre, coming out the other side with a fancy whip of the wheel.

"Give it me back!"

Baby and Manchester United were both laughing but had clearly put distance between themselves and the deranged kid. Markus's eyes were wild, spit came from his mouth like a rabid dog. He ran at Leader and kicked the bike from under his feet. Leader stumbled but did not fall. His hat came off and the handlebars stabbed him in the ribs.

His face went red and his mouth looked different.

"Right that's it."

He threw the bike in the dirt and stormed over to Markus, blasting him full in the face. A white light flashed in his head and the world went silent. The floor pulled him down and he was on his back. It went black for a few seconds. His mouth began to fill with a hot coppery taste.

Three featureless figures stood over him, blue sky in the background.

A voice came from one of them.

"Fucking hell kid I only wanted a ride on your fucking bike. Didn't have to make a fucking drama out of the whole fucking thing!"

The voice echoed and Markus could only really make out the word *fucking*.

"You've got issues," another one of them said.

They all laughed.

"Now," Leader said, his tone measured and definite. "I'm taking this bike. It belongs to *me* now. I'm doing this to teach you a lesson."

Markus's senses were beginning to return. He was starting to understand what was being said to him. Anger reached down and lifted him to his feet. The boys were walking away with Mongoose and Markus charged at them with a war-cry.

"What the fuck?!"

He remembered his dad teaching him to punch. *Follow through*, he always said, don't punch with your fist, not even your arm, but with your *whole* body. Manchester United was nearest and Markus landed one clean on the jaw.

"Oooooooohhh!" They all cried.

One of them even laughed. Man U stumbled back, hurt, embarrassed, then anger. He grabbed Markus by the collar and punched him on top of the head several times only this time it didn't hurt. Markus was taken over by something. He kicked and felt a chin bone *thock* on the end of his trainer. Man U's grip came loose and Markus began to overpower him, only the other two had joined in and Markus was on the floor again. Kicks running over his back like a stampede of buffalo. Again it didn't hurt but Markus couldn't get up this time.

By the time he could the boys were gone and Mongoose was gone and his head was bewildered. The reflection off a green beer bottle twinkled in the grass. It wasn't until he heard the traffic above that he realised where he was, *Brown Bowl*. Markus ran, over towards the opposite exit. He wasn't sure how much time had passed but it couldn't be that long. They couldn't have got *that* far. He ran down the bank, jumped a wall and began fence-hopping through a line of backyards.

A woman was hanging her washing out, "oi!"

Out the other side onto Graffiti Square, vaulting a shopping trolley. All the time his eyes darting around in front of him for a stick or a house-brick. Something. Anything to arm himself with. The edge of the estate appeared before him and he had to take one of the three streets: Curzon, Milner or Fox Hill. Markus dropped his head and went straight down the middle: Milner. The sound of his own footsteps echoed through the terraced street where three boys and a bike sauntered idly over the tarmac.

"Oi!" Markus yelled.

Led by Leader the three heads turned. Disbelief all over their faces.

"Give *her* back."

They stood silent. Leader stepped forward. "Her?" he said, mystified.

"She's mine."

Manchester United stepped alongside Leader, face twisted into an ugly scowl. At first Markus thought all his spots had popped because there was blood down his face. Only he realised that this is what his punch had done.

Man U took the bike from Leader and looked like he was going to do something to it.

"Give him the bike Reg."

"What?" Man U said.

"Give the boy his bike."

Respect enlivened Leader's eyes, lighting up his face. Man U conceded at last, sighed, slowly nodding his head.

He walked Mongoose over and put the handlebars in Markus's hands.

"How old are you?" Leader said.

"Why?"

Leader laughed. "Are we back on that again?"

All the boys were laughing now.

"Just tell me how old you are?" Leader said with a handsome smile.

"Eight."

"Eight!?"

The three boys looked at each other in shock.

"Fucking hell you're big."

"I'll get bigger," Markus said, his expression unchanging.

"Your mum must be feeding you good."

For the first time Markus let go of Mongoose. He stepped forward.

"Don't you *ever* talk about my mum."

Leader held up his hands in surrender. "Hey. Alright. Fight's over. You win."

Markus picked Mongoose up and climbed back on her. It was far too big for him and he wobbled up the street, until the three boys couldn't see him anymore.

The day had dimmed and it was almost twilight. The buildings and cars looked clear and defined, like a film-set.

Back on his own street, Markus looked at the blood on the wall. Only it wasn't real blood because real blood was in his mouth, and in his heart, pumping all around his little-big body.

FUCK THIS WORLD. FUCK LIFE.

He knew what those words meant now, and he will carry them around with him, forever.

Mel

Dear Self-Esteem Diary,

First off, like, You're this little sky-blue book with a white teddy-bear on the front. It's a bit babyish but kind of cute too, in a way. They gave You to me as a way of Letting Out my innermost thoughts and feelings. A way of releasing all The Dark Stuff so I don't bottle things up and get suicidal and stuff.

So I guess this is it. I guess this is like My First Official Entry EVER and tbh I'm not really sure what I'm supposed to do. They said to write like whatever is in my head at the time. They said to not think about it Too Much but just say whatever comes out. They said I'm supposed to write like I'm talking to a friend so ...

... here We go ...

... Tbh I'm not gonna Lie but there's probably no point to Any Of This and it could ALL just be a TOTAL waste of Your time and mine but hey ...

... suppose there's no harm in trying, right?

First off, like, I don't remember The Past, only what They tell me. And like, there's only so much past a 13-year-old girl can have isn't there? Like, I remember the last year, easy. I remember the last year because of like, everything that's happened and stuff. But before that it ALL becomes pretty much blurry more or less. The One Thing I can say is that there's only EVER been the three of us. There's only really been me, mum and My Sister Adele. I can't remember anyone else EVER being around. There was a grandma once, I think. But she's dead and gone now and isn't coming back. She's at peace. She's Somewhere Else, somewhere else for good.

... FEEL like I'm starting to ramble so I better start at the beginning before I lose myself completely ...

First off, like, I was born in the June of 2001, around midnight. It was either just before midnight or just after. I don't remember which. mum calls me the Midnight Child and says that's why I have trouble sleeping. And it's true, I do. I mean I must be like a vampire or something because I much prefer sleeping in the day than at night. Like, it takes me ages to drop off but when I do there's no waking me at all. Like, I can sleep past midday, easy. Sometimes even later, like 2 o' clock in the afternoon or something. I get SO deep and sometimes mum or My Sister Adele has to shake me or pour cold water in my ear and that's when I wake up mad and chase them off and then I'm irritable for the rest of the day or even longer.

SLEEP.

I love sleep.

Adore sleep more than anything else in the world.

Tbh I'm not gonna Lie but sleep is about the only time I'm truly happy.

Because, like, in sleep you get to have a break from life and stuff. Like life doesn't really exist in sleep and I like that loads. No one tells you what to do in sleep and there's no rules or anything. People don't shout or ignore you and there's not all the stress-stuff that happens in life.

Getting into bed FEELS like The Best Thing EVER. Laying in the dark with all that lovely softness around you. MMMmmmm. You can lay there and your mind can do what it wants and it's like some kind of bliss. Especially when the world winds down and you feel yourself drop off and little bits of dreams begin to flash and pull you down, way down into that gorgeous spiral of oblivion. I love that ... I love that bit ... I love that bit the mostest. That Just Before Sleep Bit.

I'd say that was The Best Bit EVER.

See.

So.

Getting into bed I have no problem with, it's just The Waking-Up Part I don't like.

That cold shock of reality and then you realise you've got to start all over again ...

... I'm rambling again so I'll go back to the beginning again...

13

First off, like, I don't like My Name and never have. Even Before The Beginning when I first learned it, I never liked it. It just didn't FEEL right. It didn't sound right and didn't fit me at all. 'Melanie' didn't belong to me. It belonged somewhere else and to someone else and I wanted Them to take it back. I wanted mum to take it back and give me a Different One but I knew she wouldn't do that because she's selfish as always. My name is the First Thing I hated her for. Hated my mum. Melanie/Mel seemed like an old person's name. Like it doesn't fit my generation at all but more like when my mum was growing up, like in the 1980's or Somewhere.

Now My Bestie Mia has got the coolest name. I like it cos it's kind of sexy and sounds like a cat. The name Mia purrs, it whispers. It sounds like it's of The Night.

If I had to choose my OWN name I'd pick something like that. Or maybe Keira or Kyra. Something definitely starting with a K at least.

But.

Your name is Your Name when all said and done so I guess I'm stuck with Mel for Life.

Mel forever.

First off, I want You to forgive me for my punctuation but I'm just writing to You how They told me. All free-flowing and natural and stuff. Suppose This isn't like homework so it doesn't really matter. It's not like I'm being graded or judged or anything so I guess it doesn't really make a difference in The Long Run.

Overall I think This is going quite well. Like, I think this Self-Esteem Diary Thing seems to be working out. It's weird cos I'm only on the Second Page but already I FEEL better. Like some kind of weight is being lifted off my shoulders.

So I guess They were right!

It really is like I'm ACTUALLY talking to an ACTUAL friend so thanks for listening. HA!

Whatever happens it HAS to be better than taking head-meds because tbh that is Officially The Last Thing I Want To Do EVER. Avoid that scenario at <u>all</u> costs.

So ...

Overall My Plan is to write This as a kind of a life-story, like a biography kind of a thing. Starting when I was a kid and leading You right to where I am NOW.

13 years old and <u>very</u> unhappy.

That's what I want to do.

Write about it ALL.

Tell You how it is so You get to know the TOTAL me, The Real Melanie Ellis.

I mean, there's absolutely LOADS. Loads to do with my dad and him leaving and him not being allowed to see us anymore and stuff.

There's all THAT.

But ...

Suppose there's no real rush is there? I mean it's not like You're going anywhere, is it? And I'm certainly not so ALL in good time.

Anyway.
Either way.

Think I'll stop now, quit now. Think I've said More Than Enough for like, My First Official Entry EVER.

I'll probably write tomorrow, or the next time I feel stressed or suicidal and stuff. Which could be as early as tonight. HA!

Anyway.
Either way.

Like, I'm happy I've met You Self-Esteem Diary and I FEEL that this relationship could work. Like, I think We could go A Long Way. I like how You listen and don't judge me and it's good to know You've got my back.

So ...

Speak soon,

Yours, Mel.

Or ...

The Girl with No Name.

P.S. I'm going to HAVE to keep You hidden under my bed because The Last Thing I want is mum or My Sister Adele reading You and trust me they will. They are nosey and won't let me have <u>anything</u> to myself.

So …

Under the bed You go.

Where The Heart Was

Markus

The house had gone quiet and Markus didn't know why. It was as if something bad had happened and everybody had left, forgetting to tell him. He wandered over to the window and looked outside. Hard wind moved through the bushes in the backyard. He quite liked its sound, moaning through the house, between the walls and in the roof. A plastic plant pot toppled off the wall, rolling over the concrete in circles and half-circles. Markus stared at it, fascinated. Electricity everywhere. It was August although it looked like autumn weather. A ladybird dead centre of the window and Markus was amazed how it could stay there in all that outrageous wind. The curtain flapped, throwing one of his birthday cards to the floor. It hit the linoleum with a *slap,* landing face-down. Markus bent down and picked it back up. It was a card in the shape of a red football shirt. It had the number 5 on the back. Markus had turned five two-weeks ago only no one had bothered to take his cards down.

Suddenly the sound of a door behind him, followed by soft footsteps on the carpet. Markus turned to see his Auntie Tara stood in the hallway. She appeared taller than normal. Her brown hair tied back into a pony-tail. Her eyes were puffy, like she had just woken up.

"Aunt Tars," Markus said.

He normally ran into her arms and she would squeeze him and pick him up, spin him around. Only something in the way she looked made Markus stay where he was.

"Markus," she said in a thin voice. "Come and sit with me soldier."

Saying *soldier* stuck out. She never called him that.

Aunt Tars wiped an eye like she was tired and then sat. Her shiny black skirt moved up her leg and a knee stuck out. He looked at her knee. It was pink with a tiny white scar in the middle. Markus sat next to her, up close so he was touching her. His side of the sofa was broke and he could feel a spring stick in his back. Outside the wind had stopped and everything was still.

"Markus," she said his name again, looked at him and gave a fake smile.

Markus knew the difference between real smiles and fake smiles by now. Something was wrong. Something had happened. For some reason he stuck out his tongue only this time she didn't laugh. Just looked right at him. Markus noticed some small wrinkles around her eyes that he hadn't seen before. He thought of spiders.

"I have something to tell you Markus."

"Yeeeaaahhhh," Markus said, laying his head to one side.

He opened his eyes as wide as they would go and pulled a face.

"This is serious Markus," she said. "You know the word *serious*?"

Aunt Tars was struggling with this. She wasn't doing a good job at all. The kid was five, not fifteen. But she was having a tough time herself and just wanted it over with.

"Yeeeaaaahh," he said again.

She didn't like this face he was pulling. It was all ghoulish and weird, like his head was made of rubber.

"You know that your mum has been poorly don't you Markus? You know she hasn't been very well?"

"Yeeeaaaah."

This time he said it different. There was a disturbing intensity in there now.

Aunt Tars didn't know what to do with her hands, so she kept them where they were, clasped in her lap.

"You know that she's been living in the hospital don't you?"

Markus didn't say anything now, he just stared at her, into her, past her, through her.

Aunt Tars felt like he wasn't listening anymore.

She put her hand over his two little ones and tried looking into his eyes. Then she looked at his hair instead. Markus was known for his 'good head of hair.'

"Markus listen, your mum has left us. She's with God now, up *there*."

She said it fast and it didn't sound right. Aunt Tars had promised she wasn't going to do this, lessen the blow by this bullshit god/heaven thing. She had chickened-out and gone for the soft option, the easy way out. She couldn't bring herself to give it to him as it was.

"Mum's dead?"

A sudden stab of pain, like the five-year-old was delivering the news to *her* for the first time. A tear filled her eye and popped over her cheek.

Markus stood, Tara's teary eyes never leaving the boy's face, waiting. Markus then did a strange thing. He bent his knees and flopped forward like a weird dance. He did this two or three times before a smile came to his face.

"Mum's dead," he said with a giggle. "Dead."

He put a finger in his mouth and did a three-sixty turn on the spot, before doing that knee-buckle thing again. Aunt Tars was crying. She had been crying all morning over the death of her sister and now it was back, silent floods of tears that seemed to turn her stomach inside-out with grief. Markus was laughing now, crazy red-faced laughing. He turned the other way and looked at the opposite side of the room. His *good head of hair* was pointing at the ceiling as if he'd put his finger in an electric socket. It was then Aunt Tars realised he was still wearing his pyjamas. Four in the afternoon and Markus wore blue and white PJ's with a racing car on the front. He was still laughing.

"She died. Mummy died."

He threw himself on the floor and did a forward roll, before running from one end of the room to the other. He jumped onto a beanbag, landing on his chins and Aunt Tars winced as it looked painful, only Markus was back up.

"Why did she die?!" Markus said. "Why did she die?!"

It didn't sound like a question, more like a mantra that was sounding off in his head. He laughed again and then pounced on Tara, laughing, laughing.

"Why are you laughing Markus? Why do you think it's funny?"

"I don't," he said, pulling a face. "I just do."

Spit hit her eye and then Markus kissed her face before laughing some more. He kissed her hard and at first she thought the boy had bitten her. A small wet circle imprinted on her cheek.

He's a kid. This isn't the reaction I expected. But, it is 'a' reaction. Go with it. Stay with it. He's a child. Markus is a child. He's just a boy. A little boy.

He ran around the house for several minutes more, sometimes laughing, sometimes silence, sometimes this strange purring sound. At last he stopped and stared at the shelf where his mum had a collection of thimbles from different holidays of the past: Scarborough. Yarmouth. Dorset. Cardiff. It was a silly little tradition her sister had picked up from their mother. Thimbles. Markus was staring at them. Aunt Tars could see his face from a mirror on the wall. It was a Liverpool Football Club mirror, smeared with fingerprints and tiny dots of rust. It framed Markus's face perfectly, like he knew the right spot to stand in. Underneath in green font: *You'll Never Walk Alone.*

"Are you okay Markus?"

Markus stood staring at the mirror. He looked exhausted, yet there was still a hint of amusement in his face.

He's a strange boy, Tara thought. But he's my responsibility now. She felt a sense of duty, to both her sister and the boy. She knew what the rest of the family was like and she knew she had to be there, in some way. But she also felt unease. He's a strange boy, she thought again, or maybe she said it out-loud this time.

Because Markus was now looking right at her.

Markus didn't go to school for a long time. It could have been a few weeks, or a month, or even a year. Since Mum died things had been a blur; time, memory, experience. Everything was all jumbled-up. He spent a lot of time on his own, playing with his toys. When he finally did go back he realised the teachers treated him different. He was always sat at the front, near their feet, and he never seemed to be able to get into trouble.

Couldn't get into trouble, even if he tried.

"You get away with things," a boy said. "You get away with murder."

It was true. He did. He picked on a girl in the sand-pit one morning, pulled her hair and pushed her in the back only he didn't get into trouble for it, the girl did instead. Markus wondered if this was because Mum had died and this meant the teachers *had* to be nice to him. Did he have special powers over them, he wondered? Markus did more things. He wanted to see how much trouble he could get away with. When he pushed a glass off the table in the lunch hall a teacher did shout. The teacher didn't want to shout, he could tell, but, she did. After that Markus felt his special powers begin to slip. In the end the teachers did tell him off. They did shout at him, take him out of class; send him to the wall. Markus knew things were changing, almost like it was the end of an era.

Teachers began to notice something else too. Markus never called anyone by their name. It was always Him with Black Hair, Fat One, Glasses Boy; Blonde Girl. Even teachers were Tall Man, Old Lady, Big Feet. The teachers tried to help him with names but Markus insisted he couldn't remember.

"I don't remember names," he said, flatly.

At home his brother Ryan was always crying and this made Dad mad.

"Stop crying for fuck's sake. Stop! Your brother's three years younger than you and he doesn't cry. *Be a man.* Your mam wouldn't want you crying all the time like a big baby. Like a fucking *girl.*"

This only made Ryan cry even more. Markus liked it that he didn't cry but his brother did. It made him feel older and stronger. Only this feeling didn't last. When the two boys were alone things changed.

"You get away with murder," Ryan said.

Markus had heard this phrase before at school, although he didn't know what it meant.

"You get away with murder and I hate you."

Ryan wasn't that much taller than Markus but he was three years older and that was loads. Ryan seemed like a man.

"Think you're so special. Just because Dad loves you more, you think you're so clever."

"No," Markus said.

"Well Mum loved me more and if she was here she'd make things right."

Markus stared at Ryan's face. He was so pale and he always had a snotty nose. His hair almost covered his eyes and there was a little scar under his lip that looked like saliva.

"Give me your hand."

Markus would give Ryan his hand and he would pull his fingers back until they cracked.

Aaaaaahhhhhhh.

He would do every finger on both hands and the pain would be unbelievable.

"Tell dad and I'll do your toes as well, and your ears and your hair and your arms and legs. I'll break your whole stupid body and you won't be able to move!"

Ryan hit Markus most days, whenever he could. Literally anytime the two boys were alone there would be pain. Sometimes the pain was so great Markus wanted to die. Ryan's presence became a conditioned response. As soon as he saw, heard, or smelled his brother he would break into sweat. He tried spending more time with Dad.

"Let me alone for a bit kiddie. Go play with your brother."

At first Markus didn't know why his brother hated him so much, and why he had to hurt him. After some time Markus came to understand: favouritism. Dad favoured the younger over the older. Markus tried to turn this around. He tried to get into trouble with Dad but it never worked. He even pretended to cry and sulk like his older brother but it just didn't wash. Dad hated Ryan the way Ryan hated Markus. Markus saw the way Dad treated his older brother and it wasn't fair. Ryan always seemed to have a bad cough, a dry cough that wheezed in his chest. He would cough for hours and Markus got tempted to ring 999. Ryan would cough while Dad watched TV and this got him mad the most.

"For fuck's sake lad. Can't you go in the other room ... or die or summat?!"

In the end he would pick his brother up and put him over his knee, slapping his back. Only it wasn't a slap on the back like Aunt Tars did. It was more of a smack, a *whack*. Sometimes Markus thought he saw a fist. A hollow *thud*. By the end the cough got worse and his brother was done-in, tear-trails glistening his cheeks.

His pulpy voice squashed in the back of his throat, "stop! Please dad, stop!"

An hour later it would be Markus in pain.

Ryan would corner him in his room.

"Give me your hand."

By now Markus had learnt the words, "fuck off."

Ryan rushing him, grabbing at his hands. Only two years had passed and Markus was nearly eight. He was about the same size as Ryan and he would struggle to get the boy under his control. Still he'd bend his fingers back until they cracked.

"Why won't you cry?" Ryan shouted. "Why don't you *ever* cry?!"

Markus wondered this himself. He wondered why he didn't cry like other people. He'd seen pretty much everybody cry, at some point. Aunt Tars, kids at school. He'd seen his teacher Ms Gaskell cry. Even Dad, around the time of Mum dying. His brother cried at least once a day, if not more. So why couldn't Markus cry? He'd often pretended to cry but he wanted to *really* cry. Real tears. He wanted to know what it felt like. He thought he was missing out. Even when Ryan was bending his fingers back or beating on him, he never cried. The feelings he had were overwhelming but it was a different kind of emotion, *hate.*

Markus did hate Ryan. He used to feel sorry for him but now he just hated him. He began to think of ways how to kill him. Stab him with the kitchen knife that Dad used to cut meat on a Sunday. Push him in front of a bus. Maybe put poison in his dinner.

"Dad can you buy poison from the shop?"

"What?"

His older brother always had a blue lollipop in his mouth. Kind of like a habit and it was something else for Dad to pick on him for.

"You had a dummy till you was ten and now this fucking thing!"

The lollipop made his lips purple, like he was always cold, or ill. When Ryan was beating on him Markus would think about smacking it down his throat so he would choke to death. That way it would look like an accident and he wouldn't have to go to prison.

"Dad, can kids go to prison?"

"What you going on about this time ya little nutter? On about poison, now prison. Not wired up right, you. Definitely take after ya mam."

Markus didn't know what that meant but he knew he didn't like it. Dad often said things about Mum and he wondered if he should kill him too. He could kill them both and then chuck them on the bonfire. Then he can live by himself and be happy. Although he didn't really see Dad all that much. He was always at a place called *pub.* Sometimes he brought women friends home and that's when Ryan would cry the most. Dad was big and blonde, kind of like golden hair that was thinning on the top. He had a reddish face with cracks in, and watery blue eyes like he'd been crying, or was just about to.

Markus remembered him having a massive argument with Aunt Tars. He had a hold of her wrist and she was saying something like,

"I'm your wife's sister you sick bastard!"

Markus didn't know what that meant. He didn't know what lots of things meant and he couldn't wait until he got older so he could. Maybe then he could join in more.

*

The worst beating ever came after dinner one night. Again it was because of something he didn't understand. They were having chips from the chip shop. They used to sit at the dinner table because that's what Mum liked but *all that* had gone now, so they just sat on the sofa with trays on laps. They were plucking away at their chips when Markus saw loads of scars on his brother's arms. His sleeve came up without Ryan knowing and Markus noticed all these marks on his skin. Some were thin, like scratches, and some were fat, like slugs. There were red ones and white ones. Markus didn't even stop to think, just blurted out, "what the hell is that?"

All eyes went to his arms and Ryan froze, like he had stopped breathing. The shock on his face screamed through the room. His dad's eyes were half-closed, and he kept swaying from side to side, missing his mouth with the chips. From nowhere his hand shot out and grabbed Ryan's wrist.

Markus expected him to say something like, "what the fuck?"

Instead Dad just held it there while he carried on eating. His thick greasy fingers pinning his scarred arm to the arm of the chair. He ate on, silent, disgusting, filling his mouth, vinegar dripping down his whiskered chin. Then he stopped and looked down at the scars.

Again Markus didn't know what any of it meant. He didn't know what the scars meant or how they got there. He couldn't understand this human behaviour. His Dad carrying on the way he did, while Ryan silently cried, pale horror all over his face.

In the end his dad threw away his arm, like he was throwing trash into the bin. Then he launched the rest of the chips at the telly, leaving a greasy imprint on the centre of the screen. *Casualty* was on, and Markus thought it was strange to see all the doctors and nurses covered in chips.

Dad took himself upstairs to bed, without saying a word.

Markus thought he heard a door slam, but that could just have been in his head.

That's when *the beating* happened. It was a beating like no other, a beating like no other at the hands of his older, tormented brother.

"Ryan no."

He punched, kicked, bit. It went on. And on. Increasing in intensity. Markus tried to shout but no sound would arrive. He pulled the fingers back so hard that the little one cracked. Not just a crack like it normally did but a *break*. He felt it separate from the rest of his body. He felt it go away, like it may as well have been on the other side of the room. Pain roared in his skull, and through the rest of his being. He felt fire. It's when he heard his brother filling up the kitchen sink he knew he was truly going to die tonight. Somehow his brother had him on the worktop, his neck in Ryan's vice-like grip. His face could feel heat from the water, the rising steam. A reflection appeared before him. Two faces; one of terror, the other of rage. The sibling's heads came together in a dark, broken blur. Markus opened his mouth to scream *help* only for it to be filled with water. His head was dunked, a rush of sound, blast of panic.

He's gonna see this through to the end.

He tried to fight against it but couldn't. The water had him, his brother had him. Death was winning. He seemed to be under forever.

He's gonna see this through to the very end, until there is nothing left, nothing left but black.

Images began to flip through his head like a catalogue: his brother's face, his dad's face, chips, vinegar, fishcakes, *Casualty* on telly. Liverpool FC. School. Teachers. Kids. The girl he bullied. He saw thimbles on a wall: Scarborough, Yarmouth, Dorset; Cardiff. He saw Aunt Tars. She was telling him Mum had died but now he could be with her because he was going to die too. They could be together in heaven and that was the best place in the world. All of a sudden he felt quite nice, a light-headed surrender and the pain seemed to vanish. His head got so light he could feel it rising to the surface, almost like something was pulling him back up. Sound returned and light came to his eyes. He saw the kitchen again and a face before him. At first he thought it was Mum, or Aunt Tars, or Ms Gaskell. Only it was a man-face, a boy-face. It was his brother. It was Ryan. Only Ryan didn't look mad anymore. He looked scared. His face had some kind of love in it and Markus was confused. Maybe he was dead and this is how things looked in heaven, like real-life only love there instead. His brother was holding him, then he tried kissing him. The kiss was weird. It was an open-mouthed kiss and he wondered if his brother was being gay. Only he was breathing into his mouth and it felt weird and nice at the same time. He knew that his brother didn't really know what he was doing. Markus could feel pain everywhere, mostly in his little finger.

"I'm sorry Markus I'm sorry! I went too far. I didn't mean it. Please don't die."

"I won't," Markus said.

Ryan sat him down and tried to give him a glass of water but that was the last thing in the world he wanted. There was blood on his pyjamas. In the background he could hear the *Casualty* theme music and again he wondered if that was in his head because Casualty had finished *ages* ago.

His brother wouldn't stop crying.

"Ryan I'm alright. I just want to go to bed."

It was then that Ryan looked at him in this mystical way. It was like he was confused but admired him at the same time. It was like he looked up to his younger brother. Like he was a king, or a famous person or something.

He just said, "you're not real."

At school using crayons hurt his hands. He could use his fingers, just not the little one. Then Ms Gaskell noticed and asked him what was wrong.

"Nothing," the boy mumbled.

Ms Gaskell took his wrist and looked at his hand. Markus noticed how big her eyes were through her glasses, like goldfish magnified in a bowl.

"Trapped little finger in door," he said, realising he was speaking strange.

She looked closer. "Oh my goodness it's broken."

All of a sudden he had loads of fuss again. It reminded him of Mum dying. They took him to the staff room and all the other kids watched on. He'd never been in the staff room before and it seemed like another world. There was the smell of what he knew to be coffee. It was bitter and sharp and made his head hurt. There was also the faint smell of cigarettes. His dad smoked and Aunt Tars did too. Did all grown-ups smoke? Did they *have* to smoke? Did you have to smoke to become a grown-up? Would Markus have to smoke to become a grown-up too? In the tiny window was a plant. It was small and covered in spikes. Markus thought it looked like some kind of weapon.

They sat Markus down and went to get the school nurse. He liked the school nurse because she was blonde and pretty and reminded him of one of the girls on *Emmerdale*.

While waiting he looked at one of the paintings on the wall. It was a snowy picture of matchstick men and women. It was weird because it seemed to be good and crap at the same time, like he wondered if one of the clever kids had done it in class.

The nurse came and said his little finger was broken. She felt it with her fingertips and he liked that, even the painful part. He couldn't believe how soft her touch was. He thought of snow.

The school nurse then noticed all the other stuff, cuts, bruises, a lump of his shoulder. Markus had to take his clothes off in front of the nurse and that made him dead embarrassed.

"He needs to go to the hospital."

Markus put his clothes back on and then another teacher came in that he had never seen before. He was blonde and thin and had a red nose. Markus noticed all this flaky skin on his face. Made him think of the flour they used when baking cakes in class. He looked younger than the other teachers and his voice was posh. He had this really gentle way of talking, almost like he had magical powers.

He kept saying, *you won't get into trouble.*

Markus wasn't a snitch. He'd never tell on Ryan, but the way this man talked … he kind of *pulled it out of him.*

"It's my brother, Ryan."

Markus told him the whole story. He told him about all the times he could remember. He told him about the kitchen sink and how he thought he was going to die and see Mum again.

"And does your dad know about this?"

"No."

"Does he ever see this?"

"No."

"Does he ever help Ryan?"

"No."

After that things got really jumbled up again, just like when Mum died. Markus went to hospital. Then he went to Aunt Tars' for a bit. Maybe he stayed there a night, or two. They went to the cinema and ate ice cream. What Markus loved the most about staying with Aunt Tars' was the bed. It was big and comfy and he liked not having to share his room. She also lived in a bungalow and that felt kind of cool too.

When he finally did go home to Dad and Ryan things had changed. There was a seriousness to everything. Dad was clean-shaven and the house looked clean too, or, *cleaner.* There was a new picture on the wall of Mum. It was a picture Markus had never seen before and it was like she was alive again, watching over everything. Ryan had shrunk. He appeared smaller. He'd had his hair cut and Markus could see his face now. He didn't cry as much as he used to but it was like he was holding everything in. Markus thought he looked like a dog, or a baby deer. His eyes were large and moist and lost. He knew that the beatings from his older brother were over. Not just because he had been in trouble, but because he *couldn't* beat him even if he wanted to. Markus was bigger now, taller by an inch and probably half a stone heavier. It was then he realised he might have stayed at Aunt Tars' longer than he thought.

It was around this time that Dad came home with Mongoose. He fell through the backdoor laughing. Uncle Nigel was laughing too. Both of their faces were beaming red. Markus couldn't believe how red they were. They looked like a pair of traffic lights on Stop.

"Got you a Christmas present kiddie!"

It was July. They had ambushed him from a sweaty sleep and had him out on the backyard. A washing line cut across it, taut like tightrope and almost decapitated the tall staggering brothers who wrestled the bike between them. Markus still waking, looking up, adjusting his eyes to the half-moon light that fell across red-bricked wall terrace.

"Down here kid, down here!"

A silver bike crouched in the darkness. Dad was holding one handlebar and Uncle Nigel was holding the other. The word *Mongoose* stamped on the frame in faded yellow lettering.

"What's mongoose mean?" the child asked.

This made Uncle Nigel laugh. "You're right. Your lad int wired up right."

"Fucked if I know," his dad said, leaning forward, almost toppling. His blue eyes swimming in the tops of his head.

"It's like half-monkey, half-rat," Uncle Nigel said, propped on the outhouse, sparking up a fag. "It kills snakes."

Both men were surprised to see the child jump on without caution. "Steady on kid."

The bike was way too big and Markus couldn't get on properly. He felt the cold of the frame through a hole in his PJ's. He winced as his little scrotum fell out and touched the aluminium. This made Dad and Unc Nige howl with more laughter.

Dad held the back of the seat while Markus did laps around the small yard. He was having a great time and this was the best present ever. Laughter dizzied the night air and the little backyard became a hive of humming joy.

Up above Markus could see a Ryan-shaped silhouette in the yellow square of light. Mongoose was far too big for Markus. Really it should have been given to the older brother and Markus knew this. Even though the silhouette was featureless Markus could see a set expression in his mind's eye. There was a lots of things in there: Blame, shame. Hatred, revenge.

Only by now there was nothing he could do to Markus. He was out of reach.

Markus was untouchable.

Mel

Dear Self-Esteem Diary,

Like, I only wrote inside You yesterday. Like only 14 hours ago to be EXACT but tbh I'm not gonna Lie but I haven't stopped thinking about You since. Having You here is a great comfort and the thought of filling myself with You is so exciting!! It's weird, cos technically, like Officially You're not even a Real Person. I mean, there's no one really HERE, is there? Like, it's just Me writing on THIS piece of paper. But, like, I don't know, it's like there really IS someone out there. On the other side of this page, listening in and being with me and stuff.

It's like You exist but You don't exist ... if that makes sense? Lol.

Anyway
Either way.

Tbh not much has happened since We last spoke. Cos the 14 hours between us has been filled with sleep. Perfect, pure sleep. I got in bed Last Night and closed my eyes and my head felt unusually calm and kind of empty. Like, my thoughts broke up and sleep slid into me. It kept me there and it was a good break from life and that, and it was a good break for my brain and my bones and stuff. I'd say it was Officially The Best Sleep EVER. I think this is because The Usual Stuff that is inside me wasn't there anymore. It was OUT. It was out of me and onto the page. Out of me and inside of You. It's like You took it ALL away and stuff. You took it away by letting me write inside You so thanks for that!

Anyway.

It's Saturday today so no school. No school and stuff. I do have homework but that can wait. It's just some history stuff anyway, about the Native Americans and that but who cares about history anyway? What's gone is done and what's done is gone. I never understand why we have to think so much about The Past and stuff. Suppose EVERYONE'S got a history though, and history is like something you carry around on your back, I suppose, like a rucksack kind of a thing. It weighs you down and stops you from going forward. I mean we all carry The Past on our backs only some people have a Light Load and some people have a heavy one. Like, I'd say I have a heavy one. Definitely. Definitely a heavy one. A heavy one for a 13- year-old anyway. Like My Bestie Mia says she has a heavy one too but I listen to her upbringing and I can't BELIEVE how easy she's had it. I mean, like, she makes out she's had All This drama in her life and stuff but she doesn't know the half of it. Like her Mum is really nice but Mia makes out like she's this really Controlling Bitch but she doesn't know the half of it. She should have my mum for a day, or even a minute. Then she'd know what controlling REALLY is. Mia's mum's like really beautiful too. She's got long black hair like an Italian Person and she drives a car without a roof on. She gives Mia lifts everywhere which is so cool. My mum doesn't even drive.

Anyway.

Like I said at The Very Beginning. I want to tell You about my life and stuff, start when I was a kid and lead You to where I am now. 13 years old and <u>very </u>unhappy.

So, like, first off, I don't really remember my dad completely. Only bits and blurs and stuff. I remember a face and maybe a smell. I think he wore glasses and I think I remember him picking me up and doing This Thing where he got me to walk on the ceiling. Like putting me upside down. So he must have been tall to be able to put me on the ceiling and stuff. I think I remember the house although you'll have to bear with me because there's already been so many. So many houses. I think we lived in a house near trees. Well, maybe not trees but definitely loads of hedges and stuff. Y'know, like a cul-de-sac kind of a thing. The house was small but then they always are.

Either way.

I remember a dad. I remember there being a dad. I remember the feeling of four. Of there being the four of us because like, My Sister Adele is only just younger than me, like by only a year and four months so she's always been around. I think my Dad smoked because I remember that smell too. I remembered it on his breath when he used to pick me up and do That Ceiling Thing. I remember him being dead-nice only he couldn't have been cos he left, or mum threw him out, or both.

Then we moved out to an EVEN smaller house and then there was three. Just me, mum, and My Sister Adele. It was here I remember The Shouting start. I remember a lot of shouting and swearing and stuff. I remember being Picked Up and put into other rooms. Other rooms where there was no shouting but still I could hear it. Dad would come back and bang on the door. Bang on the window and he would be shouting and crying and looking really upset. They talk about Earliest Childhood Memories. Well I have one. I remember the image so clearly. Of my dad and the window. He had his arms out and his hands were flat on the glass. And his head was tilted Way Back like he was looking at the sky and I remember thinking how he looked like Jesus on the cross. Because you see he had no top on as well and his body was dead-white and full of weird ribs and he had a diamond of patchy hair on his chest that was kind of gross too. And there were loads of tattoos that shocked me, like, strange tattoos, like, scruffy ones; blobs and dots and words you couldn't really see. His neck was scary too, like the throat-part was all yellow and mashed-up. mum was sat with me. I think, in the kitchen, hiding from him. She had her hands over her ears and perhaps she was on the phone too at some point. It was horrible, like a nightmare kind of a thing. And as much as he was crying and I did FEEL sorry for him I knew I didn't want him in the house, or anywhere near me. It was the First Time too that I knew mum was right and telling The Truth for once ... dad was a bad man.

Then we moved again. This Time it was like a house but more like a big place with lots of other people there and stuff. The three of us all stayed in the same room. Me, mum and My Sister Adele. mum said this wasn't for long. We weren't staying here for long, she said. What I DO remember with this place is that the food was really good. I remember there being big pans of stew and stuff and we could refill our bowls as much we wanted. Don't think My Sister Adele liked it but then she never does. Probably cos like she's a vegetarian and always has been for as long as I remember. mum was right, it wasn't for long. She was telling The Truth for once and we didn't stay there long at all. Maybe only a week or something like that. Next we went into a caravan kind of a thing. At least I think it was. It was the smallest place yet and there were others just like it, to the left and to the right of us. It felt like a holiday kind of a place. It was Here I got to understand what had happened with dad. I was older now. I was older now so mum could tell me. She said he was a bad man. Like, he was a bad man that shouldn't be around children. Said he took things called Drugs that make you do bad and crazy things. At the time I remember being really confused. Although I remember that day I saw him on the window and I think it made sense. All of a sudden I got really scared, like REALLY scared. Like he was going to come and kill us and stuff. I thought about him All The Time and saw him All The Time. Like, EVERYWHERE. Even though I didn't really know what he looked like I saw him. Felt his eyes on me. Felt his crazy druggie eyes on me like All The Time. I remember getting lost one day. We went to some toilets while we were out and somehow mum and My Sister Adele left me and I couldn't find them and I got like hysterical. This Man came over and kneeled by me and I swear it was HIM. Swear it was my dad. My OWN dad had come to kill me so I got even more hysterical, so like eventually more people came and The Dad Guy looked upset but I didn't care because I felt I'd been saved. After that I HATED my mum for leaving me. She said she was sorry but I knew she wouldn't leave My Sister Adele that way. Never, EVER. Not in a million years or more. After that I had nightmares, nightmares All The Time. Yet mum STILL told me things about dad and I wished she wouldn't but she said she HAD to. It was for our own good, she said. I don't know. To me it was wrong. All wrong. It's like she liked scaring us, or should I say, liked scaring ME. Cos My Sister Adele didn't seem to care. She never does. She's always so clever and calm and not affected by ANYTHING. It drives me nuts.

Anyway.
Either way.

I was finding it hard to understand what mum was saying about dad because tbh I'm not gonna Lie she was doing EXACTLY the same. All the things dad did mum was starting to do, too. SHE shouted. SHE threw things. SHE threatened. SHE lied. All the time Lying. But more than anything it was The Shouting.
    Always The Shouting.
    She always mostly shouted the word COPE.
    Cope, I remember the word Cope. mum kept saying it and saying it. Shouting it and shouting it. Cope, cope, cope. I can't cope! She'd shout that word over and over and her mouth and eyes looked like

really weird and stuff. Like they got dead-big, especially her mouth. It looked like a big black hole. Me and My Sister Adele would run around this small caravan kind of a thing and mum would yell till her voice cracked and broke. I CAN'T COPE. I think me and My Sister Adele must have found it funny in a way cos it made us laugh and then mum would go REALLY crazy and chase us and grab us and then maybe one of us would cry.

There was a time though when it changed and got serious. Like, REALLY serious. I remember this too. I even remember The Day cos my favourite cartoon was on at the time. It was Wednesday and SpongeBob SquarePants was on but like, I couldn't watch it properly because the colour on the telly wasn't working properly. It was all Black and White, like how things used to look in the olden days. I kept trying to tell mum but she was busy making our dinner and stuff.

I'll see to it in a minute, she said.

I must have been crying or shouting or something cos mum just flipped. Like, TOTALLY flipped. Like worser than ever. Like something I'd never seen before. Like it must have been bad cos even My Sister Adele looked shocked and scared and that NEVER happens. I remember mum's face. It went like dead-red and full of spit and teeth and a vein came out of her forehead like a big thick slug. She had a wooden spoon in her hand with a dollop of mash potato on the end and At First I thought she was going to whack me with that. My Sister Adele moved back and her eyes went wide and her hair blew back and the next thing I saw a flash and felt this MASSIVE, mad pain rush into my cheek and into my jaw and through my skull and I fell off the chair and landed on the floor and I'm almost sure I was kind of Knocked-Out for a few seconds or more. When I Came To mum was still hysterical only it was a different kind of hysterical, like a sad/guilty/traumatised kind of hysterical. Like she knew she had done something wrong and felt TOTALLY, utterly remorseful and that. She had me in her arms and kept kissing my head and my face and stuff. Only every time she did it hurt cos like, she must have really given me a good whacking cos my face was on fire. My Sister Adele looked TOTALLY shocked and tbh kind of scared too, and I was scared and mum was scared and it was like that WHOLE caravan was an awful place to be in That Moment. Then mum did a strange thing. She got totally obsessed with making SpongeBob SquarePants colourful again but by This Point I didn't care and was like, more bothered about my face because I was almost *completely certain my jaw was broken, or worser. mum put a bag of peas on it, then a slab of ice.*

I'll fix it, I'll fix it. That's all she kept saying. I'll fix it, I'll fix it.

And I really didn't know what she meant. I didn't know if she meant fixing my hurting mouth or fixing the colour on the telly. Or fixing our dinner or fixing something else, like a bigger something else, like maybe fixing Life Itself or something.

Either way.

After that she was on the phone for a Long Time and I heard that word again: COPE.

I heard it again and again and the next thing, like that very night, some people came to our caravan and me and My Sister Adele were taken away. Like mum was too. She was taken one way and me and My Sister Adele was taken the other way and what was Truly Amazing is that I saw My Sister Adele cry for like The Very First Time EVER. Like, Officially. And that made me cry cos it must have been serious like it was all MY fault.

Like, ALL my fault.

Like if I hadn't of made all that fuss none of this would have happened.

Like what did it matter if SpongeBob SquarePants wasn't in colour?

Like there's way worser things in life and stuff.

So …

I never watched SpongeBob SquarePants EVER again. And still haven't to This Very Day.

So,

Like, I can't remember what happened after that. Like, I mean, what happened straight after that, like that very night. I remember being treated like stupidly well. Like ridiculously good. I think we stayed in a hotel kind of a place but I couldn't enjoy it cos I was scared of mum. Well, not scared OF her. But scared of what was happening TO her. I thought like, maybe she was locked in prison and that she'd be there For Life. Or for like twenty years or something. My Sister Adele kept saying things about prison and that scared me more. There was a blonde woman that kept telling us that Everything Was Okay and that all we needed was a holiday.

After a time we saw mum again. Like it might have even been the very next day. She hugged us and hugged us and sat us down and told us stuff. Said we were going to live with a nice woman called Mrs Stubbs. Said she was like an aunty kind of a thing and I was confused because I didn't think we had an aunty, or a grandma, or any other family. She said she was a Foster Parent but I didn't know what that meant. She said we're having Time-Out. Time to fix things and make things good again and I liked the sound of that. Mum said that we will be able to see her just not live with her for the time being. I cried but I was kind of glad and excited too. Probably more than My Sister Adele, who was just like dead-sad and stuff. She said she wasn't mad with me but I could tell she was. She went dead-quiet and didn't talk to me as much as she used to do. Although mum and pretty much everybody told us how important it was that me and My Sister Adele stick together.

You two must always have each other, they said.

At <u>ALL</u> costs.

And tbh I can't tell You how many adults there were. There was loads. Loads of adults that were all so dead-nice. We got loads of nice things too. Loads of toys and teddies and sweets and clothes and stuff. More than ever before. It was like a Christmas kind of a thing. Like Christmas and birthday rolled into one. Like it was on the same day and stuff. I wondered if this happened to ALL kids. I had a feeling it didn't.

So.
Anyway

I was just turned 7 now and I was off to live with Aunty Mrs Stubbs.
   Do I call her Aunty Mrs Stubbs? I asked mum.
   No, she said, just call her Janet.

Janet opened a big red door that had all this ivy stuff on and I liked that because it reminded me of a Harry Potter kind of a place or a Lord of The Rings kind of a place, all magical and faraway. The Blonde Woman was with us too but mum wasn't. Why isn't mum coming? I asked.

She's having a rest and getting better, she said.

Is she poorly? I asked.

The Blonde Woman didn't answer properly, just told me not to worry and that's when My Sister Adele nudged me in the side and told me not to ask too many questions all the time.

So we lived with Mrs Stubbs in her magical house and it was magical in a way because it was big and had loads of books. And even some cats and a pond in the back garden and I liked it although I could tell My Sister Adele didn't all that much. She was still being dead-quiet.

Mrs Stubbs was older than mum and really she looked more like a grandma than a mum. Her hair was white and her bum was big and her boobs were big and her voice was posh and she was kind of gentle and strict at the same time and tbh I think I liked her from the moment she opened the door. Even though I had just turned seven like I said I knew she was going to be good for us. I just had that FEELING, like an instinct kind of a thing. Like I had a FEELING that dad was bad and mum was kind of bad I knew that Mrs Janet Stubbs was good.

And she was, is.

So we went to a new school. We ate new stuff, better stuff. We did new things, like read and play games and bake cakes and listen to music and stuff. Sometimes we didn't want to do them and we would throw a tantrum but Mrs Stubbs had a way of winning without The Shouting. She was firm and fair and clever and strong. I'd say she was powerful, like she had this silent power, like it was a power of goodness. She was always talking about nature and stuff. She always used to say that nature was god and I didn't know what she meant.

God is not a man, she said. Not even a woman. God is all around. God is just a word, she said. Maybe it's the wrong word, she said. Nature is the right word. Nature is truth. Nature is love. Nature is everywhere, trees and sky and earth and water and fire and stuff. Nature is you, and all the stuff inside of you. Nature is you and me. Nature is also that space between you and me. If you close your eyes you can feel it, and if you listen to it, very carefully, it will show you the way to go.

I was young so I didn't really get it, but I listened and didn't forget and now it all kind of makes sense.

It's no secret that My Sister Adele is cleverer than me, like WAY cleverer than me so sometimes she would ask her questions, about life and stuff.

What about heaven?

Heaven is nature too, Mrs Stubbs said, Heaven is here.

Well what's up there then?

Sky.

What's past the sky?

More sky.

What's past that?

Space.

What's past space?

More space.

What's passed that?

Skegness.

They would smile at each and I wondered if My Sister Adele was going to take her too??

mum couldn't visit us but we could visit her. mum looked better and seemed better and she told us it wouldn't be long before the three of us were together again. But to be TOTALLY honest with You I wasn't sure. Janet's house was better. It felt safer, it felt smaller even though it was bigger. Smaller in that it kept a hold of me, like cosy and warm and stuff. Like a cuddle or a hug kind of a thing. I wasn't sure if I wanted to leave Janet. I just ... wasn't sure.

I couldn't tell what My Sister Adele was thinking or feeling cos she got on with Janet too. I really didn't know if she wanted to stay or go.

Either way.

Our Time was up. We stayed with Janet for what I thought was three years yet ACTUALLY it was only six months.

We went back to the place where ALL this started, some officey, housey place on the outskirts of town. The Blonde Woman was there again. mum was on her knees with her arms out. She was smiling really big, so big her eyes were shut.

Come here my babies! She shouted at the top of her voice.

My Sister ran, so I followed and we both charged into her arms and she squeezed the life out of us. She hugged us for ages and I was kind of happy in That Moment. I say 'kind of' cos even though I WAS happy and smiling there was also a little weird feeling inside. It was that instinct-feeling Janet always talked about, that Nature-Feeling deep within. And this Nature-Feeling wasn't happy. It was kind of dark and uneasy.

I guess you'd call it ... Dread.

Anyway.

We moved again.
   A new house.
   A new home.
   A new hope.
   A fresh start.
   A fresh start, mum said.

She always said that, those words; Fresh Start. I'd heard that so many times in My Life.

We're having a fresh start.

It was another smallish house, on a cul-de-sac kind of a thing. There was a McDonald's not too far away so I guess that was good. It's the First Place we went actually, McDonald's.

It was there we talked about The Future and mum made her promises.

mum said that EVERYTHING was fixed now. Everything was fine and fixed and going to be alright from Here On In. I believed her and My Sister Adele believed her.

No more shouting.

No more The Shouting

No more bad stuff.

No more dad.

No more past because The Past was done and gone.

No more moving house again.

I was glad to hear this because moving house was terrible, TOTALLY horrible. It was awful and stressful and never made you believe that you belonged anywhere.

Already I felt like I had lived in a thousand places and I was only nearly eight years old.

As I've got older the town has gotten smaller. I used to think it was big but it's not so big at all. Small people with small minds. No one leaves, no one comes. Apart from Polish People and Romanian People and Other People from Other Places. People moan about all the foreigners coming in but I don't mind it so much. Why They want to come here though I'll never know. Nothing here, nothing beautiful except maybe the wide, wide river of the Clementine Channel.

Welcome to Kimble Wells!

So.
See.

They say that Home is Where the Heart Is, but sometimes I wonder if I had a home in The First Place. Sometimes I even wonder if I had a heart. Or maybe TOO MUCH of one. Sometimes I FEEL as if my whole body is a heart, ready to burst.

Anyway.

Maybe THAT is something to talk about At A Later Time.
Yes. A Later Time cos I need to stop writing now. Need to stop, quit. I'm TOTALLY exhausted and I can't see straight. My handwriting is all squiggly and crazy and I'll NEVER be able to read this again. HA!

So ...

finished now bye.

Mel

P.S. Just slept, snoozed. For maybe an hour, or more.

Now I have re-read what I wrote and I'm TOTALLY shocked at where All This came from?? I don't remember any of it and I'm TOTALLY weirded-out ... but like, in a good way.
CAN'T believe I've written 7 pages that is insane! Like it's almost TRIPLE the amount of Last night. I know it's not a competition or anything but it does show that I'm opening up to You and stuff.
My finger is on fire and there's a big red circle there now, like a blister kind of a thing.

P.P.S .Going out with My Bestie Mia tonight. Saturday Night after all. They're replaying the last Twilight film at the cinema. Mia's like obsessed with these films because like she thinks The Main Guy is like dead-fit and gorgeous and I kind of agree but she goes Way Over The Top like she does with everything. Her mum is picking me up in an hour and I don't know why but Her Mum always makes me nervous for some reason. Probably cos she's an adult, and beautiful and confident and stuff. She always asks me LOADS of questions (unlike my own mum) and that kind of makes me sort of shy too.

Anyway.
Either way.

I'm excited by the night.

Later ... xxx

Blank Portraits

Markus

"Did you kick my door?"

"What?"

"Did you kick my front door?"

Markus pulled a screw-face, and then turned it upon his little mate. "What you on about?"

They were sitting on a wall at school. T was eating from his lunch-box. Markus's eyes hovered over all the lovely food he had; salmon sandwiches, chocolate bars, yoghurts, a big shiny apple.

"There was a massive footprint on my front door. Mum thinks it was you but I told her it wasn't."

T's voice had gone considerably weaker throughout the last sentence.

"Your mum needs to watch her fat mouth. I didn't kick nothing."

"That's what I thought," T said, putting his head down.

Markus's stare seemed to have no end.

After a while he put his eyes on a bunch of girls playing a ball game on the grass.

"You wanna come round tonight and play?" T said, resuming.

"Play?" Markus said, with a sudden spreading smile.

"I mean come over?"

Markus's smile stayed there, mocking his friend. "Well that depends?"

"On what?"

"On whether you're gonna be in."

"I'll, I'll be in," T stuttered.

"And on whether your fat mum can keep her fat mouth shut."

"She will."

"That's alright then," Markus said. "I'll *play*."

Markus laughed and T turned red.

"Now give me one of them yoghurts."

Their friendship stayed for the next two years, until they were ten years old. Although they didn't really see each other at school. Markus played football with the rough kids while T was in the Computer Club with the wimpy kids. Markus didn't want to be seen with him, only catching him at the beginning of lunch, where he would take food from his lunchbox. In return Markus made sure T never got bullied. Markus didn't even know T's real name, just assuming it was short for something. It was after school or in the holidays Markus would see his friend, coming over to his house. Kicking off his shoes. Part of the furniture now. He loved all the big dinners and new toys. He also got to go to cool places like Fantasy Forest, the cinema, the zoo. They even went to Alton Towers once and Markus never had to pay. He never needed any money. It was *all* free.

The only thing Markus had to *put up with* was watching the way T's mum treated her son. It was sickening. The way she mollycoddled him was cringing. She wouldn't let him do anything, go anywhere. Bikes were too dangerous. Football too rough. Inside was better, inside was safer. So she built him a palace he would never have to leave. T had *every* toy, every computer game. He had a PlayStation *and* an Xbox. His bedroom was like a fortress. He had slides, dens; a ball pool. It was incredible. Although his mum was always interfering. She was up every twenty minutes, checking on him, making sure he wasn't doing anything too dangerous, making sure he had his asthma inhaler.

"Doesn't your fat mum ever leave you alone?"

T shrugged and put his head down, ashamed.

One day they were watching YouTube on his iPad when his mum came in.

"Is it okay if you boys have a run out with me to the cobblers?"

"Oh mum we're playing!"

T's mum was leaning over. Markus noticed a massive crack in her chest that made all her skin look weird.

"I know love but I really need to get this backdoor key cut. It's kind of an emergency, son."

T looked at Markus and rolled his eyes.

"I'll go do it for you," Markus piped up.

T's mum stood back. She was wearing an apron around her middle part. She didn't know what to say for a few seconds. Markus was staring at her red lipstick.

"No. No it's okay Markus. It's all the way up Hockley Top. No, we ... "

"It's not far," Markus said, shaking his head. "I'll go on Mongoose. Only take me twenty minutes."

T had his head down. He always got embarrassed when his mum spoke to Markus.

"Well ... "

"Really. I'll go. I don't like being inside all the time anyway," he said, getting a dig in.

"And your mother doesn't mind you going *all* that way?"

T's head sprang up and he glared at his mother. She went red and Markus watched her lips twitch. "I mean, doesn't your *dad* mind you going all that way?"

Markus said nothing, just carried on staring at her, slowly shaking his head.

"Well, okay Markus. If you're sure you don't mind? That would be a big help. Thank you. I'll have some nice lunch waiting for you when you get back."

"Can I go with him?" T said from nowhere.

Her face went into sudden panic. "Well ... "

"You haven't got a bike dozy; you're not allowed one," Markus said, getting in another dig. "I'll be twenty minutes, tops. I don't see what all the fuss is."

T's mum looked at Markus like lots of adults looked at Markus; a mixture of trepidation and disbelief. Suppose the word was *awe*. Markus was a bad-un, a wrong-un. From the wrong side of the tracks. But you couldn't help admire how *quick-on-his-feet* he was. He spoke roughly, impolite and abrupt. It was obvious that the boy wasn't going to take to education yet at the same time he had an unusual eloquence for a boy his age. It's like he always knew what to say and when to say it.

"Money," he said, putting out his hand.

T's mum gave him the key and a twenty-pound note and told him to be careful on them roads.

"Want me to pick anything else up while I'm out Mrs?"

T's mum didn't like him calling her that, *Mrs*. It was rude and a little out of date. Why couldn't he *ever* remember her name?

"No it's okay Markus, just the key."

Markus liked the feeling of the twenty note in his hand. It was new and crisp and he enjoyed the *crinkle* it made as he slipped it

44

into his pocket. It made him feel kind of rich too. He pulled Mongoose out of her place in the hedge and began pedalling up Edwards Lane. Mongoose was the right size now. Markus had shot-up in the last two years and Mongoose fit just perfect. She looked as good as new too. Most nights Markus had her under rag and polish, working away until she gleamed like a diamond. Apart from a few punctures and a scratch on the frame she was as good as the day Dad bought/stole her.

Markus Venner worked the hill, pedalled up by Mighty Bites and smelled all those bacon and egg sandwiches being devoured by the workmen outside. He couldn't wait to get back to T and dive into an epic lunch. Markus was surprised T wasn't the size of a cow with all the grub his mum slung down his neck. How he got to remain a scrawny little shit is beyond me, Markus thought. Not like he gets any exercise either.

He was at the cobblers in no time, only a little red-faced and out of breath. His *good head of hair* was all over the place and Markus tried to pat it down before he got in the shop. There was no one in the queue and he liked that. Fucking hate queues, and crowds and people, he thought. An oldish man shuffled out from the back, wearing a small pair of glasses and a large moustache. His face was tanned with loads of lines and cracks in it. I'd hate to be old, Markus thought. Nothing worse than being old. Being all weak and slow. Not being able to run or fight properly or climb trees. Not being able to *escape*. I mean what's the point of that? What chance have you got? I'm never getting old, Markus thought. I'd rather kill myself first.

"Alright mate," Markus said.

"What can I do for you?" the man said.

"Do key-cutting?"

"We do."

Markus held the key in the air. "Can you cut that?"

"We can."

We, why did he keep saying *we*? There was no one else around. The old man was on his own.

Markus placed the key in his big, thick, wrinkled hand. His hand looked too big for his arm. Come to think of it his ears looked too big for his head. All his features looked out-of-proportion, like Mr Potato Head or something. Yeah, definitely don't want to get old, Markus thought.

45

"Just the one key?" the old man said.

He now had his back to him.

The question turned Markus silent. Suddenly he felt a little explosion of excitement pop in his stomach. His mouth went dry and his palms got hot.

"Sorry," he said, pretending not to hear.

"Just one of these keys need cutting?"

"Two!" Markus shouted, feeling the unnaturalness of his tone. He steadied himself and answered again. "Sorry, I need two."

The old man put his hand up and nodded from the back.

From nowhere Markus got one of those hard-on things. He had started getting them more and more recently and he hated it. It was always when he was in a public place. That's why he had started wearing jeans lately instead of joggers. He would have to grab *his thing* when no one was looking and tuck it into the elastic of his boxers.

The sound of the key being cut screamed through the shop while Markus turned and looked outside. It was windy, brown leaves blew in a clockwise circle outside the door. A mother and two daughters were crossing the street. The mother was holding the younger one's hand while the oldest lagged behind. She had her arms folded and her head down and she looked sad. He tried to catch her eye but couldn't. She was about the same age as Markus.

"There you go," the old man's voice broke his daydream. "Two cut keys."

"Thanks," Markus muttered.

"There's your original and here's the cuts."

He put the cuts in a little envelope and sealed it, before taking the money and then handing Markus the change.

"Thanks Mr," Markus said cheerily. "Have a good day mate."

"You too," the man replied, a little smirk appearing under his moustache.

Outside Markus popped the envelope and put one of the keys in his other pocket. He jumped on Mongoose and that hard-on thing came back. But it didn't matter because he was moving now. No one could see him.

At the dinner table T's mum wouldn't stop thanking him. It was as if he had trekked over the Himalayas barefoot.

"You pedalled *all* the way up that hill. You must be a really strong boy."

"The strongest," he said with a cocky smile.

He looked at T and T put his head down.

They ate a feast. After, while T's mum took the plates away Markus leaned over and whispered to his little mate. "I've made a decision."

T sat up instantly. "What?" he said, eyes shining with anticipation.

"I'm going to kill myself on my thirtieth birthday."

Markus watched T's face change, scared and a little disturbed. "Why?" he said.

"Who wants to get old."

The small boy thought for a few moments and then shrugged, as if it seemed to make sense.

His mum came back with pudding, a big chocolate Elephant's Foot smothered in cream.

"I know there's cream in the middle but I know you like it on top too."

Markus couldn't take his eyes off it.

"Can Markus stay the night Mum?" T said from nowhere, surprising Markus just as much as his mother.

"Oh I don't know about that Trevor. You know it's a school night. But ... seeing as though Markus did me a *massive* favour today ... I think I could bend the rules, *just* once."

Markus had a mouthful of Elephant's Foot but he talked through it anyway.

"It's alright Mrs. Gotta get home."

Disappointment rinsed through T's expression.

"Got to make sure dad and bro and all that is alright. Think my Aunt Tars is coming round later too."

His mum sat down opposite and started eating her Elephant's Foot. She got it all around her mouth and had to guide some of it in with her finger.

"And how are things at home Markus?"

T rolled his eyes and looked away, crippled by embarrassment.

"Oh alright, y'know. Same old."

Again she was charmed by his mature ways and confident manner.

After Markus thanked T's mum. He thanked her for the food and for offering him to stay the night. He complimented her on her cooking and her home and she even wondered if the child was starting to flirt with her a little. She was laughing so much she hadn't noticed that Markus didn't say goodbye to her son, or even acknowledge he was there.

He climbed on Mongoose and started his journey home.

"Ride safe now," she sang from the top of her voice, waving at him.

Markus took his hands off the handlebars and held them in the air, partly so he could wave back, and partly to show-off.

Aunt Tars was already there. He could see her and his dad sitting in the illuminated window of the kitchen. Markus put Mongoose in the outhouse and stepped inside. The kitchen was swamped in heavy cigarette smoke. Bottles and half-empty glasses littered the worktop. Nub-ends were crushed into an ashtray and Markus wanted to be sick. I might do many wrong things in life, Markus thought. But I'll never smoke, never, ever. Aunt Tars was drunk. Dad was too. By now Markus knew what drunk was. He could easily distinguish between drunk people and sober ones. Adults were nearly always drunk, especially in the night time. He could tell mostly because they were nice to him. They did things they'd never do sober; pick him up, cuddle and kiss him, give him things. Markus knew it was all fake so he didn't take it too seriously.

Aunt Tara had her arms out the second she saw him. "Alright Soldier."

Solider. The word knocked the breath out his chest, floored him proper. A dark chill ran up his back and into his shoulders. *Soldier*. She hadn't called him that since the day she told him about Mum. *That* all-fated afternoon when he learned his Mum was dead. *Soldier*. Saying it now was weird and out of place, almost like a trick, or a test. It reminded him, took him back like some cruel déjà vu.

Her arms were still out, a silly drunken lipstick pout, "gimmie a kiss ... or a hug at least."

Markus reluctantly put his body into her embrace. She was all over him. Her hand found its way to the back of his head and she brushed it. "Such a good ... "

" ... head of hair," Markus groaned, finishing her sentence. "I know."

He moved away.

"Oh what's the matter with you sulky pants?" she said.

She had rips in her tights and her eyes were half-closed. Dad's eyes were too, his red face aglow through the moving walls of smoke. The kitchen was tiny and the smoke filled it like a gas chamber. Markus coughed and wanted to get out of there.

"Must have had a bad day at school!?" Aunt Tars speculated, crossing her arms and legs messily. She frowned with some faraway sympathy, like she was trying to work something out. The backend of the boy disappeared into the hallway, taking the stairs.

His dad spoke for the first time since Markus got there.

"He's been round that posh lad's house. Seen how the other half live and probably thinks he's too good now."

What his dad said wasn't a million miles away. Spending a day at T's put this little shit-hole into perspective. Being back here was a massive come-down. A cold reality-check.

Markus plodded the stairs, rolling his head with each heavy step. For some reason the image of that girl popped into his brain, that sad-looking one outside the cobblers. The pretty girl wearing glasses, who seemed so disconnected to the rest of her family. Noises were coming from his brother's room. He looked at his door and saw the word *Ryan* in gold garish lettering. His older brother barely came out of there these days. Always cooped up, building them stupid planes. Pointless seeing as though he never goes outside to fly them. It was Ryan's birthday next week. He was going to be a teenager.

He kicked his bedroom door and it swung open, soundlessly like a yawn. His room appeared before him. More hard comparisons were made to T. Where lived and what he had. This unjust balance of everything. How can some have so much and others so little? He looked around at his room. The sheer smallness depressed him. Markus stepped into it and closed the door behind him. The room was small but it'd be *even* smaller if not for Markus's fanatic neatness. It was the only clean and tidy room in the house. Markus didn't have much but what he did have was carefully stored away.

Everything had its place. Everything had its compartment.

Markus pulled off his hoodie, hanging it on the rail. He then went over to the window and peered outside, up at the moon which was pretty big tonight. There was a light wind too, which moved the branches of a small tree on the main road. On the whole Markus preferred night to day. He liked the calm and mystery of it all.

Things looked better in the dark. Things *felt* better in the dark. Life was slower and more interesting.

The feast at T's kept his appetite away and if he was lucky he would fall asleep before he got hungry again. He didn't want to go downstairs and see the adults, not when they were drunk. He loved seeing Aunt Tars, but not when she was drunk. She said the same things over and over again and always ended up talking about Mum.

When he lay down *that thing* stabbed his side and he remembered, *key*. Need to keep this safe, he thought. So he took it from his pocket and went to put it in the Liverpool FC tin he hid under his bed. *All my secret stuff.* Only the shine of the key caught his eye and kept it there. He was amazed by how bright and new it was, by how cold it felt. *A perfect thing.* He held it up and examined it, turning it slow in the soft light, against the smudge of the moon. It made him think of a piece of ice, or a shard from a broken mirror. Markus saw his face in the wink of its reflection. *Here I am.* Before running his thumb over its cool smoothness. A key to another world, he mused.

Oh, the places we'll go.

Around midnight Markus heard noise downstairs. A bump, then a smash. Voices were under his floorboards. Two of them, a man one and a woman one. His Dad's and Aunt Tars'. He couldn't tell if it was laughter or crying, or if one was laughing and the other was crying. Or maybe his brother was down there with them? Although that would *never* happen. Ryan was normally asleep by ten. Then another sound, something sharp and shrill, a squawk from outside and Markus wondered if he was dreaming. He sat up straight and listened, his ear open to the wild dark. Nothing, silent. He lay back down and pulled the curtain across all the way – just then a creak in the stair. He turned quickly and faced the wall, pretending to be asleep. Next there was a whisper, a *shush*. Gentle footsteps were outside his room. He opened his eyes and looked over his shoulder, feet breaking the beam of light at the bottom of the door. Outlines of his Stevie Gerrard poster looked down on him from the wall. He closed his eyes as the doorhandle began to twist. Hopefully they will see him fast asleep and leave him alone.

They were on the inside now. He felt heat from another body. Eyes were on him, boring into his back. One step, two step – slow and careful. A large shadow covered the wall. They were over him, an inch away. The bottom of his bed suddenly began to sink. One of the springs popped and made him jump.

"I know you're awake," came the voice.

Next there was breath, and a kiss on his face. Hair fell into his eyes and Markus sat up, mad.

"Fuck you doing?"

"I only wanted to see my favourite nephew."

Her voice wriggled through his ear. Cheap perfume entered his nostrils and burned them. Her face hovered over his, freakishly in the dark.

"I was sleeping."

"No you wasn't soldier, I can tell."

"And stop calling me *solider*. I don't like it."

She gave him a salute and then snorted into laughter. "Whatever you say my favourite."

"And don't say that either cos it's not fair on Ryan."

"Oh and like you care," she laughed again and Markus didn't know what she meant.

Aunt Tars then tapped the switch and light invaded the room, stinging Markus's eyes. He had to squint through his fingers.

"You know," she slurred. "Your mum would be *so* proud of you."

"Oh god, you're fucking drunk."

She giggled and fell off the bed and looked younger than she was.

"You will too," she pointed, circling her finger. "When you're older ... now pull me up."

Markus did, his aunt shocked at how easy the child did this.

"Never!" Markus blasted. "I'll never get drunk like you and dad and all the adults."

"That's what we all say," Tars said sagely, her laughter slow and soft.

"I fucking hate adults."

"You swear like one," she said. "See, you're halfway there and you don't even know it."

She got on the bed properly and tried to steady herself.

"Oh come on tiger why so miserable?" Slapping his knee. "I only came to say hello."

"Hello," Markus said, defiant. "Goodbye."

He put his head deep into the pillow and covered himself back up.

"Ooohhh-waaa," Aunt Tara sang.

She tried to rip the duvet back but couldn't, too strong was the boy.

"I've got school in the morning," he said, finally. His voice muffled from the other side.

"Pleeeaaassssee," she said.

Her voice so fucking irritating. He was being worn down.

His head came poking from the duvet. "Really. I have school."

She waved him off. "You don't care about school. *Kids* don't care about school. That's the *whole* point."

Markus's eyes were growing accustomed to the dark. He was starting to feel really awake and he didn't like it. Defeat was falling in him, moment by moment, until eventually he was in her loving bearhug.

"Baby baby I knew you'd come around."

He sat up with his Auntie Tara. She linked his arm and started talking, mostly shit from her life. She talked long and dreamily about the past. Eventually it got to her sister, his mum. As always her phone came out, tapping the screen, locating *photos,* then *gallery.* Her purple fingernail tap-tapping away. *Albums: My Big Sis.* Her starey cross-eyes trying to focus on the little square of indigo light. Her coordination was shot, so Markus had to hold the phone as she swiped through a nostalgic narrative of snapshot memories. *Your mum as a baby. Her first day at school. 16th, 18th, 21st. Our first time abroad. You and Ryan. That prick downstairs.*

"Why he never married her I'll never know."

Markus had seen them tons of times before, and he felt as he always did – not much, nothing. To him pictures were always a let-down, not real, not the real thing, a lie perhaps.

"She doesn't half look like you y'know?"

Markus smiled thinly.

"Oh don't let these photos fool you, she does. Like in real life she looks *just* like you. I should know, I was there. I see it. I see *her* in *you*. Every time you talk. It's in your mouth mostly, in that scowl of yours. You have her temper."

"Mum had a temper?"

He already knew this. He just liked hearing about it. It was the thing he liked hearing about the most. Her temper and the times she put people in their place. Times she fucked people up.

"Oh yeah," Aunt Tars smiled triumphantly, gazing out at a memory.

"Half the shit that arsehole pulls downstairs," she began, throwing her arm sloppily at the door. "Would *never* happen if your mam was around. *Uh uh.* No way. Wouldn't fucking happen mate."

A huge smile dropped on Markus without him realising it. Beaming and brilliant. His mum suddenly seemed alive, wickedly alive and at his side.

"She'd whip that prick into shape in no time."

"Ha."

"Nobody fucked with your mum. *Nobody.*"

Markus was now widened into wakefulness, utterly engrossed. The drunken woman suddenly found new ways to tell old stories, keeping her young listener gripped. Hours and hours floated away until dawn began to press hard at the window. Tara was winding down, dying out like a faulty toy, stooped into sleep.

Markus too was on the wane, a sickly adrenalin dump moved in his guts, consciousness caving-in. Every now and then a dream would kick him awake and he'd see his aunt still there. An impossible lump at the edge of his bed. In his delirium he saw his mum. His aunt's body hosting his mum's soul. He wanted to talk to her. He wanted to say something.

Mum, mam, mama, mother.

The next time he woke she was gone, and minutes later he heard a knock on the door, followed by his brother's timid voice on the other side.

"Markus. You going school?"

"No."

"Okay."

When he woke again he could feel how much later it was by the tone of the sky, the fullness of that mid-morning light.

His first thought: Shit I missed school.

His second thought: Fuck it.

Downstairs was trashed.

Ain't nuthin new for trash like you.

He walked about and hated every part of this small shit-tip. He thought of T's house and knew he had to clear it all up and make it as tidy as his.

He thought of T's House ...

In the sudden grip of furious excitement, he was upstairs and back in his room, under his bed to his red and gold Liverpool FC tin ... that silver key gleaming with just as much intensity as the night before.

Ain't nuthin see for trash like me.

He vaulted the stairs, leaving the house unlocked. Took Mongoose from the outhouse, running alongside her, before leaping on the saddle like a horse.

Skidded to a stop at the end of his street.

FUCK THIS WORLD. FUCK LIFE.

He didn't put Mongoose in her usual parking space, but rather took her out back and hid her behind T's dad's shed. The weather was cold but Markus was hot. He was hot and excited and a little uncertain. Standing in front of the backdoor he took out the key. He knew no one was in. T was at school and his mum was at work and his dad had some job that only had him home at the weekends.

He slid the key into the lock and kept it there. Closed his eyes and waited a few seconds before giving it a light twist. It was a little stiff but it worked. The sound of the bolt sliding back gave him that little hard-on feeling again. He pulled down on the handle and the door clicked open without him having to try. Warmth slipped through and Markus felt it on the tip of his nose, and then on the rest of his body as he stepped inside ...

... and closed the door behind him.

He stood with his back to it and looked at the kitchen. As bright as ever, with those big windows and lemony walls. His eyes crawled all over and it was like the first time he'd been here. It looked different, new. It felt like it was his. *All* his.

It belongs to me now.

Markus liked the kitchen but it was kind of cheesy too. There was a big sign on the wall saying *home sweet home*. The bread bin was in the shape of a loaf of bread and the egg basket had little chick patterns on. Alphabetical magnets colouring the fridge: *trevor loves mum 4eva*. The word 'love' represented by a heart, half pink/half red.

"So gay," Markus whispered, rolling his eyes.

Markus had to fight off his first urge, which was to trash the place completely, dismantle the whole house room by room. Starting at T's bedroom and then work his way through, ending with the kitchen on his way out. He wanted to do that so much but he had to hold back. He wasn't here for a quick thrill, but rather to savour it all in the long game.

This was his house and he had to enjoy it *all*.

A car door outside made him jump. He ran to the front window and ducked, spying through the lacy nets to see that nosey neighbour carring a bag of shopping to his porch. He put down the bag and let himself in. Markus let out a huge, cunning smile.

If only he knew.

If only T knew, and his fat stupid mother.

If only they all knew.

If only they could see me now.

Above all he liked this feeling the best. He liked the freedom and power of it. *Go where I want, do what I what.* He was like The Invisible Man, or some kind of ghost, evaporating through walls, floating upstairs.

Markus caught his reflection in the big mirror on the landing. The glass was clear and shiny and had a gold frame around it. It made the house look even bigger. Markus gazed into it and was a little startled at what gazed back. It wasn't him but somebody else. Markus moved and tried to catch himself out.

Is that really me?

His face was too big and his eyes were too wide. He looked Chinese. He had no top lip and the bottom one was red, too red, like it was sore or something. Markus didn't look right; his skin didn't look right either. It looked hard, wooden. He looked like a spooky doll. He looked like a girl, an alien, another boy. Markus didn't want to look at himself anymore so he moved on …

… into T's room.

He looked at all the toys but didn't play with them. It wasn't the same playing on your own. On your own it seemed babyish and dumb. Again he wanted to break them all and had to stop himself. What he really wanted to do was go in mum's room. That excited him the most, mainly because he had never been in there before. He stood at her door and put his hand on the knob only he didn't *feel* to go in there yet. Not now. Not today.

So he went back downstairs and decided to do *one of everything*. One slice of bread with one slice of ham washed down by one glass of milk. He actually got temped to make a cup of tea even though he didn't like hot drinks. He wanted a cup of tea because that's what adults had. Markus felt like an adult today. He played one game on the PlayStation and watched one cartoon on the T.V. After he sat and watched the goldfish. There were four of them and they all looked the same. Markus didn't like pets. He couldn't see the point of them.

It was getting on for three o'clock. In half an hour T's fat mum will be picking up her drippy son from that shitty school. Better get going, he thought. He retraced his steps and checked all the rooms. Making sure he'd left everything as he found it.

He looked at the kitchen on his way out.

"I'll be seeing you again," he said.

He put the key in his pocket and took Mongoose out the back of the shed. The key and Mongoose were now his two favourite things in the world. They are both silver and they are both shiny. And they both take me where I need to go. He took the long route home, going the opposite way.

No one can see me, he thought. I have to stay invisible.

Markus needed to get Ryan a birthday present otherwise he wouldn't get one. Dad wouldn't get him one and Uncle Nigel wouldn't. Ryan had no real friends so there wasn't much luck there either. Aunt Tars will but it would only be something crap.

I need to get him something good, he thought.

Markus decided to leave Mongoose at home today and go on foot. He had a slow walk into town. It was almost spring and Markus noted the change in weather. There were more colours and it was much warmer. Despite the blue sky and the sun being out Markus still had to wear a coat. Ever since Ms Gaskell had said, "put your coat on otherwise you'll get pneumonia and catch your death of cold."

Pneumonia.

The word was like a bomb going off in his head. Pneumonia is what took Mum away. It had killed Mum and Markus didn't want it to kill him too. Since Ms Gaskell said that Markus had developed an obsession of always wearing a coat, no matter what time of year it was.

Springtime was pretty and Markus enjoyed kicking off the daffodil heads outside the old people's home. He took aim, ran over, closed his eyes and then swung his foot as hard as he could ... he liked the sound it made; *slap, snap* – decapitating the flower cleanly.

He imagined he was taking penalties as he did it. Markus missed playing football. He used to be the penalty-taker but he got kicked off the school team for smacking Elliot Cooper in the mouth with his football boots. Who needs the shitty school team anyway? I'll play for Liverpool one day.

Kelman Shopping Centre was an ugly grey block. Markus thought it looked like a giant plug, like someone had stuck it in the centre of town and left it there. He wandered around the perimeter, trying to remember where Toy Box was. He hadn't been there in ages, not since all that fuss at school. His dad and Aunt Tars took him there to buy some wrestling figures. Markus had a feeling it was upstairs. He walked towards the stairwell. Sun came through the building and lit up the path in columns. Markus looked at the shadows and light and thought of stripes on a zebra. He then thought of bars on a prison cell. By the top entrance a group of older kids were doing skateboard jumps off a step. Markus stood outside Greggs and watched them. After a while a security guard came over and told them to go away.

Adults, Markus thought, always spoiling things. Always sticking their noses in. Always getting *involved*. Fuck them.

The smell of greasy sausage rolls was making his head hurt so he walked away from Greggs, taking the iron stairwell to the next floor. He was right, Toy Box was here. It had a picture of a clown on the window with a speech bubble saying: "welcome."

So gay, Markus thought.

He stepped inside and collared the first employee he saw. A tall, thin man with loads of teeth. Markus noticed he looked a bit like the clown outside. His body was long and looked like it was made of rubber.

"Do you have planes?" Markus said.

The man stopped and looked up like it was the most complicated question in the world.

"Like planes you build yourself?" Markus added, trying to help him out.

This floored the man even more and he had to close one eye to think.

"Yeah," he said. "This way."

The man was so tall it gave Markus neckache. They walked aisle after aisle until they came to the planes. Markus noticed there was a Katy Perry song playing in the background.

"You know," the man said with a large smile. "I didn't think they did these anymore. I thought they only did these when *I* was a kid."

Now the man was really smiling and Markus could see that his teeth were bad. They had little brown cracks in them.

Ugh, Markus thought, he eats shit.

"You build these all by yourself?" the man said, bending down.

"It's for my brother. It's his birthday."

"Oh," the man was still smiling. He must be really happy, Markus thought. "Do you know which one you want?"

Markus had his neck tilted right back, looking at all the planes. A shadow of his *good head of hair* hovered on the tiled floor. "I want ... the biggest and the best!"

The planes were high up, almost to the ceiling, but the man was so tall he didn't even need a stepladder. His spidery arms reached up and plucked a box from the top. On the front was a big red fighter plane. He read out the name of the plane but Markus didn't hear right. It was two words with loads of numbers after it.

"Yeah," Markus was nodding his head. "That one."

"Do you want me to take it to the counter and gift-wrap it for you?" the man said.

"Nah," Markus replied, smiling back this time. "Gonna have a look round for a bit."

"Okay," the man said.

He left, his giant feet slapping across the tiles.

Markus struggled to hold onto the box. It was massive and Markus wondered if there was a real plane inside. Like, what if there is, he thought? Then me and Ryan can fuck off and leave dad to it. He suddenly imagined him and his bro side by side in the cockpit. Perhaps there's a little hole in the floor where you can put your legs, so you can run down a hill and take off. He'd seen hand gliders on T.V and wondered if that's what was in the box. He imagined flying over his house, over the estate, out of the town, the country. Maybe he'll live in America, where all the girls are pretty and you can buy guns. Think I'll go on my own though, Markus thought. Ryan is a pussy and he cries too much. He stays in his room all the time and I still hate him for what he used to do to me. I haven't forgiven him and I'm only getting him this plane because it's his 13th birthday.

Markus couldn't carry the box properly with two hands, so he put it on his head like how women carry their shopping in Africa.

He knocked something off a shelf and heard it slap on the floor behind him. He carried on, taking the long way. Brown Teeth was already talking to another customer, dumb and distracted. Markus walked right by him, through the checkout, passing the trollies, passing the baby ride by the window and then straight through the exit. He took the stairwell extra slow, planting two feet on each step. At the bottom he realised how far home was, and how long he'd have to walk with this thing on his head.

Oh well I'm strong, he reminded himself, *the strongest.*

At the edge of the shopping centre he heard a voice. At first he didn't think the voice was for him because he couldn't see anyone. Then he heard it again, clearer. The voice reminded him of a teacher, only more serious. It was a man's voice. Its tone was calm and strong.

"Put that thing down boy."

Markus did, feeling the instant relief in his neck. He couldn't see a thing, eyes full of sunlight. It lit him up like he was on stage. Another tall man was here. Only this one wasn't smiling. He wasn't frowning either. He was just sort of *normal.*

"You know you didn't pay for that don't you?"

"Yeah," Markus said.

"Is there a reason you didn't pay for that?"

"Yeah."

The eyebrows on the man's head went up, "which is?"

Markus noticed he had a moustache. Not a moustache like his dad used to have, but a small, thin moustache.

"I haven't got any money."

There was the smallest movement in the man's face, "get inside," he said.

For half a second Markus thought about running. But there was no point. Markus wasn't a very fast runner. He could fight and he could throw things. He could climb and he was quite good at jumping. But, he couldn't run. Markus wasn't born to run away.

He now knew that the man was an undercover detective. He dressed like normal people so he could blend in and catch you out. Markus could tell he was good at his job because he didn't even need to hold his wrist. Just followed Markus back up the stairwell, one step behind. At least he didn't have to carry that plane on his head this time. Detective held it with his long fingers. Toy Box said *welcome* again as they moved past the clown on the window and stepped inside. He was amazed to see all the staff waiting for them. A sea of serious faces. Markus hadn't noticed they were all wearing the same clothes, a uniform. They each had these little green waistcoats and red trousers. Markus tried not to laugh, as they looked like elves at Christmastime. The first face he saw was Brown Teeth. It was sad because he looked at Markus kind of hurt. Like he had done something to him *personally,* like he had betrayed him in some way.

"Follow me," Detective said, free of emotion.

Markus put his head down and followed, every eye in the shop was on him and he felt kind of famous. He noticed a Justin Bieber song playing in the background.

Detective opened a door at the back and stood there. The door was kind of camouflaged, as if he had just opened up the wall.

He pointed into a lighted room and Markus followed his finger. He heard voices behind him, murmurs. Detective led Markus to a small room with a table and chair, nothing else. Maybe there was a clock on the wall. He told Markus to sit and he sat. He couldn't help but notice how cool Detective was. He didn't do much and he didn't say much but he meant business. He was *smooth.* He also didn't give a shit that Markus was a kid, that he was only ten. Detective thought Markus was scum and Markus could tell. This made him boil inside and he wished he was the same size so they could have a fair fight, one on one.

"What's your name?" Detective said.

"Markus."

"Surname?"

"What?"

"Second name?"

"Venner."

"Markus Venner," Detective said, pulling out another chair from somewhere and sitting opposite the boy.

"Done this before Markus Venner?"

"Nope."

"I'll rephrase that. Got caught for this before Markus Venner?"

Markus wondered why he kept saying his name in full.

"Nope."

"Who'd you live with?"

Markus suddenly imagined Detective with a toothpick in his mouth.

60

"Dad and brother."

Detective sat silent for a while, just looking at him. He wore a black leather coat. I'm not the only one who wears coats in the sun, Markus thought. Maybe he's terrified of pneumonia too.

"Okay," Detective said.

He had been looking at his face and it was like he was making a decision.

"Okay," he said again. "We're going to call your dad."

He looked at Markus for a reaction. There wasn't one.

"What's your dad's number?"

Markus was staring at him blankly.

Detective pulled a funny face as if to say, *am I talking to a fucking ghost?* Markus knew that was the sentence that went thought his head. He heard it.

"Dad's number?" he said again.

Markus shrugged.

Detective shrugged back, annoyed. The first bit of real emotion Markus had detected in the man. "What's that?" Detective shrugged again and his jacket leapt and the zip part hit the plastic chair.

"I don't know it."

"Well take out your phone and look for it."

"I haven't got a phone. I'm only ten."

Detective looked shocked like all adults looked shocked. Markus looked twelve, easy. Maybe even older.

Detective squinted and Markus thought he was quite handsome. Bet he gets loads of girls. Only he looked scruffy too and can't imagine that he showered much.

"What's your dad's name?"

Markus didn't answer straight away and Detective pulled that face again. He was about to speak but Markus got there first, "Lance."

"Lance?" Detective said with an open mouth.

"Lance," Markus echoed.

Detective shook his head, "are you even being serious?"

"Why would I not be serious?"

Markus often got this with adults too, a sway of power. Like they couldn't work him out.

"Your dad's name is Lance Venner?"

Detective stood and was about to leave the room.

"No."

The boy stopped him mid-step. Detective took his hand off the handle.

"What do you mean *no*?"

"Venner is my mum's name."

"What?"

"Venner is my mum's name."

Detective sat back down, truly irritated. "And where is your mum?"

"Dead."

Detective took in a breath and leaned back and couldn't work out what was going on.

"She died of pneumonia."

Detective's face was blank.

"Are you scared of pneumonia?" Markus said suddenly.

Detective pulled another face, "what?"

"You wear a coat in the sunshine. Just like me."

"What's your dad's name?"

"Lance, I told you."

"His surname?"

"His what?"

"His second name?"

"Oh. I don't know."

Detective was on his feet again, leaning over the boy. "What do you mean you don't know?"

"I forgot."

"How can you forget, it's your dad?"

"It's been ages. I don't remember."

"What's been ages?"

Markus went to answer but Detective waved him off. Markus read the words in his mind: *forget it.*

"Right," Detective had lost it now. "I've given you a chance but you've fucked me about so I'm calling the police."

Again he looked for a reaction in Markus that wasn't there. Detective left the room and locked it and then returned some ten minutes later. A little calmer now.

"I've rang the police and they're on their way."

Markus didn't say anything.

"You know kid you could have made this easier on yourself if you had told me the truth from the beginning. I was just gonna call your daddy and deal with it that way."

"I did tell you the truth," Markus said.

Detective rolled his eyes.

For some reason he got that hard-on feeling again. He wanted it to go away so he tried to think of T's mum but that made it worse.

Gross, he thought.

Detective was shaking his head, and maybe smiling a bit. "Want a drink?" he said.

"Yep," Markus replied.

"Tea or coffee?"

Markus started laughing.

"What's so funny?" Detective said, irritated again.

"Kids don't have hot drinks, stupid!"

Aunt Tars picked him up from the police station several hours later. She was covered in tears and her face was so upset it looked crazy. A police woman had to take her into another room and calm her down. There were two main policemen. An old man that was the sergeant and a black man that was a P.C. Markus could tell that the sergeant was brought in to try and scare him. That was his job, to scare kids so much that they wouldn't come back. Only Markus could *feel* that it was a performance so he didn't take it too seriously. He wasn't scary at all. The black man wasn't really that black but probably more white. He was mixed-race although dad called them *mongrels*.

"What's a mongrel?" Markus asked.

"Well it's half and half innit?"

Dad said they were worse than blacks because they were always angry. He said they were angry because they didn't belong anywhere. Blacks didn't want them and whites didn't want them and this made them hate the world. Even though Markus was only ten he was starting to realise that everything his dad said was bollocks. In fact he often formed most of his ideas by listening to dad, and then thinking the opposite. The mixed-race police officer wasn't angry, actually he was the nicest adult he had ever met. He was cool and funny and he even gave him a can of coke. On the way out he said, "it's nice what you did for your bro, but next time save up your pocket money."

"I don't get pocket money."

"Then get a paper round."

"You have to be eleven to get a paper round," Markus said, standing on one leg. "I'm only ten!"

This cracked the policeman up and he wouldn't stop laughing for ages.

In the car Aunt Tars was still crying. She wasn't making the noises anymore but tears were leaking down her face. Markus watched them get stuck in her wrinkles. He wanted to reach over and wipe them away.

"Is this where it all starts Markus?" she said, her voice wobbly.

Markus didn't know what she meant.

"Is this where it *all* starts?" she said again. "What next, what you going to steal next, money, clothes, a car?"

"I can't drive."

"Don't get fucking cheeky with me!" She tried to hit him with her free hand but it didn't hurt. Markus wanted to laugh. He looked at a bouncing Elvis toy on the dashboard.

"What else have you stole, hey? Come then, tell me. Cos I know this isn't the first."

Markus thought of the key but that wasn't really stealing. He'd only made another copy. He had stolen some food but then T's mum *always* gave him loads of food so that didn't count either.

Markus remembered the time Aunt Tars pretended she'd ordered more food at the Chinese. She rang them up and shouted down the phone, saying they'd got her order wrong. Then they came back over and delivered more food, free food.

Wasn't that stealing? Wasn't that the same thing?

This was another thing Markus hated about adults. They told you not to do something yet they'd do it themselves. It made no sense. He wanted to mention this but Aunt Tars looked too upset, and he didn't want her to *flip*. He couldn't be doing with listening to her anymore. She was still going on.

"It's not looking good Markus. You've been kicked out the football team and nearly kicked out of school. And you're only *ten*."

Dad always said Aunt Tars was *dramatic*. He had a feeling he knew what that word meant now.

"What happens when you get older?" she went on. "What happens when you get to sixteen, seventeen? What then, drugs, prison?"

Markus wasn't listening anymore. He was looking out the window, thinking of other things.

It's Ryan's birthday tomorrow. I'll never get him anything now. I haven't got time.

Dad was sitting in the kitchen. He had a fag in one hand and a glass in the other. On his face he wore a strange smile, which Markus found surprising because he expected him to go nuts the most. Aunt Tars didn't say anything, just put the kettle on and then went upstairs to *fix my face.*

Dad was staring into space. His face got redder every day. He took a swallow and then gazed at his son, who was standing next to the radiator even though it wasn't on.

"I don't care what you do," he said. "Just don't give me any stress with *her.*"

He nodded up the stairs, where Aunt Tars could be heard running a tap. When she came down she looked better, calmer. She forgot about the kettle and filled up a glass from a bottle on the worktop.

"You hungry?" Dad said.

Markus nodded.

"I'll fetch us some chips," Dad slurred.

"You're not going anywhere, you're pissed," Aunt Tars said, downing the glass.

"Am I fuck I've only had a swallow."

"I'm going," Aunt Tars said with wide eyes, filling up another glass. "Just let me calm down a bit."

Dad stared at Markus, his eyes the usual watery blue. His eyes sometimes looked like they were trying not laugh and this made Markus want to laugh. It was a look that said *fuck it.* Fuck life. Sometimes Markus couldn't help but like his dad even though he was a shit father and a shit human being.

"I'll fetch the fucking chips," Dad said, stumbling forward.

"You're drunk!"

"You're not doing too bad yasen gal," his dad sang. "Calm it a bit."

"Lance your ten-year-old son has just been arrested for shoplifting. Will you care a little more about that than who's fetching the fucking chips?!"

Dad gave Markus that amused look again and the two smiled at each other.

Markus went to his room for a lie down before the chips arrived. He heard Aunt Tars come upstairs and go into his brother's room. She was asking him what he wanted from the chip shop. After they started up a conversation about something else but Markus couldn't hear because their voices had ducked into a whisper. Moments later Markus began to drop to sleep but someone was at his door. He could tell from the feeble knock it was his brother.

"What?" Markus snapped.

"Can I come in?"

His voice just as weak as his knock.

"If you have to."

The door crept open and Ryan came in. His hair had grown back and was covering his eyes. He was super-thin and looked like a girl. He still wore long-sleeved t-shirts to cover his fucked-up arms.

"Is it true?" he said, slightly dramatic.

"Is what true?"

"What you did for me?"

Markus sat up, irritated. His eyes felt hot and gluey and he really wanted to kip for a bit.

"That you stole me a plane for my birthday?"

Markus felt a rush of disappointment in the failing of his mission, "yeah but they took it back."

Ryan charged at Markus and grabbed him, pulling him into a hug. "Oh thank you Markus."

Markus pulled a face from under his embrace, "are you deaf? I said they took it off me."

"I don't care. I don't care. That's the nicest thing anyone has *ever* done for me."

Markus didn't get it. He didn't understand. There was no plane. There was no birthday present. How can something be *the nicest* if it doesn't exist? His brother kept holding him and in the end he started to cry like he always did. Markus wanted to push him off, maybe even punch him in the mouth. In the end he just let his brother hold him.

So gay, he thought.

T's mum's bedroom was not what he expected. It wasn't as tidy as the rest of the house, or as clean. The bed was unmade and there was a scattering of clothes on the floor. Markus picked up a sock.

Gross, he thought.

He imagined her crusty feet and fat ankles and dropped the sock back on the floor. Even though the room wasn't up to standard with the rest of the house he liked this room the best. It was a woman's room and there was no trace of a man in here. He could tell that his dad slept somewhere else, in the spare room perhaps. Markus had only met T's dad once. He was a weedy little man who looked constantly frightened, bit like his son. Even though Markus was only ten, eleven next month, he had a nose for fear. He could sniff out when somebody was scared and what they were scared of.

Markus wandered the room. It was turquoise and white, with flecks of light pink in the wallpaper. There were no photos or pictures. Markus felt that this was a selfish room, a *greedy* room. There was a plate and an empty box of chocolates on the bed. The dressing table was littered with a collection of perfume, different shaped bottles gleaming in the dusty light. Markus picked one up and squirted it. He closed his eyes and felt the cool particles land on his face. Next he went hunting through her drawers. He explored through her bras and couldn't believe how big her breasts were. They were *enormous.* Surely they weren't this big in real life? His favourite was this expensive-looking one, lacy and lurid red. The cup so big he could fit it over his *entire* head. From nowhere that uncomfortable hard-on feeling came again.

He felt like it was time to leave the room now, so he did.

The next time he was at the house he went straight to her room. Even before food or TV and Xbox. T's mum's room excited him although he couldn't put a finger on why. The duvet stuck up in the shape of a cave. Markus got on his knees and looked into the black mouth of the hole. He imagined T's ugly mum in there, all naked and fat and grotesque. There was another empty box of chocolates inside.

Gross, he thought.

Markus stood and began to take off his clothes, slowly, piece by piece. Folding each item on top of each other until there was a neat pile on the bedroom floor. He crawled inside and felt the gigantic wave of the duvet crash down on top of him. The coolness on his naked skin was brilliant.

Best bed ever.

All this space. All this room. Way better than his own bed back home, which was as narrow as a coffin and just as hard. Here he could roll over ten times and still be no way near the edge. After a while that tumbling sleep-feeling came, lapping up against his brain like he was about to drop off and fall under. His limbs lightened and seemed to float, as if he was being carried off by the tide, downstream ... downstream ... where the fishes are ... over rocks ... over rocks ... tadpoles, ducks, daffodils.

Nature and stuff.

Markus knew he was dreaming cos he heard a girl's voice in his head, small and sudden: *nature and stuff.*

... downstream ... carrying on downstream until something stopped him ... a pool of red, swimming before his eyes. It seemed to be all over him, like he was tangled up in it. All over his body and around his head, pressing against his skull from all sides. It was then that he knew what it was ... *in dream* ... he realised it was the big red bra from the drawer. *That* bra. Her bra. His mum's bra. T's mum's bra ... *still dream* ... and that hard-on feeling came again only this time it was different. Bigger. More powerful. Too powerful and overwhelming, like it was *everywhere.* Everywhere. His whole body and being ... it was as if something were trying to *get out.* A force trying to break out of his rib-cage. It was an awful, scary feeling. Doom. Like the world was about to end, like the world was about to end because it was too big ... too big for him to hold so it *had* to explode.

Markus gasped and kicked-out and woke up. He looked around the room, frightened, bewildered, on fire.

Oh.

He took deep breaths, eyes still moving around the walls of the room. When he looked down his could see his little penis standing on end, poking up. At first he thought he had wet the bed because there was *something coming out.* It was like wee but thicker. Markus dabbed it with his finger and it stuck and stretched, warm, sticky, like glue. Whatever it was confused and frightened him and all of a sudden he felt a massive need to leave this room, this bed, and never come back.

Markus was taking time out, taking time out from T's house. He was taking too many chances. Coming here too often, eating too much food and messing with things too much. He was amazed he hadn't been caught yet. He was taking too many chances with school too. Too many days off. Dad was receiving letters, threatening court.

Markus decided to take time out.

Next time he came back was a month later, a month to the day. He came back on his 11th birthday, the first of August. He made some beans on toast and sat on the sofa to watch *The Big Bang Theory*. He liked this show although he didn't totally understand it. It was about a bunch of geeks that hung-out with a really hot chick. He didn't get most of the jokes but he liked watching it anyway. He especially liked the Asian lad with the funny voice. He was smart but stupid at the same time. Markus watched him and laughed and tried to copy his accent. When the break came on Markus got up and walked over to the fish tank and looked at the fish. Now he had spent time studying them he could just about make out the difference between them all. One was bigger than the rest. He had a black nose and angry eyes. Markus liked him the best. Next was the one that looked like it had yellow hair. Markus liked this one too. He could tell it was a girl and it reminded him of the woman on *The Big Bang Theory*. The next one reminded him of the tall man who worked at Toy Box. He was long and thin and had brown cracks on him that made him think of the man's bad teeth. The last one he hated. He was the small wimpy one. He had a certain lost look and he was always floating around at the back. He reminded Markus of two people: his brother Ryan, and T.

Markus took the little fishing net that was clipped to the side of the tank and plunged it into the water. He stirred it like he was stirring a bowl of soup and it made the fishes go crazy. They were hard to catch, apart from the wimpy one he hated. He was easy. He was easy to catch because he always did the same thing, swim to the corner and cower. Markus took him out the tank and watched him breathe. When he looked at his face he saw the word *gormless*. His little mouth was gasping like mad, eating up air, and his eyes seemed to be staring dead hard and wild. He wanted to crush his face between his thumb and forefinger. Instead he put him on the carpet and watched him flap about. Markus found this bit really funny. It was strange seeing *a fish out of water*. It's like it shouldn't really be happening, like it was against *nature and stuff*. Probably the same as humans being in the sea. It's not natural. That's why we need goggles and tanks and wet suits. We're not supposed to be there the same way as this goldfish isn't supposed to be on the carpet. He lay down next to it and watched him flap. His flaps got less and less and Markus could feel him dying. Then as there was almost no flaps at all Markus threw him back in the water. He could feel the relief of the fish, like when humans burst out the bath after holding their breath. The fish would just drift at first, like he was dead, but then he would twitch and go back to swimming normal again. That's when Markus would grab the net and pull him back out, repeating the process. He did this again and again. Sometimes he did it for only a short time and sometimes he did it for longer. He was surprised that the goldfish didn't learn and keep out his way, but then Markus remembered that they only had a seven-second memory. He was also amazed by how long the fish could last. Sometimes he would watch for seemed like a whole episode of *The Big Bang Theory.* The fish had stopped flapping and looked dead on the carpet, but as soon as he was back in the water he would come back to life again.

Ultimately though he didn't want to kill the fish. He didn't want *anything* giving him away and stopping his fun.

With T's house at his fingertips he almost didn't mind the shit-hole where he lived. For T's house was a refuge. It was freedom and solitude and luxury. It was a place where he got to play and exercise some of the impulses that were growing and taking shape inside him. It was a place he called *home.*

One night Markus couldn't sleep. There was a full moon pressed at his curtain, illuminating the whole room. Markus needed darkness to drop off. One chink of light kept his head going. It must be way past midnight, he thought, turning and twisting in the bed. Something was bothering him. That hard-on feeling was here and it wouldn't go away. It felt like it shouldn't be there although he didn't know what to do with it. Didn't know how to get rid of it. Frustrated he lay there, wide awake. He tried counting sheep. At a hundred and thirteen he quit. What a stupid idea, he thought. *Counting sheep.* Whoever thought of that? He had school in the morning and he knew if he stayed awake one more hour he wouldn't go. Then dad *really* would be in trouble. He lay there and lay there and sleep was not even close. He sat up, adjusted his pillow, and then crashed his head back down.

That's when the idea shot into his brain like a bullet.
Home.
His mouth went dry and his palms got hot. That hard-on feeling

becoming stronger than ever. It raged between his legs and moved up into the rest of his body like fire. He sat up and smiled. The slow smile wicked in the dark. Markus got out of bed and peered under it. His little white hand reaching out for the Liverpool FC tin, the gold rim flashing as he peeled off the lid and took out the key.

Going round to play.

He was dressed. Dressed in black, trainers on, hood up, creeping out into the night. He thought about Mongoose but decided to leave her be, fast asleep in the outhouse. He took to the streets, head down with hands buried deep within his pockets. The night was vast and awesome and he was wide, wide awake. Not a soul in sight, not a sound. It was like being on the moon. Markus felt like he was the last boy on earth. Him against the world. He watched the houses pass by. People asleep in their beds, having dreams, nightmares.

Edwards Lane looked different in the night time, silent, empty. Markus almost felt sorry for it. He was already at the gate, unhooking and opening it up. Gentle footsteps down his long, flower-lined driveway. Down the side of his house, into the shadows. Markus couldn't believe he was here; couldn't believe he was doing this. He felt like another boy. He felt like someone had taken over his body. Always that rush of feeling as the key slid into the lock. Door silently opened. The dark kitchen had him standing there; standing there for a while, absorbing the interiors.

"I'm here," he whispered.

The house answered him back, "I know."

For some reason he was directed straight to the kitchen drawer, a drawer he had never used yet he knew exactly what was inside, *knives.*

A tray of blades.

They gleamed in the dark, long, shiny and silver. He saw the word *shark*. Their different-sized handles bunched together. Markus closed his eyes and picked one. It felt right in his hand, perfect weight and shape. He held it out in front of him and felt the air cling to it like it had a magnetic pull. He waved it around slowly, slicing up the space around him; smooth, fluid, like water.

Again he didn't know quite what he was doing and for a moment he wondered if he was trapped inside a dream. I'm still in bed, he thought.

Only he wasn't.

He was upstairs, outside T's room. The door was ajar and he could hear the soft purr of his sleep. Markus put his toe on the door and pushed. It opened with an agonising creak. The objects of the room appeared miraculously before him. Markus took a step towards the bed, over his little mate. He could see the ginger of his hair poking out the duvet. Markus knelt beside him. He watched on, the swallow rhythms of his body rising and falling. A foot stuck out. Markus put the blade near his toes, hard metal and soft flesh, with just a millimetre of space between them. He traced the weapon up the side of his body, ending at the dark dot of his ear. He kept it there and imagined slowly inserting it, twisting it like a screwdriver until he got to the soft pulp of his ridiculous brain.

Markus felt alive, exhilaratingly alive.

Just then T stirred and rolled over. It was like the boy had opened his eyes and was looking right at him; his pupils large and liquid black. Too scared to move or say anything.

"You awake little boy?" Markus whispered.

No answer came so Markus smiled. "You stay sleep," he said. "It's safer there."

Next he was in his mum's room, so quick, almost as if he had melted through the walls.

She was lying on her back, dead to the world. The first thing he noticed was that her mouth was open, wide open wide. The sound of her breathing reminded him of Darth Vader from that Star Wars film.

"Man," he whispered.

He noticed her nostrils too. They looked massive. Along with the mouth there was three gaping holes in her head like a bowling ball. She almost didn't look human, Markus thought. She is a sleeping monster, something from outa-space. She reminded him of a mound of hills, a set of caves. She looked like landscape. She was bald too, or she had some kind of hairnet on and Markus couldn't work it out. He stood and studied her, his head to one side, amazed and curious. Taking a step closer he lowered the knife, pointing its point between the two large lumps in the bed. Again he traced upwards, slowly, stopping at her exposed throat. Her throat was so white and so large. If he looked close enough, under the flab, he could about see a pulse. He tapped the knife to the movement of her heartbeat, her life. In this moment he felt like he controlled her life. He felt like he controlled *all* life. Like all he had to do was press down and end it all.

There. Done. Over.

If only they knew.

They are asleep, but if only they knew.

He was gone. He was gone again. Out the kitchen and gone. Out the door and gone. Out the driveway and gone. Out the gate, the street, and gone. He was back in his house before he knew it. He was back in his bedroom and again he wondered if it had all been a dream, a fantasy; the inner workings of his insomnia imaginings. He lay in bed unsure of what was real, yet still, he was maliciously awake, alive.

He lay there and lay there, turning thoughts over, and thinking some more.

It wasn't until he rolled over and looked down and saw the knife laying in the dead centre of his bedroom, that he realised, it had indeed, *all* taken place.

The very next day he saw his little mate sitting on a wall, his lunchbox open with all those delicious goods lying face-up at the sky. Markus came over and planted himself next to him. Put a hand in and plucked out a chocolate bar. As always T showed no resistance and didn't seem to bother at all.

There's no limit to what I can do, Markus thought.

Only something was bothering T, it was in his face. Markus thought of the face of the fish, the goldfish he played with on the carpet. He saw the word *gormless* again.

"What's up with you?" Markus said, almost an accusation.

A tear was in his blue eye.

"Mummy's scared, so I'm scared."

Normally T tried to act tough in front of his superior mate, but this morning there was none of that, just a sacrificial honesty that Markus found bewildering.

"Scared of what?"

"Mum thinks we have a ghost in the house."

Markus was staring at him. "What you on about you freak?"

"She thinks someone has been coming in our house. She's thought it for a while now."

T paused and looked down at his lunchbox. So far he hadn't eaten a thing.

"Things move," he said. "Things go and then come back. Food goes missing and even our goldfish has died."

"It died?" Markus said, without thinking.

T turned and looked at him. He had the same chin-wobble his brother had. It was uncanny, and for a moment Markus couldn't distinguish between the two faces.

"A knife has gone missing," he said. "A kitchen knife has been taken from the drawer and now she's scared to death. She's called the police and dad has had to come home from work. She's even had the locks changed."

Markus felt his chest tighten. "What?" he said, angry. "Your mum's dumb."

For the first time T actually looked mad at Markus. "Why?" he said.

"Because he's a ghost. It doesn't matter if your mum changes the locks. He'll get in anyway."

In the following weeks T kept asking Markus to come around and *play* and Markus kept saying *no*. He had no need for him now. After all the liberty he enjoyed there was no way he could go back with *other people* there. It just wasn't right. In the end he told him straight.

"I don't wanna be your friend anymore."

Shock slapped his face. "What? Why?"

"Because."

"But why?"

"Just because."

"Just because why?"

"Just because you're not my kind of person."

Just because you're not my kind of person.

What ten-year-old talks like that?

T didn't understand.

"So go away," Markus said, smiling.

T broke down. He broke down and bawled like he was a girlfriend being dumped. Markus put his face up close to his little mate. He seemed fascinated by T's heartbreak, fascinated and amused. The pain in T's expression was quite remarkable and Markus enjoyed what he saw. T tried to hide his face but Markus kept looking at him and looking at him. In the end he shook his head pathetically. "So gay." he said.

After that he never saw him again. It was time to go to big school. T went to one big school, the posh one. And Markus went to the other.

Mel

Dear Self-Esteem Diary,

So.
See.

Like, the One Thing I'll always have on my side though is Truth.

*Truth in that I tell it. I will always tell The Truth no matter what. At
ALL costs. No matter how messed-up things are, or how angry I get,
or ill I feel, or mad I become, I will always say it as it is, or how I see it
to be.*
   At least then I know I've done My Part.
   *Because without THAT, without Truth, the Whole Thing collapses.
I mean, like, the bottom end of the world falls through and everything
is lost.*
   Lost for good.
   Lost forever.

*Cos, like, Tbh, I've never met A Single Human who hasn't lied to me
at Some Point.*
   Mum.
   My Sister Adele.
   My Bestie Mia.
   Dad.
   Even my Other Friends like Campbell, Suzie, Neve and Joshua.

So.
See.

I've learnt that humans lie.
   Humans don't do Truth.
   Humans aren't pure.
   Not pure, EVER.

*The Only Things that are pure if you think about it, are animals. Like
pets and stuff. They never lie. But that's not cos they're Good like
people pretend, that's just cos they're dumb and primitive and don't*

have evolved brains and that. So it's not a Moral Thing with animals but more of a Biology Thing. It's not something you can really admire about them, it's just, like, the way they are built and stuff.

Anyway.
Either way.

The Truth Thing is SO important to me and I just wanted to let You know that. Just wanted to get that off my chest before we move onto the Biography Bit again.

Anyway.

A part of the Biography Bit, I suppose, is telling You what I look like. Suppose it's only fair. Suppose it's only right seeing as though You're getting to know My Mind and My Head and My Thoughts and that ... suppose it's Only Fair that You should get to see what I look like too. Although tbh I hate This Part cos I REALLY hate the why I look and always have. I'd say that is a part of the problem and maybe The Biggest Part of the problem.
The way I look.
Like, my appearance and stuff.

Either way.

I should really let You know what I look like cos it seems only fair ... and honest.

So.

Here We go ...

First off, like, we'll start at the top and work our way down. Start with my hair, which isn't blonde or brunette but is kind of like in the middle, like a mousey kind of a thing. It used to be long but now it's short. Well not short, but shortER. It's not too short, not like a lesbian kind of a thing but more shoulder-length. Although people mostly said they prefer it long, like dead-long so I'm thinking of growing it back again.
Next is my face which I REALLY don't like and never have. mum

says I look like my Dad and I hate her for that cos that must mean he's ugly cos I am, kind of. I mean My Bestie Mia thinks I'm dead-pretty and some boys say I'm dead-pretty and even My Sister Adele says it but she's a Liar and not to be trusted.

Anyway I'm not pretty so don't listen to them.

I mean, like, suppose I'd say I'm photogenic. I kind of take a good picture but only when my glasses are on. But photos aren't Real Life anyway. In Real Life my face is kind of weird. Like, the Left Side and the Right Side don't match COMPLETELY. Like, they aren't TOTALLY equal and that gets me depressed.

Like, I just wish I could be more symmetrical and stuff.

See.

So.

My face isn't good and I want Them to take it back.

I want a new face.

A different one.

I want to be a different girl.

Like, if I could have a New One I'd have one like Mia's Mum. Even though she's probably like 35 or something she's still Stupidly Stunning. I'd love to look like her. Or like That Girl from Twilight cos she's dead-beautiful too. Only she's beautiful in a natural sort of a way, not like in an obvious, too-beautiful way, not like Beyoncé or Nicole Scherzinger or Someone like that. I wouldn't want to look like Them cos then everyone would stare and scrutinise and that'd be Hell. Too much attention. Boys would be All Over you and girls would hate you and then I could see how beauty would be a curse like they say. I think I'd just prefer to be subtle and stuff.

Anyway.

Next is my skin, which I don't like either. This is because I'm far too pale and always have been. Like, sometimes I even think my skin looks a little yellow, or yellowish, like I'm ill or dying or something. Plus I get spots, not loads, not like an acne kind of thing, but enough, more than most, more than My Bestie Mia anyway. My skin is greasy and mum says this is cos I don't eat right. Like, I don't eat enough and what I do eat is The Wrong Kind of Food. But that must mean it's HER fault. Cos like, Officially she IS My Mother after all so ULTIMATELY it's her responsibility if you think about it???

Either way.

I think it's safe to say I don't like my skin. I don't like my skin and You wouldn't either.

Next is my eyes and that is like The Worst Part EVER.

Like, Officially.

I won't even talk about This Part cos it hurts too much and gets me depressed. I have to wear glasses and I'm TOTALLY sensitive about that and always have been. My eyes are awful. And sometimes I want to stab them out and hand them back. Basically I'm boz-eyed and always have been. The Right One is NORMAL but the Left One is all weird and wonky and wrong and stuff. When I wear glasses you can't notice as much but it's still pretty bad. Tbh I'm not gonna Lie but it was the First Thing I got bullied for. Like people said things even as Far Back as nursery. Then people said things at school and even my OWN mum and Sister have made comments in The Past. The Only Person who loves it is My Bestie Mia. She says it makes me look mysterious, like I know Something that others don't. Like I'm looking into a dimension that No One Else can see. Ha! That's kind of cool and pretty amazing, but really I think she's just trying to make me feel better.

Anyway.

My eyes are brown, at least they was when I was younger but now they are bluey-green, I think. Tbh I don't even remember. Like I say, I've made The Decision not to talk about my eyes cos it hurts too much and gets me depressed, so we'll skip This Part.

Next is my smile and suppose if I HAD to pick. Like, if I REALLY had to pick then I'd probably say this was My Favourite Part. Mia's Mum says I have a 'surprising smile' whatever that means, and says I should try to smile More Often. My teeth are quite white and straight and I've never had to wear a brace like Mia has, so suppose I'm quite lucky in This Department. Only sometimes my lips get red and sore cos APPARENTLY I'm always putting things in my mouth, but like, it's weird cos Half The Time I don't even realise I'm doing it, like a subconscious kind of a thing. Either way, I'd still say my smile is My Favourite Part. Cos, I remember too. When a man came up to me in Tesco and said I have a Beautiful Smile, only mum quickly pulled me to one side and told him to go away. He was dead-handsome as well.

I think, if I'm being Honest, mum just being dead-jealous and stuff.

Next is my body and I don't like that either and never have. I think there could be something wrong with my back cos it curves, like a stoop kind of a thing. Like my spine is bent at the top. Not big time.

Not like a disabled kind of a thing but just a little. mum says I should just change my posture, sit up more and walk like a lady.

Like she can flippin talk! She's got a body like a man half the time anyway!

Anyway.

Either way.

My front side isn't much better either cos I haven't got boobs yet. Mia says not to worry cos they will come, EVENTUALLY. Easy for her to say cos she's got a pair of sexy ripe apples and All The Boys look and make comments and it's really not fair.

See.

So.

My body is still growing, I think. I'm 5ft4 the Last Time I checked, which is about average for a girl my age, or maybe a little above average if I'm being Honest. I'm way taller than Mia and only about an inch shorter than mum. I'll catch up with her soon and Take Over and I can't wait for that! I'm kind of skinny too, or maybe Slim is a better word. Although I have put a little weight on my bum in the last few months which I kind of like, but am kind of scared of at the same time. I never know what is in fashion and what is not. Some boys like big bums I've heard, and some don't. Either way my Bum Bit is better than my Boob Bit definitely.

Anyway.

mum called me Gangly the other day and I wasn't sure what that meant, but I GUARANTEE it is something negative. She also said I was ALL ARMS AND ALL LEGS and that sounded negative too.

Anyway.

Either way.

She can't really talk when it comes to This Department.

Cos.

Whatever happens, I really hope I don't inherit my mum's looks cos she IS funny-looking. Like, REALLY funny-looking and weird-looking and looks like a disabled person half the time. I know that sounds cruel but I'm just telling you The Truth. Her face is all wonky and I definitely get my horrible eyes from her so thanks for that mum!!!

mum says I look nothing like her. She says I don't take after her at all. She reckons My Sister Adele does but The Only Reason she says that is because she wants to be seen as pretty. Cos, like, My Sister Adele IS dead-pretty and tbh I'm not gonna Lie but I wish I looked like her instead. I wouldn't go so far to say she's beautiful but she is cute, very cute, like dead-cute. Like ALL the adults say so. They say words like ADORABLE and GORGEOUS. And they're always pinching her cheek and trying to touch her and cuddle her and like pick her up and stuff, and tbh I don't even blame them. The Thing that stands out most about Del is her hair. She has these UNBELIEVABLE locks that tumble down her back, and her hair is always so shiny and smooth and soft and perfect. It's like the colour of chocolate. What makes Her Looks even worser for me is that she's never big-headed or arrogant about it, so that makes people love her EVEN more, like she's kind of oblivious and people just love that. She's bubbly and charming without trying to be. Like she's not self-conscious in the slightest, and you'd never get HER writing in a stupid Self-Esteem Diary cos she's not a loser like that!

Loser like me.

Also. Another Thing I forgot to mention about My Sister Adele's looks is her teeth. She's got this little gap in her front teeth that people love too. I always thought having a gap made you goofy, and I liked that cos it meant I could beat her at something, I could have better teeth, but Turns Out she's even betterer than me at that too ... !!!

Anyway.

I'm going off on one now.

And I know all I've done today is go on about People's Appearance and how they look and stuff.

Which is kind of shallow, I know

But.

But suppose it's important, right? I mean, You need to know what We All look like so You know what You're dealing with.

So now you know.

I've not done the Biography Bit today but I'll Come Back to that next time, promise!

Anyway gonna stop now cos I FEEL tired again.

Feel tired all the time now and not sure why??

There's no doubt that The Anxiety is starting to come back. Maybe You can tell?

I felt quite happy when We started this Self-Esteem Diary but tbh I'm not gonna Lie that has faded a bit. Like, I do FEEL shit again. Like shit and stuff.

Deep Down I think this is cos of mum and My Sister Adele.

They just get closer and closer while I get further and further away.

Sometimes I just want it Over With. Just want to cut them out completely, like with scissors, clean and simple.

Snip.

Gone.

Then I wouldn't have to live in their shadow All The Time and could just go and do My Own Thing.

Hmm.

My Bestie Mia seems to think The Answer is for me to get a BF. But I dunno. Think I'm WAY too young for a BF at This Stage Of My Life. Although sometimes it would be nice to share my problems and have some arms to hold me tight. But a BF is also like so, so scary.

Scary and stuff.

Like I wouldn't even know where to begin.

Anyway.

Catch ya later bye.

MEL.

P.S.

Cinema yesterday was good. Mia's Mum didn't ask me too many questions and the last Twilight film is extra-good and Even Better on the big screen. The sounds were amazing, so real and raw. Like the vampires were all around me, but I couldn't see them.

Eeeeekkk!!!

YIKKES!!!!

Heavenly Creatures

Markus

Mongoose was gone. She wasn't there. The outhouse door slammed against the red-brick wall in an October wind. On the floor lay the busted padlock. Markus stepped in and looked around the damp, spider-webbed walls. All that was there was a battered, fold-up table and a flat Liverpool FC football.

Markus stood and stared into space, heartbroken.

He had never felt anything like it before.

He had not rode Mongoose in months. He was too big for her now, twelve-year's old and five-foot-seven but that didn't matter. Still he cleaned her daily and she was his. They had been through so much together.

He gazed around the small yard. There must be some mistake, he thought. His mind went into overdrive, considering all possibilities:

Dad must have something to do with this, maybe he's had to borrow her? But then why the busted lock? Perhaps he couldn't find the key? Nah. Makes no sense. Maybe he busted the lock to make it 'look' like a robbery? But why would he do that? To sell her. But why would he need to sell her? Cos he's a fucking alcoholic and hasn't worked in months. Maybe the person who Dad stole her from all those years ago had stolen her back? Maybe they had tracked her down at last and have taken what was rightfully theirs. Mm?

Just then another thought swooped in. The Taylor Brothers from three doors down. They were always going on about Mongoose and had wanted her for years. Several times they had tried to buy her off Markus, offering all kinds of swaps: PlayStation, new Liverpool shirt, mountain bike, DVD player. They had even offered booze and fags and Markus had to tell them, "I don't get drunk, or smoke. Anyway, she's not for sale. She's mine!"

Markus didn't know what they wanted with her anyway, they

were thirteen and fourteen and way too big for her. Only Mongoose was vintage by now and Markus had a feeling they had a buyer for her elsewhere. The Taylor Brothers were street entrepreneurs, and had already earned the nickname, Mini-Krays.

The heartbreak feeling subsided and another one replaced it: rage.

He stormed out the back and headed down the alleyway that connected all the yards. Three gates away was the house of The Taylor Brothers. He kicked it open and Ewan, the oldest brother, was on his back step, smoking a fag. His eyes went wide when he saw the oncoming figure of Markus Venner.

"Markus what the fuck?"

Ewan had his school uniform on, red and grey tie hanging loose down an open shirt. He wore a black bubble coat over it and had cherryade all around his mouth.

"You nick my Mongoose?"

"Fuck you talking about you little prick?"

Markus wasn't little. He was the same size as Ewan and two years younger.

"My Mongoose has been nicked."

Ewan pulled a screw-face and stepped forward. Markus detected a look of genuine surprise and could tell he had nothing to do with it, "coming round my yard making accusations?"

"Your brother in?"

As if on que, the younger, Stewie, stepped psychically out the back door. He wasn't as fiery as his older brother, but had a much worse reputation.

"What's this?" he said, pushing down the black curls on his head.

"This prick's accusing us of nicking his baby bike."

Stewie looked confused, and a little bored already, like he had other things on his mind. Markus was looking around the yard. The outhouse door was open and Markus was inside. Ewan let out an incredulous laugh and Markus saw the word, *audacity*. He held his hand out to his younger brother.

"We gonna let this nob look round our house like we're criminals?"

"You *are* criminals."

Ewan grabbed Markus by the collar and straight away he felt the twelve-year-old's body stiffen like wood. Stewie joined his brother and looked at Markus right in the eyes.

"Mate, what is this?" he said.

Ewan let go and all three stepped back.

The Taylor Brothers could batter Markus if they wanted. It was two against one and they had three years on their side. Ewan couldn't lose face and his younger would back him in an instant if a punch was thrown, but deep down they didn't want that. Markus was a nutter and they knew he'd be back the next day with a brick, beat him with that and he'd be back with a bat, next day a broken bottle, next day a knife. And it would go on and on until one of them, if not all three of them, was dead.

Markus was beginning to relent himself, not through fear but because he could tell the boys were innocent, well, not innocent, but innocent of *this*. They had nothing to do with Mongoose. He could *feel* it.

"Alright," he said with a nod.

Ewan was still snarling but his younger brother now had a smile on his face, a look of slight admiration.

Markus nodded again and turned around.

"Yeah you better walk away!" Ewan said.

Stewie threw back the curls on his head and stood on his tiptoes. "Hey, anyone in your year smoke yet? We got some knock-off fags."

Markus was already out the back gate, yet Stewie shouted after him.

"You should come and work for us!"

School better not piss me off today, Markus thought, as he approached its gates. Teachers better not either, and Mazie Vickers *definitely* better not. The bell rang in his ear and he threw his bag through the door. Registration passed, maths passed, break passed, History passed, lunch passed. Mongoose was on his mind the whole time. He thought about the day he got her, dad and Uncle Nige pissed up in the early hours, teaching him how to ride it around his small yard before the eyes of his envious brother who watched on from his bedroom window. He thought about the time he fought for her, snatched from his grip and beaten unconscious by the estate bullies yet still he got her back. All the trips to T's house on those weird and wonderful afternoons. He thought about the adventure to Skegness he made on his own, thirty-six miles there, thirty-six miles back. Mongoose and Markus had been through a lot, and now she was gone.

"Are you with us Markus Venner!?"

His daydream was broken by the voice of Mrs Meeks. The German teacher stood at the foot of the class with her hands on hips. Markus blinked hard and the room came back into focus.

"I said are *you* with us?" her voice was rough, like she smoked too much.

"Yes," he said.

The loss of Mongoose had taken some of the sting out of his tail. Markus sat deep in his chair and hugged himself.

"Your turn," Mrs Meeks said. "What is your name?"

A question mark formed in his expression, "Markus," he said.

The whole class erupted into laugher. The laugh he recognised the most was from Mazie Vickers. She sat erect on the front row, looking back at Markus, her blonde explosion of corkscrew locks and the troop of freckles on her nose and cheeks burned into him like the sun. Markus saw the word, *spiteful*.

"Yes I know your name is Markus. And thanks for telling us that," Mrs Meeks said. "Now could you try telling us that in *German*, seeing as though this is a *German* lesson?"

Markus was hating big school. He wasn't fond of little school either but big school was just shit.

"Repeat after me...*ich heibe Markus*."

He felt the classroom grip him like a fist and squeeze the life out of him. Mazie began to look and smile at everyone, gathering every pupil on her side, before directing all her ridicule at him. Markus saw the word, *gloat*.

He stood silent. He stood dumb. He felt his face go red. When he went to pull the collar loose from his neck he saw that his hands were shaking.

Sympathy came to Mrs Meeks' face and he could see that she regretted singling him out like this.

"Take your time Markus and simply say the words with me, one at a time, *ich*."

"Ich," Markus managed that. It sounded fine. It sounded just like how Miss said it but still Mazie laughed. She nudged the mate beside her and pointed at Markus like he was a circus freak.

" ... *heibe* ... "

Miss was on the next word but Mazie had fucked with his concentration. Sniggers had already started to crawl around the class.

"Class," Meeks said, telling them off.

Markus felt utterly alone.

"*Heibe*," she said again, nodding.

"I can't," he said. "It won't sound right. It will come out wrong."

He didn't realise Mazie was laughing so much until Meeks said her name. "Mazie. Behave."

The teacher looked at him again.

"Yes you can Markus, c'mon ... *heibe*." She nodded again like it was the easiest thing in the world.

And maybe it was but Markus had choked and there was no coming back from it. He stared at the red of her eye and tried to block out Mazie and Co but he couldn't. The longer it went on the harder it was getting. Like he had built it up too much. Like even if he did say it right they were going to laugh anyway. *Heibe*. The word sounded like fizzy pop drink *Tizer*.

"*Heibe*," she said again.

Markus felt like she had said it a thousand times and was amazed at her patience. The two-syllable word teetered on his lips but would not come loose. Markus felt like he had a stutter, or some other speech impediment.

Will you just fucking quit and leave me alone.

In that moment Mrs Meeks must have read his mind, because at last, she did.

"It's okay Markus."

Markus breathed a sigh of relief. He felt to sit down but then realised he already was. It was the longest five minutes of his life. Mazie was staring right at him, along with everyone else in the class. She had them all on her side. She pushed her tongue against her bottom lip and pulled a face like a retard. Markus looked back and in an instant a decision was made.

You've done it now. You pushed the button. It's on.

After the last lesson Markus rushed to the front gates and waited. He sat on a wall obscured by a bush and waited for that unmissable blonde hair. She appeared, her entourage not far behind. They stood and messed about for a bit before starting their walk home.

Markus leaned over the wall, sucked up and spat out a string of phlegm, and then began to tail them.

A quarter of a mile in the group split into two. Those who caught the bus broke off onto Lincoln Avenue while Mazie and the rest carried straight on along Fairmount. Markus was sixty metres back. He walked close to the gardens, ducking in one of them whenever anyone turned around.

More dropped off the pack, went in other directions. Eventually there were three: Mazie, her mate, and a boy. Markus was tempted to run up behind them and ambush. He would lay into the boy and batter him. Give him such a bloody beating, all the while looking into the eyes of Mazie Vickers. *Any more of your shit bitch and you're next.* Only the police would come knocking and he'd probably be kicked out of school. Got to be smart, he thought. By now they were in the new housing complex, each building was exactly like the next. Markus liked this estate though, something about it felt like he was in another country. There were cute little lawns and a park with a skateboard ramp. It didn't feel like his shitty little town at all.

Didn't feel like Kimble Wells.

The boy hugged the girls and turned off at another close and then there was two, two blonde girls walking arm in arm. Markus had to admit he did kind of fancy her mate a bit. Her name was Janine, he thinks. He would even go so far as to say she was beautiful, but like Mazie she was stuck-up and the only time she ever paid Markus any attention was to take the piss out of him.

Well we're gonna do something about that, he thought.

The two girls lived only doors apart.

Markus crept behind a camper van and watched on.

The blonde dots waved at each other over their lawns, and then went inside. The sound of one door closing, and then the next.

In his mind Markus took a photograph. *Gotcha.*

He didn't feel to go home yet. He was still wound-up and wanted a little more time on his own. He probably had another three hours of daylight before the dusk would begin its descent.

He decided to go to his den, The Den.

Markus had found a den, or rather he had found a den-place and then built one there. He had stumbled upon it by complete accident when he was out one day taking a random, aimless walk. He had wanted to get away from the claustrophobia of the estate so he ventured out in the fields, over the bridleways and into the countryside, the near-wilderness that faced the east of the county. Most of it was farmland that he wasn't allowed to be in. He stared at cows and cows stared back. All around there were sounds. Running water whooshed from somewhere. Something squawked, something twittered, something cock-a-doodled. A tractor growled in the distance. Nature moved. It was peaceful here, open. He enjoyed the solitude and liked not having to talk to anybody. All the dark impulses that normally bullied his mind were gone and what was left was a clear, blue place, like the sky which he walked under.

On instinct he took a left behind a berry bush and slipped into a downward trail that led to an opening. At the bottom of it lay a giant tire, and just beyond that a large wooden board under a fallen tree. All these objects lay scattered and tucked away next to a small wooded area. He saw the word, *yours.*

It's mine, Markus said. A den. He stayed there for an hour or two, checking the place out. It was so hidden no one would ever find him here. On the way home he took photos in his mind, snapshots of landmarks so he could find his way back. Over the next few weeks he moved in, brought little Markus-things and made the place home. Bits of food and drink, loads of sweets and chocolate and a big bottle of Coke. He brought a patch of carpet and a rug, clothes, a towel, rope, string, torch, a hammer. He brought a pocket knife, kitchen knife, bread knife, Swiss army knife, flick knife, lock knife, fold knife, his Liverpool FC tin with all his secret stuff in. He brought a sketchpad, a notebook, a porno mag. He stuck a Stevie Gerrard sticker onto the tire and attached a St George's flag to the tree. A camo canopy was used to shelter it all. At the end of it he stepped back and looked at The Den, admiring what he had built. Now he had a place *all to myself.* He made a vow to never bring anyone here, no one ever gets to see this, *no one.*

So he went to The Den that evening, the evening after following Mazie Vickers home. It was cold so he slipped on an extra layer when he got there. He climbed onto the tire and lay back, looking at the gathering dusk and the slow rising of the moon. He replayed the German lesson through his head. Why couldn't he say that one simple word, *heibe*? All he had to do was simply repeat after Mrs Meeks yet he had humiliated himself, or rather, Mazie had humiliated him. Ever since she had caught him staring at her on the first day she had made it her mission to belittle him and turn the school against him. He used to think she was beautiful, but now he thought she was ugly. By the time he had stopped thinking about it, it was dark. So he took out his torch and began the long walk home. As always The Den had made him feel better, gave him some calm and perspective. It was night time when he got back to the estate. He made some beans on toast and got in front of the telly. Dad was at the pub and his brother Ryan was in his room as always. There was a horror film starting at midnight and Markus decided to watch it. Normally he didn't have the attention span for a whole film but this one looked good. Besides, he could stay up late tonight because he didn't have to be up in the morning.

Markus was bunking school.

Tomorrow was the beginning of his new mission.

Mazie's house didn't feel as safe as T's. The neighbours were too close and there wasn't much room. He stood by the camper van over the street, sizing it up. He breathed in, on the exhale two words floated out from his mouth, *Fuck It.*

Fuck life.

There were no cars in the drive and he could feel there was no one in. He strolled down the side of the house and went straight around the back. A shiny green washing line bowed across the centre of a small, square lawn. On each corner was an ornament in the shape of a red and white toadstool.

His eyes searched on.

Mm. What am I looking for?

A key, of course.

He checked the usual's, doormat, plant pot, underneath a garden table.

Nothing.

Markus peered through the windows. The interiors were dark and he couldn't see much. It was no way near as big as T's house but it seemed just as tidy. On the windowsill was a pink comb covered in blonde locks. He thought of Mazie's spiteful, gloating face and his blood began to boil. Just then a noise came from his left, a sharp scratching sound way down below. A little wooden cage hidden in the corner of the yard. Markus spat in the grass and walked over to inspect it. He got down on one knee and looked in. A pair of pinkish eyes glared back.

"Perfect," he said.

At first he thought it was a rabbit, but after giving the water bottle a few squirts a guinea pig appeared on the other side of the wire mesh.

"Hello boy," Markus said.

He had never spoken to an animal before and he thought people who did were stupid, like a dog or cat or cow can understand the English language? Although maybe they understand *tone* and that's why Markus was trying to sound pleasant; hoping to gain the creature's trust.

"C'mon boy."

He had to fiddle with the latch for a good minute before he got the door open. The guinea pig was white with a brown face. It was fat and Markus knew there was no chance of it running away. It waddled forward, taking tentative steps, his nose twitching, trying to sniff out what was going on. Markus had never been in contact with these rodents before, so he covered his hand with his sleeve in case it tried to bite him.

"Here boy."

Cradled in his forearm, he stroked it for a few minutes with his thumb, before lifting it up and looking at his face. It made him think of T's goldfish for some reason, *gormless*. On standing up Markus lost his grip, its back legs slipped and his arse felt out but Markus managed to catch it.

"There, there, boy. Let's keep you safe."

He opened his school bag and dropped it in. He saw the panic of the creature and it went crazy for a few seconds. Markus stepped back and watched his black Adidas rucksack shuffle forward to the movement of the animal inside. A slow smile crept onto the boy's face. He looked around the yard, then at the neighbours either side. He popped up the hood on his hoodie and then took out one of his shoelaces, before tying the zip part of his bag. Checking it was secure before roughly throwing the bag over his shoulder. Already he could feel the guinea pig running around his back.

Feels fucking weird, he thought.

He decided to leave the cage door wide open. That way when Mazie Vickers looks through her kitchen window, she'll see …

Markus left the house. He walked brisk, with his head down. It's times like this I wish I had Mongoose, he thought, because The Den is miles away.

The farmer's daughter was taking the dog for a walk. She was crossing the top field when she saw a boy in the distance. It was unusual to see anyone out here, if ever. Her first instinct was to shout out, tell him to go away, but then she realised that part of the land was not private property.

He was standing with his legs apart, swinging something around his head. It looked like he was throwing the hammer in the Olympics.

What is that? she thought, squinting.

He brought the object downwards onto the ground. He did it again and again, for about a minute. The wind was howling and the bushes behind her made an awful noise, but through it all she swore she could hear the boy screaming.

The foot-part of his P.E sock was drenched in blood. Markus could hear the rattle of broken bones as he walked back to The Den. He turned the sock inside out and the mangled corpse of a guinea pig fell in the mud.

I'm going to deliver this mush back to its owner, he thought, I'm going to deliver this back to Miss Mazie Vickers. He wanted to put it back in the P.E sock and leave on the doorstep, or maybe tie it onto the cage with his school tie. He wanted to display it, send her message; let her know who it was, without telling her who it was.

He wanted to shut her mouth.

He wanted to shut her mouth, *for good*.

Only he'd watched enough crime shows to know that they could trace his D.N.A from the sock and the tie.

Would they really do that, Markus thought, would they go to all that trouble for a guinea pig, a pet?

Either way, he didn't want to take the chance, so he wore gloves and got a piece of string instead, sneaking over to the Vickers residence at midnight. On the way he nipped to the chip-shop for a small tray of chips and a fishcake.

"Anything to drink?"

"Can of coke."

"Pepsi alright?"

"No, coke."

"We only have Pepsi."

"Nothing then."

The greasy-faced Greek looked at the boy a little strange and

Markus wondered if he knew what was in the rucksack on his back. Markus felt a wave of paranoia and wanted to get out of there.

Mazie Vickers in the night time.

All the curtains were closed and he could feel everyone in bed. One of those security lights came on and he almost ran away. Only he'd been through enough gardens to know that no one paid attention to those things anymore. *It's just a fox.* Round the back the cage door had been closed and locked. He imagined all the fuss it must have caused, the panic, the loss. He knew what it felt like because he had felt the same thing only yesterday with the death of Mongoose. He knelt down by the cage and opened his rucksack, took out a Morrison's shopping bag and pulled out the Guinea pig, which by now was nothing more than a ball of bones, blood and fur. Some of the intestines dropped to the floor.

He tied it neatly to the dead centre of the cage, using a bow as a knot.

The security light had gone out by now, but was activated again, on his way out.

Mazie didn't come to school the next day, or the day after that. Markus was loving it and moved around with a silent sense of power. Then news broke, one of her mates let it slip and a rumour slowly started to spread through school: *Mazie's murdered pet, hung out to dry like Jesus on the cross. Psycho on the loose.* Most people didn't believe and waved it off, or else it was just a grand exaggeration. *Mazie is a drama queen.* Markus wouldn't stop smiling to himself, what he really wanted to do was tell someone, shock someone. Only Markus had no real friends at the school, besides, you can't trust anyone in life, only yourself. He admired his work, satisfied that his mission was a success. It had been bold and brilliant and clever. He was also thankful for that little rodent being placed in his path; a golden opportunity taken. He realised how crucial returning it was. Left it could have been dismissed as a runaway, the door not being shut properly, or maybe someone had stolen it. But hanging it out like that was perfect. It was apt. He saw the word, *trauma.*

Now she knew she had an enemy, an enemy not to be fucked with.

Mazie Vickers had been taught a lesson.

When she finally did come back everybody made a fuss. Markus thought at least some jokes would go around but there was nothing. Everybody loved Mazie, all the girls wanted to be her friend and most of the boys fancied her. Markus kept quiet and stayed out of her way. In German she sat quiet at the front, her head down. Her hair no longer had that eye-catching radiance. If anything it looked sad. Can hair be sad, Markus thought? She didn't shout out all the answers like she used to. Her best friend Janine linked her arm the whole time. That kind of thing wasn't normally allowed but the teacher made an exception. At the end of the lesson, on the way out, Markus caught her eye. He wanted to smile but he didn't want to make it that easy, instead he smiled with his eyes, the way Dad did. He felt the smile. It was his turn to present the word, *gloating*. His eye-contact was unmoving.

Mazie broke down, and ran off.

"Mazie what's the matter?" the teacher said.

Markus nodded ever so slightly, then shrugged his shoulders innocently to Mrs Meeks.

Two days later the headmaster called Markus to his office. There was something different to Mr Donoghue. Mostly he looked irritated, like he couldn't be bothered to be here. Only today his expression was more solemn. Markus saw the word, *troubled*.

He coughed and cleared his throat, asking Markus to sit, which was rare. Most of his 'telling's off" were done with Markus standing up. The light from the office bounced off his bald head like a disco ball.

"Markus."

"That's me," he sang.

Donoghue peered seriously over his glasses.

He coughed and cleared his throat a second time, "according to the register you weren't at school on Wednesday."

"Today?"

"Last Wednesday."

"I don't know sir. It was a long time ago."

"You wasn't in on the morning, or the afternoon, and your parents didn't call the school."

"No sir."

Donoghue carried on looking at him, wanting more.

"Dad was ill sir. I had to stay with him."

Headmaster found this hard to believe, but he'd heard worse.

"I *will* be checking with your father Markus."

"That's okay," he said in a breeze, almost taunting him.

Markus went straight down to his next lesson, P.E. He was a little late so he explained to the gym teacher he had been with the headmaster.

"Nothing new there then."

A few classmates giggled. By now Markus already owned the rep of a bad-boy. Pretty much everyone in year7 knew him. He got changed into his P.E kit. When he stepped out into the gym hall he only had one sock on.

"Where's your other sock Venner?"

He looked down at his bare ankle, then back at the teacher. Most of the class were swinging badminton rackets in the air.

"Sorry sir, my guinea pig ate it."

Markus laughed and then the rest of the class did. Only for him, the joke had a completely different meaning.

School seemed to settle for a while. Mazie retreated into her shell and that had an effect on the rest of the pupils. Markus did his own thing and there was a period of calm. That was until he noticed the new girl in school. At first Markus thought it was a boy because she had short hair. She sat beside him and Markus thought he could smell perfume. He glanced over and when she looked back he was shocked, not just to discover her gender, but also because of her eyes. They were the most unusual eyes he had ever seen, striking, speckled. Eyes which blazed with an intense greenness. Markus saw the word, *cobra.*

Over the weeks he became hypnotized by her and couldn't understand why. She wasn't even beautiful, not like how Mazie Vickers and her mate Janine were anyway. She was tall and thin and had no tits. *None whatsoever.* Her nose was long, like a hook. She was dark and people said she was Jewish. Markus thought she was foreign and expected her to talk in a different language, or with an accent at least. She hung around with no one and he couldn't recall her saying a single word, except maybe to call out at register.

"Carmen."

"Here."

Her silent confidence towered over everyone. The way she walked and looked around. It was as if everything was beneath her, as if she didn't really have to be here and was doing us all a favour.

She moved slowly, with ease and grace. All the time in the world. There was something cold and cruel about this new girl in school, detached yet at the same time achingly magnetic. Markus wanted more of her. He would look at her and smile. A smile which was never returned.

When he got home one night his brother Ryan was crying again. Markus could hear him from the backyard. The door was ajar and he saw him move about in the vertical beam of light. Markus walked over and pushed the door but it was stuck. He pushed it harder and felt it bounce against something soft.

"Don't, you'll hurt him!" his brother shouted.

"Who?"

"Dad."

Markus couldn't be doing with this shit tonight. He was cold and absolutely starving. He pushed again and was about to power on through.

"Markus no!" Ryan yelped. "His head, his head's there."

He sighed and put a hand through his *good head of hair*. "Well what the fuck's wrong with him?"

Ryan was up on the worktop, looking out the window. "I don't know Markus. He's just lying here. He won't move. I'm scared."

"He's fucking drunk," Markus said. "Go and tip some cold water on him."

Ryan wore a white vest. Markus noted how pathetic his arms were. "I'm not doing *that*," he whimpered.

"Just wake him up. I'm fucking starving and need to get in the house."

"Markus this is serious, he could be dead."

"You'll be dead if you don't wake him up."

"Markus he could be bleeding on the inside or something. His face don't look good."

"Neither would yours if you'd been on the piss all day."

"I'm going to ring nine, nine, nine."

"Don't you fucking dare!" Markus was becoming infuriated. "You're not embarrassing me Ryan. Now get a grip and pour some water on his face and wake the prick up. I'm starving and cold and need to get in *my* house."

His brother didn't reply. He heard the opening of a cupboard and the running of the tap.

Markus put his ear to the door. "You doing it?"

"Shall I just pour it on his face?"

"Pour it on his face Ryan."

"All of it?"

"Pour *all of it* on his face Ryan."

"He might hit me if I do this."

"I'll hit you if you don't."

There was silence, then the sound of water hitting flesh. Markus had to hold in a laugh.

"Oh Markus," Ryan's voice wobbled with fear and Markus started to laugh out-loud.

"Is he moving?" He could hear his dad spit and moan. "See, told you he ain't dead. Dad move the fuck out the way I need to get in!"

Markus rammed the door and it hit something hard.

"Markus that's his head, you're going to knock him out again."

"Is he moving?"

"Not really."

"Fuck this!"

Markus started to walk out the yard.

"Markus where you going?"

"To get fed."

The streets were dark and Markus walked through them with a growling stomach. A fox ran across his path and he instinctively reached for his slingshot but it wasn't there. He thought about lifting something from the Polish shop only he couldn't be bothered. Markus dug into his pockets and felt change. He fingered around and prayed for a few pound coins. Nope, there was only a fifty and a few tens and fives.

Broke as a joke.

So he headed in the direction of Aunt Tars. Auntie Tara lived on Norman Close. It was a big circular street that reminded Markus of an athletics track. She lived at number seven, which was right around the other side. He could already see *Look North News* flash from the telly so he knew she was in. He crept behind a bush and then walked on his hands and knees until he was directly under her window. Counted to three before leaping up and banging on the double-glazing as hard as he could. He heard his aunt before he saw her. A scream ripped through her chest and covered the lounge. She fell back against the sofa, both hands pressed at her heart. "You little bastard!"

Markus was doubled-over with laughter.

His aunt at the window, white-faced and furious. "You nearly gave me a fucking heart-attack!"

"Let me in," he mouthed, pointing to the back door.

She met him at the side of the bungalow. "Don't *do* that Markus. Don't *ever* do that again."

"It was only a joke."

"Things like that aren't funny. You need to grow up."

He followed her inside, patting down his hair.

"What do you want?"

"Nice way to greet ya favourite nephew."

"I haven't got any money."

"I'm not after your fucking money."

"And don't swear."

"You fucking swear."

"I'm a fucking adult."

"I hate fucking adults."

"So you say."

Markus slumped in the armchair and looked at the news. Some kids had been terrorising a disabled man in a park not too far from here. The man was looking into the camera with tears in his eyes. Then he put his head down and said, *I just can't take it anymore.*

Aunt Tars lit up a cigarette and opened a window.

"Do you have to open that it's freezing."

"It's my house I'll do what I want." She blew a jet of smoke out the window but the wind knocked it back in. "Besides, you're wearing that big coat, anyone'd think you've got pneumonia."

Aunt Tars regretted using that the word the second it left her lips. She looked away and hoped he hadn't noticed. Markus put his eyes back on the TV. Sport. Football. Lincoln City had lost at the weekend, so did Boston and so did Hull. He didn't give a shit about his local teams anyway, as long as Liverpool won that's all that mattered.

"Do us a bit of din Tars?"

His auntie crushed out the rest of her fag and closed the window. "It all suddenly becomes clear."

"What?"

"Where's ya dad?"

"Don't know."

"Pub?"

"I don't know."

"I've been trying to ring him all day."

Markus stuck his lip out and looked back at the TV. National news now. Pakis bombing each other and that black American bloke talking about it at the White House.

Aunt Tars had the oven on. "Only got fish fingers and chips. It'll hafta do."

Markus nodded, "got mushy?"

She looked at him and then shook her head, opening the cupboard and pulling out a small green and blue tin.

"In fact I may as well eat now an 'all."

She pulled out another tin.

Just before dinner was served Markus's phone went off. The word *Ryan* glowed in the centre of his screen. He was going to ignore it but he knew his older brother would panic, and he couldn't be doing with the drama.

"What?"

"Markus?"

"What?"

"Dad's not dead."

"I know that."

"He's moving, just."

Markus didn't say anything, just looked at the steaming plate of food being put down before him.

"Where are you?"

"Out," Markus grunted.

"I know *that*. But where?"

"Mate's."

"You haven't got any mates."

"Got more than you."

"Markus I'm starving and there's nothing in the cupboards, or the fridge. Nothing. *Literally* nothing but booze."

"Eat that."

"Markus I'm being serious what am I going to do?"

"Fuck sake Ryan ya fifteen."

Aunt Tars was filling up two glasses with juice.

"I was thinking of ringing Aunt Tars."

"No point," he kept his voice down. "She's out."

"How do you know?"

"I rang her. She's out. Said she doesn't want to be bothered tonight anyway. I think she's on a date."

"Oh."

"Look promise you won't ring her?"

"I won't."

"I'll pick you some chips up on the way home."

"You will?"

"Yes."

"Alright. Thank … "

Markus cut him off and then sat down.

"Who was that on the phone?" Aunt Tars said, sitting opposite her nephew. "You were very whispery."

"New girlfriend," Markus said casually, taking his first mouthful of food.

His aunt's face came alive. "Oooooh who's this then?"

"Just some girl."

"I know *that*," she said, sprinkling vinegar. "What's her name?"

Markus yawned and looked over at the TV again. "Carmen," he said.

"Carmen," she echoed. "Very exotic."

Markus shoved his fork into a fish finger. "What's exotic mean?"

The question floored Tars for a few moments and she had to think. "Means different," she said.

"Yeah," Markus said with his mouth full. "She is."

The two ate in silence for a bit. When Markus picked up the juice he looked at the coaster beneath. It was cream-coloured with pink lettering that read, *Enjoy the Little Things in Life.* He downed the juice and then covered it up again, the words magnified under the glass. Near the end of the meal Markus found his eyes surveying his aunt. He looked at her hands and her wrists, her arms and her neck. He looked at her face and then made a little cough.

"Banging the weight on a bit aren't you Tara?"

Markus only ever used her Christian name when he was making a point of something, when he was being cruel. Tars stopped eating her food and then stared at it. She closed her eyes and took in a breath, "thanks Markus."

Her tone was sharp and Markus shrugged.

An awkward silence passed.

"Don't you think I don't know I've put on weight?"

Markus shrugged a second time. "Don't know," he mumbled.

She put her knife and fork down delicately and looked at her nephew. "You're rude."

He wouldn't look back, kept his head down. "Truth innit," he said with a mouthful of fish finger.

"You don't have to say *everything* that's on your mind y'know? Some people do have *feelings*. Just cos you don't."

She picked her cutlery up and continued to eat, still shaking her head. Markus said nothing. He became aware of the ticking of the clock.

"Rude," she said again. "No manners. You come here and I feed you and all I get back is insults."

"Alright. Calm down."

Markus's face had gone a little white.

"You know what you are?"

He looked up, briefly.

"You're *a taker*. You take from people and give fuck all back."

Markus turned back to the telly. Those gay-boy One Direction lads were on. He watched them dance about and wondered which one was the hardest. I could fight them all, he thought, all at the same time.

Aunt Tars didn't finish her dinner. She took it into the kitchen and moments later Markus heard the drumming sound of chips being scraped into the bin.

I could have had those, he thought.

Aunt Tars had poured a glass of wine and was smoking out the window again. Markus had his coat on.

"Right Tars," she was facing the other way. "I'll get gone."

She never answered.

"Let myself out," he said.

At home Ryan had somehow got Dad onto the sofa. Most alcoholics go thin and weak, not Dad, still he maintained the physique of an aging rugby player. He lurched forward, swaying; his head in his hands. Markus looked at the red of his face and the blonde of his hair through his thick, ugly fingers.

"Get us a can, lad," he slurred.

Ryan's face opened with horror. "Dad, no. *Enough*."

"Get us a fucking can!" he howled.

"Dad, *please*."

Markus shook his head and marched to the fridge, pulled open the door and yanked out a can, cracked it and watched some of it spill on the carpet before putting it inside his dad's grip.

"Markus!" Ryan cried.

"Here. Drink it. Quicker you die the better."

Dad slurped hard at the beer and then rocked back with his eyes half-closed. "Watch your lip son or I'll ... "

"What?" Markus stood rigid, fists clenched and ready. "You'll what? You couldn't fight your way through smoke. You're a fucking embarrassment."

Ryan had already moved himself away.

"Call yourself a man."

His dad tried to get up but his legs wouldn't let him. Gravity pulled him down and laid him out on the threadbare carpet. The can toppled over and poured all over him, the more his dad clawed after it the more soaked he got. His hair was drenched in beer. Markus pointed at him and laughed. "That is so fucked up."

Markus couldn't stop laughing and Ryan couldn't stop crying. Before they knew it their dad was asleep again, snoring, dead to the world.

The brothers looked at each other and then at their dad. Ryan was drying his eyes with the back of his hand.

"You need to toughen up," Markus said. "This is the way it is."

His brother was snivelling. "We are what we are," he said in a tiny voice.

Markus stared at his dad, considering his brother's words. "Yeah. Suppose," he conceded.

Then,

"Well. That's me. I'm going bed."

"Markus," Ryan's voice was full of longing.

Markus stopped at the bottom of the stairs.

"My chips?"

"Oh," he said. "I forgot. But hey, there's a big one on my shoulder."

He pointed to his shoulder and smiled.

"But you said you'd get me some on the way home??"

"Like you said bro, *we are what we are*."

He winked and then disappeared.

Ten minutes later Markus got out the shower and dropped into bed without drying himself properly. It was still early and he wasn't even tired but that didn't matter. I'll lie here and lie here until I am. He thought about life, Liverpool, school, The Den. He thought about all the people he hated and what he wanted to do to them.

Most of all he thought about Carmen; Carmen, Carmen, Carmen.

The next day he saw her. She was on the top field by the Astroturf, surrounded by three lads. One had a hold of her bag and the other two were taunting her. When she tried to grab it he threw it to the next boy, and then he to the next. Carmen was distressed.

Markus was already running towards them, his fists and teeth clenched.

"Oi!" he was surprised by the depth of his own voice and how loud it sounded.

There was anger, but there was also a good feeling too. He felt alive and shiny and fast. He saw the word, *hero.*

He hit the bank and by the time he reached the top Carmen already had her bag back.

"Leave her alone," he roared. "Leave her the fuck alone!"

He could see his girl looking at him. Her slender figure stood against the periphery of his vision, arms-folded and curious. The boys had bunched together, preparing for some kind of defensive manoeuvre. Markus could take them apart and they knew it. He looked closely at their faces and saw that fear wasn't the only emotion there, confusion too, lots of it.

"Her?" said one.

"Leave *her* alone?"

The third one laughed and put his hand over his mouth.

Markus looked over and Carmen looked back only they weren't her eyes. They weren't striking and they weren't speckled. Nor were they green, but blue, blue and heavy, like a dopey puppy dog. Her lips didn't have the usual gloss and her hairstyle was different.

Markus tried to speak but he couldn't. Whatever he wanted to say got stuck in his throat and it was like a déjà vu of his German lesson, *heibe.* The bullies took advantage of this confusion and made a break for it – down the bank and gone, only a thin trail of noise leaking out behind them.

"Weirdo."

"Faggit."

"What the fuck was all that about?"

Markus was left alone with Carmen but it wasn't Carmen, it was someone else.

"Thanks."

The voice wasn't a girl one either but at the same time it wasn't

102

quite a boy. There were no words to say how freaked out Markus was right now.

"Bet you thought I was my sister didn't you, Carmen? Don't worry. It happens all the time. She's my twin."

He held out a smooth hand, "I'm Callum."

Markus was still in shock. Eventually he took the hand, the fingertips, and gave it the smallest of shakes. "And you are?"

The boy was smiling and Carmen never smiled and now the difference between them was startling.

"Markus," he said with a gulp.

The boy folded his arms and raised his eyes to the clouds. "Fucking hate this school."

"Me too," Markus replied, after a pause.

"We've got that much in common."

Despite his docile eyes the boy was bright, well-spoken, and like his twin owned an air of superiority which strangely excited him.

"Well," he said. "Better get gone. Don't wanna be late for *another class.*" He said 'another class' in this really dull and drawn-out voice, then he laughed and his laughter was kind of musical. Markus saw the word, *charm.*

He watched him skip down the bank and head across the football field. The further in the distance he walked, the more he looked like a girl, looked like Carmen.

Markus was happy to close the lid on this school day. He took off his tie and dropped into bed. He felt dirty and he didn't know why. He felt like he'd been cheated and there was a definite feeling of some kind of humiliation. He felt an overwhelming rush of violence towards Callum even though he hadn't really done anything wrong. He tried to work out if he still fancied Carmen and he decided that he did. In fact, if anything, the encounter intrigued him and made his girl *even* more of a mystery. *Twin.*

His head hurt and tension twisted in his neck and shoulders like knots and what he wanted to do, what he really, really wanted to do, was wait till dark and then go catch a cat.

Cats weren't hard to catch. They weren't hard to coax. But what cats were hard to do, cats were hard to kill. He only had to see the linage of the cat family to know that these creatures fought to the death, and fight to the death is what the first one did. It was a bloody mess and Markus didn't know what he was doing. He didn't know what he was doing because he hadn't planned it, hadn't prepared for it. He just found one in his arms one afternoon and then decided to murder it right then and there, kill it like he killed Mazie's guinea pig only you couldn't fit a cat into a P.E sock, it wasn't that simple. Three or four cats later though and Markus got the hang of it. He knew what he was doing. Markus knew what he was doing now. He had obtained a very sturdy, yet very thin piece of rope. With the help of Google he had learnt how to tie the perfect noose. Along with a weighted tip and a nearby footbridge the cat's neck nearly always broke instantly by the drop. If the noose wasn't fitted properly or if the cat was especially big and strong then Markus got to watch a show. He got to watch it fight for a while until eventually it would strangle itself to death. Markus didn't like cats. Markus didn't like cats because they told lies. They acted all cute and cuddly in front of a winter fire but they weren't like that in real life. In real life they were tortuous, sadistic bastards who got their kicks. So Markus got his kicks too. He looked at it as fairness, justice, karma. He was just putting himself in the food chain along with all the other beasts in the kingdom. *Food* chain. He wasn't eating the cat physically but he was feeding himself, feeding something else; a deeper, mysterious appetite. At this stage in his life Markus just saw it as a pastime. It was something he simply *did*. It relieved stress and felt good. He enjoyed the hunt, and the rewards it brought. Some kids played video games, some played football. His brother Ryan built model aeroplanes. Markus killed cats.

Cats weren't hard to catch, they weren't hard to coax. The way to catch them was simple. You had to catch them without looking like you were *trying* catch them. One whiff of an agenda and they were gone. Less was more. The more you searched the less you found. All you had to do was hold something sweet in your hand and they'll come. They always come in the end, eventually. People want pleasure, they want the promise of pleasure. And wanting is always more pleasing than having. *They* come to *you. People* come to *me.* Markus knew what he was doing.

Out of all the spare chairs in class Carmen chose the place next to him. Her perfume entered his world and he closed his eyes and breathed her in. His heartbeat quickened and he experienced an unusual rush of nerves. He really hoped her twin brother had told her all about his heroics. Through the lesson she never looked at him or showed any signs that he was there, yet he imagined there was an invisible chord, linking his mind to hers. He tried to send her words, messages.

Look at me. You're so sexy. I love you.

Markus Venner felt like this was his first love, his first true desire. *Carmen,* his mind whispered.

She looked at him and frowned. Looked at him like shit, but she had looked at him when he had told her to. It was a sign, a sign to speak to her now, at last.

He didn't want to think about it too much because the words will get stuck in his throat like they always did, *heibe* …

"Carmen," he said it out loud this time and she looked over. "You're Carmen, yeah?"

She nodded.

"Got a twin brother called Callum aint ya?"

He was aware of how common he sounded; how common he was.

She nodded again.

"Did he tell you about me? I'm Markus."

He wanted to say more but he couldn't, he'd come far enough.

She nodded her head, barely, only just. Markus felt a sudden bolt of electricity in his gut.

She knows who I am and that's why she's sat where she's sat.

Gladness was all over him. He wanted to yell from the top of his voice. Instead he waited until the class was over and then followed her, hung back and followed her, out the year block and through the library, up to the tennis courts towards the main entrance. He was going to follow her home like he did with Mazie Vickers but something told him not to.

You had to catch them without looking like you were trying to catch them.

He stopped and let her go, but two minutes later he found what he was looking for. Callum toned down his strut as he walked past the football team. He folded his arms and lowered his head, only to throw it back up when he heard his name being called.

"Callum!"

The energy of Markus took him aback. The last time they met he was so awkward, so sullen. He reminded Callum of a sulky kid. It's like he couldn't have got away quick enough, Callum thought, and now here he is, greeting me like a long-lost friend.

"How are you Callum?"

"My hero," he joked, "how are *you*?"

Callum had a slow, deep voice.

"Alright mate. Hey, I was wondering if you wanted to hang-out sometime?"

"Really?" Callum said, doubtful and surprised.

"Really," Markus was nodding his head. "See I'm like you, no friends."

Callum pulled a face. "I have friends. Just not *here*." He looked around at the school like it was a dumpsite.

"Right," Markus said.

The boy didn't look right and Callum didn't trust it. His speech seemed false, mechanical. He looked over his shoulder to see if anyone else was watching. He had this down as some kind of prank. When he realised it wasn't he began to blush with excitement. His eyes were wet.

"Yeah," he said, trying to act casual. "What did you have in mind?"

"I dunno. McDonald's."

"McDonald's?" Callum echoed with a snobby laugh. "Okay...let's do numbers."

When Callum took out his phone Markus noticed he wore nail varnish, but like it had been rubbed off.

Callum watched his eyes as the little rogue punched in his number.

"Wanna drop call me?"

"What?"

"Ring me so I have your number too."

"Oh. Okay."

He did and now both phone numbers had been exchanged.

"Okay then Markus, I'll see you around."

"You will."

Markus watched him walk away, only this time he didn't look like Carmen, as much.

Markus was going to give it *exactly* two days before texting Callum, to the hour. Only the boy beat him to it, by literally minutes. Markus found this strange and he wondered if the twins had some kind of telepathic power. There seemed to be a magic in the air which Markus couldn't put his finger on.

Callum asked if he was free to hook up today and Markus said, *yeah.* It was Saturday. Callum asked what he wanted to do and again Markus suggested McDonald's. Callum replied with *lol* and Markus couldn't understand why that was so funny. Callum told him to meet in Starbucks in an hour but Markus didn't know where that was and again Callum said *lol.* He then went onto give him directions and Markus took photos in his head. He was going to suggest bringing his sister but held back. *They* come to *you.*

Okay C U there.

Markus didn't recognise Callum until he was about an inch away. He wore glasses and a scarf and looked about eighteen year's old. Markus wore trainers and joggers and a hoodie. His hair was massive and needed cutting but he barely had any money. Even today was going to be tough. He could just about afford one drink.

"Hi," Callum sang. He tossed the scarf over his shoulder and laughed nervously.

Markus couldn't help notice Callum look him up and down and that got him mad.

"Wanna go inside?"

Markus nodded. He'd never been Starbucks because he didn't like hot drinks and really it was a place where adults went. He didn't even know what drinks they had or how you ordered them. Callum was already in the queue, adjusting his glasses, studying the menu on the back wall over the counter. The coffee machines whistled and screamed and bucked. Markus looked around in a kind of trance.

"What do you want?" Callum asked.

"I'll just have a coke."

Again Callum laughed and Markus didn't understand why he kept laughing at normal, everyday things that just weren't funny.

"You need to get one from the fridge."

"What?"

"The bottles are over in the fridge."

"Oh."

Markus grabbed one and walked back through the queue, feeling self-conscious like he was pushing in. Callum took it off him and then placed it on a brown tray.

He then gave his order.

"Can I get a skinny latte with soy milk."

What the fuck did he just say?

They then asked Callum for his name and that really confused him. Markus didn't have a clue what was going on and he was totally spun-out.

Moments later they shouted out his name, "Callum."

And then gave him his *whatever-drink-that-was-called.*

Callum led him through the busy Saturday afternoon crowd and at last they found a corner seat in the window, "is anyone sitting here?"

Two women shook their heads and moved a chair out of the way for him.

Markus was amazed at his confidence and how easy he was around adults. He felt completely out of his depth. Markus always thought he was ahead of his years but this was another level. Markus was streetwise and could play adults, to a certain degree, whereas Callum actually felt like an adult, like he was one of them. Markus opened his coke bottle and wondered if Carmen was the same, mature, too mature.

"So, here we are," Callum said, clapping his hands.

"Yeah," Markus said.

Callum suddenly found him to be the boy he met on the grass bank, confused, distracted, withdrawn.

"Good to be out of school, hey?"

"Yeah."

"So glad we got two weeks bank hols. *Bliss.*"

Markus had forgotten about that. Good job he mentioned it or he may have rocked-up to an empty school.

"Hate school," Callum said.

"Me too."

Callum ripped open two packets of brown sugar and tipped them into his coffee like a chute. He slowly stirred while looking out the window.

"Although," he said, blowing steam off his beverage before taking a sip. "You have saved me from a lot of trouble."

Markus gulped his coke and sat forward, "what do you mean?"

"People leave me alone now."

"How's that?"

"Because I'm connected to you."

"What?"

"They associate *me* with *you* so they stay away. You have quite a reputation you know? People *are* scared of you."

Markus got a rush to the head and felt some of his control come back. He sat up and smiled a touch.

"They think you're a psycho. You do know there's a ridiculous rumour going around that you butchered Mazie Vickers's pet guinea pig, and then displayed it on her porch?"

Markus let out an unvetted burst of laugher, "what?!"

It was the cage actually. She hasn't got a porch.

Callum held up the palms. Markus noticed how long his fingers were. "I know, right?" Now he really did look like a girl. "I don't mind," he mused. "The more outrageous the rumours, the more fear you generate, and the more fear you generate, the more they leave me alone. Fact. Only the other day two chavs came to pick on me and one said to the other, *Markus Venner looks after him, leave it.* It's so cool. It's like I have my own private bodyguard."

Not knowing what to say or think, Markus shook his head and gazed out the window. A funny-looking woman was trying to control a dog on a lead. It nearly pulled her over. Her two kids were walking about ten paces behind. They looked embarrassed.

"I bet your sis knows all about this as well, don't she?" he said, taking a sip of coke, feeling nervous again.

"No," Callum said flippantly, his voice going high. "I don't really tell her much."

Markus felt a stone drop. He tried to keep the disappointment out his face.

"What's the deal with you two anyway?" he went on. "I never see you together. Don't you ever talk?"

"We don't need to," Callum took his glasses off and leaned forward, making his eyes big. "We're the same person," he said, all spooky and mysterious.

They stayed for another hour and laughed the whole time. Callum said he was *off his head on caffeine* and Markus said that the coke had given him a sugar-rush too. At the bus stop Callum gave him a hug goodbye and Markus didn't think it was weird or anything. It wasn't like hugging a boy, but more like hugging one of his girl cousins or something.

"See you on Monday."

"No you won't," Callum sang, getting on the bus. "Bank holiday, remember?"

Markus smiled. "Hey thanks for paying for the drinks. I owe you."

Callum swung out the bus door like he was in a pantomime. "You can buy next time bodyguard."

Markus shook his head and thought he was crazy.

Callum's company had been like a drug, and when Markus came-down from it he felt a little low and depressed. He also felt a weird kind of guilt and he didn't know why. It was that dirty, tricked, cheated feeling again and Markus wanted to rid himself of it, so he went to Graffiti Square in the estate to see if any of the lads were knocking about. It was Saturday night and there was normally a big game on. The sides had already been picked and the match was just about to kick-off. Several beer bottles had been smashed over the gravel and everyone helped kick the scattered glass to the side. Raph who organised the games told him to 'pick a team' so Markus looked for the side which had the least amount of Man U shirts. He imagined his dad's face if he saw him passing the ball to the enemy. *Scum.* Markus wore a Liverpool top that was three seasons old and two sizes too big. On the back the number 8 had faded and half of the second R from the word GERRARD had peeled off. Markus preferred playing football with these lads than the kids at school because they were older and bigger and he could get stuck-in. Sometimes it got heated and they'd be a scuffle. If both parties wanted to take it further a ring was formed and they'd fight it out. So far Markus had been involved in three, two wins and the third was a draw against a much older black kid who wore an Arsenal top. They were mates now though.

Tonight there was none of that. The weather was getting better and the nights longer and there was a nice buzz around the game. Markus's team lost but in the last minute he scored a sweet free-kick from outside the box.

His mate Alex high-fived him after the game. "Check out David Beckham."

"Hey," Markus said. "Don't call me that Man U scum."

Alex put his hands up and shrugged. A few of the others were squirting water bottles down their necks and taking off shin pads. Another lad Kirk came over.

"Alright Venner?"

"Alright," Markus nodded.

Markus didn't like Kirk. He had a rep as being a bit of a snake, always shit-stirring and looking for gossip.

"Heard you offered-out The Taylor Bros."

Everyone turned and looked, eager to hear more.

Markus spat out a string of spit. "Where you hear that?"

"Heard you went round accusing them of nicking your bike."

"Man, mind your own business."

Kirk stepped back and stood sideways on. Markus saw the word, *jackal*.

"You should be careful," he said. "Stewie's fucking crazy. He'll shoot you, man. Don't let that friendly way of his fool you. He'll put a bullet in the back of your head."

Others watched on, their faces in agreement. Markus looked at them all and scowled, turning his attention back to Kirk. "Fuck him. Fuck life. I don't care if I die."

He looked back at the faces. Some were impressed. Some looked confused, others a little disturbed. He could tell they wanted a punchline so he gave them one.

"I'll eat his fucking heart."

Kirk smiled and shook his head. "Maybe you're the one who's crazy."

Markus held his eye until he looked away first. "Maybe I am."

The exchange had darkened the mood and he could tell the rest of the lads didn't want to be around him for much longer.

"Fuck it," he said.

He turned and left them to it. Behind his back he could just about hear them whispering about him as he walked out of Graffiti Square. He quite liked it.

Thoughts of Carmen kept him awake that night, all night. Mostly fantasies, fantasies about saving her from danger. He played them out in his insomniac head. Diving under an icy lake, pulling her to safety before giving her the kiss of life. Or jumping into a burning house when all other firefighters had tried and failed. His favourite one though was when terrorists hijacked the school, taking Carmen hostage. The SWAT team and negotiators were getting ready but Markus would beat them to it, sneaking under the police tape and heading towards her. He'd move through the corridors by commando roll, checking each classroom, looking for his girl. At last he'd see one of the armed terrorists and he'd take cover by diving into the cookery room, where he'd take one of the knives and then return to his mission. At last he'd find her.

Carmen would have a gag in her mouth and tears down her face, her eyes widening with fear on seeing Markus. Because of their telepathy he'd see the words in her head. *Markus. No. It's too dangerous.* But Markus would pounce on the terrorist's back, sticking the knife through his neck. He'd wiggle the blade about, spraying the classroom in blood. Some of it may get on Carmen but she wouldn't mind because her man had saved her. He'd play that scene over and over. He'd picture everything down to its finest detail. How her parents would thank him, take him out to dinner; give him loads of money. He'd picture the news reports and the medal ceremonies. Most of all he'd picture how Carmen would want to spend the rest of her life with her hero.

Markus thought about this for so long and hard he got depressed when he snapped out of it and realised that none of it was real.

In the morning his phone woke him up. His eyes sore and stingy as he reached out and picked it up.

"Hello."

Markus was so tired he hadn't even looked at the name on the screen.

"You asleep?"

"Was."

He knew the voice, just not the person who owned it.

"Want me to call you back later?"

Markus closed his eyes and then opened them again. Yawned and took a mouthful of coke from his bedside table. "Who is this?"

A pause. "I'm deeply shocked Markus."

Who was this? No one he knew talked like this. *Deeply shocked.* He pulled the phone away from his ear and looked at the name in the top-left-hand corner of the screen, *Callum.*

He rubbed his eyes and sat up. "Callum. Sorry just waking up."

"I gathered," his voice sounded like Carmen's even though he'd barely heard her speak. He *felt* her voice would be like that. *I gathered.*

"Look I'll call you back."

"I'm awake," Markus said, taking another swallow of coke.

"Okay," Callum said. He seemed to be breathing heavy. "Okay," he repeated. He sounded like he was building himself up to something. "I know we only saw each other yesterday but I thought we had a laugh."

Markus was now upright in bed, patting down his *good head of hair.* "Yeah we had a laugh," he agreed.

"I thought there was a spark."

"A spark?"

Markus didn't really know what that meant although he'd heard it before, *spark.* Maybe he'd heard adults say it, like on telly, like in the soaps or something.

"Forget it," Callum said dramatically. "I'm making this way too complicated."

"Callum what the fuck you on about?"

"Do you want to come over to my house on Friday?"

Markus instantly saw the image of Carmen's face. It blazed like fire from a match, briefly, and then went away again. He gulped and sat up even more. He was almost kneeling. "Your house?"

"Yeah my family have this really cheesy tradition. *Film Food Friday* we call it. The name is pretty self-explanatory."

Markus wished he'd talk normal. He didn't understand anything.

"Yeah does what it says on the tin," Callum sang. "We eat, we watch a film, and we do it on Friday."

"Oh. Okay," Markus was getting there. "So you want me to come over and watch a film and I'll get fed?"

Callum let out another one of those belittling sniggers. "Pretty much."

"Alright. Yeah," Markus was scratching his bum-hole with his thumb.

"We all kind of take it in turns to choose a film."

It was Markus's turn to laugh. "That's so gay."

There was a deadly pause on the other side but Markus didn't seem to notice. "So whose turn is it this time?"

"Carmen's. She always chooses something arty and weird so brace yourself."

Hearing her name got him a little crazy and he had a flashback from last night: The knife in the terrorist's neck. Carmen running into his arms.

"So you'll come?" Callum's voice went up, and hung with hope.

"Yeah," Markus said.

"Cool. Well I'll text you my address later on in the week."

"Alright."

"I look forward to seeing you."

"Alright. See you at school."

"Markus!"

"What?"

"You keep forgetting. *Bank holiday.*"

"Oh, yeah."

Callum laughed and hung up.

Markus was nervous for the rest of the week. It wasn't a feeling he was used to. He was going to see Carmen and it had to be done right, *all* right. He needed to be at his best and look his best. Markus wanted to be handsome and mature. He needed a haircut although he had no money whatsoever. He thought about tapping Aunt Tars up only she had given him way too much already and squeezing anymore out of her would be near impossible. *Hmm.* He went into his brother's room and nicked a handful of DVD's. *Transformers, Spiderman 3, Dumb and Dumber,* that Christmas film *Polar Express* and two of those *Twilight* films. I'll take these to the pawn shop later today, he thought, probably get a tenner for the lot. That should sort my haircut out. Next he needed something to wear. The only shirts he had were school ones and an old checked one that was ripped under the armpit. Maybe Ryan will have a spare although he's a bit too skinny these days. Or perhaps dad has one that doesn't fit him anymore? We'll see.

On the Wednesday a text came through with an address. It was in the posh end of town but Markus expected as much. He had to be there for seven o clock in the evening. He was going to ask his dad for a lift but he'd only be too pissed to drive so Markus went on foot.

He was going to zig-zag the streets and cut through the estate only he decided to take the scenic route, walk alongside the Clementine Channel. The sunset will look pleasant on the water and it will be romantic.

Put him in the mood.

Markus could smell his own aftershave as he got nearer to the address and panicked that maybe he'd splashed on a little too much. Licking the palm of his hand he tried to wipe some of it off. He then went to pat down his *good head of hair* but realised there wasn't much of it left. This got him worried as it had made him look drastically younger. *Hmm.* It'll have to do.

He took out his phone and looked at the text Callum had sent, making sure the address matched the one on the road sign, Lake

Hill Lane. He liked those words and the way they sounded on his lips, almost like it could be in a song. *Lake Hill Lane.* He walked down it. The road was covered in smooth, shiny cobbles and Markus enjoyed the sound of his heels clacking against them. In his mind he saw squares of hard chocolate being snapped and dropped into a bowl. It was the same sound, *snap, clack.* On the brow of the hill an old-fashioned phone box stood under a tree. It was red like the ones they had in London in the olden days. He looked inside and saw no phone. Nobody used it but Markus figured it must be like some kind of ornament. He was surprised no one had smashed it up by now.

Markus got to the house. Again he double-checked that the number on his text corresponded with the one on the front door. It was a black and white, semi-detached that was partially obscured by a tree. It sat back at an angle, horizontal facing, which made it look like a moving arrow, sharp and fast and at the same time slightly confrontational. Markus walked onto it and used the heavy knocker in the centre of the door, which echoed through the house. A few seconds later he heard movement on the other side, footsteps and a key. When it opened he saw Carmen and his heart stopped.

Only the boyish voice broke the illusion yet again.

"Callum?" he muttered.

The face smiled and again Carmen couldn't look any further away.

Callum went red so he put his head down and his black hair flopped forward. "You made it?" he said.

"Why wouldn't I?" Markus replied, pulling a smiley screw-face.

"Come in," Callum said.

A huge, echoing hallway took him in and Markus looked up at the ceilings and the beams that joined them. The house was far bigger than the exterior portrayed.

"Nice place," Markus said.

He thought about his own shit-hole and an anger/envy feeling stuck in his gut.

Callum wrapped his slim body around the banister at the bottom of the stairs. "You look smart."

Markus looked down at his dad's shirt, "thanks."

"Haircut too."

Markus nodded and looked at his host. Callum seemed to be in a daydream, like he was making his mind up about something.

Suddenly he snapped out of it and changed his tone, doing that *making-his-eyes-big* thing. "Mum and dad are out shopping, picking up a few bits."

"Sister?"

"She's upstairs, in her room, where she practically spends her *entire* existence."

Markus pictured her naked on the bed. Lying on her front reading a magazine. Her legs up in the air, locked at the ankles, licking her thumb as she turns a page.

"Markus!" Callum clicked his fingers in front of his face. "I said did you find it alright?"

"What?"

"The house?"

"Well I'm here aren't I?"

Callum smiled and lead him through the lounge and into a kitchen. The house was covered in books, books on shelves and on the floor, books by the sofa and on coffee tables. Kitchen full of books. There was lots of painted black wood and exposed brick and stone, yet the interiors were warmed by reds and orange. A big African rug covered the floor. Markus had never seen a house quite like it. It was like he was in another country, or had stepped back in time, or forwards perhaps.

"Drink?"

"Coka Cola."

When Callum laughed Markus decided now was the time to call him out on it.

"Why do you laugh when I say things?"

There was a certain strength to his tone that put Callum on edge.

He took that smile off his face. "Sorry. What do you mean?" He tried innocence but it didn't come across. Markus had sniffed him out.

"You know what I'm talking about." Markus was leaning on the lime-coloured kitchen wall. Under his head was a framed Oscar Wilde picture with a quote reading: *we are all in the gutter, but some of us are looking at the stars.* "You laugh when I say certain things and I don't get it. Like when I say coke or McDonald's you laugh."

Callum was a little flustered but he tried to maintain his adult way. "Oh Markus I'm not laughing *at* you, just *with* you."

"I still don't get it?"

"It's just your little ways. Anyway," he said, changing the subject.

"We don't have fizzy drinks here. What about juice?"

Callum knew that Markus was staring him out, "whatever."

Markus moved his eyes at last and carried on looking around, studying the house. He wandered back into the lounge and picked up a pink book with a woman's face on it. It was a cartoon face with blonde hair.

He read the title and said it under his breath, "The Bell Jar."

Callum came in with the juice. "Oh. That's what my sister's reading for like the tenth time," he said, nodding at the book in Markus's hands. "Bit depressing."

"Doesn't look depressing," Markus said.

"Trust me, it is."

"What's it about?"

"Suicide."

"Oh."

"And you don't get more depressing than that."

"I'm going to commit suicide."

"What?" Callum stopped and made an o-face with his mouth.

"I've decided. When I'm thirty."

"Why?"

"Who wants to get old?"

"Thirty's not old."

"To me it is."

Callum wanted to laugh but stopped himself. He was then going to ask Markus if he read but stopped himself with that one too. Instead he sat next to him and said, "I had a dream about you last night."

He handed Markus the juice and caught his eye.

"Oh," Markus said, disinterested.

"It was a weird dream and I don't actually remember it but I know you were there."

Markus didn't say anything, just put the book down and took a sip of juice.

"Ever get that?"

"What?"

"Weird dreams you don't remember?"

Markus was staring at the old grandfather clock in the corner of the room. "I don't dream."

"What?" This time Callum did laugh, a small one.

"I don't dream."

"C'mon. Everybody has dreams."

"Not everybody. Not me."

Just then the door sounded and two adults walked into the room.

Callum stood but Markus remained where he was. He wanted to laugh because he couldn't believe how much the parents looked like their kids. Nose, hair, colouring. The works. Not just similar but exact, *dead on*. Like if you put a thousand adults in a room and you had to pick the parents you'd do it in a second. What was freaky is that they looked like each other too, as if mum and dad were twins themselves and this was the product of incest.

Weird shit, he thought.

"Hello," they both said at the same time.

At last Markus did stand and shook their hands. "Markus Venner," he said.

Callum found it strange the way he said his name in full, almost like they should know who he was. As if he was a famous person, or, a *notorious* person. Callum was hit with a flash, like he had made a grave mistake bringing this boy into their home. The feeling passed and everything soon became normal again.

As for Markus he very rarely acknowledged the good in people but he recognised it in them. Right from the off they made him feel welcome. Everything about them was natural and friendly and warm. Somehow Callum drifted into the background as the parents talked while putting the shopping away. They were posh but not snobby, Markus thought. They didn't seem to judge and were actually more down-to-earth than their offspring. Mum talked a little more than dad, but dad was cool too. He smiled a lot and kept asking if Markus wanted anything.

"You hungry?" he said.

"Well dinner is ready now anyway," Mum interjected.

From nowhere a table was set and food was being put down, drinks, condiments, candles, and napkins. Markus had been talking so much he hadn't noticed it. It was as if it had all just appeared miraculously, like a magic trick.

Callum had put music on, some easy listening stuff that Markus would normally find boring, but which seemed to fit the atmosphere of this occasion.

"Where's Carmen?" one of the parents said.

"Upstairs, where do you think?" Callum said in a bored tone.

He was sitting on the sofa with his legs thrown over the arm.

"Go and knock her Cal, tell her dinner's nearly ready."

Callum jumped up and headed for the stairs. Markus got an instant case of dry-mouth, his palms got clammy and thoughts felt thick in his head.

"Is there anything I can do?" he said, trying to keep his voice steady.

"No," his dad said with a smile. "You just relax."

He tried to relax but couldn't. "Can I use the toilet?"

"Of course," his mum said, washing her hands. "Just over there." She pointed to a small door at the back of the kitchen.

In the bathroom mirror Markus didn't like what looked back. His hair was way too short and he looked about ten. Next to this Jewish family his skin was too pale too. He looked like what American's called *white trash*. An estate kid who ate too many chips and drank too much coke. His eyes were ringed with insomnia and his nose looked sore. His broken home lived in his face. He felt crude and dumb and he knew he didn't belong here, and although these people were probably the loveliest adults he'd ever met there was a part of him that wanted to destroy them, destroy it all, the table, the house, their faces, their lives.

Markus took a deep breath and tried to calm himself.

He walked back out and expected to see Carmen waiting for him but she wasn't.

"Where is *that* girl?" Dad said.

"She said she'll be down in a minute."

"If I had a pound for every time she said that I'd be a millionaire."

"A lifetime of minutes," Mum said, laughing.

"*A lifetime of minutes,*" Callum pondered. "Sounds like the title of a novel."

The four of them took seat at the table and waited for the fifth who was going to be *down in a minute*. Markus was about to tuck into the food but then realised the other's weren't. They were patiently waiting on Carmen. Markus noted how calm and civilised they were. If that was his own dad he would probably have smashed the table up by now and dragged her out the room.

They waited.

The stairs were facing him, wooden steps that cut across his field of vision. All of a sudden he heard a door open and close, followed by footsteps. The footsteps were soft and Markus pictured bare, brown feet on the carpet. A smooth, shapely foot with cute toes. She got closer, and closer. Then he saw her, a foot; a leg. He was wrong; she was wearing socks, pinks ones with white stripes. With each step she got longer and longer, the rest of her leg, her hips, her waist, torso, head. She moved like so many times before at school, slow and erect, insolent and disinterested in the world.

"The hermit arrives."

Markus didn't know what *hermit* meant. Most of the words this family used he didn't know the meaning of. Carmen didn't look at him, but he didn't feel singled-out because she didn't look at anybody and the family didn't seem to mind. It's like they just accepted that it was *her* way.

It was time to eat. Only the layout of the food and the food itself confused him. He didn't know what to do or even what the food was. There was chicken, he knew that, then there were all kinds of weird salads and veg and sauces and stuff. He'd never experienced this style of self-service before and it was a little intimidating. How much to take and in what order? Normally it was a tray of chips or a dollop of mash on a plate and you were good to go. In the end he watched Callum and then just copied him exactly, what he ate, Markus ate.

"Markus could you pass me the dressing?"

All eyes were on him and the boy panicked. He didn't know what *dressing* was. He spied around the table a little frantically, his hand poised in no-man's-land.

"It's okay," Callum smiled. He leaned over and reached out for a little bottle of something.

Markus felt his flesh go red. He looked around the table for a reaction but there wasn't one. No one had noticed.

For the next few minutes there was silence, just the tinkering of cutlery and Markus wondered if this was custom, but then Dad cleared his throat and spoke.

"So what do your parents do Markus?"

Markus looked down at a forkful of food, some of it slowly unravelled and fell back on his plate. "My mum's a nurse," he said.

"Oh," his dad said, nodding, maybe impressed.

"Is that at Central Hospital?" his mum asked.

"Er, yeah, it is," he said.

"And my dad's a driver," he said. "Like he drives wedding cars. You know, takes people to church and weddings and stuff."

"Really?" his dad said, definitely impressed. "Never met anyone who does that before."

Markus lifted his eyes and looked at the siblings who were sat next to each other. Callum had his head down and Carmen seemed to be looking right at him but not quite, her eyes just a little bit off to the left. Markus realised this was the first time he had seen the twins together, in the same room. It was trippy, almost like an optical illusion. It hurt his eyes.

They ate on in more silence. Callum and dad starting talking about something but Markus didn't understand what the topic was. Again there were far too many words that Markus simply didn't understand. Near the end his mum spoke up, bringing Markus back into the conversation. "Callum tells us that you're somewhat of a hero?"

At first Markus didn't know what she was talking about, then he did. It got him embarrassed and he couldn't believe how open this family was. It's like they talked about *everything*. No stone unturned.

"It was nothing," he said.

Markus had his head down and his voice was small, like he'd been chastised at school.

"Modesty is an admirable trait," Dad said.

Again Markus had no clue what any of that meant.

"We don't condone any form of violence in this family," Dad went on. "Insinuated violence or actual. Violence should only ever exist in the world of books and films. But, art imitates life so we're obviously not naïve to the fact that it does happen from time to time. History is made up of it and life suffers from it endlessly."

Markus was trying to cut some chicken but his knife was too blunt.

"We're what you call pacifists Markus," his dad said. "And for that we're at a massive disadvantage because sometimes in this wicked world *it* is brought to *us*. And it's then that we should be thankful of people like you."

Markus listened to the words but he didn't get them. At first he thought he was being told off but his dad was smiling so he guessed it was okay.

"So, thank *you* Markus for defending our son," his dad said with a nod.

Markus nodded back.

"See, we're not much of a physical family when all said and done."

"Oh I don't know," Mum said. "Carmen's as strong as an ox ... Lincolnshire gymnastics champion remember?"

Markus shot his eyes up at her.

"Runner up," Callum quickly corrected.

Maybe Carmen did smile this time, a small smile.

Dinner was finished and all the plates were empty. Callum went to put some more music on but Dad told him not to bother as they'll be watching the film soon.

"Thank you," Markus said. "That was delicious." He had purposefully used the word *delicious* because it was kind of long and maybe a bit fancy.

"Want me to help with the pots?" he added.

"Oh no Markus that's what the dishwasher is for. You go sit in the lounge. Put your feet up. Relax."

Markus did that and Callum followed him.

"They like you," he whispered excitedly in his ear.

"Oh," Markus said.

Some minutes later the rest of the family joined the lounge. The curtains were closed and candles lit. Even though they'd just eaten a tray of snacks were placed in the centre of the room. Markus got up and grabbed a chocolate bar.

"Where's Carmen disappeared to?" Mum said.

"Gone to get the film, probably," Callum said.

"Oh no," Dad made a face. "It's not *her* turn is it? You'll have to excuse this Markus Carmen always chooses the most peculiar films."

"Do you like films Markus?" Mum said.

He was licking the chocolate off the biscuit part. "Yeah I quite like horrors. I mean I quite like those *Saw* films. They're pretty sick."

Dad's eyes went small and creases appeared on his forehead. "I don't believe I know those."

"You won't," Callum said.

"Whose turn was it last Friday?" Mum said.

"Mine," Callum said. "We watched *Good Will Hunting,* remember?"

"Oh yes I liked that one," she said, sitting down.

Markus sat up. "Is that about killing animals?"

Callum and Dad looked at him, "what?"

"Hunting. Is it about killing animals?"

Callum noticed how excited he looked and it scared him a little. He remembered the rumours about Mazie Vickers and her guinea pig.

"On no," Dad said, laughing. "It's about a poor boy who sneaks into a top university and starts solving mathematical problems that have been left on the wall."

Markus thought it sounded boring and dad carried on talking about it. Only he wasn't listening because his attention had been taken over, taken over *completely*. Carmen walked into the lounge wearing shorts, tapping a DVD against her thigh.

"Okay what cinematic delights do you have for us this time Lady Carmen?"

Markus felt light-headed and he couldn't take his eyes off her legs. He'd never seen her legs before and they looked incredible. They were long and smooth and brown. She was a gymnast and it all made sense.

Dad took the DVD from her and read the cover. "Heavenly Creatures," he said.

"Oh no not that," Callum said. "The end is gross."

"Shush," said mum. "No spoilers."

Dad read more from the back. "So this is Peter Jackson pre-Hollywood?"

Carmen was nodding.

"And Kate Winslet pre-Titanic?"

Carmen nodded again.

"Looks good."

Carmen turned on her heels and fell back next to Markus. She put her leg up. Her calf muscle stuck-out and Markus could feel himself getting aroused so he repositioned himself. On her leg was the most beautiful troop of freckles, they looked like chocolate drops. There was a big one in the middle that reminded Markus of an eye. It was looking right at him.

Callum was looking right at him too. He was looking at Carmen with eyes of hate. She had stolen his place and he had to sit on the opposite side of the room, away from Markus. The lights were lowered and the DVD was put in. The menu page came on, a pale blue picture with an image of two girls next to each other. Markus hoped it was going to be a horror. Something with blood and guts in at least. He hoped it wasn't going to be loads of talking cos he hated films like that.

Just then a cat jumped up at him from nowhere and Markus almost leapt out his skin.

"What the fuck!"

Everyone laughed.

Markus was surprised the language didn't offend them. "Sorry," he said.

They delayed the film to watch him play with their house pet.

"Ahh bless," Mum said. "He likes *you*."

The cat rubbed the contours of its body under his palm. Markus could feel a weak pulse throb against his forefinger.

"You got a cat at home Markus?" Dad said.

Markus shook his head, "nah."

"You seem very natural with them."

He was trying to stare into the cat's eyes but the creature wouldn't look back. "I mean I don't have an *actual* cat as a pet but I spend a lot of time with them."

The mum and dad glanced at each other, a little puzzled at his comment.

"What's its name?" Markus said, cupping the back of its head.

He felt the room get slightly offended by the objectifying *it*.

"Cassy," Callum said walking over, reaching out to stroke the cat in his lap.

"*His* name is Cassius," Carmen corrected, sternly. She was pouting. Her eyes were so wide and green. Markus wondered if that was the first full sentence he had ever heard her say.

The cat remained on his lap. Markus could feel its little skull in the cup of his hand. He stroked it really hard, scraping back its scalp and face and ears until bones appeared. Apart from Carmen who was impatiently staring at the screen, the rest of the family winced. They looked at each other disturbed. Markus did it again and one of them wanted to say something.

But, they didn't.

The film was crap. Markus hated it and couldn't wait for it to end. Occasionally he would look over at Carmen in the dark. His eyes traced over her long, long leg and Markus saw the word, *river*.

The film went on and on. It was about lesbians and the only good bit was at the end when they caved the mother's head in with a rock. That was quite cool. Other than that it was the worst film he had ever seen and he couldn't understand why everyone loved it.

"Very moody."

"I'd say *edgy* rather than moody."

"Great tension, you could really feel how obsessive love spirals out of control."

"Great choice Carmen."

Markus rolled his eyes and figured he must have missed something. They must have sensed this because they never asked him his opinion. The cat had remained in his lap the whole time yet once the film was over Dad clicked his fingers and put him outside.

"Midnight already," Mum said, slight panic in her voice "Oh my Markus I'm so sorry your Mum must be worried sick. I hope you've texted her."

"I have," he said. "She's cool."

Mum and dad were looking at each other, like they were trying to communicate without speech. Markus picked up a slight nod of the head from mum and then dad cleared his throat.

"Would you like to stay the night Markus?"

Callum bolted up in his chair. He looked at Markus and Markus looked at Carmen and Carmen as always showed no reaction at all.

"Well ... "

Callum's eyes went crazy-mad, like Markus was about to decide whether the world should end.

"Well yeah if you don't mind. Thanks."

Dad nodded and Callum dropped back into his chair and smiled.

"I'll put the kettle on. Tea or coffee Markus?"

Markus didn't have hot drinks because that's what adults have but there was a first time for everything.

"Coffee," he said. "No, tea, I think."

When he looked up Carmen had magically gone. The room suddenly felt empty and he wanted to go home. He saw the word, *wound*.

Tea was crap and he couldn't understand why adults drank it. You had to wait ages for it to cool and then it tasted boring. It was just like warm water but a different colour.

"You shouldn't really drink coffee before you go to bed Callum. You'll never sleep."

"I'll be fine. No school tomorrow anyway. Another week off. *Bliss*."

Markus thought Callum had started acting weird all of a sudden and he didn't know why. He was fidgety and strange. He kept looking over at Markus like he knew a secret about something. His parents were *still* talking only Markus was bored by it now. Their attention had lost its charm and Markus had switched off. He noticed his bad mood had arrived since the departure of Carman. The only real reason he was in this stupid place was because of her. Now she was gone it made no sense.

He put the mug down and yawned.

"Tired?" one of them asked.

Instinctively he almost answered with "fucked," but stopped himself.

He nodded instead.

"Well we have a guest room or we can make you a bed up in Callum's? Totally your choice."

The way they talked was starting to irritate him. At the beginning of the evening he quite liked the calm and politeness of it all, how nobody swore or shouted and how everyone got a chance to speak, only now it seemed flat and humourless. There was no emotion, no *umph*. It's like you didn't know what they were truly thinking, or feeling. It seemed, Markus felt, fake.

"The spare is cool," he said, yawning again, hoping to hurry all this along.

Straight away he felt is mate deflate. Callum shrank back into the chair, hurt.

"Okay," Dad said. "It's already made up. So ready when you are."

All of a sudden Markus knew who his dad reminded him of now. He reminded him of that man from *The Simpsons,* the next-door neighbour who was always saying cheesy things. Markus smiled to himself and shook his head.

The family headed to bed. "Night Markus. Callum will show you the way. Let him know if you need anything."

By now Markus was even past saying *thanks.* "Right," he grunted.

Upstairs was even bigger than down, there were two more floors and Callum lead him to the top. Doors were all over the place and Markus wondered which one Carmen was behind. Callum opened one to a black room full of posters and books.

"Here we are."

Markus stood still and looked him over. "Thought I was staying in the spare?"

A blush rinsed through Callum's face and his hands got busy, picking imaginary lint off his t-shirt. "I mean, you can, if you want?"

"I want," Markus said abruptly.

"Okay," Callum was hurt, but embarrassment overrode it. "I'll take you there."

Markus thought he could smell perfume as they traipsed down to the next floor. It was the same perfume he had breathed in on so many of those afternoons next to Carmen. Callum stuck a leg out and kicked open a door. He put the light on and a clean, spacious room appeared. It was blue and white and bare except for a big bed in the middle.

"I have a spare toothbrush if you want?"

"I don't."

Markus had already shut the door in his face and had taken off most of his clothes. He looked out the window at the black night sky and a tree that reached up and touched it. Way down low he saw two shiny dots inside a bush.

"Yes ya little bastard," Markus said. "Cassius the cat had a lucky escape."

He was fully naked now and in bed. He stretched out and enjoyed the cool, white softness mould around his limbs. Carmen obviously came to mind. He couldn't believe how close he had come. She was only rooms away. He imagined her on the other side of the wall, or maybe above his ceiling. *She's sleeping on top of me.* He loved her and he knew it. First love. He loved her eyes, her lips, her short hair and her mysterious silence. He loved her long, long nose and her long, long legs and those memorable freckles. *She knows*, he thought, she knows the lengths I have gone. She knows and that's why she sits next to me at school. And that's why she sat next to me tonight. Carmen was just playing him at his own seductive game. She is making *me* go to *her*. If I just remain patient, he thought, if I just wait it out ...

... the rain came and sleep came and Markus was away at last. Sleep without dreams because Markus didn't believe he had them, never, ever, ever ...

... although tonight he thought he had. He thought he had because he heard his name being called out in the dark ... a murmur ... a whisper ... *Markus* ... he opened his eyes and saw a room he didn't recognise ... with a figure he didn't recognise standing in the corner of it ... *Markus it's me ... it's Carmen ...* did he hear that right ... *or am I dreaming ...* he didn't feel scared, but excited ... so, excited ... she stepped closer, her face in shadow, her nose, her lips, a robe fell off her shoulders, naked, moonlight on her skin. She took more steps and that unmistakable perfume swooped over him and closed his eyes. He felt a kiss on his lips, his chin; his neck. She was there for a long time, slowly working her way down. He couldn't believe this was happening. It's what they all talked about. It's what the world talked about all the time. Sex. S.E.X. She was going lower and he expected her to stop, say something; break this spell. It was too good to be true. Lower. Lower. Something wet and warm pressed into his bellybutton. Lower. It was a hard-on like he had never had before and then that scary feeling came. That scary feeling like something was trying to get out of it, out the end of it. It was an overwhelming feeling like the world was about to end or that the world was too much. It was that *the-world-is-too-much feeling*. He wanted to stop her but he couldn't. She was doing something *down there*. Something powerful. He couldn't tell what it was or what she was doing, what she was using or how she was using it. He just didn't know. All he did know is that the feeling was *everywhere*. It was his whole body, inside and out. It was his stomach and his brain and his mind and his heart and his blood. There was pressure, a tightening of pressure then a release like he was going to piss himself only it was so strong and scary and eruptive and it was *out*. It was out and it wouldn't stop coming out and it was ecstasy and death at the same time and he wondered again if he was asleep and this was his first dream ever ...

... soon everything stopped and his mind came back ... his body stopped and the night came back ... he felt an incredible hot wetness and the dread came back ... then he heard that dream-voice again ... that murmur, that whisper ... *wow* ... wow it said and he knew that voice and he hated that voice ... *wow* ... he knew that voice and he knew all along, really ... only he had to shut it up and get it away ... get it away from here ... *Markus ...* he wanted to tell him to go but he daren't. He daren't say a word so he just grabbed the duvet and pulled it over him, around him. He made himself into a ball and tried to shut him out, shut the world out, shut life out and pretend he's asleep.

"Markus are you okay? Did I do it right? Did I ... ?"

Markus gave a little kick and hoped that'd be enough. He hoped it would be enough to shut that boy up otherwise he knew something bad was going to happen. He knew that if he said one more word, one more murmur, one more whisper, he was going to kill him. *Literally* kill him and Markus knew he could do it. He knew how killing worked because he had done it before. He knew how necks worked and how throats worked and how windpipes worked. He also knew how he could make them *not* work. How you stopped them from working. He'd ended lives and he knew he could end another one, a human one, a boy one, a girl one, or whatever that thing was that had just done that *this* to him. One more murmur, one more whisper, one more word ...

Only it didn't come.

It left, it was leaving, leaving Markus, the room, this night.

He heard footsteps; the door, stairs.

He was gone and we're all still alive, just.

Markus didn't go back to sleep. Markus couldn't go back to sleep even if he wanted to, which he didn't. Markus waited in the dark. Laying in the dark. Staring at it and into it. Staring at the black. The night was all over his bed. He couldn't move without feeling something touch his skin. He didn't want to think about it so he didn't think about it. Instead he got out of bed and put his clothes on. For some reason his mind wandered downstairs and into the kitchen, into the drawer where sharp shiny things lay ...

... Markus opened the curtains and saw the new dawn. He saw that things had got lighter, loads lighter. He could see the house and the path running away from it. *I need to get out of here, out of this place.* He pushed the window further until he could fit his body out of it. Below him was grass, maybe, or concrete or stone or a conservatory? He couldn't quite tell; he couldn't quite see. He didn't have shoes on but that didn't matter, he didn't care. He climbed through and lobbed his body out, hung there, birds twittered in the tree, cool air on the back of his neck, stayed there, stretching, trying to make himself as tall as possible. It was murky and he was tired and he had no idea about distance. How high he was or what he was falling into, onto. He could break his ankle, leg, back, neck. He could break his life and never come back. He didn't care. *Just want to be out of here.* Markus relaxed and let his fingers come loose, one by one, and then he was falling. Bricks blurred by and the earth hit him hard. He felt like he had gone through it and was underground. He rolled back in the wet grass two or three times and this made him want to laugh out-loud.

"Fuck life," he said.

He stood and nothing was broken. He walked around and nothing hurt. He saw the word, *invincible.* He looked up at the window and the curtain flapped about in the morning breeze. At the same time something brushed past his leg and it felt quite nice. He looked down and two little eyes looked back.

Meow.

Days passed and Markus kept himself to himself, *totally.* No Dad or Ryan or Aunt Tars. No kids off the estate. No one. He just stayed in his room or went up to The Den. The first thing he did was block that little pervert from his phone, although he hadn't managed to block him from his mind. No matter how much he tried to force it from his head it always managed to find a way back in. It leaked in drip by drip, thought by thought, like a hole in the roof. He needed to talk about it but he couldn't do that. He needed to share it but he didn't know how.

He needed answers.

He didn't understand.

He was out of his mind.

At the dinner table his dad seemed unusually sober, clear-eyed and focused. His hair had been combed and his voice was free of the standard hiccup and slur. They were even having a curry for once, which never happened and seemed like a treat. His brother Ryan ate like he hadn't eaten in a week, concentration completely on the plate before him, licking his lips and fingers with each forkful of food.

"Steady on kid," his dad said. "You'll eat your hand off if you're not careful."

Markus had barely touched his. His mind elsewhere, prodding bits of rice with his knife.

"Dad," he said, tentatively. "Can I ask you something?"

His dad looked at him and sighed.

Markus picked up some rice, and then put it down again. "You know if you play for Liverpool. And you loved playing for Liverpool and you *knew* you played for Liverpool. But one day you put on a Manchester United shirt by accident would that still make you a Liverpool player?"

"What the fuck you going on about?" Dad said with a mouthful.

"Like if you put it on by accident?"

"Why would you put a scummy United top on by accident?"

"I mean they're both red, it's easily done."

His dad stopped eating and stared at him. "Markus son you better not be thinking about swapping sides otherwise I'll fucking disown ya."

"I'm not. I'm just saying."

"Liverpool go *way* back in our family, years, generations. You don't just *change* when you feel like it. You have your team and you stick with it. For *life*."

Markus looked over at Ryan, who was oblivious. He hated football or anything like that. Markus kept looking at him, the way he ate, his movements, his gestures. He'd always been a bit of a pussy but this was the first time he realised how *delicate* he was, how feminine. Could it be that his brother was a bandit? He thought. Markus suddenly got scared, really scared. What if gayness ran in the family? What if it was in the blood and there was nothing you can do?? Come to think of it his mum had always looked a bit on the butch side in her photos, thick-set and sturdy and her hair was short. What if she was a lesbian in disguise, he thought, I mean like deep down inside what if that's really who she was?

Maybe our whole family is gay and perverted and sick?

Markus didn't eat anymore. He went straight upstairs and climbed into bed. He had to think about this. He had to *understand*. He had to think long and hard and work it all out. He knew he wasn't gay. He *knew* it. He didn't fancy boys. He fancied girls. He fancied loads of girls at school. He fancied Mazie Vickers before she became a bitch. He fancied her blonde mate. He fancied them girls from *Little Mix*. Especially that dark one Leigh-Anne Pinnock. He had even wanted to put a poster of her up on his wall but he knew his dad would go mad with her being black and that, well not proper black, but she wasn't white and Markus would never hear the last of it. He fancied girls, *he did,* even women, like older women. He fancied that Holly Willoughby woman who was on morning telly and he even fancied one of his teachers at school, Miss Haddon even though she was like thirty or something. The more he thought about all this the better he felt. He loved girls and women and the only reason that happened was because Carmen and Callum looked alike. They were twins for fuck sake. I mean he had even said it himself, *we're the same person*. It was easily done, an easy mistake. Could have happened to anyone ...

... it was still pretty sick though ... and to say it was his first time ... *disgusting* ... no one could *ever* find out. If they did Markus would kill himself it was simple as that. He will put a noose around his neck just like he did with those cats. Then he'd be straight off that footbridge. His neck would break and there would be no more Markus. That would be karma, karma for the cats, and everyone else who had been touched by the hand of Markus Venner.

The bank holiday was almost up and he had to go back to school. The two weeks seemed to have split into two. There was the week leading up to *the event* and the week running away from it. The week before was full of anticipation and wonder while the week after was crippled with dread and humiliation and regret.

Time to go back.

He got up early and had breakfast with Ryan. His dad hadn't made it to bed from the night before and lay splayed out in the lounge, half on the sofa and half on the floor. Markus thought he looked like those criminals in the olden days who had to go in the stocks. On their knees with their head and hands trapped.

That'd be a cool job, Markus thought, an executioner.

The brothers ate cheapo cornflakes to the sound of their father snoring and slathering in his sleep. They tried not to laugh.

"Watch this," Markus said.

He put his bowl in the sink and then tip-toed up to Dad. Deftly he slipped his fingers into his pocket and produced a wallet.

"Markus what you doing?"

He slipped a tenner out and then flashed it to his brother like a victory flag. He pulled the note tight and it made a funny sound. Markus closed the wallet up and slid it back into his pocket.

"Dinner money," he said.

Ryan shook his head but couldn't help smile.

At the shop Markus bought two bags of sweets, two chocolate bars and two cans of coke. With the change he split it with his brother. Ryan was surprised because Markus never gave him anything.

He took the pound coins reluctantly. "I feel guilty," he said.

"You've got to be fucking kidding," Markus said with a screw-face. "The fucker owes us. It's as much *ours* as it is *his*."

Ryan's face remained unconvinced.

Markus held out his dirty hand. "Give it me back then."

Ryan smiled. Markus smiled back.

At school there was an odd atmosphere, kind of eerie. The sky was empty and silent. Cars drove by the gates but didn't seem to make any sound. A cat jumped down from a wheelie bin and glanced at Markus, before running off. It reminded him of the morning when they were told about the kid who had been stabbed outside the chip shop. Rumours went round for weeks that it was Stewie Taylor, but eventually two Polish lads from Boston were arrested.

Markus looked around at everybody. Kids were miserable, they looked like zombies. Markus knew that most kids hated school. Naughty kids hated being told what to do and clever kids hated being bullied. No one was happy. The teachers weren't happy. The headmaster wasn't happy. Dinner ladies weren't happy. The only person who was happy was Mazie Vickers because she was beautiful and clever and popular but even she wasn't happy now cos someone had put her pet guinea pig in a P.E sock and smashed it to death.

People stayed out of Markus's way all morning and he liked that. Only there was still this feeling that Markus couldn't put his finger on. There was something amiss. *Something in the air.* In the end he put it down to it being the first day back after a two-week break. Mentally kids were still at home, half-asleep, chewing on cereal while waiting for *Jeremy Kyle* to start.

He saw Callum only once, a glimpse of his queer body and his queer face. Markus found it tough but he had to look at him. Had to give him the death-stare to let him know what time it was, keep him away, a warning.

It was before dinner the real commotion arrived. A small crowd had gathered outside the English room. There was laughter, a cheer, yet at the same time there was something dark. Markus had always had a nose for trouble, ever since being six years old he could sense when something was *wrong*. As he stepped closer to the classroom a boy glanced in his direction and then took off. Markus felt this instant dread. There wasn't a boy in his year who could fight him so the fear wasn't a physical one. It was something else, a deeper fear, the thing he feared the most: humiliation. When Markus stepped into the room others left. Pretty much the whole class had scarpered.

He looked around and wondered what all the fuss was. He could feel something pull at him, his eyes were drawn to the chalkboard on the back wall. There in huge letters were the words:

It's Official: Jew Boy and Psycho Boy are Lovers!

Markus froze. He felt his bodyweight drop into his feet. His legs wanted to buckle and the only feeling he could relate it to, was when he was told his mum had died. His eyes stayed on the cruel words and how big and bold they were. His worst fear made real. He vaguely recognised the swirling, adult handwriting only he was too scared to take any of it in. Outside the noise continued. It sounded like a party. He looked through the smeary widows to see a crowd of people all laughing and having a good time. Boys were high-fiving and girls hugging, like something good had happened. He didn't understand it. It was all too much for him. He knew he needed to do something, so he did, He took off, almost smashing the door off its hinges. He vaulted the stairs and tried to run in the opposite direction to the crowd but they tracked him. Corridor after corridor, the library, a flight of stairs. He lost his way for a moment and ended up bursting through a fire door. He went to the Astroturf because he knew he'd be there because that's where he always was. Up on the grass bank. His little queer boy.

The crowd was still there, following at a distance. Maybe Markus thought he had lost them, maybe he had blocked them all out.

Callum knew he was in trouble the moment he saw his face. Markus attacked the bank, running into it so hard he thought he was going to penetrate the earth. The place where he had saved him from violence was the place he was about to inflict it upon him. Markus had scared people before. He knew fear and had seen what it looked like in people's faces. But not like this. Not like Callum. It was so primal it almost stopped Markus. He saw the word, *petrified*.

"Markus please. *Please*. Please I didn't know."

The crowd went silent behind him.

Markus already had a fistful of collar.

"Markus I didn't say anything. I didn't tell them. It wasn't me. They knew. They *just* knew."

Markus silenced him by smashing the words back through his mouth. He felt teeth break over his knuckles. The sound travelled down the bank and filled the rest of the school field. A feral scream cut through the sky. Markus wanted to let out his own scream. He wanted to scream into the faces of the people that were staring at him, the blank, clueless, stupid faces.

Mazie Vickers remained hidden throughout, standing at the back of the crowd. She watched Markus bolt out the school gates, a wild animal running away. Callum was on his hands and knees, coughing up teeth, quivering, traumatised. She wanted to go over and help him but guilt kept her where she was.

Markus was getting expelled for this.

His days were over.

Mazie Vickers would never have to see him again

Markus was going to commit suicide just like he promised. He was heading up to The Den to get a piece of rope. He was heading to The Cat Footbridge to end it all. Only his head was in such a state he didn't know where he was. Everything seemed to be about his face. He couldn't let anyone see his *face*. When he finally looked up he saw that he was near the old quarry on the outskirts of town. *How the fuck did I get here?* He was so exhausted he had to stop otherwise he was going to collapse. His head was light and dizzy and he couldn't control his breathing. His battered body slumped under a mud-spattered sign that read DEAD END.

He carried on taking deep breaths, trying to recover.

Breathe.

Breathe.

Focus finally came back, familiar sounds grew around him. Birds busy in the branches above. He knew he was near a main road because there was a constant hum of traffic down towards his left. There must have been a grate or something in the road because there was a drumbeat sound every time a set of wheels ran over it. The sound was hypnotic and Markus zoned-out for a few minutes.

"I need to get up to The Den and hang myself," he said, nodding, final. "That's what I need to do."

Seconds later his trance was broken by a momentary blur,

something caught his eye, a flash; a silver sparkle. The object sobered him up and brought him back to life.

He saw the word, *Mongoose.*

Never had his soul had such an arrow-like will. He was moving through the air, almost like he was flying. Mongoose and the boy on her saddle got closer and closer and Markus couldn't believe what he was seeing, that *she* was here again.

He caught them both on the corner of the dirt road, piling into him and grabbing his collar with such impact that the boy got the wind knocked right out of him. He gasped and fell in a thorn bush. In less than an hour Markus had another terrified face before him. He could see his own demented reflection in the boy's eyeballs. The boy was petrified and had not a clue what was going on, just this madman snapping and snarling like a rabid dog. The boy thought Markus's head was going to come off. How he had not hit him yet was a miracle.

"This is mine! This is mine! My Mongoose, mine! Where did you get it? Where? Where? Tell me now or you're dead!"

The boy needed to talk, he needed to explain. If he was ever going to save himself from the wrath of this psycho then he had to tell him what he knew, yet at the time same he was so overwhelmed he couldn't put two words together.

"Where?"

"My dad," he managed to splutter at last. "My dad gave it to me."

"Who is your fucking dad?"

"Terrence. Terry Moran."

Something gave way in the boy's face, a hint of recognition. "And where did *he* get it?"

Markus's voice had dropped, got clearer. The boy felt a flicker of hope. "Erm, he, he bought it from a mate, a mate at the pub."

"Who?"

"I don't know his name." Markus tightened his grip and squashed the boy's windpipe. "A bloke."

The word *bloke* got crushed in his throat. Markus had to loosen his grip if he was going to find any answers. "You seen him?"

The boy nodded.

"What's he look like?"

"Blonde. Red-faced. Always pissed."

By the word *blonde* Markus was already off, tearing down the road, leaving him there, still quaking in terror. His face felt like it had been punched even though it hadn't. When the adrenaline had come down a level the boy got confused.

If the bike meant so much to him then why didn't he take it?

It's like he was so mad he had forgotten.

He was so mad he had forgotten to commit suicide too.

He watched Markus run. He wasn't very fast but rage gave him the illusion of speed, like a bull with a spear in his back. One thing was for certain, whoever he was running to, was in deep, deep, serious trouble.

Mel

Dear Self-Esteem Diary,

First off, like, before we start, I have to tell You something ... my mum has just been out and bought a dog!

Like, a dog is living with us now! There is an ACTUAL dog pissing and pooing and sleeping in the house. Can You believe it!? mum told us she had a surprise waiting for us after school and I got so excited. Like I thought we had a present or something. Maybe like a Mountain Bike or a trampoline in the back garden or something. Only it wasn't. It was a dog. A DOG! And not a cute furry little thing like a poodle or a yorkie but like, a beast! An absolute beast. Like, a big-jawed muscular pit-bull kind of a thing. You know the sort? Those that are ALWAYS on the news for ripping kid's faces off and stuff.
    OMG!
    But, you see, this is my mum all over, <u>irresponsible</u> and crap. Putting <u>herself</u> first and her kids <u>last.</u>
    And can You believe she's only gone and called the thing Babe.
    Babe???
    What a stupid name to give a Killing Machine. Babe? Suppose she was trying to be funny, like an ironic kind of a thing but I don't find it amusing. Not at all. I mean it's only a puppy at The Moment but who knows what's going to happen in The Future when it gets all big and strong and adult and stuff. mum says we've got to show it Love and bring it up right. But how can she do that when she can't even bring her OWN kids up right??
    I'm scared of That Thing already. The way it bombs around and puts its mouth on stuff. Its eyes all wild and weird and stuff. I won't go near it, no way near it. mum says this is bad cos animals can smell fear. She says I've got to Trust it but why should I trust it? What reason do I have to trust it? I don't EVEN trust humans so I'm not exactly going to trust a stupid dog am I? Besides, like, you can't trust something that always has the same expression. Cos a dog looks the same all the time, like, whether it's happy or sad so you just don't know. Like, you just don't know its emotions and what's going off in their brains and stuff. Like, you just don't know whether they're about to lick your face or sink its fangs into your cheek.

You just don't know??!

Anyway.
Either way.

If That Thing ever does attack me I swear I'm going stick my finger up its bumhole cos that's like supposed to stop them and stuff. Or like I'd tear its front legs apart like a piece of chicken cos that's supposed to make its heart pop out. And if I wanted to, if I REALLY felt like it I could quite easily put rat poison in its food and kill it and nobody would really know it was me.

They say there's more than one way to skin a cat … well maybe there's more than one way to skin a dog too!

Lol!

She even made us take The Thing for a walk through the MIDDLE of town. Where EVERYONE could see us. She couldn't even control it, like, it was WAY too strong for her and it pulled her all over the place. Me and My Sister Adele hung back and pretended not to know her. A boy even glared at us from Starbuck's window.

It was so embarrassing.

Like, SO embarrassing.

Of course My Sister Adele has DECIDED to start warming to it, so this will be just another thing that Angel-Daughter and Perfect-Mummy can share and bond over and I'll be the outcast as always. Always.

Anyway.
Either way.

Anyway I just had to get that off my chest cos it's been a Major Thing and it's upset me as You can probably tell, and like, that's what You're here for anyway, isn't it Self-Esteem Diary? You're here to let me unload my crap.

So here I am, unloading the crap, so thanks for that!

Anyway.

Anyway I better get back to the Biography Bit otherwise I'll go off on one and lose myself completely like Last Time.

139

So.

So back to the story of Me.
   Back to the Biography Bit.

First off, like, I know They tell you about it at school and stuff ... but The Truth is nothing can really, truly prepare you for the First Time you bleed.
   Like, it's so unbelievably scary I really, Honestly thought I was going to die. Like, ACTUALLY die, literally die. Like I really thought it was The End and stuff. I didn't expect it at all. I didn't expect there to be so much, so much blood. Like there was LOADS and it happened faster than I thought and earlier than I thought and I wasn't prepared for it at all. I was going for a pee and that's when I saw it. Like I didn't even think it was blood At First cos it didn't look like blood, not real blood. Like it was all gooey and stuff. It was all thick and bright and it looked more like paint. It was in my knickers and a bit on my leg and then in the toilet and stuff. Looking back there probably wasn't all that much but it seemed so cos I was only little and it was My First Official Time EVER. I remember letting out this absolutely massive scream and My Sister Adele ran into the bathroom and I wanted her to get mum but she wouldn't because she kept on being nosey and it wasn't until I screamed EVEN LOUDER that she fetched her.
   Ring the ambulance I'm dying!
   And you never guess what my mum did, what My Own mum did? She laughed. Just laughed in my face and told me not to be silly. Like how am I supposed to know, how the heck am I supposed to know what it was!!?? She sat me back on the toilet and wiped me down and explained things again like school did. She told me this is what happened and the way it was From Now On. I was a big girl now, a young woman, she said. After that I will say she was kind of good for once. Like she did take me on a Special Trip into town where she bought me this kit kind of a thing. Like it was a Little Bag with Little Tampons and Little Pads and Little Pants and this Little Booklet where there were all these Little Stories and stuff. Like what other girls had gone through and stuff. Like there was a blonde girl and black girl and they had speech bubbles over them filled with pink crayony writing. It was a bit babyish but it was kind of cute too. I think I still have this kit somewhere actually. Because I like to keep

things, like mementoes, like cos it's about holding onto memories and stuff.

Anyway.

After that everything was fine and I wasn't scared anymore. And tbh I'm not gonna Lie but I quite liked it cos it made me feel all grown-up. Like I couldn't wait to tell people. Couldn't wait to tell My Bestie Mia.

I told her at school and At First she looked surprised. Then she looked pissed-off. Then she just sort of acted all bored like she'd been through it ages ago but I could tell she was Lying. I could tell she was Lying cos she would've mentioned it. Like she would've BROKE HER NECK to tell me. But this is Mia all over. She always has to get there First, be there First. She always has to be The Best no matter what. I don't blame her for it. She IS what she IS and I kind of accept that and love her for it.

People ARE what they ARE, I guess.

And the quicker we accept that the easier EVERYTHING is.

Anyway.

After that I started to ache, like all the time ache and the aching was all over, like mostly where my chest was, where my boobs were going to be, like where my nipples were. Like they were sore and stuff. My back hurt too, like a crampy kind of a thing. I hated it. I dreaded it. I wanted it to go away. I wanted Them to take it ALL back. I didn't want to become a woman and would have much preferred Things to have stayed where they was. I felt it change my brain too, like my mind and stuff, cos I started thinking different and then feeling different. Like the emotions got all raw and real and stuff. Like I'd cry at the most silliest things and I didn't understand why. Like I didn't understand what was happening. Like the world felt too big, like Life Itself seemed too large to live in. It was like I was too small and was being swallowed up ALIVE.

It was at this time I knew My Bestie Mia had started hers, too. I knew because she started talking about it more. Like before she was all vague and stuff, like she was guessing how it felt whereas now she ACTUALLY knew. Like she talked about EXACT things.

Her mum had bought her a Period Kit too.

I got jealous cos even though I started before her she got boobs first. She would stand sideways in the mirror and they would poke through her school shirt like little ripened apples. Whereas I was pretty much flat more or less. But what REALLY shocked me was a couple of months later when Mia showed me her bush. She just sort of released it from nowhere in her bedroom and I think I actually swore out-loud. I think I said WHAT THE FUCK.

I've had it for ages, she said.

Wow.

Haven't you got one?

No. I mean not like that. I mean I've got a few hairs and stuff.

Show us.

No. No way.

C'mon.

No. No way.

Just a peek.

I shook my head and could feel my face go red.

(*Something to mention Self-Esteem Diary, before we go on any further. I just want You to know, that just because I'm open and talk loads inside You I don't want You to get the impression that I'm like this in Real Life cos I'm not. Tbh I'm not gonna Lie but The Truth is I'm shy. Like dead-shy. Like to the point where I don't even talk and stuff. Like I much prefer to hang-back and watch, hang-back and listen. Like I come out of my shell but I come out of it SLOW, very slowly, like I REALLY have to trust You for before You get to see who I am and stuff. So it's important You know this so you know The Truth of who I REALLY am and that.

So.

See.

Me and My Bestie Mia are TOTAL opposites and You'd never put us together. We're like that Chinese symbol kind of a thing. I forgot what it's called but you know what I mean. Like the one that is black and white and has two dots. Like it's about being opposites but being the same too. Well that's like me and Mia cos like I'm an incurable introvert and she's an outrageous extrovert.)

She put her bush in my face and started laughing.

Gross put it away.

You calling my pussy gross?

Stop being a lesbian!

You know you're supposed to shave these things?

What?

She covered it up At Last.

Yeah after it gets so long you're supposed to shave them cos that's what boys like.

What's the point of that?

Well you don't shave it all off completely, just some.

So you look forward to having hair and then when you do you shave it off?

Mia nodded.

Where did you hear that?

Read it in a magazine.

Which one?

Can't remember. Anyway I know it's true cos I've seen my mum's and she shaves hers.

You've seen your mum's?

Of course, why wouldn't I, she's my mum. Haven't you seen yours?

Ugh. Yuk. No way.

Why?

Can we change the subject please?

Me and My Bestie Mia became inseparable. Like we was with each other ALL THE TIME. We were both kind of outcasts at school so we built our own Two-Girl Gang. We did have some other mates but mostly it was just us, M&M, Mia and Mel. People used to call us lesbians but we didn't care. We didn't care what people said. We didn't care about no one.

"It's not us." Mia said. "It's everyone else that's weird."

You spend too much time with that girl, mum said. It's not healthy to spend all that time with one person.

You're just jealous cos you haven't got mates.

mum flipped when I said that. Like her eyes went crazy and I thought she was going to hit me again cos I could see it in her face but I could also see that she managed to stop herself in time.

Anyway, she said, you start spending too much time with her and I'll put a stop to it.

You can't do that.

I can do what I want I'm your mum.

I hate her. I hate her and I was starting to hate her more, EVEN more. I looked at other mums and they didn't behave like that. Mia's mum wasn't like that. She loved us hanging out and even said she was glad that I was her best friend. She said I was 'a good influence.'

It's Official: Mia's mum was The Coolest Person In The World.

I liked going to her house and I liked even more staying over at night. Mia was NEVER allowed to stay at mine whereas I was allowed to stay at hers whenever I wanted. If it wasn't for my mum putting a stop to it I could probably have Stayed Over every night. I could probably have even moved in For Good. I looked at her mum and longed to have her as My Own Mum. Life wasn't fair. My Bestie Mia didn't know how lucky she was. We got to eat cool food and watch cool films. We got to try on clothes and wear make-up and Mia was always dressing up and being different people. She wore costumes and outfits and then walked around for hours pretending to be different characters and stuff. Like she really got into it and her acting was SO talented and good that it sometimes spun me out. Like I didn't even know what was Real anymore. Sometimes she was a jazz singer, sometimes she was a nurse, sometimes a man, sometimes an old woman from war times, sometimes a prostitute in Paris. She'd try and get me to do it but I was always too shy and I felt stupid and it didn't feel right. That's the whole point, Mia would say. You're supposed to feel different, be different. Leave Mel Ellis behind and create something entirely new. She'd put on an old-fashioned hat and spin around.

Don't be confined to the one thing, she said.

Ha. Half the time I didn't get what she was going on about.

The Part I loved best though was The Sleeping. Mia had a double bed and we would sleep together. She didn't know it but sometimes I would cry when she went to sleep. Cry at being so happy. Cry at being close to someone cos there's No Feeling in The World better than being close with someone. Having that warmth and love and soft skin and breath all over you. Cuddling and stuff. We'd wrap legs and she'd stroke my hair and it was Love. Like it felt just like love. Not a lesbian kind of a thing but a higher love, a deeper love. In the morning we'd lay-in till dinner and her mum never knocked on doors like my own mum did, or shout or hoover up outside or make us go to the shop but she just let us be, let us lie there until we were ready. And we'd lay on our fronts and take it in turns to draw on our bare backs with a fingertip. We'd try to guess the words we'd make. I'm a better speller so I'd write longer words whereas Mia nearly always wrote rude ones.

D, I said.

Yep.

I, I said.

Yep.

L, I said.

Yep.

D, I said.

Um, hum.

O, I said.

Yep.

Dildo?

Bingo!

What the hell is a dildo?

Oh my god you don't know??

She'd jump up and get all excited. She loved it when I didn't know things and she got to tell me. I would sit back and listen to her with a smile on my face, telling me all these things about life and stuff.

A dildo is what you use to masturbate, she said, they're guaranteed to give you an orgasm like EVERY time, without fail.

I'd heard about orgasms but I wasn't exactly sure what they were. Mia was always talking about them, like ALL THE TIME. She was obsessed with them and said she needed to have AT LEAST five a day to even function properly.

I always got so embarrassed when she talked about them.

Have you had one yet? Did you do what I showed you?

Meeeee-ya I said, stretching her name out. You know I don't like talking about it.

Mel you're a prune.

A what?

A prune.

Think she meant 'prude' but I didn't correct her. Mia liked Playing Adult so I let her have her time.

Lay on your back, she said.

Oh not again.

Mia would go to her DVD collection like she always did and pick out one of the Twilight films, normally the last one cos that had the most nudity.

In Twilight I liked Pattinson but Mia preferred the Dark Wolf Boy who always had his top off. Like he did have a hot bod and a six-pack and stuff but he seemed too posey to me whereas I liked Pattinson cos he had cold-blue eyes and death-white skin and he was all mysterious and stuff.

Anyway Mia would press Pause, mostly on this scene where Topless Dark Boy was leaning over Kristen Stewart, about to kiss her.

Think I'm gonna have a clitoris orgasm today rather than a vagina one, she announced.

I wouldn't say anything, just hide behind the other side of the bed feeling stupid.

Now, she said, taking most her clothes off. You need to warm yourself up, get yourself into it. You can't just go 'straight down there.' You need to stroke your body first, awaken yourself, tease yourself.

I'd be lying on the floor, dying, trying not to laugh. It's like, how serious she was that made it so funny.

'Tease yourself,' how stupid.

Mia would start making these noises, like little moans and stuff.

Start touching your tits.

Haven't got any, I said.

Concentrate.

I bit my bottom lip and tried not to laugh again.

Touch your nipples then, she said. Then stroke down, get to your stomach, your bellybutton, move to the inside of your thigh. It's all in the head y'know Mel, sex is in the head, we aren't like boys. We can't just 'have' orgasms we have to 'achieve' them.

Now I really was confused. 'Achieve' is what you do in an exam or like on Sports Day or something.

Then Mia starting using words that I didn't have a clue about. Like body-part words that sounded all sciencey and stuff.

Vulva, clitoris, labia, urethra, perineum.

She was just showing off and I knew it was fake. Like she'd just Googled it or something and was reading it out like a shopping list. Like if I asked her what was where she wouldn't have a clue.

That's when Mia would really start putting on a performance. Like she'd be near screaming and I'm surprised her mum didn't think I was killing her, like stabbing her to death or something.

Yes, yes, OOOooohh, ooooohhhhhkjnhhhhhhhhhhnnjnn, yes I'm coming, I'm coming, I'm going to come, I'm fucking coming ...

I popped my head over the bed and she was thrashing around on it like a goldfish out of water. Her legs were like shaking crazy and stuff, like a fit kind of a thing.

After she calmed down.

I think that was multiple, she said.

I nodded, so embarrassed, but like embarrassed for her this time.

You know what a multiple is?

I shook my head.

It's a clitoris one AND a vagina one combined, like at the same time.

Oh.

Did you have one?

Nearly.

She shook her head and exhaled, disappointed. Girl. We need to sort you out. We need to get you a BF.

Mia reckoned she had a BF. Said his name was Jacob and he was 18 years old. He had a 10 inch penis and they'd had sex like 20 times. She said she couldn't introduce him because it had to be a secret because she was underage and he could go to prison.

I won't tell, I said, you can trust me.

I know I can but I just can't take that chance.

I knew she was Lying cos I could see it in her face and tell by the tone of her voice and like she only used the name 'Jacob' cos like that's the Dark Boy's name in Twilight. Mia thinks I'm stupid but I'm cleverer than she thinks. Cleverer than a lot of people think.

Anyway.
Either way.

I never met any Older Boys but instead we went to a party with some boys our own age. It was My First Party and I was so dead-nervous that I think I had My First Official Anxiety Attack. It was ten minutes before Mia came round. I was looking in the mirror and I wasn't liking what I saw. In fact I HATED what I saw. I had nothing good to wear and I looked so revoltingly ugly and that's when this shaky, panicy, rushy feeling came on all over me. It only lasted for about a minutes but it was dead-intense and scary and stuff.

Think I just had My First Official Anxiety Attack, I said.

Don't worry, Mia said, I get them all the time. It just means you're growing up.

Oh.

147

The party wasn't even really a party. Just three boys in a room. They were all nervous and they didn't talk for the like the First Hour. Neither did I. We all just listened to Mia. Then Mia went upstairs with The Leader of the boys and I was left with the other two. Tbh I'm not gonna Lie but The Truth is I didn't even fancy any of them, not really, not one bit. One was tall and one was small and they both wore braces. Then Mia came down and said that she'd just downed a WHOLE bottle of Vodka and that she was now 'paralytic.' Some music came on and then we all kind of got rowdy and stuff and that's when I had my first kiss. Like My First Official Kiss EVER. It was outside, round the back. Near some bins cos all I could smell was garbage and stuff. It was with The Small One, Tyler I think his name was. I had to bend down to do it and it wasn't great cos his breath smelled cos he smoked loads and in fact he even had a fag in his hand at the time. I was kind of holding my breath all the way through it. It was weird cos I wanted Mia to see me yet I didn't at the same time. I didn't want her to cos like the boy was ugly and stuff but I wanted to prove I had done it. So I even kissed him again and At Last Mia came out and started clapping and cheering like I had just won a Sports Day race or something.

In the end my mouth hurt and my back hurt from all the bending down and I just wanted to go home. Now Mia had seen me I wasn't bothered about carrying on. The boy wouldn't leave me alone and in the end Mia had to push his face away and told him to Piss Off.

Back at Mia's I gargled mouthwash for like an hour and then got into bed.

We were both laughing our heads off.

How was it?

Disgusting.

We laughed more.

Why did you do it then?

I shrugged.

Why did you do it for so long?

I shrugged again.

We lay on our backs and I watched the whites of her eyes flicker in the dark.

Did you have sex with him, I said.

Who?

The boy at the party?

She paused like she hadn't heard, or like she was thinking of an answer to give me.

148

No. she said.

Her voice was different this time, like she was natural, like she was being real with me for once.

We rolled over and touched heads and our lips were close. We weren't going to kiss because we weren't lesbians but it felt like something else. It felt like kissing without kissing, almost like we were sucking up each other's breaths, like maybe our souls were kissing or something.

I love you, she said.

I love you, I said

A week later Mia had to go away.

She had to go on holiday to Spain with her mum. I thought it was only for a week (and that was Long Enough) but when I found out it was for two I nearly had My Second Official Anxiety Attack.

Mel, it's okay. I won't be long.

I stood in her driveway and Mia said how pale I looked. My hands were clasped and I had my head down and my glasses were all smeary with tears and stuff. Mia kissed all over my face and then got in the car and when I heard the door slam I thought my own heart had popped. She waved from the window and it was like she was leaving my life For Good.

Mel get a grip it's two weeks! You could do with a cooling-off period anyway.

mum was shouting at me through the noise of the hoover.

Cooling off? Cooling off from what? I shouted back.

That girl, you're obsessed with her.

It's only two weeks, god! My Sister Adele added. She kept poking her head over the book she was reading, that stupid, sly, superior smile of hers.

And YOU can stop sticking your nose in, I said, ripping the book out her hands.

Mum, she yelled, she just nicked my book!

The hoover stopped and I threw the book back at My Sister Adele before mum had a chance to interfere.

You give her the book back, she shouted, stepping into the lounge.

It's back!

I pointed at My Sister Adele who was already reading again.

You need to get a grip, mum said. You need to get out and do something, instead of moping around all day.

I could feel my nose tingle and tears began to fill my eyes. I miss her, I said. My voice like cracked when it got to the word 'miss.'

That's when I caught mum and sis sharing a secret smile and that just made me Flip, like, TOTALLY lose it and stuff. I jumped up and slapped a plate off the armchair and it smashed all over the floor. My Sister Adele looked up from her book all open-mouthed and shocked. Like her eyes went dead-big. mum chased me up the stairs and I heard her trip and smack her leg and then she flipped too. I tried to make it to the bathroom and lock her out but she caught me by the neck and pushed me up against the wall. She was so strong I couldn't move. Her face in mine. And her face had changed colour. It was all red and pink and purplish like someone had tipped a jar of beetroot over her. Her skin was all cracked too and I realised how old she was getting. I felt her nail go into my neck and I let out a little scream. My Sister Adele came to the bottom of the stairs and shouted, "No Not Again" and that seemed to snap mum out of it. Her face got scared again, like a regret kind of a thing. She put her hands in her hair like she wanted to pull it out.

You wind me up. You wind me up Mel. Don't make me do this again!

She went back downstairs and put the hoover back on and My Sister Adele just looked at me like it was all my fault. I think she was even shaking her head.

In the bathroom mirror I looked at my neck and there was a little nail mark but no blood, which is good cos I'm actually allergic to blood. Well, not allergic but a phobia. Like it makes me want to faint and stuff. I think it's the smell of it more than anything. I also got a phobia of snakes too, of worms. Anything really without arms and legs. Even goldfish aren't great.

Anyway.
Either way.

Tbh I didn't care about the nail mark in my neck cos I had a bigger pain in my heart. Cos the pain of missing Mia was greater than anything mum could EVER do. I went to bed that afternoon and it seemed like I stayed there for the WHOLE two weeks she was gone. It was like being dead and alive at the same time, like a zombie kind of a thing. Tbh I would say that this was My First Official Bout of Depression cos I couldn't eat and I couldn't sleep. I was kind of

*freaked-out by how much I missed her. I had dreams about her and
kept visualising The Moment when she came back into my life For
Good.*

The day she DID come back was unreal.

*I waited where she left me, at the end of her driveway. I kicked stones
and looked at the sky and stopped breathing every time a car came
down the street. When HER car came down the street I thought I was
going to pee myself. She jumped out the back and we charged into
each other's arms and nearly knocked ourselves out. She kissed me so
hard on the mouth she made my lip bleed. When she saw the blood I
thought she might say 'sorry' but instead she just smiled and said 'hey
we're vampires!"*

It took a few minutes to take her in properly. It was like the world
was all upside down and stuff. It really, Honestly, felt like she'd been
gone two years and not two weeks. I hadn't even noticed that she had
dyed her hair. Normally her hair was the same colour as mine, like a
mousy kind of thing. But now it was blonde, like dead-blonde. Her
skin was tan too and she looked like some kind of a Movie Star. This
made me worry about My Own Looks and I got scared that maybe
she wouldn't want to be around me anymore.

I've been doing a hundred sit-ups every morning and all I've eaten
is salad, she said.

She pulled up her top and it was brown and kind of ripped and
stuff. Not like a six-pack but definitely a four. It was pretty amazing.

I folded my arms.

In her kitchen her Mum made us lunch and they talked for hours
about the holiday.

You girls need to see the world when you're older, her mum said.
There's a whole life outside of this shitty little town. Don't stay here.
Don't stay in Kimble Wells. Get out when you can. This town is a box
and the people don't think outside of it.

Mia was nodding her head and I think I knew what she meant cos
tbh I've always wanted to leave KW too. Sometimes I wish I could live
out in the countryside, like in the wilderness, like sometimes I wish I
could have my own Secret Den which nobody knew about.

When we were alone in her bedroom Mia told me about the rest of
the holiday. The Bit her Mum didn't see. There was a 20 year old
waiter called Pedro.

I told him I was 16, Mia said.

And he believed you?

Yeah, why wouldn't he?

She cupped her boobs and laughed.

Mel he was sooooo hot. Like ridiculous. Like incredible. Like he had a body just like Twilight Man and he had this beautiful skin and he took me out on his moped to the other side of the island to watch the sunset. It was the most wonderful thing I have ever seen in my WHOLE life. And then when it was night we went into this cave and the moon was out and the sea was crashing in our ears and he slowly took off my clothes, piece by piece …

Mia told a good story. How she used words and images was quite amazing.

Her story stayed with me for days.

In the shower one afternoon I felt That Feeling in my tummy. It was a tingly magic feeling and it seemed to spread. Up and down and then back again. I had the showerhead in my hand and that's when I did the thing Mia had told me. I did feel self-conscious At First even though no one was there. I made the temperature a little hotter and then put it Down There. I moved it around in little circles and it felt kind of good, like, so good really. After a while my legs got tired so I stopped the shower and got out the bath and put a towel on the floor and laid down. I couldn't do this in my own room cos I share with my sis and besides, my nosey mum was always coming in every five minutes.

Now I didn't have Mia watching over me it felt quite natural, natural and nice. My body was still wet and like covered in watery beads and trickles and stuff. I looked at the small fold of a belly-tire and I guess I'm no Mia but that's okay. The sun was strong and it came through the window and bathed the whole room in its light. It reflected from the lime-green walls and turned my skin a similar colour. I didn't know what any of the body-parts were called but I played until it felt right, until it felt right for Me. I thought about Pattinson and I thought about Mia and that Spanish Boy that probably didn't even exist. In the end I didn't think of anything, just felt my own body For The Very First Time. After a while my hips began to roll and I didn't know if that was meant to happen but I carried on. I carried on and it was like I was carried out of myself and into another dimension. I made 'some' noise but I didn't swear and scream the house down like Mia did. And my legs didn't thrash and kick like hers either but they did wobble, a bit. I don't know which kind of orgasm it was but I knew I had one, My First Official Orgasm EVER. I had had it. I had 'achieved' it and now I really was some kind of young woman. Maybe, really, perhaps, probably not.

When Mia asked if I had 'arrived' yet I just sort of shrugged and played it down. I loved and adored her and she was the ONLY thing I had but that didn't mean I had to tell her <u>everything</u>.

I'm allowed secrets.

Some secrets, my own private world.

At least I did until I started this Self-Esteem Diary.

Until I met ...

YOU.

Man of The House

Markus

Markus was sick of eating chips. He was sure it was the grease and fat and vinegar that was giving him spots. He picked up an ugly one from the tray and stared at it between his fingers, before throwing it down the back of the radiator. A two-litre bottle of coke sat in the space between him and his brother Ryan. It was the month of May and the backdoor had been left open. The state of the house had deteriorated over the last few weeks but no one seemed to notice. Neither of the siblings were also aware that their dad had been missing for three days.

"Need to borrow your laptop in a bit," Markus said, putting a chip in his mouth.

Ryan took a gulp of coke.

"Ryan!" Markus said. "I'm borrowing your laptop in a minute, where is it?"

Ryan shook his head.

Markus spat out a chip and pulled a screw-face. "What ya shaking ya head for?"

"No."

"What do you mean *no*?"

A kid was screaming outside on the estate. Markus got up and closed the door.

"You're not borrowing it," Ryan said.

"What!"

"No more. I'm not having that sick shit on my laptop."

"What sick shit?"

"You know what I'm talking about."

Just then a figure appeared at the back window. The door was opened and in stepped a woman. It took a few moments for the boys to recognise their aunt. They had not seen her in over a month and she looked different. Her hair was longer and she'd lost weight. She was dressed in new clothes and there was a glow in her face, like she'd been on the sunbed or something. She stepped forward and looked around at the house.

"Oh. My. God," she said without moving her lips.

"Tars where the fuck have you been?" Markus said.

Her face was frozen, only her eyes moved, looking around at the junk and decay.

"Tara we've missed you," Ryan said, a little helplessly.

Markus rolled his eyes.

"Yeah," Tara said, still in shock. She stepped forward and heard cubes of broken glass crunch under her shoe.

Suddenly she seemed to snap out of it and went into business mode.

"Let's have a sit down," she said.

"We're sitting down," Markus said smugly.

Tara searched for a space. At last she found one in the lounge.

"Come here," she said.

The boys were glad to leave their chips. They sat opposite her. She had a skirt on and Markus noticed how smooth and shiny her legs looked.

"You're coming to live with me," she said.

Auntie Tara had decided to dive straight in, tell them how it was.

Markus smiled. Ryan frowned, concern wrinkling his face. "Why?" he said.

"Cool," Markus said. "You still got Netflix?"

"Your dad has got himself into trouble. He's had to go to prison."

"Oh god," Ryan put a hand over his mouth.

"Surprise sur-fucking-prise," Markus sang.

"Now it's nothing serious. I mean he hasn't killed anybody or anything. He just needs ... help."

"He needs to sober-the-fuck-up," Markus said with a grin on his face.

Aunt Tars put some large eyes on him. "Markus. Language."

Ryan was crying.

"Oh for fuck's sake Ryan are you even surprised?" Markus said.

Tars went over and put the boy in her arms and squeezed him, stroking his hair.

Markus sighed and took his phone out and started texting.

"Everything is going to be alright," she said. "He just needs time. He needs help, support. And he's going to get it. You know we all deal with things different and to be honest he never recovered after your mum."

Markus stopped texting. His face went red.

"Oh don't fucking bring *her* into it. That was ages ago. Bout ten fucking years!"

"Seven. Seven this August," Tara corrected.

"Seven. Ten. Twelve. Whatever. It was fucking time ago and you all need to get a fucking grip."

Aunt Tars let go of Ryan and spun around on her heels, thrusting a finger into Markus's face.

"First off. I'm not one of your little arsehole mates on the estate, so you better start talking to me with some fucking respect."

Markus laughed. "You swear. You just fucking swore."

"We all need to stick together at a time like this, so just think on."

"Stick together?" Markus said, standing up. "Where have you been in the last month? Eh?"

Tara breathed deeply and focussed. She knew she needed to be calm. She knew she needed to deal with this different. With Markus you couldn't meet fire with fire because then they'd be a bigger fire, the *biggest* fire.

"You're coming to live with me now. You're staying with me. Okay? Okay?"

Ryan nodded his head, wiping away tears.

"Things are going to be different. But listen."

Markus was texting again but this time Tars took the phone out his hand. "Listen," she said.

"Tut."

"I have my own life to lead, alright? I have my *own* life so you two need to buck up and help me. There's going to be new rules. New ways of doing things. I have my own life to live."

"Yeah. You said," Markus said.

"I've just got a new job at the hospital and I'm also in a relationship now."

Markus pulled a face. "Oh yeah. With who?"

"It doesn't matter right now. You'll meet him soon enough. But I need *you* to help *me*."

Both boys looked at her confused.

"I know we can do this. I know we'll get along. But Markus ... "

A scowl was set deep in his face.

"I need you to go to school."

He looked out the window.

"Look at me." She took his chin and pulled his face towards hers. "Go to school. Now there's no point getting you in till after the summer holidays but you *need* to go. I've already got to go to court for this and there's a lot to sort out but when you go, *go*. And *stay*. Don't get into fights and don't get expelled. I'm not expecting you to be a professor. I know it's not your thing but just go and keep your head down and get through it. That's all I ask."

Markus found himself nodding.

"And Ryan."

Again she made him look at her. "We're gonna be honest. We're gonna be open. We're gonna talk about things. No secrets in this house. Well, *my* house. The three of us will talk about *everything*. Now let me see your arms."

Markus looked over at his brother, then at his arms that were hidden under a jumper.

A jumper in May!? Markus thought.

"I haven't," Ryan said in a small voice.

"Let me have a look." Aunt Tars was already rolling up his sleeves.

His arms were covered in loads of white scars but no red ones, no new ones. "Good," she said. "Good boy."

She felt like she was getting somewhere, with both of them. Her mood had lifted.

"What did dad go to prison for?" Ryan asked.

"Lots of little things. He didn't pay fines. He didn't go to Community Service. He's in prison for being drunk Ryan."

Ryan nodded, happy with the answer.

"Now one last thing," she said. "Some people are going to be talking to you over the next few days. Lots of different people. I don't want you to worry. Just tell the truth. *Always* the truth. If we want to help dad they need to know everything, alright? There's nothing to be scared of. Nothing bad is going to happen. The worst is out the way."

Ryan was nodding and seemed to be happier too. Markus looked bored. But then he thought of something and his face changed. "I'm getting the bigger room though yeah? I mean I'm bigger so I need the bigger room."

"We'll see," Aunt Tars said smiling. "We may have to toss for it."

"Tails I win. Heads you lose." Markus was smiling now and Aunt

Tars always thought he had a good smile even though he rarely used it. A good big smile and a good head of hair.

"And you still got Netflix?"

"Yes Markus," she said "I've still got Netflix."

The brothers moved in. Markus got the bigger room. Although he was hardly in the bungalow anyway. He was always out. Checking out his new stomping ground. He liked it here because there were less people, less houses, less traffic, less noise. The sky above seemed bluer and he loved walking by the Clementine Channel. He only had to cut through an alleyway that was nestled in the corner of the horseshoe-shaped close, across an inclined patch of grass, and then he was up over the water. There were always people out walking. Old people and people with dogs. They nodded and said *hello* and it was much friendlier than the estate. Sometimes Markus would walk for miles, a whole afternoon, waving a stick in the long grass or throwing rocks into the water. He felt like he didn't need The Den anymore.

When he got back one day Aunt Tars was out, probably with her new boyfriend although Markus hadn't met him yet. Waiting until the time is right, she said. Markus didn't see what the big deal was. People were always making a drama out of everything. Just let me meet the prick, he thought.

"Ryan you in!?" he shouted.

He leant over the sink and ran the tap into his mouth, "Ryan!"

He went into the toilet and took a piss. On washing his hands he saw a drop of blood in the sink. He put his finger in it and tasted it. "Little bastard," he said. He tore through the bungalow and charged into Ryan's room. Ryan jumped up and a white, stringy bit of bandage unravelled off his arms. Markus grabbed it and pulled Ryan onto the bed and held it there for both of them to see. "What the fuck is this!"

"It's nothing," Ryan said, surprisingly calm.

"Doesn't look like nothing."

"Oh so what."

"You know what Tars said. No more of this shit."

Spit hit Ryan in the face and he had to put his head down. "Like you give a fuck about the rules."

"Why do you do it anyway?"

Ryan took his arm back. "Cos I like it, okay. I *just* like it."

"Why?"

"I don't know why."

"It's fucking weird."

"No weirder than the sick shit you look at on my laptop."

Markus blushed and turned away.

"*How to tie a noose. Cat off a block of flats. Cat off a bridge. Cat suffocates.*"

"That was last year," he said. "And I was just fucking about."

"Not to mention all that sex shit you watch."

Now it was Markus on the back foot. He stormed out the room and slammed the door, his brother's victorious voice chased after him. "Like you always say. *We are who we are.* So stay out of my business and I'll stay out of yours."

They ate a pasta dish that night. It was silent around the dinner table. Markus had his head down and Ryan sat upright with an unusual grace and calm, twiddling the pieces of pasta on his fork before slowly placing them in his mouth.

"Quiet tonight," Tara commented.

Silence followed more silence.

"Anyway," she said. "You'll get to meet Cog on Wednesday. He's coming over for dinner."

"Cog?" Markus said.

"It speaks suddenly," Tars said.

"What kind of a fucking name is Cog?"

"Language."

"Cog though, really? What's his surname, Wheel?"

Markus laughed and looked at his brother for support. None came.

Aunt Tars finished chewing what was in her mouth. "You laugh now," she said, smugly. "But you won't."

Her words squared-up to Markus like a challenge. A dumb animal hurt flickered in his face, like he'd been betrayed in some way. "Who is he? The Big Bad Wolf?"

Aunt Tars said nothing, amusement played lightly on her face.

After dinner the boys did the pots, Markus washed, Ryan dried. All the time Cog was on his mind. He was pissed-off. He was intrigued. Markus was a little nervous.

Markus woke to the voice of a child. It came from outside on the close. Moments later he heard the mother telling him off.

Eventually both voices got carried off by the wind.

He thought of his own mum. What would she be doing if she was still alive? What would think of Markus if she could see him now? Would she still love him? Would she be disappointed; tell him off, shout at him?

His daydream came to an end by a loud knock on the door. He waited for his auntie to answer but the knock came again, twice as hard. He thrashed his legs in the bed, pissed off about having to leave it. Having threw on a pair of blue Adidas joggers he went to the back door where the knocking continued.

There were two figures on the other side. Their images distorted by the pixilated glass. Markus leant forward and took a closer look. He vaguely recognised the hair of one of them, a tight mop of black curls.

When he opened he drew in a breath as the visitor's identities became clear.

"Alright Markus."

It was The Taylor Brothers.

Markus stepped back and prepared for some kind of physical onslaught. Stewie was smiling, Ewan was not. He realised they were linked by an orange mountain bike that filled the space between them. Emblazoned on the frame was the word *Mustang* in thick, black lettering.

"What do you want?" Markus said.

He kept himself out of reaching distance, his eyes glued to their chests. Any sudden shoulder movements and he'd hit first.

First in, first out, his dad always said.

As always the younger Stewie did the talking. "We want to give you a present." He let the mountain bike roll forward an inch. "We know how cut-up you were over that mongoose."

Markus was still expecting some kind of trap.

"Thought you could use this for your rounds," Stewie added.

Markus pulled a screw-face. "What rounds?"

Ewan was glaring at him like he didn't want any part of this.

"We want you to come and work for us. Work this side of town. We run the estate; you cover this side."

"Doing what?" Markus said, his lip was out and his hair was massive.

"Make drops. Pick up payment. Build custom."

Markus pulled another face and looked back into the bungalow for a second, making sure his aunt was out.

"Why me, what about ya other scabs?"

Ewan made a *tut*. Shook his head and looked the other way.

"You live this side innit," Stewie said. "Think we can trust you and we *know* you can handle yourself." He let out a little laugh. "Look mate I ain't gonna beg."

Stewie could already read the answer in his face. Markus was just testing and Stewie liked that.

"How do you know where I live anyway?"

Stewie replied by a gentle smirk on his lips.

"How much?" Markus said with a scowl.

"Put it one way," Stewie said. "You won't need to get a paper round."

Stewie nodded to his hand that was out before him, and five seconds later Markus took it.

Wednesday rolled around and Markus hated these unusual nerves that were rattling inside his body. He just wanted the night to arrive so he could meet this man head-on and see what all the fuss was about. Aunt Tars said seven so he had a few hours to get back to the bungalow and prepare. He didn't like it when he saw a rusty, pick-up truck in the driveway. He wondered if it was maybe the neighbour's or something but then he saw Aunt Tars through the kitchen window, and a dark figure sitting in front of her.

Markus put his hand on the door and breathed, mustered up something from his gut and then walked confidently into the kitchen. A pair of green eyes caught him and knocked that confidence straight back out.

"Markus, my favourite nephew," his auntie sang, yet there was a hint of something uncertain in her own voice too. "This is Cog. Cog ... Markus."

The introduction felt forced, like Tars had played the lines over too many times in her head.

The man's eyes landed on Markus and wouldn't move. Markus nodded and the man maybe nodded back. On meeting anyone new Markus always gave them The Eye Test. A little stare-off to establish who was boss. Markus never went into it to see who would win; he knew who would win: Markus. He did it to see how long they would last. See what kind of enemy I'm up against. Only this time

Markus didn't even engage. The Eye Test wasn't even an option. The man wasn't very big yet his presence took over the whole kitchen; bungalow, street. He was everywhere. He was all over Markus's world and there wasn't room for much else. His eyes followed the boy. His eyes hurt him. When Markus finally did look at him he looked annoyed, like he had an *explode-at-any-time aura*. His face was sharp and dark behind a small shaped beard. Thin, black hair was centre-parted on top of his head. He didn't know if his jaw was clenched or if it was always like that.

Markus was in the fridge although he didn't know what he was looking for.

"Markus what are you looking for?"

"I don't know."

"Come and sit down. I'll make you a cup of tea."

Markus had lost some of his basic motor skills and Tara had to help her nephew to the table with a guiding hand.

The man had still not said a word and the silence, for Markus, was unbearable.

A mug of steaming tea was put before him and Markus stared into it. He could still feel the man's eyes on him yet when he glanced over he found that they were not. Cog was just simply looking ahead, blank.

Moments later Ryan came into the kitchen, whistling. He had already met Cog and seemed totally at ease in his company, as if he could be any random person off the street. Ryan didn't get it. He didn't realise how dangerous this man was, how lethal. Ryan was oblivious. Maybe because he was too passive, too weak. His energy didn't clash with Cog the way Markus's did.

They ate. A family of four. A big steak dinner with peppercorn sauce and loads of veg. A jug of purified water was on the table and that was a new feature too. People talked over dinner but Markus couldn't remember what was said. He was stuck in his head and he couldn't get out of it. Cog talked, eventually. His voice was like his eyes, calm and penetrating. Choosing each phrase carefully, no sentence was superfluous, not a word wasted.

Towards the end he looked over at Markus.

"So Markus," he said, putting a neatly cut square of steak in his mouth. "How do you live?"

What a weird thing to say, Markus thought. Not *what do you do* or *what are you into?* But, *how do you live?* Markus couldn't help but feel that the question was a threat, a threat masquerading as pleasantries. He looked to his aunt and bro for a reaction but their faces remained neutral, like it was a perfectly ordinary question and then Markus wondered if he had heard it right.

"I dunno," he mumbled at last. "Just … "

Cog's eyes widened a touch, waiting for an answer.

"Day to day," he managed to say.

Cog nodded. "Best way."

It was then Markus noticed his neck. He'd never seen a neck like it before. It was full of muscle and sinew. It's like it was made up of bits of twisted rope.

While his auntie cleared the pots she addressed the boys.

"Just letting you know. Cog is staying the night. That alright with you guys?"

Guys? Tars was acting weird too. She would never use a word like *guys*. Cog was having an effect on this family and Markus didn't like it.

Aunt Tara looked at Ryan. "Sure," he sang.

She didn't look at Markus. She knew he wouldn't give her an answer but that's okay, she didn't need one. That little exercise was purposefully to establish; who was man of the house.

It was strange to be back on the estate again. In The Taylor Brothers kitchen talking business. Tea stains were splashed up the walls and fag ash treaded into the carpet. Mum nagging in the background while a toddler played fetch with a staffy.

"Mum either sort the kid out or sort the dog," Ewan shouted through. "They're doing my fucking head-in!"

More indecipherable nags sounded from the other room.

Stewie was sat smoking, calmly flicking ash into a tray while Ewan opened a case full of weed and knock-off cigarettes. By his feet was several crates of cheap cider.

"You don't drink or smoke do ya?" Stewie said.

Markus shook his head.

"That's what I heard."

Markus didn't understand.

"Well that's perfect. Just what we're looking for. Too many kids getting high off their own supply. Just why we choose *you*."

Markus could see Ewan shaking his head while he set up shop.

"That kettle gone yet?" Stewie said to the older.

Ewan didn't answer.

"Right," Stewie said, holding up a twenty bag of marihuana. "There's a stoner called Neil. Lives your end. He's seventeen but a right drip. Right pussy. You'll have no probs with him. Always has these studenty parties. Two or three times a week. Him and his mates buy a shit-load only he's always ringing at Stupid O' Clock in the morning so keep your phone on. There's these kids too, your end again, bout your age. Always getting wrecked on the rec. Only none of them can get served. Give them a crate only charge them double. Few of them smoke too. So you might shift a few ten bags. There's a couple of regular lads and there's Georgie who always buys on tic. Now he does pay eventually but you might need to give him the odd slap to hurry him along. A girl too, always wandering the Channel with her boyfriend. Probably does fifty's worth a week. Like I say Markus they're all kids so nothing you can't handle. Your name alone should keep them in check."

Your name, Markus thought, what was wrong with my name, what is he on about?

"There's an old fella that buys an Oz every month but I ain't trusting you with an Oz yet. See how we get on for a few weeks first."

What's an Oz, Markus thought? He saw the word, *Australia*.

He was finding all this a bit too much and felt out his depth.

"You keep all the dollar in this wallet," Stewie pulled out a huge black wallet. "I know *exactly* what should be coming back at the end of the week so I expect that number, no less. Don't let anyone haggle. Price's fixed. We've also got one of those ultra-violet machines so if any fucker uses those dodgy notes that's going around we'll know."

Markus nodded, a little dumbly. He was used to buying football stickers and playing on Xbox and all this seemed a little unreal.

"Now you got a place to stash this?" His fingers tapped on the different-sized bags

"Can't I just keep it in my bedroom?"

"Live with your auntie innit?"

"Yeah."

"She cool with that?"

"No she'd go fucking mad."

"Then *no* it's not alright in your bedroom it stinks to high-heaven."

Ewan turned on him. "Don't let your auntie be throwing it away or calling the police otherwise it's *your* head."

Ewan eyeballed him so Markus eyeballed him back until he looked away.

"That tea ready yet?" Stewie said to his brother.

Ewan sighed and went over to the kettle.

"He's right. You need to keep it in a safe place."

"I've got somewhere," Markus said, suddenly remembering The Den.

"Somewhere dry?"

"I've got somewhere."

"Somewhere safe?"

"I said I've got somewhere."

Ewan came back with the tea. He handed his brother a mug with the word *Benidorm* across it. In front of Markus a Manchester United mug was put down. Markus went to pick it up. On seeing the iconic badge his hand shot back as if he'd just been zapped by an electric fence.

"What the fuck!"

Both brothers glared at him. "What?" said Stewie.

"I can't drink out of that."

Stewie's eyes surveyed the mug. "It's clean you cheeky bastard."

"No it's not it's dirty."

Ewan was clearly offended and clenched his jaw.

"It's got scum on it," Markus went on.

Stewie clicked first and started to laugh. Ewan didn't get it and still thought he was talking about hygiene. "Coming in our house ... " he muttered.

"Forgot you a Mickey Mouse," Stewie said.

"A what?" Ewan said.

"A Mickey Mouse. A scouse. He's a Liverpool fan."

Stewie laughed more. "You're a funny lad Markus, a funny lad."

Markus still wouldn't smile. He stared at the mug like he wanted to smash it.

"Get him another mug Ew."

Ewan shook his head and took the cup. "Liberties," he whispered under his breath. "Fucking liberties," he said louder, pouring the tea from one mug into another.

On the way out Stewie invited him to a party on Saturday night. Some lad called Titch was having a party at his house. Some good lads were going to be there and there should be some bitches too, he said.

Markus nodded, only half-interested. He left The Taylor's with a rucksack of gear. Stewie slapped his arm, giving him some final words of encouragement/faith/veiled threats.

"I *know* you'll do us good."

Markus knew the score. He knew what he was getting himself into. Only he liked the risk, the edge. He liked the buzz and the newness of it all. It would give him an identity too, an image, status. It was like he was a character in a film. He was becoming *a somebody*. For Markus money came second. Money he could take or leave. He'd never had it anyway so what's the fuss? Although he could do with a new pair of trainers, his old ones had been talking to him for the last few weeks and it was kind of embarrassing. *Money*, maybe he could buy his Aunt Tars something nice to say Thank You for all that she's done. Although he had to be careful, stealth-like. Aunt Tars didn't miss a trick. It was kind of spooky how she knew things. Markus often wondered if she was psychic. The only thing that didn't appeal to him in all this was having to spend time with them pair of arseholes. The Taylor Brothers were scum, there was no two ways about it. One of them even supported Man U. Fuck it, he thought. I'll just do it over the summer. Something to do. Something to fill the time. Have a laugh. Save a bit of cash. Fuck it all off before I go back to school in September.

He had to walk past his old house on the way out. It seemed empty and he wondered if anyone else had moved in. It had only been two months yet it seemed ages ago. It was July and the estate was very different in the summer. In the summer the estate was buzzing. It felt like a carnival whereas in the winter it was a funeral. Markus only really remembered the winters. He stood at the fence and looked into the backyard, through the windows. He imagined his dad slumped in one of the corners. Ryan flapping over him like a hysterical woman. Nah, not missing much, he thought, moving on.

Tara and the two boys were sat in the living room watching the soaps, Emmerdale then EastEnders. He preferred Emmerdale because the women were better-looking and the people seemed marginally happier. EastEnders was intense. The characters were either hysterical or suicidal. Soaps were supposed to portray real life. People were fucked up, Markus knew this by now, but not *that* fucked up.

All the way through Markus made comments and Aunt Tars had to keep telling him to shut up.

"I'm watching this," she said, not taking her eyes off the screen.

Ryan played on his phone and never looked up once. Since moving into Tara's Ryan spent more time out of his bedroom. He seemed happier too, he talked more and didn't seem so timid.

Just as they were getting ready for bed Tara said, "so, what did you make of Cog?"

"Cool," Ryan said.

"Bit of a twat," Markus said.

Markus hoped the comment would offend Tara but it didn't. It's like she was expecting it. She smiled and this infuriated Markus more.

"Prick didn't talk."

Tara put on a pair of glasses and picked up a book, one of those *Fifty Shades* novels. "He likes *you*," she said.

Markus stopped pouring coke into his glass and looked surprised.

"Night," Ryan went into his room.

"Night love," Tara shouted after him.

"How can he like me he doesn't even know me?"

"Says you remind him of himself, when he was your age."

Markus made a *pisssssst* sound but she could see he was secretly flattered.

"Anyway," she said. "Nanite."

She turned off the light and left Markus in the dark.

Markus had two-hundred and eighty quid in his pocket. The most money he'd ever had at one time. It was in the big black leather wallet Stewie had given him.

At the party Stewie took it off him and counted it out. "Nice one. So, you should still have a couple of twenty-bags left, yeah?"

Markus nodded.

"And the knock-off fags?"

"Not sold."

"And the crates you picked up in the week?"

"Selling them on Wednesday."

"Nice one."

Ewan stood next to them, he seemed half-drunk and happy for once. He put a hand through his red hair and nodded at Markus. "Nice one," he echoed.

"Here," Stewie gave Markus two twenty-pound notes. "For now."

Part of Markus was happy and part of him was unsure. He had no idea if he was being ripped-off or not. Stewie put his hand on his back and lead him into the party. Most of the people Markus recognised from the estate. There were a few girls too. A tall mixed-race girl and a busty brunette with her hair slapped back into a bun. Both of them were drunk and loud. They were about two years older than Markus. There was another girl too, a blonde pretty girl who was sitting in a lad's lap. Markus thought he could smell something. He put his nose up and sniffed out the room. It was the same scent he had been carrying in his rucksack all week.

When Stewie introduced him to the girls Markus got nervous. He wasn't used to talking to girls and he became cripplingly self-conscious. He said something stupid and everybody laughed.

"Who is this little man?" the mixed-race girl said.

"He's my boy, Markus. Markus Venner. Craziest fucker you'll ever meet."

Stewie slapped his back like that was a good thing, like it was his label. *Markus Venner: Crazy.*

The mixed-race girl looked him up and down. "Don't look crazy."

"Looks about twelve," the other one said, laughing.

Markus didn't like being introduced like this. It was like he was a freak and everybody was looking at him.

An hour passed and Markus really wanted to leave. They were all drunk and stoned and the music was so loud he couldn't hear himself think.

Then a boy stepped forward and shouted into the room. "Guess what lads, Crystal Palace is on her way!"

All the boys started cheering and going nuts. One lad grabbed his balls with one hand and high-fived his mate with the other.

Markus was confused, he thought Crystal Palace was a football team.

The only people who didn't look happy were the girls. The mixed-race girl stood and cocked her head to one side. "You lot are sick!" Her earrings swung and she did these gangster signs with her hands. "What you do to that girl is bordering rape."

"Fuck off," a fat lad shouted. "She loves it."

"She's fucking retarded and you lot take advantage," the brunette girl added. "Got a good mind to report you."

"Just jealous," Ewan said, who by now was really pissed and staggering all over the place.

"Please!" Both girls said at the same time.

Ten minutes later there was a cheer and Markus saw a chubby blonde girl walk down the driveway. The party got quiet all of a sudden, like something bad was about to happen. A dark curiosity came over Markus and he decided to stay a little longer.

All the boys mounted at the door. Ewan's drunk-flustered face turned to Markus and said, "honestly mate, you wanna get on this. She'll do *any*thing to *any*one at *any* time."

He turned back to the door and waited for the girl to walk through it.

Markus was still confused. He had an idea what Ewan was talking about but he wasn't entirely sure. All this was new to him.

Eventually a girl stepped into the room and Markus thought it must be the wrong person; that they were talking about someone else. She looked sweet and polite and the description didn't fit.

"Hi," she said. She almost sounded posh, only the girls had called her a *retard*? Markus sat and waited for another girl to step in, some estate trash wearing a mini-skirt and crop top. This girl was dressed quite nice. She wore a long floral dress and had sparkly bracelets on her arms. She wasn't pretty, or even attractive. Her face was peculiar, her mouth was big and she had a square-shaped jaw. Her eyes were a little too close together and she looked around the room like she didn't belong here, and knew it.

She spoke to the girls first, "hi Candice, hi Skylar."

"Alright Crystal," they both said, part mocking, part sympathy.

Markus watched on, intrigue growing.

Somebody had put a can in her hand and already the boys were jostling for position.

"That's our cue to leave," mixed-race girl said.

She shook her head and Skylar followed.

"What's up girls?" Ewan shouted. "Fucking off now the competition's here?"

Candice did another comical gangster sign with her hand, and left.

Somebody had taken Crystal's hand only Markus couldn't see

who. There were so many boys crowding her it was hard to tell. He traced the arm until it ended on the shoulder of Luke Beadman. Luke was disgusting. He was fat and pale and always had a fag in his mouth and the same multi-coloured baseball cap on his head. He had a hair-lip and spat everywhere when he talked. And when he talked he nearly always talked about sex. There were rumours on the estate that he used to have sex with his younger sister. Whenever he was asked about it he'd just pull this grotesque face and laugh. Markus looked at his face and wanted to destroy it. There was something about Beadman that made his blood boil. He was everything he hated in life.

"Steady Beady," Ewan shouted. "Not having her all to yourself."

Ewan stuck his hand up the back of her dress and began moving his arm up and down. Markus couldn't believe what he was seeing. Beady grabbed a boob and then another lad joined in. Another one kissed her and more boys tried to get in on the action. Markus felt like he had to do something only the girl didn't seem to mind. She didn't seem to be enjoying it either. It's like she was just *there,* blank, neutral. Like she was doing something totally ordinary, waiting in the queue at McDonald's.

Soon the mass began edging towards a brown door. He looked at them and thought of one of those wildlife shows on telly, like when a pack of hyenas were on a zebra, all attached onto a different body part, trying to bring it down. Someone kicked the door open and they were almost inside, Beady leading the way. Just then Markus heard his name being called.

"Markus kid!" It was Ewan. He had one hand holding the door and the other full of breast.

"Markus man c'mon, get in!"

The whole party was looking at him.

"C'mon kid." Another one shouted. "It's all for free."

The only lad not in the mass was Stewie. He was sat in the opposite armchair with a spliff hanging out his mouth. "Go on Venner," he said "Go and wet your whistle."

Terror hijacked his body and Markus didn't know what to do. None of it felt right and his primal instinct was to take off, bolt straight for the front door. Instead he dropped his head and stared at the crusty carpet and prayed it would swallow him up.

"Fucking hell man what's wrong with you!" It was Ewan again. "You gay?"

The insult smacked him in the face and brought him back to life. Markus was on his feet before he knew it. "Fuck you say to me?"

Ewan saw the screw-face and the demon in his eye. "I said are you a *virgin*?" He was playing it down and trying to laugh it off. The door was almost closed. The moving mass of a sex-monster almost out of sight. Markus felt some fingertips lightly pull at his jeans.

He looked down to see Stewie looking up at him. "It's cool," he said. "Sit."

The brown door slammed but Markus still glared at it.

"Sit," Stewie said again.

Markus did, reluctantly.

The only people left was Stewie and the couple. The girl was still sat in his lap where she'd been all night. Markus couldn't even see what the boy looked like. He was just arms and legs with a blonde girl for a torso. They were passing the spliff around between the three of them. Markus sat back, still boiling. Eventually the rage was overtaken by unease, unease then by fear. All packed into a neat box of paranoia. What if they all knew about The Carmen Situation, the story of the twins from his previous school? What if the rumours had travelled this far and everybody knew? Markus looked at Stewie, then at the blonde girl. They both looked pretty wasted and their faces were hard to read. Just then the boy under the girl leaned forward and handed the spliff to Markus. The gesture suddenly brought Stewie to life. "I'll take that," he said, taking the spliff.

"You don't smoke?" The lad said, brushing back a curtain of blonde hair from his girlfriend. Before Markus opened his mouth Stewie answered for him. "No he *doesn't*. And no he *won't*. Not having my best earner getting *the taste*."

The stoned boyfriend accepted the answer and then disappeared back behind the blonde veil of his girlfriend.

Markus sat back and his head felt light anyway, just from the passing vapours. He thought he could hear noises from behind the brown door, or maybe that was in his head? Either way, it was time to leave.

"I'm off."

He thought Stewie may contest this but he didn't. He did catch him at the front door though, his movements slow and his eyes doped and heavy.

"Hey Markus."

He turned and faced him.

"Don't mind Ew. He was just joking."

Markus nodded.

"Pop round in the week. Give you some more contacts, and gear. You did well."

He slapped Markus's face lightly and that angered him. Stewie was supposed to be The Hardest Kid on The Estate but right now he knew he could take him. One blast in his mouth and he'd be straight through that door. And there'd be no getting back up. Then he'd take his older brother out, then Beady, then the rest of the perverts in this shit-hole crack-den.

Markus nodded, and left.

He was glad to be out of there. The moon was full and high in the sky. It was like a spotlight following him home. He could hear the faint flow of the Clementine Channel. He headed towards it and couldn't wait to get there, near nature, away from people. Only he wasn't free yet because he heard two female voices from the bushes, down by the park. A triplet of Adidas lines streaked through the dark.

"Oi."

Markus ignored it and carried on walking.

"Oi kid come here."

There was no escaping. He felt like the night had a grip of him. He recognised the voices even though he'd only heard them once. It was from Candice and Skylar whom he'd met earlier. They were sitting on a wooden beam eating a cone of chips.

"Want a chip?"

Since moving out of his dad's Markus had developed a hatred of chips. The thought of eating just one made him feel sick.

"The wolves still in Crystal Palace?"

Markus had forgotten about the girl's nickname and for a moment he thought Candice was talking about football.

"Don't talk much do ya?"

She was chewing gum *and* eating chips which Markus found weird.

He shrugged.

"You wanna stay away from those lot they're bad news."

Moonlight slipped over her bare brown stomach and cooled it. Her belly-stud winked under its glow. Candice had a piercing above her lip too, to the left. The more he looked at her the more she looked like the girl he fancied from *Little Mix*. The girl he had wanted to put a poster up of but daren't because of what his dad would say. *Take that nigger off my wall.* He couldn't understand why his dad hated black people so much. *Don't ever let me catch you going out with a spook. It's not right. Shouldn't mix.* Markus didn't get it because black girls were beautiful. Leigh-Anne Pinnock was, Beyoncé was, and Candice was.

"How old are you anyway?" she said.

"Old enough."

That burst the girls into laughter and they almost dropped their chips.

"Okay then," she said.

"You're a runner for Stewie aren't you?" Skylar said.

Markus nodded, feeling a rush of pride.

"Big man, hey?" Candice said.

"No," Markus replied with a scowl.

"They'll rob you y'know," she said with an air of certainty.

"What do you mean?" Markus suddenly got interested.

"They'll rip you off. It's standard. They always get little yewts to do their dirty work and then *they* pick up the green. It's standard."

Markus knew he had to fight his corner, and maybe his boss's too. "It's *their* gear," he grumbled.

"*You're* taking the risk. It's *you* carrying. It's *you* who'll get busted. It's *you* who will go down. I've seen it before."

She put a finger to her own brain. "Think about it," she said.

Her sidekick Skylar was nodding.

"I know what I'm doing."

"I'm sure you do." Candice smiled, rolling her eyes. "Ever been to a Y.O.I?"

"What's a Y.O.I?"

"Young Offenders Institute innit."

"Nope."

"You will if you carry on running for them scumbags."

"You hang around with them," Markus said, still clinging to some kind of defiance.

"Not really," Candice said.

"We just pass the time," her mate added.

"Anyway little man, don't say we didn't warn you."

It pissed him off why Candice kept calling him *little man*. He was the tallest lad at the party so why did she keep calling him *that*?

Perhaps Candice could see straight through him. It's like she had something. It was more than just street wisdom. It's like she *knew things*.

"Whatever." Markus bit the air and moved on.

"Charming," she sang, laughing, not a hint of being offended.

As Markus walked home he was confused at why he was so rude to Candice. It was obvious that he fancied her like mad and all she had done was show concern and care for him. Markus hated the way he behaved. Sometimes, he just didn't understand himself.

Markus crept into the bungalow as quietly as he could. He kept the lights off and went into the fridge, reaching for a carton of apple juice.

"Thought your auntie said to be back by ten."

His heart stopped first and he dropped the carton second. It exploded all over his feet.

"What the fuck!" he gasped.

The faint outline of a human form sat in the corner of the kitchen. When he turned on the light he could see a topless Cog eating a whole chicken with his bare hands. The light blinded Markus for a few seconds and at first he had it down for a hallucination.

"Is that you?"

Cog never answered, just carried on eating. His fingers shiny with grease.

"Look at the mess you've made," he said.

Markus was on his hands and knees, mopping up the juice with a pack of cloths.

"Want some chicken?"

"No, thanks," he said.

How he was planning to give him any was a mystery. The carcass was pretty much stripped.

"What bad shit have you been getting up to tonight?" Cog said in his calm tone.

Anyone else and Markus would have told them to mind their own fucking business but his green bottomless eyes levelled him. Markus had seen these eyes before in a different face. He saw the word, *Carmen.*

"Nothing," the boy said at last, sheepish.

"Hmm," Cog pondered. "I don't believe you. I don't believe you cos it takes one to know one and I know you."

He was talking in riddles and Markus didn't get it. When Cog moved out from the table Markus was shocked to see his physique. It was totally ripped, not an ounce of fat. It was impressive but at the same time it looked freaky and gross. His skin was covered in scars and scar tissue. His torso was brown and hairless. He looked like a machine.

"How old are you?" he said.

Markus considered giving Cog the same insolent answer as he did to Candice, *old enough.* Only he didn't. "Nearly thirteen," he said.

It was the first time he saw him standing and he couldn't believe how small he was. Well not small, but short. He was short, shorter than Markus. Markus was 5'9 by now and this man was a good two inches shorter yet he still felt massive. Markus was tiny beside him. It's the way he carried himself, the way he held himself together, all relaxed and powerful. Full of purpose and poise. His head was over his hips, his chest sunk and his back seemed to expand, spread out to each corner of the room. His head remained still and his arms were coiled and ready, like he could spring into action at any given minute.

"Nearly thirteen," Cog repeated, his lips sticking together.

He was now stood quite close to him, studying the boy, like he was making his mind up about something. "Heard you did your daddy?"

"What?" Markus said with an intake of breath.

"Did him. Fucked him over. Beat him up."

Markus nodded his head slowly as the memory swam in.

"Yeah I chucked a mug at his eye. Gave him nine stiches," he said, proud.

"Why'd you do that?"

"He sold Mongoose."

"He sold what?"

"Mongoose. My BMX. He sold her to go and buy some booze."

"He did that?"

"Yeah."

"Well that's a shitty thing to do. Selling your *own* son's bicycle. Disgraceful."

"So I fucked him up."

"You did?"

"Yeah."

"You punch him?"

"I tried but he was too big so I threw a mug at his eye instead."

"Show me how you punched him."

Markus tried to get into a fighting stance but the kitchen was too small.

"I tried for a right hook, a haymaker."

Cog was looking right into him. "I said *show* me how you punched him."

Markus suddenly got nervous and he didn't like this feeling. "What do you mean?" he said.

Cog leaned forward and put the palm of his hand out like a boxing trainer. "Show me how you punch."

Markus moved his body around, feeling a wave of pressure. "Here, in my kitchen?"

"Yeah," Cog said.

Markus shifted around more, skittish, trying to get into position. Again he looked into Cog's eyes and felt his usual aggression diminish.

"Go," Cog said.

He unleashed a right and felt his knuckles sink into Cog's palm with a slap.

"Good," said Cog, genuinely impressed. "Again."

He let off another bomb and this time he felt his knuckle hit something sharp. A gold ring gleamed on one of his greasy fingers.

"Again," Cog said.

He wanted to ask Cog to remove the ring but that would be a definite sign of weakness. He launched another but it wasn't as strong as his previous two shots.

"You hit well," Cog said.

Telling me what I already know, Markus thought, smug.

"You follow through but there's something missing," Cog said.

Markus felt his pride pop like a balloon.

"You follow through but you follow through *too* much. You give yourself away."

Markus was confused and it showed in the lines of his face.

"Let me show you."

Cog now took to Markus's side of the room, creating more space. "Punch again," he said.

Markus paused this time, feeling the aggression build up like a fire. He wanted to make this one count. Only this time when he went for it he felt his legs go from under him and he went crashing to the floor. His head was spinning and the world was upside down. He thought the noise may wake the bungalow up but for some reason it didn't. Cog's dark figure loomed over him. He held out a hand and hoisted Markus back onto his feet like he was an inflatable doll. As easy as he had him on the floor was as easy as he had him back up.

"What the fuck was that?" Markus said, genuinely perplexed. "You sweep my feet?"

Cog shook his head.

"What then?"

"You borrowed too much energy. Gave yourself away. All I had to do was take it. Watch."

Cog told him to do it again only this time he slowed it down, showed him the mechanics of his own physicality and framework. "You need to remain rooted. It's good that you use the whole of your body but the punch needs to snap."

"How do you do that?" Markus felt alive with intrigue, like he was about to be revealed some great secret.

"I'll teach you."

Markus's eyes widened.

"But it's late. Another time."

"When?"

"Whenever I'm around."

Markus wanted to ask when that was but he knew not to push it. Cog noticed Markus was breathing a little heavily. "Take your shirt off."

"What?" A blankness washed over Markus's expression.

"You're a strong boy but you're out of shape. Take your shirt off."

Markus pulled off his t-shirt. The boy noticed the drastic contrast to the man's body, especially the complexion. Markus was so white he glowed.

"You're out of condition," Cog said. "Big time. You've got boobs. Terrible for a boy your age. What shit has your dad been feeding you?"

"Chips."

"You need protein," Cog said. "You need eggs, and chicken."

Markus had never felt so self-conscious and pathetic.

"Before I teach you anything you need a strong engine. You can't go into battle without anything other than a tank."

Markus nodded, holding his t-shirt with both hands.

"Put your top back on."

Markus did.

Cog looked at him again, long and hard. He nodded. "Yes," he said. "You've got it inside. It burns."

Markus didn't know what he meant and he wanted to ask but knew he shouldn't. Cog walked away, to Tara's room, which was at the other end of the bungalow.

Markus got in bed and thought about the night. It rolled right through him in reverse: Cog's claw dripping in chicken. Candice's moonlit, midnight skin. Crystal's lost expression trapped behind a jungle of savage faces. Markus was slowly being taken over by sleep and these images kept flashing in his head. Markus didn't dream but if he ever was going to tonight was the night, here, now.

The Den, at one time, was at the centre of his universe. Now it was just a place to stash his gear. He'd taken down all the personalised décor and regarded that as an immature phase, *a boy and his den*. Now he was a man with a plan. Plus he couldn't afford the risk of bringing it to attention. He kept the rucksack hidden, in a patch of undergrowth beneath the fallen tree. It was dry and safe and impossible to find. The only way of being robbed was if someone had followed him and was watching with a pair of binoculars.

Markus only had four more twenty-bags to shift and then he was out. Stewie would be over-the-moon and Markus might get paid a bit more this time. He took the rucksack and headed out The Den. It was warm but overcast and Markus liked this kind of weather the best. It was all moody and tropical like something big was about to happen. He picked his bike up from his house and then cycled down towards the precinct. He dismounted Mustang and pushed her for a bit. Just then he saw someone come out the pet shop and cut across his path. He recognised the girl, the walk, the face. She turned and looked at him and Markus tried to put his head down and ignore her. Her dirty-blonde hair got tossed up by a breeze and then that big-jawed mouth moved. "Hi," she said.

Markus pretended she was a stranger.

"Eyup," he said, only just.

"You were at the party the other night, Markus, right?"

He was amazed she knew his name and couldn't recall ever giving it to her. He wanted to deny it. "Yeah," he said.

"Crystal," she said her name all wide-eyed and happy like they were long-lost friends. She surveyed his face, probably wondering what number boy in the queue he was.

"Yeah," Markus grunted. He couldn't be ruder if he tried.

"Yeah I remember you," she said, all sing-song and her behaviour tripped him out. It's like she had no idea what she had done. It was as if she'd been to a normal, civilised dinner-party.

"You left early, right?"

Irritated, Markus nodded fast and was moments away from screaming down her neck STAY AWAY FROM ME YOU DIRTY SLAG.

"Just been pet shop," she said. "Get my guinea pig his din-dins for the month." She clapped a plastic bag with her fingers and giggled. Then she looked up at the sky and squinted, made a sun-shade with her hand. "Think it's gonna rain," she said.

"I hope it does," he said.

She got really excited and pulled a big face. "Hey me too I love the rain! I love any weather that is different. Like rain, snow, sun, wind. When it's extreme and makes the world look different. Does that make sense?"

Markus found himself nodding. "There was a rainbow over the Channel yesterday, see it?"

"Oh no wow, really?" Crystal said. "I should walk that more. It's beautiful out there. I know I should make more of an effort."

"I walk it most days, nights too," Markus said. "Clears my head."

"Bit of a thinker, then?" she asked.

"Dunno. Never thought about it."

When he realised what he'd said they both laughed. They talked on and before they knew it they were outside a house and Markus wondered how he'd got there. It's like he'd done the whole journey on autopilot.

"Well, this is me," she said, standing outside a shithole of a house. Two of the windows were boarded-up and the lawn was so overgrown you could barely see the door. It was even worse than his old house. Only Crystal didn't seem embarrassed by it at all. Markus saw the word, *oblivious*. He looked at her face and it was like it had changed throughout the journey of the walk. He had begun to notice more things there, a mole, a squint, a dimple on her chin.

"Hey well if you ever want company walking the Channel then I'd love to go."

She had this unusual front, a confidence and glow that was impervious to others. Like she didn't care what the other person was thinking.

"Yeah, sure," Markus found himself saying.

Before he knew it she had a hold of his phone and was punching in her number. Not once did he think to look around to see if anyone else was watching. That realisation only hit him a few minutes later when he was walking away.

What the fuck are you doing, he said to himself? Suddenly paranoia came in and he couldn't cycle home fast enough. He got there and fell on his bed and searched through his phone until he came to the name *Crystal* with a number after it.

He went onto the Delete option, his thumb hovering over the red button.

A few days later Markus had a pair of Liverpool football shorts on. He tied up his trainers and began doing stretches. There was nothing more he hated in the world than running.

"Strips fat," Cog said.

Markus sighed and was praying to God that no one saw him.

"Half-hour three times a week and those boobs will be gone."

Markus just wanted to get to the fighting bit. He wanted to be like Anthony Joshua, not Mo Farah. Cog lead the way. They cut through the alleyway and took the usual route up to the Clementine Channel. Five minutes in and Markus was already dying. His face was burning and his chest stung and it was like someone had smashed his ribcage in with a sledgehammer.

"Careful," Cog said.

Sensing it before he saw it, a pit-bull came bounding around the corner, attached to a girl. The girl was no way near strong enough to contain it. Cog stopped running and walked straight towards the dog. Markus was too tired to take any of it in. He spat out a string into the grass and took the opportunity to stop. The dog did too, under the glare of Cog. The girl had her head down and seemed embarrassed by the whole thing.

"Sorry," she muttered.

As soon as they were gone Cog started up again, and Markus had to follow. Back home Markus lay sprawled out on the driveway.

"Terrible for a boy your age," Cog reminded him. "When I was thirteen I used to cover the county in one afternoon."

Markus made pained grunts and tried to get up.

"Your next run will be easier, one after that even easier. Soon you'll be on it, then we'll fight."

"Show me that punching thing," Markus managed to say.

"Not yet."

Cog had his top off and Aunt Tars looked at them both from the kitchen window.

Over the next few weeks Cog had whipped Markus into shape. Now he began to show him some basic fighting techniques. How to punch and where to punch. He showed him how to *snap* without giving himself away. He taught him framework and bits of combative psychology. They played out a few confrontational scenarios, doing a drill called *touch and go*. Where an attacker makes a move and then the would-be victim has to respond. Over the dinner table they talked about it and Markus said the words, *thank you Cog.*

Aunt Tars suddenly lifted her eyes up from her dinner plate. She made a little cough and then addressed the table. "In all the years I've known you nephew, never have I heard those two words come from your mouth. *Thank* and *You*. Wow. Miracles."

Cog showed no reaction.

Markus had his head down. "Don't be daft. Course you have."

"Really Markus," she said. "Never. The times they are a-changin."

Markus shook his head, smiling. "Hey Ryan you should come training with us?"

Everyone looked at the older brother, who pulled a face and smiled. "I would but I'm washing my hair," he said.

Everyone laughed, and even Cog managed to pull a slight smile.

Aunt Tars looked around the table. It's taken a while, she thought, but these are good times.

Markus was in shape. The boy-boobs were gone and his stomach was more or less flat. He had muscle, definition. He lay on his bed and looked at the Leigh-Anne Pinnock poster now on his wall. His hand had found its way into his boxer shorts but then suddenly, from nowhere, another thought came to mind. He sat up and reached for his phone, scrolling down to the letter C. He was going to call but decided to send a text instead.

It took only two minutes for him to receive a reply.

Ten minutes later he was on his way to the Clementine Channel to meet a girl.

Twenty minutes after that Markus was no longer a virgin.

The first thing he wanted to do was leave, get the hell out of there. He scrunched his eyes and hoped by the time he opened them again she was gone, that all of this was imagined. He did that but Crystal was still there, laying on her back, that vacant look on her face, her massive jaw sticking out in the twilight. He moaned and rolled over, wondering what he was going to do.

"You okay?" her voice was gentle, nurturing, like she had picked up that something was wrong.

And something was.

He was here, in this room, this bed. He'd just lost his virginity to Crystal Palace, the town bike. The girl who was known as a slag, a tramp. A girl who was called by other girls, *retard, Mongol, flid.*

All the boys had been there but that was different. That was done in a pack. It was a party-trick, something to laugh about. It wasn't serious, just a joke, a piss-take, mockery. They didn't actually fancy her. They didn't actually like her. They didn't choose her from other girls because she was pretty, cool, sexy, fun. They just did it cos they could. Because she was *there,* available, convenient. They didn't take her number and text her and meet her and go to her bedroom and lose their virginity with her. It wasn't a one-on-one, intimate thing, like a boyfriend and girlfriend deal.

Markus shivered in the bed, repulsed by his own actions. His head was in bits. He couldn't believe how fast it had all happened. Only an hour ago he was in his own bed, ready to have a little tug after his work-out to the gorgeous Leigh-Anne Pinnock but then something crazy came over him. This irrational sexual force. It was almost like he had no free-will, like it was someone else, a madman acting on his behalf.

He was confused by how different the two feelings were, the before and the after, *that* and *this. That* was driven to Crystal almost like it was a bodily need, like hunger or thirst. He had no doubt or hesitation when he met her at the Channel. Kissed her straight away.

"Anyone in at yours?"

She shook her head dumbly and he almost led her to her own house, no different to the pervs at the party who lead her through that dirty brown door. He got lost in the kissing. The close proximity blurred out her features and he got so carried away he found her to be pretty, beautiful even. He's not a hundred-percent but he may have even told her, said the words out-loud.

"You're beautiful."

She stopped and looked at him weird, shocked. She looked at him like he was mad; stupid, blind. "Really?" she said.

He couldn't remember what he had said but he nodded anyway and carried on, taking her clothes off. He put it in for the first time and he couldn't believe how good it felt. Although it wasn't like how people described. It wasn't tight nor was it wet. She didn't scream like they said either. In fact she didn't make any noise at all. It was silent. Silent the whole time. Her face was still so close and all he could see was the pink of her nose and the blue of her eye and the blonde of her hair and for a moment he tranced-out and it felt like he was with Mazie Vickers. Mazie Vickers, that beautiful enemy of his.

"Sure you're alright?"

That and *this*. *That* felt all of that but *this* felt all of this. Regret. Guilt. Humiliation. Inadequacy. A self-hatred so loathsome he wanted to hurt himself. He imagined *their* faces if they could see him now: Crystal Palace laying in his arms. Oh my. If this ever gets out I'll do myself in, he thought, suicide for definite this time. Fill my pockets with rocks and walk out to the Clementine Channel in the middle of the night.

"Markus you alright?" she seemed worried now, really concerned.

He found himself nodding, staring into space. He was so lethargic he couldn't move and after twenty minutes or so the come-down dropped off and he began to feel a little better, not much, but a bit. He began to take in his surroundings, the bare cube-like room. No carpet just squares of newspaper, cut-up linoleum and a rug on the floor. No wallpaper either, just pictures of nature-scenes blu-tacked to the wall, rivers, mountains, sunset fields and a rainbow.

Bit gay, Markus thought.

The window had no curtain or blind and it was like the whole world could see in.

It was dark, by now.

Their legs were still wrapped and Markus wanted her to take them away yet at the same time he liked it. It felt quite nice. Her legs were big and smooth and unusually warm. It was the closest he had ever been to another human being.

"I'm hungry," she said from nowhere.

Her voice winced when she said it, like she was in pain.

"Me too," he said, realising his own hunger.

"I got no food."

"Where's your parents anyway?" he said.

She shrugged. "Mum at her boyfriend's I imagine."

She put her forearm across her stomach. "There's never any food."

He noticed a birthmark on her pink forearm. It was a brown patch with blonde hairs sticking out of it. He turned away in disgust and then got that overwhelming feeling to take-off again.

A few moments passed and he heard the rumbling of a stomach, hers or his he couldn't tell, maybe both?

"Fancy a pizza?" he said.

She closed her eyes and purred. "You read my mind. Because if I could choose anything in the world right now it would be that. A big, fat pizza with hot melted cheese."

She opened her eyes again. "But got no money."

Markus had to pause and take in a breath before he decided to turn these next words loose. He had to think about it because they could get him into trouble.

I really should go, he thought, I really should get out of here while I can. I've already been here long enough, too long, far too fucking long.

"I have money," he said. "I'll get us one."

Straight away she sat up and looked at him with eyes of love, as if it was the nicest thing anyone had ever said to her. "Really?" she said. Her eyes glittered like she had diamonds in them. "You'd do that?"

Markus was already putting a sock on, his lip out. "It's just a pizza, it's no big deal. What flavour?"

Her hands were clasped, a cheesy smile spread over that epic jaw. "Any. I don't care. Maybe ham and pineapple."

"Hawaiian then?"

"Any. You choose."

Markus thought about the diet Cog had given him. Fuck it, he thought.

He stepped out into the night. No longer a virgin. Thirteen years old and the V-sign was off his neck. He walked the still, silent streets. Dominoes wasn't far, just in the corner of the precinct. Five minutes away, if that.

The lights from the precinct hurt his eyes. The yellow and red neon cut into the summer dark. Two drunks were holding each other up by a bin and a kid wearing glasses kicked a can against Lidl wall, its metallic sound echoed through the flat, concrete square. At the florescent counter Markus ordered a Mighty Meaty thick crust and a Hawaiian thin. He also got a two-litre of Coke and some wedges with a garlic dip. The smell of the food was driving him insane as it wafted up from the boxes and he was tempted to pop it open and steal a slice. Only he wanted to wait. He wanted to wait, wait for Crystal. As he passed a line of parked cars he suddenly heard his name being called out. He recognised the voice only it bewildered him.

"Venner!"

One of the cars had a window down with a face in it. The face had sunglasses on even though it was night. It wasn't until he saw the stringy black hair and the smile that he realised it was Stewie Taylor. Horror came all over him in an instant.

"What you doing out here at this time of night?"

"Pizza," Markus replied dumbly, holding up the box.

"I can see that," Stewie said. "But you live on Norman. Pizza Hut just round the corner."

"Fancied the walk." Markus felt his voice go up a notch and he was becoming flustered.

Only Stewie seemed to accept it. "Jump in we'll give you a lift."

Markus stood there, not saying anything.

"Just waiting on Beady. He's making a drop." Stewie popped the back door. "Get in."

Markus's palms were sweating like mad and his brain had stopped working altogether. A muscle in his leg tensed and he jerked towards the car. *So Close.* So close and it'd make life so much easier. Only Crystal's face floated in his mind. He felt her hunger through his own. He saw how happy she was, how moved, how touched that someone was doing something for her, buying her something, if only a pizza, a pizza with ham and pineapple on it.

"I'm gonna walk," he said.

Stewie pulled a screw-face. "Ya mad?"

"It's a nice night."

That cracked Stewie up. "You an old man or something? Only old people say shit like that and only old people *enjoy* walking. No one our age walks if they don't have to. Ya mad? Besides, your pizzas will go cold by the time you get home."

"Microwave."

"Ya mad? Who wants a microwaved pizza?"

Just then the hairs on the back of his neck pricked. Beady waddled into his peripheries. That blinding multi-coloured cap of his ducking into the car.

"Alright Venner?" he leered.

Markus nodded. The entrance of Beady made him even more determined to stick to his guns. Markus was not getting in that car. He was going back to Crystal.

"Suit yourself weirdo," Stewie said.

The engine started and hip-hop music blasted from the car. "Party Friday," Stewie shouted through it. "Same house as before. Be there at eight."

Markus showed no expression, just nodded.

The car beeped twice and Beady thought it was funny to stick two fingers up as he drove away.

Cog unzipped a bag of knives.

"Whoa!"

Markus's face shined like the collection of bladed instruments before him. He reached inside and took one of the handles.

"Careful," Cog said. "That'll have your finger off."

There were outside in the back garden.

He took the six-inch blade off the boy. "Stand back."

Markus did and then Cog broke into a rapid knife pattern, carving up the air in front of him. His movements were fluid and devastating, the weapon shimmered so fast it appeared like there were ten separate blades rather than the one.

"Whoa!" Markus said. "What the fuck is that?"

Cog stopped, twirling the knife into a leather sheath which was tied to his waist. "Piper," he said.

"What?"

"Piper Knife Fighting System. It's a criminal art used in the ghettos of Cape Town."

Hearing the words *criminal* and *art* next to each other sounded strange.

"Show me," Markus said with passion.

"Give me some circuits first," Cog replied, the usual plainness in his voice.

"Oh Cog c'mon," Markus pleaded. "I'm bored of that shit."

Cog whipped the knife back out and threw it in the bag, zipping it up.

"Alright," Markus said.

Cog took his top off and by now Markus had no embarrassment in taking off his. He was stripped and lean, fighting fit. Before they started Markus noticed something.

"Hey you religious?"

Markus could tell that Cog didn't like being asked questions. He always wore the same expression whenever he was, *back off.*

"Why do you ask?"

"You got Jesus on your arm."

He pointed to a bearded portrait inked under his bicep.

"That's not Jesus," he said.

"Who then?"

"Rasputin."

"Who?"

"Grigori Yefimovich Rasputin."

Markus pulled a silly screw-face. "Who the fuck is that?"

Cog looked up as if he was receiving the words from the sky. "Mystic. Peasant. Seducer. Magician. They couldn't kill him. They couldn't keep him down."

"Who?"

"The Russian aristocracy."

Cog went into a history lesson but Markus had switched off. He just wanted to get the circuits out the way so he could go and play with the knives. They did five sets of press-ups, burpees, crunches, lunges and sprints.

Cog unzipped the bag of knives again. "Just get the blunts, the training knives."

Cog showed the boy some simple, slow patterns and then sped them up. After they went through some strikes, switches and strips. Markus seemed to pick them up quite quick.

"Good," Cog said. "You got natural coordination."

They ended the session with a sensitivity drill and Markus wanted to carry on. He was back in the bag, pulling out a weapon he had not seen before. It was black and the blade looked like a shark's tooth. The handle had a hole in it and it fitted onto the finger like a ring, with the handle running across the palm, the blade sticking out like a hook.

"Whoa this looks fucking evil."

"Give it me back," Cog said with his hand out.

"What is it?"

"A karambit. They use them in South-East Asia."

"How does it work?"

Cog sighed a little, then gave a small demonstration. "The blade goes in and then it is used to manipulate the limbs."

"*Cool.* Show me more."

"You can't do too much too soon. It's no way to learn."

"Next time?"

"We'll see."

Mr Wheatley took a step back so they couldn't see him. He looked through his bedroom window down at his neighbour's back garden. It was a strange sight to see. A topless man teaching a topless child how to harm somebody with a knife. Mr Wheatley was old and times had changed and people amused themselves differently to how they did in his day, but Mr Wheatley would have to be a fool not to know that this was wrong. And that nasty bag of tricks, surely half of the stuff in there had to be illegal! He wanted to tell his wife but he didn't want to cause her any alarm. He wanted to call the police but he didn't want to put himself in danger. I'll have a little word with Tara, he thought. He had known her for seven years and he'd never had any problems. If anything she had been the perfect neighbour. Hope she isn't getting herself into any kind of trouble, he thought.

Cog could feel someone watching him so he glanced up and the shadow in the window tilted back.

"Let's go inside," he said to the boy.

"Hey have you got a gun?"

Markus's enthusiasm hadn't dropped and it was the most animated Cog had ever seen him.

"Maybe," he said.

"You hunt? You go hunting?"

"Sometimes."

Cog picked up the bag of knives and slung the strap over his shoulder. They walked into the kitchen. Markus pulled open the fridge and took out a carton of apple juice, filling up two glasses.

"What do you shoot?"

Cog shrugged. "Deer. Fox. Pheasant. Rabbit. Anything that moves."

"Humans?"

Cog smiled with his eyes and shook his head, put his shirt back on and then Markus did too.

"Can I come with you one day?" he said, handing Cog his juice.

Cog took a swallow, straightening his shirt with the other hand. "One day," he said.

Markus nodded his head, excited. Then he thought of something else. "Hey where's the best place to stab someone?"

"In the voice box," Cog said, without having to think about it.

"Why's that?"

"So they can't scream."

"Come!" Beady screamed down the phone.

Everyone laughed and Beady had to place a fat finger over his hair-lip to silence them.

"Come!" he said again. "It's a great party. *Everyone* is here." His eyes slowly crawled around the room, magnified behind his bottle glasses. "Yeah the girls are here too … Candice, Skylar … yeah they both wanna see you babe."

He was lying. The girls weren't there at all. Again people started to laugh and Beady had to hush them.

"Just come!" Spit flew everywhere, just like it always did when Beady talked. "Crystal babe this party just ain't the same without you."

Markus sat with his head down, staring at the same crusty carpet with the same swallow-me-up feeling. Why did he do it, why did he have sex with Crystal?

Beady listened on, his mouth open, face twitching while the girl on the other end talked on. "Alright babe cool. See you in a bit."

Beady ended the call and put his hands up in the air like he was lifting the F.A Cup. "Nailed it!"

The party cheered. Someone whistled. Beer got sprayed everywhere.

A voice whispered in Markus's ear. "You getting on it this time kid?"

Beady was first at the door when she arrived, ushering her in like she was royalty. He winked at Ewan and then put a can of lager in her hand, sitting her in his lap. Someone thought it was funny to play the old Prodigy song *Smack My Bitch Up*. Markus couldn't believe it but the stupid bitch was looking right at him. She kept looking and it was so fucking obvious only no one seemed to notice, *yet*. He had told her straight, told her on his way out, after he'd fed her pizza and had sex with her again. Keep this between us, yeah? Don't say nothing. I don't want people knowing my business. She had nodded and understood and he had even made her promise. Only now she is looking at me, smiling at me, making it so fucking obvious, Markus thought. He couldn't take the pressure so he got up and began pacing, brushing his hair back with his hand, taking himself to the other side of the room where Stewie and a few others were.

"Markus my man," he said, slapping his back. "Another good week."

Even though Markus had shifted twice as much gear Stewie had still given him the same forty quid.

"C'mon Stew man, I doubled-up."

Stewie smiled, leaned back against the wall. "I know. Probation period in it."

His mate laughed and Markus got the feeling he was a part of some joke.

"What?" he said.

"No serious mate. Next week I'll give you a raise."

The mate laughed again and Stewie lightly slapped his face and Markus felt himself burn-up. He felt himself burn-up even more when he turned to see Beady put his fat hand inside Crystal's jeans. Markus decided to go back to where he was sat, opposite her. She was looking at him again only this time he didn't mind. He wanted her to see his face so he could let her know what a disgusting slag she was. Another boy had joined them and was whispering in her ear. Crystal didn't take her eyes off Markus. She looked at his face like she didn't know what to do. Markus downed a can of coke and shook his head. Beady took her face and pointed it to the dirty brown door and Markus could tell that this time she didn't want to go behind it. A third boy flew down on them like a vulture. Then a fourth, a fifth. Ewan came in too. Taking both of her hands and pulling her onto her feet. Beady got pushed out and had to fight his

190

way back in. It was fucking disgusting and Markus wanted to set fire to the whole house and burn everybody inside.

All the while Crystal never took her eyes off Markus but no one noticed because no one was looking at her face. They were too focused on her body-parts, her tits, arse, between her legs. She was up and moving, almost frog-marched. Markus held eye-contact, until it was broken by the slam of the brown door.

"I'm off," Markus said, standing.

He looked around the grubby flat like he was too good to be there. Stewie tried to catch him at the door again only this time Markus didn't want to hear it. He was already through it and out of the yard, the street, the estate. He walked away from it all with an angry stride, the lights, the noise, the people, heading towards the dark-blue night, the silent dark.

Markus woke up with blood in the bed. It was like the *Godfather* scene with the horse only Markus didn't scream, he just sat up confused, rubbing his eyes. It was on the duvet and the pillow. His t-shirt was covered too. His first thought: is this my blood?

It was only when he saw the gash on the outside of his wrist he remembered ...

... *knife.*

It wasn't self-harm cos that's only what girls and pussies do. It's what his brother did. For Markus this was a war scar. He got in from the party last night full of naked rage. He wanted to hurt someone, so he went into the kitchen drawer and took out a knife. Up until now Markus had only played with training knives but now he had a real one, a sharp one that could actually cut. He kept the kitchen light off and began some of the patterns Cog had shown him, twirls and side-stabs. The blade looked glorious in the dark, like a silver bat flying through the night. Markus felt like a ninja, an assassin. He imagined returning to the party, kicking down that dirty brown door and saving Crystal from the clutches of those evil perverts. Markus carried on with the knife drills until his arms got tired and that's when it happened. He heard it before he felt it, a skin tear in the silence of the kitchen. Then the pain came in. Markus had to admit it felt quite nice, even more so because he couldn't see it. A searing pain that took all his thoughts away and for a moment he got to experience the process his brother Ryan went through. When he turned on the light a bright red rose of blood was blooming from his wrist. Markus felt faint but there was no doubt the sight pleased him. He wanted to let it run, flow right out of him only he couldn't be bothered to clean it all up, or explain to Tara in the morning why her kitchen looked like a murder scene. He quickly grabbed a nearby tea towel and placed it over the wound, applying pressure. He took it into his room and replaced the tea towel with clean t-shirt. He kept it there until he thought it had stopped. Hours passed and soon Markus was ready for sleep, ready to be taken under by it.

Now there was a messy disk of dried blood, bits still oozing from the cracks. He must have caught it several times in the night, hence all the mess. He lay there and could quite easily sleep some more. Thoughts of the night came back and Markus felt another kind of pain, a deeper pain that wouldn't just heel with a scab. He couldn't understand why he was feeling this way cos Crystal was just a slag, nothing more. So what if she took his virginity and they'd had a cute little night eating pizza and listening to music. It didn't mean anything. Means nothing, Markus thought. Either way he took out his phone and went down to her name, then to the Delete option only this time he *did* actually press the red button.

There. Done. She's gone.

His phone felt clean again, apart from a fingerprint of blood.

He lay there longer. Normally Markus couldn't lie in, couldn't sit still and he definitely couldn't stay in the house but today was different. He had no motivation whatsoever. There was this sad, heavy feeling like the world was pointless and nothing made sense. Markus often got angry about things but this was something else. He saw the word, *depression*.

Just then he heard voices, or rather, *a* voice. It was Tara and Cog arguing but he could only hear one side of it because Cog didn't shout. He didn't *need* to shout.

"I know Cog but he's thirteen years old!"

He could tell his aunt was trying to keep her voice down so Markus couldn't hear but she was doing a shit job.

"Yeah ... yeah it's good you're teaching him to defend himself although he doesn't really need it ... I mean, it's not like he's the class wimp is it? ... but knives Cog KNIVES ... all the shit you hear in the news and then you're teaching him how to stab someone ... I don't care ... no I don't care ... not in this fucking house ... not under my fucking roof you're not ... no ... no ... it doesn't matter which neighbour told me ... well alright go ... GO ... fucking go then ... fuck off!"

Markus couldn't be doing with this shit, he thought, not this morning. He'd heard enough shouting when he lived with dad. Markus was starving and could do with some breakfast but there's no way Tars could see his hand because then she really would flip.

So Markus got up, got changed into some fresh clothes. Opened his bedroom window and climbed out. There were some benefits to living in a bungalow. There wasn't far to fall.

Somehow he found himself outside her front door. He wore green and brown and it's like he was camouflaged by the long grass which seemed almost as tall as the house. How did I even get here, he thought? He was just taking a walk along the Clementine Channel, clearing his head only the scenic surroundings didn't do its job. Not this time. He kept thinking about things and thinking about things, anger and confusion pushing those thoughts onto further thoughts. In the end he had too many to handle and he knew the only way to release them was to get answers so here he was. Her front door staring him in the face. He knew she was in and knew she was in alone. He could sense her there, almost see her through the bricks. Cleaning up, tidying. Keeping herself busy.

The door was thin and the knock came loud, reverberating down the street. A black bird flew overhead and made a screeching sound.

Moments later he heard the jangle of keys and the bolt slide across.

Her big face full of surprise at seeing him. "Markus!"

Her behaviour was odd, it threw him. She was either in some kind of denial or she really was a retard like the girls said. Or perhaps she had a twin, some other girl that had no qualms about going into a bedroom full of lads.

"Markus," she said his name again.

Her hair looked damp like she had just gotten out the shower.

"You gonna let me in?" he said, taking a step inside before he was invited to.

"Yeah, course," she said.

The boy's big frame loomed over her. He was wrong about the cleaning because the house was a shit-hole, trashed. Clothes, papers. When he saw the pile of beer cans he half-expected his dad to come climbing out of some corner.

"Good night last night?" he said, sarcasm dulling his voice. He took the only clear space the sofa would allow.

She pulled the sleeves over her wrists, hunched her shoulders and went onto one foot. "Yeah it was alright," she said innocently.

"Enjoy yourself?"

"Yeah it was alright," she said again.

A silence passed that wasn't all that awkward, just a silence with no need to fill it.

"Want a drink?" she said.

Markus nodded.

From nowhere Crystal pulled out a two-litre of coke. Markus recognised the bottle and the little rip in its label. It was the same bottle from the night he was here, the bottle from Dominoes.

Markus snatched it from her and took a gulp. It was flat but Markus didn't mind. He actually liked flat pop and sometimes left the top off on purpose. He felt a sugar rush and sat deeper into the sofa. "You gonna sit or what?" he said to the girl. "You're making my eyes hurt."

Crystal sat. Sunlight revealed a galaxy of dust particles that orbited her head. God she's ugly, he thought, studying her gormless face with that big stupid jaw hanging from it. Why am I even here? Markus knew girls were starting to take an interest in him. Girls at his old school acted funny when he was near them; half fear, half intrigue. They were attracted by his size and his brooding aura. His piercing eye contact and the way he moved around like he didn't give a fuck. Even the gorgeous Candice the other night. She was a lot older than him but he felt it from her ever so slightly, there was *something*.

And now I'm getting bent-out of-shape by this clown. Markus looked at her wondered why this was. Protective, maybe that's what it was? I'm protective over her. No it was more than that. He felt like he *owned* her.

Time to say it, he thought. Metaphors that adults used began to swim around in his head. No more ... *beating around the bush,* got to ... *take the bull by the horns.*

He sat forward and took another swig of flat coke. The liquid slid down his throat, warm and sugary and smooth. "Why do you do it?" he said.

"Do what?" she said, eyes wide, genuinely confused.

Markus rolled his and got nasty. "Are you mentally retarded?"

"At the party?" she said.

"Why do you let them do that?"

Her face went red. She went to say something but stopped.

Markus stared at her, demanding an answer.

She shrugged.

He stared more, wanting more. Like he'd stare forever until she gave him the truth.

"They just like me, I guess."

Markus let out an artificial laugh.

Crystal had her shoulders up, tense.

"Do you believe that?" he said.

Her eyes were still big and she looked as clueless as ever. "I don't know."

"Do you like it?"

"I don't know."

"Do you even know what goes off in men's heads?"

Markus didn't know why he used the word *men* and not *boys* or *lads*. Maybe he was looking at the bigger picture.

Just then Crystal got distracted. Her attention seemed to shift to Markus. "What's that?" she said, her voice full of motherly concern. She got up and walked over to Markus, took his wrist, which was covered in twisty streams of red and black dried blood.

"It's nothing," he said with a pout.

Crystal's eyes crossed as she put his wrist at the centre of her focus. "We need to get this cleaned," she said, not even interested in how he got the injury.

Markus let her lead him into the kitchen, which was surprisingly clean compared to the rest of the house. She let the tap run and then put his wrist under it. Markus felt a slight sting and winced. She pulled out a little green box with a white cross on the front. Put it on the worktop and popped it open. Crystal no longer seemed like a dumb teenager but more like a capable adult, almost like she was an actual nurse at the hospital. She washed the wound, cleaned and dressed it, used antiseptic cream and a bandage. "You should have stitches but I guess this will be okay."

Markus got that feeling again. He felt it swoop in. It was the same one he got the other night when he went out to buy her pizza. It was a powerful, vulnerable feeling and Markus wasn't sure he entirely liked it.

"Just don't ever do that again, alright?"

"What?" Crystal went back to being dumb.

"Those boys, Beady, don't ever go behind that brown door again, promise?"

Crystal smiled, like she had all the power now. "What are you my boyfriend or something?"

She cut the bandage and tied the last knot.

"If you want," he said, surprising himself.

"Okay," she said, nodding, looking at him with those peculiar blue eyes.

There was an air of indifference that bothered him.

"Okay," she said again.

Markus looked away and wondered if he was going to regret this later but right now his chest felt like it was on fire.

"Want to go and walk The Channel?" she said.

"Maybe tonight, when the sun goes down," he said, looking at her face. "It's prettier then."

There must be some mistake. His hands ferreted into the undergrowth, chin resting on the mossy ledge of the fallen tree. He bent down to take a look but there was nothing there. No rucksack. No gear.

"There must be some fucking mistake," he said out-loud. "Can't be, can't be, fucking can't be!"

He searched through The Den, or what *was* The Den over and over and tried to work out what had happened. Mind playing tricks on me? Perhaps I sold it all? Perhaps I got spooked and tried to hide it somewhere else and now I can't remember? Had a lot on my mind lately.

Nah, the rucksack has been here the whole time and I know it.

In the end he settled on the only possible explanation: he'd been robbed. Good and proper.

But that lead to the next question, robbed by who?

The first suspect that came to mind was his dad but then he remembered that his dad was *inside*. So who else, Cog, Ryan, Crystal? Whoever it was had stalked him and tracked him and taken his gear and now he was in a whole world of shit. Now he had to go back into the estate and explain all this to The Taylor Brothers.

He knocked and waited and both bros came to the door like they were expecting him.

"Markus my man, step inside."

Markus didn't want to be inside the house so he came straight out with it.

"Your gear has gone."

"Sold up already?" Stewie said with a nod. "Nice one. We've got some … "

" … nah you don't understand," Markus interrupted "It's *gone*. It's been robbed."

Shock slapped Stewie in the face and his older, red-headed brother was by his side in an instant. Less surprise in his.

"Say this again," Stewie said, robotically.

Markus put his feet firmly in the ground and turned sideways. "Someone," he said with a pause. "Has robbed all your weed."

"I knew it! I fucking knew it," Ewan shouted. The colour in his face matched the colour of his hair. He looked so mad Markus thought his head was going to come off. Stewie put a hand up, signalling him to calm.

"Tell me where it has been robbed from?" Stewie said in a measured, but simmering tone.

Markus kicked the step and looked at Stewie. "My den."

"Den!" Ewan shouted. "What fucking den? This isn't a game you c$nt!"

Markus felt his pulse quicken. A seed had been placed.

"What fucking den?" Stewie said, still cool, but focused.

"I got this place out in the fields. A place where I stashed it."

Ewan threw his head up at the ceiling. "Stewie I told you. I told you from the fucking start. Don't trust this kid. Don't trust this little shit and what did you do?"

"Oi," Markus said. "Watch your mouth." He felt his chest sink and his arms coil.

Stewie seemed to notice this transformation and got weary.

"You fucking what?" Ewan moved forward onto his brother's shoulder.

"You asked me what happened and I'm telling you. No need for insults."

Just then Markus saw Stewie clock something to his left. He remembered there was an aluminium bat propped up against the door. Markus knew what was coming next although Stewie seemed to be hesitating, like something was holding him back. Markus was trained now. He knew what he was doing and it's like Stewie knew this.

"Let's just take a second and work this out," he said.

"What is there to work out bro he's stiffed us."

"If that's what you think then beat me now," Markus shouted, looking up at the sky. "Take that bat you're eyeing up and wrap it around my skull but I'm telling you I GOT ROBBED."

"You know you owe us?" Stewie said.

Things calmed and Markus nodded. "I know that."

"You know you owe us big."

Markus nodded again.

Ewan had walked off. Markus wondered if he was going to get another weapon.

"There was about an Oz there."

"Yeah," Markus agreed.

"You owe us three-fifty."

Markus's features knotted into a question mark. "Thought you said an Oz was one-eighty?"

"Three-fifty." It made Stewie's mouth big to say that, *three-fifty*. He said it clear, like there was no negotiation or wiggle-room. His eyes were big too. It was the first sign that Stewie was capable of real violence and it took Markus aback, a bit.

"So get me that by Friday and then we'll think what to do next."

Markus wondered what day it was and tried to work out how long he had. Before he had a chance to say anything else the door was shut in his face.

Crystal made noise this time. She made noise when they had sex. She made noise and it was so different to the first time. It seemed slower and she held onto Markus. She touched his face and looked into his eyes. Put her hand through his *good head of hair*. There was music in the background, playing from a cheap bubble CD player in the corner of the room. CD's were old-fashioned but Crystal was old-fashioned, somehow. She seemed not of this time, or *any* time. The music didn't have any singing in and Markus thought it was crap and weird at first, but then he quite liked it. It was gentle and powerful at the same time, like music you heard in a film and Markus imagined he was in one. A romance film with bad people in as well. The CD case lay next to him on the floor and the cover was a nature scene. Crystal loved nature-scenes and she had them all over her bedroom wall. Afterwards they didn't say anything, just listened to the rest of the album, and to the rain outside. It was funny because they didn't say anything for the rest of the night. Even when he left her at the door, all was silent. He just hugged her and kissed her eye and then disappeared into the night.

Through the bungalow window Markus could see the flickering colours of the TV. Cog was sat in front of it watching American Football. The Oakland Raiders were playing the Miami Dolphins. Cog had tried to make the boy watch this before but Markus found it boring. Too many rules. Too stop-start and Markus thought it was stupid because it was called 'football' but they didn't even kick it. English football was better. English football was proper football. Give me Stevie Gerrard any day! The only thing Markus liked about the American version was the colours. They were bold and lurid and Markus found himself trancing out when watching it.

He got a coke from the fridge and slumped into the chair next to Cog. Cog took his eyes off the screen momentarily and looked at the boy.

"You've been fucking," he said, plainly.

An eerie pause filled the space between them.

"What?" Markus said, freaked out but he didn't show it.

"I can smell her," the man said.

Instinctively he put his fingers to his nose and watched Cog smile through the dark reflection of the television.

"What you doing Friday night?" Cog said after the silence.

Supposed to be paying The Taylor Brothers three-hundred-and-fifty quid, he thought.

"Nothing," he said.

"Wanna watch a fight, a real fight?"

Markus was pouting, distracted, thinking how he was going to get hold of that kind of money. "Sure," he said, at last.

He felt Cog nod his head.

Markus tried to watch the game but it was too boring. Even the hypnotic colours couldn't keep him in his seat. "I'm going to bed," he said.

The man's voice collared him at the door. "Hope you bagged-up."

"Bagged-up?"

Cog took a swallow of beer.

"Rubbers. Johnnies. Condoms. Don't wanna be catching a kid when you're just a kid yourself. Not to mention all those nasty diseases knocking about."

Oh, Markus thought, leaving the room. It never crossed my mind.

Markus was going to get ambushed and he knew it. It was all over Stewie's voice on the phone, in his tone and in the words he used. He was *too* normal, too casual. And the fact he wanted to meet him at The Rec and not his house was a giveaway itself. A wide-open space. No one around, no people, no witnesses. Nowhere to run.

Not that Markus *would* run. He wasn't the running kind.

Fuck them, Markus thought. Fuck life.

Markus had had time to think about it and he knew it was The Taylor Brothers who had robbed him. It was kind of obvious. Candice had even warned him all those weeks ago, *they'll rip you off. It's standard.* They'd stolen their own gear and now Markus was expected to pay for it.

Only he wasn't going to.

He took a kitchen knife from the drawer and tucked it into his sock. Outside he was surprised to see Cog in the driveway, washing Tara's car. His top was off and he watched his abdominal muscles press against the suds on the window.

"Where you off?" he said.

Markus glanced down at his sock, making sure the weapon wasn't on display anywhere.

"Just off to meet some mates," he said.

Cog looked at him with an air of suspicion, cogs turning in Cog's head. Markus watched his glassy green eyes give him the once over.

"Mind if I join you for a bit? Could do with a stroll."

Cog didn't wait for an answer. He threw the soapy sponge into the water and some of it splashed onto the paving.

"Yeah, alright," Markus said, his hands uncharacteristically in his pockets.

Cog picked up the bucket and tipped it into the drain. He went into the bungalow and returned a few minutes later wearing a white t-shirt and a light beige jacket even though it was probably the hottest day of the year.

The day was brilliant and blue and dazzled by sun. Its intense rays shimmered off the tarmac like glass. The two walked through it in near-silence. After fifteen or so minutes they got to the entrance of The Rec. A purple ribbon was tied to the gate to commemorate a girl that was murdered there two years ago.

Markus wondered why Cog was still with him, by his side.

"Alright man, just meeting them down there so I'll catch ya back at the house in a bit, yeah?"

Cog was looking at him knowingly, a slight smile in his eyes.

"C'mon," he said, nodding assertively towards The Rec, where Stewie and Co were waiting in ambush. At the top of a grassy mound a small gang of five hovered in the distance like matchstick men.

"That them?" Cog had his hands in his pockets and a breeze brushed over his curly thinning hair. Markus nodded with that pout of his, unsure about this whole thing. He really didn't want this shit. He didn't want *anyone* fighting his battles but most of all he didn't want people knowing his business. The last thing he needed was Aunt Tars finding out about this.

"Cog man I'm alright. I can deal with it on my own."

Cog was already walking towards them and Markus noticed the gang change shape. He watched them move around and reform uneasily. He could tell they didn't know what to do. He could almost hear them talking, planning, plotting. They probably thought Markus had brought another kid along. Cog was short and from that distance they wouldn't know he was a man.

But the way he walks...

Something was amiss because one of them had bottled it. Markus recognised the plump figure of Beady hang back.

Typical Beady, Markus thought, fat fucking coward.

Markus and Cog were side-by-side. Any pre-fight anxiety Markus may have had had slipped away.

Now he could see faces, clear and distinct. Stewie moved some hair from his face and Ewan was talking. That nasty, flustered, twisted expression of his. Soon the two met in the centre of The Rec.

Some kids were playing on a climbing frame about a hundred metres to the left.

Markus felt an unsettling tingle of déjà vu. It was the same feeling he had on the day he met Cog for the first time. That wild, silent, aura of his.

All five looked at Cog and then looked away, like even *looking* at him for too long would send him over the edge. They put their attention back on Markus. Stewie stood at the front while his mates moved restlessly behind, not wanting any part of this.

"Alright Markus?"

For the first time Markus detected a quiver in the leader's voice. Markus nodded.

Cog had the whole gang under his green stare.

"Yeah about that thing," Stewie began. "Forget it, yeah. Shit happens," he said with a plastic laugh.

Markus nodded, not changing his expression.

"I'll catch up with you in the week with some more."

Markus looked at each face, until he got back to Stewie. "Nah," he said. "Think I'm done mate. Not really my thing."

He could tell Ewan was fuming but there was nothing he could do.

"Alright," Stewie said. "That's cool. I mean like whatever."

Markus wondered why he had started talking American all of a sudden.

"Well. I'll see you around then."

Markus nodded and then left, Cog slowly following him.

Back at the bungalow Markus took out two glasses and filled them with juice. Cog sat on the sofa and began to take his shoes off. "The fight starts about eight," he said.

"What?" Markus said. "What fight?"

"It's Friday."

"Oh. Yeah," Markus said. "We telling Tars where we going?"

Cog looked at him like he was stupid.

"Well what will we tell her then?" Markus said, handing him the glass of juice.

"Leave her to me."

Markus headed to his room for something.

"Oh and Markus," Cog shouted after him. "You might wanna put that knife back. You won't be needing it."

The mud-spattered, rust-encrusted pick-up veered off the country lane and headed down to a deserted woodland.

"Where the fuck we going?" Markus said.

Neither wore seat belts.

Cog never answered, just bounced up and down to the bumpy rhythm of the truck. Soon civilisation appeared, an abandoned warehouse, caravans, dots of people and cars. The cars were big, four-by-fours and small trucks. Most had tinted windows and dodgy number plates. Another car pulled up minutes after. A unit of a man stepped out, bald, scarred, gold tooth winking inside a smile.

"Fucking hell Cog haven't seen you for a bit, how's tricks?"

As always Cog didn't answer verbally, just gave a nod and then shook the man's claw-like hand.

"That your lad?"

Cog nodded and then the man waded over to Markus and shook his hand. Markus felt something in it.

After the handshake Markus looked down to see Queen Elizabeth the II looking back, a crinkled twenty-pound note.

"Nice to meet ya Cog's lad. Your old man was the best."

Markus was glowing, more from the title than the money. *Cog's Lad.*

Cog put his palm on the small of the boy's back and lead him towards the abandoned warehouse. People everywhere said Cog's name and Markus could hear the respect in their voices. A small stocky man was doing some shadow-boxing with his top off, stopping every few seconds to fix the tape on his fists.

"Alright Cog?" he nodded.

"Who you fighting?" Cog said.

"Some Mick."

"Worth putting any on ya?"

"Maybe to lose," the man said with a toothless smile. "Getting old and fat now Coggy. Scrapping with a hangover int wise eivver."

Cog smiled and walked on.

"That your lad?" the fighter shouted after him.

Cog nodded.

Every time someone asked that Markus had money put into his hand and he didn't know why. Must be a gangster thing, he thought.

Markus didn't like being so small. Wherever he went Markus was nearly always the tallest, if not the tallest then the biggest, the broadest, the bulkiest. He liked the feeling of physical superiority only now he was surrounded by giants, muscle men, bouncers, fighters. The only other kids who were around were at the caravans with the women. The only woman around the men was a tall, old-ish woman with a big gob. She shouted things out into the crowd and took money off people. She had bottle-blonde hair and a shocking orange face, loads of make-up, fake nails, fake tits and knee-high boots.

Everyone called her Queenie.

"That your lad Cog?"

Cog nodded.

"Must have his mum's genes cos he's better looking than you ya c£nt!"

Everybody laughed and Cog shook his head with a smile.

Queenie was the only one who didn't give him any money. Instead she planted a pink kiss on his cheek and Markus felt the lipstick cling to his face.

"Yeah, handsome lad. Give us a call when ya legal son."

She laughed crazy and Markus noticed her teeth and tongue were yellow and it made him feel sick. Money seemed to be everywhere; taken out of pockets, wallets, sleeves, hats. Passed from hand to hand and back again. It was in bundles, rolls, envelopes, those little see-through bank bags. Money on tables and in the air. Plucked from shoes and socks and the ground. No one seemed to care where it was going or where it came from. There was gold everywhere too. On fingers and thumbs. Around necks and wrists. In ears and eye-brows and teeth. There were dogs everywhere too. Big dogs and little dogs. Dogs chained up and dogs roaming free. Markus watched a dog with one ear piss up a car. Some men drank beer, some ate burgers and hotdogs by one of the caravans. One man held a key up to another man's nose while he sniffed hard and then nodded his head. There were half-smoked cigarettes stubbed out on the wasteland and that faint trace of weed lingered in the air, a scent Markus was now familiar with. There seemed to be this changeable atmosphere. Sometimes it was loud and riotous like a party then with a click of the fingers a deathly quiet would swoop down and everybody would go into their own worlds. People communicating in some secret, silent code. Then they'd be muttering, a word, some joke would set things off again and laughter would sweep through the men, jaws rattling, and everything would be back to normal.

Markus stood by Cog and absorbed it all, watched it with wide-eyed wonder.

The fighting took place in a ring made up of haystacks. Markus thought it looked like five or six giant Weetabix stuck together. It wasn't like boxing on the telly. They didn't wear gloves and when they punched you could hear bones break and the slap of knuckles against flesh. Markus saw the word, *pounding*. The crowd got so wild Markus thought there was going to be a massive gang fight. The last fight was the best. A little man battered a big man but the big man wouldn't go down. Despite the avalanche of punches is face absorbed he just wouldn't drop. Markus respected him even though he lost. It's how he would have been this afternoon if he would have met Stewie and the gang alone. I wouldn't have gone down no matter what. Never go down, Markus thought. Fight to the death. After the fight they all picked the loser up like he was the winner. A big beaming smile shone through his bloody face. His face was so bloody and deformed and the fight was so long Markus couldn't even remember what he looked like at the beginning.

They stayed around after the fight.

"You Cog's lad?"

Markus nodded and got more money. He could probably afford to pay Stewie back only he didn't have to. No one could fuck with him now Cog was his dad.

"Your daddy was the best," a man with an Irish accent said. He stunk of booze and for a moment he thought about his own dad, his biological dad, the one who was away in some prison somewhere.

"He doesn't talk about it cos he's not much of a talker, see." The red-faced man slurred on. "But he could knock-out any man."

Markus looked over at Cog, who stood in the middle of a ring of men.

I'm gonna be like that one day, Markus thought. People will know my name and they will pay me respect.

Cog glanced over at the boy, and winked.

Two weeks later, Markus was awakened from a late afternoon snooze by the ring of his phone. He picked it up to see the name *Stewie* flashing in the centre of his screen. He had not seen or heard from him since that day on The Rec, the day of the botched ambush. He wanted to let the call slide but something told him to pick up.

"Hello."

Stewie was outside. Wind scraped through the phone and there was a murmur of voices in the background. Markus could barely hear him.

"Markus."

"What?"

"Markus you there?"

"Here."

At first he thought Stewie Taylor was going to ask him to work again. Markus got ready to stick to his guns. "Hey the strangest thing has just happened."

"Oh?"

There was a pause, more interference on the line.

"We're not far from you actually," the voice came back. "Just up along the Channel. There's about seven of us chilling, smoking, drinking ... and you never guess who we bump into ... ? That retard Crystal Palace."

Panic thumped in Markus's chest.

Stewie let out a sly giggle. "Anyway we get on *it* as normal, you know how Beady is, only this time she knocks us back. She *actually* says 'no.' I mean when does that bitch *ever* resist?"

Markus was burning up.

"Only reckons she's gone and got herself a BF! But we're like *what-the-fuck*. I mean, who in their right mind is gonna go out with that ugly slag? Especially seeing as though she's had half the town in there. You'd have to be desperate, right?"

Markus stood up, then sat down. He didn't know what to expect next.

"Anyway we don't believe her cos no one would stoop *that* low so we push on. I mean Beady is practically raping the bitch and that's when she blurts it out ... blurts out the name of her boyfriend. She says ... "

Markus couldn't take the pressure anymore. "She's fucking lying!" He yelled out, denying the charge before he had even been accused of it.

Laugher crashed in from the background and Markus realised he was on Loud Speaker.

"And then it all makes sense," Stewie said slowly. The interference on the line dissolved and Stewie became alarmingly clear. "It all makes sense now," he repeated.

Markus caught his face in the mirror. It was white. "What makes sense?" He noted the tremor in his own voice.

"You're a sneaky fuck Markus I'll give you that," Stewie began. "Pizzas," he said.

"What?"

"Night I saw you with the pizzas. Thought it was a bit weird you all the way out there when there's a Pizza Hut next door. And how you were behaving, all shifty and that. And to think you were right outside her yard and I didn't even think about it. Like I say Venner, *it all makes sense."*

Humiliation was eating Markus alive, from the inside. "Fuck off!"

"No wonder you never went into the room with her. No wonder you always fucked off early too. Couldn't stand to hear your missis being banged senseless by the boys!"

"Fuck off!" Markus was now shouting down the phone.

"Like I say," Stewie let his words hang viciously. "It. All. Makes. Sense."

"You're full of shit."

More laughter tumbled into the phone.

"Is she full of shit too, then? Cos she's telling us everything … "

Markus went to say something but Stewie cut him off.

" … I suggest you get down here mate. Nip it in the bud and clear your name before the news spreads."

Markus couldn't. Markus couldn't do that. There's no way he could face this. Again that suicidal drive took over his whole being.

"You go into hiding Markus you're gonna look guilty as fuck."

Markus had his fingers pressed into his forehead like a gun.

"I'm telling you this as *a mate,*" Stewie said. "You need to come and meet this head-on."

Markus killed the call and kicked his trainers on. He was out his bedroom window and moving, running, sprinting as fast as his legs would go. Through the alleyway and up onto the Channel. By the time he got there he had talked himself into it so much that he actually *believed* that he hadn't done anything. That it was all lies. The faces turned when they saw him. Some concerned, some amused, some, like Stewie, had a combination of both. He was straight on her, straight at Crystal. She wore tacky black leggings and a denim shirt. Her hair was everywhere like she had been trying to fight someone off.

"Markus babe I know you told me not to say anything but they were trying to … "

His hand slapped her across the face so hard the rest of the sentence never arrived. She stumbled back, sideways, towards the edge of the water. His first feeling was to chuck her in the Channel. Pick her up from behind and dump her in. No chance of her saying anything then, he thought. Instead he took a handful of her dirty blonde hair and yanked her to the floor. Dragged her bare knees across the stony path. A yelp ripped through her chest. "Markus *don't.*"

"What are you lying for?" he roared. "Why are you telling lies about me?"

Rage put her at the end of his tunnel-vision. The rest of the crowd were blocked out.

"I don't know," she said in the smallest murmur.

Markus liked that. It sounded convincing.

He grabbed her face and squeezed her cheeks until her lips sprouted like a deformed flower. "Tell them you're lying," he said. "Fucking tell them!"

Tears dripped onto his fingers. She moaned through them, trying to make her words audible.

She made a sound that was close enough and that seemed to satisfy him. He let her go. It wasn't until he looked down he realised he had a fist held up to her face. When the red mist cleared Markus could see that the others were truly entertained, standing by, laughing their heads off. The nearest was Beady, his mouth a contorted black hole, trying to hold himself upright from the hysteria. That stupid multi-coloured cap lopsided on his melon head.

Markus felt a second wave of rage wash through him and he turned that fist towards him.

He was already low to the ground and when he pushed up from it a punch followed. Clean on the jaw and Markus felt the breakage of bone across his knuckles. Beady's legs buckled and he dropped silently to the floor. He had punched loads of people but he had never knocked anyone out. Cog's tutelage had worked. The root, the framework, the twist and snap. Markus knew how to punch like a man.

The laughter stopped and the world seemed to, too. Everything around him. The breeze, the water, nature. It all stopped. The knock-out shocked the gang of lads, a mixture of fear and anger with a sprinkle of admiration on top. Beady's body was decked-out, half on the bank, half on the path. It was the first time he saw him without that cap and the sun shined off a bald patch. A perfect pale circle planted in the middle of a thick, black mop. His piggy face squashed between the grass and the tangle of his broken glasses.

Markus stepped over his body symbolically and faced the gang.

Its leader had to say something so he did. "You know you're fucked," he said in his usual calm.

"You're fucking dead!" Stewie's older brother added in a cracked scream.

Markus couldn't understand why they hadn't rushed him. It was seven, (he looked back down at Beady) no six against one, but they didn't move.

The violence was cathartic and Markus suddenly felt a bizarre urge to confess. To unashamedly admit that Crystal had indeed been his girlfriend, for a time. He looked at the cowering girl and wanted to say sorry. The rise and fall of his chest slowed as he began to calm.

He was glad she had seen him knock-out Beady.

She was on her knees, looking up.

Mascara-tears streaked her face and her legs were cut.

Her expression was strange and almost prophetic, like she knew what was going off in his head. He thought he detected some kind of smile; a smile he couldn't see, a secret smile. Like she was smiling on the inside. The sun was beginning to set and it turned her big jaw a certain kind of orange.

When he got back to the bungalow Aunt Tars was sitting sideways in the kitchen window, lighting up a cigarette.

"Smoking again?" he said, pulling open the fridge to grab a carton of milk. "Thought you'd quit?"

The milk plopped into a tall thin glass. She didn't answer.

Tars took her first drag, a big long pull. Pleasure swept over her face as she exhaled.

"Where's Cog?"

Still no answer.

"Fuck sake Tars will you say some ... "

"He's gone," she said, suddenly.

"Gone where?"

"He's *gone*. Gone, gone."

Markus was still confused.

"We've split up Markus. He won't be coming back here anymore."

Markus felt his mouth go dry and his face go white. He put his empty milk glass in the sink and stared at it. "Look if this is about the knives, it's not his fault."

"It's not about the knives," Tars said.

"Because I heard you arguing the other morning."

"It's not about the knives Markus," she repeated.

There was a pause, a heavy silence hung over the kitchen.

"What then?" Markus said at last.

Tara finished her cigarette and then took each leg off the windowsill.

"We're just not right for each other," she said. "Maybe I'm not right for anybody, right now."

Markus stared back into the sink, then looked at the straw chair where Cog normally sat.

"There's no hard feelings between us," Tara said. "It was mutual."

"Mutual," Markus said under his breath, feeling milk still on his lip.

He looked at Auntie Tara who was at the sink washing Markus's glass without thinking about it. The features on her face arranged into a stoical mask. Markus began his walk down the corridor towards his room. When he got halfway he decided to stop. He looked down, to his left, and then turned back around. "*He* ended it didn't he?"

Tara couldn't hide the surprise in her face. She had given herself away to the boy. She didn't need to give him a verbal answer.

"Probably because you let yourself go."

That familiar spike of cruelty in his voice.

"You what?" her mouth twitched and her eyes shrunk to slits.

"Well," the boy began. "We have banged some of our weight back on haven't we Tara?"

Tars stepped forward like she was going to lunge at him. "You hurtful, hateful little bastard!"

She picked up the milk glass she had just washed but Markus didn't flinch. He knew she would never throw it.

"What did you expect?" he continued. "Cog's an athlete, man. He doesn't wanna be seen with some beach whale waddling off his arm."

Tara put the glass down and touched her lip, stopping any more words from coming out. She let out a strange smile and shook her head, like she had realised something for the first time.

"You're sick," she said. "There's something wrong with you."

Markus stared her down the whole time, smiling.

"Just get out," she said.

Markus did, he stepped out of his aunt's bungalow, closing the door softly behind him.

Mel

Dear Self-Esteem Diary,

Turns out Babe is The Man of The House. All this time I thought it was a boy because of her name and stuff but ACTUALLY it turns out she's a boy. A boy and not a girl. A boy and not a bitch. I caught him humping the sofa one morning and I was like OH GROSS and ran to tell mum and My Sister Adele but they just called me Stupid.

  How can you not see it's a boy you spacker look at his penis!!!

  Don't call me a spacker! I said to my sis.

  She laughed in my face and mum joined her and they both just thought I was dead-stupid.

  They even thought it was funny when Babe tried to hump my leg. My Sister Adele even videoed it on her phone and then threatened to post it on Facebook and YouTube and stuff.

  DON'T YOU DARE!!!

  What d'ya reckon mum? Shall I post it for the world to see?

  And mum just looked at me all leering and spiteful and stuff and said … depends if she behaves??

  My Sister Adele never did post it but I was like Scared to Death for the WHOLE week. And tbh I'm not gonna Lie it was a pretty traumatic thing, wondering if the WHOLE school was going to see an ugly dog trying to have sex with my leg, not to mention how utterly gross it was.

  And can You believe I even had to take That Thing out. mum made me. She ACTUALLY made me take that beast out for a walk <u>all on my own.</u> I took it up to the Channel and I totally hated it. I mean it almost yanked me off my feet and pulled me into the water at one point. This man and this boy were out jogging and Babe got spooked and I thought she was going to like attack them and stuff. Only the man had these weird green eyes and he sort of stared at it and Babe calmed and cowered and that was bizarre. It was like the man had supernatural powers, like a horse whisperer kind of a thing, only with a dog.

  Dog whisperer! Ha!

Anyway.
Either way.

211

I HATED That Walk with the dog and I vowed to never do it again, not on my own anyway.

I don't even like the effing dog, I said. Adele likes it I don't. She should take it!

Oh stop being a drama queen, mum said. You're the oldest and the strongest, you should take him. (Actually this wasn't true. I might be older than My Sister Adele but I wasn't really stronger.) The Last Time we fought I sort of felt her overpower me. Although I could never admit this, not out-loud anyway.)

At least make her walk with me then! I said. It's not safe taking that thing out alone.

And stop calling him Thing and It, mum screamed back. His name is Babe!

Yeah and it's a stupid name for a dog, especially a boy-dog. Why do you always do embarrassing things?

Me and mum argued loads that day. And tbh we've been arguing more and more lately and I'm not even sure how much more I can TAKE.

Anyway.

Breathe.
Breathe, Mel.
Breathe and stop.
Ah. Ahh.

See.
So.

So I just had to get that off my chest and stuff.

Think it's time I took You back to the Biography Bit.
Back to the Biography Bit before I lose myself completely

So …

It was about this time my Dad came back.

It was at this time Dad came back into My Life and like, I can't even tell You how shocked I was. Like, there's no amount of words

In This World that can tell You how utterly shocked I was.

And suppose it was Fate, like a destiny kind of a thing. Cos You see I was in the house On My Own when he knocked on my door on some Random Tuesday Afternoon.

It was in the School Holidays I think cos mum and My Sister Adele was out shopping and I was home alone. Like I was just doing my room when this strange knock came on the Front Door. I say it was strange because it was like a half-knock. Like it had a pause in the middle of it. At First I thought I was hearing things and stuff. Or maybe like it was from next-door or something. It was kind of awkward and weak, like maybe whoever was knocking didn't REALLY want to be there. Like they was selling something or maybe like one of those Jehovah Witness People who everybody tells to eff-off and stuff. Anyway, the Second Knock was really loud, like REALLY loud. Like it made my heart jump and my feet come off the floor and it about Scared Me To Death. I even dropped this piggy-bank thing I was holding and I thought it was going to smash and cover my room in like a million, trillion coins and stuff.

Anyway, I ran downstairs and looked through one of those spy-hole things we've got in the door although I couldn't really see nothing. I was going to shout and ask who it was but I was kind of shy so I didn't. It was in the middle of the day and like broad daylight so I just opened up and then there was This Man, only he had his back to me.

Even when he slowly turned around I didn't know who it was. Cos like, well like I've never REALLY seen My Dad before. Not since I was like about four years old or something.

(Actually that is a Lie and I MUST correct that cos My Bestie Mia did MAKE me find him once on Facebook. I typed in his name and this face came up that I sort of recognised.

Ugh gross, Mia shouted. Is that him?

Think so, I said.

Says he lives in Boston so it must be, Mia said.

I stared at his eyes and tried to work it out.

He IS creepy. Mia was yelling and it was The First Time I hated her. Look how creepy he is. Looks like he's on The Sex Offender's list or something...

How can you tell he's creepy, I said. It's just a face? You haven't EVEN met him so how can you judge him like that?

Mia was bouncing on the bed. He's creepy you can tell. I can tell. You can tell EVERYTHING from a person's face, didn't you know that? There's even a word for it.

No there isn't, I bit.

Yes there is. It's physiog … something.

You're full of shit! I said.

Mia stopped bouncing. Hey don't get ratty with me just cos your dad's a freak.

He's not a freak! You don't even know him!

You don't know him either.

So?

Hey I don't even know my dad either. It's no biggie. THAT'S just what dads DO. They LEAVE. Get over it.)

Anyway.
Either way.

My Dad was here. At the door. In front of me. He was so nervous his face was shaking a bit, like his lips and stuff. I remembered about the drugs and wondered if he was still on them. Tbh I'm not gonna Lie I was so happy when I realised it was him. Only I got nervous too and I couldn't even talk. None of us talked. We just stood there in silence. A neighbour walked by but they didn't even look over. It was amazing cos he looked nothing like how I imagined, or remembered. Like, he didn't even look like the Facebook pic either cos like his hair was all short and stuff. And his clothes were all smart, like he wore this kind of shirt and jacket, like a suit kind of a thing. And tbh it's a million miles away from that horrible image I have in my mind. Like my Earliest Childhood Memory. The one where he was topless and screaming and scratching down the window like a psycho.

He stood, calm and quiet and his eyes were all soft and moist like he was ready to cry, like an emotional kind of a thing. He wore glasses, just like me.

It was My Dad after all these years.

At last one of us HAD to talk and it was actually Me, believe it or not.

Hey, I said.

Melanie, he said.

It was weird to hear my name being said in full and For Once I actually didn't hate it, my name. Melanie.

Melanie are you alright? He said.

I just sort of nodded and then looked down at my white socks with pink toes.

Is your mum in? He said.

No. I said.

Your sister?

I shook my head again.

So you've been left alone?

He seemed mad by that and I was kind of glad that he was mad. It felt like a protective kind of a thing.

We went quiet again and I could hear traffic from the main road.

Can I see you? He said.

I was still looking down and I shrugged my shoulders.

I'd like to see you again Melanie. Is it Melanie or can I call you Mel?

Mel, I said.

I Hated 'Melanie' but for some reason I liked him saying it and wished I'd have stuck with that.

Can I see you again, Mel?

I shrugged again. Didn't think you was allowed, I said.

I wasn't, he said. But that was a long time ago and things are different now. I am different now. I'm clean, he said.

I didn't know what he meant by Clean. Like maybe he showered more now and stuff.

Okay, I said with a nod.

You'd like to see me again?

Now he was smiling and it was strange to see him smile. Like it changed the WHOLE of his face completely.

I guess, I said. I guess it would be alright, I said. Like if it's alright with mum and stuff.

He stopped smiling again and so did I.

Well I'm gonna do something about that, he said.

Suddenly I got really panicky cos I imagined mum coming back Right Now. Like I pictured her walking down the avenue and seeing me talking to My Own Dad at the door. I visualised just how nuts she'd go, like I know she'd Just Flip. So I tried to hurry the rest of the conversation along.

I'll talk with her, I said.

Dad nodded but I could see he was unconvinced.

Well maybe let me do that bit, he said.

You can't come in, I said.

I said that kind of forceful and he looked surprised.

I didn't mean today, he said.

I let out a sigh of relief and nodded, okay, I said.

There was more silence and I could FEEL how happy My Dad was. Like a ton of bricks had been lifted off his shoulders.

Thank You Mel, he said. Thank you for giving me the chance to make things right again.

I shrugged and looked back down at my socks. I wiggled my toes around and thought of something else to say.

It'd be nice to see you, I said.

For A Moment I could tell he wanted to hug me but was holding himself back.

I'll be in touch, he said.

I nodded and then watched him walk away. Something in the way he walked reminded me of a small boy.

After I went to my bed and laid on it, face down on the pillow. I was kind of happy but kind of scared too. Like, I really didn't know. Like, I really didn't know how this was going to go.

For some reason I didn't tell mum when she came back.

Mel, she shouted, come and help your sister put this shopping away.

I came downstairs like everything was normal and I quite liked having knowledge that they didn't. They carried on in their own worlds and had no idea that something BIG had just happened.

What you been up to while we've been gone? mum said.

Nothing. I said.

You can't do nothing, stupid, My Sister Adele said. Otherwise you'd be dead.

She wanted a reaction but This Time I didn't give her one. Just stood silent, kind of smug. My Sister Adele turned her head fast and hit me in the face with her long hair. She always did this and then tried to make out it was an accident. Again I showed no reaction.

mum stood in the kitchen holding a box of Frosties. Tony the Tiger's big orange and black face smiling his head off.

What's up, she said, look like you've seen a ghost?

Maybe I have, I said.

Freak! My Sister Adele shouted in my ear.

I went back upstairs.

When mum DID find out she went mad. Like, TOTALLY insane but that was always going to happen. She said some solicitors had been in touch and that dad NOW had the right to see us again, if we wanted to.

My Sister Adele didn't want to. She didn't even give a shit.

Loser! She said. Why would I even wanna see that loser?

I went quiet and thoughtful and this made mum shout.

Trust you, trust you to want to see him again after ALL he's put us through.

Because she's a loser herself, My Sister Adele said. Losers stick together.

Don't you remember? mum was shouting so loud her voice cracked.

You don't have to shout, I said. I'm sat in front of you. I'm not in China.

My Sister Adele took her phone out and started texting.

mum sat opposite me.

Don't you remember how he was, how he scared you?

I remember how YOU scared me, I said.

She sighed and rolled her eyes and sat back.

Don't you remember all the moving we had to do, the shelters, the refuge, that damn caravan?

I remember YOU smacking me in the face and having to go and live with a foster parent.

That trapped mum. Whenever I brought that up it trapped her cos it's like she couldn't lose her temper cos then it would prove my point.

She put her hand to her head.

You're never going to let me forget that are you?

No, I said.

And you know it will torture me to the day I die.

I didn't say anything.

I've said sorry a thousand times. There's nothing more I can say.

I didn't say anything.

There's nothing more I can do. Mel I even reported MYSELF for god's sake. I got help and I'm doing my best! The best for you and Adele and I can't let that man back into our lives he's toxic. Toxic and dangerous. He's an addict Mel. A drug addict don't you understand?

Well he looked fine to me!

I had both hands on the armchair and I put my face forward when I said that. But as soon as I did I knew I'd messed up. Made a mistake.

Shit.

Her face went blank with shock.

What? She said.

Nothing.

I tried to act normal but it was no use.

Even My Sister Adele looked up from her phone.

You've seen him? mum said.

I sat back and looked out the window.

He's been round here? She said in her normal dramatic way. IN THIS FUCKING HOUSE?

Not IN this house, I said. Just AT this house. But so what, how was he supposed to make contact, smoke signals?

mum was on her feet, going mad.

I couldn't even hear what she was saying anymore so I just went upstairs.

See.

So.

So time passed and Dad's solicitors must have won or whatever because it was Official: I Was Allowed To See Him If I Wanted To.

And, I did.

Like, if nothing more than to piss mum and My Sister Adele right off.

I was given Dad's number and we started communicating by texts and the odd phone call.

We arranged to meet at a pub called The Falcon. It wasn't a pub-pub but more like a Family One. One where kids were allowed and stuff. Tbh it wasn't even that far from where I lived. Pretty much on the same road more or less. mum insisted on walking me there, even though I had been WAY further On My Own. But like, now all of a sudden she cared about my safety.

Yeah. Right. Whatevs.

She walked me down Kings Road and then even waited around in the pub car park For Ages.

I don't want to see him, she said. Don't let me see that druggie arsehole for one minute.

But like, she was TOTALLY Lying cos she wouldn't stop looking around, like in a nosey, trouble-causing kind of a way.

Go then! I said.

Her arms were folded tight across her chest and her eyes had gone all small and venomous, like a snake.

Just then my phone bleeped and Dad had texted, telling me he was Inside.

He's in there, I said. Nodding to the pub door. I'm fine. You go.

mum didn't even say nothing, just stormed right off. Her shoes making gravelly scratches across the car park.

She looked kind of ridiculous and all I could do was smile to myself.

It was a Saturday afternoon I think cos there were loads of people around, like families and kids and stuff. Everyone was eating and I could smell all these lovely dinners. Wish I could eat out sometimes, instead of the crappy food mum does. I walked around the pub looking for Dad, through the first big room and then into the second. Then I saw him. He was sitting alone at a corner table. The First Thing I noticed was how sad he looked. Like he looked dead-sad and I was surprised by that. Cos I thought he'd be happy to see me and stuff. I also noticed how upright he sat. Dead-upright like a cardboard statue or something. I had to admit I'm not even gonna Lie but Mia was kind of right. He was sort of creepy. Not creepy in a dangerous way but more like a lonely way. He looked up at me and then sort of shuffled around. He put his hand through his hair and stood and then we did an awkward hug kind of a thing.

Mel, he said.

Dad, I said.

Want a drink? He said.

Yeah, I said.

So I told him I'd have an Apple and Melon J2O and that sort of confused him. Like he didn't know what they were so I went to the bar and helped him. He bought a bottle of beer for himself. I don't know why but he was quick to tell me it was Non-Alcoholic.

Just Becks Blue, he said, no booze in this.

Okay, I said, nodding my head.

We sat back down. Only I had my back to the noise and people and tbh I can't sit like this at all. I can't sit like this and never have. Like it's a bit of a thing with me. Almost like a phobia kind of a thing. Like it makes me want to have a Panic Attack and stuff so I got up and sat next to Dad but that made him REALLY uneasy. Like it freaked him out. Like maybe it was too intimate or something.

It's okay, I said. I just can't sit with my back to people. I like to see everything in front of me.

Dad smiled a big smile and then put his head down.

Ha, he said. You take after your old man for that. I'm EXACTLY the same.

Now I got to see My Dad properly, for like the First Time really. His face was thin and pointy and he looked kind of tired. Like his eyes were puffy and baggy behind a pair of sharp, silver glasses. And his skin was kind of red and patchy and stuff, like an eczema kind of a thing. I guess you could say he looked old, like too old to be my dad. Like I thought of other dads but he was WAY older. But then mum was old too so I guess they must have had me Late In Life.

Dad had bad teeth too and I could tell he smoked loads. Cos, like, one of his fingers was yellow and brown with nicotine. It was kind of gross and I tried not to look at it.

Just nipping out for a fag, he said.

I could tell he was nervous cos he kept 'nipping out for a fag.' He kept moving his beer bottle around too, like picking it up and putting it down without drinking it. He also kept rotating it on the beermat, twisting it in circles and half-circles. After a while though he started to relax and that made me relax. We talked about things and it felt quite natural. Although there was still things about him that were odd, little things. Like he'd go dead-quiet all of a sudden and stare into space and not remember a thing I'd just said. Or sometimes he found things to talk about that got him mad. Like stuff to do with work or politics or things from The Past.

Your sister don't wanna see me then? He said, from nowhere.

I paused and didn't know what to say. I didn't want to hurt him but The Truth is The Truth and I always tell It.

No, I said. She doesn't.

He was picking some of the label off his beer bottle and flicking it.

Suppose your mum turned her against me?

I just shrugged.

Did she try and turn YOU against me?

This made me feel a little mad cos tbh I didn't really want to talk about Them, EVER.

I've changed, ya know? He said.

He began to get nervous and emotional again, like his face did that shaky, twitchy thing of his.

Suppose your mum's told you about my habit?

I nodded.

He turned and faced me and I could tell this was A Big Moment For Him.

See ... I need to explain ... see, I only took that stuff cos I was in pain. In pain because I couldn't see you. In pain because I missed you so much, because ... because your mum wouldn't let me see you. She kept me away and the pain was so great I needed medicine to take the demons away.

I didn't know what he meant by 'demons.' I thought demons were things you watched in horror movies and stuff.

You only have your mum's side Mel. He went on. You never got mine, My Side. Now I wasn't perfect but your mum wasn't either. She did a lot of bad things.

I knew she had something to do with ALL THIS. I began to feel that hate-feeling again right in the pit of my stomach.

But the medicine has gone now. He said. I don't take that stuff anymore. I'm CLEAN. I've changed and I want to prove to you that I've changed. I know this won't happen overnight but maybe if we just start slow we can build a relationship. We can be Father and Daughter again.

His eyes got like teary and I think that maybe mine were too. More than anything I was hoping this might give me a chance to get away from mum and sis. Maybe I can live with Dad in The Future and get away from Them.

We had another drink and lightened-up a bit. Dad asked me about my life, about school and stuff. He even asked if I had a BF and I felt myself blush and go dead-red. I shook my head and told him No.

Good, he said. You're far too young anyway.

We talked and occasionally he would bring up mum again. It was clear he hated her just as much as she hated him. And that made me sad cos for the First Time I realised I was born out of hate. I was built on a foundation of hate from two people that hated each other and I was the end-product.

I was a disaster from the start.

A bad thing waiting to happen, like a curse kind of a thing.

Anyway.
Either way.

Our two hours were up and it was time to go. He reached under the table and pulled a purple card from a Morrison's shopping and gave it to me.

Open this when you get home, he said.

We had another hug only this time it wasn't so awkward and he held onto me for longer.

I didn't want to go Straight Back to mum yet so I took the long way home, by the Clementine Channel. Most of the way I didn't even really think. Just walked alongside the water. Occasionally I would throw stuff in and watch it get taken by the current …

… so like, I managed to avoid mum for a few days but it wasn't easy. She was sniffing around, so nosey, trying to get information. She acted like she wasn't bothered but I could tell she was. She was dying to know what happened, what was said, what HE said, how he looked, EVERYTHING. She asked me little things At First, casual stuff. She even yawned in the middle of questions, pretending she didn't care, pretending it was all trivial and beneath her. But I could see just how eager she was, how desperate. Eventually she couldn't take it no more so she sat me down and pretty much demanded that I tell her.

It's my business, I said.

It's MY business too. I'm your mum.

It's my business.

I'm your LEGAL guardian. I have a RIGHT to know. I'm RESPONSIBLE for your welfare.

I smiled at that, whatever.

Mel, tell me!

It's my business. It's my life. He's MY dad.

My Sister Adele sat opposite, engrossed in her phone as always.

Oh so he's your dad now all of a sudden? mum went on.

mum always did this weird wink thing when she was getting mad. Like her eyelid began to throb and flicker. She looked like a spacker.

Did he blame me? She said, standing in front of me with her hands on her hips. She wore this stupid apron around her waist that said, HEY GOOD COOKING!

I'm not saying anything.

Bet he blamed me?

Don't ask me things cos you know I can't lie?

Bet he thinks I turned you against him?

You DID turn me against him.

mum's face went even weirder than normal. She bit down on the next sentence and the words scraped through her teeth, how fucking dare you!

Adele got up and moved to the other side of the room, her eyes not leaving the phone. I remember thinking how cool she looked doing that. My Sister Adele is always cool and it's infuriating. Even in the most heated situations she always manages to look cool.

How dare you say that Mel. Mum wasn't cool. I had good reasons to turn YOU against HIM. He was a druggie scumbag.

I didn't want to be drawn into it but I already was.

Yeah well everybody deserves a second chance!

mum was in my face. Her breath all over me, that oniony smell of hers. He's had a second chance. She said. And a third and a fourth and a fifth and a thousand!

A second chance with ME mum, with me! I was aware how high my voice was. It's not all about YOU ya know?

mum shook her head and turned around.

I didn't dare tell her about the card with the money in cos she'd Just Flip.

Bet he didn't even mention your sister?

Adele popped her eyes over the phone for a second. Don't even bring me into it, she said.

He doesn't take drugs anymore, I said.

Ha.

He DOESN'T.

Heard it before.

He's CLEAN.

A leopard never changes its spots.

He's not a leopard he's a human being with a human brain.

mum seemed surprised when I said that.

Anyway he only took them cos he was missing us. It was do deal with the pain of missing us. It was his medicine.

Adele WAS listening cos she smiled when I said that. That sly smile got me so mad. I wanted to get up and knock her stupid teeth out.

Oh Mel, mum said, sitting down. Did he tell you that?

I didn't say anything. I was hugging my knees by now.

Darling he's always taken drugs. He took drugs before I met him. He took drugs when I met him. He took drugs when we were married and he took them when you were born. He didn't take drugs BECAUSE he lost you, he lost you BECAUSE he took drugs.

I was crying a little now, and mad. So mad my teeth were hurting.

That's his trouble Mel. He blames everybody but himself. He's the victim and it's ALWAYS someone else's fault. This woe-is-me bollocks. He loves it when bad stuff happens cos then he's got an excuse for taking that shit.

I was snivelling and I hated snivelling cos it was like SHE had won … yet again.

Well then why did you get with him, if you knew that's what he did?

mum held my hand, which was strange cos she NEVER showed affection, EVER.

Cos I was young and stupid, she said. It was a mistake.

My glasses were steamy and I couldn't see the world right.

Yes, I said. You're right. It WAS a mistake. You and him should never have got together and I should NEVER have been born. I'M the mistake.

I got up fast and left the room.

Mel I didn't mean it like that, she shouted after me.

My Sister Adele was still smiling to herself as I passed her. Heading upstairs I heard her mutter, God she's melodramatic.

That made me fly back into the room and snatch the phone out her hands. Looking at her dead in the eye. I'll fucking kill you one day bitch.

Oi! mum yelled.

My Sister Adele put her hands up and opened her mouth like she was all innocent and stuff.

What? What? What did I say?

I dropped the phone in her lap and headed back upstairs.

I took out MY phone and wanted to text Dad. I wanted to call him. I wanted him to come and pick me up, take me somewhere, anywhere. Anywhere away from HERE.

mum and My Sister Adele had obviously talked about this and had decided to make some kind of pact. Cos from here on in they didn't talk about it. They didn't ask about it. In fact they barely spoke to me for weeks. They pretty much ignored me more or less. They didn't look at me and they just spoke to me in one-word answers. At the dinner table they talked over me like I wasn't even there. I was confused and sad and angry and tbh with You, I can Honestly say that there's nothing In The World worser than being ignored.

I'd prefer anything, shouting, screaming, noise. I'd even prefer mum to smack me in the face again or grab me round the neck. I'd prefer Adele's sarcasm and that superior smile. I'd take anything over being ignored. Cos, like, if you're ignored it's like you don't even exist, like an invisible kind of a thing. It's like you were never born.

Me and Dad met up a few more times, once to go for a walk and another time we went to the cinema to watch a vampire movie. Not a Twilight film but another one. It was kind of crappy and Dad agreed.

Things were good and he was right, we were Father and Daughter again.

Thought maybe we could go to Skegness next week, he said.

Yeah, I said, excited.

Not quite the season but it'll be something different.

Yeah that'd be cool.

Think your mum will mind?

I put my head down. Nah she won't mind, I said. She doesn't care what I do anymore.

It was weird but I could tell Dad was disappointed by that. It's like he wanted to get under her skin.

Dad picked me up in his car. It was an old blue car with old-fashioned windy windows. He touched my knee and kissed me on the cheek. Hello princess.

I didn't like being called Princess cos it was kind of gay, or maybe like what you said to an 8-year-old or something.

Your mum in? He said, staring up at the house.

Can we just go? I said. Pulling the seatbelt around me.

Yeah, he said, still staring at the house. Yeah we'll go.

I'd not been Skeggy for ages and it was kind of weird going in the winter. Like there was no one around and stuff. Just old people and drunk people and miserable people that lived there. The fair was still there but nobody went on it. I watched the rides go round and thought how sad it looked. The clock-tower looked sad too. Normally loads of people sat around it eating ice creams but now it was just deserted and boring and stuff. Dad bought me some candy floss but eating it in the drizzle felt weird and tbh I just wanted to go home. Especially when Dad started to act weird. Like his behaviour got all strange and suspicious and secretive and stuff. Like he kept lagging behind, or walking ahead, or disappearing into the toilets every five minutes. Sometimes he was dead-talkative and happy and then he seemed a little out of it and distracted, like he wanted to be somewhere else.

Hungry? He said.

I nodded.

I was starving, apart from the candy floss we'd not eaten a Single Thing all day.

Let's go eat then kiddo, he said. There's a great little pub up on the seafront, does some great chips.

He took me there only he didn't eat. He just drank from a Becks beer bottle only This Time it didn't have the words 'Non-Alcoholic' on it. He downed about five of those while I ate and then his words got all slurry and stuff, and he kept repeating himself. He kept talking about mum only this time there was something darker in his eye and he swore more. He said the eff-word in like every sentence and I didn't like it. After the pub he took me down onto the beach. It was almost dark and the beach was freezing and blustery and awful. I hated it. Why would ANYONE want to walk on a horrible, empty beach in the middle of winter? The wind was so strong it was like I was walking on the spot, not getting anywhere. Dad had his eyes closed and he was acting really freaky and stuff, muttering under his breath and making all these noises and I realised My Bestie Mia was right. He WAS creepy,

This is where you were made, he said.

We were under this mouldy pier and I didn't know what he meant. He was talking in all kinds of riddles and tbh I'm not gonna Lie but he was starting to scare me. My Own Dad was scaring me just like he did when I was younger.

Under the pier was eerie like a horror film, There was long grass and decaying wood and broken glass and even a shopping trolley was under there. I could hear the wind howling through the planks above and it also sounded like the tide was coming in. From nowhere Dad's hands were on me. He grabbed me and pulled me into him and his breath was all over my face and he stunk of so many bad things.

She'll never take you away from me again … never, ever take you away from me again.

His voice was croaky and evil. It seemed to crawl into my ear like a bug.

226

Dad can we go home now, I said? I'm cold and tired and I really want to go home.

My voice seemed to snap him out of the weirdness and it was like he didn't know what was happening.

Yes, he said. Yes baby we can.

I didn't like him calling me Baby either cos like that's what you call your BF or something.

He looked scared himself, like he was scared OF himself. Like he didn't know who he was or where he was.

Let's go home, he said, all longing and tender.

The drive home was even worser. It was pitch-black and he was driving like a madman, bombing all through these country lanes at like 100MPH or even faster. It's like he was running away from someone, like he was being chased, or maybe like he wanted to die or something. The night zoomed by, towns and villages slipped past my window and the road unravelled under us at a blurry, break-necking pace. When I looked over at him I could see he was driving with one-eye-closed and I was like WTF! It was like he was really trying to concentrate on staying inside the white lines of the road.

I never in my life thought I'd say this, like EVER. But it was the First Time in my WHOLE life I couldn't wait to get back to number 5 Lawson Avenue. I couldn't wait to get back there. Couldn't wait to get back Home.

We pulled up and it was like Dad knew, like through all the fucked-up-ness he knew how wrong all that was. Cos he like slammed his head against the steering wheel and kept it there for ages. I just sat silently next to him. A Christmas Tree air freshener was still swinging from the rear-view mirror. I stared at it until it stopped. Even though I'd just been sitting I felt out of breath, out of breath and exhausted like I had just ran a marathon or something. I wanted to move but daren't. I wanted to move but the chaos in Dad's head kept me there. Like I felt if I tried to move he might grab me or something worser.

I thought I better talk first so I did. Okay so I'll see you then.

Gently I began to sneak out of my seatbelt. When I looked at my hand there were red marks from where I'd been gripping on so tight.

Dad didn't say anything, he just stayed where he was. Head on the steering wheel. His eyes were scrunched up and there were loads of lines all over his face.

As I got out the car I knew I'd never see him again. That was it. This was the Last Time, Officially.

Mum was right. My Sister Adele was right. He was a loser.

He was a loser and so was I …

The Boy Who Throws Chairs

Markus

Markus got into a fight on the first day of his new school. It was two against one and Markus was the one. Some boys took the piss out of his dated Liverpool top.

"What's up, mum can't afford to buy you the new one!"

Markus blasted the mouthy lad straight in the nose and blood pissed out. His mate tried to help but got the same in the ear. Two boys wobbling over the school field with their arms up in surrender like the way they did in the films.

News spread and within a day Markus was back where he started: a kid with a rep.

But Markus liked the rep. He pretended he didn't but secretly he revelled in it. Notoriety kept his engine running. People left him alone. They didn't look him in the eye. They crossed to the other side of the street. Yet his name was on everybody's lips and he was never too far from their minds. They were always waiting to see what he was going to do next.

The Kitts Academy was smaller than his previous school yet it seemed bigger because of its minimalist lay-out. It had been renovated over the summer to keep up with the surrounding schools in the area. The new Americanised academies were popping up all over the country and had now reached Lincolnshire. The classrooms were bright and airy, linked by locker-lined corridors. Through the windows you could see alternating squares of lawn and tarmac and rubber. It was all symmetrical and precise and colourful. The headmaster liked the change and thought it was important to *move with the times* whereas mothers stood in flocks outside the school gates and complained.

Markus didn't give a fuck; school was school, no matter how you dressed it up school was shit. Full of pricks and twats and c+nts and bastards and arseholes and wankers. The quicker I'm sixteen the better, he thought.

At home he took off the gay blazer with the gay badge that had the letters KA linked like a set of keys. Ryan didn't have to wear a blazer at his school.

"How was your first day?"

Markus turned his head slowly and looked at his brother with a scowl.

Ryan smiled a weak smile, and said no more.

"Dare you knock on that door?"

Markus, The Taylor Brothers and a couple more were loitering outside Elizabeth Court. It was getting dark.

"Dare you boot that door full-pelt?" Stewie said again, pointing.

Markus followed the direction of his finger to the second floor. Between two baskets of dead flowers was a dirty white door.

"They're granny flats," Markus said.

The lads were looking at each other, trying not to laugh. As always Stewie was deadpan, giving nothing away. "Go boot that door," he said. "And I'll give you a tenner."

Markus was off, moving towards the iron stairwell.

"He's mad," one said.

"Not right in the fucking head."

"He does *anything*. Not scared of *nothing*."

Markus could hear them, and the comments only fired him up even more. By the top of the stairs he felt that addictive rush of invincibility. He didn't give a thought to the owner of the door or who lived behind it. Just grabbed the disability handle on the wall and gave the door two massive blasts with his foot. He heard laughter after the first kick and then a cry from inside after the second. He must have kicked hard because the whole front of the flat seemed to shake. Markus ran off, back down the stairs. His footsteps sounded musical as they clanked down each rung. At the bottom he heard the door open and a figure loomed above him.

"Crip!" one of his mates shouted.

"You fucking kids are gonna die!!"

Markus was being chased. When he looked back he saw a crazy sight. Some man wielding a walking stick in the air. The figure wore a bright red beanie hat and his dressing gown was gaping open to a stick-thin torso.

"Sparky you're mad."

Sparky was Markus's new nickname. He'd earned it due to his

new passion for setting fires, notably after burning down the shed in the churchyard. The event had even reached the local newspaper.

"Sparky-Marky strikes again!"

The man wasn't giving up, he limped towards the gang of lads like a madman, spinning the metal crutch in the air like a Kung Fu master.

"Little bastards," he spat, almost falling over.

That cracked the boys up.

"Steady on Crip."

"Hey Crip ya might wanna do ya dressing gown up mate. Not really appropriate, flashing to schoolboys."

The gang were backing away onto the churchyard, where Markus had set the fire less than a week ago.

"And don't think I don't know it wasn't you who set fire to that shed," Crip cried, pointing to a patch of black rubble on the grass. "So disrespectful! Little termites, that's all you are."

Stewie did a cheeky dance and Ewan tried to spit at him.

"I fought in Afghanistan you arseholes. You don't frighten me."

The man did more moves with his walking stick and the boys cheered. "Check Jackie Fucking Chan out here."

"You weren't brought up; you were dragged up." Crip carried on. "Bet half of you haven't even got dads. Mums probably don't give a shit either!"

Markus stopped backing away. "Hey watch your fucking mouth."

"Oooh hit a nerve have we?" Crip said, coming closer.

Markus set his scowl on him.

"Got mummy issues have we?" Crip leered, rotting teeth inside a dirty smile.

"I said *watch it*." Markus warned again.

Crip took his walking stick and held it in two hands, drawing it back like a baseball bat.

"Sparky man c'mon," someone said from behind.

"What's up? She fuck off and leave you? Ah poor baby."

Markus had his fists up and was moving forward.

"Or maybe she's dead? Yeah that's it, isn't it? Mummy's gone and died on her little brat."

Markus screamed and charged at the man but was met with the swing of the walking stick. An inch higher and the boy's face would have been off.

"You wanna play orphan-boy?" Crip screeched. "Oh I'll play with you alright."

He swung and missed but shoulder-barged the boy into the gravel. He brought the stick down again, glancing him. Realising he was out-matched Markus had to retreat.

"Sparky man leave it."

"That's it fuck, back off!"

Crip had the stick pointing at him like a rifle. It gleamed in the dusk.

Markus was shaking and disorientated, still he had his fists out. "If I was your age I'd batter the fuck out of you," he gasped.

"Yeah, well ... ." Crip was out of breath too, leaning forward, letting the stick take his weight. " ... you're not are you?"

"I will be," Markus said. "One day."

There was a little smile on Crip's face, sensing he had achieved some kind of victory.

"You boys come round here again and you really will get it. I got a gun inside and I've got no qualms about putting two in you. So stay away!"

His shout echoed like a dog bark.

He turned and limped away. Night had fallen and the man looked like a silver ghost floating back up the hill.

The gang re-joined Markus, who was still staring at the departing figure.

"You're lucky he didn't kill you," Stewie said.

"He's lucky *I* didn't kill *him*," Markus answered back.

"Nah," Stewie said. "He's too much, even for you."

Markus didn't like that. Made him madder than ever.

Another boy joined in. "Fucker was in the SAS."

"Got honourably discharged."

"Killed so many people he lost his mind."

"Man is crazy."

Markus turned to them all. "You lot believe anything. Rumours that go around here. So stupid. Man I hate this fucking town. Hate Kimble Wells."

Markus stormed off and the gang watched him.

"Hey Stew he didn't even ask for the tenner. You dared him for a tenner, remember?"

Stewie kept his eyes on Markus, his curls moving in a slight autumn breeze. "Venner don't give a shit about that. He doesn't do it for money, he does it for something else."

They watched him turn the corner and disappear out of sight.

"Hey what happened to his mum?" one of them said.

"Think she killed someone."

"Nah I heard someone killed *her.*"

"Nah she definitely killed someone."

"She's in prison."

"Fucker carries on the way he is. He'll be joining her."

They all laughed at that one.

Markus hadn't seen Ryan for ages. He'd gone into hibernation again and the younger brother was surprised to hear him knocking on his bedroom door.

He opened it. "What?" he said, irritably.

He was taken aback to see his older brother sporting a new hairstyle, a drastic side-sweep with blonde flicks.

"What the fuck!"

"What?" Ryan said innocently.

"Fuck's that on your head?"

Ryan threw his big blue eyes upwards. "My new style."

Markus walked around him, looking at it from all angles. "You look like one of those gay-boys on X-Factor."

Ryan shook his head and sighed. "If I knew I was going to be insulted I wouldn't have even bothered."

"Bothered what?"

"To see if you're ready."

Ryan had started doing this limp-wrist gesture and it made Markus want to be sick. "Ready for what?" he said with a screw-face.

"Ready to go and see dad."

Markus could smell perfume, luckily it was coming from his auntie, who was getting ready in the next room. "Come on Markus," she shouted. "Visiting is between one and three."

Markus looked at his brother like he didn't know what he was talking about.

"You've forgotten?" Ryan said with an open mouth.

He did the limp-wrist even more and Markus wanted to snap the fucking thing off.

"I forgot to remember," he said.

Ryan went red in the face. "You said you'd come this time."

Ryan had this bitch-whiney voice and Markus thought about imitating it.

"It's been five months and you've not been to visit him *once*."

Markus didn't say anything, just smiled.

"He *misses* you," Ryan said dramatically.

Markus wanted to laugh. "I'll come next time, promise," he said, robotically.

Markus couldn't believe that Ryan didn't know he was taking the piss. His people-reading skills were crap.

"You said that *last time*, and the time before."

Aunt Tars must have been listening in. "Oh Ryan just leave him."

Ryan stood, hurt. His lip quivering.

"Send him my love," Markus said with a restrained smile.

Ryan shook his head and went to leave, but then spun around on his heels and faced his brother again. "You need to let go of your blame and anger, Markus. You need to forgive dad and stop harbouring all this resentment."

That did crack Markus up and this time he didn't hold it in. Laughed right in his face. "You don't get it do you?"

Ryan stood, his knew hairstyle wobbling on his head, waiting for more words off his younger brother.

"I'm not harbouring nothing." Markus mouthed the words as slowly and clearly as he could. "There is no blame. I just don't give a shit. I'm not visiting him because I'm upset." Markus was staring at him hard. "I literally, just, can't be arsed."

Aunt Tars was waiting at the door. Markus thought how fat she looked in that skirt. He was going to tell her but he couldn't be arsed with that either. "Ryan," she said "C'mon!"

Ryan did that stupid catwalk turn of his again, and strutted away.

Fucking families, Markus thought, wish they'd all die

The only person Markus really had any communication with at The Kitts Academy was a gobby emo-girl who sat in front of him at registration. Markus tried to ignore her but she was always dancing in front of him, doing cartwheels or speaking in this weird put-on accent that sounded half-Pakistani and half-Italian. Most of the time he managed to block her out but then she started bending down in front of him. Literally just a few inches away. Markus had to admit she probably had the best arse he had ever seen but that didn't matter. She loved herself and he couldn't truly fancy someone who loved themselves, especially as much as she did.

"Yo New Boy!" she said, pulling a strawberry lollipop out of her red mouth. "What's your name?"

Markus produced that pout of his, and then slowly turned his eyes on her. "Why?" he said.

She didn't seem phased by his Eye Test at all. "Pleased to meet you Why," she said, holding out a hand. "I'm Mia."

"Dare you knock on Crip again?" Stewie said.

All eyes were on Markus, more expectancy on him this time. It was a dare, a challenge. Markus *always* had to accept. He had a rep now and a rep came with great responsibility.

"Go on Sparky, fucking dare you."

"Nah man," another said, goading him. "Not after last time. *Even* you're not that mad."

Markus glanced over to Elizabeth Court, that dirty white door where the madman with a walking stick lived behind.

Markus was ambushed by a sudden attack of nerves. They beat around in his stomach like bats. He looked around at the gang, the line of faces that were watching him, studying him intently, looking for a flash of fear or a crack of unease, anything to give him away, show that he had bottled it. Only Markus hadn't bottled it. Markus would never bottle it, ever. A wicked smile spread across his face and his eyes came to life with a malicious sparkle.

His mates made happy animal noises as he began walking.

It was earlier in the day than last time. The grassy courtyard was lighter and Markus was much more exposed. He took another look behind to see the gang reposition themselves, getting ready to run. Stewie Taylor had picked something up to lob at Crip and his older brother Ewan moved onto his shoulder.

"Go on Sparky!" one of them shouted.

Adrenalin began to spread over the boy's body as he got nearer to the iron stairwell. The October sun escaped the shade and lit Markus up momentarily, blinding him for a second. Just then Markus saw movement, a blur, a body, a face. Someone was stepping out from the stairwell, waiting for him behind the wall. The sun was still in his eyes and he couldn't see properly. There was a flash and a shape moving towards him. Markus tried to duck but it was too late. It smashed him in the side of the face.

"Got ya you little bastard!"

Sound crashed through his ears and it was like life had been sucked right out of him. Everything was upside down, inside out. Everything was spinning, coming undone. Markus staggered back not knowing where he was. He could feel the man on him, grabbing at him, clawing at his face. But it was the initial blow that had done the damage. He could feel his brain vibrating in his head. The lights were beginning to dim but the need to get away was primal. It felt like a matter of life and death. He was running, or what he thought was running. Crip was still in pursuit, on his back, that scratched voice all around him.

"Fucking get here orphan-boy I'm not done with you yet!"

The ground rolled under his feet, like he was trying to walk up the escalators the wrong way.

"Ha, ha, ha!" Crip was close by. Markus felt that lethal walking stick wafting behind his ear. "Got ya, got ya!!"

Markus was waiting for help from his mates. Stewie Taylor or one of the others to come to his rescue, pick him up, cover him, attack Crip or distract him at least. Only nothing came and Markus got desperate. He was even tempted to cry out that word he had never used in his whole life, *help.*

Somehow he had gotten away, he had made it. Escaped to a safer place, under the shelter of a bush. He doubled-up and spat-out blood, maybe a tooth. Pain was everywhere, splitting through his skull and taking over the bones of his face. He'd never felt anything quite like it. He was dizzy and it felt like he was about to pass-out, like he was being pulled under by something. He couldn't stop, he thought. I have to keep walking. I have to get *home.* Markus stood and tried to get his bearings. The sign for Apple Tree Lane was shining to his left. He tried to walk it only he couldn't remember it being this steep. It was as if he was wearing boots filled with sand, each step felt like ten. Moving but not getting anywhere. He imagined it was what being drunk felt like, weak and handicapped and nauseous. He felt like he was going to be sick, collapse. Part of him wanted to fall at the nearest house, bang on the door and ask for help but he knew he could never do that. Push on, he thought, must push on.

At the summit of the hill he touched his face and more pain blitzed through it and he knew that something was broken. *Had* to be.

At last he reached Norman Close, so happy to see that line of bungalows to the right. He prayed that Tars was out, and Ryan in his room. Don't want them to see me, he thought, don't want the fuss. The questions. The hassle. His prayers had been answered because he managed to get into his room undisturbed. He looked in the mirror to see the side of his face ballooned like *The Elephant Man*. Fuck, he slurred, holding onto it. That bastard, that bastard cripple is going to pay for this. He's going to get his comeuppance if it's the last thing I do.

Markus dropped into his bed and it swallowed him whole. He lay there for a while before turning onto his back. Stevie Gerrard looked at him from one wall and Leigh-Anne Pinnock from the other. The room began to swirl and the ceiling was swinging back and forth about an inch from his nose so he turned back over again.

Markus knew you shouldn't go to bed with concussion. He'd heard that before. Go to sleep with a bang to the head and you might never wake up.

Wake up dead.

But Markus didn't care, Markus didn't care at all. Might not be a bad thing, he thought, closing his eyes.

Fuck life.

Markus did wake up. Markus woke up alive and that disappointed him, a bit. He had got his vision back and his bedroom was still again. The world wasn't a-swirl and upside-down anymore. The only thing that was different was the bloody golf ball he had in his mouth. It was thick and throbbing and gave him trouble breathing. It was sometime in the early morning because he heard the birds in the tree outside and Aunt Tars pottering around in the kitchen at the far-end of the bungalow. Markus smacked his lips and sucked on a mouthful of blood. He was thirsty. He was dying of thirst. A thirst so powerful he felt his insides crack with dehydration. Fuck it, he thought. I've got to face her at some point. As predicted Aunt Tars freaked-out when she saw it.

"Oh my god."

"It's nothing."

"Who hit you?"

"No one."

"Who you been fighting with?"

"I haven't been fighting."

Tars was up close, her head to one side. "What then?"

She went to stroke his hair but Markus flinched her off.

"I took an elbow in football."

His aunt just rolled her eyes, not believing a word he said. Once he applied ice, showered, gargled with mouthwash and popped two Anadin Extra it looked no way near as bad. Just a half-inch cut along his lower gum. It was still noticeable though.

"Hey Markus, dad sends his love." Ryan said, entering the kitchen. "Oh my god what happened to your face?"

Markus couldn't let anyone else see this, least of all Mia.

"How do you feel?" Aunt Tars said.

"It did make me feel dizzy at first. To be honest I'm a little scared of catching it again."

"Alright I'm keeping you off school for a few days."

Bingo, Markus thought.

"Maybe get you in at the doctors."

"No doctors," Markus said. "A few days rest, that's all."

Ryan looked at him from behind the fridge door. Shook his head, envious that his younger had managed to skive school.

So Markus enjoyed having the bungalow to himself for a few days. He watched films and ate junk, managed to find Ryan's laptop where he spent hours on YouTube. He watched fighting mostly, street fights, school fights, gang fights, girl fights. He favourite was that big black Kimbo Slice. He was a bad boy. He let people punch him for a bit before battering them senseless. Then he went onto murder stuff, school shootings, suicide bombers, serial killers. He watched documentaries and interviews on Ted Bundy, Jeffery Dahmer, Ed Kemper and Arthur Shawcross. His favourite was The Night Stalker, Richard Ramirez. He'd dress in black and then go hunting in the night. His court case was the best because he wore sunglasses and looked cool, blowing kisses to the girls.

On the third day Markus got bored. There's only so much of this shit you can watch, he thought. Kind of sticks in your mind and you can't get rid of it. Even when he went out walking along the channel, all he could see was bloody bodies and evil eyes. Stuff fucks with your head, he thought.

Nope, he was ready to go back to school, definitely. To be honest he kind of missed Mia, or rather, he missed the flirty attention she gave him. He found a picture of her on Facebook. She had her mouth open and her tongue out, that cocky pose of hers. She was pulling her school shirt up, belly-button dimpled into her taut, pale stomach. Markus enlarged the image and slid a hand into his boxers...

... after he floated in a pool of guilt and was kind of disgusted with himself. He didn't even like Mia, not when he really got down to it. Her body was fit yeah but he didn't like her face, that arrogant expression of hers. He didn't like her hair, which she was dyeing every five minutes. Most of all he didn't like her personality. She didn't feel real to him and wanking over her felt like she had taken some of his power. He didn't like this feeling and vowed to never do it again.

"Where you been hiding?" she was leaning over his desk, squeezing her little breasts together.

"Out," he snapped.

His aggression didn't put her off. If anything it made her flirt with him more.

"Out where?" she said, chewing gum. Markus suddenly got paranoid about his injury. He didn't want her seeing his misshapen jaw-line. He didn't want her having *anything* over him.

She was looking at him in a certain way, like he was being studied. Her head to one side, curious. It was like she was searching for something. He remembered tossing off over her and that made him squirm. What if she knows, he thought? What if she can see it in my face? What if some girls can sense things like that?

Markus did his usual when in a tight spot: best line of defence, attack.

"Fuck you looking at?" he snarled.

"Not much," she said with a wink, turning on her heels, lowering herself slowly into her chair.

Markus pictured yanking the chair from under her and smashing it over her head.

Bitch.

After class she was on him again. Over him again with another button undone so he could see even more. Doesn't this girl *ever* quit, he thought.

"What you doing for lunch?" she said.

"Eating," he said.

This made Mia smile. "Well," she began. "I normally spend it with my bestie but she's off sick, *yet again.* Swear she's a hypochondriac."

"Bestie?"

"Yeah my best mate Mel."

"Oh."

"But hey," she sang. "You can be my bestie today."

She was weird but he was starting to like that. Her persistency was strangely charming. If she wasn't careful this girl might grow on him, like a tumour.

"Wanna go and get chips?" she said.

"Nah," Markus said, looking at the ground. "I fucking hate chips."

"Canteen then?"

Markus nodded, and then followed her there.

His first thought was fire. Only fire was too risky, too dangerous. Plus Crip lived in granny flats and he didn't really want the early cremation of a dozen OAP's on his conscience.

Conscience.

Markus waited until bang-on 10pm, threw on a black Adidas cap and then crept out his bedroom window.

Markus was on another one of his 'missions.'

The Close where he lived was silent and empty and it felt a lot later than ten. It had that early hour quality to it. Markus liked the night, the dark. He enjoyed walking around in it and it was like no one could see him. A nocturnal cloak of invisibility.

Night-time felt like freedom.

You can do what you want here.

He walked the channel until he saw the spire of the church poking out between the trees. Taking a few alleyways and avenues he found himself outside Elizabeth Court. The journey had taken him no longer than fifteen minutes. Markus pulled the cap lower over his face, surveying the area. There was no sound, or movement. Only his own stealth-like motion as he crept to the edge of the courtyard, sneaking along the shadowy bushes at the side of the wall. At the foot of the iron stairwell he raised onto his tiptoes and then began to ascend the steps as slowly as he could. At the top he took a moment, breathed in deep and then headed to the ghostly white door that seemed to hover in the darkness. He took hold of the disability handle like he did the first time and waited. Maybe he heard the faint murmur of the television on the other side. He gave it a second and then booted the door twice; *boom, boom.* Crip was on it straight away. That demented war-cry of his.

"WHAT THE FUCK!"

Markus dived into the dark corner at the top of the stairs.

The sound of Crip's limped footsteps getting closer and closer, *thud, drag, thud, drag.*

Markus heard the chain being unhooked and the key rattling in its lock. The door was open and here was Crip. Red beanie hat. Open dressing gown. Manky sandals. That infamous walking stick ready to take the world on.

"C'mon ya little bastards!"

Markus had to time this right. Go too early and Crip will see him. Go too late and Markus will end up being trapped, cornering himself into a dead-end.

"Where are you fucker?"

Markus waited for one more *thud* and *drag* and now he was lined-up just where he wanted him. Right at the top of the iron stairwell with his back facing. Markus made his move only Crip must have heard him. The boy was shocked to see the cripple move so fast. He'd managed a one-eighty turn and now they were head-to-head.

They caught eyes for a split-second.

"You," Crip said.

Only Markus had the advantage of already being in motion. Doing as he'd been trained he used the floor for maximum power and pushed off, not giving anything away. Keeping the framework of his body he hit the man full in the chest and he toppled back. Crip seemed to balance at the top for ages, like a cartoon. He seemed to hang there and hang there, a fifty-fifty chance whether he was going to go or not. Markus was going to charge again and take that other fifty percent away but he didn't want to ruin the aesthetics. He liked watching this desperate act, his face full of savage horror. Then his leg went, the good one. As if the top step was covered in ice it just slipped and then the whole lot went. Crip was falling. He almost did a full backwards somersault like that gay-boy Tom Daley at the Olympics. Markus heard his neck break when he landed. A *snap* and then a *crunch*. Markus watched the rest of his body crash down after it and roll over another two or three times until there was a dark corpse sprawled out at the bottom.

Markus was a little stunned by just how crazy all that was. He never expected such a show. He stood there, looking down, and now it was all silent, as if nothing had happened. No one stirred.

There was no sound from any of the neighbours. They were all probably in their ancient sleep, oblivious, dead to the world.

Markus was certain this man wasn't going to move but there was no way he was going to step over him anyway. He'd seen way too many horror movies to know that they always caught your leg on the way out, one more twist of drama before it all ended.

Markus didn't want that.

So he climbed over the balcony and let his body hang, before letting go and landing on the grass.

It was time to get back home, back to his bungalow.

Another mission accomplished.

School was the same and he carried on like it was a regular day. In fact he had almost forgotten about it until Mia said something at lunch.

"What did you get up to last night?"

At first he had to think, then he remembered. *Oh just pushing a cripple down two flights of stairs. You?*

A wave of paranoia crashed in on him. *Why is she asking me that?*

"Nothing," he said defensively. "Why?"

"You look tired. Look like you haven't slept a wink. What's up, up all night thinking about me?"

"Yeah, right," Markus said, aware he had gotten a little hard under the table.

Mia smiled, slid in next to him and began to unpeel a banana.

They ate in silence. Markus drifted off into his own world until he was snapped out of it by two kids talking on the next table.

"Yeah that Crazy Crip Guy died this morning."

"Who?"

"That nutter who was thrown out the army. You know him. He's always hobbling around naked, scaring kids with that walking stick."

"Never heard of him."

"Anyway someone found his ass frozen in the mud."

"What you on about frozen? It's not even that cold."

"Well not frozen but you know that stiff-thing that happens to dead people."

"No."

"God you don't know *anything*. Anyway, he's dead."

"Oh."

"Watch football last night?"

Markus had stopped eating and was staring into space. His mouth was dry and he needed a piss. He was only vaguely aware of the girl who was chewing his ear off.

"So I told her, Mel ya better snap out of it there's nothing wrong with you. The only disorder you've got is hypochondria."

Markus got up slowly.

"Venner are you even listening?" Mia said.

"Yeah," he said, clearly not. "I just need a piss."

"That's polite dinner talk. Alright well I'll catch you at the gates. I think you should do the gentlemanly thing and walk me home tonight."

"Yeah," Markus said, again not listening.

"Suit yourself weirdo. Hey you've not even finished your lunch."

Markus was already gone.

When Markus did find out that Crip was actually dead he went into a silent panic. The paranoia got unbearable. He got paranoid about everything, footprints, fingerprints, DNA, eyewitnesses. He got paranoid by the fact he had googled it on his brother's laptop. He'd never been able to figure out how to delete the browser and was convinced his brother was going to see it and then shop him to the police. A week later and one small newspaper article eased his mind. It said that he had fallen, that he had suffered from mental health issues and had a history of falls. This suddenly made him feel better and the fear and paranoia was replaced with another feeling, that familiar invincible glow of being able to get away with *anything*.

He lay in bed at night, replaying the scene through his head.

"You." That was Crip's very last word, *you.*

He had said it with this sort of whispering acceptance, like he could sense his own death.

"You."

The 'you' was *me,* Markus thought. *I* was the last person you saw, the last *thing* you saw. I was the thing that took you away. You were taken away by *me.*

Markus was wondering if he was going to dream at last. Perhaps an event this momentous would stir up something inside him, open up his subconscious, pushing his deeper feelings to the surface, a flashback, a face, a nightmare. Anything.

It didn't.

He slept as sound as ever.

Back at school Markus sat in the canteen and looked at the other kids. They all had their lives, the things they did, their achievements, their goals, their hobbies, their plans.

Markus enjoyed that *if only they knew* feeling. He liked watching them move around him, oblivious of his deeds.

What he had done was massive and shocking, something beyond their experience and this put him above them.

He was separate to the rest.

He was an outsider.

It was strange to see Stewie Taylor by himself, without his older brother or one of his other cronies. He stood at Markus's back door and Markus couldn't believe how small he was. Without his entourage he looked even smaller. How can someone of this size command such respect, Markus thought?

"Markus," he said.

Markus had just finished eating a bowl of Cheerios and had milk all over his mouth. "What do you want?" he said, grumbling.

Stewie wore a certain smile and it unnerved Markus, a little.

"Hear about Crip?"

"Who's Crip?"

Stewie had his head to one side, studying Markus's reaction. He found something there.

"Ah c'mon man, you know Crip. Nutter with the walking stick. Lives up on Elizabeth Court. *You* used to terrorise him, remember?"

"Hey *we all* terrorised him," Markus said quickly.

Again Stewie picked up his reaction, he was collecting them, gathering information.

"Yeah well he's dead."

"Yeah so I heard," Markus said without thinking, putting a hand through his hair.

"Thought you said you didn't know him?"

Fuck. Markus felt his brain crumble. He stared at the wall and hoped to find an answer there.

"I ... you just told me who he was."

"Yes ... " Stewie said. There was a clarity to his tone that was

244

frightening. " … but before I did you said you didn't know who he was. So if you didn't know who he was then how do you know he's dead?"

Markus put on his scowl-mask and stepped back. "You're talking shit man."

He went to close the door but Stewie caught it with his foot. "I know you had something to do with it."

Markus pulled a face. "Yeah right." He struggled with the door but Stewie had him.

"I *saw* how mad you were that day. Calling your mummy and then that little blast in the chops he gave you. Knocked you out, man. He beat you and you didn't like it. That pride of yours Venner. It was always gonna get you into trouble."

"Like I say, I don't know about any murder."

"Who mentioned murder?"

"You did."

"Did I, when?"

"Well he died didn't he? And you're thinking I did it."

"I said you had *something to do with it*. Who knows what happened? Maybe he fell, maybe he was pushed. I don't know. I'll leave *that* for the police to find out."

Markus felt his blood run cold.

"I mean, I can only tell them what I know. That you used to go up to his door and kick it. That he used to chase you and try to hit you with that crazy walking stick. That you and Crip became enemies, that you had *beef*."

"I'll deny it," Markus said flatly.

"I'm sure you will. But I got witnesses. About a dozen."

"I'll still deny it."

"Oh c'mon, man. I managed to trip and tie you up and them there *pole-leese* is a lot cleverer than me. You're fucked Venner and you know it."

Markus did know it. He *was* fucked and he was feeling his world come apart. Stewie Taylor had taken his world apart in minutes.

Markus switched tactics. "You know I'll kill you."

"Ha. So now you're admitting it all."

"You know I'll kill you," Markus said through his teeth. He was so angry he felt like he was going to explode.

"You won't be able to," Stewie said calmly. "You'll be in prison, serving life."

Markus stood upright and breathed. "What do you want?"

"Just what you owe me, three-fifty. The three-fifty you owe me for my stolen gear."

"The gear *you* stole."

Stewie shrugged. He didn't admit it, but he didn't deny it either.

"In fact round it off to five."

"Five-hundred quid?"

"Beady wants a little compo. After all, you about broke his jaw."

Markus kicked the doorframe and suddenly realised his brother was in the next room. He prayed to god he hadn't heard all this. "Fucking hell," he said.

"C'mon man I only want what's mine," Stewie said. "You should think yourself lucky, I could squeeze you for a lot more. I mean this is some serious shit. This is *murder* man you even said so yourself. I could get *a whole lot* more from you but that's just a scummy thing to do. Plus, I kind of like you, man."

Now Markus had both hands on his head in defeat.

Stewie wore a Man U track top and Markus knew he had chosen this on purpose. It was symbolic, to antagonise Markus, let him know this was war. With Stewie it was all about the details.

"It's *only* five-hundred quid," Stewie went on. "It's fuck all. A drop in the ocean."

"If it's fuck all then why do you want it?"

"Principle," Stewie said, stepping forward. "Because something's are above money, and drugs, and any of that other bullshit. Because your stepdad or whoever he was has gone now and you have *no one* to watch over you. Because you thought you could beat me but you *can't*. And never will. Because I have you by the balls and you can't go anywhere. I will always have this over you and there is fuck all you can do. So pay me, in full, by Friday. Otherwise I'll be straight down the cop shop and then you'll be proper fucked, *for life*."

Stewie was gone, not another word. And Markus got to answer his own question, that's how Stewie Taylor commanded so much respect.

That's how.

Markus had no idea how he was going to get hold of five-hundred quid in two days. He thought of places he could rob or people he could borrow from. There was nowhere and no one and nothing. In the end he came back to the place he always did: Aunt Tars.

It was only yesterday though they'd had their worst argument yet. Markus let rip, got real. Pulled out all the stops and said some unbelievably cruel things. Worse than ever. Even worse than his usual jibes about her weight. Markus had moved up to the next level. He actually said these words:

"Just because you can't have kids yourself, Tara dear, doesn't mean you get to play mummy with us."

He had even found it funny, how it broke her and how upset she got. He couldn't believe how words could do that, how sounds from a mouth could totally destroy someone.

Now he needed her, he needed her help more than ever before.

They sat in silence. Ryan kept flicking that stupid gay-boy hair of his.

Does he know how fucking stupid he looks, Markus thought. He imagined taking a handful of it and yanking his head into the dinner before him.

Auntie Tara kept glancing at Markus over the dinner table. She knew something was wrong with the boy, reading his troubled mind with a maternal psychic power. She knew he needed her help, lingering in the kitchen after washing the pots, waiting for his older brother to leave so he could ask her something.

"Tara can I ask you something, *for* something."

She sat sideways in her window and lit up a cigarette. Tara was the only person Markus knew who could start smoking *and* put on weight at the same time. With Tara there was no in between, she was either an alluring MILF or a bland frump. In the last two months she had dramatically swayed to the latter and Markus couldn't imagine her ever getting *it* back.

Markus found it sad and embarrassing.

"Go on," Tara said.

"I need some money."

Tara blew out smoke and Markus watched her clouded expression unchanged.

"I need five-hundred quid."

"No chance," she said flatly, not even pausing for thought.

"You haven't even heard me yet."

"I've heard enough."

"I'm in trouble."

Tara smoked in silence. "What kind?" she said.

"I can't tell you."

"So yesterday I was an interfering infertile bitch and now you want half a grand at the drop of a hat." She let out an angry downward jet of smoke. "World doesn't work like that Markus."

Half a grand sounded more than *five hundred*. Tara could be very clever in how she used her words.

Markus stood dumb, not knowing what else to say. Tara noted the worry-lines streaking across his forehead and was surprised to see that something had perforated his bullet-proof bubble.

"Drugs?" she said.

"What?"

"Are you into drugs?"

Markus shook his head. "Nah. Nah it's nothing like that."

She got down from the worktop and faced him. "You bring *any* shit to this house Markus and you'll be straight into care without a conscience."

Tara normally found it uncomfortable holding eyes with the boy but this time she stared at him without a blink. "Get into shit. Get expelled, arrested. Kill somebody for all I care but don't bring *anything* to this house."

Tara didn't mean that and Markus knew it. She was just playing tough woman.

"So you can't help me?" Markus said.

"No," she said. "No I can't. Not if you don't tell me what it is. Five hundred quid is a lot of money and I'm not just going to *hand it over* without any explanation."

She was clever, trying to tease the truth out of him.

Markus held onto it. It wasn't going anywhere. "I can't Tars. I really can't tell you."

"That's that then," she said, brushing her hair back like she was still attractive.

Markus wanted to hurt her, say something to fuck her up only this time he didn't.

"Okay," he said, switching tactics. "I understand."

He put his head down and walked solemnly to his room. He expected his aunt's voice to collar him at the door, give in like she normally did.

Only this time.

Markus was fucked and he knew it. He's going to prison. He's going to prison for a long time for pushing a crippled war-vet down a flight of stairs and killing him. He didn't sleep that night and in the morning he was straight up and out the bungalow, walking the Clementine Channel with a headful of ideas. I could run, he thought, pack a rucksack and go into hiding, steal food, sleep where I drop, live on the run. It could be quite exciting. No one to answer to, do what I want. Plus I'd be famous, picture in the paper, face on the news. Everyone would know my name. Everyone would know *Markus Venner*.

By the end of the walk he had dismissed it for what it was, *a stupid idea*.

This isn't a film, or a book. This isn't TV. This is real life.

Part of him thought about going to Stewie Taylor, ask him for more time, or to pay less money. Only he hated the idea of grovelling to that wannabe-gangster arsehole. Not on my deathbed, he thought. If I go down I go down with dignity. I'll just have to face it. Face what's coming and accept the consequences. Prison might not be so bad. Can't be any worse than school.

Markus returned to an empty home, Tara and Ryan must be out on one of their little daytrips. She's probably buying him some new clothes right now, or eating at a restaurant.

Markus got a drink and then slumped into his room with his head down. He went to take a drink from his glass when he noticed something on the bed. His bed had been made and a manila envelope sat in the centre of it.

There was nothing written on it and Markus wondered if it was even meant for him.

He got on his knees and picked it up, turned it over, looked at it. It felt quite chunky, like there was something inside. He peeled it open with his thumb to find five small bundles of twenty-pound notes, separated by little white strips of paper. Behind the money was a note written in Tara's handwriting.

I don't need to know what this is for. I don't care. You don't have to thank me for it and we never need mention it again.
  Whatever is going on, I trust and believe in you, Markus.

Your Auntie Tara.

P.S. Maybe you can pay me back when you become a famous footballer.

Markus picked up the money and stared at it, a massive smile growing on his face. He couldn't believe it.

"Cool," he whispered.

He screwed the note into a ball and tossed it into the air, heading it into the bin. The money he scooped up and slid into his wallet before heading into town. The first place he hit was Sports Direct, treating himself to the new Liverpool Home top. After he made his way to McDonald's, ordering a Big Mac meal with extra fries. He sat in the window and pulled off his jumper, replacing it with the Liverpool shirt. The price tag still hanging off its neck. After munching through the burger he whipped out his phone and called Stewie Taylor.

"Alright you blackmailing bastard, I've got your money."

The voice on the other end was surprised and glad.

"Bout sixty-odd quid short though," Markus added, after arranging to meet.

The silence told Markus that Stewie wasn't happy, but fuck him, you can't have it *all* your own way. Markus was satisfied he wasn't giving him the full amount. He felt the sway of power tilt his own way a bit.

After the call he sat and finished the rest of his meal. He admired the bold redness and crisp fit of Liverpool through the window's reflection. Markus nodded to himself as he slurped up the last dregs of his shake.

Overall he'd done alright out of the whole thing.

He'd come out on top.

It was another school in another German lesson with another teacher trying to make him say another stupid word in front of another stupid class. Trying to make him do something he didn't want to. Trying to embarrass him, take away his power. Only he was bigger and sure of himself now. He'd learnt from the last time and here he was, flat-out refusing to play ball.

"Markus everyone else is participating so say the word after me..."

"No."

The teacher stood in front of him, shaking his head.

"C'mon Markus it's only right you get involved too. It's only *fair*."

All eyes were on him only this time he didn't give a shit. Markus sat stubbornly silent, head down, unmoving.

"Markus I'll wait all lesson if I have to, into break time if I have to..."

The class groaned and somehow the teacher had turned them all against him. It was a nasty trick and Markus Venner felt the full force of rage build up inside him. He felt his face change.

"Man I ain't saying nothing."

"You're not saying *anything*." The teacher corrected with a snigger. "Maybe we should teach you to speak English before we do German."

That made everybody laugh and Markus found himself on his feet. His chair flipped, leaving its legs sticking up in the air like a beetle on its back. The laughter dissolved and an uneasy hush replaced it.

"Markus sit down."

Markus could tell the teacher had shit it, a little dorky fuck with glasses.

"You fucking make me sit-down, prick." Markus roared. "Do you know who you're fucking with? I've killed a man."

Markus shocked himself by saying that. He watched the teacher's confused face whiten another shade. "Markus get out."

His voice cracked and all the shitting-it symptoms were in full view.

"Get out!" he said again, pointing to the door. Markus watched his hand shake in mid-air.

Markus lowered his head and smiled, preparing for attack.

"Philip go and get Mr Melvin."

A fat kid ran out and Markus kept on staring at the teacher.

"Markus you just need to calm down."

"You started this," Markus said in a low voice, a near whisper.

"Markus ... "

Before the teacher could say another word Markus grabbed the legs of the chair and launched it across the room. Surprised by the force of his own throw he stepped back and watched the chair spin through the air, crashing into a filing cabinet at the back of the class. The sound split through the room and put everybody into a panic. Some kids ran out, some put their head down and pretended it wasn't happening. Others stood with their backs to the wall, open-mouthed.

One kid didn't though, she just sat calmly and looked at him, adjusted her glasses and looked at him some more.

Mel

Dear Self-Esteem Diary,

Straight into the Biography Bit ...

First off, like, I didn't fall in love with Mr Dukes straight away. Like it wasn't a Love-At First-Sight kind of a thing. In fact at the beginning I thought he was a bit weird, and funny-looking and geeky and stuff.

It definitely wasn't love-at-first-sight but tbh it wasn't far off.

Like, maybe it took An Hour or something like that.

It ALL took place in that first lesson anyway, My First Official Lesson with Mr Dukes.

He wasn't even a proper teacher. He wasn't EVEN a supply either, but one of those student ones, like he was just Starting-Out, like he was still learning and stuff. Maybe it was his nerves that attracted me in the First Place. Cos like, I'm nervous too so I know what it FEELS like and maybe I thought we had a lot in common from The Start.

He wore glasses and had black curly hair. And the black curly hair was like the hair that black people have, like an afro kind of a thing. And he had it on the back of his neck too and that was just SO cute, too cute, dead-cute. Like they looked like little curly cookies and I wanted to eat them all up. Yumyumyumyum!

I liked his clothes too cos he didn't dress like a Proper Teacher. Like his clothes were dead-cool and unique, like he wore waistcoats and chinos and sometimes I saw him wearing a hat on the way to school. And he rode a bicycle to work and he even wore a cute helmet too. And that was so different cos all the other teachers drove cars. So I guess you could say he was a Free Spirit. It's like he didn't belong anywhere.

And he was only dead-young too. Like he wasn't old like all the other teachers but like he was maybe only twenty or something like that. Maybe only ten years older than me, like when I'm twenty he'd be thirty and that's not so much of an age gap at all, not really.

So you're Mel, he said.

They were his First Words to me and tbh as soon as he spoke to me I just fell under his spell, but like in a good way.

Cos.

See.

Like I'm always dead-nervous when I meet someone for the First

Time but there was something about Mr Dukes that just made me all soft and relaxed. It felt like there was a glow between us right from The Start. Like, if you put your hand in the space between our bodies you'd feel it, an electric current; a warm and safe energy, like the sun or something.

I guess they call this Chemistry.

He smiled this big beaming smile and Straight Away I knew everything was going to be okay whenever he was around.

He's so gay! Mia said.

What?

Dukes, he's so gay.

That made me laugh.

He is, Mia said.

How do you know?

Cos I have a strong gaydar.

What's a gaydar?

It's a special power only certain people are born with, it means you can read when people are gay.

I laughed even more.

Besides, she said, only gay people wear waistcoats.

That is just ridiculous, I said.

And the biggest reason I know he's gay, she said, looking out at the sky like she was an angel or something. Is that he hasn't looked at my arse ONCE.

Now I was cracking up.

It's true, Mia said with a serious face. EVERY man looks at my arse. Teachers are the worst.

That's gross, I said.

Mr Melvin does, Mr Abbott does, Mr King does, and Mr Walsh is the worst. He doesn't even try to hide it. It's like he WANTS me to see him.

Urgh gross, I said, he must be at least fifty!!!

Honestly Mel you don't even know the half of it. It's not even a joke. My arse is constantly covered with eyes. They crawl all over me and I HATE it.

Mia didn't half exaggerate although she did have a good bum. But you see I didn't have that problem cos I didn't even have a bum for teachers to perv over. I mean mine was still flat and boring, just like my chest.

Mia said that it will ALL come soon but tbh I'm not gonna Lie I was sick of waiting! Where are you lumps and bumps and curves and stuff!!!???

So now I did wonder if Mr Dukes was gay. What if Mia was right? Even though there is like zero % chance of me ever marrying him I REALLY hoped he wasn't gay cos that would just ruin EVERYTHING. I didn't think he was cos like I'd seen gay people on TV and stuff and he was nothing like them at all. Not one bit.

After that First Lesson with him I went home and fell on the bed and said out-loud ... I'm In Love. I'd never been IN LOVE before but I'm sure this was it. I mean, IT HAD TO BE. It had to be cos he was in my head and wouldn't leave. It was like he was EVERYWHERE, attached to every thought and feeling. It was crazy. I sat at the dinner table and there was this like weird, exciting numbness all over me and stuff. Like if you got a mallet and smacked me over the head I wouldn't even feel a thing. Even when mum and My Sister Adele kept trying to wind me up I didn't feel that either. It's like nothing outside of this bubble existed.

So ...

I was dead-nervous about the next lesson with Mr Dukes, cos of all the build-up and stuff about seeing him again. Only when he came up to me with That Smile everything was alright.

How's your work going Mel? He said.

It was weird cos it was like I calmed him too. Cos I watched him with other kids and he seemed nervous, like he didn't really know what he was doing and stuff. Yet with me he changed, he got all soft around the edges and his smile only seemed to grow.

Work is going okay Mr Dukes, I said. How is your new job going?

That was a dumb thing to say and I knew it, but he just laughed in a cute way.

It's going okay Mel, he said, nodding slowly with that lovely, lovely smile.

He had the softest voice ever. It was calm and gentle and reminded me of a cool summer breeze stroking across your ears.

We looked into each other's eyes for ages and I just know that something truly amazing happened in That Moment. It's like we made our vows to each other without saying a single word.

He moved onto Mia only he didn't spend as long with her, and there wasn't the same intensity and I knew he had singled-me out.

Plus Mia was right, he didn't look at her arse, not even once. Not even when she got up and strutted to the toilet with that stupid catwalk thing of hers. And he didn't look at her because he was gay, he didn't look because he wasn't like other men. He didn't look at her in That Way cos he was real and true and pure, like snow.

Back at home I thought I was going to die. LITERALLY die. Die for good. Before I kind of wondered if I was IN LOVE whereas now I KNEW.

And it was the most amazing feeling EVER.

All the films and songs were right. It really was the greatest feeling. It was EXACTLY how They said. It felt like fire. It felt like rain. It felt the sky, space. It felt like rockets taking off into it. It felt like nature; waterfalls and rivers and oceans and stuff. Being in love made you float, fly, soar! It made you feel invincible, invisible. It made you feel like you lived in your own world, on you own planet with your own rules.

It was true. It was The Truth: Mel was Officially In Love For The First Time, in love with Mr Dukes!

I didn't tell anyone, not even My Bestie Mia. And tbh she would be The Last person I'd tell anyway. She'd be the worst. Cos like she'd just make it all about Her Self. All about Mia. The Mia Show. She'd probably try and make me jealous or something like that. Probably try and flirt with him and that would just drive me like TOTALLY insane and I'd probably end up killing her. Or she'd do something crazy like tell him or tell someone or even blurt it out in front of the WHOLE class and then I'd just DIE for good.

No.

No.

This One I'm keeping to myself, I thought. Keeping it just between Mr Dukes and me.

Our secret.

Our silent secret.

Our silent, special secret.

And I thought about him At Night, all through the night. I thought about him in bed and tbh he just added to My Insomnia even more. He was with me at night. He was with me in bed. Only I didn't really think about him in 'that way' so much. I didn't really think of him Like That. I mean I didn't really think about him the way I thought about say, Pattinson in Twilight. But I imagined different things, other things. A Different Kind of Closeness. Like I imagined him wrapping me up in his strong arms and holding me, holding my head and stuff. Or tangling his legs with my legs and we'd be all safe and lovely, like a womb kind of a thing. I imagined that soft voice in my ear, saying things about life and stuff. And he'd touch me everywhere and like love me with this great, deep love. I knew this was kind of wrong cos he was an adult and stuff, like a full grown man. But tbh Our Love felt like it kind of broke the rules with everything, like it was above age, above what people thought. It even felt like it was above Physical Appearance if that makes sense? Almost like we were just two forces blending into each other.

Are you alright Mel? My Bestie Mia said.

Yeah why?

You're acting weird, she said. Like you've been acting weird for ages. It's like you're not even here, like you keep staring into space. What's up, are you in love?

No, I said with a gulp. I felt my face go white.

I had to be careful cos Mia would pick this up. It was strange cos Mia was dumb in some ways but like a genius in others. Like she was dumb at school stuff, lesson stuff, like English and Maths and That but she was super-clever at Reading People, especially at finding out secrets and finding out weaknesses. I had to be careful.

So.

See.

I liked it when she went on holiday again and I got to have Mr Dukes ALL TO MYSELF.

What I loved about him the most, like my Favouritest Part of all was how he made me laugh. Like he was SO funny. Like it was Official: he was The Funniest Person I'd Ever Met in My Whole Life. He did this really clever thing where he'd mix words up and change sentences, and it confused people but it liked cracked them up to. And I loved laughing This Much cos it like made you stop thinking and stuff, like it put you TOTALLY In The Moment and all there was in life was laughter. And laughter is a good thing. Cos it's like the highest form of happiness if you really think about it. And I liked laughing at Mr Dukes cos I could tell he liked it. Like he would look at me in this certain way and then try to make me laugh even more. And then it would FEEL like there was just Me and Him in the room, the school, the world.

And it wasn't just the Happy Stuff he was good at but he was good at the Sad Stuff too. Like he was there for me when I was feeling down. Like All This was happening just after the time with my dad. Cos You see mum and My Sister Adele were still giving me a Hard Time about it all. And on top of that I was starting to get down about my appearance too. Like My Looks were really starting to get me depressed. Cos You see my boobs and bum had still not come. And I had to wear these really ugly chunky glasses cos my others had broken. And tbh I'm not gonna Lie but I Officially felt like The Most Unattractive Girl in The World. And it's like Mr Dukes knew this cos he came up to me one day and said, You worry what people think about you, don't you?

I had a tear in my eye and I nodded a bit.

The truth is Mel, no one is thinking anything. You know why? Cos they are too busy worrying what you think about them.

It's all a trick, he said.

He put his hand on my shoulder and squeezed it. The squeeze made me close my eyes and I drew in a breath. His hand felt like it was there for ages.

I couldn't believe he had touched me like this. It truly felt like Heaven.

For Ages after I felt that squeeze on my shoulder. It's like it was always there. If ever I missed him I would focus and put All My Attention onto my right shoulder and it was like Mr Dukes was here again.

Tbh, after a while, I started to feel low again. It's like I had come-down from the high of Mr Dukes and ended up frustrated. The class wasn't big enough, the lesson not long enough. I wanted MORE. More of Mr Dukes. I wanted him to see me after school. Take me away somewhere, ANYWHERE. Get on the back of his bike and cycle to another town; city, country. Somewhere far away where no one knew us.

Cos I couldn't do this I imagined things instead.

I imagined his house, where he lived. I imagined what his Real Life was like, how he lived. Y'know, just like the little things and stuff. Like what he had for breakfast and what newspaper he read on a Sunday. I pictured what his bedroom was like and I REALLY prayed that he didn't share it with another woman, like a girlfriend kind of a thing. Or even worser, a wife! If he did have one I knew she would be dead-beautiful and dead-clever. She'd be dead-mature too and tbh I tried not to think about This Part cos it only spoiled things. Besides, if

I DID think about it too much it would only drive me TOTALLY insane and make me want to kill her in a jealous rage or something ...

Ah. Just wild.

Anyway.
Either way.

The Thing I wanted to do more than anything was tell him. Tell him what I felt. Come clean. Let him know my TRUE TRUE feelings that were DEEP DEEP inside. I wanted him to know The Truth. I wanted to write him a note, a letter, like a Love Letter kind of a thing. I thought a Valentine Card would be a good idea but that was like ages away and I was getting too impatient! Like, I had all this love and craziness inside me and I felt like I was going to burst if I didn't tell someone soon. Tell someone NOW. I was SO close to telling My Bestie Mia but I knew that was TOTALLY out of the question. I know Her. I know Mia. I know what she's like. When it's just us she'd be all cool and stuff. She'd make a MASSIVE promise to keep it a secret. Like she'd be really nice and say the sweetest things. Like she'd go out of her way to help me and stuff. But as soon as she was at school it'd be different. As soon as she was in front of an audience all that would change. She'd HAVE to show-off and get attention and blurt it out to the WHOLE school. Then she'd cover her tracks by pretending it was an accident. Like she'd say it just slipped-out or blame someone else.

That's the kind of thing she'd do.
That's how she operates.
Like the famous saying goes, "Who Needs Enemies When You Have Mia as A friend."

See.
So.

I can't tell My Bestie.

And I couldn't tell mum or My Sister Adele either cos they'd just be worser. Like they'd just laugh in my face and stuff. Like they'd make my life a misery I just know it.

So you see I was pretty much trapped more or less.

I guess I took this out on Mr Dukes cos tbh I'm not gonna Lie but for the next few lessons I was kind of cold with him, and maybe a little rude too.

How you feeling today Mel, he said?

Fine.

You sure?

Said I was didn't I?

Okay, he said, moving on.

As soon as he walked away I regretted it and wanted him to come back. He was talking to another kid but I could tell he Knew Something, cos he liked looked up and gave me this thin-lipped smile, like an awkward kind of a thing.

And I also knew because we were telepathic and could read each other's minds All The Time.

So at break I went into the library and wrote him a love-note.

Dear Mr Dukes so sorry for being rude but The Truth is I'm totally in love with you and have been for absolutely ages and it's starting to drive me like totally insane and I just need to know if you feel the same. ???. Anyway, like, I know you're like way older and stuff but I am ready to wait for you. Like wait till I'm older and left this school and then maybe we can be together for good, like forever. If you just tick the Yes box (underneath) then I can relax. If you tick the No box then of course I'll be totally heartbroken and totally DESTROYED and DEVASTATED but at least then I can TRY to move on and get on with my life. So the decision is yours really.

Yes   No

P.S. For security reasons I'm not putting my name although you know who it is anyway and if you don't then that's kind of an answer itself.

I took the note to his desk at lunch only I was way too chicken to do it. My hands were shaking and I was so paranoid about anyone seeing me, especially Mia. So in the end I just put it down as a Dumb Idea and ripped it up into a trillion pieces and threw it in the bin where it belonged.

259

Oh Mel you're spending too much time with that girl again, mum said.

My Sister Adele was eating spaghetti in that totally annoying way of hers, Ravelling it around her fork and then sucking it up. The sound she made was disgusting and it went right through me.

What are you talking about? I said to mum.

I wasn't hungry. I'd eaten about two mouthfuls but didn't want anymore.

Because you're not eating, you're not talking. You're just MOPING.

Adele, I said, will you just eat like normal people.

Adele looked up, but I'm not like normal people, she said, I'm superior.

She broke the word 'superior' up into loads of parts, soup-pear-ree-ah.

I shook my head. Anyway, I said to mum. What's Mia got to do with it?

mum slammed her own plate down and sat opposite it. Cos you always get like this when you spend too much time with her, she said. Or when you fall out with her. You MOPE. You don't eat, talk, do anything.

What do you care what I do? I said.

Can we just eat in peace, pleeeaaase, Adele said.

You stay out of it, I snapped.

Mia's an attention-seeking snot and I don't want her around here again, mum said.

That made me laugh my head off.

She never comes here anyway. I said. And why would she?

What's that supposed to mean? mum said with big eyes.

We live in a dump.

You ungrateful little bastard.

I laughed again cos I knew that wound mum up the most.

It's not even about Mia, I said. I don't know why you're mentioning Mia. There's LITERALLY noting happening with Mia.

Now 'I' was starting to lose it.

You're crying all the time, mum said. You never want to talk about it. Then WE have to suffer from your shitty moods.

I don't suffer, Adele said, sucking up a string of pasta. I don't even notice.

Shut up! mum said to Adele in a Rare Moment of conflict between them.

I'm just saying ... Adele said, putting her hands up. Don't say WE when you mean YOU.

I loved it when Adele and mum argued although it rarely happened. I liked it cos Adele was way too smart for mum and she showed her up for what she was, a thicko!

mum never got into it with Adele cos she knew she'd lose so she always turned it back on me.

Is it cos of your dad?

I got up and left the table, stood at the door and shouted as loud as I could: It's nothing to do with Dad and it's nothing to do with Mia. I wish you'd both just leave me alone!!

After an outburst I nearly always stormed to my room but This Time I found myself going through the front door for some reason, like I was running away For Good. I didn't even know where I was going. I walked for miles, along the waters of the Clementine Channel, almost to the other side of town. By the time I got there I WAS starving. Like, proper starving, like a feeling faint kind of a thing. When I looked in my pocket all I could find was a fifty pence piece and a five. Great, I thought. Not much I can eat with that.

I thought it was getting dark but it was hard to tell cos the red and blue neon of the Tesco sign was dead-bright, lighting up the massive car park I walked through. I could smell food from the cafeteria and it smelled just like the food from the cafeteria at school and it made me hungrier even more. I stopped at the Magazine Aisle and had a look through some. I don't know why I did this cos looking at magazines always got me dead-depressed. Seeing all these Beautiful Girls everywhere and stuff. All these slim and shiny girls with perfect bodies and faces and that. It just wasn't fair and it made me as self-conscious as ever. The one I picked up had Leigh Anne Pinnock on the front, that dead-pretty dark girl from Little Mix. She was on the beach in a bikini with her new footballer boyfriend. She looked dead-happy like she knew the secret to life and stuff and it kind of got me mad that I didn't look like that. And to make it even worser I caught my reflection in the plastic that was holding up the magazines and I couldn't believe how funny-looking I was, all boz-eyed and pale and disgusting and stuff and tbh I felt like punching myself in the face!

I looked at her body then I looked down at mine. I was all flat and stooped and horrible and stuff. Her body was amazing and I imagined how hard it would be to get like that. Like all the work you'd have to do. I remember doing a workout with Mia and her Mum once and it about flipping killed me. Like, I couldn't walk for a week, or even longer. Never Again!

Anyway my tummy growled and I remembered The Real Reason I was here: hunger. It was so intense I had gone past it in a way. I remembered that I only had 55p to my name so the Only Thing I could really buy was two packets of cheapo Tesco crisps. I got one Salt and Vinegar and one Cheese and Onion but when I went to leave through the electric doors I got a bad instinct-feeling cos there was a gang of lads outside. Some of them were on bikes and some of them were on foot. They were kicking a football around and the Security Guard had just told them to go away. It was Officially Getting Dark so I tried to walk quite quickly but my nature-instinct feeling was right just like it always is cos one of the boys shouted after me.

Hey girly, come here.

His voice was slithery and slathery and creepy and I just knew I had to get away.

Hey girly don't ignore me. He shouted again.

All of a sudden I really regretted storming out the house and walking This Far.

Girly!

He was following me and he wouldn't stop following me. I put my head down and folded my arms and tried to walk as fast as I could.

The boy was on a bike and I heard the wheels clicking to my left and I realised it didn't matter how fast I walked he was always going to catch me.

Girly!

His voice was dead-spluttery and I felt spit hit my ear.

Why you covering your tits girly there's nothing there.

That Bit got me mad so I stopped and faced him. He was vile. A fat, hair-lipped thing hanging off his bike, he wore glasses and had a ridiculous multi-coloured cap on his head.

I only wanna talk, he said.

Leave me alone!

Just then one of his mates shouted up after him: What's up Beady, caught yourself another rape victim?!

The word RAPE cut right through me and made This Thing real. I wanted to run but realised that the only thing at the end of the car park was a red underpass and that would just be the Worst Place in

The World to Be. Panic set-in and I didn't know what to do. The fear was overwhelming and I heard the wheels of his bike get closer and closer. Then headlights from a car lit me up and I seemed cornered. Someone had gotten out of the car and was standing over me, a man-sized figure.

Mel.

I looked over but couldn't see his features, only the smell of a familiar spicy fragrance.

The voice came again, Mel are you alright?

He stepped into the light and the face of Mr Dukes appeared before me.

The First Thing I wanted to do was run into his arms.

Is this boy bothering you?

I nodded, joining his side. Mr Dukes took off his glasses and the gentle teacher seemed to transform into something else.

What's the problem mate?

His voice had changed too, like the one on the street was different to the one in the classroom.

The boy was already cycling away. Nothing, he shouted, putting his hand up in the air. Just making sure the girly was getting home alright.

Go on, fuck off.

Hearing him swear was weird too. Mr Dukes looked mad, like dead-mad, like he was ready to kill that boy.

You alright Mel?

I nodded my head, realising I was smiling a bit.

You know that boy, any of those boys?

I shook my head this time. I hadn't said a single word yet.

Mr Dukes looked around him, you alone?

Nodded.

What are you doing out here at this time?

I got hungry, I said.

Yeah I can see that, Mr Dukes said.

He pointed at my jeans and hoodie that were covered in crisps.

Oh, they must have popped while I was running away, I said, dusting myself down. It must have been the Salt and Vinegar bag cos the smell was everywhere.

I should go and get those guys, Mr Dukes said, heading back towards them. They need reporting or something, he said.

They'll probably be gone by now, I said.

We stood in the car park and it seemed really dark and quiet. A sudden gust of wind carried an empty can of coke across it.

C'mon, he said, get in.

I couldn't believe I was sat next to Mr Dukes in his own car. Sat next to him and we were all alone. I felt the world warp around me and I became ecstatically alive. Like part of me thought it wasn't real, like a dream kind of a thing.

It was even dreamier when he pulled into McDonald's drive-thru and ordered two Big Mac Meals.

We sat in the car park and ate them. At first we didn't talk. Then we did.

So, he said with a mouthful of burger. Why are you hungry? Why didn't you eat at home?

Had a blazing argument with my mum and left the dinner table, I said, plainly.

Mr Dukes smiled and nodded his head, like he knew what I was talking about.

Ah. He said. One of those.

Yup.

You don't get on with your mum?

I hate her.

Mr Dukes stopped eating, surprised by that.

Hate, he said. Hate's a strong word.

It is, I said. But the right one.

My glasses felt like they were steaming up and I hated it when that happened.

What did she do that was so bad?

For some reason, in That Moment, I couldn't answer that and it made me think that maybe this was ALL MY fault.

I shrugged.

Anyway, I said, changing the subject. I thought you didn't drive.

Mr Dukes was onto his fries by now. Watching him eat McDonald's was weird. I expected him to only eat posh food.

What do you mean? He said.

Your bike, you cycle to work.

Oh. He said, smiling. That's just for exercise. Man of my age needs to watch his waistline.

This got me really curious about his age and I was dying to ask him, only maybe I didn't want to know.

What about your dad? He said.

What about him?

Is he around?

He was, I said. Then he wasn't. Then he was again. Now he isn't, again. It's complicated.

It always is, he said putting his head down. When he put it up again he let out a MASSIVE burp and it echoed around his small car and it totally shocked me.

What the …

I almost swore.

I watched his lips suck up more strawberry milkshake and he did it again. He was laughing and he told me to do it.

Go on, he said. Your turn.

What? No way.

Go on.

No. No way.

Now I was laughing.

Do it, he said.

You're mad.

Do it. He said again.

He was smiling so much and I noticed this cute dimple on his chin that I had never noticed before. There was some pink milkshake on the red of his beard and I wanted to touch it.

No way, especially not in front of you.

What do you mean, 'especially not in front of me?'

That made me blush and he smiled at catching me out.

Belch or I won't take you home, he said.

That's fine by me, I said.

He raised his eyes and I was dead-impressed by how good I was at flirting.

Okay, I said. Only for you.

I burped but it was only a Little One so he made me do a Bigger One. We both began burping about ten times and it was kind of weird and I didn't know why we were doing it but it made us laugh like crazy, like a hysterical kind of a thing.

In the end he had to drop me home so he did. I got him to drop me at the bottom of the Avenue so he couldn't see the dump of a house where I lived. And also so my nosey mum wouldn't see. Later I realised that this was a MASSIVE mistake because what if he wanted to send me a Love Letter one day, or a Valentine's Card or something.

Either way I said Thanks and looked at him For Ages. Although what I REALLY wanted to do was lean in and kiss him only I knew I couldn't do that ... Just Yet. When I finally did leave his car I decided to run. I ran cos I was so excited. It was Officially The Best Night of My Entire Life. I ran so fast, faster than ever before, like a Usain Bolt kind of a thing. Even faster than Mia and she came third on Sport's Day. I bombed right through my front door, bounding up the stairs without gravity.

Hi mum. Hi sis. I shouted through the walls.

I heard mum say, sure that girl's schizophrenic, or bipolar at least.

But I didn't care what They thought. I didn't care what ANYONE thought.

I had my man, my husband to be. The Love of My life.

I couldn't believe he showed up the way he did tonight.

What a coincidence, a miracle, like a destiny kind of a thing. It's like God had placed us together at EXACTLY the right time and place.

He was my hero, my saviour, like a Guardian Angel kind of a thing.

I got in bed and pulled the covers over me and lay there in bliss. TOTAL bliss.

An hour later mum came up and put My Sister Adele to bed, sitting on the edge of it combing her long brown hair. Every time she caught a lug Adele would grimace and grit her teeth.

You know you shouldn't run off like that Mel? mum said. You haven't eaten, bet your starving now aren't you?

Nah, I said. I'm full. I'm totally full.

When mum turned out the lights and closed the door I opened my mouth and let out a MASSIVE burp.

Urgh, gross, My Sister Adele said. A few seconds later she said something else: That smells of McDonald's.

For the next two weeks Mr Dukes had the class to himself. Like, he wasn't just wandering around talking to kids anymore but he Actually ran a WHOLE lesson all by himself, like a promotion kind of a thing.

I was dead-proud of him.

Like, I could tell he was dead-nervous at The Beginning and stuff, cos he kept stumbling on words, and I could tell he was out-his-depth but I just looked at him right in the eye, nodded my head and told him with our telepathic powers ... You Can Do This.

And it must have worked and he must have heard me cos he got better, like Straight Away. Mr Dukes became a great teacher, and he was so funny, like a proper comedian on the stage, like, teaching us stuff but making us laugh too.

Sometimes he'd do a private joke, like Just For Me.

Like he'd let out a burp and pretend it was an accident, like burp into his fist and say Excuse Me and everybody would laugh but I just put my head down and blushed like crazy.

When I looked up again Mr Dukes gave me a cheeky wink and all I could do was shake my head.

At the end of his third lesson Mr Dukes caught my arm on the way out.

Mel can I have a word?

He almost mouthed the sentence without sound and I got really excited. What Could It Be, I thought? I wondered if perhaps he wanted to see me again, like take me for another McDonald's or something. All the kids went out and I was alone with him. The butterflies in my tummy were going crazy and tbh I don't think I'd Officially been this nervous, EVER. Then I got even more nervous and maybe a little scared when I saw how serious his face was, like dead-serious, like something bad had happened, or was about to.

Mel.

I loved him saying Mel, the shape it turned his lips into. His tongue hitting the top set of his teeth as my one syllable name tripped from his mouth.

He smiled that big smile again and I got a flashback from Our Time in the car.

Mel I'm leaving soon and I just wanted to tell you in person.

His words didn't seem real and At First I didn't know what he meant.

Leaving? I echoed.

Shock was all over me. I felt the weight of the world drop into my feet.

I'm leaving this school, your class. Guess you could say I can get a proper job now, he smiled.

I went to say something but stuttered so I tried again: You could get a job HERE.

My voice sounded desperate, and Mr Dukes made this sound that was half like a laugh and half like something else, a sad something else.

Ah. Mel. It doesn't work like that.

I couldn't hold it in and I cried a bit and it made me feel so stupid and pathetic.

But I don't want you to go, I said, my voice breaking.

I wiped tears off my face with my sleeve and now Mr Dukes looked all blurry and stuff.

He touched my arm and I thought I could see tears too, in his eyes, but That Part could just all be in my head.

You're the sweetest girl, he said. You have something special inside you, I can see that.

But no one else can, I said, crying more. No one else knows me like you.

I wanted to dive on him, hug him, kiss him forever and tell him not to go, to stay here with me.

I love you, I said.

I said it from nowhere but it's like I HAD to. Like I knew The First Time I said IT had to be for him. I mean I'd said it to Mia before but this was different. He was my First Love. Mr Dukes was Officially My First Love, EVER.

He smiled again and didn't seem shocked, or bothered that I said it. Like he knew anyway.

Mr Dukes took a turquoise band from his wrist and put it on mine. He seemed to hold my hand for ages and the contact was incredible. Like it had electricity running all through it. He didn't say anything cos he didn't have to. He didn't need to say I Love You back cos giving me this turquoise band did that.

It was A Moment I'll never forget.

I left the classroom and left Mr Dukes, looking at him One Last Time through the little squares in the glass. In his face I saw the words … I'll Come Find You One Day.

And I still believe he will.

P.S. That part of the Biography Bit was pretty intense and I feel a little drained and emotional, reliving it all. Like I've even been crying a bit and some of my tears are ACTUALLY on the paper and stuff. Makes me realise how much I still love him. Makes me realise how alone I still am too.

Most of the details I'd like totally forgot and now I see just how powerful Writing is. Like a supernatural kind of a thing. Cos like the pen starts to glide across the page and then magic happens, like all these secrets and hidden places just unfold before you and by the end you're like TOTALLY amazed and stuff. Where did this come from? How did this happen?

I still have the Turquoise Band on the side of my bed. It's the most beautiful colour and it takes me places, takes me to a tropical lagoon on the other side of the world. Sometimes if I'm really low I'll put it on and FEEL Mr Dukes with me and it makes everything that bit better.

It also has a word on it that I didn't notice when he first gave it to me.

It says, AGAPE.

I don't know what that means and I keep meaning to look it up.

P.P.S. Anyway. mum is shouting me now, (literally as I write these words.) She wants me to take that stupid dog out for a walk again.

P.P.P.S. I've just read this over and noticed I mentioned God earlier. "It's like God placed us together."
For the record I don't believe in God and never have. Saying that was just a Figure of Speech kind of a thing.

P.P.P.P.S. A boy threw a chair in class today. I didn't see his face.

Unformed Personality

Markus

Markus was going to his first Liverpool match. It was supposed to be a present for his thirteenth birthday but it was over two months late. He was going to Anfield with his Uncle Nigel and Cousin Charlie. Markus was nearly sick with excitement when he opened the belated birthday card and a ticket fell out. He watched a gold and red flash as the ticket twirled through the air and lay face-up on the carpet. When he saw the word *Liverpool* his eyes almost fell out his head. On bending down to retrieve it he saw the date stamped across the top in bold, black letters and digits, *October 4th, 2014. KO 3pm.*

It was only against West Bromwich Albion and Markus couldn't help but be disappointed by this. He would much rather it have been Manchester United or their other rivals Everton, or maybe even another big club like Chelsea or Arsenal.

Oh well, Markus thought, West Brom will have to do.

Auntie Tara had never seen her nephew so animated. It was a weird sight to see, an almost six-foot teenager bounding around the bungalow, punching air and howling at the ceiling.

"Alright Markus calm down."

There was something in his eye that unnerved her, a manic edge that made her uneasy. Maybe it was because she wasn't used to seeing this kind of emotion from the boy. It was odd, out of place, over the top.

And all over a game of football, Tara thought.

He hadn't shown this depth of feeling over his mother's death, or over his dad being incarcerated. Now he was going to his first Liverpool match and Markus was about ready to tear the house down.

"I can't believe it. I can't fucking believe it."

"Alright Markus calm down," she said again, slowing and strengthening her words.

Markus *couldn't* believe it. The only games he'd ever been to were when his dad took him to see Boston United. *Boring bottom league Boston.* They'd lost both times in a crappy little stadium that had just a couple of thousand in attendance. Now he was going to see Premier League giants Liverpool FC, the love of his life, the club he'd supported since he had any conception of what football was. He was going Anfield along with fifty thousand others, sitting in the famous Kop stand too!

His dad's brother Nigel and his twelve-year-old son Charlie came to pick him up at nine on the Saturday morning. Markus answered the door, all small-eyed and wired from a sleepless night before.

"Fucking hell Marky didn't you get no kip last night?" his uncle said, stepping into the kitchen. "Eyes like piss-holes in the snow."

Like Uncle Nigel could talk, he looked permanently wrecked. He was a big man with a big red face, eyes bloodshot and watery like his old man. Even though they had different colour hair people could tell that Lance and Nigel Venner were brothers. They had the same square head and the same sharp nose, a signature comical mouth apiece that was caught between smirk and grimace. The two brothers were roughly the same height too, Lance 6.1, Nigel 6.2. Both men had a thirst for booze and this lived in their faces; that flushed leathery complexion that was indicative of hard drinkers. The Venners had been drinking heavily since age seventeen only older brother Nigel had managed to hold it together over the years. He was considered a 'big drinker' whereas Lance owned the label of 'alcoholic.' Although both probably drank the exactly the same, difference only being that older Nigel managed to hold down a job and a family whereas Lance had come undone.

"Alright Nige?"

Tara stepped into the kitchen and gave her brother-in-law a peck on the cheek, before turning her attention to the boy by his side.

"That's never little Charlie is it?"

The boy smiled and Tara suddenly got really excited. "Oh my god he hasn't half grown-up." She bent down and hugged the boy but Charlie froze a little with shyness.

"Handsome boy," Tara sang. "Gonna break some hearts you are, aren't you?"

His dad rolled his eyes. "Oh don't make his head any bigger for fuck's sake."

Markus noticed his uncle's hands were shaking a touch. He'd seen this with his own dad too, especially in the mornings.

"Hey he looks like that actor," Tara said.

Charlie blushed but he was loving it all the same.

"Oh what's his name ... ?"

Markus felt his mood drop. It was like a stone had been plopped in his chest.

"Him out the Spiderman films ... ?"

This was supposed to be Markus's day but Tara had turned all the attention onto Charlie, who was standing there smug, soaking it all up.

"Franco!" Tara said clicking her fingers. "James Franco. He looks like a little James Franco."

"Alright Tars ya embarrassing yourself now," Markus snapped.

"Little fucker's only been scouted too," Uncle Nigel said, the booze from his breath was all over the kitchen now.

"Scouted?" Tara said.

"Was on holiday in the summer, down Devon. Having a kick about with some kids on the camp and the little fucker only got scouted by Southampton. They're signing him next week."

Markus was hating this. He wanted to stick his fingers in his ears to stop him from hearing anymore.

"Oooohhh." Tara made a silly noise. "Gonna buy us all a new house when you're famous then?"

"Maybe," Charlie said, a victorious grin spreading across his too-handsome face.

Markus couldn't take anymore and was terrified in case Tara asked him what he thought, which he knew was the next thing to come from her mouth. Markus wouldn't be able to conceal the intense jealousy he felt so took himself to the bathroom and began cleaning his teeth. In the mirror he noticed how small his eyes were and how white his face was. He looked ghoulish and weak, not right. Like he was ill or something.

Fuck Charlie, he thought. I'll be famous one day, and I'll be more famouser than he ever will. I'll be on front of all the papers and on every news program, then what will they all say?

Markus cleaned his teeth, and as he did he heard the adults talking through the walls. They were talking about Lance, his dad.

"You been to see him?"

"Last week. You?"

"Bout a month ago," Nigel said, an edge of guilt in his tone. "How's he doing?"

"He's doing alright," Tara said, her tone rising with a lilt of hope. "Reckons he'll be out in two months, six weeks perhaps."

"He'll be alright," Nigel said. "Done him good I reckon."

"While ever he's not drinking Nige, he's doing good."

Markus listened on, mouth full of paste and brush.

"Yeah I agree," Nigel said, hypocrisy in his voice now. "Kid been to see him?"

Tara said nothing but Markus saw her face in his mind's eye, slowly shaking her head, face full of disapproval.

"Don't worry," Nigel said. "I'll sort him."

Markus spat toothpaste angrily into the sink and felt his blood boil. *I'll sort him.* Who the fuck does he think he is? Markus wanted to tear into the kitchen and confront the gossiping adults. Tell them to mind their own fucking business and stop being such hypocrites. Only he remembered the big day, the big game, and how an outburst might fuck all that up. So Markus calmed himself down, breathed, emptied his mind, and walked back into the kitchen as if nothing happened.

"Alright Stevie Gerrard!" Uncle sang.

People did say he looked like Stevie Gerrard and Markus loved that. Better than looking like some Hollywood queer-boy anyway, he thought, glaring at his younger cousin.

"Even got the new top an' all," Nigel said, pulling at the badge.

Charlie wore the new Liverpool Away but the Home was better.

"Where did you get that?" his aunt said.

Markus suddenly remembered that the person asking him the question was the answer to it, *you did.* Tara did. *Tara* is the answer. I scammed you.

"Oh…" Markus was stalling.

Tara waited.

" … I did a swap at school," he said, suddenly.

Markus was normally a master liar but this time he couldn't help think he'd landed flat on his face. Tara eyed him with cold suspicion.

He wanted to get out the door but Tara wasn't letting it go that easy.

"Swapped it with what?"

"Something. I can't remember now."

Luckily his uncle gave him an inadvertent helping hand.

"Anyway. Enough gassing. Merseyside isn't next door, y'know?"

The three boys left the bungalow, Tara giving Markus one last kick in the teeth on the way out. "Hey Charlie, not long before we're coming to watch *you* at Anfield."

His cousin turned and smiled at her, while Markus stared at the floor; his shoes, a piece of dog shit that was by the car.

They stopped at a service station about halfway, stretching their legs and taking a piss. After Uncle told the boys to wait by the car while he popped into the shop to 'pick up some bits.'

Markus wanted to hate his cousin. He wanted to hate him because he was stupidly good-looking and stupidly talented and life wasn't fair. He wanted to hate him but he couldn't because his cousin Charlie was too nice. He was too friendly and cool and that, weirdly enough, made him hate him even more. While they waited for Nigel Charlie took out a football from the back seat.

"Heads up!" He lobbed the ball over a row of cars and it landed exactly at Markus's feet.

When Markus looked up his cousin was grinning, a glow of self-confidence radiated through him, acknowledging his own gift. Markus passed the ball back, uneasily, praying it got there.

"So you're playing for Southampton?"

Charlie nodded, playing the ball modestly back, no tricks this time. "Uh-huh."

"Not quite Liverpool is it?" Markus said.

Each time the boys said something they passed the ball, almost like they were passing their words too.

"No," Charlie said. "But it's still a Premiership club."

"So?"

"Adam Lallana started at Southampton, and he's on the starting line-up today. Bet he'll score too."

Charlie was right. Markus knew he had a shit argument and was making himself look stupid, making himself look jealous and bitter. The next time Charlie got the ball he did a fancy flick and the ball spun in the air. His feet moved so quick Markus couldn't see how he had done it. Now Charlie was doing kick-ups, effortlessly keeping the ball up like it was a balloon, defying gravity. Next it was on his head, almost like his cousin had a blob on glue on it. The ball rolled left to right as Charlie's neck swayed from side to side. Markus had to say, it was pretty amazing.

"Tackle me," Charlie shouted to him.

Markus tried but there was no way, Charlie had him inside-out. Markus didn't stand a chance. Some kids on the estate were good but his cousin Charlie was a different class. After a while Markus began to enjoy his talent rather than question it.

"Fucking hell man," Markus laughed. "Alright then I get it."

"I'll play for Liverpool one day," Charlie finalised.

Markus nodded, not challenging him once.

They played a bit longer and Markus managed to get it off him a few times but he had a feeling Charlie let him on purpose. He could see that the young prodigy was a bit weary of Markus and probably didn't want his legs being taken out.

That was a consolation, Markus thought, that I could beat him in a fight, and that's all that mattered really. It's all that mattered when you got down to it.

"Where the fuck is your old man?"

"Probably necking a can in the toilet," Charlie said.

"Oh," Markus said.

"Hope he brings us some sweets."

"Hope he doesn't crash on the way. I really wanna see this game."

"Nah," Charlie said. "He'll drive safer *having* a drink than *needing* one."

"Adults are fucking stupid," Markus said, booting the ball at a nearby car.

"I know," Charlie said. "We'll be one ourselves, one day."

Uncle's hands had stopped shaking as he popped a stick of chewing gum in his mouth and began driving again. An hour and a half later they were there. As they drove through Liverpool the colour red started to appear, almost as if the city was bleeding from the inside. Markus was amazed by how big the buildings were, how vast and busy the streets were. He was totally overwhelmed by how many people there were. He was shocked to see how many different colours the people were too, black, Indian, Chinese, just loads and loads of dark people. In some areas there were even more dark than white and this shit Markus up a bit. Do they *actually* live here or are they just on holiday? Markus wanted to ask but he didn't want to look stupid. Suddenly he felt an overpowering vulnerability, like the city was too big for him. Like he was out his depth. Even though he'd only been away from his town/bungalow/auntie for a few hours he was experiencing a weird sense of homesickness.

Anfield was rammed and manic. Cars beeped. People shouted. Someone banged a drum. Already there were songs and chants and the roar of a crowd.

Cousin Charlie seemed unfazed by the whole thing while his uncle managed to find parking space he called 'Secret Spot.'

"Been using this spot for the last twenty years!" his uncle said.

As they walked towards the ground Markus felt a fear of being lost. He didn't have his uncle's or his cousin's number in his phone and he got paranoid about losing contact with them. He stared at his uncle's leather jacket and made sure it didn't go out of sight. They had a hotdog and then Nigel bought Markus a program and a match day scarf, half red of Liverpool and half blue and white of West Brom. He tucked the Brom bit into his hoodie and exposed the red of his team. Markus wedged himself between uncle and cousin and the three entered the Kop End at the south side of the ground. The noise was incredible but this time the thirteen-year-old boy met it with exhilaration rather than trepidation. They were sat close to the front and Markus was hypnotised by the green of the pitch and how unreal all this looked in real life, before his naked eyes. So weird having watched so many games on TV and now here I am. There was a cheer each time a Liverpool player was announced on the Tannoy, starting with goalkeeper Simon Mignolet right through to Rickie Lambert. About halfway through the team sheet the name Steven Gerrard caused the biggest cheer and Markus felt himself wee a bit in his pants. His mouth felt dry and he shivered with a sudden attack of nerves. After he regretted not getting the number 8 and his hero's name tattooed on his new shirt.

Why didn't I think?

The players ran on and a wave of cheers whipped up through the crowd. A northern breeze found its way in from the Mersey and glanced across Markus's face. Songs and chants broke out from different corners of the stadium. As one eerily died-out another began. The game kicked-off at the stroke of three pm. Liverpool in red, Brom in white. The home side attacking the goal that Markus stood behind, maybe five metres to the left. The sun was out and cut the pitch in two, Liverpool lit up as they applied some early pressure. Markus was shocked at how aggressive the fans were, almost like they were about to fight someone. When the ref called a free-kick for Brom one bloke lost his head.

"You wanna go to fucking Specsavers ya c^nt!"

Most of the voices had this really funny accent and Markus had to remind himself he was in Liverpool. Sometimes he'd stop watching the match and gaze around at the crowd, in awe. Markus felt this peculiar insignificant feeling, he felt small and worthless and the only other time he remembered feeling like this was when he looked up at the stars.

At the stroke of halftime something happened. Adam Lallana skipped forward, playing a sweet one-two with Coutinho. From nowhere he was on goal and the crowd drew in a collective breath, holding it, before the Liverpool number 20 fired, burying the ball smoothly in the bottom-left-hand-corner of the net, no more than ten metres from where Markus, cousin and uncle were sat, who were now going crazy, along with another twelve thousand fans in The Spion Kop stand.

The rush was intense, through the frantic blur of the fans Markus watched the players celebrating on the pitch. Just then Markus felt a little pull on his shirt. It was Cousin Charlie.

"Told you Lallana would score."

He winked and then turned his attention back to the celebrations.

Seconds later the whistle blew and the first half was over.

During the interval the three queued at the toilets before going to the refreshments bar. Uncle Nigel sank a pint of lager from a plastic cup while Markus and Charlie sucked on a coke and munched a Mars bar each.

"You wanna watch that," Charlie said, pushing his finger into Markus's belly. "Keep eating them Mars bars and you'll never play for Liverpool."

Cheeky bastard. Markus's instinct was to lay one on him, a dead-arm at least. Only the crowd was tight and he couldn't pull his fist back.

You can have that one for now, Markus thought, but I'm saving it.

They missed the first few minutes of the second half because Nigel was downing his third pint.

"C'mon dad fucking hell!"

Luckily no one had scored, but just after the fiftieth minute something happened. A Brom player got brought down just outside the box, at least it looked like it was outside the box. The ref pointed at the penalty spot and the crowd went mad.

"What the fuck!"

"C!nt."

"CNUT."

"WANKER."

"You've got to be fucking kidding."

"You must be fucking blind ref."

"It was a mile outside ya cnuting retard."

Markus felt his face go red. He couldn't believe it. He couldn't believe the referee was going to spoil his *whole* day by giving the Away side a penalty. The captain Steven Gerrard was in the ref's face. The fans shouted more stuff.

"You tell him Stevie lad!"

"Nut the c%nt."

Gerrard must have said something bad because the next thing the ref had a yellow card out and Markus's day just got worse.

"No way."

"No fucking way ref."

"Get out of it."

The fans were going so wild Markus wondered if they were going to kill the ref after the match. Maybe kidnap him in the car park, shove him in the boot, drive him somewhere and then tie him to a tree, set fire to him and then chant at his burning body, *you're not singing, you're not singing, you're not singing anymore, you're not singing any ... more.*

A player called Berahino stepped up in the fifty-sixth minute for Brom and placed the ball on the spot. He looked down, nervous. Markus had his eyes closed and his fingers crossed. The noise crashed in around him and he waited for it. He heard a whistle and then the crowd got angry again. When Markus opened his eyes he saw white shirts celebrating and Markus wanted to punch something, someone. He wished a West Brom fan was nearby so he could kick the fuck out of them. Uncle Nigel was shaking his head and Cousin Charlie looked ready to cry. *Wimpy Little Bastard.* He'll never make a professional crying like that.

Markus suddenly wanted to go home. I'm not coming all the way out here for a crappy little draw. A draw is pathetic. A draw is not a win therefore it was the same as a loss.

The game got boring for a bit, not much happened.

Then at the other end he could see his team pushing forward, and then the crowd cheered again. It took a few seconds for the hysteria to reach this side of the ground. It was good old Jordan

Henderson. His name flashed in lights on the screen up above. His teammates crowding him.

Markus liked his cousin again; they were hugging and dancing around and life was suddenly alright.

Markus was so happy when the referee blew his final whistle and the game was over. Liverpool had done it. Liverpool had made his day. His first game and his birthday present and the reds had done it. They had won 2-1.

They were just about to leave but Uncle stopped them. "Eyup, ya mate's coming over."

Gerrard and a few others were jogging up the pitch towards The Kop. They stood next to the goal and waved at the fans. Markus waved back, catching Stevie's eye. The Liverpool captain was looking right at him, and Markus couldn't believe it. He nodded at the boy and moved on. Markus wanted to say something, he wanted to tell Uncle and Cousin but he knew they wouldn't believe him. They'd think it was corny and probably think he was making it up.

Markus Venner decided to keep it to himself.

On the way home they stopped at the famous Harry Ramsden's and had a massive fish dinner. Markus wolfed all of his while Charlie only ate half. Uncle Nigel didn't eat all his either but managed to fit about four pints of lager in.

"Tell ya something lads," Nigel said, belching into his fist. "You think today was good you should have been around in the eighties."

"Dad," Charlie whined. "Stop always going on about the olden days."

"Dalglish's boys: Rush. Hansen. Grobbelaar. McMahon. Beardsley. Barnes. Little ginger Nicol at the back. Unfuckingstoppable lads."

Markus knew this script verbatim because he'd heard it from his old man a thousand times. The glory days of old. Markus had to agree with his cousin, it did get boring after a while. Who cared about 1987, this was 2014! Suddenly he thought about his dad, how much he would have loved today. He imagined what he was doing now, *in this moment.* Probably being fucked by some big black man in the showers, Markus mused, a light smile on his face. That'll teach him to be a racist, being raped by the enemy ... ha.

The rest of the way home they listened to the other results around the country. Man City had won. Leicester drew. Hull had beaten Palace but most of the big games were on tomorrow. Arsenal. Chelsea. Man U.

Markus really hoped Liverpool would beat Manchester United this season. Now with that old c*nt Alex Ferguson out the way there might be a chance.

"Hey Markus, your mum still going out with that bloke?" Uncle Nigel said from nowhere, breaking his thoughts.

"No," Markus replied.

Charlie had fallen asleep.

"Why what happened?"

"Don't know." Markus didn't try to hide his irritation. He was bored now and just wanted to get home.

Uncle Nigel stunk of booze and the car wobbled around a bit.

"She not seeing anyone?"

"Ask her yourself," Markus said. "I don't know what she does."

Uncle Nigel nodded, trying to focus on the road.

When they pulled up at the bungalow Charlie woke up. "We home?"

"I am," Markus said, grabbing his hoodie, opening the door.

"Hey let's swap numbers," Charlie said eagerly.

"Why?" Markus said, looking at him like he was stupid.

"I can let you know how I get on at Southampton."

No voice this gay was ever playing in the Premiership, Markus thought. He ignored him and stepped out the car. After today I won't see these pair of twats again, he thought. Weddings, funerals, the odd birthday bash, that's it.

Uncle Nigel was just a pisshead like his dad and Charlie was a cocky, show-off little shit.

"See ya," Markus sang in a high cold tone.

"Oi Markus," Nigel shouted.

Markus had a feeling his uncle was going to make him say *thank you*. Adults always did that. They took you places and gave you things and then expected A Thank You at the end of it. Sometimes Markus wondered if that's the only real reason they were nice to kids. So they got to have praise for it after, a way of making them feel better about their shitty lives.

Markus still had the back door open and his uncle was leaning over the seat.

"Go visit your dad, ey?"

Markus never answered, just slammed the door in their faces, and headed back towards the bungalow.

Mel

Dear Self-Esteem Diary,

This is The Part where shit got real. This is where Life got messed-up and effed-up and stuff. This is where EVERYTHING just TOTALLY spiralled out of control!!!

With Dad gone and Dukes gone I got horribly alone again. My Bestie Mia didn't give a shit anymore cos she'd got this new BF and I was just COMPLETELY out the picture.

As for mum and My Sister Adele, well, they were just getting worser by the day. Sometimes they were nasty to me and sometimes they just ABSOLUTELY ignored me. And as I've said before, that is just THE WORST THING IN THE WORLD, like a Hell kind of a thing.

So I decided now was the time to run away. It was either that or it was Suicide, like I was more than ready to kill myself, kill myself For Good.

First off, like, I rang this Emergency Number that They gave me ages ago. It's like a place I could call if I ever needed to.

I'm ringing cos I think I'm ready to commit suicide, I said. I've just packed my rucksack and I'm running away for good.

Okay dear I just need you to calm down a minute, what's your name love?

Mel. Melanie. Mel Ellis. Melanie Ellis.

I said that weird and it sounded like I was four different people.

Okay Melanie, why don't you talk to me and tell me what the problem is?

I want to live with Janet again.

I don't even know why I said that ... and tbh I don't know where it came from. I just sort of BLURTED it out.

Okay who is Janet, dear?

I could tell the woman on the other end of the phone was black. Cos like, she had a black voice. I could also tell that she was fat. Cos like, she had a fat voice. She was a fat black woman and she sounded dead-nice.

Janet was my Foster Mum when I was little and I want to live with her again. Like I want to go there NOW.

Okay Melanie where are you?

I'm walking up Lawson Avenue, it's where I live. Like I snuck out my back garden and I'm heading to the park. Can you come and pick me up cos tbh I'm not gonna Lie but if you don't I think I might try and kill myself for good.

Melanie it's okay, the voice said. Just keep talking to me dear.

Can I come and live with you?

Sorry?

I just want to live with my old foster mum Janet, is she still on the list?

What list dear?

Like the foster list.

Okay Melanie we need to take one step at a time. We need to slow down and just focus on one thing at a time. First off, is there anywhere you can sit?

Sit?

You need to stop and sit down so you can talk to me properly. You sound really out of breath Melanie and I need you to sit and calm.

Well … yeah.

I stopped. I sat.

Where are you dear?

I'm at the park now. And I'm sitting like you told me, like I'm sitting on a climbing frame kind of a thing.

And where is the park?

Well it's just around the corner from my house, like only two minutes away really, like it's just opposite the chip shop.

Okay dear.

The woman said her name was Monique and My Guess was right cos that is kind of a black name if You really think about it. Anyway, she was dead-nice and dead-good at her job and stuff, the way she calmed me down was kind of amazing. When I was calmed she asked me if there was any chance I could text my mum and let her know where I was and I said:

NO. NO WAY. There's no way I can have ANY contact with her EVER again. Like I would rather kill myself for good.

Okay so just stay where you are Melanie and someone will be coming out to you soon.

This confused me.

What do you mean? I said.

Someone is coming.

Here? I said.

Yes.

To the park?

Yes.

To this ACTUAL climbing frame.

Just stay where you are, and keep talking to me.

Suddenly I kind of regretted it all, like regretted packing my rucksack and walking out and calling Monique. Like it all seemed a bit BIG. Like I had caused LOADS of trouble and wasted loads of time and stuff.

Who is coming, I said?

It's what's known as a Crisis Team Melanie, they're just here to help.

Okay.

I asked Monique if she had kids and she told me she had two little boys.

Haven't you thought of being a foster mum? I asked her.

Oh no, she said with a big laugh, I already have my hands full with those.

Are they naughty, I said?

Nah, she said, just very energetic.

I couldn't believe how nice Monique was, like, she didn't even sound like an Official Adult but more like a mate or a dead-cool auntie. I wish she could be my mum. Even if she was black and our skin didn't match I wouldn't care, Monique would fit me I can tell. I was even laughing now and in a good mood and I wanted her to call the WHOLE thing off.

Just then a car pulled up and two people got out, a woman and a man.

Okay they're here, I said.

Okay Melanie just tell them what you told me.

Are they going to find me somewhere else to live?

The man and the woman was crossing the grass, heading towards me.

Just be calm Melanie and tell them how you feel, tell them what's happened. You're a bright, intelligent girl Melanie and you have the world at your feet.

That was such a beautiful thing to say and it gave me a lump in my throat.

Thanks Monique, hey can I ring you again?

I work here Melanie.

But can I ask for your name?

There was a pause on the other end of the phone.

Just talk to The Crisis Team Melanie, they know what they're doing.

The man and the woman were now standing over me, smiling.

I said goodbye to Monique and ended the call. Cos she had made me feel better I felt like all this was fake now. It's like I wanted to be upset again so ALL THIS meant something.

Melanie, The Man said, smiling, lowering his head.

I wiped away a tear that wasn't there. That's me, I said.

The Man and The Woman was dressed smart, but in a casual kind of a way. They were both quite tall and attractive and that made me feel EVEN uglier. The Man did all the talking and The Woman hung back.

They introduced themselves although I couldn't remember their names. The Man was fat and confident and handsome and he had an aftershave-smell that took me Straight Back to Mr Dukes, like they wore the same cologne or something, and this was powerful and it kind of made me fancy him a bit, which was ridiculous cos it was like totally the wrong time and place.

The Woman had still not said a word but her face was dead-pretty and calm, like she had big eyes and looked kind of owlish. When she walked over I noticed how much she reminded me of My Bestie Mia, all graceful and slow and upright, like a swan.

So I told them EVERYTHING. I told them that I'd been into care before. I told them about mum and My Sister Adele. How mum was always angry and Adele was always arrogant. How they worked as a team and broke my spirit daily. I told them how they both ganged-up on me during the whole 'Dad Period.' I said that I was depressed and sometimes even suicidal and that today was the First Day I actually thought about killing myself For Good. I told them that I wasn't a very good swimmer and that I was thinking of putting LOADS of rocks in my pockets and walking out into the Clementine Channel like Virginia Woolf.

You like reading? The Man said. You ever read Virginia Woolf?

No. But I just heard about her life at school. She must have been really depressed and I know how she feels.

I looked up at The Man and he smiled a gentle smile. He had lines on his face and his tan looked fake, like maybe he used one of those stand-up sunbeds. The Woman was shivering a bit and I guess it was getting late and cold.

Have you read Virginia Woolf, I said?

Well yes. The Man said. Yes I have.

I should read, I said. I've never read a book in my WHOLE life. Not one. Not even at school.

The Woman was looking at the man, as if she wanted to move This Thing along.

What do you say we go and have a little chat with your mum? The Man said.

No. No way. I've made a vow to cut all contact with her forever.

It doesn't work like that. The Woman said, firmly. We need to talk with your mum.

It was the First Words she had said. There was something powerful in her tone, not bad or aggressive, just powerful and certain.

Okay, I said.

I got in the back of the car and they drove around the corner to my house. I saw My Sister Adele's stupid, nosey little face in the window when we pulled up. They let me lead the way into the house, a few paces behind. The Man kept telling me that everything was going to be alright. Sis had obviously warned mum cos she was already up on her feet and at the door, hugging me in this really fake way but This Time I wasn't letting her get away with it.

Oh mum stop putting on an act when people are here, it's pathetic.

Adele was smiling like she was really enjoying all this, like it was a Soap Opera or something.

mum offered drinks but they didn't want any.

Love?

I just rolled my eyes

So we sat and we talked and mum acted all innocent like I knew she would.

She's just so sensitive, she said. I know teenage girls are but she is just SO sensitive. I feel trapped because I can't say anything or do anything without her breaking down, or kicking off. Sometimes I feel as if I'm trapped, as if I just can't COPE.

And there's that word again, COPE.

Trust mum to make it all about her, as if she's the victim in All This.

I said that in front of the Crisis Team and in fact I started shouting.

The Man had to calm me down, okay Mel, okay. No one else is shouting.

Adele was trying to hide her face.

And you can stop laughing, I said to her. This isn't a joke you know, it isn't A GAME. It's MY LIFE.

Okay, The Woman said. I think we're going to need some kind of ongoing intervention here. Melanie I think you need some independent help so we're going to introduce you to CAMHS.

I'm not taking medication, I said. Never!

No it's nothing like that, The Woman said.

Mel will you just listen to the lady. We're all just trying to help you.

It was stuff like this that got me the maddest. The way mum singled me out and made it look like I was the bad one, the crazy one.

The Man and The Woman told me about CAMHS, what they did, how it worked, and tbh it did sound quite good. Like it was Somewhere I could go and ACTUALLY talk instead of being shut out all the time. They made me an appointment for the following week and gave me loads of leaflets and stuff.

I could see My Sister Adele shaking her stupid little head but I tried not to look at her. Tried to block her out. mum said she was there for me and would take me to the appointment but I know all this was just a performance in front of the Crisis Team.

Anyway.
Either way.

They left and I was back where I started, in a house with The Family from Hell. I didn't get to live with my old Foster Mum Janet and I didn't get to live with the lovely Fat Black Monique either.

I did what I always did, went to my room and got under the covers.

About an hour later I was starting to drop to sleep when I heard a voice in the dark.

I'm sorry Mel for being a shit mum, but I'm trying my best, you have to believe I'm trying my best.

I was so tired from all the emotions I didn't know if that voice was from Real Life, or from a dream I was having.

mum thought the answer was church. She wanted me to start going back to church with her and My Sister Adele. She thought it would be a good way for the three of us to bond again. Tbh I'm not gonna Lie I HATED church. Apart from the pure boringness of it all I couldn't stand the people who went there. They were just these fake people, all serious and silly and stuff. Both mum and Sis were in the choir and they went to church every Sunday and Wednesday. Sunday was obvs the Main service and Wednesday was The Midweek Club, which was kind of gay cos they played games and had quizzes and did little theatre plays from the stories of the bible and stuff. But like, mum didn't even read the bible, she didn't even know A Thing from the bible. Like, I know WAY more bible-stuff than her and I'm not EVEN religious. But mum wasn't religious either, not when you really got down to it. She just pretended. She wasn't religious cos she was always doing Bad Things and taking the lord's name in vain. I mean she wore this gold cross around her neck but that didn't mean nothing. I could wear a crash helmet, doesn't mean I could ride a motorbike.

Why don't you believe in god? She would ask.

I don't believe in god cos there's too much bad in the world, I said. Like people are horrible and do the most horrible things, like murder and lie and rape and cheat and steal and stuff.

Well that's just people making the wrong choices, she said. That has nothing to do with god.

Yeah well what about nature-stuff, I said? Like earthquakes and tornados and floods and diseases and stuff?

mum couldn't answer that so she stormed off instead.

Another thing I couldn't understand about the Religion Thing is how come there are so many? Like Muslim and Hindu and Buddhist and Christian and stuff? All arguing about The Truth yet no one really knows what The Truth is, not when you got down to it. I think it was all just pretend. Like, it MUST just all be pretend cos if it wasn't there would be just one religion instead of like a zillion. Makes no sense. And people are only mostly the religion they are cos of where they're born. Like the only reason I go to a Christian church instead of a Sikh one is cos I'm in England, not India. So it doesn't really count. Like it doesn't really count if you think about it. Like it's nothing to do with choice of faith but more like luck, like a random kind of a thing.

Like I say, none of it makes any sense.

Anyway.
Either way.

My Sister Adele doesn't believe in god either cos she told me.

Why sing in the choir then, I said?

I like singing, she said. Plus they give you all that free buffet food.

Ha!

That was My Sister Adele all over: a clever taker. She reminded me of a vulture.

The church we went to was just this crappy little one on the other side of town. Why we had to go ALL that way I'll never know. Someone had burnt the shed down in the yard and they hadn't even been bothered to get a new one. People reckon it was haunted too. Some crazy person who lived opposite had died not long ago but there were rumours that he was murdered. They say the man escaped from an insane asylum and used to walk around the church naked. People said that when it was dead-quiet you could hear his Walking Stick clattering against the church walls.

To me that was a load of rubbish cos there was no such thing as ghosts, or god or Jesus or any of that crap.

The Only Thing I believed in is what my Foster Mum Janet used to tell me all those years ago. That the only real force was your instinct, like that nature-instinct feeling deep inside. Cos like I believed in that cos I had seen it and felt it. Like when my mind was dead-clear, and dead-empty of noise and stuff I get this voice, this pull, this drive that guides me and takes me to places and stuff. Sometimes I didn't listen to it and things would go wrong. Or I wouldn't listen hard enough and again things would go wrong. But when I did listen, like REALLY listen, then I was sure to be alright.

So really, that's the only thing I believed in.

It was as close as I got.

Life got EVEN more complicated when a man flashed at me at the bus stop. It was dead-early and dead-foggy and I didn't quite know what was happening, just heard this creepy voice say:

Hey, look!

I wasn't taking it in properly and it didn't really mean anything At First. Just this person by the bushes, opening up its coat. Tbh At First I thought it was an old woman with a deep voice cos its body was all bumpy and stuff, like it had loads and loads of rolls and the top set looked like a pair of boobs.

Do you like it, It said?

Then I looked down and saw this tiny thing standing on end. It was dead-small and pink and again I thought it was a woman. Cos tbh it looked more like a Girl Bit than a Boy Bit. It wasn't until I noticed all of its body-hair that I realised it was a man. The hair was grey and it made his body look all shiny and silver and gross and stuff. And the hair Down There was even longer than his ACTUAL penis and it was all just too freaky and scary and REALLY, REALLY disturbing so I screamed out loud …

OH MY GOD!!!

And I was running away like so fast but his voice and laugh was running right after me.

Hey don't go!

And tbh I'm not gonna Lie but I really thought I was going to be raped or maybe something even worser. The bus went by and I tried to scream at it but it just carried on into the mist and disappeared For Good. To my left I saw the yellow lights of Morrison's Supermarket and I knew I had to get in there and get safe only the voice had gone now. I turned and he was nowhere in sight and for A Moment I even wondered if I had imagined the WHOLE thing.

I didn't go Morrison's but went home instead. Ran into my mum's arms and cried, telling her what had just happened.

Oh Melanie, she laughed.

She was laughing right in my face, like it wasn't a serious thing at all.

Oh Mel you JUST got flashed. ALL women get flashed at, at some point in their life. It's what happens.

She stroked my head and wiped my tears and it felt kind of nice, like a soothing kind of a thing. Can't remember mum EVER doing this before.

It's okay, she said. It's okay, she promised. Men are awful, I know.

I was upset for pretty much ages. Like, I kept replaying it in my head and I didn't know why. Like I kept thinking about it and thinking about it and it made me feel kind of dirty and kind of guilty, like it may have been My Fault in some way. And I could never walk past that Bus Stop again and this made My Bestie Mia suspicious and she kept calling me a Weirdo. And it's like she even picked up that something had happened cos she kept saying things like: I Think Something Happened There, I Think You Lost Your Virginity There.

And a part of her was right, cos I did FEEL that I was muddied in some way, like I wasn't pure anymore, like a drop of oil had polluted something deep inside me.

Anyway.
Either way.

What I'm trying to say, is that I was kind of weary of boys and men now.
  Something in me had changed, For Good.

The CAMHS Thing was turning out to be really good. It was nice to get to talk about my problems for once. I saw a few people and filled out a few things, like questionnaires and stuff before being given My Own Counsellor. Her name was Mualja, (said like Moo-al-ya.) Mualja was dead-slim and dead-pretty and dead-ginger, like she had this shock of orange hair that burst from her head like an explosion. She had a foreign accent although I had no idea where she was from, probably Poland or somewhere like that. She was dead-good at her job too cos like she got me to open up LOADS. And they must have had contact with my school cos like they knew about the Suicide Notes me and Mia had left on the teacher's desk, notes about jumping off a bridge or a tall building, or popping loads of pills or opening our veins up in a warm bath.
  Do you want to tell me about that, she said?
  We was just joking, I said.
  And they must have talked to Mr Dukes too cos they knew all about my depression and my body-conscious issues and stuff, and like, Mr Dukes was the Only One who knew all that, what with us being able to read each other's mind and stuff.
  Mualja asked me to describe what living at home was like and I said it was like living in a big freezer. I could tell that Mualja thought it was a strange thing to say and tbh I didn't even know what I meant either.
  I mean, it's just like cold and empty, I said. I feel like I can't move.
  Sometimes I liked seeing Mualja and sometimes I didn't. Sometimes I was more effed-up than I realised cos I'd just cry all the way through it.
  One Time I got so bad Mualja said, you need something to calm you down.
  This got me scared so I looked at her and shouted, No, No, I'm not going on head-meds!

After they put me on a Watchful Waiting Period, which meant they were just going to see what happened, so I really tried my best to be happy cos The Last Thing in The World I wanted was to go on meds. If my Panic Attacks and depression didn't stop then they strongly recommended I try Fluoxetine. It would just 'take the edge off' they said. It would just 'carry you through,' they said. They told me it wasn't as bad as people said. They told me that it had a bad stigma but in actual fact it had been proven to help people beat depression and 'lighten the load.' They promised me it wasn't addictive in the slightest. mum thought it was a Good Idea but then she would say that, anything to keep me doped-up and out of her way. Tbh I'm not gonna Lie but I didn't want to go on Fluoxetine, or any other drug. I'd heard Mia's Mum say once that doctors get you on That Stuff as a way of making money. They're all on commission, she said.

Mualja could see I didn't want this so we stuck to CBT, for now. She also showed me loads of breathing techniques, and a meditation technique called Mindfulness. She tried telling me about how The Mind worked and stuff but tbh I just didn't get it.

I kept all what was happening to myself. I kept it all a secret. Like, I didn't tell anyone at school cos I didn't want them to think I was An Official Crazy Person. I didn't tell My Bestie Mia just like I didn't tell her about Mr Dukes, or anything else in My Life cos she'd just gossip and make drama and be selfish and stuff.

So I kept it to myself but that's okay cos I preferred it that way.

The Next Time I went Mualja gave me … You.

She gave me THIS sky-blue book with a white teddy-bear on the front.

This is a Self-Esteem Diary, she said. Write in it whenever you feel down. Write in it whenever you want to let off steam. Write in it whenever you feel lonely. Think of this diary as a friend, a best friend, a soul-mate. Write in it the way you would talk. Don't think, just talk. Say EXACTLY what's on your mind. Don't hold back. Be natural and direct and honest. This Self-Esteem Diary will never judge you. This Self-Esteem Diary will always listen, no matter what you have to say.

So this is it: Here YOU are. Here WE are.

HERE we BOTH are NOW

I've brought You up to Present Day and tbh this is The Official End of The Biography Bit.

That's pretty much all there is.

Of course there's LOADS more little things I could have put, but like, you can't write EVERYTHING otherwise we'd be here all day. But, like, I'd say all the major events of My miserable, effed-up Life have been covered more or less.

So we're in THIS MOMENT with only the future ahead of Us. Of course there will be more Biography Bits to come and tbh I haven't got a clue what's going to happen next, which is kind of exciting, but kind of scary too.

Anyway.
Either way.

I'm glad You're here, walking alongside me. It's nice to have a friend that I can REALLY open up to cos I haven't been this Honest with anyone, EVER.

Not mum. Not Dad. Not My Sister Adele. Not My Bestie Mia.

Not teachers. Not counsellors. Not anyone.

YOU'RE The First.

And what else is special about Our Relationship is that I know we'll last Forever, like an immortal kind of a thing. Cos as soon as these thoughts and feelings are put down on paper it's like they'll always be there. Like even after I die they'll still be around. Like Anne Frank, she may have died in War Times but her spirit and stuff is reborn every time someone opens her diary, and I want My Diary to be the same. So, like, even when my body goes into the earth my soul can live on ...

... cos, see...

... there's nothing worser than being forgotten ... there's nothing worser than people not knowing you ever existed ...

P.S. Today, two boys Shouted Something at me outside the chip shop. I had just bought a battered sausage and was on my way home when one of them said:

Now that ... is a nice arse.

His mate was sitting on the wall and he added in a stupid American accent:

I agree, a mighty fine ass!

I turned so fast my glasses fell onto the tip of my nose. I had to push them back on to see properly.

Fuck off creeps! I said.

When I got home I waited until mum and My Sister Adele went to Midweek Club before slipping into mum's room. Normally I hated the sight of myself in the full-length mirror which stood on the back wall.

I replayed the boy's words in my head, "Now that ... is a nice arse."

There was something in the way he said it, something in the pause between the words, it's like he REALLY meant it and stuff. Like he really thought I was maybe kind of sexy. I may have looked angry when I said "fuck off creeps" but The Truth is I was kind of glowing inside, like a dead-flattered kind of a thing. Cos this had never happened to me before and this kind of thing only ever happened to Mia.

A smile lit up my face as I turned to see a definite curve and shape of a bum.

I was happy for once.

Maybe I was a woman, now.

Fancy Like Mad

Markus

Mia stood between a girl and a boy and introduced them to each other.

"Mel, this is Markus. Markus, Mel."

Mel wouldn't give eye contact at first, instead she looked at her shoe, and the bright green grass it was standing on. When their eyes finally did meet it was like a bomb going off. Something happened straight away. It was as if the world had stopped turning, like one life had ended, and another had just begun.

Mia was talking but neither the girl, or the boy, could hear a single word she said.

"Whoa. Alright. Maybe you two wanna go and get a room. Cos you look like you're about to fuck each other, or kill each other. Only I can't tell which."

They were caught in some kind of trance. Neither one of them blinked once.

"Okay one of you *needs* to say something," Mia said. "Cos quite frankly this is getting weird."

A moment later the spell was broken as one of them smiled, Markus.

Mel followed.

When she smiled back, it was like everything went back to normal again.

Markus was looking at the world from space. He zoomed-in closer, the reflection of his *good hair of hair* dimmed the screen of his brother's laptop. He zoomed-in again, watching Europe swell before him. Google Earth was kind of amazing, Markus thought, technology was fucking weird. How the human race had gone from drawing on cave walls to being able to see *everything* from a satellite in space. He zoomed-in again until he could see Britain, England, Lincolnshire, his town, his close; the bungalow he was sitting in *now*.

He thought about *the girl* and zoomed back out, looking at the four corners of his little town.

I wonder where she lives, he thought. "She's somewhere down there," he said out-loud.

His eyes traced along the Clementine Channel, and back.

There was no doubt this girl had got into his head. Girls had got into his head before, but not like this. *The way she looked at me.*

He wanted to know more about her so he clicked off Google Earth and went onto Facebook. Only he didn't know her second name so he was kind of stuck. He contemplated texting Mia to find out but he knew that wasn't a smart move. Mia was a loud-mouth gossip and within twenty minutes the whole school would know his business. Instead he went on to Mia's profile and then scanned down her friends list.

There she was, a cool black-and-white profile pic of a beautiful girl wearing glasses. He clicked onto her and enlarged the photo. She had her hood up and Markus thought she looked like some kind of model, her hair artfully falling out of the hood, flopping over her right eye and stroking the outlines of her face. There was a smile, but only just. She looked older and more confident than she did in real life.

What was odd is that her cover photo in the background was of the kid's film *Minions.*

Markus didn't think the two images looked right next to each other.

There wasn't much information on her profile at all. Only that her second name was *Ellis.* Melanie Ellis.

He liked her name and the sound it made in his mouth. There was a certain musicality and rhythm when he said the name in full. She sounded like some kind of famous person, Markus thought.

He looked at the rest of her pictures and she was beautiful in every one and he just knew that one day, one day soon, she was going to be his girlfriend, his first ever proper girlfriend. Markus felt his arrow-like will point straight in the direction of Melanie Ellis.

I'm coming for you.

He went through each photo twice, studying her face, her expressions.

The only one which had somebody else in was the colourful image of Mel and a younger girl playing at the park.

She looked similar to Mel but with long hazel hair and Markus had her down for a younger sister.

Markus clicked onto *message* and a rectangle box of white space opened up before him, a cursor flickering in the top left-hand-corner. His mind drew a blank on what to say. People always said Markus *had a way with words.* Aunt Tara had often said he was *too smart for his own good sometimes.* Only writing words was different to saying them and it was here that the teenager had come unstuck. He had typed in five words but the rest of the sentence just wouldn't arrive. *Hi Mel I was just …*

Thinking of you?

Wondering what you were doing?

Adding you on Facebook because?

In the end he sacked the message off altogether and clicked the friend request option instead.

Yeah that's better, Markus thought, can't go wrong with that.

Afterwards he closed the laptop down, only he was thinking about *the girl* so much he forgot to put his brother's laptop back under the bed. Markus was so distracted by thoughts of Melanie Ellis that he hadn't even noticed the new poster of Ryan Gosling above his brother's bed. Markus enjoyed thinking about her, he was excited by the space she had filled in his head. He got a strong urge to share all these feelings so when he heard his aunt step into the kitchen he quickly joined her.

"I met a girl today Mom."

Aunt Tars hated it when Markus called her *mum*, especially using that mocking Americanisation.

"Markus," she scowled. "Stop taking the piss."

"But I did meet a girl."

Tara could never tell if he was being serious or not. "Really," she said. "And what's her name?"

"I don't remember. But I think she's the most beautiful girl I've ever seen," he said, nodding.

His words seemed to clash against his masculine energy and Tara decided he could be bullshitting. He often 'made stuff up,' if nothing more than to test Tara or entertain himself with some kind of psychological game.

Tara put out her cigarette and stared at the boy's expression, trying to find the truth there.

"So beautiful you don't know her name?" she said.

"I didn't say I didn't know her name, I said I don't remember."

"And there's a difference?"

"Of course."

Tara was sometimes perplexed by her nephew's sudden change in mood. He had these peculiar transformations that came out of nowhere. One minute he could be closed-off, sullen and brooding, dragging himself through the bungalow like a big bear. The next open-hearted and breezy, whimsical, playful, almost a spring in his step. When he was like this Tara thought there was a trace of femininity in him, something girlish in his smile. Of course Tara would never tell him this, not only because he would kick-off, but because she liked having something on him that he was naïve about. She found these characteristics untouched and pure, and she hoped no one else would notice and tell him because that would just spoil *everything*.

The more he talked the more Tars thought there could be someone of interest. Tara had seen this look in people's face before, especially a teenager experiencing it for the first time.

"Tell me about her then?"

Markus thought about his words for a few moments before turning them loose.

"She's wild," he said, making his eyes big. "Like me."

Aunt thought it was a strange way to describe someone, but she kind of expected this kind of thing off Markus by now.

"God help us," she said.

Just then Ryan stormed into the kitchen. "That's it I want a lock putting on my bedroom door! *It's* been on my laptop again, probably looking at sick shit."

Markus raised his eyes at the older, who was standing with his hands on his hips, head cocked petulantly to one side.

"First off yeah, call me *it* again and I'll knock that fucking queer head straight off ya queer shoulders."

There was that drastic transformation again.

"And second off, yeah. I don't know nothing about no sick shit I was just using Facebook if you must know."

The song had been knocked all out of Markus and rage had replaced it. Tara had to restore some harmony otherwise she could have a casualty on her hands. The brothers had been clashing a lot lately and older brother Ryan had no idea how close he had been sailing to the wind.

"Markus do you want me to get you a laptop for your birthday? It'll have to be a cheap one mind."

"What I want ... is for him to stop accusing me of shit."

Ryan took a bottle of water out the fridge only he couldn't unscrew the lid. "I don't mind you borrowing my lappy Markus, I just don't want you going in my room."

Lappy, Markus thought, who the fuck says *lappy?*

Markus took the bottle from his brother and pulled the top off with one sudden twist, handing it back to him. Tara smiled a touch, thinking how symbolic that gesture was. Neither brother broke the rhythm of communication while that happened and Tara found this endearing. They were chalk and cheese, the Venner brothers, but sometimes the two moved on autopilot and it was comical to watch.

Over dinner Markus passed Ryan the ketchup and Ryan passed Markus the salt.

"Hey can you believe," Ryan said, "That this time next week Dad will be home?"

"He'll be *out.*" Markus corrected. "Not home."

Ryan raised his eyes and did that camp wrist thing of his. "Yeah," he said. "That's what I said."

The Kitts Academy was now an exciting place to be. Markus didn't mind going there and he was conscious he was making an effort to keep his head down and not get expelled. There was little or no chance of violence, as most kids made a point of staying out his way. The Chair Throwing Incident had earned him a week's suspension from school. Markus never understood why being suspended was supposed to be a punishment, *get in trouble and we'll give you a week's holiday.* Made no sense. Either way the outburst had made teachers weary. He was bigger than most of them and like the pupils, they stayed out of his way. Especially that nerdy little fuck of a German teacher, condescending prick won't even look him in the eye now. Nope, Markus was good, he was left in relative peace. As long as he kept his head down, he could do pretty much as he pleased; turn up late, leave early, not do homework, not wear proper uniform. One teacher had pretty much let him know this. *Keep a low profile Venner, that's all we ask.* Markus wasn't here to learn, he was here to *go through the motions,* turn up, get ticks on the register and keep his aunt happy. That was it. That was all.

Although The Kitts Academy had suddenly thrown in a new reason for him to be here now:

She stood knocked-kneed and uneasy against the back wall. Doing that impossibly cute thing of hers, stroking some fallen hair between her ear and the frame of her glasses. Next to her was an equally shy Indian girl and without her 'bestie' Mia, Mel looked even more fragile. Markus walked towards her, feeling his own brand of uneasiness. Just like the time he went to message her on Facebook his brain went to mush and there was no chance of words. So he found himself veering off towards the glass door to her left.

"Alright four-eyes."

It was the captain of the football team, Finley Cox, along with three or four others. Mel had her head down but the boys surrounded her.

"Think you need some window-wipers on them specs Mel, you look a bit steamy."

The sun made a massive Markus-shadow that put half the room in shade. He stood over the boys, staring at them one by one, singling them out; breaking their collective power. Heads went down and Mel was left alone.

"Alright Markus?" Finley said, trying to smooth things over. His voice had dramatically diminished in spirit. "You playing five-a-side tonight?"

Markus's attention was only on Mel. Between looking at the floor and glancing at the bullies she caught his eye in return. He didn't know what to say to her so he said nothing. The silence gave him added menace and the boys moved on. There was something strong in her eyes now. He imagined a fire going on behind there. A fire that no one else knew about.

A bell rang above them and kids everywhere scattered like cockroaches, upstairs, down corridors, into classrooms.

Markus and Mel stood for a few moments more, before she went in one direction, and he another.

Markus Venner always walked the Channel when he had something on his mind, no matter how much of a detour he had to take. That evening he had Mel on his mind, this mystery girl from the classrooms and the corridors. He couldn't believe he hadn't noticed her before. Mia was always in and out of groups, flitting from one clique to the next. She had introduced Markus to a hundred of kids, loads of dicks and dickheads, pricks and posers, bastards and bitches. Markus didn't like people and he had told Mia no end of times, *you're wasting your time, I don't give a shit.* Now he had met her Mel. Mia said she was her 'best friend' but Mia had introduced about five other girls with the same title so Markus just rolled his eyes.

"Markus, this is Mel. Mel, Markus."

He felt like he had met her before. She was a familiar stranger, close but a million miles away. Not a word has passed between them yet she had not left his mind.

It was summer, or at least summer was on its way. The first week of May had been full of sun, even though it had quickly turned cool in the evenings. Daffodils lined the calm waters that he walked along and a red twilight reflected of it like fire. Markus enjoyed the changing of the seasons, when one thing ended and another began.

As he got near home he saw two figures way up in the distance, playing near the water. Throwing things in and play-fighting up the bank. At first he thought it was two girls, a pair of slim blondes being silly in the late spring evening. Only one of them seemed frighteningly familiar. It was her walk and the way she threw her arms in the air. Markus kept his distance, moving alongside a thorny berry bush. He quickened his pace a bit more so he could see them a little clearer. Now the two were holding hands, showing affection, even a few quick kisses had passed between them. Markus had them down for a pair overly tactile friends, girls flirting with the idea of same sex romance. He saw the word, *experimenting.* As he drew even nearer he realised that one of the girls was actually a boy, in fact both of them were, as he got closer still he saw that one of the boys was a boy he knew, a boy that was his brother, a boy that was Ryan.

What the fuck.

Now the two were full-on snogging and this made Markus want to be sick. It was one thing to watch a couple of bandits lip-locking, he thought, but to see *my own brother.* Markus fought off the instinct to do what he always did when something made him mad. *Attack.* Go over and batter the bum-boys for being disgusting and shaming his family. Markus thought of the shit this would cause. Markus had a rep and the last thing he needed was that rep being tarnished by being associated to gay-boys, having that queer gene in his family. He wanted to confront them but something was holding him back. Truth was it kind of scared him, the whole thing was weird and alien and even being near it felt wrong.

Or was it that alien? He remembered that awful time in his life with those fucked-up posh twins. A time that shamed him so much he thought about committing suicide. Markus never thought about the past, or people from it. Only sometimes deadly reminders swooped in and turned his life upside-down.

Maybe this was one of those times?

Maybe he knew his brother was gay only *seeing it* made it all too real?

Maybe *everyone* already knew and it was Markus in denial?

Maybe it was living in this town that was the problem? Kimble Wells was way too small and he detested everyone knowing your business. He hated being talked about. He hated being boxed-in.

Markus watched Ryan kiss his boyfriend goodbye, before skipping into the underpass. Markus tailed him through Tesco car park and onto Victory Lane. Soon they were on Norman Close, his brother having no idea that he'd been followed for the last hour. Markus liked following people. He like watching people without them knowing. I'd make a good spy, he thought.

After Ryan stepped into the bungalow Markus gave it a few minutes before he followed.

Dinner was already being placed on the table, a steaming hot vegetable lasagne.

"Perfect timing," their auntie said.

The Venner brothers sat opposite each other. Markus suddenly got an urge to out his brother. Ask him who that boy was, that other little queer boy he was holding hands with along the Clementine Channel. Markus went to say something only his auntie beat him to it.

"Any more news on that love of yours?"

Ryan went bright red, only when the boys looked up it was the younger sibling who was being addressed.

"You remember her name yet?" Tara said smiling, laying out the cutlery before him.

"Yeah," Markus said, his face a little blank. "Yeah I remember her name."

Hey Mel.

Markus was so over-the-moon she had accepted his friend request he decided to message her straight away.

Hey Markus, she replied.

What you up to?

Not much. Like, just been taking my Stupid Dog out for a walk and stuff. Lol. Funny … swear I saw you earlier. Was u up the channel? Lol.

Markus suddenly got paranoid. Hope she didn't see me spying on my bent bro.

Yeah I was. Lol. Where was u?

Bout hundred metres behind you. Lol. That's mad.

Yeah mad.

That was weird, he thought, she was following me, following someone else. Markus didn't like that.

Was gonna shout you, lol. But like, didn't know it was you like 100%.

It was me. Lol.

It would have been weird if I had of shouted you, lol. Cos like, have you noticed that we haven't OFFICIALLY spoken one word to each other yet? Lol.

I know.

Why is that?

Dunno.

You shy?

No. You?

No.

Really?

Well … bit.

Ha!

Ha.

Well Mel, we're speaking now.

This doesn't count. Cos like, it's not a Real Life kind of a thing.

Suppose.

Do you think we'll EVER speak?

Probs.

Probs?

Course.

Ha.

Lol.

Maybe our WHOLE life could be this, just talking on messenger, a cyber relationship.

Relationship?

No I didn't mean it like that!!

Ur cute.

Am I?

Yup.

Really?

Really!

Ha, well, I'm just a swaggy badass.

WTF!

Ha. I am random sometimes, Markus.

I like that. I like random. I also like it when you say my name.

MarkusMarkusMarkusMarkusMarkusMarkusMarkus.

MelMelMelMelMelMelMelMelMelMelMelMelMelMel x

Hey did you just kiss me?

Yes I did. Lol.

We've kissed before we've met ???!!! Lol.

What u talkin bout. We've met!!

I mean like properly. I mean like where we've talked and stuff. Lol.

Maybe we'll talk properly tomorrow??

Maybe we'll kiss properly 2 ??

Don't push ur luck boy.

Lol.

Anyway, gotta go. Mum is shouting me for dinner.

K.

Speak soon Markus.

Speak soon Beautifulness.

Hey! I like that! Is that my pet-name? Lol.

Yeah. What's mine?

Hmmmmm???

Go on?

I'll have a think about it and tell you tomorrow.

K.

Right. Really gotta go now. Mum is going CRAZY. Says she'll kill me if I'm not down in 10seconds.

No one will kill you. Not now I'm around.

Awwwwwwww xxxxxx

Xxxxxxx

Xxx x x
Xxxx xx XXXX XXXX X x X
XXXXXXXXXXXXXXXXXXXXXXXXXXX
XXXXXXXXXXXXXXXXXXXXXXXXXX
x
x

Markus woke up late, later than usual. He lay there and tried to guess the time. He figured around 10.30am, 10:33, he thought. He also tried to *feel* who was in the bungalow ...Tara was out, Ryan in. He closed his eyes and imagined what Mel was doing. She was in the shower, her hair darkened by the water. She looked funny with her glasses off, eyes scrunched as she washed her face under the showerhead. Markus lay in daydream until he felt it was about eleven o'clock, before swinging his legs out of bed, slipping his socks and jogging bottoms on and plodding heavy-footed to the kitchen. No sign of Tara and he could hear his brother move about in the adjacent room. Markus pulled open the fridge and a weak light lit up the already sun-filled kitchen. A lawnmower moaned from two gardens down and Markus could feel all the things that made up the season of summer. In the fridge a packet of bacon lay on the top shelf. He reached in and took it out, pulling off the plastic cover.

"Ryan."

"What?" his brother's voice was tight and defensive, like he was expecting some kind of conflict.

"Fancy a bacon sandwich?"

There was a long pause, as the younger brother was already pouring oil into the pan.

"Err ... yeah, sure."

Ryan came out his room, looking at Markus a little dumfounded. In the almost fourteen years Ryan had had him as a brother not once had he ever offered to do something for him like this. A smile was on Markus's face and a song must be in his head as the boy was singing something under his breath.

He kept the pan on a low light, flipping the bacon before laying it onto a slice of bread that had been buttered in advance.

"Sauce?"

Ryan nodded, still stunned. Markus flipped a bottle of brown and squeezed two perfect trails in and around the bacon.

"Juice?"

Ryan nodded, again staring and shocked and open-mouthed.

Markus had the fridge open, almost a little dance as he pulled out a carton of tropical and loaded it into a tall sparkling glass.

"Bon appetite."

He lay his older brother's breakfast out onto the kitchen table and then started on his own. Ryan sat and began to eat, still spooked by his younger brother's behaviour. When Markus sat opposite Ryan had to ask what was going on.

"What do you mean?" Markus said with his mouthful, brown sauce falling down his chin.

"The way you're acting, all nice and that. It's weird."

Markus shrugged. His behaviour hadn't changed that much, Ryan thought. He still ate like a pig.

"It's just with dad coming out and that," Markus said. "Makes you put things in perspective."

"Perspective?" Ryan almost coughed out his bacon.

"Yeah, y'know. Like life's too short."

Ryan was amazed. "Well that girl must really have got in your head."

Markus shook his. "Nah. Nothing to do with that mate."

"Okaaay then," Ryan said, eyes wide. Yet part of him was starting to believe his brother.

"We all just need to let go."

Again Markus was talking with his mouthful and Ryan couldn't hear him properly. The mower outside got louder too and sounded like it was in their own backyard.

"Let go?" Ryan said. "What do you mean?"

Markus had some trouble swallowing, but he wanted to make sure his mouth was empty before he started talking again. He was nodding his head, trying to make the food go down. Once it had he looked at his brother earnestly. "You need to come-out."

The sudden bluntness made Ryan's face go white. "What?" he said breathlessly.

"Ryan. *We* know. We *all* know. I've even seen him."

Ryan went to deny it but then didn't. "When?"

Markus began eating casually again. "Just around."

"But ... "

"You're nearly seventeen."

Ryan was perplexed by his brother's mature and direct behaviour.

"Ryan we always say it, *you are what you are.* If this is who you are, then it is what it is. You shouldn't be scared."

Ryan now had his head in his hands, looking like he was about to cry. "I'm only scared of dad," he said. "Auntie Tara, Auntie Tara knows. She's known for ages."

This time Markus seemed a little surprised, and a little pissed-off that he wasn't the first.

"Dad's going to be out of prison on Friday and as much as I'm excited to see him, I'm also terrified of him finding out."

Now Ryan did cry, it was like his insides burst and all the fear was pouring out of him in torrents. "You know Markus. You know how much he *hates* it all. You know how much he is *disgusted* by all that."

Markus now had his brother in his arms, holding him tight. Ryan was crying so violently his whole body was trembling in his embrace.

"He'll disown me I know it. And I've already lost mum. I've already lost one parent Markus and I can't bear to lose another."

"You won't," Markus said. "You won't lose anything or anyone. We'll get through this bro, promise."

The mower outside had stopped and the bungalow became powerfully silent, except for the undying sobs of Ryan Venner.

Big Bear.
What?

After yesterday's bonding moment Ryan had no issues with his younger brother using his laptop.

Big Bear.
Big Bear?
That's ur pet-name. Lol.
LLlllllooooooooooooooooooL!!!!!
Lol.
Why big bear?
I dunno. Cos like, ur kind of big and cuddly and stuff.
Ha!
Lol.
But I mean how do u know? We haven't cuddled yet. We haven't even talked.
I know. Lol.
U didn't talk today.

U didn't either.

I know. Lol.

Maybe u r just as shy as me only ur 2 shy 2 admit it??? Lol.

Probs. Lol.

Anyway it's hard 4 either of us 2 talk with rent-a-gob around.

Tell me about it. Lol

Like, I do love My Bestie but she does go on and on and on and on …

Is she really ur bestie?

Yeah why?

Just.

Just what?

Just never seen you around is all. Lol.

Probs dint notice me.

Trust me I'd notice u. Lol.

How?

Don't make me say it. Lol.

Say what? Lol.

How beautiful you are.

Yeah right!!!!!?????

You ARE.

I HATE the way I look and always have.

Noooo.

You really think I am?

Absolutely.

Hmmmm???

From the first time I saw u.

Hmmmm???

That's probs why I haven't spoken to you yet. Lol.

Gosh.

Yup.

I'm not used to this. Feels weird and stuff.

What does?

Attention and that. It's normally Mia that gets it all.

She's a lameo.

She's alright.

Ur more beautiful than her, easy.

Noooo.

Anyway mum not shouting you for dinner 2nite?

Nope. Had it. Now she's out with Babe.

Who?
Oh. Our dog.
Ur dog's called babe lol?
Yup. Dumb I no.
Ha.
I hate it.
Mum or babe? Lol.
Both.
Oh.
And my sister adele 2.
U got a sis 2?
Yeah but don't talk about her.
Why?
Cos you'll probably fall in love with her and stuff like everyone else does.
No one is more beautiful than you.
Oh stop!
It's true.
What about ur mum?
What about her?
Get on with her?
No.
Why?
Cos she's dead.
What?
Dead.
Really?
No I made it up.
What?
Yes she's dead.
Oh I'm sorry. X
Why sorry, u didn't kill her?
?????
?????
Ur humour is weird.
Dunno.
U live with ur dad?
No.
Who then?
My aunt.

U get on?
Not really.
Why?
I hate adults.
Me too.
Fuck life.
Why u say that?
Just ... lol.
Yeah, suppose.
U not happy?
Am now.
Why?
I like talking to u Markus.
Love it when u say my name.
MarkusMarkusMarkusMarkusMarkusMarkus.
MelMelMelMelMelMelMelMelMelMelMelMel.
Ha. Lol. Knew u was going to do that. Lol.
U told Mia we chatting on FB?
Noooooo.
Gud.
Drama queen.
Gossip girl.
Lol.
Lol.
Hey can I ask u something?
?
How come u always on your own?
When?
Like, at school and stuff?
People are dumb.
People are scared of you.
?
At school and stuff.
Oh.
There's rumours u killed someone?
WTF!
I know, right!
Killed who?
Dunno.
Lol.

Lol.

So how many schools you been b4 Kitts?

Couple.

You get expelled?

Man u ask a lot of questions.

Oh. Sorry.

Lol.

Just interested in you.

Why?

Dunno.

X

X

I'm interested in u 2.

X

Think ur dead beautiful.

So u say.

It's true.

Hey thanks 4 stopping Finley and that from picking on me the other day.

U always change the subject when I call you beautiful.

Do I? Lol.

Lol. Anyway yeah Finley and all that football lot are a bunch of pussies anyway.

Lol.

Think they're tough but they wouldn't last a day on the estate.

U live in the estate?

Not now. But I'm from there.

Is it rough?

Not really.

Where do you live now?

Norman close, by the Channel.

I live not far from the Channel too, but further up.

Where?

Lawson Avenue, not far from McDonald's.

Oh.

Do you still see ur dad?

Sometimes.

When was the last? Sorry I'm being nosey again. Lol.

Bout eight months ago I think, can't remember.

Wow that's a long time.

Yup.

I don't see my dad much either.

Oh.

How come so long?

Dunno. He lived abroad I think. Seeing him on Fri but can't be arsed to be honest.

Families are strange.

Families are shit.

Suppose. Lol.

Lol.

Anyway Big Bear it's almost midnight.

Fuck.

Wonder if we'll speak tomorrow at school??

Let's not. I like this. It's kind of exciting.

I know. I know what u mean, like a different kind of a thing.

And I like Mia not knowing 2. She thinks she's so clever.

If only she knew.

Ha.

Lol

Night Beautifulness.

I can't tell u how much I like u saying that.

Beautifulness?

Uh-huh.

Well I like my pet name 2.

Big Bear?

Yup.

Speak to u tomorrow Big Bear, or rather, SEE u tomorrow Big Bear.

Lol. Night Beautifulness.

Night. X

x

x

Putting up *Welcome Home* banners and balloons was just the most stupid thing Markus had ever heard of. He couldn't believe they were doing it. That kind of thing was for war heroes, or adventurers who had explored the Antarctic, not for alcoholic scumbags who had done a stretch for breaking the law.

"I'm telling you Tars ... you make me go live with him again and I'll proper kick-off."

"For the hundredth time Markus, you're not going to live with him. How many more times!"

She was standing on a stool with her back to him, tying a blue and yellow banner across the curtain rail. "Is that straight?"

Ryan walked in with a pink balloon, and then walked out again.

"Too much to the left," Markus said.

Tara adjusted the banner. "Now?"

"Straight," Markus affirmed.

Tara stepped down from the stool and faced her nephew. "You know, you might wanna try a little forgiveness sometimes. You may need some yourself one day," she said.

She had this certain look on her face like she could see into the future.

"What's that supposed to mean?" Markus said with a scowl.

"Whatever you want it to mean," Tara replied with a smile on her face.

Auntie Tara was looking fit and well again. She'd been back to the gym and some of her old confidence had returned. Markus preferred her fat. She was too up-herself as an attractive woman, too smug and sure of herself.

"Now blow up this balloon," she said with a cocky sparkle in her eye.

"Yeah right." Markus shrugged her off, before taking himself to his room.

He slammed the door and fell on his bed, the room flipped as he landed on his back. Markus thought about Mel and wondered if she'd messaged him again. Really he should get a new mobile sorted instead of fucking about with his brother's laptop all the time.

Mel. Mel. Mel.

Mel Ellis.

She's all tangled up inside me.

Markus must have dozed off because when he opened his eyes again he was all disorientated. There was a commotion outside his bedroom door; noise, a rumbling of feet, a door, a voice.

"Markus, Markus dad's here!"

Ryan's voice high and vital, like it was the most important thing in the world. *Dad's here.*

Markus blew out a breath between his lips and slowly got up from the bed, rubbing his eyes, standing up, leaving the room.

Through the kitchen window he saw a tangle of bodies, both Tara and Ryan hugging a big man in the driveway. Dad's brother Nigel stood nearby, watching the sentimental reunion, an uncomfortable smile glued to his face. When the three-way embrace let go Markus could see that both Ryan and Tara had been crying.

"God," Markus said under his breath, watching the homecoming party make their way to the back door. Markus could already see that his dad had put on weight, more meat to his bones and he appeared much healthier. His face looked less red, which made his hair look less blonde. Altogether he looked like a different man.

"Son," he said, stepping through the back door.

Their eyes met and straight away there was a hint of confrontation, that slight smirk in the older man's mouth.

"Dad."

Everyone else stood around watching them, like they were expecting something to happen.

"Ain't giving me a hug like the rest of me family?"

Markus traipsed over and placed his body rigidly into the man's arms. Dad didn't hug him back properly either and Markus knew that his old man was testing him in some way.

As soon as it was over Markus took himself to the other side of the room.

"Thanks for the visits son," his dad said. "They really kept my spirits up."

The atmosphere was tense. Nigel and Tara were both looking at the floor, Ryan out the window, the late afternoon sun lighting up his bottle blonde hair.

Markus shrugged.

"Thirteen months," his dad said. "And not a peep."

Markus was shocked it was that long. He thought it was about half that, at least.

Markus shrugged again, pulling his best *not bothered* face.

"Anyway," Lance Venner said. "I'm here now."

"Want a drink Lance?" Tara said.

"Fucking hell Tars I've just come out … now you're trying to feed me the stuff that put me there."

"I meant a cup of tea?"

Lance was laughing and Tara was too. He had his big hands on her shoulders and his face was all screwed up with joy. "I know you did love. I'm just joking. It's nice to be able to have a laugh at last. Some serious bastards in that nick y'know!"

Markus let out a silent sigh. He knew his dad was going to be spending the whole night, if not year, telling his prison war stories.

"Markus put the kettle on," Tara said, smiling at him. "Nigel you having a cuppa?"

"I'm alright with these Tars," Uncle Nigel said, lifting up a bag of cans.

That's this family all over, Markus thought. Dad in recovery and his own brother getting steaming in front of him on his first day of release.

Older brother Ryan stood at the edge of the kitchen, so far his dad had barely acknowledged him. When he did it wasn't pleasant. "And what the fuck have you done to your hair?" He pointed aggressively at his oldest son. "You look like Jedwood."

That made Markus laugh, and he joined dad and uncle, who were cracking up and pointing at a red-faced Ryan. Humiliation whitened his face.

"Seriously pal," his dad went on. "What the fucking hell is going on?"

Ryan's mouth wobbled as he tried to say something.

"Alright," Tara said, shouting from the other end of the kitchen. "Leave him alone."

She whipped some foil off a spread she had made earlier. "Come and eat then."

The boys bolted over and began tucking into the food. With a mouthful of chicken leg Lance started on his stories. "First night in man, and I've got this junkie-fuck in the bunk below, clucking, rattling, squirming about like a dying insect. Fucking screaming out at one point, screaming out for his mum. Saying all kinds of weird shit. Gotta tell you, lads. For a first night in, it was pretty fucking hard-core. Next night a little easier, week after easier still. After a month it was a piece of piss. Did me bird standing on me fucking head."

Markus had heard this term used before, *standing on my head,* mates from the estate who had been in YOI said it, *I did it standing on my head.* It was to show how hard they were, that prison time was easy. Markus thought it sounded like a stupid thing to say.

If I ever go prison, Markus thought. I'll never say that.

"Yeah I got in with some good lads." His dad was still going on. He'd always been full of bluster and bravado only now he had turned it up a notch. "You know what amazed me ... is how all the wogs and pakis and whites stuck to themselves."

314

"Lance!"

Tara stared him down. "We're not having that kind of talk in this house."

Dad looked at her gone-out, like he thought she might be joking. "It's not a house, it's a bungalow."

"Whatever Lance. Not that kind of talk around the boys."

A Dorito was hanging out of his mouth. "Since when did you start getting Mrs Political Correct?"

"Things have changed," she said, a stern finality in her tone.

Nigel was half-pissed by now, moving onto the hard stuff, pouring vodka into a Liverpool glass he had brought himself.

Mel was right, Markus thought, families *are* strange.

Throughout the evening both Dad and Uncle took turns in checking Tara out; sly, sleazy glances every time she bent down or reached up for something. Markus knew what they were doing and it made him feel sick.

"So overall prison was a piece of piss, an experience if nothing else," his dad announced. "It's straightened me out and sobered me up. Gave me some time to think, realise what's important in life."

Everybody listened on intently, giving Lance Venner his moment. Markus sat bored, switched-off, not buying into the bullshit for a second. I know how people work, he thought.

His dad carried on. "Met some new mates. Read a few books, and did a bit of queer-bashing when I really got bored, hahahaha."

Markus looked up at that remark, shot his brother a sharp glance and Ryan looked back, his face full of fear. Again Tara sighed only this time she didn't say anything. Markus noticed she squeezed his brother's arm for reassurance, a sign that Ryan had indeed told her.

"Hey Markus, you heard about little Charlie?"

"Yeah he knows." Uncle Nigel slurred.

"Little Charlie is down Southampton for the summer, signed up to a Premiership club. Not bad ey? It's nice having talent in the family. He might play for our Reds one day. Do us all proud!"

"Little shit's getting homesick though," Nigel said. "Wants to come home already. Told him to stop being a puff."

Again Markus looked over at his brother.

"C'mon then Marky boy tell us what's been going on?"

His dad had started acting weird and Markus wondered if Nigel had been sneaking him booze. "You still a hard little fucker?"

Markus shrugged.

"Still ya dad's little pit bull? Hey I heard you're in a new school. You the hardest or what?"

"Course."

"That's my boy!!"

Lance rubbed his son's head. All the food was gone and Tara was tidying up, Ryan helping her by sweeping bits of food into a dustpan. Markus watched him closely and noticed he had been playing down his *gayness* since his dad's arrival. He'd deepened his voice an octave and that limp wrist thing had gone altogether.

"Got a bird on at this school then Markus?"

Markus had his head resting on his fist, bored. "Her name is Mel."

"Mel," Dad said with a smile.

"Hey at least you get a name out of him." Tara shouted from the next room. "He hasn't told us a thing."

His dad rocked back and touched his chest. "Ey that's cos he tells his ode dad everything!"

Tara came back into the kitchen.

"Is she fit?" his dad pushed on.

"She's a thirteen-year-old girl dad."

Lance let out a laugh. "You know what I mean. Is she fit for *you*?"

"She's beautiful."

"Yep he's in love," Uncle Nigel said, sniggering.

"Beautiful?" his dad said. "That's no way for a hard man to talk?"

Markus stood up and stretched. "Why don't you ask how Ryan is? Why do you have to talk to me all the time?"

Lance Venner pulled a face, like this was the first time it had occurred to him.

"Yeah," Tara agreed. "You haven't spoke to Ryan once."

"Haven't I?" Lance said, looking over his shoulder, trying to see where his other son was.

Ryan had his lip out. He looked like some pathetic wounded animal and this irritated Markus. Now was the time, he thought.

"Why don't you ask about the love in *his* life?"

Something suddenly swooped in and took hold of the bungalow. Tara was looking at him, glaring at him, her face white with shock. Not as shocked as Ryan, who was wondering if he'd heard it right. Something gave way in his dad's face, like he knew what was coming.

"Oh," he said. "Never knew you were courting kiddo. What's her name?"

316

"I ... "

Tara wanted to step in and say something but she didn't know what.

"*His* name," Markus said, clearly.

"What?" his Dad said. Some of that signature redness returned to his face.

"Oh you don't know?" Markus, who had been in slouch-mode all evening suddenly stood tall. "Well dad, you're not the only one who has recently come out. While you've been coming out of prison your oldest son Ryan here has *at last* come out the closet. He's gay dad."

Uncle Nigel's mouth dropped open.

The first person Markus looked at was Tara, who was glaring at her nephew with eyes of pure hatred. The second person Markus looked at was Ryan, but all he could see was the back of his head, as he ran out the back door, a sob choking in the back of his throat.

"Well," Markus said, slowly looking around room. "That went down well."

Markus lay there that night, with his hands behind his head, listening. He listened to the world around him. Listened to Tara, Nigel and Dad talking into the small hours of the morning. Sometimes the voices were raised, sometimes they were hushed. He knew they were talking about serious things, deep things, troubling things. He thought he heard his mum's name being mentioned. He heard cupboards and glasses and cans being cracked. At some point someone went out and returned some fifteen minutes later. He knew that his dad was drinking again. He recognised that laugh and hiccup of his, sounds he only made when he was on the bottle. He'd been out of prison less than twelve hours and already he was back on it. Markus listened out for his brother but he was gone for the night, probably hiding out at his boyfriend's. He heard the kitchen window opening and closing every twenty minutes and he knew his dad wasn't the only one who had let an addiction overcome him. His aunt had too. She was smoking again. Now there was shouting, mostly from his dad. Only his voice was too washed with alcohol for Markus to hear what was being said. A bottle smashed and a door slammed and then there was silence. Silence that stretched out for ages. Silence that came to an end by the sound of crying; long, deep, muffled sobs that seemed to reverberate through the walls. Markus thought it sounded like some injured animal and he suddenly experienced a flashback from his *days with the cats*. His brain told him he should maybe go and see his Auntie Tara, comfort her in some way. Only he couldn't. Or, he *wouldn't*. Part of him blamed her. Why does she even bother with us all, he thought? She has no biological ties so why does she even care? All we are is Venner scum, he thought. Two alcoholics, a queer, and me. And what am I? Nothing but a hurtful, hateful little bastard. Aunt Tars had even said those very words herself, *hurtful, hateful little bastard*.

Ha.

Fuck life.

Markus listened to the sobs and wondered if they were ever going to stop. She carried them to her bedroom and continued there, crying into her pillow until the night waned and the sun came up.

Markus wasn't tired so he listened on until they did stop, and finally she fell asleep. After that there was just the sounds of the bungalow, sounds of insects outside and the occasional car, a dog bark in the distance, and the creak of his bed, every time he turned over.

Hey how was The Time with your dad Big Bear?

Ryan hadn't been at the bungalow for two days so Markus could use his laptop as freely as he wanted.

Beautifulness! Yeah it was gud thanks.

Where did he go travelling?

Travelling?

Yeah, like, U said he goes travelling and stuff?

Oh. Yeah. He went America.

Oh wow!!

What u up 2?

Not much. Just chillin. U?

Same. Just chilling.

I'm bored.

Wanna meet?

What!?

Meet, wanna?

When?

Now.

Now?

Now is always the best time to meet. Lol.

Eeeeeekkk.

What?

I can't. Lol

Why? Lol.

Not yet.

Why?

2 scared lol.

What of?

It's 2 scary lol.

?

Feel like we've built it up too much. Like, like I like this No Talking Thing but it's kind of like there's loads of pressure now. Lol.

Lol.

Oh and I've got to tell u sumthing BTW.

?

I think Mia knows about us.

Us?

Markus could see his own smile in the reflection of the screen. Mel took ages to respond to this one.

Well, like, I think she knows something's going on?

Going on?

Okay Markus stop playing games.

Markus typed out *playing games?* But then deleted it. He didn't want to spin her out too much. Instead he put: *love it when you say my name.*

MarkusMarkusMarkusMarkusMarkus.

MelMelMelMelMelMelMelMelMelMel.

Lol.

So Mia knows we chatting on FB?

No but she thinks I Fancy You Like Mad. Lol.

What makes her say that? Lol

Dunno.

Lol.

Probs cos how quiet we are around each other and stuff. Lol.

Lol.

Anyway she's dead-clever, like a detective kind of a thing.

So you DO fancy me like mad?

I never said that! Lol.

Yes you did. Lol.

Hey stop catching me out. Lol.

Aw bless. X
Now I feel stupid. Lol.
Ur cute.
Stop!
Lol.
What about u?
What about me?
Do you, like, fancy me like mad?
Kind of.
Kind of?
Course!
Phew.
Told u. Think ur the most beautiful girl I've ever seen!
I'm rolling my eyes right now. Lol.
It's true!
You don't think I'm more beautiful than Mia surely!
Now I'm rolling my eyes. Lol.
Hmmmmm???
Lol.
So what we gonna do?
Maybe we should be BF and GF then?
Really?
Yup.
Wow.
Lol.
Maybe u should ask me out then, so it's an OFFICIAL kind of a thing?

Markus could feel his insides burn as he typed in the next message.

Will you go out with me Mel? Will you be my GF?

He erased the shorthanded *GF* and went for the full title.

Will you be my girlfriend?

Send.

Markus waited. He waited for her reply. While he waited he caught the reflection of his face in the laptop again. He was amazed by how serious he looked. Everything seemed to be so crucial all of a sudden. Even though he already knew the answer he glared at the screen until that little three-letter word was there.

Yes.

Mel

Yes.

First off, from The Start. From The Moment we met I knew. Just TOTALLY knew. Just knew that something BIG had to happen. It did. Cos, like, it was that Nature-Feeling all over again. That Nature-Feeling I always talk about. The mysterious instinct-feeling that leads and shows me The Way. It was in the air that day, and all around like a hurricane. You know what I'm talking about. You should know what I'm talking about By Now. That force, that drive deep within. Our eyes met and locked, and there was a buzzing in my head and daylight didn't look the same anymore. Mia melted away completely and was just another feature in the landscape, like a tree or a bin or a hill or something. Just. There was just. There was just his eyes and my eyes. His heartbeat and mine. It was kind of like magic, You know? Like sparks and spells and stars and stuff. Chemistry and that. Big Bear had come from the woods, You see? Big Bear had come from the moon. Things weren't the same now and wouldn't be, wouldn't be ever again.

Big Bear had come from The Past. Big Bear had come from The Old, Old World. I remember. I remember knowing that he had always been there. There from The Start. Cos, like, tbh I'm not gonna Lie but I've always felt him there, see? Felt him there, here, somewhere. Somewhere out there. He was always hanging around, on the outskirts of town. I had seen him before, known him from That Time before. Had seen him out on street corners, through shop windows, crossing roads, climbing over gates, kneeling by the river's edge. He was always alone, I think. Always alone and wandering, alone and waiting. Waiting for something to come along. Waiting for something good to come along. Waiting for me. Cos, like, we were always going to happen, tbh. It was only a matter of Time. Time before we met. Time before This Town brought us together. It was always going to happen inside of Kimble Wells, You see. We were always waiting. Waiting to happen. Like being drawn-in, drawn-in together, almost like we was on a piece of string or something, an invisible chord, always together, always connected.

Connected and stuff. His mind and my mind.

Cos, like, he was always hanging around on the outskirts of my mind, too. He was always pushing against its walls, trying to find a way in, step over, come inside. He used to visit me in the Night Time, see? At nights, in dreams. Only I never knew, never knew all that. Never knew that at all. Just felt it there. Although back then I didn't know what it was, but Big Bear was crossing worlds and oceans and skies to reach me. Find me here. I felt his shadow always. Towering over me. He'd walk the waters and climb a beanstalk to my window, tap three times to let me know he was there, here. Big Bear was from underground, an underworld where the giants live.

Big Bear was from The Future. Big Bear was from space. Always up there, always looking down on the rest of us. He was taller than everybody else. Bigger than everyone too. He was taller than an adult and bigger than a mountain. He filled me up. Filled up the room, filled up the room in my head. He filled up this diary too. THIS diary I am writing in. The one I am writing in NOW. The diary you are reading, the book you are reading NOW. Big Bear lives in your head. He lives there like he lives in mine. And in my heart and veins and lungs and stuff. I breathe him in, and out. Cos, like, I fancy him, I do. I admit. I admit it. I admit that I fancy him like mad. And he does too. Like, he fancies me like mad too. Says he does. Says he does and I kind of believe him cos like, I can tell. I can read it. Read it in his face and in the words he uses. And in the words he doesn't use too. I can read it in the silences we have, in the moments we take, in the looks we share.

Big Bear.

Big Bear.

Big Bear is hanging around the outskirts of the summer we're about to have. The blue sky we're all under. The green grass we lay upon. Cos, like, we break up from school soon and the summer is all ours, there for the taking. We break up from school soon and I can't effing wait. Can't wait for all that freedom we're going to have. Of slow, slow days. Long, slow days with nothing to do. Days of nothing. Nothing at all. Days with no classes and corridors and lessons and stuff. Days with no alarms in the morning or bells in the afternoon, screaming down your ear like the way teachers do; telling you to listen, sit down, sit up, sit still, sit straight, look straight, think straight, don't move, don't talk, don't do anything unless They say first, do your classwork, homework, lifework, wear uniform, button up, follow the rules. Always the rules. Rules. I hate rules and always have. The world is full of them. Rules that THEY make up. Make up as they go along. School and teachers and mums and people in high places and stuff. Everyone has to follow. Everyone has to follow Them. Everyone has to follow them but Big Bear.

Big Bear. He doesn't care. He doesn't care and never has. Not one bit.

Big Bear is from the Estate. From the big bad estate where It All goes down. Big bear is from These Streets. He's rough and tough and does what he wants.

Big Bear is there for me. Says he's there for me now.

Says he wants to look after me and I believe him, I do. Cos, like, he protected me once before I remember. I remember. Like when the bullies were bullying me he just put a shadow on the wall and looked at them once. Once was enough. Once was enough and now they know. Now they all know to leave me alone, At Last. Leave me alone for good. Cos, like, I'm not alone anymore. In this world. Like, I don't feel like I am, anyway. Cos, like, I always have been in The Past. It's no secret that I've always been a Lonely Girl. A lonely girl from The Start. A lonely girl when all said and done. But now I'm a new girl, a new girl for sure. A new girl now cos he asked me out. Big Bear asked me out, like an Official kind of a thing. I even remember the exact day and date and time and stuff.

It was a Saturday. At 19:13 on May 23rd 2015.

He asked me out.

He asked me out and I said: Yes.

I said yes and we are Officially GF and BF, now.

And.

And all of a sudden Things are different, like TOTALLY different, now. Different and stuff. I feel like a Real Person, At Last. I feel like a WHOLE person and not just half of one. It's like I have something to live for, now. Something to breathe for. Someone to love and something to die for. If that makes sense? Songs and movies talk about it All The Time and now I get it, now I TOTALLY understand. Cos like, it's about life and stuff. Love and that. So I have a purpose now, I do. A direction. A direction I am heading in. A new thing. A new thing to look forward to. A Real Reason to get out of bed and stuff. Like for the first time EVER it feels like something truly exciting is about to happen. Like, like it feels like the First Chapter of My Life is finally over, like the First Part is over and now I can start a new one. Just. Turn over the page and see what happens next ...

Part Two

"In the midst of winter, I found there was, within me, an invincible summer."

Albert Camus

Slow Days, Fast Food

Markus

"Wonder what we'll be doing this time next year?" she said.

She was curled up on his chest like a cat.

"Dunno," he said. "Don't think about the future."

She turned her head and looked up at him. "Think we'll still be together?"

He pulled a screw-face. "Course."

She closed her eyes and a dreamy smile appeared.

Up above a tightrope of foam scarred the blue sky. The plane had gone but its sound remained. "Ever been abroad?" he said.

When she didn't answer he sat up and looked down. She had fallen asleep. Great, he thought, now what do I do? He moved some hair that lay across her glasses and decided to watch her, until she woke up.

Tara Haywood had never experienced her nephew so calm; so easy and tranquil, so *well behaved*. It was almost like he had been hypnotised, or drugged, like he was under a spell, or coming down with a bug, a bug that made him docile, dreamy, *not with it*. Markus was often quiet but his silence had always been intimidating, unnerving, that brooding menace which put everyone on edge. Whereas now he was just mellow, zen-like, almost peaceful to be around. Tara wondered if it was something to do with this new girlfriend of his. If so she was dying to meet her, intrigued to meet the only human who had ever managed to *get inside* and settle him. Tara also wondered if it had anything to do with breaking up from school. She knew her nephew wasn't fond of The Kitts Academy, or any school for that matter. Maybe the promise of a six-week break had chilled him out and brought about this change in mood. Lastly she considered that maybe it was because his brother Ryan wasn't around anymore. Since *that night* the siblings hadn't spoken a word, Ryan had pretty much moved into his boyfriend's and now

Markus not only got to be *the man of the house*, but, *the only man of the house.* Markus didn't have to put up with his dad either and this too could have been a factor. Lance Venner was back on the booze, a full-time job where his only obligation was to walk to the off-licence and back. He had moved in with Uncle Nigel and the two were into all kinds of scams and schemes, his dad on incapacity while his brother picked up a pay cheque for being his carer. It was a joke, and Markus found the whole thing shameful. He didn't want to be associated to any of it. Instead he spent time with his new girlfriend, or taking long walks alone. As far back as Tara can remember, her nephew had always enjoyed time by himself, out walking in the wilderness, a rare thing for a teenage boy.

Today he walked up to the new houses that were being built over the old donkey field. Big town-houses that were colourful and pleasing to look at. The estate was called Ocean Hill. There was no ocean and there was no hill but Markus liked the name, made him feel like he was somewhere else; somewhere warm and tropical and vast. A different town, country, continent. He wandered around and purposefully got lost. He liked the feeling of being lost in a place that was no further than a mile from his house. *So near yet so far.* Having his senses jumbled. The disorientation was delicious, exciting, exhilarating. Almost like he *was* somewhere else, and was *someone* else, another boy in another life with another past. Markus revelled in the freedom of having no identity. He imagined he had a different face, different skin colour. He imagined he spoke a different language. Had a different name.

Suddenly he recognised a certain landmark, a bus shelter which led to a road he knew, which had on it a shop he went in daily. By now Markus knew where he was. He was no longer lost. No longer in his little fantasy world. Reality was here again.

Mia did a cartwheel through McDonald's and the woman at the counter told her off.

"This isn't a park."

"Free country."

"It's a public place."

"So is a park."

"Stop being cheeky or you can go."

"I've got ADHD, *chill.*"

Mel got so embarrassed when Mia started performing like this.

She could never go anywhere or do anything without her bestie acting up, showing off. Mel loathed the attention this created and put her head down.

Why can't she just be normal for once?

Markus came out the toilet and joined them. He grabbed Mia's burger and bit into it.

"Hope you washed your hands," she said with arched eyebrows, thrusting her pelvis forward.

"No," Markus said, trying to put a finger in her mouth.

Mel *hated* it when they flirted like this. It drove her mad and she wanted to scream and run out or tip a whole cup of strawberry milkshake over their heads.

Mel was next in the queue, "Big Mac Meal and a portion of chicken nuggets please."

Mel could feel Mia and Markus push and play-fight behind her.

The woman behind the counter pulled a face. "Sorry darling you're going to have to speak up."

Mel felt her face burn-up and flush red. "Like, just a Big Mac Meal and a portion of chicken nuggets please."

The woman sighed. "Darling can you tell your mates to stop messing about there's other customers here."

Mel made a half-turn and tapped Markus on the arm, "guys," she said.

"Forget it," the woman said, rolling her eyes. "What drinks do you want with that?"

"Err, like, one strawberry milkshake and one chocolate."

Seconds after the woman handed Mel her order, Markus snatched the bag from her grip, plunging his hand in and pulling out a clump of fries. He tipped his head back and opened his mouth, eyes staring up as Mel, Mia and others waiting in the queue watched the food disappear down his neck.

"Ugh ya tramp!" Mia shouted at the top of her voice, making *even more* of a spectacle out the whole thing.

Markus laughed and Mel put her head down again, inching her way to a spare table by the window. She was almost sat when Mia's piercing voice cut through the room.

"Mel, where you going?"

"Sitting here why?"

"Have you seen it outside?" Mia had her hands on her hips and her legs crossed at the ankles, revealing an impressive calf muscle.

"It's like fucking Spain out there and you wanna sit indoors. Trust *you*."

Markus suddenly switched, taking his attention off the food and putting it on his girlfriend. He took her hand and stood in front of her. "Oi, fucking leave her," he said to Mia. "If she wants to sit inside then *we're* sitting inside."

Mel smiled a bit. "Nah. Mia's right. It is a beautiful day."

Markus and Mel were looking at each other while Mia carried on talking to herself.

"I'm always right," she said, her voice fading through the glass, as she moved through the doors and stepped into the sun.

It was blazing, perfect, rare weather. A heatwave that seemed to have dropped on the town from nowhere. Yesterday was mild, if not a little overcast, yet today the sun was out in full force, burning from a cloudless sky of blue. The three teenagers walked through the Saturday streets, people idly walking by them in summer clothes and sunglasses wedged to their faces. Expressions caught between pleasure and a slight irritation at just how hot it was. Mia led the couple to a grass bank.

"We better make the most of this," she said. "Supposed to be pissing it down tomorrow."

Markus and Mel weren't listening, too busy lagging behind, whispering silly things into each other's ears; pinching, kissing, fooling around. They didn't even know Mia was there, no matter how loud and theatrical she got. Mia was background noise, at best. When she took to the grass she upped the ante, slowly rolling up her t-shirt bit by bit, settling to sunbathe, showing-off her toned, tanned stomach. Through Markus's playful embrace Mel watched her seductive ritual. She watched her with unease, the unease slowly swelling into full-blown panic. *Mia was trying to get his attention.* Only it wasn't working because her boyfriend was oblivious. He hadn't batted an eyelid. His attention was for Mel and Mel only.

The three sat on the bank and ate in silence, an uncomfortable silence. The awkwardness coming from Mia as her exhibitionism had failed to cause a reaction. She gave it a few minutes before trying a more direct approach.

"Can I ask you two something?"

Her tone alone was confrontational. The couple looked down at her from the top of the bank.

"Have you two, like, had *one* day apart since you got together?"

Markus pulled a screw-face like he didn't know what she was talking about. Whereas Mel shuffled around a bit, put her head down and shrugged.

"It's not healthy, y'know?" Mia continued, sucking up the last bit of milkshake. "Spending all that time together. Couples like that never last."

Fear flickered across Mel's face. She thought about it for a few seconds before hitting her back. "Yeah, and how would you know?" she said.

"Read it in a magazine," Mia said haughtily. "Plus, my mum told me."

Markus spat in the grass and laughed.

"What?" Mia said, opening out her hand, almost as if she was holding the fresh air like a ball.

"She's just jealous."

"Oh please," Mia said, turning the other way.

"You *are*," Markus said, mouthful of big mac.

"Of you?"

"Of *us*."

Mel kept her head down, but she knew what Markus was saying was right. Their friendship hadn't been the same since they'd got together.

"Markus you're full of shit," Mia said, posing. "If I wanted you I could have had you."

Fury kicked off in Mel's gut straight away, moving upwards inside her, through her chest, into her throat, almost like she was about the choke on it. *How fucking dare she.*

Markus was laughing.

"No Mia," he said, holding her blue eyes with his brown ones. "I could have had *you* if *I* wanted to."

Mel didn't know what that meant and she felt the rage sway towards her boyfriend now. She didn't know what any of it meant. All these head games. All these clever mind games and sly insinuations. Why couldn't people just be straight for once? Why couldn't they just speak *the truth*?

"Yeah right," Mia said, stroking her own stomach, more protectively than seductively now.

Markus was smiling an unusually large smile. "I could have had you if I wanted to and you know it. Only I wanted Mel instead."

Mel suddenly found her voice. It took hold of her, impulsively. "I am fucking sat here you know?"

That silenced both Mia and Markus, who turned and looked at her a little shocked.

Mel rarely swore. In all the years Mia had had her as a bestie she very rarely swore, if ever. It was always *eff* and *effing,* never the real word. Mia had always liked this about her, found it cute; innocent, endearing. So hearing a full *fucking* come from her shy sidekick was a peculiar thing.

"Check you out?" Mia said, moving her head around like a swan.

"I'm just saying Mia, like, like sometimes you talk like I'm not here and stuff."

Mia bounced to her feet, acting all silly and light of heart. "Bestie I'm just joking! I'm just messing. I know you and big lad there are meant to be. I'm nothing to do with it. Nothing to do with it at all. I was just playing. I'm just having a laugh. Sorry I touched a nerve."

Mel felt a flash of regret. She felt foolish and guilty yet at the same time she was still suspicious of her. Mia was clever and she was more than aware of what she was doing, the games and the power plays. Mel wasn't sharp enough to keep up and never had been. Her head was a-spin and half of the time she didn't know what was real. She looked over at Markus to see what he thought only he wasn't listening anymore, totally switched off. Too busy concentrating on a small colony of ants, which he was crushing one by one with his thumb.

"Bestie I love you," Mia said, throwing herself into the arms of Mel. "I'd never come between you and your man."

"Lesbos," Markus said.

"Anyway," Mia continued, sitting in her lap, leaning back. "Thought you were taking *him* to your mum's for dinner tonight?"

"I am."

"Then why'd you let him eat that massive big mac meal then?"

"I could eat again," Markus said, wiping a black smear of dead ants on his jeans.

Mel smiled. "He's right. Honestly Mia. He can eat like a horse."

When the three stood Mia looked Markus up and down and smiled. "Bet he's hung like one too."

The rage returned and this time her face couldn't hide it.

"Mel I'm joking, *chill.* Jesus this relationship is really sucking the life out of you. Why are you taking everything so seriously all of a sudden?"

Mel didn't answer. She was too tired by now.

The three started a slow walk towards the Clementine Channel. Over the trees the sun lowered and it had gotten a little cooler. Tomorrow's predicted downpour suddenly didn't seem like an inconceivable thing.

They cut through a small field where a gang of smaller kids were just finishing up a football match. Markus watched them while chewing a blade of grass, swaying his head.

"Can't believe you've been going out a month and you've not met my second mummy and my second sister yet," Mia said.

"You haven't got a first sister," Mel said.

"I've met them," Markus said. "In passing."

They were almost at the top of Lawson Avenue.

Mia caught Markus up and took his hand. "Hey and don't let Mel fill your head with ideas that they're this family from hell. They're nothing like that at all. They're totally lovely. Her mum is just this quirky dinosaur and her sister Adele is just this beautiful genius. She has the most beautiful hair in the world and is most definitely the brains of the family."

Mia turned her head and shot Mel with a cunning glance. In her eye was a slice of spite that Mel hadn't really noticed before. She called Mia her *bestie,* but she felt that title slowly start slip.

Markus met the Ellis family for real. They were called *Ellis* but that was her Dad's name. In fact it was her Mum's too and Markus couldn't understand why she kept it when they'd been divorced for like a hundred years or more. Mel was nervous, Markus could tell. He could also tell that Mel didn't really want him to meet them and Markus didn't either. He couldn't be bothered. Adults were all the same and meeting one more wouldn't make much difference. Her mum was a bit weird. She shook his hand which was weird and she had a weird face. A very weird face, Markus thought. Her voice was weird too, almost like a man's voice, deep, with some kind of accent, maybe Scottish or Irish or something. Markus couldn't tell. He didn't say much, just nodded at both the mum and the sis and then sat down in front of the telly. Mia was right about her sister Adele, she was pretty and smart and her hair was long and shiny but overall Markus didn't like her. She was a cocky little shit who thought she was better than everyone else. Mel sat next to him on the sofa and they watched an episode of *The Big Bang Theory*. Her sister Adele kept laughing out-loud at all the clever jokes and Markus found her irritating.

"Hear ya like footie then Markus?" her mum said, setting the table. She really did sound like a man.

Markus nodded.

"I'm a Rangers fan, me," she said.

"Oh."

"What about you?"

Markus felt Mel tense up from the squeeze in her hand. She was embarrassed. He saw the word, *cringe*.

"Liverpool," he said, at last.

"Hey they did alright last season, didn't they? Second, was it? Or was that the season before? Hey what do you reckon about Gerrard retiring?"

"Depressing, we'll never be the same again."

Mel was surprised her mum knew so much about football. She was amazed she had somehow managed to gain a little rapport with Markus. She combed some hair behind her ear with her fingers and sat up a bit.

"Why do you support Rangers anyway?" the boy asked.

"Well I'm from Glasgow originally, aye." Her mum paused, put down a bottle of ketchup on the table and let out an embarrassed laugh. "Hark at me," she said. "One mention of the homeland I'm already back saying *aye*."

Markus smiled.

"Why Liverpool anyway, from there?"

"Nah. Just my dad," Markus said, adjusting himself on the sofa. "He's always been a mad supporter so I have to be too."

"Ever been to Anfield Markus?"

Mel's head was ping-ponging between her mum and her boyfriend.

"Yeah, once."

"Who did they play?"

"Can't remember now. We won though, I think."

The four sat at the table and ate. Mel couldn't believe that Markus and Mum continued to talk, about football, school, other sports. He talked about growing up on the estate and Mum talked a little about her own upbringing. Mel had never seen Markus like this around an adult. Normally he went out of his way to be rude to them. Teachers, shopkeepers, Mia's mum. He never gave them the time of day. Mel looked over the table at her own mum like she was looking at her for the first time. The word *proud* was not too far from her mind. Adele seemed different too, like she was really paying attention for once, listening and looking at faces, instead of rolling her eyes and making clever remarks all the time. After Mum served up some ice cream for pudding and then took Markus out back to meet Babe the dog. The family pet didn't take to her boyfriend as warmly as her mother. He was cagey and wouldn't stop barking.

"Oh he's weary of you," Mum said, smiling. "New man in the house."

Markus smiled and tried to stroke him but he kept running off. Mel leaned on the wall with her arms folded, watching. It was almost dark in the back yard. A wind picked up and the full moon was out. Adele was jumping up and down the step backwards.

"Anyway Mrs Ellis, I better get going."

"Oh, alright."

"But thanks for dinner. It was nice."

"You're quite welcome. But no Mrs Ellis. Call me Erica."

"Alright Erica."

Markus put his head down and in a rare moment he seemed kind of embarrassed, if not a little vulnerable.

"And don't worry about Gerrard," Erica added. "I'm sure they'll find someone new."

"Nah," Markus said. "There's only one Stevie Gerrard."

Mel walked her boyfriend to the front door. Once there Adele came walking down the stairs towards them. The flush of the toilet still rumbling through the pipes in the walls around them. "See ya Markus," she said in a sweet voice. "Nice meeting you."

"Yeah you too Adele. See ya."

Mel felt light-headed and she suddenly got an attack of something. What if Mia was right? What if they're not the *family from hell* and all this is in my head?

What if it was me all along??

Markus broke her reverie by locking his fingers with hers and kissing her forehead, then on the lips.

"Nice family," he said.

"Ya reckon?" A ring of excitement chimed through her voice.

"Yeah they're alright. Better than mine anyway."

Mel bit her lip and bent her toes back on the carpet. "When can I meet your auntie anyway?"

"We'll see," Markus said, stepping into the night.

"Hey shall I ask mum if I can walk you back?"

"Ha."

"What?"

"Girls don't walk boys home, silly. That's not how it works."

"Oh."

"If you did then I'd have to walk you back. And then we'd spend the whole night walking back and forth between our houses."

"Might not be such a bad thing." She kissed him again.

Markus looked up. "Moon's out. It's dark."

The teenagers were looking at each other right in the eyes. Markus looked at her bad eye, the one that wasn't quite straight. I've never met a girl like this before, he thought. She's all brand new.

They kissed again and then he headed off, up along the shiny, moonlit tarmac of the cul-de-sac.

She was closing the door when he shouted one last thing. He said it fast and Mel couldn't quite tell what it was, if it was a three-syllable word or three separate ones? She was sure it was the latter, and she was pretty sure it was the three words she had been waiting for, waiting for all her life.

Markus stepped into his bungalow half an hour later. All the lights in the living room were off, just the flash of the television. Tara was sat up watching that *Kill Bill* film. He wasn't sure if it was the first one or the second. Markus preferred the first because there was less talking and more fighting. He shuffled forward and dropped into the chair next to her.

"Alright?"

Markus nodded.

He watched the film with her for a bit. It was the second Kill Bill because it was the scene at the end, the part where Bill was talking about how the difference between life and death was a goldfish flapping on the carpet, and a goldfish not flapping on the carpet.

"Hungry?"

"Nah," Markus said with a yawn. "I've eaten, twice."

"Twice?"

"Maccy D's and Mel's."

"Met her parents?"

"Yeah."

"What they like?"

"Bit weird."

Tara pulled a face. "Coming from you, that's saying something."

Markus dropped his arm off the chair and let it swing. "What do you mean?"

Tara never answered, just smiled, carrying on with the end of the film, where Uma Thurman ends Bill by the five-point-palm strike.

As the credits came up Tara coughed and cleared her throat. "So?"

"So what?"

"When are you returning the favour, when are you bringing Mel for dinner?"

Markus pulled a face like it had never occurred to him.

"When am I going to meet this special young lady?" she added.

Markus pulled another couldn't-give-a-shit face.

Tara shook her head. "Try not hurt her Markus."

"*Tut.* I know what I'm doing."

"I know," she said. "That's what I'm afraid of."

Markus wasn't really listening. He was staring into the television, even though Tara had turned it off.

There was something moving by the water. Something small. Markus squinted as he stepped down from the grassy bank, his heavy heel crushing stones into the earth. It was something alive, a living thing. It was furry and feeble and all by itself. Markus got on his hands and knees and took a closer look at the little duckling. It twitched and bobbed and then made a pained whimper that made Markus jump. He laughed out-loud, *little fucker*. He watched it some more and then stood back up to see if anyone else was around. The Channel seemed to be moving fast today, a strong current running away to his left. The duckling was now by his foot, pecking at his trainer. When it moved again he could see that it had a limp, some kind of injury to its left leg. It made another sound, this time louder, like the animal was trying to get his attention. Markus bent down again, looking at its little beak and a pair of black eyes. He put his hand on the bed of stones and was surprised to see the duckling limp right onto his palm. It stayed there. It felt weird, Markus thought. The feel of it, so warm and helpless and fragile. A soft pulse in his fingers. Its head popped out between Markus's knuckles, knuckles beat-up and misshapen from years of punching walls and busting heads.

Now what do I do?

He cupped it in both hands and tried to climb back up the bank, which was hard not having his arms for balance. Markus kept it close to his body and could feel it move around. It wasn't moving fast and wild, just little movements that tickled his skin. His next thought was hoping that no one saw him. How would he explain why he was walking like this? How would he tell someone he had rescued a baby duck from the river's edge? Markus almost dropped the thing as he let his legs carry him down the grassy hill, which ran right into the alleyway that led to Norman Close. Luckily Aunt Tars wasn't in, so he elbowed his way through the back yard, into his garden. At the bottom was a flowerbed that Tara only half-heartedly attended to. Most of the flowers and shrubbery was overgrown so Markus managed to find a little hiding place right at the back. He put down the duckling, which moved around rapidly at first, getting its bearings at the new surroundings, but it wasn't going far anytime soon. It was clearly in pain and let out a few of those screechy sounds. Now he had more space Markus observed the thing more closely. It was brownish with a darker head, two white marks near its rear. Its beak was tiny, like a fingernail. Its leg was clearly broken, an ugly swelling where the bone had come apart. When the duckling sat Markus ran to the garage and got an old skateboard he had nicked from the estate. Putting it on its side against the back wall he boxed-in the wounded animal and built a little den among the undergrowth. He padded it all down with leaves and plants. Next he wondered what the thing would eat. Markus thought about Googling this information but then remembered that his brother had taken his laptop with him.

Either way the duckling seemed happier now. It was away from the rushing water and predators that might want to eat him for lunch. He was less scared and he wasn't making those freaky sounds anymore. Markus picked it up one last time, rubbed his thumb over his tiny, papery skull. His ribcage felt like matchsticks. Never had he held anything so fragile.

In all, there were eight houses on Lawson Avenue. Markus and Mel hid in a bush, staring at the fifth one along. They were waiting for her mum and sis to go out.

"C'mon man, fucking hell."

"I know, like, they should be gone by now."

Another ten minutes went by and then a figure blurred through the vertical rectangles in the door. "That's Adele," Mel said.

Markus bit his lip and ducked lower into the bush. An ice cream van chimed away in the next street. The door opened and both mum and sister stepped out. The road was white with sun. Mum wore a turquoise t-shirt and a pair of pink shorts. Markus let out a nasal laugh. "Your mum looks gay."

"I know," Mel said, blushing a bit.

Adele wore a headband with a plastic visor on the front.

"Your sister even gayer."

"I know. Embarrassing."

The teenage couple got as low as they could. A twig was digging into Mel's side but she tried to ignore it. They listened to the footsteps until they faded. When the two looked up again they could see Adele pulling her mum in the direction of the ice cream van.

"Typical Adele. Always wanting something. Greedy bitch."

Markus smiled and shook his head. "I don't know why you hate your sis so much. She's alright, man."

"You don't know her. You've only met her like three times. She's evil."

Markus didn't understand why Mel was so ashamed of her house either. That was alright too, quite big really. She should see where I lived with dad, in the estate, then she'd know hard times. Now the coast was clear the teenage couple crept out from the bush and batted themselves down. Mel pulled her t-shirt up to see a deep scratch across her side, almost drawing blood.

"Ouch," she said through her teeth.

"Let's have a look."

Markus traced his finger along it. "Can't believe how soft your skin is."

"Tickles," Mel said, flinching away from his touch, laughing.

He did it again, chasing her down across the road. They were outside her house now.

"Hope number nine didn't see us hiding in that bush," Mel said.

"She's like a proper nosey neighbour and stuff. Doesn't miss a trick. Probably grass on us."

"Hope for her sake she doesn't," Markus said, finality in his tone.

"Why what you gonna do Big Bear?"

Markus smiled and then drew a finger quick across his neck.

Mel rolled her eyes and the two went inside.

Markus couldn't believe how soft her skin was. They started snogging more or less straight away. They snogged all the time now and couldn't get enough. They seemed to be getting good at it too, like they were really starting to get to know each other, like they had their own rhythm. Two bottles of J20 had been placed on the kitchen table but Mel and Markus had started snogging before they had a chance to open them. Snogging, necking, kissing, making out, getting off. Markus had to bend down to reach his lover's lips. At first he thought Mel opened her mouth too much so he had to slow her down and show her the way. Now it was perfect. They started gentle and then it got faster and harder. It got quite crazy and they fell over and crashed onto the sofa, which made them laugh. Markus put his hand to her face, stroked behind her ear and onto her neck.

"I like that," Mel said breathlessly.

"Do you?"

She closed her eyes and nodded dreamily. Mum and sis were on her mind, thoughts of them came in paranoid stabs. What if they've forgot something, what if they came back? She knew mum would go mad and probably ban Markus from the house for good. Markus pulled her on top of him and slipped his hand up the back of her t-shirt. He really couldn't believe how soft her skin was, how warm and smooth, so, so soft it didn't feel real. Do *all* girls have skin like this? It was as if he could put his hand through and feel inside. She must use special creams or something, Markus thought. He ran his palm and fingertips across the surface of her back, feeling the dip of her spine. Their tongues were going so crazy and for so long their jaws began to ache. When they pulled away they looked at each other, amazed by how red and swollen their mouths were.

Wild.

"J20," she said.

Mel popped them open and handed one to Markus. They drank

in silence, looking around the room impatiently, drinking kind of fast, eyes catching each other constantly. Once the beverages were done they were back on it. Markus on top of Mel this time, between her legs, kissing, kissing like mad, furious. Psychically opening their eyes at the same time, locked and staring, dizzy, fuzzy faces, breath everywhere. He was surprised how strong his girlfriend was, thin arms pulling him down, gripped on, never letting go. Markus moved his hips back and forth like he was having sex for real, sex with clothes on, dry humping. The friction was intense and he watched her face blotch-up and go blank. She looked lost, like she wasn't there anymore.

"You alright?" he said.

Her eyes nodded so he carried on, pushed on. Holding her wrists behind her head. Her body was going weird and Markus didn't know what was happening. He didn't know if he was hurting her or not. She kept tensing up and relaxing, like she was building up to something. Every time he slowed she gripped him harder, forcing him to carry on. After a while her legs began to shake a little, tiny vibrations in her hips. Markus didn't know that hard-ons could last for so long. It had been here for the last hour and he was beginning to ache. He felt damp, hot and sticky and kind of frustrated. At last they ran out of steam and collapsed back, holding each other, exhausted, out of breath. The room didn't look the same, the dimensions were all out of proportion and Mel thought she could see two of everything. She had to readjust her glasses, which were all steamed and smeary.

"That was mad," she said.

Markus agreed and held her head in his arms, kissing her hair a thousand times.

"Want another J20?" she said.

"Yeah," Markus replied, sitting up, playing with his paints. "And then you can shut that fucking dog up!"

Only now did Mel realise that Babe was barking. "You heard him?"

"It was going crazy the whole time. Didn't you hear?"

The blotches in Mel's neck were beginning to fade. She shook her head. "Nope. I didn't hear a thing."

Markus smiled. Mel smiled.

Then she disappeared into the kitchen and Markus could hear the fridge door being pulled open and the sound of two bottles clinking. By the time Mel opened the back door the dog was already quiet, the barking had stopped.

Silent.

Markus didn't see the point of giving him a name but he still felt like a pet. His walking was still a bit fucked-up but the duckling was definitely getting better. The first night Markus just chucked in whatever food he could find, as far as he knew ducks didn't have teeth so he avoided anything too tough. He threw in bread, popcorn, grapes and a crushed-up banana. He also put in a bowl of water. The next morning the bread was gone and maybe a few of the grapes. *Ha, as if he would really eat popcorn!* What Markus really needed to find was some worms. Ducks eat worms, he knew this. I see it at the Channel all the time, beaks pecking through earth, pulling up stringy things for snacks. He watched the duckling for ages. He liked watching him and found it soothing. Markus liked nature because nature didn't pretend. Nature just *was.* There was no doubt that his leg was getting better, he limped less and seemed more confident at walking. He considered making some kind of splint but thought he might end up doing more harm than good. *Let nature take its course.* When Tara came back from work he left him alone, only seeing him again once his aunt had gone to bed. He wasn't sure why he was keeping it such a secret. It didn't really matter, Tara wouldn't care; if anything she'd probably find the whole thing admirable and endearing. Maybe that's what Markus was afraid of. He didn't want the fuss. It was *his* thing, his project, his duckling.

He found a few worms and bugs, also some red berries from the bush at the bottom of his close. That evening, before Tara came back he planted a little feast for him.

"There you go mate, tuck in."

In bed Markus couldn't sleep for some reason, something was bugging him, poking at his mind. Then at two a.m. it swopped in and caught him as he was dropping off. He sat up with a gasp, like he'd just crawled out of an icy lake. *What if the berries were poisonous?* His aunt had drilled it into him for as long as he could remember. *Don't eat those red berries they'll kill you.* The warning had been embedded in his mind ever since. He even thought of it as a way of committing suicide if he ever needed to. Markus got out of bed and opened the window, imagining his little friend laying on his back, foaming at the beak. *Tried to save it but now I've killed the thing.* He threw on some clothes and climbed out, moving along the outside of the bungalow's perimeter until he was around the back. He squatted at the den and spied around the shadows, no sound or sign of him. Markus looked closer, adjusting his eyes. There he was, in the corner, unmoving. Some of the red berries were there, but some were gone. He prodded the duckling and the duckling moved. Markus let out a sigh and then laughed.

"Thought I'd killed you mate, ha. But then I should have known. You're a duck, not a human. You can eat what you want. Different digestive system and that, ha."

He picked out the red berries and flicked them away, just in case. The duckling looked up, his eyes twinkling in the dark.

"Bet you think I'm a mad-head, don't ya? Ha."

Markus thought he saw the animal nod.

"Anyway I better get back to bed," he said. "Better get some sleep. Gotta see my girl tomorrow. Taking her to the cinema for the first time although I don't really know what to see. I know she likes those Twilight films so I better find something with vampires in. Anyway mate, I'm going now. See you in the morning."

Talking to the duckling reminded him of when he used to talk to his Mongoose BMX all those years ago. Overall Markus had probably had more conversations in his life with things that couldn't talk back. He was beginning to fall asleep when something woke him up again. *Rain. What if it rains? Really I should have built some kind of shelter, some kind of canopy!*

Markus laughed at how ridiculous he was being.

Ducklings live on water. They don't care about rain. And they don't care about red berries either. Just go to sleep. Go to ...

Mel and Markus, and most of the time Mia too, ate at McDonald's. And also Greggs, Burger King, Subway, Noodle Bowl, Cookie Jar, Wimpy and Kimble Snacks. Over the summer Markus had gained a bit of a belly, Mel too. Mia never put on an ounce of fat no matter how much junk she tipped down her neck. It wasn't fair. Life wasn't fair.

The three would hang out, sit in the park and put all their money together. See how much they could afford. Mia always had the most to contribute, Mel hardly any, and Markus always found a way of turning up with something although the other two never knew how.

I have ways, he said with a wink. Even though they'd been going out nearly two months Mel still found Markus a complete mystery. He never gave anything away, and she still hadn't been to his house, met his auntie or his brother or anyone in his life. There was so much she didn't know but every now and then secrets would slip through unexpectedly.

Once some rough kids came over on their bikes and shouted, hey we know what you did to Crip! Markus had to chase them off with a stick.

"What are they talking about?" Mel said. "Who's Crip?"

"Just some bullshit rumour that's going around."

"Tell me."

"It's nothing."

"C'mon."

"I said forget it."

When Markus got this look in his eye she knew not to push it. There was a short temper he had lost his grip of on a few occasions. Once when some boys jumped the queue in McDonald's and once when Mia tried to humiliate Mel in front of a group of Goth kids. He'd rear up in seconds and silence everything around him. Mel found this scary but protective too, especially the time with Mia. No one had really stuck up for her before and it felt kind of nice. As long as this rage wasn't directed at her, Mel strangely liked it. She found it a turn-on. Most of the time he was sweet, playful, moving around without a care in the world. Nothing but Mel. He loved her; she could tell. She could tell by the way he looked at her and the way he touched her, by the way he talked to her. It's like they had their own world that no one knew about. Like an energy kind of a thing, Mel would say.

They text constantly, sometimes frantically, smiles glued to their faces, staring at their phones like zombies, falling over their thumbs, numb to the outside world.

Mel get off that phone. You've been on it for three hours straight! It's not healthy!

Markus your dinner's getting cold.

So many texts they couldn't keep up, as one beep would finish another would arrive, so many they would lose the thread of conversation. Senseless language but that didn't matter, as long as they were here; connected, linked, together. Even though they saw each other every day Mel would still experience that dopamine rush every time she heard that buzz and saw his name flash on her screen. Markus felt just as crazy. When they were apart he would try to guess where her mind was, what she was thinking about. He'd *feel* her doing the same things he was throughout the day, showering, eating, using the toilet, feeling horny, hungry, tired, excited, sick in love.

He thought about introducing her to his aunt so she could stay with him, sleep over. He imagined cuddling up to her all night, talking, whispering, wrapped up, arms in arms and legs in legs, two hearts beating together as one. He pictured a sweet sexual bliss, laying naked in these summer nights. He knew Tara would let them, *eventually*. He had a way of wrapping his auntie around his finger and he knew he could win her over, *in time*. Tara wouldn't be the problem; Mel's mum would be. Erica Ellis had always been cool with Markus, on the four or five times they'd met. Only behind closed doors she was different, according to Mel anyway. She was supposed to be dead-strict, spiteful, a religious nut who would not let the couple be alone together. Markus hadn't seen any evidence of this so he wasn't entirely sure. We'll cross that bridge when we come to it, he thought.

"Show me your bedroom then," he said.

They had snuck into her house again while mum and sis were out. Right away he could see his how nervous his girlfriend was. It flickered across her face and he saw the words, *oh no*. Was now the time? The time to take her virginity away. They'd had this conversation. They talked about it at length like they talked about everything. I want the time to be right, she said. I want it to be special. I don't want to be worrying about mum coming back and catching us. I don't want there to be any pressure. I want losing *our* virginity with each other to be sacred. *Our*. Markus didn't mean to lie to Mel. It just sort of happened. It just sort of happened because he had quite literally forgot. Forgotten that he had had sex before. Sex with that retarded girl last year. He had even forgotten the girl's name. Something beginning with a C, I think? It had completely slipped his mind because Markus didn't really think about the past. So when Mel asked him if he was still a virgin he said, *yes*. Her face lit up and he could see how happy she was, how glad and relieved that she was going to be *his* first too. It was only an hour or so later that he remembered, *oh yeah*. I have had sex before. I'm not a virgin after all. Markus thought about telling her, coming clean. Only he had seen how happy she looked, how pleased. Telling her now will ruin that. It will also catch me out as a liar. Best keep shtum. It was said and done so Markus didn't feel the need to make a U-turn and go back on it. We'll keep it like this, he thought. What she doesn't know, won't hurt her.

They were in her bedroom and Markus could tell that now was not the time. He could *feel* that Mel wasn't ready so he stayed away from her.

"You share with your sis?"

Mel nodded.

Markus looked at the two beds. "Bet yours is the one by the window?"

Mel nodded again. Her arms were folded.

"I'm psychic," he smiled.

"More like psycho."

He realised there was no carpet under his feet. The floorboard creaked.

"You should have taken your shoes off," she said. "Mum finds footprints everywhere."

He smiled again, looking around the room.

"It's a bit babyish I know," she said. "But like, most of this stuff is Adele's anyway."

Markus looked at a basket full of colouring books and toys. He picked up a figure from the pile. "Who's this?" he said.

"Jesus."

"What?"

"Mum and Adele go to church. Midweek Club it's called. It's kind of gay."

"You don't believe in any of that crap do you?"

Mel shook her head. "What about you? Do you believe in god?"

"I *am* god," Markus said, laughing.

"Whatever."

Markus looked at a *Minions* poster on the wall. "You can relax. I'm not going to try and have sex with you y'know."

He felt Mel breathe out and relax.

"Good," she said. "Not here. It wouldn't be right."

"Why? Do you think god is looking down on us?"

"You know what I mean."

"I know what you mean."

He stepped up towards her and took her hands, kissed them both, one at a time. "It'll happen when it happens. There's no rush. We have all the time in the world."

Mel looked at Markus. "You always know."

"Know what?" he said.

"Know *exactly* what to say and when to say it."

"Told you," Markus said with a shrug. "I'm god."

She rolled her eyes and poked him in the stomach. He winced and took her in his arms. "Wanna go Maccy's?" he said.

"No dollar."

"I got a bit. Maybe enough for a shake each."

"Cool." She nodded.

"Shall we text Mia?"

"Nah."

"You know she'll go mad if she finds out we've been without her."

"Fuck her."

Markus let out a wild laugh. "Since when did you swear?"

Mel shrugged and smiled and then panicked a bit, as she swore she'd just heard the front door go.

What the hell is he up to now? Tara thought, watching her nephew pace the back garden. She stood back from the kitchen window and continued to watch. He kept disappearing into the little garden at the back of the yard, ducking down low to his hands and knees. He was looking for something, in that, he'd *lost* something. The first word that shot to Tara's mind was *drugs*. He was stashing and selling drugs. Made sense. All that money he seemed to have last summer and now he was up to the same tricks. She moved behind the fridge, making sure she was hidden. Now he was talking to himself, the sound of his voice drowned out by the double-glazing, "Where are you, where the fuck are you mate?"

Mate?

Tara pulled a face. A knot of confusion crumpling her expression.

Where are you, *mate?*

If it was drugs then why was he talking to it like it was a real person?

Markus was looking everywhere, along the walls, down by the bush, in plant pots and over next door's fence. He stood in the centre of the lawn with his hands on his head, exasperated.

When he caught his aunt's face through the window his face dropped and he started acting normal. Came back inside, making a feint yawn.

"Alright Tars?" he said naturally.

"I am," she said, drying a fork. "You?"

"Yep," he said, drumming on the worktop.

"Lost something?"

"What? No. Yeah just looking for my football. Fancied a kick about."

"Oh," she said.

That could explain it but she doubted it. She looked closely at her nephew's eyes. There was a rare pain there, a strain, concern. He was preoccupied.

"Mel still coming tomorrow?"

"Uh-huh," Markus said, nodding. He was sat on a barstool Tara had not long purchased, spinning around in circles and half-circles.

"You looking forward to it?" she said.

"Uh-huh."

His mind was elsewhere, she could tell.

"Be good to finally meet her."

"Alright then stop going on about it Tara."

"I'm just saying."

"You're building it up more than it needs. Just let it be."

"All-*right.*"

They shared a long silence in the kitchen. Tara drying and putting away the rest of the pots. Markus, staring into space.

"Anyway," Tara said. "Your brother is going to be coming back home soon."

This burst Markus's daydream. "Oh fuck."

"Markus!"

He let out a large sigh and shook his head.

"Well he does live here."

"Thought he'd moved in with that other bandit."

Tara stopped what she was doing and faced the boy, hands on hips. "You need to stop that kind of talk. You're not living with your dad anymore y'know?"

A bored expression dulled Markus's face, putting his eyes on the ceiling.

"You want to live like a philistine then you can go and move in with the rest of the Venner arseholes."

Markus didn't like that. He was ready to kick-off but Auntie Tara beat him to it.

"Just be nice," she said.

He spun around a few more times on the barstool.

"What does philistine mean?" he said.

Tara smiled. "It means just that."

"Just what?"

"The fact you don't know."

Markus didn't care, his mind had moved onto something else: that his brother was back which meant his laptop was too.

Tara put the kettle on. She thought about adding that Ryan was delicate about the break-up so Markus should tread carefully, only she didn't want to give him any more ammunition. Markus was still preoccupied, thinking, standing up every once in a while to look outside. Tara didn't have a clue what was going on or what he was looking for.

"I'm going out," he suddenly said.

"Where?"

"Channel."

"What for?"

"Find something."

"What?"

Tara didn't get her answer, just a closing of the front door.

She was small, not short, but small. There was something fragile about her, Tara thought, delicate, gentle. She had her head down most of the time. Kept adjusting her glasses every time she looked up. Much prettier than she had anticipated, much more timid too. Tara tried a little conversation but Mel was just way too shy to talk. Tara didn't mind. She didn't mind the girl only giving her one-word answers. She could see that it was through nerves rather than rudeness. She could see she was a good kid, sweet, self-conscious, maybe a little sad inside too.

Overall Tara liked her. Although she was struggling to picture her with Markus, as a couple. They didn't seem like a match. Not at all. It seemed an unlikely pairing for a teenage first love.

"Got any brothers or sisters Mel?"

"Sister."

"What's her name?"

"Adele."

"Do you get on?"

Mel said nothing.

Markus wished Tara would shut the fuck up and leave her alone, analysing her in that know-all clever way of hers. He never wanted this stupid meal anyway. Why was it so important to meet parents and win them over and fit in? Markus hated adults and their stupid rules. He just wanted to get to sixteen so he could move out and live his own life, put all this crap behind him.

"Markus tells me you like the Twilight films?"

Mel put her head up and looked at Tara in the eye for the first time, smiled for the first time too. She nodded her head quite emphatically. "Do you?" she said.

Tara was a little flawed by how big and beautiful her smile was. It seemed to come out of nowhere and beam across the table. She was also taken aback that the girl had turned the same question onto her.

"Erm ... I don't think I've watched any of them Mel, not all the way through anyway."

Mel was excited all of a sudden. "You should. You should watch them. There's more to it than you think. It's kind of like another world and stuff. You'd like it."

Mel brushed some hair behind her ear and then began to eat properly, rather than just play with it like she had been doing. It's like bringing the Twilight films into the conversation had suddenly put some life into her. Tara could now see them as a couple. There was more to Mel than meets the eye, she thought. The girl was strange, intriguing.

Another thing that was peculiar, Tara noticed, was that Mel seemed to *vibrate*. At first Tara thought she was seeing things, or maybe that it was the lighting of the room, but when she looked really closely at Mel she seemed to have this shimmering effect, a quiver. She noticed this more when she looked at her hair, a strand of it curled out and seemed to blur, almost like it was a spring that had been flicked. Tara had no idea what this was. It was odd.

"Want me to help with the dishes?" she said, after the meal.

Tara's first instinct was to say the done-thing; *no it's fine, you sit.*

But Markus had already disappeared into the lounge and put the telly on, so Tara thought this would be a good opportunity to have some alone time with the girl.

"Yeah, okay. Thanks Mel."

"I like washing pots anyway," she said, stepping in front of the sink, which surprised Tara as she assumed the girl was going to dry.

"Oh. Do you?"

Mel rolled up her sleeves and plunged her hands into the water. "Yeah, cos like, it's quite soothing, like a meditation kind of a thing."

"Yes," Tara said, again a little perplexed by the randomness in which the young girl spoke. "I suppose it is. Do you always wash the pots at home?"

Mel didn't answer, she just stared into the sink, looking at her hands covered in soap. "The bubbles are kind of amazing too don't you think? If you look really closely, you can like see all these swirly colours and stuff. Look … "

She held a hand up to Tara's face.

"Oh yeah," the auntie said, noticing it for the first time.

They washed the rest of the pots in silence. The two stood side by side and the quiet didn't feel strained, but rather natural and easy. Towards the end Tara spoke.

"Oh. Apologies for Ryan earlier, you know, not wanting to eat with us. He's just feeling a little down at the moment."

"That's okay," Mel said, drying her hands, adjusting her glasses once again. "What's wrong with him?"

Tara untied her hair and then retied it, talking with the hairgrip between her teeth. "He's a little broken-hearted," she said with a sympathetic wink.

"Oh. Did his girlfriend leave him?"

The question gave Tara a little blank in the brain and she didn't quite know how to answer that. She assumed Markus would have told her.

"Yes," she said, an uneasy break in her voice. "Something like that."

"Oh," Mel said. "Well, like, I hope he gets over it and stuff."

"I'm sure he will Mel."

They looked at each other and smiled. The eye contact went on and something passed between them, something good. It was like they were meeting each other properly. This was broken by noise in the next room. Markus was banging around moodily, making exaggerated movements, letting the bungalow know, he was getting impatient.

"What the fuck were you two talking about anyway?"

Markus was walking her home along the channel.

"Couldn't we have like, walked the street way?" Mel said. "At night this place is creepy."

Markus was pulling her and walking fast. It was pitch-black and it was almost as if he could see in the dark, like he knew the route like the back-of-his hand. There was just the sound of his heavy foot trampling through the grass in front of him. Mel felt they were walking a little too close to the water and she was scared.

"I said what were you two so cosy about anyway? What were you talking about in the kitchen?"

"We was, like talking about your brother."

Markus went quiet for a few moments before asking the next question. "What did she say?"

"Just, just that he was heartbroken and stuff."

Markus left it alone, said no more. Eventually Mel's eyes got accustomed to the dark. They weren't as close to the water as she first thought. She was still confused as to why they had to walk this way, along uneven paths and through long grass, stopping every five minutes to climb those annoying bridleway gates. Made no sense when they could have just walked through the lighted streets.

She followed Markus.

To her right she thought she could make out the dark outlines of a horse in the depths of a field.

When they reached Lawson Avenue he let go of her hand. He seemed bothered by something although Mel didn't know what.

"I like your aunt."

Markus didn't say anything.

"She's special, I can tell."

Markus pulled a screw-face. "Yeah, special needs," he said.

"No I mean it," she said. "I *feel* it. She reminds me of someone. She reminds me of my old foster mum."

That was the first time she had ever mentioned that to him, first time she had ever mentioned that to anyone. Mel thought Markus may ask about it.

He didn't.

"Your mum's waiting," he said.

Mel turned around and looked at the house. "Where?"

"The curtain just moved."

"I hate living there. The thought of going back in makes me depressed."

Markus didn't say anything.

Mel looked down at a piece of mud on her trainer. "Are you alright?"

"Yeah why?"

"You didn't seem right tonight, like, not your usual self and stuff."

Markus looked at the black starless sky, then back at her face.

"I just prefer it when we're alone. I don't like it when adults are around. I just prefer it when there's only us. No one else."

"Aww Big Bear."

She put herself into his arms and he wrapped her up, feeling her head nestled on the ledge of his chest bone. The curtain flickered again and her mum's face was now clear in the window.

Markus stared at her, until she was gone.

Mel

Dear S.E.D,

First off, I NEED to apologise to You BIG TIME for like not writing inside You and stuff. Like I know it's been ages. Like, it must have been AT LEAST Two Months or more … ? So I am, like, really, really, so, so sorry and stuff. But like, The Truth is I've Fallen in Love. And quite literally My WHOLE Mind has been taken by THAT and writing in THIS Self-Esteem Diary hasn't even occurred to me once. And I think tbh it's cos I haven't NEEDED to, which can only be a Good Thing, right?

So …

Don't take it personally and stuff. Cos at The End of The Day, even though I call You A Friend … You are Officially only plastic and paper and ink and stuff, whereas Markus is an Actual Human Being, made up of skin and bones and blood and stuff. So really, he is ALWAYS going to come Out On Top if You really think about it …

Anyway.
Either way.

mum just went flippin mental when she caught Markus in my bedroom, like she just TOTALLY flipped only she didn't do this in front of him, (of course). In front of him she acted all cool and that. Like you couldn't even tell anything was wrong. She's always polite and nice in front of other people. She carried on talking to Markus like she wasn't upset, carried on talking to him about football, being all friendly. But The Second I came back that evening she flipped-out. HOW DARE YOU SNEAK YOUR BOYFRIEND IN HERE WHILE I'M OUT. SO FUCKING DISRESPECTFUL. She put her weirdo face up to mine, spitting like a crazy rabid dog. Did you have sex, she said? Did you have sex in your OWN sister's room? It's my room as well, I said. So you did have sex in there you dirty bitch! No I didn't. I put my hands over my ears and ran upstairs. I could hear her weirdo muffly voice going on about being pregnant and stuff. I DIDN'T DO NOTHING, I shouted back. I slammed the door but she kicked it open and The Thing nearly came off its hinges. Don't you dare sneak him in here again, she said. Otherwise I'll stop you from seeing him. GOT IT?!

I lay on the bed and tbh I'm not gonna Lie but I didn't care anymore. Love gets You like that. Makes you all dumb and numb to The Outside World, like an anaesthetic kind of a thing.

mum still had to try and get The Last Laugh in though. Cos there was some pictures of me in the living room that I had made her take-down before Markus ever came over, pictures when I was a kid and stuff. Awful, grotesque pictures of me looking all hideous and horrible. mum had taken them down, but the Next Time he came over I saw she had sneaked them back up. Although Markus didn't notice them. He didn't even look at them once. So really the joke was on her!

Ha.

It was my 14TH bday in June and mum and sis got me a new mountain bike which wasn't so bad. It was pink and girlish and a bit too small but I liked it all the same. mum also got me some cool clothes which I was dead-surprised at cos normally she hasn't got a clue, no taste at all. My Bestie Mia bought me the ENTIRE Twilight Box-set which I was just thrilled about. I have the First One and the Third One lying around somewhere but to have them ALL in an Actual Collection is just the best EVER. I keep meaning to show them to Markus only we always end up snogging instead and never get round to it.

He. Ha. Eeeeek.

Markus actually didn't get me Anything for my bday. I mean he got me like A Girlfriend Card with the words MY GIRLFRIEND on which was TOTALLY cute but he didn't get me An Official Present. But to tell You The Truth I don't mind. I don't care. Cos tbh there are more important things in life than Things, more important things than Stuff and Objects and Goods. Emotions and Feelings and Love and Cuddles are WAY more important and when it comes to THAT I am Officially The Richest Girl in The World cos Big Bear gives me LOADS.

He's also a TOTAL gentleman too cos he's been so patient and respectful when it comes to The Virginity Thing. Not once has he pushed or been pushy or tried his luck and stuff. And I really do believe that he's not like other boys at all. It's like he can read when I *feel anxious or when I want him to Slow Down and stop cos he just does, without me even needing to tell him. It's like he has this weird Nature-Feeling that can read my brain and body and stuff. And he doesn't even fall under Mia's spell either, which is like TOTALLY rare cos ALL The Boys do. Even though it's the height of summer and she practically walks around with nothing on his attention is always on ME. Which is weird cos in the summer I hate my bod more than EVER cos people can see more and it makes me feel uneasy and stuff. Mia wears less whereas I want to wear more. She loves her bod whereas I hate mine. Yet Markus says he prefers me and he even says that in front of her, which she hates.*

I think what I'm trying to say Self-Esteem Diary is that I've Officially met The Boy of My Dreams.

His bday is next month and I'm going to buy him something extra special.

He never talks about The Past. He doesn't talk about The Future either.

He doesn't remember people's names and he gives them strange nicknames.

Sometimes he says Racist Things and I don't like that but most of the time it feels like an accident.

He's the biggest boy in the school.

He's fat and fit at the same time, like a wrestler.

His eyebrows almost touch, like a wolf.

His hair is the best.

He very rarely smiles, if ever, when he does it looks too big for his face.

I wish he'd smile more.

I wrote a kind of a poem for him once:

Big Bear,
He feels the sun warm through his good head of hair.
It makes his scalp tingle fair.
I squint at the same time cos I care.
It's like the world has ended, and there's just us two there.

I know it's a bit crappy and stuff but it's just how I feel, like a summer kind of a thing.

I'll tap three times on your window, he said.

Where will we go? I said.
Just sleep, he said.
Where? I said.
By the Channel, he said.
All romantic and stuff?
Yeah.
Okay.
What time does ya sis fall asleep?
Bout nine, maybe ten.
I'll come at ten.
Kay.
You got a sleep bag?
Don't know, I mean no. I might have somewhere.
Just bring your duvet.
Kay.
I'll tap three times on your window and then you come and climb out your bathroom.
It's a big drop.
Nah. You got that outhouse under it.
Oh yeah.
Ha.
Ten o'clock?
Ten.
Kay.
Don't fall asleep.
I won't.

I watched Adele fall asleep about half-nine but then I got dead-tired too, and tbh I'm not gonna Lie but I felt my eyes begin to go. I looked at my watch and it said twenty-to-ten and I wondered if I was even gonna make it. I got this Habit Thing where I have to straighten up my bed and I'd already done that but I thought about doing it again but I didn't want to wake My Sister Adele up. Twenty minutes later he was there, here. Heard his light tap come three times on my window. I got excited Straight Away. Grabbed my duvet and dragged it to the bathroom. Saw his pink face through the blur of the window. Opened it up and met him there. He was squat sideways, holding onto the windowsill with both hands. Beautifulness, he said, and then leaned in and kissed me. Even though he's like kissed me a trillion times, tonight felt different. A new kind of electricity. He took the duvet off me and I was kind of embarrassed cos like it had Minions on and I thought that was dead-babyish but he didn't seem to care. Took my hand and helped me climb out the window. He was right. The drop wasn't big at all and I could just pretty much step down. I had got mum to keep Babe in the kitchen tonight which was good cos if he was outside he would be barking his stupid head off. I still had my PJ's on and Markus thought it looked cute, especially wearing trainers as well. To me it felt weird and I laughed out loud. Shush, Markus said. We must be like ghosts. What a weird thing to say, I thought. We opened the gate and sneaked out the back yard, cut through the alleyway which lead to the field, which lead to the Clementine Channel. Again it was spooky and stuff and I could never do this on my own. I imagined mum asleep and sis asleep and all the neighbours asleep and Mia asleep and everyone asleep. I told this to Markus and he just laughed in my face. No they won't, he said. It's only half past ten. Oh, I said. We walked along the water for about five minutes and then Markus pulled my hand and lead me to the right, through some bushes and suddenly the dark was gone and light was here. Candles flickering through the black. It almost took my breath away. What's this, I said. Big Bear never said nothing, just lead me there. A shiny black sleeping bag was opened up in the grass, surrounded by these little candles. Next to them was some food and drinks, like bags of crisps and chocolate and a sandwich and two bottles of pop. Markus was smiling his head off, and he sat and crossed his legs. Wow, I said. This really is dead-romantic and stuff. I put my duvet next to his. I looked around and it looked like magic, like something from a film, or a dream. I could hear the water rushing and could see a bit of it gleaming through the trees. You did all this for me, I said? Again he never answered, just took my hand. We lay back and looked at the stars and I'm not gonna Lie but it was probably like My Official Happiest Moment EVER. We didn't eat the food or drink the drink but just started kissing instead, only this time the kissing was different, real different. Like I knew what This Kissing meant. We kissed and we lay down and we took our clothes off and not once did I even feel nervous or ashamed of my body. And not once was I scared of him hurting me. Cos Big Bear was the most gentle creature ever. He kissed me again and I knew that NOW was the time. I held him tight, feeling it begin to happen. Now it was happening. IT happened. It was Officially inside me. He was inside me and I felt him there, everywhere. Everywhere, everywhere. And they always say that your First Time was like dead-crappy and stuff but mine wasn't. I gasped and the Night and the World and Heaven and Markus soared right through me and made my mind stop. Made it stop so like all The Pain and The Problems of The Past just went away forever. I was having sex with my BF for like the very First Time. When he moved, everything moved. Like the trees and the water and the moon and the earth and the summer, all moving as one, inside of me. I felt like I could see all colours too, like green and blue and red and orange and black and silver and yellow and stuff. I don't know how long it lasted cos like time didn't seem to exist anymore. I just closed my eyes and kept them closed. I felt my blood move, like waves of a sea, motion and circles and spirals and stuff. It's like he'd been here before, done this before. He stopped moving and the feelings stopped but he was still inside me, slowly coming away, away from me. But even when he was outside he still held me tight, still held my body and stuff, like for ages and that. We was silent, silent and breathing, side by side, looking up into the blue-black star sky. His hand and my hand, fingers locked, palms pressed. It was weird cos I was totally naked but still warm. Like it was the perfect temperature, cool but snug, free but still wrapped-up. Like nature had put an invisible sheet over my skin. I imagined it's what babies felt like. Then I felt the rain, and saw the rain too, cos like it floated down in little particles and seemed to melt right into me. I put my glasses back on so I could see it all properly, the speckles of rain were so light and fine they seemed to drift horizontally, like feathers swaying, lower and lower. When they landed on my face it felt kind of hot, like a pins n' needles kind of a thing.

What time does your sis wake? He said from nowhere.

What?

It was the First Thing he said after Our Time and I thought it was a bit weird and wrong. Like why would you even mention My Sister Adele at a time like this??

Erm, I dunno, normally before me.

What about your mum?

She's the earliest.

We can't be too late, he said.

But we just got here, I said.

We've been here for two hours, he laughed.

Oh.

You're tired, you sleep. I'll wake you when it's time.

358

What about you?

What about me?

Aren't you tired?

He lowered his face and kissed my eyes shut.

I was asleep by the time he took his lips back. ZZZzzzzzzzzzzzzzzzzzzzzzzzzzzzzzzzzzzzzzzzzzzzzzzzzzzzzzzzzzz zzzzzzzzzzzzzzzzzzzzzzzzzzzzzzzzzzzzzzzzzzzzzzzzzzz when he did wake me I didn't know where I was. Things didn't look the same now. It was all light and creepy and murky and bizarre. C'mon, he said. It's dawn. All the stuff had been packed away and he had me on my feet. My eyes hurt and my head was made of wool. What about the stuff, I said? I'm coming back for that, he said. Right now we need to get you home. I can't remember walking this far the night before. Getting home took me ages. We were back on Lawson and to my gate. My flower was still tingling and stuff was pouring out and I didn't quite know what it was. My whole body felt new, different, changed, alive. He had my bum in his hands and was pushing me up the outhouse, through the window, back into my house. In the bathroom and it was like I'd never left. Like the WHOLE thing was a dream, made-up, not real and stuff. Markus Big Bear was smiling right at me. We did it, he said. I nodded and felt kind of embarrassed. He went to leave but I caught his wrist. Beautifulness, he said, you need to get back in bed your mum will be up soon! Can I ask you something, I said? I wasn't even sure myself what was about to come from my mouth. You sure it was your First Time too? I said. He paused and looked down, then right back at my face. We were glowing a light green colour from the rising sun on the bathroom walls.

Course, Baby, course you were.

I liked him saying that and we kissed.

Then he was gone.

Back in bed and stuff was really starting to leak out like I was pissing but without the pissing feeling. I thought maybe that's just what happens when you have It for the First Time. I went back in the bathroom and mopped it up with tissues and then flushed it all away. The flush made My Sister Adele turn in the bed. I was no way near tired so I just watched her sleep. She was restless and seemed to be moving around a lot. She turned more, moved, twisting. I leaned in and saw her face twitch, like she was dreaming. She calmed down a bit but then started again. This time more, like she was having a full-blown nightmare. My Sister Adele was having a horrible time on the Other Side and I knew I had to wake her from it. Adele wake up, I said, she was crying now so I grabbed her arm and shook it but still she wouldn't wake so I did it harder and harder until she did. She screamed in my face and I'm not gonna Lie but it really frightened me too and I jumped back. She was white and shaking and looking around the room. It's alright, I said, you were like nightmaring and stuff. I was freaked out cos I had never seen my Sister Adele like this before. She was always so strong and in control and I didn't know how to deal with it. Just watched her with my mouth open, watched her until Reality came back.

It was awful, she said. So real, so terrifying.

What happened?

She looked so scared I wasn't sure I even wanted to find out myself.

Someone was on top on me, she said. Her eyes were wide with the memory of it. He was pinning me down, she went on, and I couldn't move, couldn't breathe ...

She dived into my arms and that freaked me out too. Cos, like, she had never done this before. She hugged me to tight and it felt dead-nice. Cos like, she had never needed me before. Cos like, even though I'm the older big sister I had always felt like the little one. Having this protective feeling was all brand-new. She was in my arms for ages, until we could hear mum start to get up, and even then I still carried on holding her. Her famous, long, hazel hair was all over me and for the First Time ever, I actually quite liked it.

A History of Feelings

Markus

He liked to lay on top of his bed with the light off but the curtains open. He enjoyed watching squares of light slide across his walls and over his ceiling every time a car passed outside. He found it soothing, hypnotic. It made him think, not-think, switch-off. It made Markus drift away.

It was almost September and he knew what this meant. It meant the summer holidays were almost over. No more late nights or lay-ins. No more doing what you want. No more long sunny days of freedom and peace. It meant going back to school. He was about to start year ten. Another year ahead. Markus was dreading it. Thinking about school put an angry feeling at the pit of his stomach, which always lead to an eventual headache. Markus *hated* school. He loathed it. He detested the teachers, the pupils, the rules, the homework, bells ringing in your ears; another lesson, another classroom, another bossy teacher in front of another group of sniggering kids. Sometimes Markus wanted to destroy the whole thing. Plant a bomb somewhere and blow it all up. He got this idea after watching documentaries on American school massacres on his brother's laptop. His favourite one was Columbine, which happened two years before he was born. He'd forgotten the killers' names but they were crazy bastards who said *fuck life*. One was supposed to be a psychopath and the other was depressed and then one day they just decided that *enough was enough*. They got a bag of bombs and guns and went into school one April day and killed the whole lot. In fact they only manged to kill thirteen, twelve kids and one teacher, before turning the guns on themselves. They were supposed to kill more but the bombs didn't go off as planned. Something went wrong. The documentary said that if they had have gone off then more than a hundred would have died. That part always disappointed Markus. The story was big with just thirteen, imagine a hundred! Markus thought about his own school, The Kitts Academy. He thought of all the teachers and kids he'd take down first. He played it all through his head, *exactly* how it would go down. He'd get them in assembly, take them out in the main hall, come in from the front entrance and then corner them, trap them, before spraying them all with several rounds of bullets. Wow. What a rush. If only you could get guns easier in this country, Markus thought. After his daydreams about massacres Markus remembered his little duckling and wondered where he had gone that day. He half-suspected some revenge by his gay-boy brother for revealing his *secret*. He thought about it long and hard before dismissing the notion. *Nah, it wasn't in him to do something like that.* Duckling just got strong and moved along. I did my part, Markus thought. I saved him. Markus then moved his mind onto his older brother Ryan. After *that day* his dad had pretty much disowned him, didn't want to see him or be around him. He found the whole thing *sick, ill, disgusting.* He's no son of mine. *Not natural* he said. It's Adam and Eve not Adam and Steve! Markus found it pretty gross too but he couldn't understand why his dad hated it so much. He literally thought it was the same thing as having a disease, like cancer or something. Then one day Markus overheard Tara and Ryan talking. They didn't think he was in because he had started using his bedroom window as a front door. That way he could sneak in and out without being asked a thousand questions about where he was going or where he'd been.

"You might not know this about your dad, Ryan, but he was abused as a kid."

The sentence stopped Markus dead in his tracks, who was on his way to the kitchen to get a drink. He crept back and stood near the glass door, not believing his ears.

"What?" There was shock in Ryan too, saying the word *what* had taken his breath away.

"You can't ever say anything," Tara said in a low voice.

"I won't," Ryan whimpered.

"Especially not to Markus."

"Definitely not." There was a venom to Ryan that Markus found surprising. "I'll never tell him anything *ever again.*"

Markus wanted to laugh; just how dramatic the gay-boy was.

"I don't know the details," Tara said. "But I think it was pretty bad."

Markus put his ear closer to the wood wall.

"You mean, like sexual abuse?" Ryan said.

Tara must have nodded her head.

"Shit," Ryan whispered.

Markus could visualise his brother all teary and wide-eyed. "By who?" he muttered.

"A family member, I think. Like I said I don't really know the details."

"How do you know this?"

Markus couldn't believe how gay Ryan was being. Now it was just him and Tars it's like he was being extra gay, over-the-top gay.

"Your mum told me," Tara said. "Years ago."

Hearing his mum being mentioned put a sudden shiver through his spine. It was like she was here, watching over him. She hadn't been talked about in ages and it put Markus on edge, made him feel low and uneasy.

"What I'm saying Ryan," Tara said. "Is that there's a reason for everything in life. The way people are, the way they think. It doesn't just come out of the blue. It's normally because of something that's happened in the past."

"So you're saying that dad hates me because he was abused?"

"He doesn't hate you Ryan, he's just scared of you."

Markus suddenly stepped on a floorboard that creaked. The sound silenced the other two in the next room. In his mind he saw their faces, big eyes, panic. Markus quickly tiptoed soundlessly to his room, before sneaking out his window. In no time he was out the driveway, the close, up to his Thinking Place. The Clementine Channel.

Dad abused? What a load of shit, Markus thought. Typical Tara, trying to smooth things over by one of her fanciful stories of the past.

Markus didn't believe a word.

Markus Venner back in his bedroom, staring at his wall and the slow square lights sliding across. Now he thought of his mum. Wondered what she would think. Wondered what she would think about *all this*. Sometimes he felt her, especially when he was up to no good. He felt the ghost of his mum get angry with him. If he ever hurt himself, cut his finger by accident or fell off his bike, he felt that she was here, speaking to him, letting him know that she was pissed off with his behaviour. He felt her most whenever there was a storm. There she is, he would think. Up above in the slashes of electricity and the rumbling force of thunder. *There she is.* He missed his mum even though he didn't really know her, couldn't even remember her face anymore. It was such a long time ago. I was five years old, I think, maybe six. No memories really, just those flashbacks of her putting a coat around my shoulders. In fact there was one memory he had although it wasn't a good one. She was taking him to nursery one morning and Markus wouldn't behave. He was playing up, throwing himself around, wouldn't put his coat on. It was windy and Markus kept thrashing around while she was trying to zip him up. He pulled at the coat and the zip caught her finger, drawing blood. Having a temper his mum smacked his legs but it didn't hurt and the boy just laughed in his mother's face. Eventually the coat was on and Markus went into nursery. Every morning Markus would go inside and wave at his mum through the window. Because of the drama Markus doubted that she would be there this morning but she was. Smiling at the window like nothing happened. Only Markus didn't respond the same way. On instinct he drew a fist and put it up to the glass. The hurt on his mum's face shocked him. She opened her mouth and looked like she was ready to cry, before walking away, into the wind, disappearing into a sea of other mums. Markus still had his fist in the air, kept it there, regret rushed through him and made him feel awful. He wanted to run back out; catch his mum, hug her, say sorry. Only it was too late. The teacher had closed and locked the door and Markus just stood staring at it, sadness swelled up inside him and he thought he was about to cry, nearly, almost.

Markus had to get a grip. He didn't like thinking about mum and he wanted to move on, or go to sleep for a bit. He thought about texting Mel, take his mind off it.

Another car circled the close outside, slowly lighting up his room again. It lit up the Leigh-Anne Pinnock poster before sweeping across onto Stevie Gerrard. The man who had not long left his club. His hero who no longer played for Liverpool anymore. Markus looked at his face, that steely scowl full of fight and determination. What a player, Markus thought. Wish I could be like him, wish I could be like Steven Gerrard. Although people did say that Markus looked like the football star, having that same *good head of hair,* they said. He was also like Gerrard in that he was a tough street kid who didn't take shit from anyone. The only difference is that Stevie had put it to good use and got rich and famous. Markus wanted to be rich and famous. He wanted money and cars and a big house. He wanted everybody to know his name, know who he was. He wanted to be stopped in the street and asked for autographs. If only Markus could have some kind of talent that would take him there. The only talents he ever had seemed to get him into trouble, fighting, lying, stealing, and getting people to do what he wanted. That was about all he was really good at. Oh, there was sex too, now. Markus had a feeling he was really good at sex because Mel was starting to make loads of noise. Sometimes she screamed out-loud and that made Markus feel like a man. Not just a boy, but a proper man. Most of the lads at school were still virgins whereas Markus was getting it all the time, every day, sometimes three or four times a day. Whenever he could. Although he had to wear one of those stupid condoms now and it wasn't the same, didn't feel as good at all. He had to wear them until Mel starting taking *that pill thing*, which couldn't come soon enough because nothing was as good as that first time, by the channel. That was the best feeling, *ever*.

It must have started getting late because cars no longer came onto the close, the lights had stopped moving through his room. It was dark.

Now his roaming thoughts moved onto Mel and stopped there, his head was full of her.

He loved her, he did. He loved Melanie Ellis because she was his first ever girlfriend. He loved Mel Ellis and he wouldn't want to be with anyone else. Most girls were stupid, Markus thought. Most girls gave him a headache. Most girls changed their minds too much and played games. But Beautifulness wasn't like that. Beautifulness was better than them. Beautifulness was better than them *all*. Beautifulness was the best GF ever and he was going to stick with her for good. He liked being her boyfriend and would do anything for her, anything at all.

Now it was pitch-black so he knelt on his bed and closed the curtains, cut off the outside world completely.

Mel

Dear Sed,

Ugh, ah, just knew I shouldn't have told Mia! Why didn't I listen to my Nature-Feeling and keep it to myself??

The First Thing she did was jump up and down in McDonald's shouting OH MY GOD YOU'RE NOT A VIRGIN ANYMORE. YOU'RE OUT OF THE V-CLUB AT LAST!!!

Jesus! I said. Why don't you like, just tell the whole flippin world and stuff??!!

Mia was clapping like she was giving me a round of applause and two black boys in the next booth turned and smiled.

I put some fries in my mouth and looked down, wanted to die.

Mia sat back down and leaned right into me, you actually did it??? She whispered into my face. She was so close her forehead made my hair move.

I nodded.

Wow, she said.

It was weird cos when I looked at her I could tell that she had been Lying all along. Like she reckoned she'd had sex LOADS but her face told me otherwise. Cos like, I'd seen This Expression before. Seen it when I told her about My First Period. And seen it when I told her about going out with Markus. It was a fake, twitchy smile, big eyes, pale skin. It was a jealousy face. A big mask of envy kind of a thing. She was a virgin and had been All Along.

Of course she went into a trillion questions but I said nothing.

Where?

How?

What poz-ish?

How long?

Was he good, big, small, average?

Who was on top?

Did it hurt?

It didn't hurt, I said.

Must be small then, she said, rolling her eyes, sucking on milkshake.

I shrugged.

It didn't hurt at all? She said.

No but something weird happened, I said.

The black boys in the next booth had gone so like, I didn't mind talking about it now.

Something weird? Mia echoed. What do you mean?

Well, like, after, some stuff came out.

I must have been kind of nervous and hot cos my glasses were doing that annoying steamy-up thing again. I had to take them off and wipe them so I could see Mia properly. She had her knee resting on the table.

Stuff, she said. You mean jizzum?

What?

Cum?

I don't …

Spunk?

No I mean it was coming out of ME and stuff.

Mia let her jaw fall open. He did wear a condom, didn't he?

Well yeah, well like I think so.

Mia took her knee off the table and sat up straight. Please tell me he wore a fucking condom!?

Yeah he did.

She was staring at me so hard it was like she wanted to fight me.

Well then why did you say 'I think so.' And why the fuck have you got jizzum leaking out of you Melanie!?

Hearing her say my full name got me scared.

Jizzum?

Cum, spunk. He fucking came inside you Mel. You let him ejaculate inside you you dumb bitch!

Suddenly I was scared to death. Can you stop shouting, I said.

What the fuck did you think it was?

What?

The stuff leaking out, she said. It wasn't fucking milkshake was it! She slammed her beaker on the table and some of it squirted out the straw.

I dunno, I mumbled. I thought maybe it was ME.

Mia was shaking her head, annoyed. I'll kill that prick, she said.

What? No it wasn't his fault.

You know you could get pregnant?

What? No. I'm too young and stuff.

Mia put her head in her hands. No Mel, you're not. As soon as you bleed you're old enough. Jesus doesn't your mum teach you anything!?

I shrugged.

We did this shit at school, wasn't you listening?

I was ill remember, didn't do it did I?

Mia still had her head in her hands, she let it go and her forehead dropped onto the table with a thud.

When was this? She said. When did it happen?

Saturday night, I think, no Sunday.

Mia didn't say anything.

Like, could I get pregnant already, like as early as this?

For once Mia didn't know something, her face went blank although she tried to hide it.

When are you due, she said. When are you due to come on?

My period?

Mia did this long, wide-eyed nod of the head like I was the most Stupidest Girl in The World.

My mind was in bits and I tried to think. Soon, I said, like next week, I think. End of next week some time. In a few weeks' time, I said at last.

Good. We'll wait till then. If you don't bleed then we're in the shit, big time. So is that arsehole cos I'll cut off his fucking balls.

I didn't say anything. Suddenly the world seemed too big.

Mia wouldn't stop shaking her head.

You need to tell your mum, she said.

NO!

You need to.

No fucking way.

We need to tell mine then.

No Mia.

We need to tell an adult. An adult needs to know.

Mia please.

We'll tell my mum. She'll know what to do.

No cos she'll tell my mum and my mum will just kill me. Like LITERALLY kill me and then she'll never let me see Markus ever again. Mia please don't. Let's just see if I bleed first.

Mia went back to shaking her head again.

Well you need to tell your mum anyway cos you need to go on the pill.

I just looked at her.

Bet you don't know about that either?

368

Some older girls sat where the black boys were.

Yes, contraceptive pill, I'm not stupid y'know!?

Mia pulled a face. You need to go on the pill, she said.

We can just use condoms.

You can't trust condoms, they break. And you definitely can't trust that arsehole to wear one.

Will you stop calling him names? I said.

What do you expect? He gets my bestie preggers at age thirteen and I'm just supposed to be cool?

I'm fourteen, and he hasn't got me preggers!

Yet.

God Mia.

If you don't bleed next week we're fucked.

I know, you've said.

Well I'm saying it again. I don't think you understand how serious this is.

It's my problem, not yours.

Mia looked right at me. Hey you might push everyone else away but you won't push me away. You might push your mum and sis away but I'm your bestie and I'm not going anywhere.

I looked at Mia and saw how serious she was. Half of me loved her and thought she was The Best Bestie Ever and the other half just thought she was an attention-seeking bitch who was making it ALL about her. I just didn't know. I just couldn't tell. Tbh I'm not gonna Lie but as You've probably gathered By Now I don't trust people and never have. And when You look at things, at like my past and stuff. You can see why. I mean, it makes sense, right?

I bled. I bled when I was supposed to and it was The Best Thing Ever. Like, I even put my finger in the blood and held it up to the light and shouted out-loud. I was happy. I was so happy. I was so relieved I cried and there was no way I was EVER going through this again. Cos the two weeks of waiting was just Total Torture, like the worrying and stress was just a pure hell kind of a thing.

<u>Never again.</u>

I hugged Mia to death and told her she was The Best Bestie Ever for standing by me and stuff.

That's all well and good, she said in an adult voice. But you need to make sure this shit never happens again. You need to get on the pill, or stop having sex.

Where do I get them from?

You need to see someone, like some kind of specialist.

Are you on the pill?

I was, she said. Mia was lying. Not anymore cos I'm going celibate for a bit.

Celibate?

No sex. I want to reconnect with myself. I want to be pure at this stage of my life.

Mia was always quoting from magazines and I was kind of used to this by now.

Well, like, where did you get yours when you was on the pill?

Just tell your mum, she'll know.

No. No way.

She'll take you to get them.

Can't your mum take me?

No. It has to be your OWN mum.

Why?

It's just the rules.

Why?

I didn't make the rules Mel, I'm just telling you them.

Okay.

And tell that arsehole to put something on the end of it until you do get on the pill.

Stop calling him names.

And make sure you watch him too. Make sure you watch him put it on.

Okay.

And tell your mum. Tell your mum you want to go on the pill. She'll be proud that you're being responsible. Your mum is no way near as bad as you think y'know. You need to start trusting people more.

Okay.

I told Big Bear. I told him about my scare. And I told him to wear, from now on. Only he didn't seem to care.

Sex is Hard Work and I'm not sure that I like it, like a complicated kind of a thing.

I was scared to death to tell mum and my Nature-Feeling was right.

Mia was wrong. mum DID go mad, like TOTALLY flipped as per usual. She was shocked more than anything. Kept talking about when she was fourteen years old. And that she didn't lose her virginity till she was eighteen. She asked me like a trillion questions and I answered none of them cos as You know I won't EVER Lie yet at the same time I wasn't going to tell her that I had unprotected sex and stuff. Anyway in the end she took me to get the pill. Said she wasn't happy that Her Own Fourteen Year Old Daughter was having sex at my age but the last thing in the word she wanted was me being pregnant. You're just a kid yourself, she said. You'd be a kid having a kid! I'm not pregnant mum, I said. That's why it's best I go on the pill, right? Even My Sister Adele came along for the trip and she looked at me like I was disgusting the WHOLE time. Both of them did, ganging up on me YET again. Making me feel like I was some kind of trampy freak.

The Pill Woman at the clinic was dead-nice and I wished she was my mum. She was soft and shiny, like she had a shiny face and shiny hair and a shiny smile. She talked about loads of sex stuff and then explained how the pill worked. How and when I should take it and that I had to take it every day without fail otherwise it wouldn't work and then I could end up with a baby and then Markus would be in trouble which I didn't really understand. She said I should set an alarm to remind me. Okay, I said. She also told me that there was side-effects and what they were, like it could make me spotty and fat and moody and tired and depressed and tbh it sounded like Absolute Hell.

I mean, AS IF I'M NOT FUCKED UP ENOUGH!!!

The side-effects are rare, she said, and would only happen in the first few months.

Okay.

mum didn't talk to me on the way home. In fact she didn't talk to me for ages after that. She said she was ashamed that her OWN daughter was on the pill at fourteen and that Adele would never do anything as irresponsible as this.

And obvs that made me feel like shit too.

All of it made me feel like shit tbh and I wished I'd never taken Mia's advice in the First Place. And I wished I'd never started a Sexual Relationship either cos it's all just WAY too much of a headache.

And stuff.

mum suddenly didn't want me to see Markus anymore. Said he was bad news. Said he was bad medicine. Said we were A Ticking Time Bomb, waiting to go off, whatever that meant. I obviously went crazy at her and we argued loads, day and night, all the time. I said what's the point of going all the way into town to get on a pill and then not to have a BF anymore. MAKES NO SENSE.

But...

Nothing makes sense, not if You really think about it. My Life doesn't make sense and never has. It's been a disaster from The Start.

From The Very Beginning My Life has felt like a Wrong Road leading to Nowhere.

I've got a mum that hates me. A sister who doesn't even know I exist. A bestie who talks to me like I'm a kid and a BF who doesn't talk to me at all!

Markus.

Like, all we seem to do lately is eat and have sex. Which is okay and stuff but he never really talks, he doesn't talk the way I'd like him to, the way a boyfriend should. He doesn't really talk things through.

But then neither do YOU, Self-Esteem Diary. I mean here I am opening my heart and soul but You never say anything back. You never help out. You never give advice. It's all just one-way traffic on a two-way street. You just sit here on the bed, all blank and white-faced and silent and stuff. A big empty nothing.

They said that having You around is a Good Thing but sometimes I'm not so sure. All it does is make me well in my own stupid, self-pity. Stirring up all these horrible emotions and memoires and that, re-living things I don't really want to re-live, revealing things I don't really want to reveal, and it's not like You even care, is it? I mean, You don't really, do you? Be HONEST. You probably just think I'm some Average Silly Girl spouting all this everyday crap about periods and boyfriends and school and hating myself, and it's all just so fucking tedious and typical and standard and stuff. Just another airhead girl in a senseless world trying to get some attention.

????????????!!!!!!!!!!!!!!!

THIS book, this Self-Esteem Diary would probably go to better use as Toilet Paper, maybe I should just rip You up and put You in the bin, or else set fire to You so I can't ever be revealed to The Outside World.

See.
So.

Sometimes I imagine how awful it would be if mum or My Sister Adele ever got a hold of You. The field-day they'd have! Using ALL this information against Me, using all my deepest and darkest secrets as a weapon. I would EVEN hate My Bestie Mia getting a hold of You too. In fact she'd be The Worstest Ever. The WHOLE town would know EVERYTHING within a week!

So.
See.
Like, Life is pretty gruesome and stuff when those closest to you are ACTUALLY your biggest enemies.

Anyway.
Either way.

I could leave You around Markus easy and I wouldn't even be bothered. He probs wouldn't EVEN open You up. He just wouldn't care. Tbh I don't even know what goes off in his head half the time. The only thing I really know about him is that he hates adults. And school too. He REALLY hates school.

Tbh I actually miss school and never thought I'd hear myself say That. It's like they say, you don't know you've got something until it's gone. And that's how I feel about school cos I'm ACTUALLY starting to miss it and stuff. I miss my other friends like Neve and Megan. I kind of miss getting up in the morning with something to do, somewhere to go. Somewhere to be. Maybe half my problem is that I have Too Much time on my hands. It's like if there's too much time and space your mind can get a little chaotic. Maybe it's good to have a purpose, to have patterns and routines and habits and stuff. Yeah. I think that could be half my problem tbh. There's only One Week before we go back and I think I'm looking forward to it. This summer has been amazing in so many ways, so much has happened. Like so much with me and Big Bear and stuff but the summer has been long. So long, too long.

Now I'm looking forward to its end. Looking forward to September and stuff. Looking forward to going back to school.

Before we go back there's something I need to do. Something that's been on My Mind a while now and if I don't get it off my chest soon I think I'll go mad, like totally insane! And that's to talk to Markus about This Virginity Thing. Cos when I really listen to my Nature-Feeling it tells me I'm not his First. That I'm not the only one. That's there's been somebody else. Somebody before me. It's been bugging me for ages now and I need to ask him. I need for him to tell me The Truth. If I wasn't his First then I won't mind, like, I won't be happy about it but I'll live. See, so. It's not so much The Virginity Thing that gets me but the Lying about it. So Officially it's more about The Lying Thing than The Virginity Thing if that makes sense?? He just needs to tell me The Truth so My Mind can go back to being Normal again.

The only time I would mind is if Mia was His First. That would just kill me. Like LITERALLY kill me and tbh I'm not gonna Lie but I would kill her. Like LITERALLY kill her. Bestie or no Bestie I wouldn't care. She'd just be dead, dead For Good. Cos like it'd be The Worst Betrayal EVER. The only reason I think this is cos I know they were mates Long Before I was on the scene. And for some reason she always kept Markus hidden from me and I don't know why. Like she'd talk about him loads but would never get around to intro-ing him to me. Sometimes I get suspicious/paranoid that there was this WHOLE relationship before we met. And that's why They seemed to talk in this stupid, secret code sometimes.

*My alarm has just gone off, time to pop my pill.

Ah. Ugh. It's probably because of These Things I'm shoving down my neck that I'm being so crazy right now, like a hormone kind of a thing.

See.
So.

Don't think S.E.D that I'm not aware that this Particular Entry has been a bit screwy and stuff. I'm aware of that, aware my pen is going about a trillion mph and my mind EVEN faster. It's like my mind and pen are having a race and my mind is winning and my pen can't keep up!

I do think that there IS something with Mia and Markus though. Something not right. Something I can't put my finger on. Sometimes *they're a little TOO QUIET around each other. Maybe I just need to listen to my Nature-Feeling more closely, cos eventually that will give me all the answers I need. Just like it always does and always has.*

Right Now my Nature-Feeling is just telling me I'm A Jealous Person.

And know that I am. I get jealous all the time and about the silliest things. I get jealous over mum and sis. I get jealous about people with money. People with looks. People with happiness. I get jealous over other families. Other mums. People who go on holiday. Girls with their dads. Girls who are good at sports. Girls with big boobs and good legs. Mostly I get jealous of Mia's legs, Mia's bod in general. In fact the Biggest Thing I've been jealous of lately, and has been driving me ABSOLUTELY INSANE is a poster on Markus's bedroom wall. He has a picture of that dead-fit girl in that girl-band Little Mix. The brown pretty girl although I don't remember her name. She wears a blue bikini on the beach and her bod is just TOTALLY ridick and her skin is just TOTALLY perfect and I get so dead-jealous that I can't even look at it, look at Her. And to make it EVEN worser it hangs right over the bed and I don't even like having sex in his bedroom anymore cos I really believe he's looking at her and fantasizing about her while he's Doing It with Me. Like I just see it as TOTALLY disrespectful and stuff. I mean before I went out with Markus I had a poster of Pattinson Twilight on MY wall but as soon as we started Our Relationship I took it down as a mark of respect, so why can't he do the same!!??

I mean why does he need to look at other girls in That Way when he has Me?

Anyway.

I thought about putting the Pattinson Poster back up but I don't think he would even care.

He wouldn't because no one really cares how I FEEL.

No one.

No one.

Not even YOU.

Runaway Train

Markus

Walked right into Yeoman's army surplus supply store, picked up the first tent he could find and slung it over his shoulder. Didn't even look around. He was so relaxed and matter-of-fact no one noticed a thing. Once out the door, an alarm sounded but *that damn alarm* had been faulty for weeks, going off at random times and the people who worked there paid it no mind.

That stupid thing.

Markus was already gone, two streets away, blending in with the rest of the Saturday afternoon shoppers. Job done. Another mission accomplished.

Monday morning, they were packed and ready to go. Two rucksacks. Two mountain bikes. Markus still had his orange Mustang from The Taylor Brothers and Mel had her birthday present, that nameless pink thing that was a size too small. They had clothes, jumpers, hoodies, t-shirts, jeans, joggers, underwear, loads of socks. They had lunchboxes and bags of food. Sandwiches, two bananas, two apples and a giant orange. Mostly it was crisps and chocolate and sweets and pop. Monster Munch. Doritos. Hula Hoops. Mars. Twix. Crunchie. Double Decker. Buttons. Skittles. Fruitella. Coke, Lucozade, and those new Monster energy drinks.

At 9am they dumped their school uniform into a bin bag and threw it over the church wall.

Won't be needing that anymore.

"Hey let's take a photo before we go," she said. "Like a memento kind of a thing."

Markus sighed and climbed back off his bike. She placed her phone on the ledge of a rocky wall and set the timer. Markus leaned over her while she adjusted her glasses and looked away. Neither of them smiled.

Markus had to wait another five minutes while she fucked around with her phone.

"C'mon man we need to get gone. School have probs reported us missing by now."

"Just wait."

He watched her face in cross-eyed concentration. "Check this out," she said.

Melanie Ellis had touched up the photo, cropping and dimming the composition, adding a spherical orb around them. Markus wasn't the type to have an eye for art but he had to say the photo looked *pretty fucking cool.* Both were peering down at the camera moodily. Markus had never seen his girlfriend look like this before. It's almost like she was another girl, a crueller and cooler version of herself. Head cocked and indirect, looking at the world from the corner of her eye. They looked kind of famous, or infamous. It reminded him of that film, *Natural Born Killers.* An old movie about a blood-thirsty couple on the run. The girl in it was kind of weird but incredibly hot and the man was a badass, cool as fuck.

"I want that photo on my wall," Markus said.

"Good," Mel replied. "Like, you can replace it with that Little Mix poster I hate so much."

"Deal," Markus said with a smile. "Anyway," he said. "No more photos. In fact you need to turn your phone off completely."

Mel had climbed back onto her bike, foot poised on the pedal. "Why?" she said.

"They'll be able to trace it."

"What?"

"I've seen it on TV. It's how they catch criminals."

"We're not criminals though."

"Just turn it off."

"What about Mia?"

"What about her?"

"Shouldn't she know?"

"Are you fucking dumb!"

Mel recoiled, hurt. The *femme fatale* from the photo had long gone and the wimpy teen returned.

"She's the *last* person to know cos she'd be the *first* person to grass," he spat with a screw-face.

Mel was nodding now, realising he was right.

"She'd do anything to have the attention back on her. Be the hero."

"Heroine."

"What?"

"Heroine. She's a girl."

"Whatever. Just do as I say and turn it off."

"Kay."

Now their bikes were moving, the weight of their rucksacks giving them a slight sway as they cycled up the lane. Mel had to get off and push it up the bank which led to the Clementine Channel.

"If we follow the river will it take us to the sea?" she shouted to her boyfriend.

An October wind blew her own words back into her face. Markus couldn't hear a thing. He was a good fifty metres ahead and Mel got scared that if he got too far he would lose her. Already she was struggling to keep up.

They decided to run away because Erica Ellis had put a stop to the relationship, or was trying to at least. Markus wasn't allowed at the house anymore and she was doing everything in her power to keep her daughter away from him. She grounded her for the smallest of things. Made unplanned trips into town. Insisted that she walk the dog with her sister. Anything to take up her time so she couldn't see him. When things got really heated between mother and daughter there were even threats to move her school. All this was because on the last day of September a twenty-pound note had been swiped from the kitchen worktop and Mel's mum was convinced that Markus Venner was the culprit.

"Mel you can stand there till you're blue in the face and tell me it wasn't him but I know it was. It *has* to be. There's no one else. Think about it. Not *once* has money *ever* gone missing and then all of a sudden ... "

Mum threw her hands up and pulled an even weirder face than normal.

Mel wasn't backing down. "Maybe, like, you just misplaced it and stuff?"

Erica Ellis tightened her chin and shook her head as Adele stepped into the kitchen half-asleep. "Can you two stop shouting I'm trying to nap?" She walked back out.

"So come on then!" Her mum pushed on. "Who else? Who else would have taken it, you?"

"No."

"Adele?"

Sister shouted from the next room, "keep me out of it," before knocking up the volume on the telly.

Mel went quiet for half a second.

"How dare you! How dare you blame Adele?"

Mel marvelled how mum always managed to do this, move the argument around until she had Adele on her side.

"I'm not ..."

"She's never stolen a thing in her life!"

"I'm not saying that." Mel stuttered. She was so mad and exasperated she wanted to cry. "Like, I'm just saying you could have misplaced it and stuff?"

Her mum was mad too, and she had to do something physical to save herself from lashing out so she reached out for the back door and let Babe into the house. The black beast bounded in and started sniffing both humans like he'd never seen them before. Those wild eyes and that wagging tail freaked Mel out. Babe had been a part of the family for a good five years now yet the oldest daughter had still not warmed to the thing. Erica began fixing his dinner.

Mel stared at the dog, looked at his teeth, his throat, its bloated belly.

"Maybe, like, Babe ate it." Mum put the tin of dog food down on the exact same spot where the money had been lifted and shot her daughter with a venomous stare. "Like an accident kind of a thing," Mel added.

"Are you taking the fucking piss?"

The sleeves of her grey cardigan hung over the teenager's wrists.

"Are you really taking the piss out of this whole thing?" Mum went on. "Either you are or you're plain fucking stupid."

"Don't call me stupid," Mel said. "And don't keep swearing at me either."

Mum was trying to calm herself down, tipping the tin of dog food into a bowl. Mel slowly looked around at the kitchen. It was a total mess, ditched, a dump. Loads of dirty dog-stuff. Paw marks and chewed-up toys and bits of dried saliva glazed across the floor and cupboards. I need to get out of here, she thought. I need to get to sixteen and go. Two more years of hell and then I'm gone. Gone for good. Gone for life.

Melanie and Erica Ellis watched the dog eat his food; their argument unresolved. Mother and daughter remained silent throughout. Their eyes firmly fixed on Babe as he licked up the dark chunks of slimy meat, thick pink tongue and black gums slobbering around the grimy bowl.

"Anyway Adele doesn't trust him either," her mum said from nowhere, a superior finality to her tone, as if Adele herself was talking through her. She was calmer now. "She gets uneasy whenever he's around. Says his eyes hurt, whatever that means. But overall she agrees with me, thinks he's no good."

Mel took her eyes from the dog and put them on mum. "Well there's a first."

"And she should know cos she's a better judge of character than you, always has been."

Mel noticed a twitchy vein in her eye. "I don't have to listen to this."

"Don't then, *go*," her mum said, knowing she'd won. "But I'm telling you Mel, you bring that thief around here again and I'll kill him."

A smug smile crawled across Mel's face. "Yeah. Right," she said with a shallow exhale of breath, looking at a kitchen knife drying in the drainer. "I'd like to see you try."

Erica didn't expect that kind of reaction and it confused her, feeling some of the fight fall out of her. She wanted to say something else, get a last word in but she couldn't think what. By the time she did her oldest daughter was already gone, out the back door, probably on her way to *him*.

Markus didn't care. Just shrugged and said three words, said them slow and monotone like he was reading out the end of a shopping list. "Stupid. Ugly. Bitch."

Mel agreed but it felt weird him saying that. "What should we do?" she said.

She was crying a bit and what she needed right now was a big Markus hug. Telepathically he drew her into his arms and squeezed her tight.

"We'll run away," he answered with the nonchalance of a monk.

"Oh yeah. Where to?"

She was smiling and feeling better and not really taking him seriously.

"Skegness," he said, plucking it from his head at random.

At first Mel really did think he was joking. She smiled again and shrugged it off but then her boyfriend starting talking about it more. Said that Skeggy was only thirty-six miles away and that he had cycled it as a kid. Said they could get there in an afternoon. It'll be an adventure, he said. It will piss the adults off and make them sick with worry. It will tell the world that we are serious about each other and that a few stupid rules and punishments aren't going to keep us apart. It will be a statement, he said. A way of saying, *fuck life*.

The more Mel listened the more excited she got. He made it sound so thrilling and free, to take to the open roads, one village and then the next, one town and then the next, city after city. Shit we might even make it to the coast and then we can hop on a boat to France, Spain, wherever you want. Prove we're more than just kids. Plus we wouldn't have to go to school anymore.

"Where will we sleep?" Mel said.

"Wherever we drop."

"It'll be cold."

"Not if I wrap you up."

"What if it rains?"

"I'll nick us a tent."

"You're mad."

"We nearly there, Big Bear?"

He was almost a hundred metres in front of her now. She couldn't keep up and the gap was getting bigger. If she wasn't careful she might lose him and then what would they do? Markus had told her to keep her phone off so she wouldn't be able to call him. She put her head down and cycled faster. Even though her rucksack was far lighter than his it was still killing her back, going uphill was the hardest, it was so heavy she thought it was going to drag her off the bike.

"Big Bear wait!"

The Clementine Channel was almost gone now, just a shimmering strip of silver to her far left. Skegness sounded such a long way away. Mel remembered going there with her dad. She remembered how long it took and that was in a car, let alone a bike! The seat was already hurting her bum and her shoelaces kept wrapping around the pedals. She had barely left the town with her mum and here she was cycling away from it with no other adults around. Kind of scary and stuff.

"We nearly there Big Bear?"

Markus had stopped at a lock, resting his leg on the black and white gate. He ripped open a Double Decker, filling his mouth with the whole bar in one swallow. He watched his red-faced girlfriend push up the hill. "You what?"

He couldn't tell if her expression was a smile or a grimace?

"Like, are we nearly at Skegness?"

"Are you a fucking mong?" he spluttered, still chewing.

She dismounted the bike and pushed it up the rest of the slight hill.

"We've not long left town," he said. "Probably not even quarter of the way to Boston yet."

Shock slapped Mel across the chops. "Well, how many miles we done?"

Markus gave a dirty chocolate grin before giving her the answer. "Bout six."

"Six, is that it!?"

Markus nodded, tossing her a Twix.

"And Skeg is how far?" she moaned.

"Thirty-six. Thirty-six point two. Probably further cos we ain't going direct."

Mel was struggling with the Twix, the gold wrapper winking in the sun. "What do you mean we ain't going direct?"

"Well we're not in a car are we? And we're not on the road are we? Probably be about forty by the time we're done."

"Forty miles!" Mel's face had pain in. "But my legs kill!"

Markus ignored her. Threw the Double Decker wrapper into the canal and started cycling again. An old man shouted from a hut at the top of the lock. "Oi don't throw litter in there!"

Markus never looked up, just launched two fingers up into the air. The old man turned his scowl onto Mel. "Sorry," she said, barely audible.

It got easier. The next seven or eight miles were practically downhill and the two rode side-by-side, letting the gravelled declines do all the work. They talked and whistled and sang songs, taking it in turns to sing lyrics while the other had to guess. Sometimes Mel would sing old songs and Markus wouldn't have a clue.

"Runaway train never going back. Wrong way on a one-way track."

"What the fuck is that?"

"Soul Asylum I think they're called."

"How old?"

"Nineties."

"You're lame."

They stopped and ate lunch in a field. Pretty much clearing all of their food in one sitting. When they counted how much money they had between them it wasn't much, far less than they imagined. Each thought the other was bringing more. Mel and Markus had just over twenty pounds to their name. Mel got worried but Markus told her not to. I'll just nick something when we get to Boston. Like what, Mel asked. Markus shrugged. It was getting colder and it was also the first time they realised this too. At this time they were normally indoors, either in McDonald's or at Markus's house, or maybe even at Mia's. It was October and there was a chill in the air, dampness had seeped through the earth, leaving muddy dregs on their trainers and jeans. It had rained two days ago, giving the grass and trees an autumn sparkle.

"Can we put the tent up here?" Mel said. "I don't want to cycle anymore. My legs like totally kill and stuff."

Markus washed down half a sandwich with a mouthful of coke and then belched in the air.

"Gross," she said.

"You're such a fucking pussy," he said.

"Why?" she said, hurt.

"Let's make it to Boston at least?"

"Oh Big Bear no more my feet are throbbing. Here is fine, there's some trees just hidden over there," she said, pointing.

Something about the word *hidden* got him aroused. An unexpected pang flipped in his stomach. His eyes traced up the inside of her legs. The switch had been switched and now it's all he could see, tunnel-vision without room for anything else.

"Okay you win," he said.

She smiled and threw her arms around him. Something wet landed on his cheek and Markus didn't know if it was spit from his girlfriend or a raindrop from the sky.

The tent was hard to put up. Fucking infuriating, Markus thought. He bit back angry feelings that swelled against his chest. *Fucking thing.* He was getting mad at Mel who was doing more harm than good. Moving things, putting pegs into the wrong places. Just go and stand over there, he said. It was the first time he'd really lost his temper at her and she was frightened and offended at the same time. But she did as he asked, sitting down on the grass with her legs crossed. Picked the last remaining daisy in the field and flicked it. Sorry, he said after a while. But I think I better do this on my own. He looked at the tent and all the tent-bits. Maybe he'd only stolen parts of the tent instead of the whole thing, he pondered. The instruction book called it *easily erectable* but there was nothing easy about it. Mel watched on. Slowly, bit by bit, Markus had the thing up, into something that looked kind of like a tent. As it took shape Mel grew happy, relieved. She hated seeing him stressed and on the edge of his temper. It reminded her of mum, and dad, and all the other angry adults she'd experienced throughout her life.

"Can you hold this?" he said.

He wanted her help now and she was glad. Sitting dumb in the grass made her feel like a waste of space. After a few more minutes they had a tent. A bit wonky but it'll do.

"Yay!"

"Let's go inside," he said.

The colours of the tent made her naked body look different, Markus thought. The setting sun came through the material and changed her skin into green and dark blue. He kissed her everywhere and then entered her. Mel found it weird, having sex outside; well, not outside but almost outside. She felt exposed, like eyes were on her. Like perverts had creeped out from the bushes and were looking through spy-holes in the top of the tent. After a while these thoughts dissolved and she began to let go. No sooner was she into it did she hear that Markus-noise, he tensed up suddenly and she felt him come inside her. Her conditioned response to this was always the same, panic. Even though she was on the pill and had been for the last two months there was still a feeling of dread. Her mum and Mia had drilled this into her by going on about it and going on about it. *Pregnant. A kid having a kid. Your life would be over.* The fear and unease always managed to outdo the pleasure and spoil the sex itself. Most of the time Mel didn't see the point.

Markus rolled off and collapsed back, out of breath. This was another thing that was making the sex crap, she thought. He always seems to be having sex for himself. It's always the same. He gets on top. Pounds away with his eyes closed and then rolls off. Mel had watched enough TV to know that this wasn't the way it was supposed to be. Twilight was no porno, but there were scenes in there that got her excited. And it always looked so long and sensual and amazing. Maybe if she got Markus to watch Twilight he might pick up some tips.

He had his eyes closed and Mel was sleepy too. She picked up his arm and draped it over her. Often she preferred this part to the sex, lying here wrapped and snuggled and safe and stuff.

When they woke it was full on dark. The sound of nature swarmed around the tent.

"For a moment I forgot where we were."

"Me too," she said.

"Fuck, the bikes."

"What?"

"We left them outside."

"Uh? Of course. Where else? They won't fit in here."

Markus sat up and looked at her like she was the most stupid girl in the world.

"I know. But we need to hide them more."

He knelt and unzipped the tent. "Still here," he said.

She knelt and stuck her head out too. "Wow look at the stars."

Markus gazed up. "I know. How come there's more here?"

"What do you mean?"

"How come there's more here than at home?"

Now it was her turn to look at him stupid. "Pollution," she said. "Like, cos we're out in nature and that. There's no traffic and stuff."

Markus didn't say anything for a while, then, "I'm fucking starving."

"Me too."

"We got any food left?"

"Some fruit," she said, putting her glasses back on.

"No real food?"

"Think we ate all the chocolate bars."

Markus pulled his screw-face. "Let's go and buy some chips?"

Mel looked at him a little gone-out. "Didn't think you liked fish and chips. Thought, like, it was bad memories. Like it reminded you of your dad and stuff. Cos, like, he used to make you eat them all the time and that?"

Markus shrugged, opened up the tent more and looked back at the stars. "Dunno. Just fancied some."

"Okay."

They didn't know where they were going but they walked. The night was black and vast and covered the earth in a blanket of sky. Dark outlines of fields rolled downwards into a valley. They must have slept a long time because Mel's legs didn't hurt anymore. She felt rested and revitalised. After a while they came across a small collection of lights in the distance.

"Is that Boston?" she said.

"Nah. Not big enough. And too close. Boston is about another hour away. It's probably just a village."

"Bet they'll have a chippy there."

"Probs."

They held hands as they descended a steep muddy bank. The moon was small and high. The stars were still out and weren't going away anytime soon. It's great out here, he said. Running away was Officially The Best Idea Ever, she said. No adults or parents or sis or Aunt Tars. No time for bed or school the next day. No being grounded or banned from the house. No people. No kids. No Mia. Just the two of them. They could do what they wanted. They had all the time in the world.

It rained in the night. Not much, but enough to make the bottom of their tent wet. Mel had not zipped it up properly when she went out to pee. She had also left her chip tray in the tent and gravy had spilled all over Markus's sleeping bag.

"You fucking mong look what you've done!"

He smacked her on the back and she woke up scared and disorientated, reaching out for her glasses. Her hair was wrapped around her neck like a noose. The smell of the gravy was sharp and sickening and had given the pair a headache. Both of their throats scratched with dehydration.

"Why did you leave this in here you twat? Now my sleeping bag's fucked."

He pointed to a dark patch near his leg.

Mel was still half-asleep. The frame of her glasses was bent and didn't fit her head properly. She was struggling to see. Markus held the dried gravy tray up to her face and for a brief moment she thought he was going to hit her with it.

"Sorry," she said at last, a bare mumble. "I need some water."

He sighed and tossed the tray out the tent.

"I need water," she repeated, smacking her lips.

"We ain't got any," he snapped. "Just pop. Here."

He threw her a half-bottle of Dr Pepper into her lap. She uncapped and swallowed and pulled a face like she'd just taken medicine. "Yuk."

Birds tweeted around the tent, sounding like they were pecking their way inside.

"Can we sleep more?" Mel said.

Markus was already rolling up his sleeping bag and packing his rucksack. "No, *up*. We've slept enough. We should be in Skeg by now. This is pathetic."

"Thought, like, you said we had all the time in the world Big Bear."

He pulled out pegs and the tent began to collapse on top of her. "Markus!" she cried.

He smiled and pulled more of it down. When she went to move a yelp ripped through her chest. "Ah!" Her eyes went wide and she froze, braced, gasping; not daring to move another inch.

"What the fuck's up with you now?"

"It's my legs." She held her knee with both hands. "They won't move."

Markus yanked the groundsheet from under her and this time she really did scream. Markus laughed. "What you going on about?"

She lay on her side, crying. "Markus don't it's my legs. There's something wrong with them."

He rolled his eyes and knelt down beside her. "One leg, or both?"

"It's like, everywhere. Like both legs and my bum and stuff. My bum hurts the most, ouch!"

He touched her and she flinched.

"You're just stiff is all. You need to move."

"But what is it? I don't get it."

Markus now started packing her things away. "It's cos you're unfit. Not used to exercise. Using muscles you don't use. Basically a lazy bastard and yesterday was a shock to the system. You need to move, jump back on the bike."

She was still on her side, in the foetal. "No that'll make it more worser."

"Come on."

He picked her up slowly and told her to stretch, move about, shake. "I used to get this all the time with football. When I hadn't played for a bit." He rubbed her legs and arse a bit until she felt better.

"Do your legs ache?" she said.

"No. Just my head."

"What?"

"Nothing."

He hugged her and held her and told her everything would be alright.

"Do you think people will be looking for us yet?" she said.

The sky had blackened from yesterday.

"Probably," he said.

She wanted to ask him something else but he was already on his bike and moving.

"Here we go again," she said to herself.

The village looked way different in the daytime. It was smaller than she thought. They passed the chip shop they went to last night and then headed straight along the main lane. People of the village looked at them as they cycled by. Some smiled. Some looked curious. Mel wondered if they knew they were on the run. Perhaps one of them will call the police.

I've just spotted those missing kids. What's the reward again?

Mel got tempted to turn on her phone while Markus wasn't looking. Just for a few seconds. Just to see if mum or sis or Mia had called. Just to see if anyone cared.

Markus cycled on without a care in the world. Just as fast and purposeful as the day before, good head of hair blown back as he bombed into the heading wind.

"Big Bear slow down. My legs hurt remember?!"

Actually they didn't anymore. Markus was right, within half an hour of cycling she didn't feel a thing. The sky darkened even more and a few scattered drops of rain were beginning to fall on the runaway teenagers.

They were back on the canals again and the yellow gravelled paths which ran alongside them.

"Why don't we stay on the road Big Bear, that way we can just follow the signs to Boston?"

"Cos people might see us stupid. We're on the run, remember?"

"Oh."

Mel was hungry although she was too scared to tell Markus. He was on another one of his missions again and nothing was going to get in his way. Best just wait till we get to Boston, she thought. Can't be far now. Although something caught her eyes that bothered her. It was an old house which looked familiar. It looked recent, like they had only past it yesterday. She remembered the door with diamond shapes in the wood, and the funny-shaped roof with tiles missing. Markus was way up ahead and she was bored of shouting after him, especially seeing as no reply ever arrived. After that certain other landmarks came into her view, landmarks she saw only twenty-four hours ago. The lock. A barge. A bin with a blue sticker on. She also recognised a hill in the distance that looked like a giant breast. Still Markus cycled on oblivious. All of a sudden she felt dread as the wasted miles began to unravel under her wheel. They were going in reverse.

At last there was a crossroads and her boyfriend stopped at them, his head turning left and then right. From the side-shot of his face she could already see puzzlement begin to distort his features. Eventually her pink bike rolled up beside his orange one. She stood silently beside him, not daring to say anything yet.

"Think we go this way?" he said, nodding to the path on his left.

Melanie Ellis knew her boyfriend well enough to detect the fake confidence in his voice.

"Yeah," she said, in breathless doubt.

He bit his bottom lip and then shot his eyes to the other path on the right. "Mm. Maybe this one?"

He looked left and right again, weighing them both up. Markus clearly wanted help.

Mel's lips twitched, looking for the right word to start this off with. "Like, err, you don't think we need to take like this path?"

She nodded backwards and Markus frowned deeper. "What you on about?"

"I don't know."

"Which path?" he said.

"Like the one behind us. The one we just been on and stuff."

Markus scraped his bike across the gravel and gazed up at the long path they had just been on for the last hour. From this angle it looked different, familiar. Too familiar. Frighteningly familiar, like they had only been on it yesterday. When the realisation dawned on him his face began to change. His eyes went small and colour drained from his cheeks. His rough hands found their way to his head, his hair, in which he grabbed like he wanted to yank it all out. "Nooooooo. God noooo please!!!"

Mel backed up on her bike, wheeled back a few inches and looked at her boyfriend.

"Please don't tell me we've gone back on ourselves. Please!"

Markus got off his bike and kicked it to the floor. The force was so great the frame bounced off the ground and landed in a bush. He charged back up the path like a bull and screamed. His guttural cry filled the sky like the rain that was falling from it. Mel's nature-feeling was *to take off*. Get out of here while she still had the advantage of wheels over feet. She put her foot on the pedal but Markus caught her with his eyes.

"You knew," he said.

"What?" The word stuck in her throat like a hiccup.

"You fucking knew."

"No."

"Yes you did."

Mel realised she was lying, that she wasn't telling The Truth.

"No I … "

"You knew that's why you nodded backwards."

"No I was just wondering, like … "

"You knew *all along* yet you let me cycle on this path for a whole hour like a c*nt!"

He took strides towards her and she flinched. There must have been something in that flinch that stopped him. She looked down and saw a fist.

"Big Bear I … like I tried shouting but you was too far in front. You're always too far in front and you can never hear me and stuff."

The rain was now heavy, hitting them diagonally in a combative torrent. It was as if the rain was getting involved, like nature was telling him to calm down. Markus seemed to hear it because his face changed again. He stopped and looked up, looked back. Looked at Mel. Smiled a touch, a certain smile Mel had never seen before.

He touched her wrist, then her face.

"I'm just hungry. That's all. I just need to eat."

Mel nodded. "I'm hungry too," she said. Although she didn't really know if she said that out-loud. Or just in her head.

By the time they finally did reach Boston it was dusk again. It had taken them two days to ride just sixteen miles. The rain was unrelenting and everything was soaked. Their clothes, their rucksacks, their bikes. Mel's long hair was drenched and she hadn't brought a towel. She had to dry it on the only t-shirt of hers that wasn't wet. They set up the tent faster than last night but it seemed longer because of the rain. And the field they were in wasn't as remote either. Only a hundred or so metres out from the town. From this spot they could see the train station and a nearby school.

"I don't like it here Markus it doesn't feel right," she said. "We're too close to stuff. What if some bad people stumble upon us? I'm scared."

"It'll have to do," Markus said. "It's too dark to find anywhere else."

They had a tenner left and the only thing they bought was two BLT sandwiches and a big bag of Doritos. Markus had a bottle of coke and Mel flavoured water. Back at the tent they ate them but was still hungry. Rain drummed on the roof and one of the plastic poles fell down and that's when Mel wanted to open her lungs and scream out loud, scream her head off that she wanted to go home. Back to Kimble Wells, her town, her close. Back to her mum and sis no matter how bitchy they were cos *nothing* was as bad as *this*. This Hell of being tired and cold and wet and hungry.

"You alright?" Markus said, putting his arm around her.

She nodded, her eyes far-off and trancelike.

"You're shaking."

She didn't say anything.

"It's been a bad day is all. Yesterday was good. Today bad. It's what happens. That's life. We took a wrong turn. Mistakes happen. Tomorrow will be good again, you'll see. We'll have a big breakfast and the weather will be sunny again. We'll spend the morning in town, freshen up, and then we'll follow the roads. No more of these paths and canals but the roads! We'll be in Skeggy by late afternoon, promise! And then we've made it. Our mission complete."

"How we gonna get breakfast, we haven't got any money?"

"I'll figure that one out."

Mel couldn't help it. She found his words comforting. In a few sentences he had made it all sound colourful and adventurous again. Sometimes she felt like he owned powers, like a mind-magician kind of a thing.

The arm around her suddenly pulled her in tight. As he pulled she felt his hand. His hand was going somewhere, somewhere south.

Great, she thought, despite *all this* he still wants to have sex. Again.

He was right. It was sunny in the morning and she did feel better. They had more of a lay-in and Markus seemed gentler in spirit. They packed up leisurely and headed into town. It was still autumn-cool but at least that bruised sky had lifted, leaving an endless expanse of blue. Mel and Markus chained up their bikes outside the big ASDA and then took their soap-bags into the disabled toilets and spruced up, cleaned their teeth and had a full-body wash. It made all the difference and they felt brand new. After Markus lead her straight to the breakfast bar. He loaded everything onto two plates and then handed Mel their final fiver, before casually sitting down without paying. Mel stood in the queue, petrified, while her boyfriend munched away naturally.

"Hello love." A big fat smile flashed at her from the woman at the till. "Hungry are you?" she said, nodding at the epic meal.

Mel couldn't say anything, just let out a weak, guilty smile.

"Small gal like you." The woman pushed on. "Eating *all* that. Where does it fit?"

Mel's forehead burned and her palms were sticky as she handed over the crumpled-up five.

"Large brekky is five-fifty," she said. "But *they* don't have to know that," she mouthed, winking a wrinkled eye.

Mel liked the woman at the till and wished she was her mum.

By the time Mel sat Markus was nearly done, mopping up the sauces with the crust of his toast. He belched like he always did after a meal and an old man looked over. Mel put her head down and began to eat. As the food went down she felt better, stronger, more centred. They had been gone for two nights now and she wondered if her family had finally got the message, *I will be with Markus at any cost.*

"We need to hit Skeggy today Beautifulness."

He hadn't called Mel her pet-name for ages and she liked it.

"We need to get to Skeg cos this is embarrassing."

Mel didn't understand what he meant. "Embarrassing to who?"

He looked at her and rolled his eyes, yawned, stretched. Markus had this presence. He had a way of making the atmosphere all about him. He drew attention wherever he went, mostly without realising it.

After breakfast Markus lead her into the store. They stood-out a mile, two teenagers carrying massive rucksacks through all the shopping aisles. In the clothing department Markus grabbed a packet of socks and pulled it open, stuffing the three or four pairs into his pockets.

"Markus what the eff!?"

"Moaning about your wet feet weren't ya?"

Mel looked around frantically. "Well, like, yeah, but I didn't mean ..."

"Well then."

Next he grabbed a fleece and bit off the security tag.

"Markus you're gonna get us arrested and stuff."

"We're out of dough. This is how we're gonna have to live from now on."

He was talking like they were going to be on the run for the rest of their lives.

They were in the bread section, filling bags and bags of croissants and doughnuts and pastries. Mel was too stunned to say anything else. She just followed her boyfriend around while he casually took what he wanted. He took fruit off the stands and ate while he wandered. Unpeeled a banana right in front of her and then tried stuffing it into her mouth. She was scared but laughed at the same time.

"Swallow bitch," he said.

"No. I'm full!"

She was red-faced and charged with adrenalin as they left the big double electric doors at the front. She waited for an alarm or the big hands of a security guard but neither arrived. Back on their bikes she felt good again. Felt like outlaws, wild, free. Ready to move on.

"Look at that boy," she said.

They were poised at the roundabout, a sign for Skegness hung over them.

"I think he's lost," she said.

"Fuck him we need to get gone."

"He's crying," she said.

Markus got back on his bike whereas Mel put hers down and walked over to the hysterical toddler who was climbing up a step. The word *fuck* hissed through Markus's teeth but he eventually followed. "Mel seriously, we don't make Skeg today I'm committing suicide. In fact I'll kill us both!"

She was already down on her knees, tending to the child. His crying slowed to a stop as Mel put her face up to his. "Hey. Hey. Are you lost?"

His face was snotty and red and his blonde hair was everywhere. Mel noticed how good his clothes were, crisp-fitted and immaculate. Each item a designer label. She took his hand and looked him up and down, then looked all around her, searching for a mother.

"Are you lost little boy?" she said.

"Why you talking to it?" Markus snarled. "It's too young to talk. What is it, like two or something?"

"He's a baby."

"It's a mong."

"What?"

"Look at its eye. It's all retarded and shit."

The sun had been on the boy's face but when Mel moved into the shade she could see that Markus was right. The little boy had a strange eye. It was colourless and odd, smaller than the other eye.

Mel put her head to one side and looked into it. "What's your name?"

"I've told you he's too young to talk. Can't we just drop him in that shop or something and go. It's freaking me out."

Mel closed one eye on the sun and looked at Markus with the other. "What's freaking you out?"

"That eye man. It's fucking weird."

"He's a little lost boy for eff sake."

Markus let out a long sigh and put his hands on his head, locking his fingers.

"What's your name?" Mel asked again.

The boy made a noise and a small bubble of snot burst over his face.

"Fucking sick," Markus said with a screw-face.

"You stay with the bikes and bags. I'm going to find his mum."

"No!" Markus's reaction stunned Mel. "We stay together at *all* times. No splitting up."

"O-kay."

Somehow Mel managed to carry her rucksack, roll the bike and hold the boy's hand all at the same time.

"Hey let's kidnap it," Markus said. "Might get a reward."

Mel didn't hear him, was too focussed on the boy.

From nowhere Markus experienced a peculiar kind of jealousy. A feeling he had never had before. He didn't like how this two-and-a-half-foot piece of shit was getting all her attention of a sudden. Met a kid for a few minutes and now she thinks she's some kind of mum.

"Hey this way," Markus said, nodding towards a gap in the buildings.

Mel turned and looked at Markus, the boy gazed up too, that weird eye and his little pink o-shape of a mouth.

"If we wanna get to the centre we should take this alleyway."

"Oh. Okay," Mel said.

Markus moved to one side and let Mel and the kid go ahead. They stepped into the alleyway, which cut off the sun and ran along the back of Asda. Mel was still talking to the thing although it never talked back. Markus pushed his bike and watched them inch along, their shadows sliding across the orange-bricked walls.

At the other side crowds of people moved around in the Boston town centre.

"Maybe we should find the police?" she said.

Markus put his bike up against a wall. "Are you fucking stupid?"

Mel looked at him, about to speak until a woman burst upon the scene, all hair and shrill voice. "Oh my goodness Jack!"

She was straight on the boy, hugging and covering him with kisses like he'd been missing for months. "Jack, Jack, Jack."

Markus stepped away and put his head down.

"Jack wherever did you go? Oh Lord thank you, thank you." She looked up at the sky as if God had thrown him from there like rain.

Mel let go of Jack's hand. "He was like, on the other side," she stuttered, pointing at the alleyway. "Like we found him there and stuff."

Mum didn't care, she just hugged the boy like crazy; who ironically, had started crying again. After she grabbed Mel, pulling the teenager into a teary embrace. Markus watched Mel's face whiten with shock, eyes swimming and magnified behind her glasses. Moments later she too closed her eyes and hugged the woman back. Markus watched the boy step away, looking up at them in wonderment.

If you're not careful lady, you're gonna lose the little fucker again.

All this sentiment was giving him a headache. He was getting tired of this bullshit and wanted to go. "Mel!"

His girlfriend didn't hear him, too locked onto her special little moment.

"Thank you, thank you love," the mum was saying. "I literally turned for half a second and he was gone. It's not like him. It's not like *me*. It's not like me at all," she said, seeming the need to justify herself to the teenager.

Mel just shrugged, her face still dazed and overwhelmed from the hug.

"Like, we, I just saw him and stuff. Like crying and that. We were on our way out of town, see, and – "

"We?"

Up until now the mother hadn't even noticed Markus. She looked at him and mouthed *thank you* over and over again, waving him over. Reluctantly he waded towards them.

"You two. I owe you the world!"

Mel couldn't hide the pleasure in her face whereas Markus found it cringing. "Where are you going?" she said. "What are your names? Is there anything I can do?"

She fired a hundred questions at them and Mel didn't know which one to answer first.

"We're alright," Markus mumbled.

"I'm Mel, and this is my boyfriend Markus."

The mum shook their hands and repeated their names. "Mel. Markus. Thank you. Thank you *both*. Can I give you a lift anywhere? Let me give you some money at least!"

Markus spied at all the gold dripping off her hand; rings, bracelets. "Well," he said.

"It's okay." Mel piped up. "*Please*, like, we can't accept a reward for just like, looking after Jack and stuff."

The mum's eyes were full of tears as she looked at her son, then back at the teenagers.

"You're such a beautiful little girl," she said to Mel. There was a raw intensity to her expression that scared Mel a little. "Bet your Mum's so proud."

Mel's face gave way and she looked at the ground.

"Thank you. Thank you," she said for the millionth time. "You hear so many horror stories on the news. I can't thank you enough."

No shit, Markus thought.

396

"I'll never let him out of my sight again."

She hugged Mel again and then looked over at Markus and smiled, before taking her son in one hand and her shopping bags in the other, disappearing back into the crowds.

Mel watched her until she was gone, when she was Markus was up by her.

"You really are fucking dumb!"

Mel turned slowly and faced him, only half-listening. "What?"

"Telling her our names. We're on the fucking run, remember? We're wanted!"

Mel didn't say anything. Everything seemed to be moving in slow-motion.

"And money," Markus added. "We're as broke as a joke and some rich bitch offers us dollar and you turn her down. Where's your head at Mel?"

Love.

"Sometimes, you just don't think," he said in her ear.

"She was nice."

Markus picked his bike back off the wall.

"No one has ever hugged me like that before," she said.

He pointed his bike at the alleyway. "Can we go now?"

"Wish I had a mum like that."

"Mel c'mon."

"Hey do you think we'll have kids one day?"

"What?"

"I'd love to have a son like Jack. I'd be a good mum, don't you think?"

Markus pulled up beside her. "What are you going on about now?"

"I said do you think we'll have children one day?"

Markus pulled his biggest screw-face yet. "No!"

A little choke cracked at the back of her throat. "Why not?"

Markus nodded at the crowds that moved around them, all the people zigzagging across their view. "Why would we?"

They were on the roads now with road signs leading the way. There were no wrong turns today, no real chance of error. Although it was getting late again and sunset wasn't too far away. The blue of the sky had dimmed to an ominous grey and rain looked like it was about to make a reappearance. They cycled in a straight line. Sometimes cars or lorries beeped at Mel's unsteady riding. Overall it was a smooth run. One road in particular ran on for miles, sweeping past villages, taking them to the edge of the woods. As the road steepened Mel got off and pushed.

"Mel c'mon."

"No I'm resting for a bit."

Markus sighed and joined her. They walked for a good fifteen minutes up the rest of the hill. From behind the trees an eerie sound droned away. When the line of trees abruptly ended something else towered above them, made them jump a little.

"Whoa!" Markus cried, excited.

Mel looked away, scared. "Ugh I don't like them."

"Wind turbines?"

She wouldn't look up. Kept her eyes on the front wheel.

Markus laughed. "You're a fucking freak."

The sound got louder, an awesome waft filling the sky.

"It's like they can see everything," Mel said. "It's like they know what we're up to."

"You mean like god?"

"Yeah," Mel said. "Like, kind of."

Markus laughed again and looked up at three more white towers looming over the hill, the propellers silently rotating in the distance.

"You're mad," he said.

It was getting dark again. The rain came down and both teenagers didn't expect this sudden attack of hunger. They hadn't eaten since breakfast and now they were in the middle of a random field without food. The feeling ached through their bones and made their heads light. With a trembling hand Markus ripped the tent from its bag.

"We'll just have to fight it off until tomorrow. There's nothing we can do now."

"Big Bear I can't! Feel like I'm gonna pass-out."

"Yeah well you should have thought about that before you insisted we come off the road! We literally had another half hour, if that."

Markus had the tent spread across the bumpy field.

"We've been riding all day," she said, arms folded. "I can't believe we didn't make it. Like, maybe we've got lost again."

"Hey I told you not to bring that up. Besides, we ain't been cycling all day. Cos we spent most of it with that retarded kid of yours."

"Hey don't call him that!"

Markus shook his head, throwing the tent pegs down in front of him. "What time is it anyway?"

"I don't know," she said, holding her tummy like it was a baby. "Too dark to see my watch. Look at your phone."

He shot her a look. "I've told you, no phones!"

"Okay. AALRIGHT."

"You better not have put yours on."

"I haven't."

"Not even for a second."

"I didn't."

"They'll trace us."

"I haven't alright."

"Do you want to get caught?"

Mel went silent.

Markus leaned in and rested his forehead on hers, staring her down, "what?"

"Well, like, don't you think we've made our point and stuff?"

Rain covered both of their faces.

"Point?" What point?"

"We can't run forever."

"It's been three fucking days. I mean this is only our third fucking night!"

"Stop swearing at me all the time. And stop calling Jack a retard. Sometimes you don't know how to be a human."

Screw-face. "What?"

Mel felt so desperate she didn't try to hide it anymore.

"I've had enough Big Bear. I'm tired. I'm cold. I'm dirty. And above all I'm hungry. I'm so effing hungry Markus. I'm hungry all the time. I want to go home."

Markus took a large step back and glared at her. "Home? Home!" He roared. "You mean home to your c$nt mum and bitch sister?"

Mel hated them but she didn't like him saying that.

"Home with *them* instead of out here with *me?* You'd prefer them rather than your own boyfriend?"

"It's not like that it's just … "

"You hate your mum," he reminded her.

"I know I do."

"She's the causer of *all* our problems."

"I know but ..."

"She keeps us apart."

Mel nodded the smallest nod.

"Well by going back you're picking her over me."

The rain got harder and a nasty wind hit them in the side of the face.

"I hate it when you play these head-games Markus. You remind me of Mia."

"What head-games? What's Mia got to do with it? What the fuck you even talking about?"

From nowhere they had the tent up. Only it wasn't straight. They were pegs missing and one half of it flapped open. Mel looked at the tent and then at the rain and wanted to cry. She was just about to but something caught her eye. A human form by the gate.

"Hey see that man over there?"

Markus was trying to fix the tent. "What?"

"By the gate, there's a man."

Markus came up from behind the tent and walked around it. When he looked the figure had gone. "Where?"

"Swear, like, I just saw a man in the mist, by the gate."

"'Man in The Mist'" Markus giggled. "You're tripping. Think this hunger has you hallucinating."

"No, like, there was a man. I saw his bald head. He was tall."

Markus had made better work of the tent but it still wasn't great. Somehow he had managed to rip part of it. Rain dripped in and Mel was dreading the night. A stomach growled and they couldn't work out who it came from. Probably both of us, one of them said.

"Hey there he is again," Mel said, pointing,

Markus followed the wobble of her shaky finger to the direction of the fence and indeed there was a man. Stood erect at the gate, a wolf by his side.

"I told you. I told you!" she said, almost excited.

"Alright you told me," Markus replied, under his breath, staring, weighing it up. "Who the fuck is this?"

His long figure blurred from behind the drizzle, his German Shepard obedient at his side.

"Markus I'm scared."

The man stared, thin and unmoving. She noticed he was

carrying a stick too, which looked like some kind of club. The mist thickened and neither teenager could see his face.

After a few eerie moments Markus sprang decisively to his feet.

"Big Bear, what you doing?"

Markus said nothing, just strode straight towards the man. Wind howled from the trees in the top right-hand-corner of the field. His clothes were cold against his skin and mud squelched under his trainers. The man remained still; his hands cupped gently on the top bar of the gate. Getting nearer Markus could see the balding grey of his head, almost like he was wearing a silver swimming cap.

"Hey old man what the fuck's up?"

He didn't seem to hear the boy so he said it again. "I said what's up?"

"You should be careful," the man said in a clear, calm voice.

"Why?"

"That's private property."

"So?"

Now Markus was a mere metre away, only the gate between them.

"What's it got to do with you?" he pushed on.

Despite the oncoming aggression the old man and his dog remained unfazed.

"It's got nothing to do with me," he said.

"Why don't you piss off then?"

"Cos I'd hate to see you in trouble."

"What you talking about?"

The man rearranged his fingers on the gate. "The farmer will be up in a few hours. And I'm afraid he'd be rather enraged at you camping in the middle of his field. He's somewhat of a tyrant, you see. And he owns a rather large gun."

Markus changed the expression in his face to something else.

"I've never liked the man, you see. He and I have never really got on."

Markus noticed that the dog was staring at him, two black eyes twinkling in the dark, swirls of white breath trailing from its jaws and the wet of its nose.

The old man wiped his mouth, which seemed to be full of two large front teeth. "Hey is that a girl with you?"

Silently Mel had joined Markus's side. "What's going on?" she said, uncertain.

"This man was just leaving," he said.

"Hello," he said to Mel with a slow voice.

"Hello," Mel replied, flinching.

"I was just telling your friend here."

"Boyfriend," Markus corrected.

"I do apologise, *boyfriend*. That the field you are standing in belongs to a rather disagreeable farmer. Who is, shall we say, very territorial about his property. He won't be happy when he sees you in a few hours."

Mel looked at Markus to do something, say something.

"I would advise that you move along."

Markus's face was set into a deep scowl but he couldn't think how to react.

"How old are you two anyway?" the man asked. "Thirteen, fourteen years old? No age to be all the way out here alone."

Mel was about to answer with The Truth but Markus came in with A Lie. "We're sixteen and we're not alone. We have each other. And what do you mean *all the way out here*. You don't know where we're from, do you?"

The man never answered. "Very well," he said, giving a courteous nod. "Just thought I'd give you the *heads up*, as they say."

"Thank You," Mel said, smiling.

The man returned the smile and went to walk away. "Look," he said, turning back around again. "I live just over there." He pointed towards the trees. "If you wish you can stay the night, in the warm. I have a huge bowl of stew that needs eating and you're quite welcome to join me."

Markus felt a sudden squeeze on his fingers from Mel.

"Nah mate. We're sound," he said.

Mel squeezed again. Markus looked at her.

"Okay. Well, the offer's there."

The man walked on, another few yards before turning one last time. "I live in that turquoise cottage by the bridge in case you change your mind. I'll be up for the next few hours. Feel free to knock on if you have a change of heart. The name is Mr Eagle," he said.

The old man and his dog disappeared into the darkness of the lane.

All Mel could taste now was the salt and veg and meat of a hot, wholesome stew. It entered her mouth and slipped down her throat and filled her stomach, bringing her being back to life.

"Markus," she said, eyes wide and locked fiercely onto his.

"What?" he said, making his way back to the skeletal tent, which was almost caved in by the nocturnal elements.

"Markus," she said again. "Let's go."

"Are you mad? I ain't going to some pervert's lair."

"Markus I'm starving."

"I'm starving too but there's no way we're going. He's a fucking nonce, man!"

"Big Bear he's fine. He's okay. My nature-feeling says he's safe."

"Your what?"

"My instinct."

"You ain't got no instinct. You're naïve. You don't know these streets like I do."

Mel had a gentle hold of his collar. "These aren't the streets," she said. "It's a field. A cold, wet, miserable field and that farmer is going to be up soon and I don't want to be here when he does. I'm going even if you're not."

Markus grabbed her and glared into her eyes. "I don't think so. You're my responsibility now. If you want we can go walk and find an all-night garage but we ain't going to some pervy paedophile palace on the promise of stew. It's a trap."

"My nature-feeling says it isn't and my nature-feeling is *always* right."

"It isn't your nature-feeling that's talking, it's hunger. All-night garage, that's where we're going. End of."

"We haven't got any money!"

Her scream made Markus jump, ripping through the night, filling the sky and echoing from the trees.

"*Please*," she said, tugging his collar so hard it was like she was trying to bring him down. "Please. I can't take anymore. I can't take another night. I can't take this hunger and cold. Please let's go to Mr Eagle's turquoise cottage by the bridge."

That bit made Markus laugh inside. *Mr Eagle's turquoise cottage by the bridge.* It all sounded so far-fetched, like some dumb fairy-tale you read in a book. Mr Eagle wasn't even a proper name. I mean who even had a name like that, only a paedo would have name like that, Markus thought. He didn't know how she did it, but Mel always seemed to get her own way somehow, in the end. When she wanted to stop and push their bikes, they did. When she wanted to stop and set up the tent, they did. Now she was insisting they go to some old man's house in the middle of nowhere, a man they had never met, a weird stranger lurking around in the dead of the night.

"My nature-feeling says it's safe Big Bear, *Please!*"

She said *please* a thousand times and she would carry on saying it until Markus broke and gave in and gave her what she wanted.

"Okay," he said, at last. "You win."

He expected her to smile and jump up and down, clapping, some kind of celebratory display, but, she didn't. Just turned and headed back to get her rucksack, while Markus started taking down the tent, which was almost blown down anyway.

Mel watched Markus's beat-up knuckles knock on the dark hollow wood of Mr Eagle's front door. The bark of the dog didn't come and the teenagers wondered if they had the right place. Markus stepped back and looked at the cottage. He couldn't even see if it was turquoise or not. All colours are the same in the dark, he thought. It was the only place by the bridge though so this had to be it. He knocked again, louder. There was no sound of footsteps or the turning of a key or bolt, but the door just silently opened and Mr Eagle's wizened face appeared, the blaze of his blue eyes and the glare of his big white teeth lit up the space before them.

"Ah. You made it," he said, as if expecting them.

"We did," Mel said, already grateful.

She stepped forward but her boyfriend placed a hand on her chest and pushed her back.

"Before we step in," he said. "I want you to know something." Markus prepared his voice, gathering his words carefully. "Anything happens to her and you die. Simple as. Even if I have to come back from the dead to kill you."

Mr Eagle didn't say anything, just opened his door and let the teenagers inside.

They were met with warmth and candlelight and the strong smell of cooked food. The dog raised her head for a second or two before going back to sleep.

"Your dog," Mel said. "Is like, so well-behaved and stuff."

"I groomed her well." Mr Eagle said with a smile, gazing down at his sleeping companion.

Markus had not taken his eyes off the old man the whole time. He studied his every move and gesture. Mr Eagle could sense this and turned his attention to the boy.

"It's good that you do this."

"Do what?" Markus said.

"Protect her this way. Shows character."

Mel didn't really get what was going on. She was still staring at the dog, admiring her shiny coat.

"Yeah. Well. Who else will, if I don't?"

Mr Eagle nodded and then opened his hand at a beat-up settee by the fire. "Please, sit."

Mel sat. Markus gave it a few moments first, still surveying the house. It was old, like olden-times. Like houses you saw in museums, he thought. Like from days in the war or something. It was bare and dark, brick and iron and dirty gold ornaments. Yet the huge blazing fire and the candles gave it a homely feel. The flickering flames lit up Mel's face as she too was looking around, blank wonderment in her expression. She hugged herself into a ball, her whole soul pointed at the food and where it was coming from.

"I'll get the stew," he said, at last.

Mr Eagle moved slowly. He was older than Markus first thought and he liked this. He watched his thin, frail gait hobble across the living room and knew he could snap him in a second, if the man tried anything funny. Once he was out the room Mel leaned forward with a big happy face. "I told you Big Bear, I told you he was safe. My nature-feelings are always right."

Markus didn't say anything, just waited for what was going to happen next.

Mr Eagle retuned with two large bowls of steaming stew; several slices of buttered French bread placed around the perimeter. He handed Mel hers first, then the boy.

"Where's yours?" Markus said.

Mel was already into it, blowing and sipping and sinking the silver soup spoon in again and again.

"I've already eaten," he said. "But you go ahead."

Markus eyed him again before staring at the spoon poised at his mouth, he waited, like that moment before a bungee jump, at last taking his first mouthful of the homemade stew. In no time both bowls were empty and the bread gone too.

Mel slumped back and gazed at the wooden ceiling. "That was like, *officially* the best dinner ever!"

A silent burp rumbled in Markus's chest and he looked into the fire, nodding in agreement.

"More?" Mr Eagle said.

Mel nodded and then Markus did too. Mr Eagle smiled and got up, his bony-veined arms shaking as he pushed up from the chair.

"Hey I'll help you Mr Eagle," Mel said.

No matter how many times Markus heard that name he could never get used to it. It sounded so ridiculous he had to ask about it.

"Your name," he said. "*Eagle*. That's not like your proper name is it? Like your actual family name?"

The old man stood, a gentle smile spreading across his ancient face, those gaping tombstone teeth almost at his chin. "No. No it's not. It's what's known as a nickname around here."

"Why can you fly or something?" Markus said, laughing.

Mel didn't get it.

The old man chuckled too. "Only in my dreams," he said.

Markus thought the old man talked strange, he was posh and cryptic, almost like his words carried a hidden meaning.

"What then?" Markus said.

Mel waited too, although she was more eager to tuck into the second bowl of stew rather than solve the enigma of the man's mysterious name.

"Nothing that enchanting, I'm afraid," he began. "Just that I used to own a pair of rather majestic eagles. Somewhat of a rare thing, and not precisely legal either. Somehow I managed to get them over from South America in the seventies. Had my boys for years. Everyone knew me as The Eagle Man, Mr Eagle. People of the village called me that and I have to admit I rather liked it, so much so that I decided to keep it, so the name stuck around much longer than they did."

"They?"

"My boys, my eagles."

"What happened to them?" Markus asked.

"They passed, like all things eventually do."

Mr Eagle looked down at his dog curled up in the corner. "Now there's just me and the old girl there."

Markus felt his guard began to slip. He now saw the old man for what he really was, lonely.

"Do you have any pets?" the old man asked.

Mel wiped her glasses from the condensation the fire had caused. "I got a dog," she said. "A stupid boy-dog with a girl's name. But like, it's nothing like your dog Mr Eagle. It's all wild and silly and stupid and stuff."

"What about you?" he said to Markus.

He got tempted to mention his little duckling from the summer only it sounded lame. Plus it was kind of a secret, something Markus wanted to keep to himself.

"Nah. Not much of an animal person."

"He's not much of a human person either," Mel said.

"Oh I don't know," Mr Eagle said, wiping his mouth again. "He seems to be very fond of you dear."

Markus looked down and Mel smiled and blushed and looked dead happy.

"Anyway I'll go and get that second stew," Mr Eagle said, moving across the room. "I also have an unopened bottle of dandelion and burdock. I'm drinking beer myself but obviously you're too young for any of that."

While Mel and Mr Eagle fetched the food and drink Markus thought more about the man. He was surprised that he never asked anything about them. No questions at all. What they were doing, where they'd been? He couldn't recall the man even asking their names. It's like none of that mattered, the details or deeds, like he wasn't interested in putting labels on things. The three of them were just *being* and Markus liked that. Adults were normally always asking questions or telling you what to do.

Eagle and Mel returned. They must have been joking about something because both were laughing, Mel especially. For the next hour there wasn't much talk. The teenagers ate slower this time, really savouring the food. They ate while Mr Eagle drank. Markus was surprised how fast he did drink, long wide-eyed tugs on the can, seeming to empty each beverage in four or five swallows. And then he was onto the next, yanking at the ring-pull, that hiss and crack before slurping again. Markus looked over at Mel and noticed her eyes were beginning to go. She was well-rested and fed and the heavy, cosy atmosphere was making her drift. Markus was tired too but he knew it would be a long time yet before he slept. Wherever he was, and whoever he was with he was always, *ultimo hombre de pie* – Last Man Standing. Now it Mr Eagle's turn to drift, but not drift to sleep like his girlfriend had, but drift off to another place. As he supped he began to ramble, his ocean-blue eyes far-off and remote as his mouth moved. Markus had seen this before with his own old man, his dad. Lance Venner had spent many a night in an alcoholic mantra, speaking to a son he didn't know was there. The old man probably sunk four or five cans in that final hour, his words slurring and blurring in repetition.

"It's a good life. Always a good life, when all said and done. As one thing ends, another begins. Because really, it was never about *me* anyway. It never was, or is, about us. But the bigger picture, you see. Like all of it moving as one. Because it's all connected, somehow. But I knew you'd come here tonight. Even before I saw you there. I knew I'd find you, at last. So little and dangerous you are. Only the eagles know. They're the only ones who can fly. But. It's late now, or early. Depending on how you look at things. It's all just a matter of perspective, you see … or not."

Markus watched him, half hypnotised, half amused. He couldn't believe how vulnerable he was. He had doubts about coming here earlier, only now he realised it wasn't the teenagers taking the risk, but the old man.

Suddenly he was up on his feet, wobbling, looking around at the room and then at Markus. His eyes flickered and refocussed, surprised to see him there, the boy, trying to work out where he'd come from.

"Oh. You," he said. "Yes of course. Well."

"You're a bit steaming aren't you old man?"

"What?"

"Banging back that sauce a bit too much wasn't ya?" Markus felt a certain sense of cruelty and disdain in the tone of his own voice.

"I … "

"Better get to bed." Markus finished off his sentence for him. "Before I take a nasty fall and end up hurt."

Mel squirmed in her sleep and rolled over.

Mr Eagle looked at the girl, then at the boy, again trying to work out where they'd come from. All of a sudden he seemed to snap out of his trance and sober up a touch.

"Yes," he said. "You're right I really should go to bed. I'll let you children sleep. Sleep like the babies you are. You know, you're only ever innocent when you dream."

"Yeah, right," Markus said. He was lying on his side, propping his head on his hand.

"Tessa sleeps in the kitchen," he said. "And the embers will die out when they're ready. Just let them burn out on their own. There's a toilet downstairs, as you know. I normally wake up around seven but I've had a rather lot of alcohol tonight so it could be a trifle later. Feel free to help yourself to anything. *Mi casa su casa.*"

"What?"

"My home is your home," he said, bowing.

Mel smiled in her sleep and Markus smiled too.

The old man left, the dog following at the click of his fingers.

Mel stirred and inched herself into Markus's lap. "I told you he was nice."

"Yes alright," Markus said. "Your nature-feeling wins again."

"Landed on our feet didn't we?"

"Suppose."

Outside the wind howled and rain battered the window.

"Can't even imagine what outside must *feel* like now," she said in a thin voice. "So glad we're not there."

Markus nodded even though her eyes were closed and she couldn't see him. She was right. It was bliss to be warm, on dry solid ground with solid walls around them. The room slowly darkened as the fire died out. Big Bear wrapped her up, and as always, she fell asleep first.

She was being rocked back and forth. A hand was on her, pushing her one way and then the other.

"Mel wake up. We need to leave, *now.*"

There was nothing so he pushed again, almost crushing her into the settee. "Mel!"

As soon as she woke her first words were, "it's my sister Adele's birthday today."

"What?"

"I'm still dreaming."

Mel was awake and Markus was in her face. "Up!"

She sat and looked around her, scared, disorientated, not a clue where she was. It took a full minute to remember Mr Eagle's Turquoise Cottage by the Bridge.

She turned back around and groaned. "No. More sleep."

"Mel we need to roll, now!"

A deep whimper smothered her voice, "it's still dark outside."

"Mel I'm serious, you don't get up now and I'll drag you out with my bare hands."

"Why are you always on a mission? We're nearly at Skegness anyway. You said so yourself, half an hour. Why can't we sleep more and have breakfast with Mr Eagle?"

"Cos I've found this, that's why?"

Markus held out a scrap of newspaper in front of Mel's scrunched-up sleepy eyes.

He kept it there while she put her glasses on. Still she couldn't see it properly so she took it from him and read:

Teenage sweethearts aged just 14 run away together with only a tent for shelter: Police appeal for help after parents raised the alarm when duo failed to attend school.

- *Parents worried after pair failed to return from school on Monday.*
- *Police are now involved and are appealing to anyone with information.*
- *The two teenagers have taken a tent with them, as well as bikes and food.*

Police are appealing for information after two teenage sweethearts aged just 14 ran away together.

Melanie Ellis and Markus Venner, both just 14, have not come home since Monday and were last seen on their way to school in Kimble Wells, Lincolnshire together.

It is believed they are on bikes and have taken only a tent for shelter, along with some food.

Both sets of parents raised the alarm around the same time Monday when the two failed to return home.

It is understood they are in a relationship together and may be camping either at a campsite or in woods or open land nearby.

Officers investigating their disappearance are asking if anyone has seen them sleeping rough or knows where they are.

A spokesperson for Lincolnshire Police said: They may still be in Kimble Wells, Cowbit, or Crowland area and officers are urging them to get in touch and let someone know they are safe and well.

'Anyone who has seen either Melanie or Markus, or has knowledge of persons camping in the South Holland area, is asked to call us.'

410

Melanie, or 'Mel' as she likes to be called is described as 5ft 5ins tall, slim build, with very long brown/dark blonde highlighted hair, black glasses and a slim face.

Markus is described as 5ft 10ins tall, stocky build, with thick mousy hair.

Underneath, at the bottom of the page, they were there. Two smiley pictures. Mel in colour, Markus in black and white. Mel's picture was a school photo and Markus was from somewhere else.

Mel stared at the sheet of newspaper, open-mouthed and pale. She couldn't say anything for a few seconds, then in a slow whisper, "Holy eff ... I never knew ... "

Markus whipped the paper back off her. "About 5:10??"

"What?"

"Saying I'm five-foot-ten, I'm fucking six-foot!"

Mel was still staring into space, suddenly she was wide awake.

"And what's all this bullshit about 'both sets of parents.' My mum's dead and my dad may as well be. Adults, police, reporters, they all fucking lie man!"

Mel couldn't understand what Markus was getting so mad about at least somebody cared, at least they were out looking for them. She felt overwhelmed, worried, scared to death, all the trouble they caused. She never knew it was going to be like this, she never knew it would go this far, this serious, like in all the newspapers and stuff.

"That's why we need to get the fuck out of here, sharp!" Markus was already on his feet. "Knew that fucker had a motive," he said, nodding sideways in the direction on the stairs. "And this is it. He's trying to keep us here, get the reward."

"What reward?" Mel said, slowly climbing onto her feet.

"There's bound to be a reward, for catching us."

"But we haven't done anything wrong," Mel moaned.

Markus shook his head and took her hand, dragging her to the door. When he tried to open it, it wouldn't. "Bastard's locked us in! I'll put the windows through if I have to."

"No wait! Here's the key," she said, reaching out and taking it from a table.

They unlocked and pushed. Already the cold invaded the cottage from a small crack in the door. Markus was gone but Mel hung back, she looked down at the dog who was curled up in the corner of the kitchen. She raised her old brown eyes at Mel and then lowered them again. Just as she made no noise when they entered, she didn't as they left.

They were on the road again, cycling past those god-awful wind turbines; pylons, woods, the farmer's field. They rode fast as the sun rose and light leaked over the countryside. Skeg wasn't half an hour away, but further, everything was always further. Markus made out he knew where he was going but Mel doubted him. Half the time they seemed to be moving at random, this right, this left, this lane, that road. Going in vast circles. Markus blamed Mel for being slow but most of it was his fault, leading them in the wrong direction again and again. Her boyfriend always way up ahead, stopping every now and then, impatiently tapping his foot while the exhausted girl played catch-up.

He was waiting for her again, this time at a neon truck stop.

"C'mon. Let's get breakfast."

He jumped off his bike and pushed it through patches of oil, six or seven artic lorries surrounding them in the oval yard.

"Big Bear just wait a minute. I don't know what's happening."

She didn't. Everything seemed to be moving so fast. There was something so frantic and crazy about this morning. Her senses felt ambushed. It's like she was still asleep in Mr Eagle's Turquoise Cottage by The Bridge and all this was just some murky nightmare. One minute she was snuggled up on a settee and now she was stepping into a creepy cafe with big grubby men everywhere. It was still early, dead early. Barely light outside.

"Markus we can't eat here."

"Why?"

"Cos, like, we haven't got any money remember?"

"Just sit and keep your head down," he said. "We have our pictures in the paper now. People will want the reward."

She could tell that part of Markus was enjoying this, like it was all some big game. "Why do you keep talking about a reward?"

Everybody looked up when they entered, like a saloon in western films. Most of the men were tucking into food, big greasy plates with the Sun newspaper spread out in front of them. Radio noise squabbled in the background. Markus strode confidently to the woman behind the counter.

"Two large English's please."

Mel thought he had a deep voice and sounded like an adult. The scrawny woman did look a little surprised to see two customers so young and at such an early hour.

"Any drinks with that love?" she said.

"Tea," Markus said.

"Two teas?"

Markus nodded and then moved to the table in the corner where Mel was sat with her head down. "Shit," she said, opening her eyes.

"What?"

"We didn't chain the bikes!"

"Fuck it, they'll be alright."

That was Markus's answer to everything, she thought. *Fuck it.*

Mel looked around the cafe. It was old and grimy with tea stains up the wall. There was an Elvis clock under the ceiling, his hips swinging to the movement of time. Then there was another old picture on the wall opposite, a black and white photo of a man standing next to a car. A caption reading, *On the Road Again.*

Most of the pictures were of women though and Mel found this creepy; blonde women and brunette women and redheaded women. One was of a blonde lady licking milk off a bottle, winking seductively. *Have you had your milk today?* Mel didn't like any of it and she wanted to leave. She wanted to leave even more when she noticed eyes of the men in the cafe start to drift over. Mel folded her arms across her chest and looked down again.

Like, don't they know I'm only fourteen and stuff?

Just then the woman's shrill squawk sounded across the cafe. "You paying for these now love?" Again all eyes in the silent truck-stop looked up at the seated teenagers.

"Ah. Yeah," Markus said, insolently getting to his feet. Mel had seen these movements before, like so many times at school when teachers had asked him to move or sent him out of class. Once at the counter a hand was slipped into his pocket and he pulled out a small clump of notes, extracted a ten and then handed it over to the woman. Mel could feel herself get mad, a bubbling of anger from the bottom end up. When Markus sat she shook her head and her long hair moved across her face.

"You stole from Mr Eagle," she said flatly.

Her boyfriend said nothing, sat back with his hands wedged in the front pocket of his hoodie.

"I can't believe you did that?" she continued.

Still the reaction was nil.

"After all he did for us?"

Markus's face moved at last, sitting forward an inch. "Fuck him."

"He took us in from the cold," she said with a voice that had a crack in it. "He fed us, gave us shelter. Was dead-kind and stuff and then you go and stab him in the back."

"No more than he was going to stab us in the back."

"How?"

"He only wanted us for the reward."

"Like, that's just BS and you know it."

Markus yawned.

"Why didn't he just ring the police straight away then? Like he would have just done it last night and stuff."

Markus remained silent.

"Admit it. Like, you only wanted to leave this morning because of the money you stole from him. He probably hadn't even read that article."

Markus gave a weak smile and shook his head again. "You might wanna keep your voice down."

"It's wrong Markus and you know it."

Markus couldn't stop smiling only now he wasn't trying to hide it. "He was a fucking nonce Mel, a paedo. Why else would he want us in his crib? The only reason he didn't try touching us up was because I threatened him at the beginning. And he *had* read that paper cos you didn't hear all the drunken weird shit he was rambling after you fell asleep. Stuff about *how he knew he'd find us.* He knew, okay. *He knew.* Besides, I don't give a fuck about him or anyone else. The only two people I look out for in this life are the two people sat at this table. And if I have to steal, cheat, or kill for us then I will."

Mel closed her eyes and opened them again. The world seemed upside down. As touched as she was by his devotion she was still angry. Still livid at him for stealing off Mr Eagle. What she really wanted to do, more than anything else in the world, was go to the toilet and turn on her phone, see all the missed calls and texts from all the people who loved and cared about her. She wanted to ring her mum and let her know where she was. *Some greasy truck-stop a mile outside of Skeg.*

When she looked up the breakfasts were there and Markus was

already into his, pouring brown sauce all over the sausage and bacon. Mel's breakfast stayed where it was, untouched.

"Mel eat, we've got a long day."

"I'm not hungry."

"Course you are."

"I ate too much yesterday."

"Just eat."

"I'm not eating because of Mr Eagle. It's not right."

Markus said no more, he ate and Mel watched. When he looked up again she was asleep, well not asleep, but not awake either, that weird nodding thing that was somewhere in between.

Markus could just about make out the words *Welcome to Skegness* on a big blue and white sign when the police pulled them over. His initial reaction was to bunny-hop over the curb and bomb down the hill, into the field and away but Mel had already given in. She had stopped dead and the police car had cut diagonally in front of her. She couldn't get away even if she wanted to.

"Put your bike down Melanie," he said.

Hearing her name in full sounded soothing and safe. He was a tall officer with a stern face.

"You too Markus," he said, no urgency in his voice. "Your little adventure is over I'm afraid."

Mel noticed the shadow of a girl on the tarmac. As she adjusted her glasses, so did the shadow. The shadow looked too big to be Mel Ellis. She looked around for another girl but there wasn't one.

"Come here," the officer said to the boy.

"Copper can I just touch that Skeg sign? I'm literally twenty yards away from accomplishing my mission."

"Enough of your games lad. You've caused enough trouble as it is. Your parents are worried sick."

He was radioing information through while chastising the pair.

"I haven't got parents," Markus snapped.

"Try telling that to your auntie. You're lucky to have someone who cares so much."

"What about my mum, like does she care?" Mel said from nowhere, throwing her rucksack to the ground.

The officer was too busy talking into the radio to answer.

Markus was still staring at the Skeg sign, wondering if he could make it in time.

"Don't bother son. I don't want to take you back to your aunt's in cuffs but I will if you don't come here in the next five seconds. Trust me, I can run faster than you pal, and this car can run faster than your bike."

Markus wore a cunning smile, considering his luck.

"Just do as he says," Mel said, tired.

Markus threw his head down, the smile still on his face as he strolled over to the police car. "Busted!" He sang out-loud. He really does think that all this is a game, Mel thought.

The officer put both teenagers in the back and then returned to his radio. The girl and the boy could hear their names being mentioned.

"Wonder if we'll have another piece about us in the paper?" Markus said with a new excitement.

Mel never answered.

Minutes later the officer got behind the steering wheel.

"Hey what about our bikes?" Markus said.

"I'm waiting for another vehicle. Don't worry you'll get it all back."

"Hey are we arrested?"

"Markus can you just stop," Mel said.

Markus sat back and stretched whereas Mel seemed to lean forward into a ball.

"Told you Eagle was a grass," he said.

"It wasn't Mr Eagle. It was the people in the cafe. Didn't you see the way they were all looking at us and stuff?"

"Bet the nonce is rubbing his paedo hands together at all the reward money he's gonna get."

Mel shook her head and looked out the window. Two more police vehicles showed up, a car and a van. Officers stepped out and gazed down at the runaway teens. Cars passing by looked in too, craning their necks, almost bumping into the car in front. One officer had to stand in front and wave them on. The morning was awash with blue lights and commotion.

"I feel famous," Markus said.

"I feel like I want to go home."

On leaving Markus didn't know if the copper did this on purpose or whether he was just turning around in the road, but the police car did in fact pass the Skegness sign on the way out. Markus smiled and nodded his head, I always complete my missions, he thought.

Always. Always. Always have. Always will.

Apart from Markus asking if they could put the sirens on and the officer telling him not to be silly the ride home was completely silent. Suppose all the talking will come later, Mel thought. She took off her glasses and wiped them so she could watch the world pass her window. Four wheels are faster than two so the distance was cut about a hundred times shorter. It's still a pretty long way though, she thought. Long enough for me. Soon the shiny sign for Kimble Wells appeared to their right. They left here only three days ago. Three days which now felt like three years; a decade, a small lifetime.

Mel

Dear Seddy,

Remember at The Very Start, how I told You that I can't sleep at night and stuff? How I used to be awake All Night but sleep in the day, like an insomnia kind of a thing?

Remember?

Well, like, I'm not even like that anymore. In fact The Truth is I'm exactly the opposite. It's very rare I'm ever awake after 11 o' clock tbh. Tbh I'm tired all the time These Days and I don't know why??

I think there could be something wrong with me.

Like SERIOUSLY wrong with me.

Like, I LITERALLY could be dying inside and not even know it.

I'm even tired Right Now and struggling to keep my eyes open, struggling to write THESE WORDS. Only I've not written inside You for ages and I think's it's time for a catch-up. Like, You deserve to know what's been going on and stuff. Deserve to be kept in the picture. It seems only right. Seems only fair.

Of course I expected mum to go mad. Course I expected her to like TOTALLY flip when she saw me again. Maybe like slap me in the face or ground me For Life and stuff. But in actual fact she charged into my arms and about crushed every bone in my flippin body by the strength of her hug. (mum is strong. Her body is like a man.) I'd only been gone Three Days but she carried on like I had been missing for years. Like I was Madeleine McCann or that Ben Boy or someone like that. The neighbours were out and the police was there and tbh I had a feeling that mum was just showing off, a Performance Piece as per usual. Another car took Markus back to his aunt and I was here again, back where I started and stuff.

Mel babe don't ever do that again!!

Babe???? WTF!!!! She had never called me Babe in her WHOLE stupid life.

Babe was Our Dog's name and I wondered if this was her way of calling me a dog, a bitch!

She was on her knees with tears running all into the cracks of her face and that. I had to say, if she was acting it was pretty amazing because her tears were Real Ones and not Crocodile Ones and she did look pretty distraught and cut-up inside and stuff.

I've been out of my mind with worry, she said.

I had to sit in the lounge and tell her and the police where I'd been and what I'd been up to.

Did Markus make you do it, one of them said. Did he bully you into running away?

No! No way!

I shouted That Bit and got dead-angry.

I have my own mind you know? I shouted some more. We were in this thing together, I said.

Okay Melanie, calm down, one of the officers said.

I told them The Truth more or less only I missed certain bits out, which isn't really like Lying cos it's not like I made stuff up. Like I told them that we was going to Skegness only it took ages cos we kept getting lost. I told them that we slept in a tent and that. I didn't tell them about Mr Eagle and I didn't tell them about Jack the Little Boy Lost. And I obvs didn't tell them about Markus stealing all that food and clothes and stuff from Asda. The rest though, I told them.

After that the police mostly talked to mum and said that I needed to see more professionals, probably like The Psychologist Peoples I saw before. mum was TOTALLY different to how she normally was, like she was dead-nice and the Model Mum. She was confused as to why I ran away.

You know why mum don't lie!!!

I don't, she said, shrugging and pulling a face.

I ran away cos you stopped me from seeing Markus, my OWN boyfriend. Cos like you accused him of stealing that tenner even though there was no solid proof!!

mum got tongue-tied and said loads of rubbishy things.

He didn't steal it I know he didn't! I said.

In The Middle of saying that something weird happened. I remembered Mr Eagle and a stone dropped through my chest. I thought of Markus stealing His Money and all of a sudden a horrible blade of doubt stabbed through my brain.

WHAT IF MARKUS DID STEAL THAT TENNER OFF THE WORKTOP AFTER ALL?

It was an awful feeling to have. To think that in fact mum could be right and I could be wrong. That All This could ACTUALLY be

Markus's fault completely. I froze a bit and wavered a touch but had to carry on defending him.

Promise he can come here again? I said. Promise he can come to the house again?

The Police looked uncomfortable and really I knew that we shouldn't be talking about this in front of them.

Promise you won't stop me from seeing him and most of all promise you won't try and end our relationship for good?!

I was exhausted but I had to get my rant out. I had to get it out while The Other Adults were here. Otherwise they'll go and she'll just go back to being Normal again, back to being Normal Mum, Old Mum, The Real Mum, The Truth Mum.

Okay, mum said, looking about ready to cry again.

A Police Lady with a heart-shaped face stepped forward and said that we need to talk about this to the counsellors.

I've seen them before, I said, but they can't do nothing.

I think there needs to be some ongoing support, The Police Lady said, but right now you're home and safe, and that's all what today is about, she said.

All through this I was thinking about My Sister Adele. I hadn't seen her but I could FEEL her. Feel her in the room and somewhere behind me. Then I noticed her bday cards on the windowsill and over the fireplace and my heart about dropped. My dream was right, it was today after all.

Adele! I suddenly said out-loud. Where's my Sis?

I saw her Famous Hair first, it swished through the sea of big adults and came back into My Life. She was ACTUALLY crying for like the First Time EVER and that really shocked me and stuff. We hugged and the hug felt real. Like a Real Love kind of a thing and even though it'd only been Three Days I missed her like mad. Much more than I realised. Much more than I thought I would.

I'm so sorry, I said. I didn't mean to do it on purpose.

Do what on purpose? She said.

The police were making their way out now, still talking to mum about stuff.

Come back on your EXACT birthday, I said. I bet I've spoilt it and stuff?

Adele held my face and looked into it and said, to have My Sister back is the only present I want. The only present birthday present I need. The best present ever.

That just about made me crack-up and feel sick with guilt at how selfish and disgusting I'd been. I truly Hated Myself and I wanted to be out of myself. I wanted to be someone else. I didn't like Mel Ellis one bit. I didn't like who she was and what she was becoming.

Adele held me and I heard the door close and then it was just The Three of Us again.

Four, if you counted Babe the dog.

mum went straight upstairs and stayed there for ages. I wondered what she was doing and why she hadn't come to see me. I heard the flush of the toilet and the creak of her bed over the lounge ceiling.

I was pretty tired too.

We all were.

Everyone.

Everyone cept for Markus, who had left over twenty missed calls on my phone already.

Over the next few days and weeks I went to see The Head People again, the psychologisty counsellory people. I even had to go to the hospital this time. Some of it I had to go on my own and some of it with mum. We talked. We talked and talked and talked. Mostly it was about The Past, stuff with dad and growing up and school and stuff. We talked about Markus too only I didn't say much cos I know that would make him mad if he knew. Like telling a load of adults all of our intimate secrets and that. It just wasn't right. We did talk about The Pregnancy Scare though and we did talk about The Runaway too.

You never seem to plan ahead, This Psychologist Guy said.

What do you mean? I asked.

When you ran away, for instance, you never really thought about what you were doing, where you were going?

I told you we was going Skegness.

Then what, then where?

I shrugged.

You know the word 'consequences,' he said?

It was weird how I always fancied these kinds of men, I was thinking inside. Even if they were ugly I still liked being around them. Older men who were like clever and official and stuff.

Course I know what 'consequences' mean, I said. I'm not stupid.

We talked more. I even told them about You, Seddy. My

Self-Esteem Diary that I had been keeping for ages.

I tell Seddy everything, I said.

Seddy? Why the name Seddy?

Cos like, the name grew over time and stuff, I said. It's called A Self-Esteem Diary but the closer we got the more I made him personal.

Him?

Err, yeah. Mostly it's a Him but sometimes she's a She. Actually it's probably about 50/50. Half male, half female.

Okay, he said.

So like I shortened Self-Esteem Diary to S.E.D, like an abbreviation kind of a thing. Then it went to Sed, now it's Seddy.

And would you say Seddy is your best friend?

Oh without a doubt, I said.

You tell him everything?

Everything.

Do you tell him more than you tell Markus?

Of course.

More than your mum?

I don't tell my mum anything.

More than Mia?

I don't trust Mia one bit.

So your best friend is a book?

I paused and thought and looked out of the window.

He's more than that, I said, finally.

What do you mean?

Well she's like everything and everyone.

Almost like he was God, or a god?

More like nature, I said. I can't really explain it and stuff, and to be honest I don't really want to.

Okay, The Psychologist Guy said. He was looking at me quite intensely but it didn't feel weird somehow.

Hey I'm not going to have to go on head-meds am I? I said. I really don't want to. I mean that is the last thing in the world I want.

The Psychologist Guy was still thinking.

Would you ever let anyone see Seddy, Mel? Would you ever let anyone read him?

I can't quite remember how I responded to that question. I might have solemnly shook my head, or I might have just laughed in his face.

Christmas and Stuff

Markus

Mel's mum's gay, Markus thought. Not gay-gay. Not *literally* gay. Not homosexual gay like his brother was. But gay in a cringing way. Like she did gay things. Erica Ellis wore a Christmas jumper with Santa on the front. She adjusted the headband with antlers sticking out and then sang *Rudolph the Red Nose Reindeer* in her kitchen.

"Muuum!" Mel screeched through her teeth, crippled by embarrassment. "Mum please stop you're killing me!"

"I'm just having fun Mel. It's Christmas Eve. I'm getting in the spirit!"

Her sister Adele laughed and filmed the whole thing on her phone.

She sang it in a deep voice and did this gay dance, punching at the ceiling as she sang the lines. "Had a very shiny nose, like a light bulb!"

In the end Mel had to leave the kitchen whereas Markus kept his eyes on her, a slight smile curled in the corner of his mouth. He saw the word, *pathetic*.

Since the runaway life had settled and there was a rare few months of peace. From the end of October through to the end of December things had been *okay*. It was like life had been stuck into neutral. Everything on an *even keel*. Markus came around the house, not often, but every now and then. He didn't say much or do much but he was just *there*. Normally waiting for Mel to get ready. Mum and sis didn't really speak to him, just the odd few words to break any awkward silences. Erica thought her daughter seemed happy for once, or happy*ish*. There was no back-chat or bad stuff, no mood swings, no friction. No more money had gone missing and Erica Ellis was slowly starting to trust her daughter and this boyfriend of hers. Mel and her boyfriend, who yesterday celebrated their seven-month anniversary. Tonight, Christmas Eve, was the first night she was allowing him to stay over.

"He can Mel but he'll have to stay on the couch."

Mel was so happy she almost hugged her mum, instead she jumped up and down, her hands making a rapid round of claps. "Thank you, thank you, thank you!"

Adele was out at a party, leaving the other three on the sofa, watching Christmas TV. Markus found the whole thing boring, watching her mum getting pissed while those pair of little pricks pranced about on the telly.

"I can't fucking stand Ant and Dec," he said. "I'm sure it's the same person but in two different bodies."

Mel's mum was fixing some food in the kitchen.

Markus continued moaning. "At least at mine we're allowed in the bedroom."

"Is that all you think about?" Mel said.

Markus cocked his head and smiled.

"This is a big deal, y'know?" Mel said, folding her arms. "Like it's such a big deal. Like it shows my mum trusts us and stuff."

"Wow," Markus said, his eyes and mouth expanding into rings of sarcasm. "I'm honoured."

Mel frowned right in his face.

"It's alright for you, you ain't gotta sleep on the settee like a fucking tramp."

"I'll sleep on it then," Mel said.

"What and I get to share a room with your sis, *cool*."

"You're sick. I can't believe you've just said that."

"Mel I'm joking, chill."

Her mum was still doing gay dances, spinning around with a plate of food. Placing it on the coffee table in the middle of the lounge. The second it touched the surface Markus leaned over and grabbed a piece of chocolate Swiss roll.

"Mum, are you drunk?" Mel said.

"Oh maybe a little but it's Christmas!" She sipped her wine and looked back at the telly. "Aren't Ant and Dec cute?" she said.

Mel covered her face with her hair.

"I don't mean *like that*. I just mean they're good at what they do."

Markus could see how embarrassed Mel was and this amused him. "Hey why haven't you got a boyfriend anyway?" he said.

Erica Ellis pulled a face and thought for a few minutes. "You're right, why haven't I?"

Cos you're old, ugly and cheesy, that's why, Markus thought.

"I'm gonna get one this year. Make it my New Year's Resolution. What d'ya reckon Mel?"

Mel was still hidden behind her hair. Markus could see the deep blush through her strands.

Erica spun around in her chair, almost spilling the wine. "Know any single men Markus?"

The smile remained on his face throughout. He readjusted himself on the settee. "Could set you up with my uncle Nigel if you want? You've got a lot in common. He likes a bit of a drink too."

Mel went even redder in the face and tried to change the subject. "Where's this party Adele's gone anyway?"

Mel's mum didn't hear her so she had to say it again.

"Oh. What? Erm, Dolphin Square or something?"

"Dolphin Square, where the hell is that? That's not a real name surely?"

"Dolpheen," Markus corrected. "It's in the estate."

Mel sat up. "You let her go to a house party in the estate?"

Markus shot her a look and Mel put her fingers to her lips, regretting the comment.

Erica was now slurring on the lyrics to Jingle Bells. "Oh she'll be alright. She's with that Heather girl."

An hour passed and Mel's mum was starting to go. Her twitchy body movements had stopped and snoring sounds began to rumble through her nose. This embarrassed Mel too.

"Why can't she just go to sleep and never wake up?" she said.

Markus smiled and squeezed her hand, nodding at the ceiling.

"What?" she said.

"While we have a chance."

"What?" Mel repeated, dumb.

"Fucking hell do I have to spell it out for you?"

His eyes widened with mischief.

"No. No way," she said emphatically.

He was already in her ear, kissing her neck, whispering. "It'll be exciting."

"No. No way."

He had her hand and was pulling her. His strength was incredible. She was off the settee with the slightest of pulls.

"Markus no! She wakes and you'll never be allowed here again. Why do you always have to push your luck?"

"It's what luck's for. To be pushed."

"Don't rock the boat and stuff."

"This isn't a boat, it's a house."

He was kissing her and touching through her jeans.

"Stop waking my flower up," she said, trying not to laugh.

Eventually she kissed him back. Took a handful of hair from the back of his head and pushed the kiss into her, their tongues going wild. The sound of the kiss clicked and smacked over the noise of the TV.

Just then a phone lit up and its ringtone made them all jump. Markus and Mel leapt back like electricity had zapped their lips apart while Erica gasped, the sudden shock making her stare around the room, not knowing where she was. She recognised the ringtone and even though her phone was only an inch away it took her a good ten seconds to put her hand on it. She gathered herself the best she could, her eyes trying to work out the name on her screen.

"Adele," she said, her voice dulled by drink and sleep. Her brain still not in gear yet.

A deep breath seemed to roll through the centre of Mel. Markus had to pull and reposition his jeans, concealing his excitement.

"See," Mel whispered in his ear. "A minute later and we'd have been busted."

Markus's face now had a dark scowl in it. He put his hands behind his head and tried to breathe out the frustration.

Erica was still listening into the phone instead of talking at it.

"Alright Adele, calm down. Where are you? Okay ... what boys? No ... alright Adele ... hey have you been drinking?"

The conversation suddenly sounded interesting so Markus sat up and leaned in, his girlfriend imitating. The two were staring intently at Erica, who now seemed to be quite sober.

"Well just leave then," she said. "What do you mean no one else wants to? Okay, well ... well ... I thought you said her parents were going to be there ... no ... no I'm not shouting at you ... "

She *was* shouting at Adele. Mel couldn't help but take a little bit of pleasure in the very rare times that mum and sis clashed.

"Well, well, you'll just have to ... "

Erica was trying to think of a solution to something but was struggling. She had her hand in her hair, rubbing her face, still trying to wake up properly. "Yes ... yes I know it's cold outside darling. Freezing, yes ... but ... no. No. No don't walk. No.

Definitely not on your own. I'll come and pick you up. Yeah I'm aware I can't drive. Well I'll get a taxi … what do you mean embarrass you … you either want me to pick you up or not!? Okay bye. Oh. Yeah. What's the address then? Five, Dolpheen Square. Okay. Just hold on."

Erica ended one call and then made another one.

"Mum, what's going on?" Mel said, standing up.

Erica ignored her and rang straight through for a taxi but one wasn't available for the next half-hour.

"Mum what's going on?" Mel asked again.

"It's this party," Erica said. "Some lads have crashed it. Says they're making everyone uncomfortable. I thought her parents were there but they're not. Can't believe she lied to me."

"Mum, like, that doesn't matter right now. We need to go get her."

"She sounds drunk too," Erica said, staring into space.

"What boys?" Mel said. "What are they doing?"

"She didn't say. Just that they're making everyone uncomfortable."

Mel poked her glasses back onto the bridge of her nose. "Well they can't be making people *that* uncomfortable, if no one else wants to leave?? Sure it's not just Adele being dramatic?"

Erica stood up. "She's not the dramatic type, you know that."

There was an accusatory bite in her tone that Mel didn't like. She could feel an argument coming on.

"Half an hour for a bastard taxi!" she said, staring at the phone.

"Like, it's Christmas Eve what do you expect?"

"Maybe I should just call the police."

"No!" Mel said. "You'll embarrass us like you always do. Like, if it was that bad somebody would have called them and stuff. She's probably just drunk."

"But Adele doesn't drink."

Mel gave her a look. "You're not calling the police."

Erica moved the curtains and looked at all the sheets of ice that had now glazed the ground.

A deep voice came from the settee. "I'll go."

Mum and daughter looked down at the seated boy, who had already kicked on his trainers.

"I'll go with you," Mel said.

"We'll all go," Erica said.

Markus had his coat on and was stood over the pair. "I'll be quicker on my own. I know the backstreets. I can be there in fifteen. You two will just slow me down. Besides, the last thing she wants is her mum and sister polling up in front of all her mates."

The two looked at each other, realising he was right.

"Thanks Markus."

"Thanks Big Bear."

Mel kissed Markus at the door before he opened it, and stepped into the night. It was colder than he ever imagined, a vicious shock of a cold that took his breath away. He had to tip-toe across a few patches of ice before cutting across the front lawns which lead him out of the cul-de-sac. Markus ran, a light jog along Kings Road towards the estate. He thought about taking to the Channel but in this weather it would turn the short-cut into a long one. He ran on, his own ghostly breath plumed from his lips as his heartrate increased. Markus had never been fond of running and hadn't run a single step since the days he used to train with his mum's ex-boyfriend. A man, who by now, he had already forgotten the name of.

A short name, something beginning with C?

Never mind.

Ten minutes later Markus was walking through the estate, those familiar streets he had grown up in. He half-expected to see his dad and uncle, staggering out of some boozer or propping each other up on a street corner, frozen to death. It was cold. Markus had never experienced cold like it. He imagined it's what Russia must feel like.

At last he was on Dolpheen. He had forgotten what number but that didn't matter because he was directed to the house by the sound of music and screaming kids. A lighted window framed the profiles of several teeny silhouettes that moved about there. In the next window a mangled Christmas tree pressed at the glass like a deformed cactus. Markus took the hands from his pockets and made his way down the driveway. At the end he came to a door. In the centre of it was a wonky piece of plastic holly with a splatter of snow like someone had sneezed across it. He opened up and stepped in. There was noise and dark and little people running around like ferrets. Beer cans and bottles of alco-pops were strewn across the floor and Markus almost twisted an ankle as he stepped from one room to the next, batting away tawdry Christmas decorations. All of a sudden he'd forgotten the girl's name. It dropped right out of his head like names always did. *Fuck. What is it again?* Markus was searching for a girl with no name. He scanned, his head moving hawk-like through the messy tangle of teenage bodies. He barged through them, knocking one of them down. At the top of the stairs a couple was necking outside the bathroom, where sounds of retching could be heard from the other side. Markus grabbed the boy and pulled him away from the lips of his girlfriend. The boy had confrontation in his face but as soon as he recognised Markus Venner the expression rearranged itself into something more passive.

"Mel Ellis's little sister," Markus said. "Have you seen her?"

The boy silently pointed to the lower level.

Markus let him go and made his way back down, barging into another boy on the way.

Over the next few minutes Markus felt the party quieten around him. Whispers and mutterings of his own name began to circulate the house.

Shit.

Fuck.

It's Venner.

Markus Venner is here.

People began to leave. Boys went silent as their bravado diminished. Girls watched on, curious. Someone had turned the music down.

Still Adele was nowhere in sight so he grabbed a girl this time, grabbed her like she was a boy, lightly by the throat.

"Where's Mel's sister?"

She pointed to a back room. Markus let her go and found a small hidden room near the kitchen. There she was, slumped on a sofa with her head in her hands. That hair of hers almost touching the floor. There was a boy nearby, who more or less jumped against the wall as Markus marched towards him.

"Do one!" He snapped at him.

The boy was out the door by the first word of that command.

Markus gently took a handful of that hair and pulled her head back. Her face was white and she looked up at him with a pair of blurry, half-closed eyes. A drunk-smile slowly appeared. She enlivened a little when she saw him.

"Markus," she said.

"Dark horse you are, aren't ya?"

Adele didn't know what he meant, she just tumbled into his arms; *her* arms went limp across his broad back. Markus hoisted her to her feet and guided her back through the lounge, which had now halved in population. What little was left parted like the Red Sea, allowing the couple to pass through the centre of it.

Outside Markus placed her against a wall. Maybe she wasn't as drunk as he first thought. The cold seemed to waken her up and put life back into her eyes. She looked around Dolpheen Square.

"Look at all the pretty lights," she said.

Markus saw strings of Christmas lights in the street, features he hadn't noticed on the way in.

"It's Christmas Eve," she said merrily.

Her little body was touching his.

"Hey where's mum?" She slurred, gazing over his shoulder.

"Home."

"Where's my sister?"

"Home."

"Are they mad?"

Markus shrugged. He was aware that everyone was looking at them from the windows in the house. When he looked up the faces disappeared.

"Hey so you've come to rescue me?" she said, tapping his chest with a weak, half-formed fist.

That posh, fake, know-all voice of hers sounded ridiculous now it had alcohol influencing it. He didn't say anything, just took her by the wrist and lead her out the square. He could feel the eyes of the party still on him, burning into the back of his head as he walked away. Adele was talking at random, saying whatever came to her head.

"Do you love my sister? Cos she loves you."

It was strange to see her like this, so wide open and honest. It reminded him of the drunken times with his dad. People always let things slip when booze was on board. Half of the reason why he, Markus Venner, would not drink himself. He listened on, entertained, taking full advantage of the new insights he was gaining.

"I do like you Markus, we both do. Mum and me. I just think your eyes hurt sometimes, if that makes sense?"

Markus could feel the deep shiver of the girl next to him, almost convulsing against the night air. Only she seemed too drunk and

430

in-her-own-world to care. Without saying a word he took off his coat and covered her with it, zipping her up. The L-size blue, bubble coat made her disappear.

"Hey that's better," she said. "No more hypothermia. Lol. "

Adele began laughing and Markus was starting to find her irritating. "Keep walking," he said.

The journey was twice as long in reverse, slowed by a drunken thirteen-year-old girl hanging off his arm. He tried pulling her but she wouldn't go any faster.

"Hey where we going?" she said.

"Home."

"Yours or mine?"

"What?"

"Well I don't know where I am?"

Adele had stopped. Being lost had woken and sobered her up. Her hair sloped off to the left while her head cocked in the opposite direction. Markus noticed she was wearing boots, which looked strange on a kid. It was the kind of thing only adults wore.

"We're cutting through the park," he said.

"But I don't recognise this."

Worry split through her tone and pushed her voice into the back of her throat.

"That's because you live in a bubble," he said.

"What?"

"I know where I'm going."

"Oh. Yeah."

The two stood on a deserted street, staring into the dark mouth of an alleyway.

"Come on," he said, holding out a hand.

A breeze made some bushes move and Adele thought she could see snow. She took the boy's hand, which could cover hers another ten times and Adele couldn't believe he was only fourteen. He seemed like a man, a man's hand and a man's voice. He had hair on his chin and down the side of his face. Her boot scratched black ice and sent her leg sliding out, making her do the splits. A scream, and then a laugh, ripped from her chest and filled the night.

Markus sighed and picked her up. They were now halfway into the dark.

"Hey," she said, grabbing his jumper, looking up into his shadowed face. "You're not going to murder me, are you?"

"Yeah if you don't hurry up. I'm fucking freezing you know?"

For some reason she had a finger over his lips. "Why aren't you wearing a coat?" She whispered. Adele suddenly looked down at her own chest and arms. "Oh yeah," she said with a piercing giggle. "Oh you're such a Gent! Wait till my mum and sis hear about this."

She tried to step forward but slipped again. The ice was everywhere, covering all four corners of the path.

Markus said no more, picked her up like she was a doll and threw her on his back. He felt the little girl bounce off his spine and giggle again.

"Woah. Wow," she said. "Feels like I'm at Alton Towers."

Markus carried her through the alleyway and into the park. His eyes quickly got accustomed to the dark, almost like a sixth sense. Sometimes he felt like he could see more at night, than in the day. He moved through the trees and shadow, knowing when to step over twigs and swerve bins and gates and benches. Adele was asleep now, or so it felt. There was no more movement and her body seemed to slump. There was no more questions or silly remarks either, no more laugher. Throughout the journey he felt his phone go off, buzzing in his pocket, vibrating on the edge of his groin. Adele was still silent and unmoving on his back, almost like a light rucksack hanging off his shoulders. They walked on for a good fifteen minutes through the semi-dark, moonlit park. The further he walked the lighter she got. Like he was used to her being there. Like she was a part of him.

As they left the park she began to stir, wake up.

"Nearly home," he said.

Only she never answered in words, just slurred and mumbled. He felt her lips move at the back of his neck. He didn't know if it was in his head but it felt wet there, like rain, or snow. There was a sensation on his skin and he couldn't tell if it was hot or cold. He moved his head and shrugged his shoulders but the feeling was still there. Maybe it was drool from the sleeping girl's mouth, he thought? The feeling began to irritate, kind of, and he wondered if it was the damp from his collar that was chafing against his skin. He thought about putting her down and checking it out. It was small and sharp, almost like teeth, a mouth. Maybe frostbite? He ignored it and moved on, only a hundred yards away from her avenue. Adele inched herself upwards, holding him tighter, her hair tickled his ear and white swirls of breath drifted over his shoulder. The sensation went on, sucking at the bottom of his neck, on the patch of flesh that ran onto his shoulder blade. By now he realised that it felt quite nice, weird, but pleasurable. The whole world seemed to be in that spot.

Lawson Avenue flashed before him; the black lettering obscured by the frost. He was disappointed to be here already, home already. Part of him wanted to carry on walking through the night, miles and miles, with this girl asleep on his back, or half-asleep at least.

At the doorstep he let her go and she slowly slid down his back, unravelling herself from him limb by limb. She didn't look at him once. Kept her head down and her hair was everywhere. She dropped her shoulders and looked even smaller.

"Home," he said, wrapping his hand around the door handle and pushing.

"Mum, like, just don't make a big deal about it and stuff. Everyone has to have a first time at getting drunk."

"You didn't," Erica said with a hiccup.

Mel adjusted her glasses onto the tip of her nose. "Yeah but like, that's only because I've got a phobia of sick, remember?"

Markus wasn't listening to either of them. He was too busy trying to solve the mystery of his neck. He rubbed it and then looked at his fingers, before pulling his collar up over the spot, which still burned a bit.

For once Erica Ellis listened to her daughter and didn't kick off. Maybe because she was drunk herself. She swayed back and forth; her face flushed with wine. She had put the reindeer antlers back on her head. She took Adele into her arms and Mel looked away, biting her lip before putting her eyes on the carpet.

"Oh I'm so glad you're home," she said, squeezing her tighter. "Mel go and get her some water."

Mel did while Erica took her youngest by the hand and led her upstairs. Markus was still by the front door. He watched them climb the stairs step by step. At the top Adele stopped while her mum disappeared into the bedroom and began fidgeting with the bed. Adele turned and put her hand on railing. The suddenness of her eye-contact startled him and he may have stepped back. She kept on looking at him, looking at him for what seemed like ages.

433

Markus experienced a powerful adrenalin rush that came out of nowhere.

"C'mon Adele," her mum shouted. "Get in bed now. Where's Mel with that water?"

She stood there for another moment or two, before turning and stepping away like a sleepwalker.

Mum woke to the sound of someone washing pots downstairs, loud and heavy-handed. She winced and rolled over as the clattering of cutlery and cupboards continued. She sat up and groaned, before twisting herself out of bed. She put her dressing gown on and went downstairs. Markus was putting the last dish away.

"Ah thanks Markus mate. You didn't need to do that."

Boy said nothing.

"Cup of tea?"

Markus nodded, wiping some spit off his red mouth.

Erica was half-asleep and maybe still pissed from the night before. There was no feelings of hangover so she thought she must be. Her eyes were dopey and her voice full of gravel.

"Merry Christmas babe," she said, leaning over with her arms out.

The hug couldn't have been anymore awkward, Markus only touching her with the tips of his fingers. It was the first time the two had ever been alone.

"Hey sorry about last night mate, got a bit tipsy."

"Hungover?"

"Nah," she said. "Not yet. Something to look forward to, ey?"

Markus smiled a touch.

"And thanks for picking our Del up an'all. You're a lifesaver."

For some reason Markus had forgotten about that. He'd been up an hour and that was the first time it had crossed his mind.

Erica grabbed the kettle and filled it. "Sorry love you say you want tea?"

Markus nodded. Radiators slurped and swished around the draughty kitchen.

"Can tell the girls are getting older," she said, leaning against the worktop, wrapping herself up into her dressing down. "Used to be down at the crack of dawn. Now I'm up before them. Ha."

She smiled at Markus but Markus didn't really smile back.

"What's your family doing this morning then?" she said.

The kettle started up, whistling away like those old-fashioned ones.

"Dunno," he said, throwing his shoulders up. "Dad probably pissed. Brother probably crying."

"Crying?"

"He always cries at Christmas."

"Oh?"

"Cries over mum although it's stupid cos he doesn't even remember her properly. I mean he can't do it was years ago."

Erica didn't know what to say to that so she said nothing.

"Your aunt's alright though int she? I mean I've met her. She seems nice."

"When did you meet her?" he said, confrontation in his tone.

"Well, like, when you went missing and stuff."

And stuff? Markus flinched when she said that. Must have picked it up off her daughter, saying *and stuff* at the end of everything. Fucking irritating.

"Oh yeah," Markus said, his lips into a triangular pout.

"Seems nice?" Erica repeated.

Markus knew what she was doing, trying to fish-out how he felt about his aunt.

I'm giving nothing away, he thought, keeping silent.

At last there was movement upstairs.

"That'll be our Adele," Erica said, pouring the tea. "Surprised if Mel surfaces till dinner. Sugar?"

Markus stuck two fingers up at her and mum pulled a face, offended. Then she realised he was answering her question and she smiled, a bit.

"Our Mel used to love Christmas when she was little. Always up first. All that's gone now though," she said, staring out the kitchen window in a trance. It was like she was talking to herself.

Slow footsteps plodded down the stairs. Adele shuffled into the kitchen yawning. Slippers dragging off her feet and her dressing gown was only half on her shoulders. "Happy Christmas," she said in a small voice.

She never looked at Markus. It was as if last night never happened.

The click of the back door sounded and Babe came bounding into the kitchen, ambushing Adele with a wagging tail, covering her hands and arms with an assault of licks and sniffs.

435

"Merry Christmas baby Babe!" she sang, dropping to her knees before kissing the dog on the mouth.

Fucking disgusting, Markus thought.

Erica came in from doing something outside, "Del go and wake your sister up."

The girl was still transfixed on the dog, staring into its eyes.

"Del go and wake your sis. She's not sleeping in till dinner on Christmas morning."

Adele looked up at her mum, the dog's skull in the palm of her hand. "You wake her. She never wakes for me anyway."

Markus finished his tea and put the mug on the top. "I'll wake her," he said.

Mum kept her head down and pretended to have not heard him. "Go on Del," she said, tapping her daughter impatiently with her foot.

"O-kaaay," Adele moaned. "I'm going."

He saw the family of girls through a red bauble on the Christmas tree. Their reflection was all warped like those funny mirrors at the fair. The four sat in a circle and took it in turns to open their presents. At the end of it Markus sat back and looked at all the gifts he'd received. Mel had bought him the new Liverpool top, some aftershave and a Bench hoodie. Her mum had bought him a Swiss Army Knife and her Sister Adele had got him a selection box.

Mel, Adele and Mum were all looking at Markus, like they were waiting for something. They looked at each other and then at the tree, and then back at Markus again.

"What?" he said.

Did I miss something, he thought? There was something going on but Markus didn't know what? He didn't know what any of it meant.

Mel

Dear Santa,

Like, tbh, I don't really exactly know what a Love Bite looks like?? Not Officially anyway. But I'm sure Markus has one on the back of his neck!!! It's small and blood-shot, and kind of red and kind of purple and kind of black and kind of yellow around the edges and stuff. I even Googled it and a picture came up and I've got to say it looks EXACTLY the same, which means he's Officially cheated on me and that makes me want to end my life For Good. Like, I know I could never live with that. I would have to Die because I just know I could never forgive him. We'd be Officially Over and that would mean I'd lose The One True Person I Only Ever Loved.

So Seddy, as You can tell, I'm pretty Effed-Up and In Bits and I don't know what to do or who to turn to.

I even thought about asking Mia cos she will know for sure, if it is one or not??

But then what if she's The One who gave it to him in the First Place??!!

Even if it wasn't Her she will just TOTALLY love it and get off on it and will spread it around school and probably try to sabotage Our Relationship for good.

I can't tell My Bestie Mia.

My Nature-Feeling is telling me to ask him about it, only I don't want him to think I'm accusing him of stuff. He's had enough people accuse him of stuff in his life and he doesn't need it off me!! His own GF!!

But.

I know something is wrong cos he keeps trying to hide it all the time. Like he keeps wearing collared shirts and coats and stuff.

But.

Where would he have got it from cos he's been with me like ALL THE TIME?! Like every day and most nights over these Christmas Holidays he's been by my side so IT MAKES NO SENSE.

So ...

Perhaps it's all in my head after all, like an imagination kind of a thing. Maybe it's just My Issues getting the better of me YET AGAIN.

Besides, it makes no sense cos the Love Bite is like All The Way round the back of his neck, almost on his shoulder blade. Like it's not really the place, is it??

So …

I think overall it's just a bruise or a graze and all I've done is look WAY into this Too Much as per usual.
    He's always playing football and fighting and climbing trees so it's probably just something from that.
    HA.

So …

I really hope I'm not becoming one of those paranoid, jealous GF's. Always told myself I would never become one of those. Mia said that she'd read in a magazine that the Biggest Causer of people splitting up is cos of jealousy.

So …

I better be careful otherwise I'll end up losing Big Bear for good.

Anyway.
Either way.

I was going to Markus's New Year's Eve Party and I was so dead-excited. I'd never been to a proper New Year's Party before and what better way to say 'hello' 2016 than to be with my BF. It was also A Big Deal cos up until now Markus had only ever seen me in jeans and t-shirts and hoodies and stuff. I mean he'd never Officially seen me Done-Up, like wearing a dress and make-up and that.
    Oh WOW Mel you look beautiful!
    I went dead-red and his Aunty let me in the bungalow. She wouldn't stop saying nice things and I could see that she was TOTALLY truly shocked.
    Wait till our Markus sees you, she said, he'll have a heart-attack.
    Tbh I loved Aunt Tars and always had from the Very Start. Big Bear always says he doesn't have 'Proper Parents' but he doesn't know how lucky he is. I'd do ANYTHING to have Aunt Tars as my mum. So what if she's not Officially a blood mum. That doesn't

matter one bit. I tell him this All The Time but he doesn't listen as per usual.

So gorgeous Mel, never seen you in a dress before, Markus really will have a heart attack!

He DID have a heart-attack, but not in a good way. I could see it in his face from The Start. He was shocked and there was something bad in his expression.

What the fuck you wearing? He said in a nasty voice.

Oh Markus that isn't very nice, Tars said. She's made all this effort.

Too much of an effort, he said under his breath. Who you tryna impress?

All of a sudden I just HATED myself and wanted to run out the bungalow and never come back. Rip off this stupid dress and throw it in the bin. Wash all this make-up off my face and spit at the mirror.

Tars tried to lighten the mood. Got her nephew in a playful headlock, although she couldn't move him.

You! She said. She's trying to impress YOU silly, who else?

I still felt kind of stupid, standing there in the kitchen.

Markus smiled at last and came up to me.

You do look beautiful, Beautifulness. You just took me by surprise, sorry.

I think that was The First and only Official time I ever heard him say the word, 'Sorry.' He held me and squeezed me and everything became alright again.

Soon people started to arrive, knock on the door and ring the bell. I started to get dead-nervous cos I wasn't used to being around so many people, especially adults.

For some reason Markus seemed really anxious about his Uncle and Cousin Charlie. He kept going on about it.

My Cousin Charlie is a little prick who thinks he's better than everyone else, just ignore him, probably best to not talk to him at all. He said.

Okay.

I'd met his Dad a few times before, only in passing, but he was always dead-drunk and stuff. He had bright blonde hair and he kind of didn't look like Markus at all. He came in and his red-face lit up the room and I had to say I kind of liked him. He was funny and told funny jokes and did funny voices and stuff. He slammed a crate of beer on the kitchen worktop and then picked me up and spun me around.

Our Lad's done well here ... he said, dangling me in front of everyone. Right little fuckin stunner aren't ya??!!

My glasses fell onto the tip of my nose and I got dead-dizzy from all the spinning.

Fuckin gorgeous gal!! If only I was twenty years younger Mel, my son would be having some competition!!

Bit more than twenty you old perv, Tars said, laughing.

Everybody was laughing except for Markus who looked like his head was about to come off.

What's up Big Bear? I said.

That twat, fucking embarrassing. Picks you up again like that and I'll stick a knife in his throat.

Oh.

More people came and music went on. Aunt Tars had made a Proper Effort and that, like she made the bungalow dead-good with loads of food and decorations and stuff. She gave me an alco-pop and I told her that I didn't drink alcohol cos of my phobia of sick but she said 'one won't hurt.'

Just then Markus came up to me and said, Fucking hell here he is.

I was shocked how much his Uncle and Dad looked alike and you could tell they were brothers a mile-off.

Aunt Tars made a real fuss of Cousin Charlie. The Superstar is here! She shouted.

She hugged him and held his face up to the light, The Most Handsome Boy in the World, she said. She introduced me to him and told me that he was like a Footballer Player and that one day he was going to be Rich and Famous and Stuff. He didn't talk much but I guess he had a friendly face.

I told you not to talk to him! Markus grabbed my arm and pulled me near the door. What did I tell you?

Jeez Big Bear! I said.

And I told you to not call me that in front of people, it's embarrassing.

I was only meeting him, I said. You can't expect me to be rude and not speak!

Markus still had a hold of my arm. He was squeezing so tight I felt my fingers tingle.

Just don't talk to him, he said.

But he seems dead-friendly, I said.

He's a little show-off.

Markus stormed off and I didn't know what was wrong. Part of me thought it was perhaps cos there was loads of people and stuff, like an anxiety kind of a thing. Most of the time he just sat in the corner staring everybody out. Mostly he stared at Cousin Charlie, stared at him like he wanted to kill him.

Here Mel. Aunt Tars put another bottle in my hand. It was orange and sweet and once you got over the bite it was quite nice.

Sure it won't make me sick? I said.

Nah. Aunt Tars said, dancing across the room. Not if you drink them slow.

I did drink it dead-slow and I'm not gonna Lie it made me kind of relax. Like it made the room look soft and fuzzy and the people looked soft and fuzzy too and I guess I can understand why adults drank This Stuff so much.

A bit later Markus's Dad's new GF turned up. She was a big black lady with bright red-lipstick. I think her name was Dolores or something. She was dead-friendly and a dead-good dancer but Markus didn't like her either, in fact he was going mad for some reason.

What a hypocrite bastard! He said.

What?

Her!

Dolores?

She's black.

So? Are you a racialist or something? Don't you like black people?

It's not that, it's him, he doesn't like them. He's always told me if I had a black girlfriend he'd disown me. Now look at him?

Lance was snogging Dolores in the middle of the room.

I don't get it. I said. Are you saying you want a black GF?

Markus looked at me like I was dirt. Oh just shut the fuck up you don't understand what I'm saying.

For some reason the booze in my brain gave me a kind of confidence and I decided to stick up for myself for once.

You've been nasty to me all night, what have I done?

You're just dumb sometimes Mel. He said. It's like you're totally clueless about the real world.

I didn't know what he meant.

I blame your bitch of a mum, he said. She's kept you in a bubble.

I was feeling dizzy and decided to put the bottle down and drink no more.

Markus got up and walked away from me and that made me feel like shit. Tonight was supposed to be a special night. There was only ten minutes to go before New Year but Tbh I wanted to go home and wasn't bothered about seeing 2016 in with him. Everyone was having a good time but I just sat there and wanted to cry.

But then from nowhere Aunt Tars had me on my feet.

C'mon Beautiful there's only eight minutes to go!

Someone had put the telly on and there were scenes of London. Like I think it was London anyway cos I could see Big Ben and That River and That Big Wheel. There was a clock in the corner of the screen, counting down. It was on five minutes now. I looked around for Big Bear but he was nowhere. Really I wanted to kiss him when the clock struck twelve and the fireworks went off and year 2016 came in.

Five.

Four.

Three.

All the adults were shouting at the tops of their voices and for some reason I felt dead-nervous like the year was coming in and it was a really Big Deal and stuff.

Two.

One.

The room went crazy and everyone was clapping and hugging and kissing and that. Party-Poppers popped and there was Silly-String in my hair. Tars grabbed me and squeezed The Life out of me but it felt dead-nice and kind of reminded me of that woman in Boston who hugged me for finding Baby Jack and all of a sudden I thought of her. And I thought of My Own Mum for some reason. And I thought of My Own Sister and My Own Dad. I even thought of Babe the Dog. And I thought of my BF Big Bear Markus Venner but he was nowhere in sight. After Aunt Tars stopped hugging and kissing me more people did. Lance. Dolores. Uncle Nigel. And it was all so nice and it was like I belonged somewhere for The First Time in My Life.

Happy New Year Mel!

It was Cousin Charlie.

He pulled me in for a big 2016 hug and kissed me on the cheek like everyone else had.

X.

From nowhere I felt a force hit me from the left.

There was a face I'd never seen before. A face like an evil mask. It was all white and scary and full of rage and for a few seconds I didn't even realise it was my own BF. I didn't realise it was Markus.

What the fuck you doin?

He had Cousin Charlie by the throat.

That's my girl man, that's my fucking girl!

He was screaming and Charlie was so shocked and scared he couldn't speak.

None of the adults could see what was happening cos they were all still hugging and dancing and singing that New Year's Song. The one where they stand in a circle and hold hands and cross arms and bounce up and down.

Kissing my fucking girl!!!

I had never seen Markus like this before and I was scared to death. I tried to shout for help but nobody could hear me. It was like a nightmare kind of a thing.

He pushed Charlie hard in the throat and it must have been like a punch cos he fell back against the telly and that's when somebody noticed, whoa, whoa, whoa!

Adults jumped in front of him and stopped him from killing him For Good.

Uncle Nigel held out a hot finger at Markus's face. Touch him again you little bastard!

Markus slapped his finger and more adults had to hold Uncle back.

Dad and Dolores were facing the other way. They were still singing that Auld Lang Syne song and didn't have a clue what was going on. Aunt Tars was in the middle of it all, helping Charlie back to his feet. She looked at Markus dead in the eye.

Why? She said. Why do you have to spoil EVERYTHING?

The music went off, or it sounded like that anyway. Suddenly it was deathly quiet and weird and now everybody was looking at me. Looking at me like it was all my fault and stuff. That's when I just wanted the ground to come and swallow me up, swallow me WHOLE.

Charlie was holding his neck and crying a bit and I felt dead-sorry for him. He was confused and scared and as white as a ghost.

Fuck you all. Markus said. Fuck life.

He smashed something on the way out, bombing out the room, the door, slamming it so hard the whole bungalow seemed to shake.

Of course I went after him. It was like my body moved before my *mind did. Almost like someone or something had me by Remote Control. I was outside and into the black. Chasing Markus up the close, seeing the white blur of him disappear into the alleyway. I ran as fast as I could but it wasn't so fast cos the alcohol made my legs all heavy and slow and stuff. He was heading towards the Channel and my First Thought was that he was going to jump in and Commit Suicide.*

He goes, I go, I thought. I will follow him and Commit Suicide too. I will follow him there. I will follow him anywhere, everywhere. I don't care.

Only when I reached the edge I could see that the black water was unbroken and that he hadn't done it after all.

I stopped and shouted his name a million times.

The sharpness of smoke filled my nostrils and all above me and around me and in the distance fireworks popped and burst and coloured and drizzled down the New Year sky. I walked around in circles, looking for him. The adrenalin and alcohol must have been wearing off cos all of a sudden The Cold slammed into me like a bus and I realised I left my coat inside. I was shivering inside my dress and I felt naked, more or less.

Then I saw him.

At last I saw him.

Sitting on a bench by the water with his head in his hands.

I shouted his name but he didn't look up. I shouted it again but he just stayed the same. My glasses were doing that steamy-up thing again and I couldn't see right.

I walked near and nearer but then I realised it wasn't him after all.

Just a shadow of something else.

This was the first hour of 2016 ...

Suicide Test

Markus

"Let's make a pact!" Mia said, biting off the tip of the straw wrapper, before blowing it across McDonald's. Markus and Mel sat opposite with their heads down.

"The three of us," she continued brightly. "Let's make a pact right here and now. One of us goes, then all three of us go."

"Go?" Mel said.

"Suicide."

"Oh."

"I mean what is there to live for anyway?" Mia said.

It was a windy February day and Markus watched people huddled-up in their cars, passing the drive-thru. "She's right," he said. "There's fuck-all to live for."

Mia's face got really excited. She threw her arm across Markus's shoulder and switched seats, sliding in next to him. Mel grimaced, and had to rearrange herself in her chair.

"I know, right?" Mia said, Americanism making her tone go up at the end of the sentence. "I mean we've all got shit going on haven't we? My mum has that new bastard of a BF. Markus is about to be expelled from school, and you Mel, you've *never* been happy as long as I've known you. And I've known you since forever."

"Markus isn't getting expelled," Mel said crossly.

Markus was still staring at the people in the cars.

"Are you?" she said again.

"No," he grumbled, having no real idea what he was being asked.

"Either way suicide is like the perfect solution, the perfect statement," Mia sang. "We'll be immortal in this town and probs the world over. They'll be a candlelit vigil and everything. We'll be known as The Kimble Wells Three, or, The Teen Suicide Triplets."

Mia was so excited she was rocking back and forth, making the booth creak.

Mel wiped some hair behind her ear and looked up. "I've wanted to die for ages. Only I can't leave Markus behind."

"Or me, right?" Mia said, putting her fingernails to her chest.

"Yeah, or you." Mel replied in a dull voice.

"That's why a pact is the only way!" Mia said. "If you do, *do it*. And let's face it you're more than likely going to be the first, then me and Markus will follow, right Markus?"

Markus nodded with a mouthful of Big Mac. He picked his nose.

Concern wrinkled Mel's expression. "But not like, together, right? You wouldn't commit suicide together would you?"

Mia looked at her confused.

"Like, you wouldn't commit suicide without me?"

"But you'd be dead."

"I don't want you dying together. It wouldn't be right!" Mel's tone was fierce.

"Alright then we'd die separate. Markus first, me second." Mia stopped herself, put her eyes up into her head and did the maths. "Well, technically, it'd be you first, Markus second, me last."

Mel's hands were clasped tight over the table. "Why do I have to go first?"

"Well you don't *have* to go first. I'm just saying that *you're more likely to go first.*"

"Why?" Mel bit.

"Because you're a depressive."

"So, you're ADHD."

"So?"

"So you could go first."

"ADHD isn't really like that, it's not really a suicide thing, stupid."

"Stop calling me stupid. I'm sick of people calling me stupid."

There was a new rage to Mel which Mia found surprising. "Alright Mel chill, we're only talking about suicide, lighten up."

This made Mia laugh her head off and Markus followed. Both of them wouldn't stop laughing together and Mel wanted to storm out of McDonald's.

"Hey if we *do* commit suicide," Markus said biting into more burger. "Can we at least take some people with us? Seems a waste to not have a little fun on the way out."

"Like who?" Mia said, suddenly excited again. She crossed her legs on the chair and sat up. Her eyes were big.

"Her fucking mum for a start," Markus said, pointing at Mel.

"Yeeeaaah." Mia said. "And we can kill my mum's BF too."

"I can do that," Markus said, smugly.

"And a shit load of teachers too," Mia said.

Mel was shaking her head and looking out of the window. "You two aren't even serious."

"About the pact?" Mia said.

Mel nodded.

"Course I'm serious. I'm the one who brought it up. It was all *my* idea in the first place."

Mel was fiddling around with a packet of brown sugar, spilling grains onto her fingertips and then sucking them off. "But I mean how would we do it? Like, what's the best way and stuff?"

Mia had finished her food by now. She was cleaning her teeth with her tongue, thinking. "I'd say pills."

"What pills?"

"Any."

"Any pills?"

"It doesn't matter what pills it's just how many. You need a lot."

"Like how many?"

"Like twenty or something. Twenty would do it, I'm sure," Mia said, nodding decisively.

Mel was staring out of the window, her eyes far-off and trancelike. "God I've been depressed since New Year," she said. "Two thousand and sixteen has *officially* been the worst year *ever* and it's only February."

"Why cos your mum has stopped you from seeing Markus again?"

"That and everything else. Her and sis are closer than ever and I can't even breathe in that house. I've had enough."

It's like Mia was studying her face, a smile slowly spreading across her own. "God Melanie Ellis you're actually really thinking about this, aren't you?"

"Yeah," she said, solemnly. "Aren't you?"

"Well yeah. I mean, if you do, I will. I mean that's the whole point of a pact, right?"

"I've always known I'll do it," Mel said.

"I'll do it." Markus piped up. "I don't give a fuck."

Mia was looking at them both with a strange kind of awe. "You know what you two are like don't you?"

They both looked at her.

"You're like a modern day Bonnie and Clyde."

447

"Who?" Markus said.

Mel had the same confused expression.

"A man and a woman outlaws. On the run, not caring about anything, killing people on their way."

"Hey who said anything about killing anyone?" Mel said.

"Markus did, remember?" Mia said.

"Oh."

"Yeah, you two are gonna go the whole way I can tell," Mia said, looking up at the winter sky, full of enchantment.

For the first time today Mel had a smile of her face. "God Mia you're so dramatic, as always. This isn't a film or a book you know?"

"It might be one day, you never know," Mia said flippantly.

"This is real life and real life is serious. Like, suicide is a serious thing."

Markus cleared his throat. "Nah not that serious," he said licking his fingers. "It's just the body doing something. Just like eating, sleeping or taking a shit. Death is overrated."

Markus scooped all the wrappers from the table and put them on a tray, stood, and then slammed it through the swing bin.

He sauntered out casually, and the girls followed.

Ryan Venner had split up with another boyfriend and was back living at the bungalow. Still the brothers had not shared a civil word since that night of last year. Tara could take no more, she found the passive-aggressive energy of the home stifling. She had brought the boys up for the last ten years and there was no way she was going to let this silent tension dominate the atmosphere anymore. So one evening, not long after Markus came home she called them both into the lounge.

"Can I at least have a shower first?" Markus said.

"No, now." Tara replied curtly.

The thirty-nine year old aunt had never held any supernatural or religious beliefs but for the first time ever she felt her sister's eyes look down on her from some heavenly place, letting her know she was doing the right thing.

It was strange to see the same boys in the same room for more than a mere few seconds. Normally, as one entered the other departed. Ryan sat upright on the single chair while his younger brother Markus dropped onto the settee, slouching across it like he was about to go to sleep.

"Markus sit up."

No response.

"I said sit up. You're not at school and I'm not one of your teachers."

Markus did with a long, unnatural sigh. Ryan wore his hair long again. He had grown out that silly blonde and two waves of shiny brunette parted neatly from the centre of his head. His complexion had cleared and he had filled-out a bit. Overall the rough edges of his youth had been sanded-down to that of a composed young man. The wimpishness of his delicate mannerisms had now been refined, giving him an air of poise and grace. He'd been out in the world now and was hardened by it. His face had experience in it and he appeared more centred. Markus didn't get to him like he once did. He was indifferent to his troubled brother, bored by him and his antics. Still, after all his aunt had done for him he decided to give this a chance.

"I'm not even going to bring your mum into this," she started.

"Don't then," Markus said, staring at the ceiling.

"But we three have come a long way since then."

There was something staged about her speech, Markus thought. And that's what it felt like, *a speech*. Like she'd rehearsed these lines verbatim.

"It's been tough, all these years. I know I'm not your mother but I've done my best to be. I never planned this and I wasn't prepared for it. But, I think the three of us have done okay."

What the fuck is she going on about, Markus thought? He could tell her script had gone to pot and now she was just winging it.

"What I'm basically trying to say is that through *all this* the one thing you've always had is each other. You're brothers and that will never change."

Well done for pointing out the obvious, Markus thought.

"You share a life whether you like it or not and I want you to start talking again. I want you to start being friends again. If not friends then at least polite enough to clear this horrible atmosphere because I can't stand it anymore. I can't stand it when you're in the house together. I'd rather be alone if I'm honest. It makes everything shitty and I have to live here too y'know?"

Markus and Ryan caught eyes for a moment.

"Now I know you're both stubborn and neither of you wants to crack first … so I'll do it for you. Today I want you both to agree to speak, or even look at each other from time to time. I'm not going to ask you to do it for yourselves, or even for your mum. But do it for *me*. I think I deserve that much."

Markus was shaking the eyes in his head, trying not to laugh a little. Does that woman realise how much shit she speaks?

"Okay," Markus said. "I agree."

Aunt Tars was taken aback that the younger was the first to speak, and who seemed to be the more willing of the two. The fourteen-year-old bounced onto the balls his feet and stepped into the centre of the room with his hand out.

The older brother stood too, reluctantly, suspiciously, joining him in a square-shaped pattern on the carpet. Ryan looked down and thought it looked like some kind of boxing ring. He combed back his hair with his left hand before putting the right into the grubby mitt of his brother.

They shook.

They shook hands and shared eye contact.

But then Ryan felt something, *pressure.*

Markus watched his eyes flicker as he had him in his grip. Not a grip to crunch a bone or cause a scene, not a grip to give anything away. A grip just strong enough to let him know he was still there, still stronger, still on top.

"Thanks boys," Tara said. "Means a lot."

"I did some research Mel. Twenty should be enough but thirty is a def. Forty and you're a gonna for sure, never coming back."

They were early to class, sitting side-by-side on the back row. Mel turned fast and her hair followed her, almost hitting her bestie in the face. "Forty what?"

"Pills s-"

Mia stopped herself from saying the word *stupid* and slipped in *silly* instead.

"Pills?"

"Our Suicide Pact, remember?"

"Oh. Yeah."

Mel wasn't really listening, too busy trying to hide the Valentine Card between her knees. She tried inching it up her thighs but it was no use. Mia caught sight of the pink envelope and whipped it from her as quick as a cobra strike.

"And what might this be?"

Mel's face went as pink as the card in Mia's hand. "Nuff-in," she said in slang, splitting the supposed word into two syllables.

"Dunt look like *nuffin*," she mocked. "Looks like *sumffin* to me. Looks like a V-card you lil hussy."

Mia was already pulling off the envelope with her ringed thumb. She took out the card and laid it flat on the desk, gazing at the front. Dread was bolting through Mel like a storm.

"Very arty," Mia said, something cruel and final in her tone.

A surrealist picture of two people made into the shape of a love-heart. "Ah bless." Mia added, opening out the card.

Inside a single bubble-like question mark hovered in the centre. "Markus give you this?"

"I think so, yeah." Mel murmured.

The fear in her voice matched the horror in her face.

"Bullshit," Mia said plainly. "Markus would never send a V-card and you know it. Least of all one like that."

The two besties stared at the card.

"It's Harrison," Mia said. "Has to be."

"What?"

"Oh come on don't play dumb you so know it is."

"No. Well. I doubt it, I mean ... "

"It's Harrison," Mia declared again. "I told you he had a mass crush on you but you never believed me."

Mel tried to get the card back but Mia wouldn't let her have it yet. "I was gonna rip it up and stuff I swear."

Mia couldn't stop smiling. Her eyes were glued to the card in a sort of bewildered trance. "Has this little prick got a death wish?" She whispered. "He knows you go out with Markus Venner, right?"

Hearing his name in full made her see the gravity of the situation. She threw her shoulders up like a pair of tennis balls.

"You telling him?"

"Who?"

"Markus, who do you think?"

"What, no."

"So you're hiding it from him?"

"No I'm ... "

"So you *are* telling him. Nice one Mel. I mean you can't be lying to your own BF."

"It's probably not even Harrison anyway."

"Speak of the devil."

When Mia said that she thought she meant Harrison, not the boy who was walking towards them, the biggest boy in the school.

"Mia *don't*," Mel pleaded. The word *don't* broke in the back of her throat and it didn't quite make it onto Mia's ear.

She was already on her feet, waving the card in the air like a flag. "Dint know you was such a romantic Venner!"

Mel couldn't remember feeling a fear like it. It felt like two walls crushing her from either side. Confusion was already knitted into his brow as he stepped nearer to the two girls, trying to work out what was in Mia's hand.

"What's this?" Markus spat gum at the classroom window, which stuck and slid down the glass, leaving a trail.

"Getting your GF a V-card," Mia taunted. "Din't think you were the type?"

For a second Mel thought about denying it was hers. There was no name on in but then she remembered the envelope that was lying in her lap.

"This yours?" Markus asked, nodding at it aggressively. His face was already drained of colour, that primal flair of the nostrils.

"Wasn't it from you Big Bear?" she said in a silly voice.

Mia wanted to laugh out-loud.

He ripped it from Mia and began inspecting it. His eyes surveying every millimetre of the thing. "No it fucking wasn't from me."

"It's from Harrison," Mia said, throwing the name in like a spear.

"Like, you don't know that for sure," Mel said, her voice cowering.

"Who?"

His lips were out, wet and pouting.

"This kid in art who's fancied Mel since day dot."

Markus turned his eyes on Mel like he wanted to kill her.

"It's not true," she said. "He's not even like that and stuff. He's just friendly."

"Oh come on Mel," Mia said. "Who else is going to send you a card like that but him?"

Mia couldn't conceal the pleasure she was getting from all this. She could barely sit still.

"What's his name again?" Markus said.

"Harrison," Mia said, before skilfully extracting herself from the scene, sitting with some more friends at the opposite side of the room. The class was full now and everybody was looking at them.

Markus gripped the card before tearing it in two, then four, then eight. The ripping sound cut through the silence, before the pieces were flung into the air like confetti.

The teacher came in at last and the lesson began. Markus sat silently on his own, brooding all the way through it. Every time Mel tried to touch him or say anything he shrugged her off.

After a while the girl turned her eyes onto Mia. Not since her mum had she hated someone so much. *That fucking bitch is no friend of mine.* Mia stretched back and pulled a face, putting both hands up in the air like she had a gun pointed at her, *what,* she mouthed innocently, *what did I do?*

Mel knew she had to catch Markus at the end of the class. She had to catch him before he caught Harrison Daniels. She had to stop him before he did something stupid. He was already charging out the room two minutes before the bell went off. Down the stairwell and into the staff car park, his big feet slapping across the rain-soaked tarmac.

"Big Bear please!"

He was making his way to Lower Block, along the edge of the school field. She said loads of things but none of them would make him stop.

"Big Bear it's not even him."

"Who then?"

At last she had some words from him, something to work with.

"I don't know."

"You have a stupid admirer and you didn't even tell me!"

"He's not an admirer. He's just a little weird art kid."

Markus was almost running now and Mel couldn't keep up.

"Mia! It's Mia!" she shouted.

He turned and shot her a screw-face. "What?"

"My Nature-Feeling says it's from her."

This made Markus howl, a mad, thwarted laughter. "What? You saying Mia is a dyke?"

"No not that but she's trying to split us up and stuff."

Markus's feet began to slow. She had some more of his attention now. He waited to hear more.

"My Nature-Feeling says that she did it herself and then said it was Harrison."

Markus was shaking his head, his brain inside going into overdrive. "And why would that split us up?"

They were almost at Lower Block and Mel couldn't get her words out fast enough.

"Cos then you'll go and beat Harrison up ... and then you'll get expelled cos you're on your final warning ... and then you'll move schools and stuff and I'll *never* get to see you ... "

Markus had stopped. Bells were ringing around the school and kids began to pour out of doors.

"You really think she'd go to *all* that trouble?" Markus said, his voice washed with doubt.

"Def." Mel looked so small, holding herself against an iron railing.

Markus stared at all the kids, probably trying to work out which one was Harrison.

"That's what my Nature-Feeling says," she added.

"Your Nature-feeling isn't always right you know?"

"It is," she said.

"It's been wrong loads of times."

"That's because I wasn't listening properly. I'm listening now."

Markus wanted to smile. "Fucking weirdo."

Mel shrugged.

"But why would she want to split us up?"

She shrugged again. "She's just like that."

Markus unzipped his coat and took in a breath.

"If you beat him up you'll get expelled," she said. "And I *can't* have you gone. I'd never survive this without you."

Both of them were looking around at the school, at all the kids and teachers that were swirling around them chaotically.

"Promise me that you won't?" Her voice was high and desperate. She stepped forward and took both of his hands, "promise?"

"Promise," he said, at last.

There was an emptiness to him that she couldn't trust.

"Swear on your life," she said.

"Swear on my life," he echoed.

It wasn't good enough, she needed more.

"Swear on *my* life?" she said.

"I do," he said. "I swear on your life."

It was still not good enough. She had to remind herself that they were in a Suicide Pact, lives didn't matter. Her brain scrambled for something and it came at last. She couldn't believe she was about to say *this*. She couldn't believe she was actually about to turn these words loose but she had to if she was ever going to believe him. "Swear..." she began tentatively, regretting it already. He stepped forward, waiting for it. " ... on your mum's grave?"

"What?"

She felt her eyes close as she anticipated the full violence of Markus Venner. Her body braced for his body, all that weight and superhuman strength on top of her, hands around her neck, choking her to death. She knew how sensitive he was about his long-lost mum and this was the first time she had ever mentioned her.

Nothing physical came, just his voice, shockingly gentle and measured. "You want me to swear on my mum's grave?"

She nodded and he mirrored her, his huge hair rocking back and forth. "Okay," he began. "I swear on my mum's grave."

At last she was satisfied. She knew now that Markus wasn't going to touch that boy. He wasn't going to harm a hair on Harrison's head. He wasn't going to do a thing. He wasn't going to get expelled. He was staying right here with her, for good.

Tara flipped onto BBC so she could watch EastEnders. She tried focusing on the screen but her nephew was fidgeting about in her peripheries, sprawled across the settee just in his boxers and the new Liverpool shirt Mel had got him for Christmas. He kept digging downstairs, scratching and repositioning himself.

"*Tut,* do you mind?" she said.

They began watching the soap. Tara didn't like BBC because there weren't any adverts. About halfway she asked Markus if he would mind going and making a cup of tea. He refused by way of silence.

"Markus, tea, *go on.* I made dinner."

Still the response was nil. Just then something caught her eye, something outside. She looked beyond the TV, through the window.

"Markus."

"Fucking hell, make your own tea I'm watching this."

"Why has a police car just pulled up outside?"

Markus went back to the silence.

"And why are two coppers walking down my driveway?"

Markus shrugged, his eyes still on the soap.

Tara jumped up and her mouth went dry. She wrapped the

dressing gown around her and paced towards the door. "Markus what the fuck have you done?"

He sighed and sat up, rubbed down the surface of his face with his hand. Two loud knocks came from the front door. "Markus go and put some bottoms on."

She was staring right at him, wildly. "Markus put some fucking bottoms on!"

He stood slowly and traipsed through to his room while Tara opened the front door. The male and female officers wore smiles as they introduced themselves. They asked if a Markus Venner lived at this address and Tara solemnly nodded before asking them inside. Her hands were everywhere and she didn't know what to do. She asked them if they wanted a cup of tea and this amused the fourteen-year-old boy, who was taking his time putting on a pair of jeans in front of them all.

"Is this Markus?" one of them said.

"I'm me," the boy said.

There was already a sly cockiness in his face that Tara wanted to slap right out of him. She was biting her thumb, nerves swelling into fear. She knew from the demeanour of the police that it was something bad; something severe, something more than petty theft or truancy from school. She could also tell that Markus knew exactly what it was. There was nothing complicated in his expression, just the normal disregard and boredom of authority. Before the police dropped the bomb Tara felt something else, a tremendous sense of shame. It came from nowhere and crippled her completely. She felt ashamed of everything. Ashamed she was wearing this chatty dressing gown. Ashamed of the cheesy pop music coming through Ryan's bedroom wall. Ashamed of the new *Fifty Shades* book lying face-up on the arm of the sofa. Ashamed of the EastEnders theme tune sounding from the telly as the end credits rolled. More than anything she felt ashamed of her nephew, who was slouched back on the settee as before, the flies of his jeans still open.

"Markus sit up!"

She felt ashamed because the officers had walked into her world with their calm and togetherness. The lady officer was exceptionally pretty, small and compact with a gentle blue-eyed gaze while the male officer seemed to fill the room with his purpose and professionalism.

They asked Markus if he knew why they were here and the boy

just smirked and spat-out a half-formed word. Tara felt herself shrink into her slippers. Why was he like this? She had never brought him up to be so arrogant and rude. More and more shame tumbled down on her like rocks, as if his degenerate behaviour somehow reflected who she was and what she stood for. Tara felt a great urge to overcompensate and chastise the boy in front of them, only this would just add to his insolent behaviour. You couldn't compete with Markus like this because he would up the ante and take it to the next level. He picked his nose and rolled his eyes and said *the little prick deserved it. Messin with my girl!*

The female officer spoke, saying how serious the injuries were. A fractured jaw-bone and several other injuries to the face and neck. He'll be spending a few nights in hospital, she said. Her head was pulled to one side and her lips folded inwards, sympathy swimming in her eyes.

Markus showed no remorse, no guilt, no stress, nothing. It was as if the police had just read-out a shopping list. They looked at each other with a seriousness that made Tara break down and cry. I just don't know what to do, she said. The female officer consoled her a little while her colleague read Markus his rights. Tara covered her mouth. She couldn't believe she was hearing these words in her own home ... *you have a right to remain silent* ... she only ever heard this on TV, on *The Bill* or those Scotland Yard Dramas she watched on ITV. The officers told Tara that because Markus was a minor she would have to come down to the station while they took a formal statement.

"Will we need a solicitor?"

"We can discuss all that down at the station," he said.

Tara nodded tearfully before going to get her coat.

While she was gone Markus looked at the officers one by one, first the man, then the woman. "Hey do I get to wear your handcuffs?" Markus said with a flirty wink, a giant smile spreading across his face.

Her slender fingers instinctively reached for the two silver rings which hung from her belt.

The male officer said nothing, just nudged him in the back, towards the door.

Ryan must have heard what was happening because his door was open and his music off. He came out of his room and hugged his aunt before turning his eyes onto his brother.

Markus saw the words: *you make me sick.*

"See you in Hollywood brother," Markus sang on the way out.

Ryan slammed the door in his face and the younger brother experienced a strange feeling that this was to be the last time they'd ever speak.

The sound of February drizzle brushed through his ears as he rolled over and slept more. Markus wasn't getting up for school today. He didn't see the point. Even though he was tempted by all the attention he'd get he couldn't be arsed to sit in the Head's office and go through the formalities of getting expelled. Instead he turned off his phone and stayed in bed. Markus had never been a big sleeper but this morning the bed felt especially soft and comfortable. He wrapped both arms around the pillow and put a leg into the crevice of the duvet. Even in winter a window was left open, feeling a slip of air touch his skin. He could hear a kid playing football outside, doing kick-ups. Although this could have been a dream because it was Tuesday and everyone was at school. He kept drifting in and out, seeing things, hearing things. A bird in a tree, cars, rain, voices. Aunt Tars' voice, Mel's, Mia's, that kid he battered yesterday. He heard his voice the clearest, *please, please, it wasn't me, I don't know what you're talking about? What Valentine card? She's just a friend, I know you go out with her, why would I ever do that?*

At last Markus woke for real and the words, images and voices stopped. The bungalow was silent. No one was in. Tars at work. Ryan at work. Just the ticking of the clock in the hallway. Markus sat up with an angry hard-on, it bulged in his boxers and made the rest of his body hot and uncomfortable. Why do I always get these in the mornings, he thought? His first impulse was to turn his phone on, ring Mel, get her round, shag her brains out. Only he couldn't be arsed with her drama. She was no doubt going to go mad about yesterday, beating her little admirer up and getting expelled. Instead he got up and tiptoed to Ryan's room. His erection had softened a shade, slapping from thigh to thigh as he waddled off to get his brother's lap-top. He already had a porn scene in mind, a bit of brutal bondage involving a little blonde in a school uniform.

His erection regained force as he wrapped his hand around his brother's door handle. Pushed only the door wouldn't budge. Pushed again only to the same result.

Bastard. Bastard. Bastard has finally fitted that lock. C*nt.

Markus felt so horny and enraged he even considered smashing the door in. He'd seen the lock, a cheap flimsy thing that would easily cave-in with a bit of force. *Hmm?* Instead he went outside and walked around to his brother's window, hoping he'd left it open. He hadn't. Markus ran his nail-bitten fingers along the white frames of wood, *nope, nothing, no way in.* The cold bit, creating craters of Goosebumps that pimpled his bare legs. When he looked up he could see that nosey old c£nt of a neighbour staring at him from his top window. Suppose I'm a sight to see, Markus thought, a half-naked boy wandering around outside in the middle of the day, middle of winter, ha! By now his excitement had gone altogether, so he went back inside and had breakfast, a big bowl of Frosties while watching daytime TV. He sat there all morning and most of the afternoon, staring into the screen. He wiped drool from his lips and ate more, clearing the cupboards of crisps, chocolate, cakes, cheese. Back at the telly he watched a programme where a rich couple went abroad and had to choose one of three houses. The presenter took them around these massive villas and then they had to guess the prices. The first house was in the city, the second one by the sea, and the third was in the mountains. Markus noticed that the husband was a funny-looking dorky fuck, while his missis was young and fit and didn't work. The woman did all the talking and the husband just followed her around, nodding his head. The wife walked in high-heels, arms folded, criticising all the houses. The first one was too small, the second one too big, and the third was too isolated. *I like peace and quiet,* she said, *just not this much peace and quiet.* Everybody laughed and Markus couldn't see what was so funny. The husband agreed. The husband always agreed. In the end the couple (the wife) chose none of the houses. *Think we'll* (I'll) *hold on for something more suited to our* (my) *tastes.* She said.

Markus stared at the telly, totally confused.

"What the fuck was the point in any of that?" he said with a screw-face.

Just then he heard a knock at the door. It was the same knock as yesterday and Markus thought it was the police again. Maybe that little prick has died in his sleep, he thought. Only it was coming from the back door so it couldn't be the pigs.

When he opened up he saw his GF. Mel was standing there, still and pale, the sleeves of her coat draped over her hands.

"Alright?" he said.

Mel didn't say anything.

There was something different about her although he didn't know what. It took a few seconds to realise she was wearing a different pair of glasses. It changed her face completely. Makes her look weird, Markus thought. "New glasses?"

"Other's broke," she said.

Even though she looked like shit, a bit of this morning's horniness came back. "Come in," he said.

"Nah," she said.

"What the fuck's up with you?" he said. "Change your personality as well as your glasses?"

"They're old ones," she said. "Old glasses."

She was acting bizarre, like she was drunk or something. Markus was already back in the kitchen, looking for something else to eat. "Come in," he said again, his voice now spiked with irritation.

"I'm not coming in today."

"What?"

"Let's go for a walk up Clementine."

"What? Why? It's freezing out there. It's raining and shit."

"Not rain, just drizzle."

"Either way I ain't going out."

"Okay," she said, before robotically turning and walking back up the driveway.

"Whoa. Where you going?"

"I want to talk to you Markus. I just don't *feel* to come in today."

"Why?" he said, dulling his voice with sarcasm. "Your *Nature-Feeling* not telling you to?"

"Something like that."

Markus hung out the door, holding onto the frame like a crucifix. "You know you need to get that sorted out Mel. That psychiatrist of yours isn't doing a very good job. I'd get your money back if I was you."

"I don't pay," she said, walking away again.

"It was a joke."

She carried on walking.

"Alright!!" The rage in his voice made her stop. "Alright," he said again, a little calmer. "We'll go walk your precious fucking channel. Just let me get dressed."

Markus did, cursing all the way through putting on his jeans and coat. He met her at the foot of his driveway before walking the long way around Norman, instead of cutting through the alleyway. They got to the water and still not a word had passed. Mel was definitely different. It's like she was some kind of ghost, or mental patient, Markus thought.

"So?" he said. "You gonna tell me what's going on?"

She adjusted her new/old glasses onto the tip of her nose. They were thicker and more colourful than her regular ones. Markus wanted to tell her how stupid she looked but this time he didn't. Mel never answered so Markus decided to do the talking.

"It's not even that bad Mel," he began, coughing into his fist. "Police just try and scare you. His jaw's not even broken. It's not even fractured like they said it was. Tars is going over to see his parents tonight, get them to drop the charges. It's no biggie at all."

Mel was walking in the grass, which sparkled with silver droplets from the rain. The channel was covered in mist, looking indistinguishable from the dank grey sky. The waters looked like a sheet of metal, unmoving.

"And school?" she said.

Markus put his head down. "Oh yeah. I don't think there's any coming back from that one."

Markus suddenly thought of something. "Hey how come you're not there now?"

Mel let a few moments of silence pass. She was even nearer to the water now. "I didn't go."

"Yeah I can see that, but why? Because of me?"

"Yeah." Markus touched her hand but she withdrew. "And other things."

"What other things?"

"Mum has got a job there."

Markus let out a sharp laugh. "What, at Kitts?"

Mel nodded.

A thin slice of weak sun shimmered behind the grey.

"As a teacher? Nah. Can't be. Too thick."

"Dinner lady," she said.

Now Markus let-rip with a massive roar. "What? That's mad, and embarrassing. I mean why the fuck would she do that?"

"Just that," Mel said, without emotion. "To embarrass me."

Markus had picked up a stick from somewhere. He was shaking

his head while hacking away at the long grass like it was a scythe. "What does your sis think?"

"Loves it. Thinks it's a great idea. Probably put her up to it in the first place."

"That's lame," Markus said. "Bet Mia is pissing herself. Bet the whole school knows she's your mum by now," he said, throwing the stick. It wasn't until he heard the splash that he realised how close the water was. The fog was thick. Everything was grey. They couldn't see no more than a few inches in front of them.

"So you're gone and mum's here," she said, finally.

"Yup," he said casually.

Again he tried to take her hand but again she withdrew it.

"Mel what's wrong? You'll survive without me, y'know? You did before we met, before we got together. Besides you'll always have Mia."

Mel had stopped but she would not look Markus in the face. "You lied," she said softly.

"What?"

"You lied to me."

"No I didn't."

"You lied to me like everyone does."

"How?"

"Like mum does and sis does, like dad has and Mia does."

"When?"

"You lied because you said you wouldn't hit him and you did. You lied Markus. You swore on your Mum's grave and what does that make you?"

Markus was smiling again. "Ha. But you see I didn't lie. Cos, mum was cremated. There was no grave to swear on in the first place." He was laughing again. "So it doesn't even count. Technically, *officially*, I didn't lie to you at all."

A smile appeared on Mel's face, but not a good smile, one of disbelief. It's like she'd stopped breathing for a few seconds.

"Goodbye Markus."

"What?"

She walked up the bank. Markus watched the backs of her rain-soaked jeans climb through the grass, away from him.

He made his hands into a tunnel and shouted on up after her. "Beautifulness I can see you're not your normal self today so I'm gonna leave you alone. But everything's gonna be alright. You just take everything too seriously all the time. You need to lighten the fuck up. I'll call you in a bit. Maybe we can go for McDonald's. Talk about it properly ... "

The girl said nothing, she didn't even look back. He watched the outline of her fade and fade, fade until she was gone; until she was another part of the mist.

Mel

Dear You, The Living,

I guess you could say this is a Suicide Note.

I guess you could say that THIS is an Official Suicide Letter and stuff. Cos, like, by the time You read this I will be dead. Gone for life, gone for good. Seeing as though Seddy has been with me from The Start I may as will use 'The Very Last Entry' to say goodbye.

So this is it.

First off, like, before we get into the final things that pushed me Over The Edge I just want to get the Funeral Stuff straight. I just want to make it all clear so you can AT LEAST grant me my wishes. If The Pact goes as planned then My Markus Big Bear should be next. I mean, in my heart I know Mia won't even Commit Suicide anyway. She is full of BS and I don't believe a word she says anymore. However, if she does, I don't want her connected to My Funeral in any way, not one bit. KEEP US SEPAERATE.

It's different for Markus, cos The Truth is he'll be In Bits and won't be able to live without me. I go, he goes, I know ...

... so ...

... the funeral goes as follows ... .

First off, we want our ashes to be put in the same jar and shook so we're all mixed together and stuff. So like, we become the same person kind of a thing. Then we want it scattered in our Special Place, The Clementine Channel. The Clementine Walk that runs through our town Kimble Wells and links our houses. It doesn't matter EXACTLY where, just as long as it stretches the WHOLE distance. I know that's a long way but there are two of us, so there should be enough ashes to cover it all. Also The Song I want playing at Our Funeral is Love Story by Taylor Swift. I know it's a bit cheesy and like, I know Markus would Actually Hate it but for me it's The Perfect Song, mostly cos of the lyrics and stuff. Because if you listen to them it's about First Love and Falling in Love and Romeo and Juliet and Living for Love and Dying for Love, which makes sense cos that is what we're Officially doing when all said and done.

Got that?

I'm not asking for much so I'm sure you can AT LEAST grant me these few wishes.

Fanks.

Other than that, there's really not much else.

I don't want peeps to be sad cos it's just the way it is and stuff. Like mum, Dad and Sis don't be guilty and think you could have done more cos you couldn't. Neither could Mia. Neither could all those psychiatrists and counsellors and stuff. Sometimes your nature is your nature and it's just The Way it is and nothing can change that. I was a disaster from The Start and always was. Madness is in me and death is the only way.

Even though I was lucky to find The Love of My Life it still wasn't enough.

mum keeping me away from him and School keeping me from him didn't help ... but hey ... it's too late now.

In Life we couldn't be together, but in Death we can be.

So Big Bear if you get to read this ... hurry up ... I'm waiting for you and your big arms to come wrap me up in Heaven! Lol.

P.S.

Also mum you getting that job as a Dinner Lady pushed me over the edge only you never realised it. You never realised how embarrassing you are, and can be. Sometimes I think you did it on purpose. I tried telling you but you just wouldn't stop. I was so mad that day you told me about The Dinner Lady Job I tried to

465

smash my own glasses into my own face and all you and Del did was laugh and call me Stupid.

Well, who feels stupid now!!??

Anyway I'm not bitter, just thought you should know these Final Details so maybe you can learn a lesson. The Biggest Lesson in Life; don't treat people like shit.

Anyway.
Either way.

The stage is set. The props are in place.

Two candles burn at either side of my room.
I'm wearing one of Markus's t-shirts and the turquoise bracelet that Someone Special once gave to me.

Twenty paracetamol stand in a perfect straight line, like a ceremony kind of a thing.

I will wash Them down with a bottle of alco-pops to numb me while I go ...

... So ...

... time to say Goodbye ...

... goodbye World and stuff ...

Yours,

M.E x

Underdogs

Markus

Markus had never been to hospital. He was lucky like that. Never really had injury or illness. Not one broken bone. (Apart from the finger Ryan broke when he was little.) Not even a filling at the dentist.

He yawned as he stepped through the electric double-doors at the entrance, took out his phone and checked Mel's text again ... *Adams Ward.*

Kimble Wells Hospital wasn't that big but it was big enough to confuse him, all these rooms and corridors and lifts and different-coloured signs. Not one matching the name on his phone.

"Scuse me."

A large smiley nurse carrying a clipboard stopped in front of him.

"Know where ... " Markus had to look at his phone again. "Adams Ward is?"

"Sure," she said. "Although really you would have been better taking the South Entrance. But it's fine." She stood sideways and put her arm out like a lollipop lady. "Just stick to the main corridor and take it to the very end. Then you need to take a left, past the canteen, into the south foyer, there you're best just asking the lady at the desk because it's very close by then. Okay?"

Markus had switched-off about two sentences in, too busy wondering what the scores were last night in the midweek games. "Okay," he said. "Cheers."

He remembered the main corridor bit so he walked that, the sound of his trainers clicking against the polished floors. All the way through he could smell old people, ill people, medicine, disinfectant, death. Fucking disgusting, he thought.

At the canteen he rushed up to the newspapers and flipped one over to the sports pages. Funny enough Liverpool wasn't the first result he looked for. *Yes ya bastard.* Leicester City had won again, putting them three points clear at the top of the Premiership. He might be a life-long, die-hard Liverpool fan but he still wanted Leicester to win. It would be a landmark in the history of football, of sport. It would be a miracle. A one-in-a-million lottery win. He wasn't alone, the rest of the country wanted this too.

World loved an underdog.

He expected to see a near-corpse with tubes hanging out so he was surprised to see her sat upright in bed, that shiny smile of hers shining more than ever. "Big Bear!" she sang, opening her arms out.

There was an old black woman to her left and an anorexic girl to her right.

She gripped his neck and hugged him as hard as she could.

"Pretty strong for a dying girl," he said.

"You're late. Get lost?"

"Yeah, place is like a fucking maze."

The black lady pulled a face.

"Fuck's up with her?" Markus said.

"Ssssh Markus, like, try not to swear and stuff."

Markus tucked his t-shirt into his jeans and looked at the anorexic girl. "Check-out Miss Ethiopia," he whispered.

Mel put a finger over her lips but tried not to laugh.

"Why am I late anyway?" Markus said. "Not like you're going anywhere."

Mel held the white sheet across her chin. "Cos, like, I wanted to see you before Mia and Mum and that came."

"Minute your Mum comes I'm fucking leaving," Markus snarled." I can't be around that bitch. She winds me up."

Mel shrugged, then smiled. "No grapes or flowers?"

Markus had meant to pick her something up from the canteen but got side-tracked by the football results. Mel was talking but his mind was still on that, *Vardy scores one more he'll break the record for most goals scored in consecutive games.*

"Missed me?"

"It's only been a day."

"Yeah, but still. I like, nearly died y'know? I mean, I really wanted to and stuff. Even wrote a suicide note."

Markus put his eyes up and shook his head.

"Yeah well we did make a pact, remember?" she continued.

"A what?"

"A suicide pact."

For a few seconds Markus didn't have a clue what she was talking about. "Oh, yeah."

"Would you have definitely committed suicide too Big Bear?"

"Yeah, course."

The black lady pulled another face, this time one of utter disbelief. Markus noticed she had a gold crucifix around her neck.

Mel locked her fingers into his. "Funny," she said. "I feel quite happy now. Like all the depression and stuff has gone."

Markus didn't say anything.

"Maybe I'm bipolar."

Markus didn't even know what that was.

Suddenly they could hear a familiar voice, three big inflatable balloons were floating towards them, attached to a piece of string, which was attached to a girl. "Mia!" Mel shouted.

"Bestie!" the girl shouted back.

She was already sprinting full-pelt towards them, almost barging into an old woman shuffling along on a Zimmer frame.

"Mia careful," her mum said, taking off a pair of sunglasses.

Mia launched into the embrace of Mel with such force the two nearly fell out of bed. The black lady next to her struggled out of bed and closed the curtain partition between them.

"It's a god-forsaken circus," she said in a strong Caribbean accent.

"Alright Markus?" Mia's mum said with a sigh.

The boy's eyes couldn't help surf over her long, full-bodied curves. "Yeah," he said. Markus pulled up a chair and sat bored for the next half-hour, listening to the girls, mostly Mia. "I can't believe you *actually* did it babe you're so brave."

"She didn't do it though, did she?" Markus said.

The girls didn't hear him. Mia continued.

"I was so gonna do it if you hadn't pulled through. Like I even had the pills and everything. I was gonna go *exactly* the same way."

Mia's mum's attention flipped between her nails and her phone.

"Here, I bought you some grapes, and a book." Mia began pulling things out of a large designer carrier bag. "It's that new vampire porn novel I was telling you about. Bit like Twilight only hotter, more adult. I mean it's not really for kids but fuck it."

469

"Fanks," Mel said, reading the book's title: *All is Wild, All is Silent*. "But like, I think I'm leaving tonight."

"Really? But it's only been a day! Is that actually safe?"

"Yeah I've only got a bit of liver damage, I think. Like my stomach hurts a bit and I was sick and stuff but other than that I'm normal."

Mia's expression was full of thought. "Shit, maybe you should have taken thirty after all?"

"Perhaps," Mel said.

If it wasn't for Mia's mum's legs Markus would have been bored shitless. He kept trying to work out if her tan was real or fake.

"Hey why isn't your mum here?" Mia said, annoyed.

"She's been with me all night. Like, she hasn't left my side since *it* happened. But I told her I needed some me-time. You know, to like, process it all and stuff."

"Makes sense," Mia said.

"She should be back any minute now though," she said, pushing her glasses back from the tip of her nose.

"Hey you've got new glasses?"

"Nah. Old ones."

"What happened to your others?"

"I got mad and smashed them."

Mia nodded her head listlessly. "Okay ... cool."

There was quiet for a few moments before Mia turned to Markus. "And how you feeling?"

He shrugged. "Alright."

"But I mean, aren't you in bits?"

Markus nodded.

"Would you have done it if she hadn't pulled through?"

"Done what?"

"Suicide, our pact?"

"Yeah, course."

"Good," Mia said with an assertive nod of the head.

Just then a girl and a woman began walking up the corridor, their movements a slow spaced-out shuffle like they'd come back from the dead. For a few moments Markus didn't recognise who they were. Their faces pale and exhausted, eyes puffed out with little dots of sleeplessness in the middle. Markus didn't know what to say to them so he said nothing, kept his head down and his eyes on Mia's mum's foot, which was streaked with orange and covered in blisters, sliding in and out of her shoe.

There was no dressing it up, The Step-Up Learning Centre was a school for naughty kids, classrooms for broken misfits with nowhere else to go.

"Give us a lift Tars."

His auntie was sat in the armchair with her reading glasses on. "No."

She had her back to Markus, who was picking at the corner of the wallpaper with his thumb. "It's all the way out in Boston for fuck's sake!"

"Should have thought about that before you beat that lad up."

"Well how am I supposed to get there?"

"Bus."

"No money."

"I've already told you. A school bus leaves the town centre at nine."

"Give me a lift there then at least?"

"No more lifts," Tara said, not taking her eyes off the page. "No more lifts and no more money. No more favours, not until you can start showing me ... "

Markus was gone before the sentence ran out, slamming his bedroom door so hard the sound travelled across the ceiling. Tara looked up, sighed, and shook her head.

Markus fell on his bed and felt a twist of regret for beating that boy up, not guilt, but regret; for now he has to travel all the way to Boston to go to this stupid, retarded school.

There were some advantages though. He only had to go there three days a week, Monday, Wednesday and Friday. And classes didn't start till ten and finished at two.

Markus figured this was because bad lads had a shorter attention-span.

A swan lay dead in the road. Markus stared at it as the bus inched along the A16. Its neck was broke cleanly in two, laying L-shaped on the tarmac, in front of a car. The accident must have happened only moments before as the driver was just stepping out, placing his head in his hands. His windscreen was damaged, webbed with cracks. A lady got out from the black convertible behind and put her arm around him, consoling him. Markus put his eyes back on the swan. A circle of lurid red expanded as blood soaked through the pure white feathers, turning it pink.

Markus thought it looked like a blob of candy floss.

The bus pulled up more or less outside the school. A grimy sign reading *The Step-Up Learning Centre* stood crooked in front of an ugly slab of a building. The school was flat and rectangular and looked more like a factory or a warehouse. Markus ducked under the red and white barrier at the foot of the car park and headed inside.

No one was there, no kids. He looked up at a clock on the wall and realised he was fifteen minutes late.

"Can I help you?" a voice said.

Markus hadn't even noticed the front desk or the elfish woman sat behind it.

"Err. Yeah. It's my first day."

"What's your name love?"

"Venner. Markus Venner."

Markus peered into her grey roots as she put her head down. Her warty finger gliding down a list of names. "Yep," she said at last. "You're with Claudia, love. Room 3. Literally just there," she said, pointing to a glass door on the left.

Markus experienced a short explosion of adrenalin as he stepped into the classroom.

A woman turned her long neck slowly and looked at him. Markus thought of the swan from earlier.

"Sorry I'm late miss," he said, putting that cocky smile on show. "There was an accident involving a swan."

A small riot of laughter sounded off behind her. Only she didn't give him the reaction he wanted.

"No need for excuses," she said mildly. "And no need to call me *miss* either. My name is Claudia. And you are?"

Straight away he saw the word *beautiful.* Not typical beautiful but quirky beautiful. She was tall and thin and blonde, a horizontal fringe framing her oval face. She had a hook for a nose which was pierced with a silver ring. Her sky-blue eyes rested on him with a quality of being both strong and soft. She wore striped hippie trousers which elongated her legs like some optical illusion, making them go on and on and on. Markus wasn't good with ages, but he'd guess she was about twenty-eight. There was no doubt she had taken him off his game.

"And you are?" she repeated, a northern accent on her sensual lips.

"Markus Venner."

Someone had answered for him. And when Markus looked over the teacher's shoulder he could see the unmistakable figure of Beady. That fat foe of his sat slumped in the middle of The Taylor Gang. He had put even more weight on, like he was ready to burst. His leering face crushed with wiry glasses. That stupid trademark cap atop of his head.

Markus nodded, affirming his name.

"Welcome," she said coolly.

She circled her arm like a windmill and put her fingers out, gesturing for him to pick a seat.

"Sparky," Beady said.

Markus had forgotten that old nickname of his, given to him from his fire-starting days. He blanked Beady and the bunch and took the nearest chair to him, on the empty side of the room. Claudia's unbeatable blue eyes came down on him for a second and she seemed to consider this.

Time passed ... his first lesson at his new school. Markus couldn't believe how calm it was. He couldn't understand how this was a school for *bad people* yet there seemed to be less rules here, less work, and the teacher wasn't as strict either. They didn't do stuff like maths or English or science but rather talk about things, question things. She'd give the class a scenario and then the kids had to write down what they thought about it, how they'd deal with it. After they got to talk about their ideas. Most of the kids gave stupid answers and said silly things, but Claudia had a way of making it funny, yet at the same time turning it around to a point of seriousness. She had *a way* that Markus had not seen in a teacher before. A control that was uncanny, a *gentle power.*

Beady was still looking over, like he wanted to be mates and Markus didn't understand this. Last they met the fat perv was eating knuckles, and then eating the ground. Some of the other boys he recognised too, lads from the estate. The rest must be from Boston and other surrounding towns. The alpha of the group was a mouthy lad who looked quite hard. He had curly hair and a big square face. One ear studded with gold and he chewed gum noisily. People called him Sniff although Markus had never seen him before. Beady had obviously given him the low-down because he seemed to be glancing over every now and then. There was only one girl in the class and Markus had her down for some kind of retard. She had a boy haircut and did nothing but suck her fingers. Her hand was red-raw and she stunk. She was the only other person to be sat on *this* side of the room. In the end Beady and Co brushed Markus off. He had clearly rejected them and there was a sudden shift in atmosphere. A palpable tension between the two sides of the room. He could tell that Claudia had clocked this.

At dinner the others took a football to a small yard around the back. Some of them looked at Markus, maybe giving him one last chance to come join them. He didn't. Instead he ducked the barrier and left the premises. He had no money so he decided to go and lift something from Greggs. Greggs was an easy place to shoplift from because all the pastries and baguettes were lined-up right near the door, plus it was always busy, loads of people to hide amongst. After he wandered around the town centre, passing the spot where he and Mel found that toddler when they went on the run, some four months ago. He couldn't remember the kid's name or what he looked like, just that something happened there. He stood in the spot and looked around. It was March and the town looked different with a modest sun shining on it, lighting up some of the streets.

Suddenly he smelt some familiar perfume and a blonde figure moved onto his shoulder.

"Alright wanderer?" she said.

It was Claudia, talking to him like she'd known him for years.

She was holding an empty salad dish in one hand and half a roll-up in the other. "You gonna turn up on time this afternoon?"

Markus returned the smile, realised he could even be blushing a shade. "I wasn't lying about the swan y'know? There really was an accident … "

Markus, who was usually, unknowingly, economical with words was finding himself starting to ramble.

She was smiling a big white smile. He realised how dumb he was sounding so he shut himself up.

They stopped by a bench and sat. She rolled-up the rest of her cigarette and lit.

"You know those boys?"

Markus nodded. "Some."

"You don't like them?"

"Nope," he said, his lips making a smacking sound, *nnno-pah*.

Claudia took an intake of breath, held it, smoke dancing under her bottom lip before letting it go.

"That Beady's a fucking pervert," he said.

A light smile played on her face, like she knew what he was talking about. "You not gonna be starting any shit in my class, right?"

She was looking right at him, still smiling. Markus smiled back and slowly shook his head.

"Good," she put her hand out towards him, the rollie poised in the tips of her fingers.

"What?" He laughed incredulous. "No. No. I don't smoke."

She shrugged and put it back in her own lips.

"Just what kind of a teacher are you anyway?" he said.

She never answered. "C'mon," she said, dunking her salad dish in a bin. "We're late."

leM tuoba klat 2 DEEN eW

Markus was hanging backwards out of bed, his hand dangling towards his phone. Mia's text was upside down so he had to flip the phone to read it properly.

We NEED 2 talk about Mel.

Markus sighed. *Always the drama.* He rolled over onto his front and replied with some half-arsed comment. Mia was always on her phone, on it more than she was in real life. Her world was Facebook, Instagram, Twitter and loads, loads more. She talked through her fingertips. Markus had her down for the fastest texter in the world, literally, as he replied another one came in.

I mean it, I'm serious, we need 2 talk about Mel. Today. Now. Meet at Maccys in an hr.

2 far, Markus replied.

Channel then.

K.

An hour?

K.

Best b there!?

Markus threw his phone under the bed and stretched.

He could see her a mile off. She must have been wearing every colour under the sun, blue hat, red t-shirt, orange cardigan, turquoise shorts with black leggings underneath, pink trainers.

"You look like a fucking rainbow."

"Ah thanks babes."

"It wasn't a compliment."

It was a windy day and she had to touch her hat a few times so save it from coming off. Everything about Mia was fast, she talked fast and moved fast. "My ADHD is worse than ever," she said, striding out in front.

"Thought you wanted to talk about Mel?"

"It's related," she said definitely.

Mia amused Markus how she thought she was an adult. She was always using quotes and phrases she had heard from somewhere else. "I'm *deranged with grief*," she said, gazing out at the water. Daffodils were now starting to appear on the banks.

Markus didn't say anything so she pushed on.

"I can't believe she tried to take her own life."

Markus stopped and pulled his screw-face. "We formed a suicide pact you donkey."

Mia spun on her heels in the gravel and faced him. "Yeah but I didn't think she was *actually* going to do it."

Markus smiled, put his head down and shook it. "You're a fucking gorm."

"I mean I just thought we were playing, fucking around. I didn't think she was *actually* gonna get twenty pills and shove them down her neck."

Markus picked something up and threw it into the water. "Well, she did."

"But I mean if she had of, would you have followed? I mean would you have *actually* committed suicide too?"

Markus shrugged. He couldn't help but look at Mia's arse, bumping up and down in front of him.

"I blame her mum," Mia said.

Markus shook his head again and sighed. "You need to make your mind up."

"What do you mean?"

"You always say her mum's not that bad."

"Yeah I know but I think she could be different behind closed doors. Like on FB she's always posting pictures and saying nice things about Mel but maybe it's all a front. Maybe she does *actually* secretly bully her."

Markus didn't say anything, he didn't really think anything either. Just noted how much Mia's voice went through him, like a needle.

"I think Mel would be much happier without her mum. I think overall she'd be a better person, less depressed."

"Probs," he agreed.

Mia had now slowed down and was walking with Markus side by side. A few times he felt her hand bump against his. They walked through a darkened tunnel of trees.

"I mean doesn't it ever bug you?" she said.

"What?"

"Going out with a depressive?"

"No."

"Doesn't it ever bring you down?"

"Not really."

Markus could smell her perfume. It spun him out a little because it was a similar fragrance to what Claudia wore. He closed his eyes for a moment or two.

"You know she's a paranoid too?"

"What?"

"She's a paranoid."

"About what?"

"Anything. Everything. She see things that aren't there. I think she could even be schizophrenic. Or in the early stages of. She's definitely on the spectrum."

Markus shook his head.

"She paranoid about us, mostly. She thinks we're secretly in love"

By now he was truly tired with Mia. *Football Focus* was starting soon and he wanted to get back and watch it, see who Leicester were playing today.

"She's paranoid about losing *you* the most. Of you finding someone else and leaving her."

They were out of the trees and in the open again.

"Fucking hell Mia you don't half talk some shit."

She stopped and swung her body lithely through the air, facing him head-on. "Hey I'm just trying to help. Our girl nearly died last week and we need to be there for her."

Markus shook his head again, totally bored now. "She didn't nearly die."

Mia carried on talking but Markus wasn't listening anymore. It was as if he had pressed the mute button on a remote control. Her mouth moved without sound. Instead he looked at all the sights in the background. The church spire. The trees rotating wildly by the changeable gusts. Two cyclists wearing matching jerseys carrying their bikes through a gate. He looked at fishermen, dog-walkers, joggers, and a mum with a pushchair. Then right at the other side of the path he spotted a girl walking towards them. Against the wind she looked like she was walking on the spot, not getting anywhere. He recognised the uncertainty of her walk, the suspicious shuffle; the stooping, round-shouldered gait carrying the world upon them. Light winked off her glasses and as she got nearer he saw a pained shock indented into her face from seeing her bestie and her BF standing so close together. From this angle it looked like Mia was standing on Markus's feet, head up, lips out, about to kiss.

Tara couldn't afford to get complacent. She'd seen this before. It had been known for Markus to knock-up two or three weeks of good behaviour, only to throw it all away again in a moment of madness. It was almost like his moods were dictated to by the movement of the tide or the positioning of the planets, the changing of the seasons or an appearance of a full-moon.

For the majority of March, however, her nephew had been tip-top, mild-mannered and bright. No outbursts, no defiance, no phone calls or knocks at the door. Tara couldn't help notice that this change had come since he'd been going to that new school up in Boston, the place for bad lads. Maybe it suited him better there, being away from *normal kids.* Perhaps he didn't feel so much of an outcast and found it easier to blend in. Maybe having other tearaways around him gave him less of a need to show-off and shock? Whatever it was, Tara thought, seemed to be working. It's like he had woken up all of a sudden. He seemed to be more involved and inquisitive about life, asking questions, bringing up the past, things to do with his upbringing, stuff about his mum. Only he didn't talk about it with that undercurrent of rage but seemed to be genuinely intrigued, almost philosophical. It was as if someone at The Step-Up Learning Centre had taken him under their wing and opened his mind up. He seemed to be making more effort with his appearance too. He actually shaved, put a wet razor to those patchy bits of stubble that plagued his face and made him look scruffy. Cut off the dirt-edged nails he got from playing outside and picking things up by the channel. He showered every morning before the days he went to school and even on the days he didn't. He wore aftershave, hair products, shoes instead of trainers.

When Tara asked him if he wanted a treat from town for his good behaviour Markus asked for a smart shirt. All of a sudden there seemed to be a sense of pride about the boy.

If Markus didn't already have a girlfriend Tara may have even suspected there was a new girl on the scene, someone he was trying to impress.

Even when his aunt asked if he wanted a lift one day Markus declined and said he preferred taking the bus. It's like he wanted to be seen as independent, not relying on his aunt for things.

It was all very strange.

Maybe it was the school, or maybe he was just growing up at last, perhaps even a combination of the two. Either way, Tara still couldn't afford to get complacent. She'd seen this before.

It could, quite easily, be just another calm before yet another storm.

Mel was walking ahead through the long grass, up the banks of the channel, when Markus sneaked a peak at his phone, checking the time, 11:43.

He still had time.

They were not too far away from the spot where he took her virginity, under a tree where an old rope-swing hung. "Mel I gotta tell you something," he said.

There was already an ominous tone to his voice which sent a chill through Mel's spine. It almost made her shiver as she turned and silently faced him. Her face whitened with dread, her eyes shrinking into little pinpricks of black.

"What?" she managed to mutter.

It was a warm, still day, almost a summer's day.

"You should sit down," he said, lowering his head.

Her head was in bits, coming undone, trying to find something, anything, anything that it could be. She looked into her BF's expression. He was always so hard to read, impossible, more or less.

She sat on the wooden beam of the rope-swing and all of a sudden her bum felt big, huge, ginormous, grotesque. She thought of Mia, and her perfect little arse.

Markus was looking at the opening, seeing if anyone else was around.

"What?" Mel said again, her shaky fingers wrapped around the frayed bits of rope.

Her glasses were steaming up.

He cupped his hands over his heart, like he was clutching an imaginary baseball. "This ain't easy," he said.

She knew it. She knew what it was. He *had* kissed Mia that day. A few weeks ago when she caught them walking together that Saturday afternoon.

"I'm splitting up with you," he said.

He said it sudden and clear and straight and Mel felt like a train had gone through her.

"What?" her lips were wobbling all over the place and Markus watched her heart go *snap*.

"Yep," he said with a solemn shake of the head.

Mel wanted to talk but no word would come.

"I've met someone else," he said casually.

Her first thought was *death*, instant death. That was it now. It was as simple as that she was gone. No bullshit twenty pills but death, real uncomplicated death. Forty pills, fifty, a hundred. She would eat them until her heart stopped. She would take the sharpest razor the world had to offer and open up her veins. Every vein in her stupid, ugly, fat body. In fact the minute Markus was gone she will be tying this rope-swing around her neck.

"Mia," she said.

She said it automatically, like her name just popped out her mouth of its own accord.

"What?" he said. "Mia? God no, ugh, Yuk."

That made only a millimetre bit of difference.

"A girl I met at my new school."

Mel had her head down and Markus watched her heart break more and more. He pulled out his phone and checked the time again, 11:57.

Cool, he'd made it in time.

His mournful expression got sliced in half by that big grin of his. "APRIL FOOLS!"

Those words were a bell going off in her head. The instant rush of relief was incredible, an overwhelming flood of life began to wash through her ears and fill her brain. She was like a junkie with a fix. Within the click of a finger she had literally been brought back to life. She gasped, whimpered. Her whole body collapsed with exhaustion. Markus lassoed his arms over her neck and she began to sob.

"Hey beautifulness, I gotya goin!!"

Next she hated him, hated him more than she had hated anyone. More than her mum or her sis or Mia. His cruelty was truly breath-taking and what was worse is that he was completely oblivious to it. She tried to slap him across the face but her arm was too weak and her fist just crumbled against his skull like a bunch of dead flowers. He was laughing, laughing. Laughing his head-off. He picked her up like a doll and spun her around. She couldn't help but laugh with him, cry, she was alive, horribly and wonderfully alive. She still hated him but she loved him too. Hated him more than ever and loved him more than ever and Mel didn't know how that was possible. He kept spinning her around until she felt sick. Colours and objects and sounds all blurred like she was trapped inside a giant whirligig. He slowed to a stop and at last the earth stood still in its axis, the sky, the trees, everything stopped spinning. She was still in his arms and now all she wanted him to do was put her down in this long grass, and fuck her.

Leicester City were only a little more than a month away from taking this title, this historical feat. If they win, Markus thought, I'm going to the victory parade. He Googled a map of Britain and realised that Leicester wasn't all that far away. I'll get my uncle to drive me, he thought. Only he remembered that they had fallen out, not spoken a word since New Year's Eve when he pushed Charlie in the throat. I'll just have to win him back over, Markus thought. Yeah. That's what I'll have to do.

It'd been happening for the last few days now, Beady perving over his Claudia. It started off as a couple of comments and gestures from the back of the class; whispers, pointing, sniggers, but now it had moved into full-blown disrespect.

"You've dropped something Claud," he said in that vile, lisping voice of his.

Claudia stood erect at the front of the class, her blazing blonde looking left, then right.

Markus shook his head, fed-up, chin propped up by his fist

"*There*," Beady said, pointing down at nowhere.

His mates were holding their sides in, trying not to laugh. Beady's eyes were fixed on Claudia, her long wavy shape behind her hippie skirt.

It didn't take long for the penny to drop. "Alright weedy Beady, joke over," Claudia said, facing him head-on. "I'm not one of your little girls. *Don't take the piss.*"

Claudia could be fierce, through her fun veneer there was a core made of steel. Another thing Markus admired her for. She kept on staring at Beady until his fat face flushed with discomfort.

Only it started back up again after lunch. Every time she turned her back Beady did things with his hands, fucking the side of his fist with a stumpy, nicotine-finger. It wasn't even funny yet his crowd all rolled around, faces contorted with hysteria. Beady leaning forward, opening his mouth, filling it with an imaginary penis. His face was fiendish and disgusting and Markus was lit with fury. More than anything he wanted to destroy that face, obliterate it beyond recognition so he could never pull those perverse expressions again. Beady sat back, rocking onto the two back legs of his chair, his grubby hand ferreting through into his joggers. He started to assimilate masturbation, pulling yet another grotesque face, mouth open and lopsided, his eyes rolling into the back of his head as the rest of his mates laughed like mad, frenzied, entertained.

Markus Venner had had enough. He'd reached the end of his patience. There was certain pleasure in letting go and letting rip. "You need to knock it on the head Beady, before I knock *you* on *your* head...*again.*"

Beady's face went blank with surprise. He held up his hands innocently and mouthed, *what?*

"Who are you her guardian angel?"

It was that kid, Sniff. This had been a long time coming. Over the last few weeks the tension between the two boys had been silently growing. Two alpha energies competing in the same room.

"Alright guys," Claudia was back facing the class, her arms arrow-shaped at hips.

"It's fucking disrespectful," Markus bit.

Confrontation enlivened in Sniff's face. "Like you can talk about respect, some of the shit I've heard about you. Pushing an old cripple down a flight of stairs!"

Screw-face, "you fucking what?"

Markus was surprised to see Sniff on his feet first. Even more surprised by his height. He'd not really seen Stiff stood-up and Markus was not used to being matched by size, and also by the same absence of fear. Markus stared at him full in the face, searching for some doubt or hesitation, a blink or a swallow of saliva. There was nothing.

Now with Sniff as a shield Beady got brave. "Oh and The Taylors send their love. Both Stewie *and* Ewan say *hello.*"

"You think I'm scared of them pair of pricks?!"

When Markus stepped forward, Sniff did.

"Guys, guys, guys."

All of a sudden Claudia's control seemed feeble as the two brutish teens waded forward, eating up the space between them.

"Whoa, whoa, whoa," Claudia yelped, rapid-fire.

Markus's world was in the other boy's eyes. They were locked onto each other. It was as if the rest of the class and the people in it had melted away. Somehow Claudia had slipped her thin figure in between them. Markus felt her there, only just. She stood facing, a blonde blur beneath him. Her spidery fingers webbed at his chest. Her voice somehow managed to perforate his swelling violence and find a way into his ear.

"Markus no, don't, don't."

His eyes were still locked onto Sniff's, the black of his pupil, the blue of his iris, the red rage screaming in his veins.

She was whispering now, for his ears only. His could feel her lips on his skin. "For me," she said. "Do it for me. For me Markus. Don't. Don't. Come. Come with me."

She had him by the hand and was leading him, feeling the silence fall over the class like a blanket, closing the door on it. Another teacher was outside, a man teacher. "Everything alright Claud?"

She didn't answer but she must have nodded her head or something because he said no more. They were over the corridor and into another classroom, a smaller one with more windows. Sun coming through them, lighting up the room, putting shadowy stripes across the carpet. Claudia still had a hold of his hand, almost like they were girlfriend and boyfriend. She jumped up and sat sideways on a desk, putting them at the same height.

"It's alright," she said. "It's fine."

He thought maybe she'd talk about what happened, ask what had taken place only she didn't. "Forget them," she said. "Forget them *all.* Forget everything. It's okay."

Her voice was hypnotic and soothing, like when you put a shell up to your ear and listen to the sea, Markus thought. "You're shaking," she said.

Markus looked down at his hands; his arms, his chest.

"It's alright," she said. "Come here."

Claudia took him into her arms and Markus got shocked. It came from nowhere and he wondered if this was happening in his imagination. Her arms covered him and he tensed up. "It's alright," she said in a velvety whisper. Slowly his breathing began to calm and his body relaxed. He closed his eyes and then opened them again. She was cradling his head, resting it on the smallness of her breast. He could see the dark pinch of a nipple through her top. Claudia had been on his mind for weeks but there was nothing erotic about this moment. He felt the side of his face press her bosom and for some reason he thought of his mum. She held him. "It's alright, Markus."

It was like someone had flipped on a switch because for a moment the boy felt something, something nameless and new, something alien and a little bit frightening. It was a build-up of pressure, a build-up of an emotion he'd not really felt before. It was crawling upwards like it had a life-form of its own, filling him up. It was like he was about to cry, cry for the first time. This is what it felt like.

"I'm alright," he said, taking himself out of her arms.

She was looking right at him, a lovely serene expression across her face; an ancient knowingness with a sparkle of mischief in her eye.

"I told you, no starting shit in my class."

She smiled, he smiled.

Up close he noticed her nose-stud was in the shape of a small elephant.

Saying anything now would be impossible. His mind was blank, calm and blank, almost like he'd been drugged.

"I can fight my own battles," she said finally, tugging his sleeve.

He nodded his head, feeling dumb.

"Go home," she said.

He nodded again. It was as if she had his head on a piece of string like a puppet, pulling it whenever she wanted. He got to the glass door. Over the corridor he could hear noise slowly start up again from the room opposite.

"Have a good weekend and I'll see you back here on Monday."

More nodding of the head. Markus pulled open the door and stepped outside.

"Oh Markus," her voice was muffled through the glass.

He opened it again. "Just remembered, not Monday. It's bank holiday. Wednesday. See you back here on Wednesday. Wednesday the thirteenth."

He looked at her one last time, and then was gone.

Mel

Dear Dearest You,

Hey You're still here! Lol. I am too. Cos like, as You can see The Suicide Thing didn't really work out and stuff. See, I'm EVEN crap at that. I'm even crap at dying. Can you believe I ACTUALLY failed at death?

Ha. I don't even know whether to laugh or cry at that? Ha.

So …

So now I'm doing The One Thing I wanted to avoid at ALL costs. The Thing I mentioned at the Very Start, like in Entry Number One: Head Meds.

I'm taking meds. They made me start taking medication and I FEEL so ashamed and silly and stuff.

I'm on that Fluoxetine I was telling You about. Only a low dose to begin with, like 10 mg or something like that. It's supposed to just take the edge off and control my urges but tbh I haven't really noticed a difference. Like, I don't really FEEL anything but then I suppose that's The Point. Lol. I've been on it for about three weeks, I think. Although They said it can take like a month or so to Kick In and work and like, get in your system and stuff. Come to think of it on Monday I did have a bit of a Spaced-Out Day but really that could have just been in my head, like a placebo kind of a thing. I have to take it twice a day. One in the morn when I first wake up and then one in Evening Time. It was quite bad at The Start cos I was so focused on taking These that like, I forgot to take my Birth Control tablets a few times!!!

Eeeeeek.

That's all My Life needs right now, a baby on board! Lol.

So I'm 14 years old and already I've got all these pills and prescriptions and potions and stuff rattling around inside me! Soon I'll be like a Walking Chemist or something. Lol. The Only Person I've told about The Meds Thing is Markus. There's no way I'm telling Mia and tbh I'm not gonna Lie but I think our friendship is Officially Over. Like, I don't think I have The Right to call her My Bestie anymore. Ever since that day I caught her and Markus up at the

486

Channel without me something inside died. Like, in my heart, my Nature-Feeling says they WEREN'T kissing, that it was just the angle they were standing in, but still, She went behind my back and arranged to meet him and that is Officially The Biggest Deceit Ever. She said she only went to talk about Me and My Suicide but it doesn't matter. What she did was <u>wrong</u> and I'd say Our Friendship is over more or less, over For Good. I don't answer her calls, and I only text her back with the shortest reply, like, with just one or two words or something.

So, I guess she is gone like everybody else in My Life, like dad and mum and sis and that.

So, I guess The Only Person left now is Big Bear.

Although tbh I EVEN thought He was gone at One Point, gone For Good. Cos like, he did The Worst Official April Fools Prank EVER. He took me out to The Spot where he took my virginity and I took his and then he said we were 'Over.' Said he was In Love with Someone Else. I thought I was gonna die, LITERALLY die. I literally felt my heart burst and my head crack. Like it was By Far THE WORST PAIN I HAVE EVER FELT, way worser than anything mum or anyone else has ever done.

Even though the WHOLE thing was a joke it did make me realise something. It made me realise that he is 'capable' of leaving. That deep within him he does have that 'potential' to just up and leave and that makes me feel terrified. It makes me feel like Life and Love is so brief and fragile, like I'm walking on a thin sheet of ice that can crack and break at Any Time.

Since then he has told me a Trillion Times that it was a joke, and that he needs Me as much as I need Him. And I kind of DO believe him cos when I look around at His Life he hasn't got anybody either. Just Me. Just Me. There's just Me, really. Mel Ellis is all that he has and stuff. He swears that he would do anything for me, die for me, kill for me. I kind of believe this too, cos like, there is this soft, romantic protective side that nobody else sees, nobody, no-one … not even You. I mean on the surface he's all tough and dangerous and detached and stuff but underneath there is a Special World with a Secret Door and only I have The Key.

Anyway.
Either way.

He would HATE me for talking like this, for saying all this mushy gooey stuff about him so I'll say no more.

On to other stuff…

At least I have my old glasses fixed now so I no longer look like the Super Weirdo. It feels good to be wearing them. I got my face back again so I get to be a little less Self-Conscious than normal. Markus said he kind of got used to The Big Thick Weird Ones, said it made me look cute and smaller but I hated them and tbh I think that was Part of The Problem and may have EVEN had something to do with The Suicide Thing if that makes sense?? Lol.

After The Suicide Thing things got okay. Okay again for like three days but then 'she' started again. Started like she always does. I thought cos I nearly DIED mum would let me see Markus again but I was wrong.

No Mel!

What do you mean No? I nearly died!

What has that got to do with anything? She said.

It has everything to do with anything. That's the whole sole reason I did it! Don't you get it??

We were outside in the Back Yard. It was Saturday morning and the sun was out and mum was throwing toys for Babe, playing fetch.

mum just let me see him again otherwise I might do it again. I said calmly.

mum got mad by this and threw the toy so hard at the back fence it cracked the panel.

How dare you blackmail me! She said. That is just an awful thing to do.

How is that blackmail, I said? Holding my hands out like a pair of scales.

You can't just run away, skip school, or take loads of pills just because you don't get what you want Mel. Life doesn't work like that.

Just then I noticed my bedroom window flip open. I pictured Adele laying on my bed, listening to the WHOLE thing.

I will not let you see that boy until this stupid little phase is over.

Phase? What phase? I said. This isn't a phase. It's like, true everlasting love and stuff.

mum made a dry snort of laughter.

Don't laugh at me mum.

mum's hand was shiny-wet from Babe's dripping saliva.

What have you got against him anyway?

mum showed a face of disbelief, like she couldn't believe I asked that.

Because he's bad Mel. He's a bad apple and everybody can see it but you. You're blind!

He loves me. I said in a high voice. He listens to me. He's like the ONLY person who has listened to me EVER. So how is that bad? What makes him so bad?

mum put a finger to her lip and did this stupid sarcastic face she does. Oh I don't know, she began, let me see. Stealing a tenner out of my kitchen. Running away from home. Sleeping in the woods for three days like a tramp. Beating people up. Getting expelled from school. Starting this stupid suicide pact. I mean tell me when to stop Mel … .

First off, like, he didn't steal that tenner, I shouted. And it wasn't in the woods. And he only beat that kid up to protect me. And … and the suicide pact was all Mia's idea anyway …

mum had stopped throwing the toys now and Babe wanted more. He slathered around her hands with his tail wagging like mad.

See, mum said, blind! You make excuses for him. You're in denial. No point talking to you at all.

I was standing against the house with my foot up against the wall. Knowing Adele was listening to all this got me mad.

Yes we've had problems, Mel. mum was saying. We've had problems. We haven't had it easy. But since he has come into our life it's got a hundred times worse. You're not good together Mel. When are you going to get that into your thick, stupid head?! You're toxic, a bad combination, a ticking time-bomb, waiting to go off.

I'd heard All This before, so I just folded my arms and rolled my head back against the wall, looking up at my open window, the curtain billowing.

mum was still going on. You can do better than that, she said.

Don't call him 'that?'

I didn't mean …

He's a real person you know? A human being. Not a thing, not an object.

Whatever Mel, I'm not talking to you while you're being like this.

She threw a toy again and it got stuck under the cracked fence.

Babe rolled on its side and shoved his snout under to get it.

When I look at you Melanie I see one thing. mum said, finally. I see your dad. Because I know that's exactly where you're going to end up. You're going to end up just like him.

I thought I heard Adele giggle from above and that made me want to fly off the handle. I thought about rushing upstairs and beating the living crap out of her.

Like dad? I said. Like dad? Now I was screaming. A drug addict. An alcoholic? A waste of space? Is that how you see me?

mum said nothing, I could only see the side of her horrible face but I know she was happy to have gotten under my skin.

You hate dad so you obviously hate me!?

Still she said nothing. Her silence gave me all the answers I needed.

I'm going, I'm gone. I'm leaving for good you stupid bitch!

I think that was maybe the First Time I called her that.

I'll pick up my stuff later.

It took me ages to open that big black bolt on the gate. I slammed it shut and heard it bounce against the frame two or three times, and I heard Babe bark and mum make a noise and Adele say something in that vile vain voice of hers ...

... I was running ... running fast ... running mad ... up Kings Road ... past the Falcon Pub at the end ... I didn't stop ... I didn't slow down ... I was full of anger and adrenalin and stuff ... it was like Cross Country at school only this time I was a winner, unstoppable. mum had done it now, pushed me over an edge that there was no coming back from ... I was onto Norman Close before I knew it ... running into the bend like an athletics track ... the tarmac was smooth and shiny and the sun had gotten brighter ... I didn't realise I was still crying but I must have been cos an old man turned off his lawnmower and asked if I was alright ... I ignored him and carried on running ... the numbers on the bungalows blurred by to my left ... 15,13,11 ... at last there was number 7 ... I didn't even go to the door, just ran around to where his window was and prayed he was in ... I knocked three times on the glass ... waited a few seconds ... and then knocked three times again ...

Part Three

"Out of the blue and into the black."

Neil Young

Saturday

Markus

The knock on his window made him jump out of bed. He waited a few seconds and then heard it again. First thing he thought of was Beady and that dickhead Sniff. Maybe they'd rounded-up The Taylor Brothers and were paying him a visit. Markus dropped to his knees and reached out for the rounders bat under his bed. Stood and drew, levelling the wooden club at the window, waiting for a head.

One came.

"Mel what the fuck!"

Fear flashed in her eyes when she saw the weapon aimed at her skull. "Markus!"

He sighed and lowered it with relief.

"What the hell?" she said, panting.

"Thought you were someone else."

"Who?"

"Never mind."

The two stood silent and still for a moment, calming down.

"Why are you out of breath?" he said.

"I ran all the way."

"Fuck off," he said. "You couldn't run a bath."

She'd been crying, puffy-eyed from tears and no sleep. Her complexion was a sickly yellow. He took her under the arm and pulled her through the window. She wore orange and red and her erratic movements made her look like a flame.

"Why'd you knock on my window anyway?"

"Cos, like, I couldn't face anyone else. Like, I didn't want to see Tars or your brother and stuff. Just you."

"What's happened?" Markus sat back down on the bed. Mel stayed stood up.

"Oh Big Bear it's my mum."

By the state of her Markus thought something truly devastating had happened, like she'd died or maybe someone had killed her.

"I can't take her no more."

"Oh?"

Mel failed to pick up the boredom in his voice, or that he was rubbing imaginary sleep out from his eyes.

"She said horrible things about you. About how you're a bad apple and how we are toxic together and how she'll try to put a wedge between us no matter what."

Markus let his head drop and smiled, rolling the rounders bat back and forth under his foot. Mel eventually sat down next to him and took his hand. "At the end she said the worsest thing ever ... she said I'm gonna end up like my dad ... and like, I know how much she hates dad. She *detests* him and thinks he's the biggest loser in the world and stuff."

"Fuck her," Markus said.

Her glasses were steamed up again. Her bad eye winced behind them. "But that's all you ever say Markus, fuck her, fuck them, fuck it."

He shrugged and then kicked the bat back under the bed.

"But what can we do?" she said, pleading.

"What do you mean?"

"We need to *do something* to make it all go away."

Markus looked up at his light bulb and thought for a few seconds. "Go McDonald's," he said.

"What?" Mel had still not caught her breath properly.

"I'm fucking starving."

They walked back in the direction of Mel's house, taking the channel route instead of the urban one. They held hands and strolled alongside the current. As always Markus had to stop every now and then to throw something into the water. Mel talked and her boyfriend listened. The girl seemed to repeat herself over and over again and eventually the boy switched off. Other things that were happening slipped into thoughts and kept Mel away. He thought about Leicester City Football Club and the race for the title. He thought about Claudia. He thought about Beady and The Taylor Gang. He wondered which flavour milkshake to have once they reached the golden arches of MaccyD's.

"Hey do you think Aunt Tars will let me come and live with you at the bungalow?"

Markus looked at her *gone out*. An expression caught in a

crossfire between amusement and screw-face. "No," he said. He said the word *no* like he was swallowing air.

"Why?"

Markus let out a ripple of laughter. "Why would she?"

Embarrassed, Mel let her shoulders bounce into a helpless shrug.

Sometimes, Markus thought, she has no grip on reality at all.

They walked on for another fifteen minutes until the park appeared to their left. They were near Mel's house. "I don't even wanna look in that direction," she said mournfully. "I don't wanna set foot on Lawson Avenue *ever* again."

Markus smiled and took her arm, pulling her into him. She looked even paler and her eyes dulled to a weak shade amber.

"We'll get out of here one day," he said. "We've only got two years and then we can do what we want. We'll move away, get out of this town for good."

"Where?" she said.

"Anywhere. Liverpool, Leicester."

"What about Nottingham? It's not that far and they've got like castles and caves and stuff."

"Wherever you want," he said, pouting.

Mel put her forehead against his chest and warmed it. "But two years is ages away."

A dull creak sounded in Markus's stomach and Mel felt it vibrate against her skull. "What the heck??"

"Told ya Beautifulness," he said. "I'm fucking starving."

She laughed a bit and the smile opened her face. Markus got onto his tiptoes and could just about see the McDonald's sign poking through the tops of the trees.

"Great," he said. "Look who it is?"

As they drew towards the entrance they could see her entertaining a small group huddled in their usual booth. Mia was performing, talking with her hands, doing a silly dance. From here, it looked like she'd dyed her hair again.

"Let's just ignore her," she said. "Pretend she isn't there."

Markus kicked the door open and walked in a straight line, keeping his eyes firmly fixed on the counter ahead of him. Mel lagged behind, fidgeting nervously on the spot. She couldn't help but glance to her right, catching eyes with her bestie.

"Mel Ellis back in the land of the living!" Mia shouted at the top of her voice.

Most of McDonald's heard her and all eyes landed on Mel, who went from pale to pink in the matter of seconds. "Hey," she said sheepishly, putting an arm-barrier across her abdomen, clutching an elbow.

Mia waved her over and Mel motioned to Markus, who had already pushed in front of the queue and was giving his order. It was Saturday afternoon and the fast-food restaurant was jammed. Mia's wave got fiercer, almost competitive. Mel didn't want to talk to her one bit but some of that old control took hold and the girl found herself drifting over, almost as if she was being pulled by an invisible chord. Mia was sat with some emo kids from art.

"Yo bitch where you been at?" she rapped, taking her into her arms. The hug felt awkward and false.

"Just. Just out," she stammered.

"Out where?" Mia countered. There was a certain venom to her tone. Her face looked different.

Mel shrugged. She was aware the other kids were listening in.

"You don't answer my calls. You can barely be arsed to text back more than two words. What the fuck is going on?"

Mel found her challenge claustrophobic. Her chest tightened and a few breaths got trapped there.

"So!?" Mia pushed on, waiting for an answer. She was loud and other people from other tables were beginning to peer over. Mel wished Markus would hurry up and come save her.

"You know what," Mel said at last, her voice small and unsure.

"No. I don't." Mia threw her head to one side and made her eyes big. "Enlighten me"

The emos began to chuckle, sending sly whispers into each other's ear.

"Like, you know why I'm not really talking to you."

"Tell me?!" Mia said with such force Mel felt a spray of spit hit her cheek.

"Cos, like, you went behind my back and stuff."

When Mel saw the emos put their heads down she knew Markus was on his way over.

"Alright Markus," Mia said, like nothing was wrong.

The boy was too focused on his burger to care what was going on. He put the tray on one of the tall tables and hopped up to a spin-stool, rotating a full three-sixty while filling his face.

"Do *you* know why my bestie is blanking me Big Bear?" Mia said.

Hearing her call him *Big Bear* lit Mel up with instant rage. She felt it cut through the centre of her body. Markus shrugged and then said something with his mouth full.

Mia ignored him and began to talk through her teeth. "We just met to talk about your suicide, stupid."

"Don't call me stupid," Mel said.

"Well you need to sort your head out." Mia hit back. "You need to sort your jealousy issues out, and your insecurity issues and your paranoid issues. All I've done is be good to you and this is how you repay me!"

A woman wearing a McDonald's work uniform came over and asked Mia to keep her voice down.

"Look, like, I don't really need this shit now," Mel said. She looked over at Markus who had moved onto his fries, washing it down by a long suck on the straw.

Mel carried on. "Mum has just pretty much disowned me and I don't need you on at me too."

"Boo-hoo," Mia said pulling a clown face. She had returned to her original volume. The woman who had asked her to quieten looked over and shook her head. "Boo-hoo," she repeated. "Poor me. You know that's another issue you need to sort, your victim issues."

Mel wanted to die. There was no arguing with Mia. She was too quick; too loud, too skilful with words. "Something happens and you expect the *whole* world to stop and give you sympathy. You've gotten even worse since you started going out with *him*."

Markus stopped eating and raised his eyes. "What?"

One of the emo kids managed to sneak out and escape.

"You feed off each other and shut the world out," Mia said. "You both need to grow-up and get a grip. This *us-against-the-world bullshit*. It's getting boring."

"You're fucking boring," Markus said, standing up.

"Oh what ... so you gonna hit me now bully-boy?"

Markus glanced around him. "Why don't you just kill yourself Mia?" he said.

Mia moved her body around like a snake. "Why don't you kill *yourself* Markus? Why don't you both kill each other? In fact Mel, why don't you just go and kill your mum *and* your sis. Put them out of their misery so they don't have to put up with you anymore."

Markus noticed a certain, strange expression sweep across Mel's face. It stayed for a few seconds, before she snapped out of it.

"And then that'll put us out of *our* misery," Mia added. "So we don't have to hear you bitch and whine about it twenty-four seven."

Mel felt a tingling sensation in her fingertips. She thrust her face forward into the girl opposite. "Mia, all you are, is an attention-seeking slut!"

Without hesitation Mia grabbed out at a handful of hair and yanked, making Mel topple forward. Instinctively she reached out for the table, rocking it onto its side, making the tray of food slide off and explode on the floor. People leapt back, looked over, gasped. The emos were gone. Markus launched a fist full-pelt towards Mia's face but missed, smashing the straw container into bits. Someone let out a scream and suddenly bodies were everywhere; teens, staff, mums holding kids. Three builders waiting in the queue watched on, laughing their heads off. Markus moved around like a bull, looking for Mia but somehow she had escaped.

"You're gonna have to leave!" the woman in the uniform said, putting a hand on the small of his back.

"Take your hand off me bitch."

Markus couldn't see Mel either. He knocked into people, looking everywhere. Just then he spotted her by the door, staggering about. At first he thought she'd been hit, a knock on the head that had sent her dizzy.

"Mel! Mel you alright?"

He joined her at the door and took her through it. Everybody was pointing and looking at them through the windows. The traffic from the main road sounded really loud.

"Mel, you hit? Someone hit you?"

She was doubled-up and breathing heavy, fast, deep. Her hair was everywhere.

"Mel for fuck's sake will you tell me what's wrong!?"

She had her arm out and her fingers splayed, like she was reaching for something.

"I'm ... I'm ... I'm having a panic ... "

Markus adjusted himself. "Look we better get gone before they ring the police. I nearly took Mia's head off!"

Mel's arm moved faster, up and down like a swan trying to take off. "A panic att ... " Her sentence ran into a breathy brick wall.

He locked her fingers with his. "I can't hear a word you're saying."

"I need ... I need to sit ... "

He guided her over to a table and sat her down. She sounded liked she was dying.

"You want me to get you a drink? Although ... I don't think they'll let me back in ... "

Mel was shaking her head but the breathing was getting faster. She put a hand up to her chest. "Mel are you dying or something?" he said in a calm voice. "I don't know what to do?"

Faces were stuck to the McDonald's window.

"Fuck you all looking at?!" Markus shouted at them.

He turned his attention back to Mel. "You want me to phone an ambulance?"

She didn't say anything so he took out his phone and dialled. Mel could hear his voice swimming in her ears. "Tara you better come quick, I think Mel's dying ... at McDonald's ... no, nothing ... nothing's happened ... we just got into a massive row with Mia and now she's spazzing out ... like she can't breathe ... she can't talk either ... "

Markus went quiet for a minute while his auntie spoke on the other end.

"An anxiety attack what's that?" Markus said. He looked back in the window and the faces were no longer at the glass. People had gone back to their food, like nothing happened. Way in the distance he could see Mia and the emos striding back towards town.

"What do you mean hold her hand and reassure her? Reassure her of what? Look Tars can't you just come? I don't know what I'm doing ... alright ... yeah."

"Tars is coming," he said, brighter in spirit.

She nodded like she could hear him and he put his hand on her head. Her breathing slowed. Eventually she looked at him, her face albino-white.

"Whoa you looked fucked-up."

He wasn't sure if she could hear him or not.

"Is that anything to do with those pills you take?"

She nodded.

"Have you taken them today?"

She nodded again.

"Maybe you should take some more?"

This time she shook her head.

"Hey you should have seen it," Markus said with a full beaming smile. "I nearly took Mia's head off!"

Tara pulled up in her white Fiat Punto. Parked in one of the only available spots and headed towards the seated teens. She wore jeans and a light denim shirt. Her hair was tied back and Markus noticed a few strands of grey he'd never seen before. Auntie pretty much ignored her nephew and put all her attention on Mel, kneeling by her feet.

"Mel," she said softly. "You alright?"

The girl raised her face and looked right at Tara. She couldn't believe how exhausted Mel looked, her eyes swollen from insomnia, lips bloodless and dry. After a few moments she nodded her head.

"You had a panic attack?"

She nodded again, slower.

Tara held her hands in the cup of her own hands, and then gave her a hug. Despite the fatigue Mel's grip was surprisingly strong, desperate, like she had drawn strength from the bodily contact.

"I think she's hungry," Markus said. "She didn't get to eat her meal. Can we nip through the drive-thru on the way out?"

"You want me to take you home?" Tara said.

The girl seemed to be awakened by that question. She shook her head, a certain horror in her eye.

"Just take us back to ours," Markus said.

"You really should tell your mum about this," Tara said in a levelled voice.

Again Mel shook.

"Her mum's a bitch," Markus said. "You should hear all the shit she's been saying about *me*."

Tara wiped back her hair and placed her palm on her forehead. "Okay you can come back to ours for a bit but I'm ringing your mum to tell her where you are."

Mel showed no reaction.

"You hungry?" Tara asked.

She shook her head.

"I am," Markus said.

Tara helped Mel walk back to the car. When they got there a

ticket was stuck to the window. Tara had parked in the disabled spot without realising it.

His bedroom window was still open from when Mel climbed through it several hours ago.

"I'm going to give your mum a little call now, Mel."

Tara's voice got slammed out by the door. "Do what you want," Markus snarled.

Mel stood there in the centre of the room. "Your room's much tidier than mine," she said randomly.

"Tidy room, tidy mind," Markus said.

Mel didn't really know what he meant so she just dropped onto the bed and took out her phone. "Mia's sent me like an hour-long text."

"What's it say?" Markus said taking off his t-shirt, replacing it with another.

"Can't be bothered to read it."

"Block the bitch."

"I will," Mel said, staring into space. "Kind of sad though, right?"

"What?"

"Losing a bestie."

"Thought I was your bestie?" Markus said half-joking, pulling the t-shirt over his belly.

"You know what I mean."

Markus was now changing his track bottoms too; pants, socks.

"She's been my bestie for like four years, now it's *all* gone, gone for good."

Markus was messing about with his room, moving things around. "Hey you should have seen it. I nearly took her fucking head off! An inch to the left and the bitch would have been sparked clean-out."

Mel was laying on the bed, staring at the ceiling. "Hey how come you haven't got a bestie?"

Markus was lining-up two Liverpool mugs next to his TV. "I did, once," he said.

"When?"

"In primary school."

"What was his name?" Mel was still staring at the ceiling. Markus thought her face looked weird at this angle.

"Erm ... " Markus put his head back and looked at the lightbulb.

" ... can't remember. He was a posh prick who was spoilt to death."

"Ha. You sound like you didn't like him."

"I didn't. Hated the little bastard."

Mel laughed but was confused. "How can he be your bestie if you hated him?"

Markus jumped on the bed next to her and it bounced. "Cos he was rich and he had loads of toys to play with. Plus his mum fancied me. She was fat."

Mel blinked and screwed up her face. "What? How old were you?"

"About eleven."

"That's, like, sick."

"Women have always fancied me," Markus said, matter of fact. "Even my new teacher at my new school fancies me."

Mel's face reddened and her mouth made a funny shape. Markus could see the discomfort of jealously in her expression. "Does she now?" she said, pretending to not be bothered. "And like, how old is she?"

"Bout thirty."

Mel shook her head, her hands cupped on her tummy like she was pregnant.

"See. You should think yourself lucky," Markus said in her ear. "All these women but *I* chose *you*."

His mouth tickled her ear and she squirmed and giggled and they began to play-fight a bit. They ended up under the covers and Mel thought he might try to have sex but he didn't. She was kind of relieved by that. In the last month or so Mel had gone-off sex completely. She wondered if it was anything to do with the meds she was on. *Reduced libido*: she wasn't sure if that was on the list of possible side-effects.

They watched one of the Spiderman films, one of the recent ones. Markus found these films dumb. The special FX were too blurry and made his eyes hurt. He thought it was stupid because all the way through Spiderman was caught in situations where he was a second away from dying, but never did. A car would be falling on him but he'd move out of the way. A train was about to hit the girl but Spiderman would catch her with his web and save her by an inch. Mel lay next to him, gripping his arm in anticipation. The scenes went on for about twenty minutes and Markus found it pointless and predictable. After they watched some American reality show and Markus preferred that because you got to watch real fights. When one of the girls started going schiz Markus thought back to the scene earlier at McDonald's.

He rolled onto his side and looked at his girlfriend. "What the fuck was that all about anyway?"

Mel kept facing the telly. "Haven't you been watching it? Like, the blonde-haired girl was talking about her behind her back."

Markus put his eyes back on the TV. "Not the telly stupid, earlier, at Maccy's."

"Oh." Mel got doubly embarrassed. "I don't know."

"I thought you was gonna die," Markus said.

"Would you have missed me?"

"Course," he said, stroking her arm with a single finger.

She sat up and hugged a pillow. They were silent for a bit.

"You had one of them before?" Markus asked.

She nodded, still staring at the TV.

"How many?"

She shrugged.

Markus picked his nose and flicked it. "So that's what your meds are for?"

"Shit," Mel said.

"What?"

"I should be taking one about now."

"Take one then."

"I left them at home this morning. Ran out the house so fast I forgot."

Markus sat up next to her, concerned. "You're not gonna have one of those spaz things again are you?" He was looking around at his room.

Mel smiled, laughed. "No, it's not like that silly. You need triggers"

"What do you mean?"

"You need, like, a stressful event and stuff. Like earlier."

"Oh." Markus sighed and seemed fine again. He looked back at the telly. "Look at the size of her tits!"

Mel gazed at the Italian girl wearing a bikini and then pulled the duvet up around her. Just then a gentle wrap came on the door. Markus sighed and shook his head and then stared at the door. "What?"

"Mel I've rang your mum and she's quite worried."

"Bet she is." Mel muttered under her breath.

"I told her you're okay but she wants you back by ten, alright?"

Mel nodded her head, but then realised Tara couldn't see her. "Oh. Okay."

The foot-shadows disappeared from the beam of light under the door.

Mel dropped her head into her hands. "I *really* don't wanna go back," she said.

They had both taken off their bottoms and his skin felt warm under the duvet.

"Don't then," he said.

"But you heard Tara," Mel said. "I've *got* to."

"Fuck her."

Markus was pulling that face, like he was up to something but Mel didn't get it. She didn't get how you could just *fuck her.*

At nine-twenty that same knock came to the door. "It's twenty-past Mel. I've decided I'm gonna give you a lift, so you don't have to walk. About ten minutes, yeah?"

"Yeah," she said, dread dulling her voice. "Fanks."

Markus got out of bed and put his joggers back on. Walked over to his door and then turned and smiled at Mel, winked.

While he was gone Mel thought maybe was using some of his persuasive powers on his aunt, making her let Mel stay over for the night. Only five minutes later Markus came waddling back into the room with his arms full of food.

"Markus what the eff ... !"

He dropped it all on the bed and the floor and then went back out, returning ten seconds later with two big bottles of pop, Sprite and Coca-Cola. Mel was sat up, dazed, leaning back on her elbows. "Markus?"

"I'm getting supplies."

"Supplies, what?"

He started grabbing things; books, his dumbbells, washing basket, a small chest of drawers.

"What are you doing?"

"Barricading."

"What?" Mel let out an incredulous chuckle.

He looked at her. "You don't wanna go home so you're *not* going home."

503

He started dragging the draws across the carpet. "Help me then."

She got up to help but made little difference, both of them couldn't stop laughing. Once the door were sealed Mel looked down at the pop. "What about water?"

"We got that," he said, nodding at the fizzy drinks.

Mel folded her arms. "I need water in the night. I can't drink too much of that stuff. Gives me headache."

Markus sighed, made a wedge in the door and slipped on through. Returned a minute later with two-litres of tap water.

Mel had her hand to her mouth, smiling behind it. "Toilet?"

"What?"

"What if I need the toilet?"

Markus looked around the room, nodded at one of his Liverpool mugs.

"Ugh. No way."

Markus still smiling.

"What if I need a pooh?" she said.

"It's a big mug."

"Gross." She slapped his arm and they laughed more.

"Ready Mel?" It was Aunt Tara. Her voice was louder this time. They could hear a set of car-keys jangling on the other side of the door.

"Yeah," Mel shouted robotically.

A soft panic in her face as she jumped up and down on the spot, not knowing what to do. Markus could see she was really excited. They held hands.

"Mel?" she said again, tinge of irritation in her tone.

"Coming."

She pulled a face at her boyfriend, *what shall I do*. He leaned in and kissed her.

"Mel!"

Mel put her hands over her mouth and fell on the bed, leaving it for Markus to deal with.

"She int coming Tars," he said.

"What?"

"She's staying here."

The couple watched the handle twist and the door move a centimetre against the solid mountain of junk. Again they tried not to laugh.

"Markus open this door!"

Nothing.

She tried again. "Oh you're taking the fucking piss."

"Just leave us," Markus said.

"You two are *unbelievable*."

"Just leave us. We're not doing anything wrong."

"And you Mel," Tara said, steadying herself. "Have I not been good to you today?"

She waited for an answer off the girl. Nothing.

"And this is the thanks I get?" There was genuine hurt in her voice.

Mel's expression changed into a serious one. She bit her lip, sat up. Looked at Markus earnestly. *Maybe we should open up. Maybe I should just go home. Maybe we should do as we're told.* "Really Mel I'm surprised by you. Didn't think you were this selfish."

Markus motioned at her to not listen but Mel couldn't help it. Tara said more things and the girl had to put a pillow over each ear.

In the end she got mad. "So you've barricaded yourself in, right? This is how you want to play it, right?"

"Right!" Markus sang.

"So suppose I go call your dad and uncle, and they come over and *force* this door open, because you know very well they can."

"They can but they won't," Markus said cockily, having it under control. "It's Saturday night Tars. They'll be pissed out their heads. But go ahead, call-em"

He knew that trumped her.

There was a few moments of thinking silence. "So suppose I better call the police instead?"

"Oh fuck the police," Markus said. "Call them an' all. Ring three nines. Sure they'd love to be spending a Saturday night on a pair of naughty teenagers, what with all the *real* emergencies out there."

He'd done her again.

Now the silence on the other side was one of frustration.

"Mel I'm really disappointed in you. I thought *you* at least were better than that."

"She doesn't care," Markus said, answering for her.

Tara was breathing heavy. "Right I'll ring your mum and tell her. Yet *more* worry you'll give her."

When Tara was gone Markus put up his hand for a high-five but he could see some bother on her face. "Oh fuck her, Mel. Fuck your mum too. Fuck *all* adults. They don't care. They just like control."

505

He was already opening a big bag of Kettle chips, shovelling them into his mouth.

Tara was back fifteen minutes later.

"And thanks for taking all the food Markus. Me and Ryan pay for it while you eat. Nice. Your mum would be proud."

Markus stopped eating; fire came to his eyes. "You fucking keep her out of it you dirty c+nt slag."

Mel was shocked by the acceleration of his temper, and the words he used. She sat back on the bed and hugged her knees.

Tara was gone but Markus yelled on. "Stupid dumb bitch. Just cos you can't have kids of your own, you pathetic miserable slag."

He threw the crisps on the carpet and then launched one of his Liverpool mugs at the wall. Mel put her head down and took cover while an explosion of red shards rained down on top of her.

"Big Bear, *what the fuck*."

He was pale and shaking. Mel wanted to comfort him but she didn't dare to. Instead she watched him crouch in the corner of the room, listening to the depths of his breathing.

After a few minutes the breaths began to slow and get shallow. When he was calm Markus got up and climbed out of the room again. *Now what is he doing?* Moments later a massive boom rattled the bungalow like an earthquake. Mel gasped, holding down a breath. She felt her own eyes widen with terror.

Markus climbed back into the room with a smile on his face. He looked a hundred times happier. In his arm was Ryan's laptop. He pulled the lead through the mess of the barricade, the black plug bouncing over it like a black mouse.

Tara was up at the door. "You little bastard," she cried.

Mel didn't like being here anymore, maybe back home was safer after all.

"He shouldn't have put a lock on it anyway," Markus shouted.

Tara had lost it, lost it completely. Mel had not heard her like this before.

"That's *his* room. *His* laptop. You've got no fucking right!"

The smile on Markus's face wouldn't stop.

"That's it I'm done with you," Tara screamed, her voice cracking at the end. "Done with you. You're no nephew of mine. No family of mine."

Mel looked at him, thinking how those words must hurt because she knew they would just *destroy* her, rip her heart in two. Only

Markus showed no reaction at all. His concentration fully on the setting up of the laptop.

"First thing tomorrow you little shit. Dad and Uncle will be round here and that door *will* be opened and you *will* be gone."

Markus already had YouTube on, drowning her out by some rock song played at full-blast.

Eventually Mel joined his side and they watched the normal stuff Markus liked; street fights, BMX accidents, documentaries on school massacres. When Markus watched this stuff he got transfixed, his blink-less eyes glued to the screen. It was almost as if Mel wasn't there.

She had to nudge his bare knee with her own. "I need a wee," she said. "And like, I'm really not pissing in your Liverpool mug."

It was meant to be funny but Markus didn't laugh, or even smile.

"Go outside," he said.

"What if your auntie grabs me?"

"What?"

"What if she like hears me and stuff and then runs out and grabs me."

"I'll punch her in the face."

"You'd punch your own auntie in the face?"

Mel had one foot out of the window.

"She won't anyway. She's probably asleep by now."

Markus could hear the mini-flood of his girlfriend urinating in the gravel.

"Hey there's a full-moon out," she said childishly, pulling her knickers back up. "Oh no, wait … it's not quite full. I think it's only like three-quarters or something."

Markus wasn't listening. He was too busy playing a maths game. When Mel climbed back in she watched him and was shocked at how good he was. When she had a go she couldn't even get past level two whereas Markus got all the way up to eighteen.

"Don't you know," he said. "There's only about ten kids in the country who can beat me at this."

Mel gazed at the numbers, not having a clue what any of it meant. Their faces lit up from the screen, hovering in the darkness of the room.

"Like, why aren't you like this at school?" she said. "You'd be in the top-set, easy."

Markus let out a small breathy laugh and shook his head,

clicking another right answer on the puzzle, moving onto the next level.

It got really late but both teens were wide awake. Markus slammed the laptop shut and lay back. "I'm bored. What shall we do now?"

"Why don't we just lay here?" Mel said.

She had taken off her glasses and was looking up at his fuzzy face, blinking in the black.

"Let's go out," he said, sitting up.

"What? Why? Everywhere is shut. There's nothing to do."

Markus looked over at the grey rectangle of the window. A wave rippled through the curtain and the tree beyond made a flapping sound as if it had a flag stuck in it. Way in the distance he could hear the water of the Clementine Channel.

"Dunno," he said. "I just like walking around in the dark."

Sunday

Mel

Sex woke me up. There was something heavy on top of me, and like, there was all this phenomenal pressure, like being buried under a breezeblock. I couldn't move. Then there was this dead-weird feeling happening Downstairs. My flower chafed and irritated, like some revolting animal was pecking at it. All over was a scary burning feeling that wouldn't go away, pressing, probing, piercing. Like being stabbed by a hot poker or something. I didn't have my glasses on and I was half-asleep so I couldn't see properly. But then as I woke up I got petrified cos there was a man's face Here, right in front of me, over me, a bright blurry oval of shocking white, like a mask, smiling, a horrible cunning smile all large and wolf-like and that's when I was crippled with like, The Biggest Fear Ever. At First I thought it was a bad dream, like a nightmare kind of a thing. It wasn't until I heard His voice that I realised it was Markus.

Morning Beautifulness.

What are you doing? I said.

Waking you with a surprise.

I tried to stop him by putting my hand on his chest, only he carried on.

Markus No.

It flippin killed cos like, I wasn't prepared or turned-on, and it was all dry and stuff.

I couldn't believe he couldn't see the pain in my face.

Ouw, I said, fighting him off.

What? He said, still smiling.

It hurts.

He stayed there and didn't move. Keeping It there, keeping It inside. After a while the pain got easier so I let him carry on but tbh I didn't really enjoy it and it didn't really feel like sex at all. It felt like Something Else.

During The Whole Sex Thing I didn't even know where I was. I didn't even know if I was at Mine or His or Somewhere Else. I had completely forgotten about all the drama of yesterday, of Last Night, everything that had happened with Mia and Tara and The Barricade and stuff.

When he rolled off his Stuff dribbled out and I remembered my pill.

Shit my tablets!

Thought you said you only needed them when you're stressed.

Not my head-meds but my baby ones.

What?

My pill, The Pill.

Oh.

I need to go get them.

Thought you weren't going back home ever? He said.

Need to, one last time.

We better go anyway. That bitch has been banging on my door all morning. Reckons Dad and Unc are on their way to kick this barricade in.

But where we gonna go?

I was yawning and still waking up, taking the room in.

Yours, we just said that.

No but I mean, like, Eventually?

We'll run away.

He said it with wide eyes like it was a new and bright idea.

But we tried that before, I said. And it didn't work, remember?

We'll do it proper this time.

Nah. No. No way. I put my foot down. I ABSOLUTELY HATED it. I can't be homeless again. It was horrible.

Markus was looking up at his lightbulb, thinking. We'll join some gypsies. He said, at last.

What?

We'll join a gypsy site and live in a caravan.

I couldn't tell if he was being serious or not.

I'm being serious, he said, coming alive with the idea. It's easy, we'll just go to a fairground and meet them. I'll persuade them to let us in. We'll work for them and travel the world.

Okay but I need my pills.

Alright.

I need my stuff.

We'll go to yours one last time and then we'll leave Kimble Wells for good.

Kay.

We started getting ready, putting our clothes on. Broken bits from that mug lay scattered all around his bedroom floor. Can you, like, tidy that up? I said. Cos if I cut my foot and see blood then I'll probably faint. Then we won't be going anywhere.

What?

My phobia of blood, remember?

Markus looked at the bits and then confusion appeared on his face. How the fuck that happen?

Really? I was looking at him.

What?

You don't remember? I said, hands on hips.

He didn't say anything and looked genuinely puzzled.

You, I said. You did it. You lost your temper and launched it at the wall.

He thought for a few seconds. Oh yeah, he said.

By the time Tara started knocking on his door again we were already climbing out the window. I stepped over the darkened patch of pee from last night, which was drying under the spring sun. As we walked out of his driveway I felt Aunty Tara's eyes on me, looking at us from the living room. I did feel a bit bad for the way we treated her. She was right, she had been good to me and all I had done was throw it back in her face. I liked Aunty Tars, she was a good parent. She wasn't like my mum. She was a good person with a good heart.

Wish I had a pound for every time I've walked this Clementine Channel. I know it like the back of my hand by now. Since me and Big Bear have been going out (it'll be a year next month.) I've probably walked it a hundred times. Maybe even a thousand. I've almost had a Full Year of it, all four seasons. In the winter the grass gets long and wet and by the time I get to His house my feet are always like dead-soaked through and stuff. And in the summer the sun reflects off the water and makes the world look extra dead-pretty, and like, there are loads of flowers lining the banks too, as well as ducks and swans and boats rippling through the water. There are also these turquoise dragonflies which I have LITERALLY not seen Anywhere Else in The World. All in all there are four bridges between his house and mine. The First One is a big wide iron bridge right near His house. We've only walked across it a few times and it makes a dead-loud sound, like hollow echoy footsteps. I think there could be a troll living under there! Lol. Further on down there are two more bridges close together. One is a normal footbridge, and the other is a disused rail line which runs diagonally, guarded by a big spiky gate so You can't get to it. Only You can get to it cos I watched Markus climb over it once and it about Scared Me to Death. He only did it cos I said he couldn't, so Markus being Markus HAD to make it A Mission and prove me wrong. Markus is a dead-good climber. I've seen him climb fences and gates and some of the tallest trees in town. It's amazing to watch him climb up to my bedroom window. He can do it in about 5 seconds flat! Then about another hundred metres down the Channel is a spot I would define as The Very Heart of Our Special Place. It's a daisy patch with two small bridges running into people's gardens. We always stop Here, like a tradition kind of a thing. We stop Here because it's almost exactly halfway between his house and mine. We once had sex Here although it was at night and in the dark so nobody could see us. (Hopefully lol.) The next bridge we call the Falcon Bridge cos it takes You back into town, and leads right to the Falcon Pub. (Another meeting place of ours.) This bridge is for cars and sometimes if it's Rush-Hour You have to wait like ten minutes before You can cross. Markus always gets dead-impatient and just dives in front of the traffic like he has a Death Wish or something. Further up Clementine You come to a small forest of Dock Leaves and seeing them always gets me sentimental, cos like, it reminds me of when I got stung and Big Bear picked one and put it on the wound and the pain just went away, like a magic-healing kind of a thing. Next comes The Park. Whenever I see The Park I always get filled with dread and anxiety cos I know I'm nearly 'Home.' A new skateboard ramp has just been built and it's made The Park like dead-busy and popular and stuff. Although they thought about taking it out cos some kid fell off his Stunt Bike and hit his head and nearly died. Loads of people had to sign a massive petition to keep it open only now they have signs everywhere telling kids to Wear Helmets. When me and Markus walk by The Skate Bowl today I get a bit sad cos Mia's graffiti is still there. She wrote in bright pink bubble writing so everyone can see.

M AND M BESTIES 4EVER.

There is a massive Love Heart in between the two M's, which, like, link us together.

She only wrote Our First Letters so no one else would know, like a secret code kind of a thing. I stare at the word 4EVER and realise it's not True, cos forever isn't always forever, is it? Not now, not anymore.

I'm telling You all this information, cos like, The Clementine Channel is Officially THE ONLY thing I'm going to miss about this town, the only thing I'm going to miss about Kimble Wells, when I leave, when I am gone For Good ...

Tbh I thought mum was gonna go flippin mental and try and stop me. So I was surprised to see her dead-calm and unfazed and that. But really all she was doing is switching tactics like she always does: implementing The Silent Treatment.

I'm going, I'm leaving, I said.

Okay love your things are by the door.

I was sort of shocked to see All My World, like all my belongings and stuff thrown into black bin-bags and left outside my bedroom. Looking at them took my breath away cos I didn't think she'd ACTUALLY go This Far.

I felt numb. I felt like a blank portrait, less than zero.

A slow headache was coming, I could feel it. It was there in and around my eye-sockets. A groggy thickness was starting to form across my skull.

Fine, I shouted.

I went through the black bags. Half the stuff I didn't need anyway so I just pulled it out and chucked it on my bedroom floor, leaving most of it across Adele's Bed.

I need my pills. I shouted.

Markus was waiting outside. I could see him pulling stuff off a tree.

I need my pills, I said again, coming down the stairs, into the kitchen. I need my pills.

I thought she'd refuse and Kick Off but she didn't and this made me shocked too.

Okay.

She reached up to the Medicine Cupboard and handed them to me in a Morrisons Shopping Bag.

Where's Del? I said.

Out. She said. Want me to tell her goodbye?

No!

I slammed the door in her face and then opened the gate.

I'm never coming back. I shouted. Never!

Markus heard me and raised his eyes in that puppy-dog way of his. When he smiled that big Markus smile I realised I was doing The Right Thing.

513

I gotta go back, he said as we walked out of my cul-de-sac.

What?

We left too quick. I need a few more bits.

I didn't like this and got A Really Bad Feeling like straight away, like never had my Instinct Nature-Feeling screamed so loud.

But won't your Dad and Uncle and That be there Now?

Probs, Markus shrugged.

I wanted to tell Him about My Nature Feeling but Markus always thought it was stupid. In fact he said he never wanted me to mention It again cos It gets on his nerves. We walked down Kings Road and my headache started like I knew it would. A dull throb pulsating in the tops of my eyes. I took off my glasses and rubbed them but it still flippin killed.

Have you got any paracetamol? I asked him.

Markus grinned and patted himself down. Not on me, he said. Letting me know it was a Stupid Question.

Oh.

Just take your Head Meds, He said.

It's not the same thing, I said.

My Nature-Feeling grew as we passed The Falcon Pub and turned back onto the Channel.

You shouldn't have broken your Brother's lock, I said from nowhere.

Markus was striding ahead and he turned and looked at me but just said nothing. Now the headache was in the top of my head too. Like there was a spike drilling down on top of me. We didn't stop at our traditional Special Place either and I didn't like that. It was like Markus was on another one of His Missions and wouldn't be satisfied until he had accomplished it.

We get my bag and we're gone. He said. No messing. No talking. No distractions.

In the alleyway at the bottom of his close my Nature-Feeling was going nuts and I was dead-tempted to say something but Markus was already out the other end. Two new cars were parked outside the bungalow, gleaming in the early April sun. Markus went quiet and put his head down like he was ready to fight. I'd seen him do this before at school.

We saw his Dad first, then Uncle, then another big man step out the bungalow and head towards us. Cousin Charlie was there too, somewhere at the back. Aunt Tars watched on from the window. The outline of her looked small.

514

I stopped still and got scared.

His Dad looked dead-violent and stuff. Right boy, time to learn the hard way. He said.

Big Bear tried to punch him but his Dad rugby-tackled him to the floor. He was going flippin insane and screaming and making all these, like, disturbing noises and stuff. He fought his very hardest but there was little he could do against three grown-men. It was strange to see him be overpowered and manhandled like this cos I had never seen it before. My mouth went dry and my hands were shaking and my head was just like totally on fire by now, like a migraine kind of a thing.

Get his phone. His Uncle said. Take that phone off him so he can't call Her.

Cousin Charlie stared right at me when he said that, looking at me like it was All My Fault. Looking at me like Dirt, like I was The Worst Scum in the World.

Markus was still screaming and now the neighbours were looking out from pretty-much every window on the close. The three men carried him inside like he was a mental patient, or like on the police shows on TV. Uncle had gave Cousin Charlie the phone and he was still staring at me like I was crap.

What! I screamed at him. What the fuck are you looking at?!

Just then another figure came that I hadn't noticed before. Mel, he said. Mel wait!

Ryan was jogging across the front lawn, his hair bouncing from one side to the other.

I was crying and mad and sad and scared, all rolled into one.

Mel c'mon, he said.

What?

This has got to stop, he said.

WHAT has got to stop?

I noticed loads of feathery dry skin on his face.

Let me give you a lift home.

He put a hand on my shoulder and that surprised me.

I'm fine. I said.

C'mon.

He already had a set of keys spinning on his finger, with the other hand he guided me towards the car. I could still hear screaming and chaos and crazy voices in the house.

Are they hurting him? I said, staring at the bungalow.

No. Ryan said. They're not hurting him.

He had the door open and guided me in. Slammed it shut and then jogged around to the other side. I thought about running back to the bungalow but my Nature-Feeling told me not to.

Ryan got in next to me and started the engine.

Hey I didn't know you could drive? I said.

He looked at me and his eyes did this kind of smiley thing. You're a strange girl Mel. He said.

I didn't know what he meant or why he said that.

Have you got any paracetamol on you? I said. Like any headache tablets?

I watched his arm spin the steering wheel as he turned out of Norman.

No. He said.

The short drive home was pretty much silent. There was an aftershave smell coming from him that I had never smelled before. It wasn't like boy aftershave yet it wasn't like girl's either. It was somewhere in between and I wondered if this was the kind of thing that only Gay People wore. Back on Lawson and that awful, awful dread came back again. My runaway attempt from home had lasted no more than an hour this time.

You both need to let this go, Ryan said, pulling up.

The engine was still running.

Let What go?

Stop playing dumb Mel, you know what I'm talking about.

I sat and said nothing.

Each other, he said. You need to let each other go before something truly bad happens.

We both stared ahead for a moment or two, watching my neighbour across the road put something into the recycling bin.

Fucker broke my lock. He whispered under his breath. Broke my door.

I looked at him.

Fucker breaks everything. And he'll break you too if you don't walk.

I pushed my glasses back and looked at him again. I'm already broken, I said.

Tara must have phoned mum cos she suddenly stepped out of the house and began waiting for me. I opened the car but Ryan's voice caught me One Last Time.

516

Mel, I like you. He said. I actually do. So don't take this personally … but … don't come to our house Ever again. Don't knock on the door. Don't even step foot on the close. It's over. Done.

My headache was now a face-ache, a body-ache, a heart-ache.

mum was still waiting, and I just hoped she had some paracetamol somewhere, to take it all away.

Monday

Markus

Melanie Ellis, quite literally, leapt from the couch when she heard the knock at her front door. Landing on the carpet she realised how sore her feet were. She'd been searching for him all morning, covering her town three or four times over. McDonald's. Channel. Falcon. All over Kings Road and the park at the top of it. She waited by the skateboard bowl. She'd even searched around the premises of The Kitts Academy, despite it being a bank holiday Monday. She was out of her mind with worry, scenarios pulling at her brain in a dozen different directions. *What if he's decided to end it with me? What if I'm not worth all this trouble? What if he really HAS fallen in love with someone else at that new school? What if his dad and uncle have beaten him up? What if the police arrested him for trying to punch Mia in the face? What if he's decided to keep to the Suicide Pact? He could be like, dead and stuff?*

She remembered they'd taken his phone off him so there was no way of contact.

Even though she was now *officially* banned from the bungalow she was tempted to go there anyway, just to see if he was alright, just to see if he was *alive.*

The leap from the couch sounded with such a crash Erica poked her head through the kitchen. "Mel what the Hell?!"

She was already at the door, hands crazy with the jangle of the keys. Babe barking in the background.

"If that's him there's trouble!" her mum said, standing in the kitchen doorway holding a wooden spoon. "That boy ... is not coming in this house."

Mel opened up and the boy appeared before her, a halo of sun against his back. She was in his arms before he could speak, squeezing him so hard she could feel his ribcage. Markus caught eyes with her mum, who stood steadfast by the kitchen door, slapping the wooden spoon into the palm of her hand.

"What you gonna do with that?" he said cockily. "Stir me to death."

Her face went white. "You're not coming in here," she said.

"I'll go out then," Mel responded, kicking on a trainer.

"Like hell you are, you're grounded."

"Grounded? What am I, like ten?"

Mel had the other trainer on. Erica knew it was a no-contest.

"Round the back then!"

"What?"

"You can sit round the back."

Markus stepped inside.

"Not through the house," Erica said, staring at his foot. "I'll unlock the gate."

"God mum this is pathetic," Mel said.

The couple turned into the sun and walked around to the back. They could hear metal against wood as she struggled with the lock.

"Want me to kick it in?" Markus said over the fence.

Mel slapped his chest and lowered her voice to a whisper. "Stop winding her up."

At last the bolt clicked and the gate fell open and the couple saw the back-end of Erica Ellis disappear into the house.

"Fuck your yard is a state," he said, looking around.

There were boxes and boards and balls and other random objects scattered around the rectangular garden. Mel led Markus to a rusty bench at the back of it. Babe stood solid at the backdoor with his tongue flopping out.

"Keep that fucking dog away from me."

"You talking about Babe, or my mum?"

They laughed, and then sat silent for a few moments. The sky dimmed suddenly; the sun being taken over by a slab of grey cloud. The weather of the last few days had gone. It was like the springtime was going in reverse, creeping back to the dark edges of March.

"What happened yesterday?" Mel began, combing hair behind her ear.

Markus was looking down at his hands. "You saw what happened yesterday."

"No, but I mean, like, after I left?"

He took his eyes from his hands and put them on the house. Her mum was moving about in the kitchen window. "We don't need to go into it really."

A breeze sang through some wind chimes next-door

Mel touched his hand. "I looked everywhere for you today."

Markus did a long spit through his teeth. "Well, you found me."

"No, you found me."

"It's all the same thing really," he said, smiling again.

They looked at each other for a long time.

"Want a drink?" she said.

Markus wiped his mouth and nodded.

"Got that J2O stuff, want that?"

"Whatever."

While she was gone her mother eye-balled him through the window. Markus held the stare but was surprised to see that the forty-nine-year-old wasn't backing down. A minute later his girlfriend returned with two orange bottles of juice.

"Wish I could kill your mum," he said as she placed the beverage into his hand, eyes still fixed on the kitchen window.

"Yeah," Mel smiled. "Tell me about it."

"You think I'm joking?" he said, raising the bottle to his lips.

"I know."

"I'm actually not."

"What?"

"I'm *actually* not joking."

Mel had nothing in her expression except blankness.

He took a second gulp, clearing half the bottle in one swallow. "And I know you've thought about it too cos I saw your face the other day."

Mel hadn't touched her drink yet. "When?" she said.

"At McDonald's."

Confusion was still tying up her face.

"Saturday," Markus reminded her. "Mia said something like *why don't you just kill your mum and your sister* and I saw this look on your face ... the same look you're pulling now."

Mel touched her chin for some reason. Markus was staring at her intensely, as if he was searching for something.

"Well, yeah," she said. "Like, life would be easier without her and stuff."

"Let's do it then. Let's end her."

Everything about Mel went slow; her thoughts, her movements, the smile which was starting to appear on her face. "What like *actually* kill her? Like, kill her-kill her? Kill her so she's dead?"

"Yes Mel," Markus said, putting the empty bottle on the floor. "That's what normally happens when you kill someone. They die. And they stay dead."

A giggle popped out of her mouth and she dropped her head onto his arm.

"What do you reckon then?" he pushed on.

"Well … yeah, like, we could. I mean, I suppose it kind of makes sense, and stuff."

"Cool," Markus said, nodding.

Erica was back in the window, washing pots. Both teens were watching her, not saying a word.

The plan was for him to get to hers at midnight, where he would climb up onto the outhouse and tap three times on her bedroom window. Like *Dawson's Creek,* Like *Romeo and Juliet.* Hearing those taps she would tiptoe through to the bathroom and let him in.

Then, *it* would happen.

Markus was sat with his auntie, waiting for her to go to bed. She normally turned in around eleven only tonight she stayed up. There was some politics show on and despite her eyes going and her head nodding, Tara seemed determined to see this show through till it's very end. Credits began to roll at eleven-thirty and Tara gathered her dressing gown and stood.

"You want this leaving on?" she said, pointing the remote at the screen.

Markus nodded.

"You ain't got school tomorrow, no?"

"Wednesday."

"Alright."

Once she was gone Markus began to move into his *mission.* In the kitchen he took three of the four black-handled knives from the wooden block on the worktop, leaving the long useless breadknife where it was. In his room he placed the blades in the centre of a black t-shirt which was laying on the bed. He stood over them, looking at the shape and light of each instrument. None of them looked right so he went back into the kitchen, pulling open one of the drawers. He moved things around as quietly as he could until he found what he was looking for. A grey and white handle with a long vicious-looking blade. He remembered cutting himself on this once in the days he used to do that martial arts training with his aunt's ex-boyfriend. He dipped his hand into the drawer and took it out, raising it ceremoniously over his head, studying it from all angles. *This is the one.* Markus walked it through to his bedroom and placed it with the rest of the family of blades, before wrapping them tightly in the t-shirt, putting the bundle in his school bag, zipping it up. Also in the bag he had a change of clothes; black socks, black underwear, another pair of black jogging bottoms.

It was already midnight. Markus was late.

He dropped out of his bedroom window and closed it, leaving a fingertip-gap so he could prise it back open. The close was empty, silent, apart from this electric wind that was starting to blow the world around.

He was off, gone, up onto the high-waters of the Clementine Channel. The wind howled and rattled and got stronger, speeding up the current as the dark waters blazed and winked with phosphorescence, rolling over rocks, swishing against the banks. An awesome whoosh from the trees thrashed above him. Markus saw the word, *force.*

There was nothing in his head, no thoughts, no real feelings, just the odd snapshot of what he was about to do. He kept facing forwards for the rest of the way, hands loose on the straps of his schoolbag, walking at a brisk, bouncy pace. Eyes growing accustomed to the dark, until the trail winding under his feet turned clear and white, leading him all the way to *her house.*

He let his legs carry him down the bank and into the park, before taking the alleyway which ran along the back of the Ellis home. Scaled the fence and then dropped silently onto the balls of his feet. All the lights were off, in the neighbours too. Although the wind was still up and those chimes were clashing like crazy. Markus didn't want this to put any attention on him so he waited. He sat on the rusty bench at the back of the yard, that empty J2O bottle was still there, by his feet. He looked into the kitchen window where her mum stood some ten hours ago. In the opaque sheen of the glass he saw parts of his own reflection; an eye, the white of his forehead, his good-head-of-hair.

He closed his eyes and felt the weight of the wind drop. The chimes only an occasional tinkle now. When his eyes were open he put them on the place he was heading, the bathroom window. He stared at the grey-dark square for so long he began to feel a magnetic pull from it. He was up on his feet, moving across the yard, cutting it in half. Onto the outhouse roof, one knee at a time, left foot, then right. Exploiting the night he kept close to the shadows, tucking into them like he was just another part of the black. Once at the window he looked through it, put an ear to the cold glass and listened.

All was silent.

Until he reached over to Mel's window and ended that silence by three soft taps.

Tuesday

Mel

C'mon girls it's about that time!

mum's voice is like, The Worst Human Alarm Clock in the World
... Officially. Adele was always up on her feet like she was in the army
or something. Having showered the night before she was pretty much
ready for school in like 10seconds flat!

I took ages and always have, dreams trying to pull me back under.
And why is it that The Bed always FEELS like extra comfortable and
blissful in the mornings??

C'mon Mel it's that time!

I heard you the first time, I shouted, smothering my head with the
pillow. I sleepwalked to the shower and stood under it for about a
minute before drying off and getting dressed and stuff.

mum was combing Adele's hair at the breakfast table while she
munched on the last mouthfuls of cereal.

I wanted to tell them BOTH how flippin Unhygienic that was but
overall I couldn't be bothered.

Your hair gets more beautiful every day, mum said, wonder in her
eyes.

I'm going to cut it off and donate it to charity.

Don't you dare!

mum looked at me, her eyes drifting over the top of Del's head.

*Any reason all that stuff from the bathroom windowsill was
moved last night Mel?*

I was slurping on the cereal although I wasn't that hungry. Never
am first thing.

What? I said.

mum's eyes were dark with suspicion. *The mirror and my basket
was moved from the windowsill. Any reason for that?*

I shook my head and filled my mouth with another spoon. *Ask Del,*
I said.

I have. Now I'm asking you.

When mum stopped brushing her hair my sister got up and went to the fridge. She snapped a four-pack of those Petit Filous yoghurts in half and then put two in front of me.

Adele, mum said, do you have to have two each? Why can't you make them last?

God mum, Adele replied, have you seen the size of these things? She held the pink pots up in her hand. They're gone in two spoons.

Adele smiled at me and then winked.

If that was Me mum would have made me put one back.

Aren't you gonna thank your sis for fetching you a yoghurt? mum said.

I'm not really hungry but yeah, fanks.

Adele was nodding her head, her eyes cross-eyed as she stared at the spoon, licking the yoghurt off its side.

Anyway I don't know what you're talking about regarding the windowsill, I said.

Okay, mum said, being like defensive. Just asking.

The doorbell went and all of Adele's friends were there, like about a hundred of them. Miss Popular!!

See ya at dinnertime Del, mum shouted.

Adele grabbed her bag and bolted back into the kitchen, kissing her on the cheek. Don't forget to give me an extra dollop of custard mum.

I won't.

The door closed and then there was just me and mum.

Would YOU like an extra dollop of custard at dinner? mum said.

I just stared at the unopened yoghurt pots, saying nothing.

C'mon Mel haven't you got used to me being a dinner lady yet, I mean it's not that embarrassing is it?

Again I didn't answer, just downed the last bit of orange juice, grabbed my bag, and left.

It was with the closing of the front door that I remembered. It hit my brain like a lightening strike. OH SHIT. THE BATHROOM WINDOWSILL. MARKUS. I HAD COMPLETELY FORGOT.

mum and sis should be dead right now.

I was in a trance as I walked to school, trying to work out what had happened, or like, what had NOT happened. He must have had a change of thought? Or maybe he was just joking after all?

I waited for him but he didn't come.

????

I must have been a bit late for school cos like, there weren't many kids around and stuff. And the ones that were there, were kind of not looking at me, like a blanking kind of thing. When one of my Besties Neve started blanking me I knew something was wrong.

Neve!

Everyone thought Neve was a lesbian, or going to be a lesbian at least. She walked like a boy and talked like a boy. Markus used to call her 'Chick with a Dick.'

I ran after her and caught her at the gates. Neve's what's up?

She stared straight ahead and her jaw went like, all tight and stuff, like she was trying not to speak.

Neve?

I'm not supposed to talk to you.

What? Why?

Mia said.

What?

Your evil BF tried to punch her in the face.

I had forgotten all about that and the Bank Holiday Monday made The Weekend feel like ages ago.

Oh yeah, I said.

Neve's arms were folded now.

But like, she grabbed my hair and yanked it, I said. What did she expect him to do, just stand by and watch? I mean, like, she got violent FIRST.

Something flickered across Neve's face and I could tell that Mia hadn't told her about That Bit. Anyway, she said, I'm late.

She took a door that she didn't really need to take and just left me there, alone.

Mia had told pretty-much the ENTIRE school and now no one would talk to me. At break I watched her re-enacting the WHOLE thing in the Social Room. She knew I was watching so she got extra-dramatic and stuff. First she played the Markus-part: punching. Then the Mia-part: ducking. All the kids she was entertaining just watched on with open-mouths. I couldn't take anymore so I just stormed off and sat by myself. Markus always hated school and I pretended too as well but The Truth is I ACTUALLY liked it. But without any friends it's not quite the same. I wanted to go over to Mia and say Sorry but My Pride wouldn't let me. I stand by what I said in McDonalds's. She

IS an Attention-Seeking Slut and I wished Big Bear Had taken her head-off.

At dinner I saw someone who I knew would talk to me, Harrison from Art Class.

Hey Harry, I said.

His face went a little white, like Surprise and Fear rolled into one. The First Thing he did was look over his shoulder. He pulled his bag close to his arm and began to walk away.

Not you as well, I said.

I can't talk to you Mel.

Why? I heard the upset in my Own Voice.

He walked faster so I grabbed his arm. Why? I said again.

He looked at me like I was stupid.

Because your boyfriend broke my jaw. That's why!

For some reason I had forgotten all about that too.

Harrison, wait! C'mon that was ages ago ... and like, he didn't break your jaw anyway ... not technically, not officially.

He was gone and again I was standing on my own.

Tbh I was so glad to hear that Final Bell at the end of the day. Like, it couldn't have come sooner. What I craved was Markus cos now I knew he was The Only Person I Had in This World. I took out my phone to text him but then remembered that he didn't have his.

Instead I made my way towards The Falcon Pub cos that's like our regular meeting place after school ...

No Markus. No Big Bear. No sign of him at all.

Again I got worried and wondered if something bad had happened. I waited for about Ten Minutes before giving-up and crossing the road, heading home, cutting through this little park opposite, well not really a park, but more of an orchard kind of a thing. I was thinking about The Day when I heard a sound from the bushes and suddenly there were two hands on my shoulders and I couldn't move. Fear hijacked my ENTIRE body and the First Thing that went through my head was Rape.

Where the fuck was you?

The voice was familiar, like, too familiar, like, The Most Familiar Voice in The World but for some reason I couldn't process it. Too scared, I guess.

Where the fuck was you? He said again.

I couldn't tell if he was smiling or frowning.

Midnight. I tapped three times on your window. Where were you?

I was so happy to see him only he wouldn't let me hug him yet. An arm kept me back.

You came? I said, surprised.

Yes I fucking came! I tapped on that window about a hundred fucking times.

Oh.

Oh?

I must have fallen asleep.

It was dark in the orchard.

Never mind, he said. Probably a good thing anyway. We didn't plan it right. We NEED to plan things properly. We need to plan everything, down to its last detail.

Okay. I said.

Let's go McDonalds's.

Now can I have a hug?

We hugged and everything became alright again.

Markus waited at the end of the cul-de-sac while I ran in and got out of my school uniform. Was gonna ask mum for some $ but there was no point. I threw on jeans and a t-shirt, and a hoodie too cos it had gotten cool again. Big Bear was sat with his bum on the Lawson Avenue road-sign.

Get money?

I shook my head.

Did you even ask?

Shook my head again.

I got two quid, he said. Enough for a small drink between us.

We could like, walk by the skateboard bowl, sometimes there are like LOADS of dropped coins and stuff. From when, like, the Stunt Riders do flips and that.

Markus looked at me with serious eyebrows. Good idea, he said.

We didn't find any coins, but we had enough for a large chocolate milkshake between us.

Why does that bitch keep staring at me? Markus said.

I looked over my shoulder and he was right. The woman sweeping the floor kept glaring over.

She must remember us from Saturday, I said.

Saturday?

When you nearly took Mia's head off, remember?

Oh. Yeah.

Hey that's gone ALL around school y'know? Mia's like told EVERYBODY. No one will talk to me now.

Markus was sucking up all the milkshake, not leaving me much.

I'll be on time tonight. He said suddenly.

On time?

I was a little late last night. Tars wouldn't fuck off to bed. Thought I was going to end up killing her as well.

That made us both laugh.

Midnight. I'll be there dead-on midnight.

I managed to get the milkshake off him at last. Some kids came in from My Year and looked over at us, a bit.

Now what about your sister? He said.

I noticed how shiny his eyes were.

What about her?

He took the milkshake back.

How do you think she's gonna react to me killing your mum?

How do you think? I said, breathing through my nose. She'll obvs wake and be traumatised and probably call the police.

Markus raised his eyes and I knew what he was thinking.

Kill her too then? I said.

Yeah.

Shall I do it?

If you want.

Seems only fair. One each.

Markus drained the last bit of the shake and the slurping sound was dead-loud.

I couldn't kill my mum anyway. I said. She's too strong.

Not for me she won't be.

I looked out the window at the cars queueing in the drive-thru.

Wow I'm kind of excited, I said. Are you?

Bit, yeah. I mean it's definitely something different.

What will we do afterwards?

He shrugged.

Suppose we should really commit suicide. I mean, like, that's what most killers do, right?

It's what Columbine did.

Who's he?

Markus got distracted by some Pretty Girls in the next booth. I slapped the table, who's Columbine?

529

American school massacre, he said.

I sat and thought for a few moments. I wish this was America, I said. Or like, that we had the same rules and stuff.

What do you mean? He said, sucking on the milkshake even though it'd gone.

With the guns and that. If we could get guns we could just shoot them and that'd be way easier.

Nah. Too noisy. Markus said. Knives is best.

Knives is noisy too. What with all the screaming and stuff.

This made Markus smile for some reason. Not where I'm gonna stab them it won't. He said with a dead-slow voice.

Oh? Why where you gonna stab them?

He pointed at the centre of his own throat. Destroy the voice-box. He said. Make it all silent.

I could feel my eyes go big. But how do you know to do that?

Markus was restless and bored. He kept putting the milkshake beaker onto its side, rolling it back and forth. Dunno, he said. I just heard it somewhere. Probably TV.

Oh.

But it makes sense really, he said. I mean just put your fingers on your throat and feel how soft it is.

Markus did this, so I followed. He was right. It was like the Softest Part Ever. Oh yeah, I said.

His fingers were still on his throat. Now, just press on your Adam's Apple, he said.

That made me laugh out-loud.

What?

Girls don't have Adam's Apples silly.

Markus looked confused. I carried on laughing.

Yeah, well, you know what I mean. He grumbled, embarrassed.

We both sat silent for a bit. I had a feeling that the Pretty Girls had been listening in cos they had gone dead-quiet all of a sudden. I looked around at McDonald's and wondered if this was like the Last Time I'd Ever be here. I looked at the people, the old people and the young people and all those in between. I looked at the kids and the people who worked there. I must have been in a trance cos Big Bear touched my hand.

You sure you wanna do this? He said.

I nodded. Yep. I'm sure. I mean, like, I know it's a bit sad to kind of take away their lives and stuff, like take away their hopes and dreams and that. But to be honest I'm only really doing it for them.

Markus had confusion back on his face.

Cos, like, it's not fair for my mum to wake up every morning and wonder if I've committed suicide or not. And I know I'm going to do it at SOME POINT. And I know she just won't be able to cope with that. So, see, she HAS to die. And then My Sister will have to die cos she'll be in bits from mum dying ... and they'll just be so much pain. So really, this is the best solution, like, it's the most logical way out of it, I think.

Markus was smiling at me and I didn't know what he was thinking.

Just promise me one thing, I said.

What?

Just promise me that you won't torture them? Like, especially not my sister. Not my mum either but especially not Adele. Promise me you'll make it quick?

Thought you were killing your sis?

Oh. Yeah. I forgot. I said. I mean, I am, yeah.

It was rush-hour and McDonald's got dead-busy. People were waiting to sit. The woman who was glaring at us came over and took the empty beaker out of Markus's hands.

Thanks for dining with us, she said sarcastically. Come again soon.

He kissed me at the top of the cul-de-sac.

Midnight, he said.

Yup.

Stay awake this time.

Yep.

Drink coffee.

I don't like coffee.

Do star-jumps then.

What?

Markus walked away. I watched him until he was out of sight.

Dear Self-Esteem Diary,

Last night the wind was howling in the black, black night. It was on the other side of my window yet it was in my head too. It felt like it was coming from the moon. It felt like it was swirling around my house like a tornado. I could hear it in the fields, off the river, through the dark hills in the distance where there was no people. No people apart from Markus who was walking with this wind. The wind was his. It was on his back and in his hair and on his shoulders. He carried the wind in his hands. His hands were made for loving. His hands were special, sacred. His hands carried the key. His hands had destiny in them. They were a matter of life and death.

Only I didn't hear his hands. I didn't hear them on my street. I didn't hear them climb my fence, my house. I didn't hear them tapping on my window.

Tonight I stay on This Side of sleep

When I came downstairs Adele was laying on mum, her head in her lap, watching that Monsters Inc. film for like the zillionth time.

Don't you ever get bored of this? I said.

They ignored me and carried on laughing.

Normally that would have pissed me right off but tonight I didn't care. Tbh I felt like all the pressure had gone, like a ton of bricks had been lifted totally off my shoulders. I sat next to them and smiled, relaxed and excited at the same time. It was like Christmas, but better.

Bedtime then girls! mum said as the film finished.

Adele was almost asleep anyway, plodding up the stairs with her head down like a zombie, mum's hand gently guiding her.

I got a glass of water from the bathroom, and looked at all the stuff on the windowsill.

C'mon Mel give us a kiss, I'm shattered. mum said.

She kissed me on the landing without really looking at me and went into her room. I watched the closing of her door.

In my room I flipped on the bedside lamp and began my ritual, like an OCD kind of a thing. I have to push my bed right up against the wall and make sure the mattress and the pillows and the duvet is properly placed. I have to do this for about an hour. It never disturbs Del cos she is always out like a light, The Sleeping Angel without a care in the world, (until tonight.)

After my ritual I went into the bathroom and had another pee, only I decided not to move the stuff from the windowsill This Time in case mum got up to use the toilet and saw it.

I was wide-awake so there was no chance of me falling asleep On

Him tonight. I checked my white watch, which was on my blue desk, next to my polka-dot soap-bag. It was two minutes past eleven ... only fifty-eight minutes to go ... I got into bed and looked over at the dark ball of my sleeping sister, silently snug in the corner of the room ... then I looked at the ceiling and waited, hands clasped on the lip of my duvet, laying on my chest. Through the sheet I could feel the steady thump of my heartbeat, and for some reason I decided to count them ... one ... two ... three ... four ... five ... six ... seven ... eight ... nine ... ten ... eleven ... twelve ...

Wednesday

Markus

There was not a person in Markus's life who he hadn't wanted to punch in the face, at some point. Brother. Dad. Uncle. Cousin. Mates. Teachers. Even his Auntie Tara. The only person not on that list was his GF Mel … until now.

He skidded up outside the main gates of The Kitts Academy. The burn of rubber against tarmac was sharp under his nose. Most pupils put their heads down or pretended to look busy, while others glanced over with edgy curiosity. *What is he doing here? Who is he after? Shit is going down!* They looked at him like he was a celebrity, or some notorious criminal taking to the witness box. One kid walked right into his path without realising it.

Markus put a hand out and stopped him, "Mel left yet?"

"I … no … I mean … I've not seen her."

Markus showed no reaction, just put his eyes back on the school gates, and the broken stream of teens that were slowly trickling from them. Mel wasn't the only person he was looking for. He also had eyes for Mia.

My fist won't miss this time.

The kids came thicker now, like ants, and Markus had to concentrate on the faces. He slouched off his beat-up mountain bike, glaring at each pupil which passed him by.

At last he saw her, walking alone with her head-down, in her own world.

He reached out and grabbed her wrist, grabbed it hard and she let out a squeal.

"You playing games with me?" he said with menacing calm.

Her face went blank and white and she looked at him like she didn't know who he was, like he was a total stranger, and not the human being she had been inseparable from for the last eleven months.

"Am I just a joke to you?" he said with the same composure. "Because trust me, I'm the last person you want to be joking with."

His grip tightened and she winced, squirmed.

It's like she was only starting to recognise who it was, "Big Bear?"

"Don't pet-name me bitch. You're taking the piss."

He noticed people were starting to look over so he rolled his bike behind a bush, taking the girl with him.

"Look, like, I must have fallen asleep again."

He let go of her arm and looked at the sky. "If you don't wanna do it Mel don't do it! Nobody's forcing you. *I'm* not forcing you. I don't care one way or the other. I'm doing this for *you*."

"I know. And I do."

"Do what?"

"I do wanna do it."

"Do what?"

"Kill mum," she said, barely audible.

"Well it doesn't look like it," Markus said in a big voice. "Making me walk *all* that way every night, *for nothing*."

She put her hands over his on the handlebars. "I'll drink coffee. I'll drink like four cans of that Monster stuff. I'll do star-jumps like you said."

Markus became slowly amused.

"I think it's these head-meds I'm on," she said.

Markus rolled his eyes, shook his head, and sighed. "Where's Mia anyway?" he said.

"Why?"

Just then a kid stepped onto Markus's back wheel by accident. When the kid saw who it was he muttered *sorry,* before running off into the crowds.

"Tonight is your last chance," he said. "Fall asleep again, and it's off."

Schoolkids were now everywhere. An ice cream van could be heard from one street and a police car from another. Together it didn't sound right.

At eight pm Markus decided he wasn't doing it. She clearly doesn't want to, he thought. Why else would you fall asleep two nights on a row? It just doesn't make sense. It's not like she's trying to stay awake for a film or a phone call, this is her own mother's death!

Fuck it, he thought. She wants her dead she can do it herself.

Instead he got a bag of Monster Munch from the cupboard and flipped on the TV in his room. He surfed the channels for an hour or so, watching bits of random crap. Then at nine a film started on C4 called *No Country for Old Men*. It was about a man with a weird hair-cut who went around killing people. Only he gave them a chance of life and death by the flip of a coin. Some of the scenes and chases were quite cool but overall the film was boring. There was hardly any talking and there was *absolutely no music whatsoever*. For the most part Markus didn't have a clue what was going on. In the end he turned it off and just lay there, listening to his auntie brush her teeth before bed. The big hand on his clock hit three, making the time a quarter past eleven.

Markus sat up and turned on the light. On his bedside table was a small sea of bronze coins. He picked out a dusty two-penny and swung his legs off the side of his bed, putting his toes on the carpet. He thought back to the weirdo in the film.

"Heads I stay, tails I go," he said to the emptiness of the room.

His thumb flipped and the two-penny blurred into the air. He caught the coin and slapped it down on the back of his hand.

Heads.

"Heads, I stay," he said.

The light went off and Markus put his legs back on the bed. He was laying on his side. When the big hand on his clock hit the six, making it half-past, a feeling washed over him, a deep drive.

"Fuck it," he said.

I got here the same way the coin did.

Markus sprang into action, following the exact same procedure of the last two nights; school bag, change of clothes, four knives from the kitchen wrapped up in the same black t-shirt. The only difference with tonight is he decided to leave through the door, rather than his bedroom window. He put his hand on the handle and felt a churning in his bowls ...

Gonna be late, bitch is bound be asleep again.

... the flush of the toilet growled around the thin walls of the bungalow, as he crept back to the door. Only by the time he got there a white hand appeared on the wall, turning on a light. The bungalow lit up.

"Markus what are you doing?"

His aunt's face scrunched with the blinding of the light. She stood in her nightie, half-asleep. Markus said nothing, one hand on the handle, the other on his rucksack. He wore the burgundy Bench hoodie Mel had bought him for Christmas.

"Where are you going?" she said.

She could see now and her eyes got clear, blue and glassy, looking right at her nephew. He looked back and their eye contact was powerful, almost telepathic.

"You know what," Tara said lightly. "Don't answer that. I don't care. Do what you want and go where you want. You will anyway."

Markus nodded, nodded because what she was saying was right. There was no expression on the boy as he opened up and stepped into the night, locking the door behind him.

He was in her backyard again, sitting on the same bench, looking at the same window. It was stiller than the previous two nights, no wind, not even a breeze. The wind-chimes were silent. This time he decided not to climb the outhouse but instead took the pole from the washing line. He stood solid with his legs apart, spacing his arms, holding it firm, before lowering it towards her window. When he thought he had control over it he gave the glass three light taps. Within a second there was movement in the dark window, the curtain pulled to one side by a hand. Adrenaline shivered through him. At first he thought he was seeing things. This girl in the window, smiling, waving.

Markus put the pole back on the line and gave her the thumbs up.

It's on.

As he climbed he heard the click of the window open above him.

"Hey," she said.

"Hey."

He passed her the bag through and then followed. Night had turned the lime-coloured bathroom into a hard, colourless grey.

"Cute pyjamas," Markus said, stepping down. He nodded at her pink PJ's with *Minions* on them.

Mel couldn't take in what he was saying. Instead she got down on one knee and opened up the bag. "Careful," he whispered, closing the window. "They're sharp." He reached down and took out the t-shirt, slowly unfolding it on the floor, revealing the blades.

"Why four?"

Markus heard panic in her voice.

"Dunno," he shrugged.

He took out his knife and then handed her another one, a smaller blade.

"Why are you giving me that?" she said, her voice stifled by heavy breathing.

Markus said nothing, just nodded at the wall, and her bedroom behind it.

"Oh. Yeah." She took the weapon tentatively with a hand that had a tremor in it.

Both teens were still crouched.

"I'll go first, yeah?" he said.

Mel bit her lip and nodded.

"You sure about this?" Markus said.

His eyes were big and his hair was big and he was staring at her with a poised intensity. Mel closed her eyes and nodded again.

"Okay then," Markus stood and crossed the landing, opened her mum's room and stepped inside.

Mel got dry-mouth, and her mind went a little mad, mad in that she thought she was going to lose it. She listened out but there were no sounds. She expected him to come back, open the door. She expected to see him again but she didn't. Mel began to wait, pace, talk under her breath. "It's okay. It's alright. Keep calm. It'll be over soon. It'll *all* be over in minutes. "

Only her words did little to help her. She felt that feeling again, that crippling claustrophobia. *Panic attack.* It was coming; swooping in, pressing down, tying her up. Everything fast, fast, faster. A hot rush raced through her head, winding up her thoughts until they were colliding into each other. Mel stopped and put a hand to her chest, slid down the wall and sat in the corner, rocking gently to the passing of time but still there were no sounds in the next room. The silence was awful. The silence was horrific. The silence was unknown and she had to find out what was happening. At last there was something, noise, a creak of the bed, something human, a word, a moan, a bump. Without really wanting to Mel found her hand pushing at the door. She stepped through it and saw a fiendish mass on the bed. At first she couldn't work out what it was. Two shapes making up one object and Mel couldn't work out who was one top of whom. Then she saw a face, Markus's. He turned and looked at her but showed nothing, just blank with concentration. As her eyes adjusted she could see that mum was on her side. There was no knife. There was no blood.

Mel thought she heard the words *get off* but she couldn't be sure if that was real.

"You okay?" she whispered.

Markus nodded.

"Is it done?"

"Getting there," he said.

He had all of his weight down and the body underneath began to twitch. When she looked closer she could see he had a pillow pulled across her head.

Mel waited. She waited for him. Maybe it was five minutes, maybe ten, but at last he let her go and stepped off the body, off the bed.

They looked at each other and he nodded. There was a small smear of red on his face.

"Is that blood on the wall?" she said.

Markus followed her eyes to the spatters over the bed.

"C'mon," Markus said efficiently. "The other room."

They left her mum's room and stood in the landing. "Where's your knife?" he said.

Mel shook her head. "I can't. I don't think I can do this."

Markus was breathing heavy. He looked quite drained. "You know we have to, right?"

"I know," Mel said. Her lips were so dry they had started to crack. "I want to but I mean … I just can't. In that, like, I don't think I'm capable. Physically or mentally or emotionally and stuff."

Mel thought he might have a go at her but he didn't. With the knife still in his hand he calmly turned and stepped towards the door in front of him.

"Wait!"

Markus stopped and sighed.

"Your shoes. Take them off. We have a wooden floor. She'll hear you coming."

Markus kicked them off one at a time, switching the knife from right hand to left, and then back again.

Mel closed her eyes as he stepped silently into her bedroom, put her forehead into the patterns of the white wall and pushed against it.

This time the silence was short.

She heard her sister right away; a gasp, then her voice clear and distinct and full of fright, shock. "I can't … "

Her voice got sliced in half by something ... and Mel found herself finishing her sister's sentence in her own head. " ... breathe."

Mel pushed her head even harder into the wall until she could feel an imprint in her skull. "It has to be done." She whispered. "It has to be done."

Minutes later Markus *was* done. He softly pushed the door open with his foot and stood before her. There was more blood this time. More on his face, his neck. His sleeves were rolled up and it was all over his hands, wrists, matted into the dark hairs on his lower forearms.

He had put the knife down on her blue desk, next to her white watch and polka-dot soap-bag.

"That smell," she said. "Blood. It's awful."

Markus shrugged, pouted. He stood there like so many times before, casual, indifferent, alone.

"Can we close the doors?" Mel said.

"Do what you want," he said. "I'm getting changed."

Markus sauntered past her and headed into the bathroom, while Mel closed both of the doors. First her mum's, then her sister's. She looked at her sister's door once it was closed. Her own bedroom door had a sticker on it that had been ripped off. Mel couldn't remember what that sticker was.

The sound of running water was deafening in the early morning hour. Markus had his top off, washing his hands and arms with soap and hot water.

"It's everywhere," Mel said.

"What?"

"Blood."

"What did you expect?"

"It's on me too," Mel said, looking down at her pink pyjamas.

Markus looked her over. "No it ain't."

She pulled at her PJ's and looked down her back. "I'm getting changed," she said hurriedly. "And start running that bath!"

Mel marched into her bedroom and for some reason it's like she'd forgot. The sight of her sister made her jump. Her body splayed out with a pillow obscuring her face. Her hair running thickly from the side of it, flowing off the bed.

Mel stared. "Her hair," she muttered.

She went into a kind of trance, everything seemed to slow, her breathing, her movements. She turned the other way while she moved the pillow from her sister's face and replaced it with a sheet. After she pulled out a drawer and took out another pair of pyjamas, yellow ones with the black outline of a lion's head inside a square.

Markus had washed most of the blood off in the sink but was still filling up the bath like Mel had asked him too. Now the light on the lime-green walls seemed extra bright.

"We *need* to get *all* this blood off."

"Will you shut up about the fucking blood?!" Markus said, irritated. "I'm the one who has it on my hands, not you."

"We both have," Mel said, stripping off, stepping into the bath. "And like, I'm just scared in case Babe can smell it ... cos like, dogs can sense things like that and he might try and attack us or something."

Markus shook his head and stepped in opposite, lowering himself into the water. "You watch too many of them vampire films."

"I'm telling you it's true."

"Well we'll just kill the dog as well then."

Markus was smiling again and as always his girlfriend couldn't tell if he was joking or not.

"Take your glasses off," he said. "You look weird wearing them in the bath."

Markus noticed that her hands were still shaking. Her skin looked yellow. Her tits looked small. Her hair seemed to be going in all directions.

"Happy now?" he said.

She paused before answering. A raindrop rolled off her nose and plopped in the bath. Slowly she began to nod her head. "Yeah," she said. "Fanks."

There wasn't much blood in the bath but what little there was, was washed down by the shower head. They towelled each other off and got changed. Mel in yellow, Markus in black. After she closely followed him down the stairs, watching his hair bounce with each step.

Markus turned on the living room light and stood there. "Has this room been decorated?"

"No, why?"

"Looks different."

His girlfriend stood with her fingers clasped, looking around. "Nah. It hasn't."

"Oh."

Markus looked at the white and red room. The framed family photos on the wall. The fake fireplace. The fake plant by the couch. A replica Oscar trophy on the windowsill, something tacky that Adele had won at school.

"I'm really nervous about Babe," Mel said, looking at the closed kitchen door. "Y'know, about him smelling the blood and that."

"I'm going in there anyway," Markus said. "Fucking starving. All this killing makes you hungry."

Mel smiled, a bit. "Well, like, I'm gonna go back up, gonna get the mattress from my bed and bring it down."

Markus nodded. "You want food?"

Mel slowly shook her head. "Not hungry."

The kitchen was black, and Markus kept the light off. He could see the dog's yellow eyes raise as he stepped in. Markus watched them for a second or two until they lowered and closed and went back to sleep. While he collected food he looked out of the kitchen window at the rusty bench, that empty J20 bottle was still there. He looked at it and thought how that bottle was a part of all this.

I was drinking from you when we decided.

The white of the fridge and freezer drew him into the corner of the kitchen. He pulled open the bottom door and vapours of cold drifted over his bare skin. He took out a tub of Ben & Jerry's and loaded it into two bowls.

Back in the lounge and there was still no sign of Mel. He thought of the time she had been up there. *How long does it take to drag a mattress off the bed?*

A minute later he heard her, the sound of something soft and big tumbling down the stairs.

"Help me with this," she said through the wall.

He put down the food and helped her set up the mattress and the duvet into the centre of the lounge. He turned the lights off and the TV on, bumping the volume down a few notches. The screen was now hovering in the centre of the dark room, lighting up their makeshift bed.

"I said I wasn't hungry."

"Eat," he said, thrusting the bowl under her nose.

She took it and prodded at the melting dessert with her spoon. "Babe alright?"

Both teens were now positioned on the bed.

Markus had a mouthful of ice cream. "Sleeping."

"You didn't, like, kill it, did you?"

"What?" Markus let out a laugh and some ice cream fell from his mouth and coloured his black t-shirt. Now he couldn't tell if *she* was being serious or not.

They sat for a while in silence, under the blueish glare of the television. Markus had full concentration on his food; ice cream, crisps, half a sandwich. After he went back into the kitchen and made some toasted teacakes.

"Remember when mum did that stupid reindeer dance at Christmas?" Mel suddenly said, shouting through. She could smell the teacakes being toasted.

"What? What the fuck's a reindeer dance?" he said, poking his head around the kitchen door.

"Well, she like, she, she put those antlers on her head and did that gay dance, remember? Del filmed it on her phone. I hated stuff like that ... stuff she did."

Markus landed back on the bed and bit into a teacake. "Can't you at least stick a film on? Fuck-all on at this time."

"Yeah," Mel said, still in the depths of her thoughts. "Yeah sure."

When she bent over to look at the DVD's Markus noticed that her bum had gotten bigger.

She turned and looked at him over her shoulder. "We could watch that box-set Mia bought for my b-day?"

"Whatever," Markus was laying back, head resting in the cup of his hand, pulling the teacake apart with his teeth.

While the disc loaded a car came down the cul-de-sac, lighting up parts of the room. Markus and Mel stopped what they were doing for a second, until the vehicle could be heard turning around, and leaving again.

"When we gonna do it anyway?" Markus said.

"Do what?"

"Suicide."

From the look on Mel's face it was like she had forgotten. "Oh. Tomorrow," she said.

"It is tomorrow."

She adjusted her glasses. "I mean, like, after sleep and stuff. I thought we could do it dead-on two 'o clock."

"Why then?"

"Just what my nature-feeling says."

Mel watched his eyes roll.

They got comfortable as the film started with the opening line, *I had never given much thought to how I would die, but dying in the place of someone I love seems like a pretty good way to go.*

"Hey do you think we should check on them?" she whispered, nodding upstairs.

"Why," Markus said with a half-laugh. "In case they've run off?"

Mel shook her head and rolled onto her side, putting her bum against his thighs. She thought she'd fall asleep but she didn't. The film kept her awake. Every now and then she would turn to see Markus sat there, staring into the screen. She couldn't tell if he was enjoying it or not. She couldn't even tell if he was watching it properly or not. His eyes were always the same, clear and unblinking and she was amazed that he never looked tired. Maybe he's a vampire just like the characters in the film, she thought? It kind of made sense because Markus never slept, or, she had never *seen* him sleep anyway. In the time they'd gone out she had not *officially* seen him sleep, *ever*. She always dropped off before he did and when she woke again he would be sat there, next to her, over her, eyes wide open.

"Wanna watch the next one?" he said as the ending credits rolled.

"You like it?" she said, excited.

"S'all right." Markus replied nonchalantly. "Bit soppy and shit."

She sat up and ejected the disk, replacing it with the next one. "You're not soppy at all are you?" she said. "Like, you don't even tell me you love me anymore."

"I do," Markus said, nodding his head, pouting. "You just don't listen."

"When, when was the last time?"

Markus sat up and looked right into her eyes. "I might not say it but I show it … actions speak louder than words."

Thursday

Mel

Big Bear was there when I woke. Sat up. Just like he always was, is. Different colours were moving about on his face, reflecting from the telly. I think he was watching The Third Film from The Box-Set, or maybe The Fourth.

I need go pee, I said.

He just kept on staring at the screen. His mouth was open, a bit.

Maybe he slept funny cos his hair was like, all sticky-up and stuff. Almost like he had horns like a ram or a unicorn or The Devil or something.

Suddenly I came off the bed, almost like a levitation kind of a thing. I was at the bottom of the stairs and the stairs looked like they were moving, like escalators in a shopping centre. I floated to the top and the need to pee was overwhelming, unbearable, like, dead-intense, so much so that I thought I might have an accident. (This has happened to me before, peeing in my sleep.)

In the bathroom I sat on the toilet and looked in the bath. There was no blood there, not anymore, no traces of it at all. I know Markus has A Thing for cleaning so maybe he came up here in the night and washed it all out, properly.

It was weird cos even though I was busting to pee nothing would come, like a constipation kind of a thing. I pushed but just couldn't go. Then I got scared about pushing, scared about Letting Go. Suddenly it felt like I was doing the opposite, Holding It In, holding it in for dear life. All around me there was like this MASSIVE fear. A fear that something bad was about to happen, or happening, or, had already happened. I guess you'd call this Dread.

And that's when I heard a noise in the next room, MY room, the room I shared with My Sister Adele. For some reason I wasn't scared even though I knew I should be. There was movement in my room, some slow shuffly footsteps, like a 'dragging-your-feet' kind of a thing. The footsteps got louder and nearer and ...

... before I knew it She was in front of me. Wearing a set of

pyjamas I had never seen before. The pyjamas were a size too big. They dropped off her wrists and covered her feet. She looked like a wizard in a cloak.

Adele was looking right at me. The outlines of her were soft and shimmering. She was pale and serious-looking, and still a lil sleepy too.

Her voice was clear and slow. You used to be an Ellis, dint ya?

What? I said.

Why are you here?

Having a pee, I replied, looking up at her.

Go then.

I can't while you're watching me.

I won't turn around.

Her hair was wrapped around her neck, covering her throat. Then she moved it and the skin there was all red and sore and stuff.

I'm sorry. I said.

Oh it's only a scratch, she said, tilting her head back so I could see more.

Her eyes had a bright, knowing light. That look of superiority that suited her so well.

I told you not to go that way, she said.

Go where?

You know.

We just looked at each other for ages until I heard a voice cry out from downstairs, Markus shouting me, shouting my name over and over again.

You better go, Adele said.

I nodded my head.

I better go too, she said. Go back to sleep. Got school in the morning.

Mel. Mel! Markus's voice was booming against my skull. I could feel my body being pulled and shaken. It was like I was beginning to swim upwards, back to the surface of something.

Adele looked at me one last time at the door, and then I woke up.

Mel!

His large, mask-like face was over me.

What? Where?

You were dreaming.

I sat up, clutching onto one of the pillows. Markus was smiling, *nearly laughing. The familiarity of the room came back. Markus touched my forehead. You're sticky, he said.*

It was my sister, I mumbled. I was saying goodbye to Adele.

Markus put his eyes back on the telly, which like, I only just realised was on.

Bit late for that, he said.

His voice was cruel and final.

I sat up more, straightened my back.

Regrets, he said?

No. I said, shaking my head. No. Cos like, I know we did the right thing, in the end.

It's not the end yet, he said.

I stood to open the curtains but he stopped me. Said we had to keep them shut.

Your mum's phone's been ringing, he said. We really need to turn it off.

Where is it?

In her room, I think.

There was an empty bowl next to my knee. Markus had already had breakfast.

How long you been awake, I said?

For some reason I expected him to say Forever but he just shrugged and looked back at the telly. Jeremy Kyle was on and it was Just Horrible to have his shouty voice in my ear First Thing. There was a woman on the show who was talking about her mum. Her mum wasn't on the stage yet, but she, she kept shouting through from the backroom. She was fat with black teeth and I couldn't tell a word she was saying. Keep it shut! Jeremy yelled back. I'll be with you in a minute! He was wearing a shiny grey suit. The daughter was upset cos she loved her mum but her mum was doing Terrible Things. Like she was having loads of men in her house and sleeping with the WHOLE town. She said her mum was proud of her behaviour even though it was dangerous.

This is sick, Markus said, smiling.

When The Mum came on stage the camera quickly cut to the crowd. People in the audience gasped and looked shocked and Jeremy did too.

Skank just flashed her fanny on national television! Markus said, pulling a face.

The Daughter put her head in her hands and looked, like, totally ashamed and stuff.

Jeremy told the old woman off. I'd say she was about 60 or 70 year's old or something like that.

The story was gross. The old woman LITERALLY let Any Man in her house and would have sex with them.

Who the fuck would fuck That? Markus said, screwing his face up.

Aren't you worried about diseases? Jeremy cried out. Aren't you at least a bit scared of these strangers you are letting into the house?

No! The woman kept saying. No, no, no! It's my life and I do what I want. Not hurting anybody.

This made Jeremy Kyle go into a full-blown rant and stuff. Not hurting anybody? He cried. You're hurting yourself! Now he was leaning right into her. You're hurting your daughter here! You're breaking her heart! Look at her. Look at this woman you're sitting next to and tell me you're not hurting anybody?!!

The camera did a close-up of The Daughter. She was like totally In Bits.

This shit is fixed, Markus said, truly entertained.

What do you mean? I said.

He looked at me like I was stupid and shook his head.

At the end of the show Jeremy asked her why, why do you have these men in?

Cos I like sex, she said.

Markus was picking his nose. Fucking sick, he said.

But I mean why do you REALLY have them in? Jeremy said, leaning over.

Cos she likes fucking moron, Markus shouted at the telly. She just told you!

Only the fat mouthy woman seemed to go quiet this time. Her daughter was holding her hand and the audience looked sad. In the end the woman Broke Down and cried … COS I JUST WANT TO BE LOVED.

This made Markus laugh the most. This shit is definitely fixed!

I still didn't know what he meant.

Jeremy was softer now. Like he wasn't shouting anymore. He told the woman that this was not Love and that these men didn't Love her and that all They were doing was using her and stuff. Then he got that bald Psychology Guy Graham from the back and said that The Show will help her.

Yeah right, Markus dismissed. The only way to help this bitch is with a bullet to the head.

I'm gonna get breakfast, I said, getting up.

The show had made me a bit upset and I was definitely on a Downer. Babe rushed at me in the kitchen like he always did and for a moment I got scared in case he could smell The Blood. I couldn't smell it anymore but I know that dogs have a stronger smell than humans, by like, a Thousand Times or something. He seemed Normal though and just licked and sniffed me and that. He must have had an accident in The Night cos I could smell wee in the corner of the room so I mopped it up and then let him out into the backyard. I stood in the doorway while he bounded about like he had rabies or something. It wasn't sunny outside but it wasn't cold either, just that grey in-between weather. After I poured a small bowl of Rice Krispies and then got back on the bed. This Morning was on now and Markus sat staring at that too. I looked at him and it felt strange to look at him. In that it was like I felt differently about him now, somehow. We had sex before I went to sleep last night and for some reason I knew it was for the Last Time. Not just cos we were Officially Dying Today but cos it no longer felt the same. It's like there had been a sudden break in the connection. It's like I wasn't even there, almost like I was watching us from the ceiling like a ghost, like a spirit kind of thing. This had kind of been happening for a while now but last night was different. It's like it really was The End.

Markus had no idea though. He carried on having sex with me like it was Normal.

Markus is clever. He's way cleverer than me, way cleverer than most. I'd say for his age he's like a genius kind of a thing. The way he reads people and knows stuff, the way he works things out. His brain is like a computer.

But.

But ...

... there are Some Things he doesn't know. There are certain things that he's just not aware of. There are things that happen Inside Me that he just doesn't understand. And never will.

Do you think Scofield is fucking Willoughby? He said.

Ugh. What? I said. No. No way.

We both looked at Philip and Holly sat next to each other.

Markus was eating a second bowl of cereal. I think he is, he said, slurping at the milk.

I couldn't agree with him on this one.

She's like, Officially The Most Beautiful Woman in The world and he's like, dead-old and stuff.

She's not THAT fit, Markus said.

I didn't say Fit, I said Beautiful. She's dead-beautiful, in a pure kind of a way.

This made Markus snort. No one is pure, he said. There's no such thing. The only people close to pure are those who don't pretend to be.

Markus spoke in riddles sometimes.

Anyway, he said. Holly's old too. She's about thirty.

No she's not she's about twenty!

We both watched her on the telly, maybe trying to work out her age. The story on the show was about a blind dog who guided a blind woman.

That's fucking stupid, Markus said. All TV is fixed.

No, that could happen, I said.

Then you're fucking stupid as well, he said.

It can, I said.

How?

Cos of like, the smell and that. Dog's sense of smell is like a Thousand Times stronger than a human's.

Markus picked up the remote and changed the channel to cartoons. He had taken his bottoms off and I noticed all these scratches all over his legs.

What the eff is that? I said, touching them.

He looked down and rocked onto his side, inspecting them for like the First Time. Oh, your mum must have done it.

Did she fight back?

Markus looked at me and nodded.

What about Del? Did she?

Nah. Markus said. She just sort of accepted it.

Oh.

Just then a vibratey phone-noise came from above us.

It's your mum again.

Shall we answer it?

Markus was already up on his feet whereas I didn't really want to go. Like I didn't want to go into her room or see her EVER again. I heard Markus open the door and his footsteps thud over me. After a while the ringing stopped but Big Bear came down with her phone in his hand.

It was school, he said.

What did they say?

Well I didn't answer it did I?

Oh.

Mum had one of those old phones and Markus began to play around with it, his face tight with concentration.

Aunt Tars rang at 8:36. He said. Aunt Tara at 8:36 and school at 10:44.

Oh.

They're the only people who've rung.

Oh.

I'm turning it off now, he said.

Kay.

Markus did, then dropped her phone into the crack of the couch.

They're gonna be looking for us soon. He said. So we need to barricade ourselves in again.

How?

Just make sure all the curtains are shut tight, no cracks or peepholes. Make sure all the doors are locked with the keys left in them, windows closed too.

Kay.

We went around the house and did that. Markus went in the rooms where the bodies were while I sealed the bathroom and the kitchen. I brought Babe back in from outside cos I thought he might run off and tell someone by barking at them and leading them back. I've seen that happen before on telly.

What now? I said.

It's almost twelve, why don't you get the suicide stuff ready.

Oh. Yeah. I said. I almost forgot about That Bit.

I got a fold-up table and Blue Bucket from the outhouse, as well as some J20'S and Bacardi Breezer drinks to wash the pills down with. I got all the tablets I could find from The Meds Cupboard as well as the secret stash of ibuprofen I had been collecting.

Last time, I took twenty, I said. This time I'm gonna take forty. Like forty should do the trick for good.

Markus nodded, cool.

I placed the table in the centre of the lounge and the Blue Bucket in the centre of the table. I dropped all the tablets in it and then placed all the drinks around the bucket, like a ceremony kind of a thing.

Shall I write a Suicide Note?

If you want. Markus was still watching cartoons.

I got this pink notepad from the kitchen and put it on the table, pen poised. What shall I write?

551

Markus shrugged.

I'm gonna put ... that we've had enough and don't care anymore. Just put ... Fuck the World, he said.

I wrote stuff but it didn't FEEL right. Like, it was No Way Near as good as my first suicide note.

Does it have to be at two? Markus said.

I was looking into the back of his head. All the colours of the cartoons were dancing around him.

I mean why two? He said. Why not just do it now and get it over with?

I still had the pen in my hand and I noticed that my fingers were beginning to shake. I was burning-up and feeling a little dizzy, a little tired. Nah. Two. I said. Two pm FEELS right. We'll die then.

You're the boss. Markus said.

I didn't finish The Suicide Note but instead sat back down next to my BF.

What shall we do till then, then? He said.

I took my glasses off and rubbed my eyes. Watch The Third film from the box-set?

Markus pulled a face. What? We watched that last night?

Did we?

I did. You fell asleep.

Oh. We'll watch The Forth then.

We put it on but I couldn't concentrate. For some reason I kept thinking about That Old Woman on Jeremy Kyle. Then I kept thinking about Holly Willoughby. I imagined what her life must be like, where she lived. I wondered what kind of mum she would be and what kind of mum her mum was. I thought about mums, all the mums I knew. I wondered what kind of mum I would be if I ever had kids. I closed my eyes and thought about My Foster Mum Janet. I imagined what she was doing Right Now. I kept my eyes closed and it was like I was trying to contact her somehow, like a telepathic kind of a thing. Like there was an invisible phone line connecting my mind with hers. I tried to focus so her Nature-Feeling could touch mine only nothing came. In the end I think I must have fallen asleep cos Markus was pulling and shaking me again, just like this morning, saying my name, waking me up.

Mel!

His large, mask-like face was over me.

Ready? He said.

Ready for what? I said, sitting up, disorientated.

Wake up so you don't have to.

What?

Where we're going you'll get all the sleep you want.

Uh?

It's two o' clock, check-out time!

The film was finishing and Markus nodded up at the Blue Bucket.

Kay, I said, rubbing my eyes.

He helped me to my feet and we both walked over to The Suicide Table.

Markus shook the bucket and all the boxes and pills made a rattley sound.

Fucking hell Mel, enough in here to kill half of Kimble Wells!

I picked up a red bottle of Bacardi Breezer and stared at it.

I shouldn't really drink alcohol, cos like, I might be sick and stuff and you know I've got a phobia of vomit.

Markus switched bottles with a J20. Drink this one then, he said.

I looked down at all the tablets in the bucket.

He must have seen the concern on my face. What's up? He said.

I held my fingers against my breastbone. Well, like, don't you think that like, this way could be a slow and painful death? Like, we could just be lying here for days, poisoned with agony and stuff?

Markus thought for a few seconds. We could slash our wrists in the bath instead?

I pulled a face and scrunched my eyes and shook my head. I don't like blood, I said.

Close your eyes.

I don't like the smell.

Markus was thinking. Well, I could stab you in the neck if you want? Get it over with quick, like them up there.

He nodded his quiff at the ceiling.

I was horrified and offended and even a little scared and stuff. You would really kill me? Like, you'd really kill your OWN GF?

Yeah but only to help you, he said.

My head was in a spin. Holly Willoughby was back on telly. This time on an advert.

Maybe we should do it tomorrow instead? I said. Plan it better.

Markus was already back on the bed, in front of the telly.

Whatever. You're the boss. But if we're gonna be around for another day we better do some shopping because the cupboards are getting bare and I'm fucking starving!

Kay.

I felt better that I wasn't dying today.

At 10 past 5 there was a knock at the door and Markus grabbed me and yanked me down onto the bed. He told me to hush even though I hadn't said anything.

In fact he said the word HUSH quite loud and that kind of made me laugh, like an ironic kind of a thing. The knock came again and again and whoever it was, was pretty determined.

It's Aunt Tars, Markus said.

How do you know?

Hush!

Again he said Hush quite loud. Babe was barking and scratching up against the kitchen door. Markus pulled a face as he stretched out towards the remote control and hit the mute button. I could see the figure move across the window. More knocks and then the flap of the letterbox shot open. It stayed open for a few seconds before it clapped shut again. Heeled footsteps, walking away ...

It's Tars dropping in after work, he said. It's about that time. Plus I heard a cough. She's started smoking again.

I touched Big Bear's face. Hey you should be a detective, I said.

We watched The Fifth and final film from the Box-Set while Markus cleared out the cupboards. Let's order a pizza, he said?

What?

Where's your mum's purse?

I was smiling and couldn't work out if he was being serious or not. He stood staring at me, licking his lips.

We are NOT ordering a pizza, are you flippin mental? I said.

Why? He shrugged.

Duh. Cos like, there's two dead bodies upstairs.

So?

I sighed and rearranged myself on the bed. Holding a pillow in my lap.

Cos like, the Pizza Guy might smell them?

Markus pulled a face and shook his head. He won't smell shit. They've not even been dead twenty-four hours yet. Bodies take ages to start smelling.

How do you know, killed anyone before?

Actually, yeah.

I just rolled my eyes at him. Stop being silly, I said. We ain't ordering a pizza. Plus he might recognise us and call the police. Plus my mum doesn't keep money in the house. Plus I don't even like pizza when all said and done.

Markus filled his cheeks with air and put his hands on his head and then blew hard at the ceiling, emptying his lungs. Let's commit suicide now then, he said. Cos nothing's worse than hunger.

This made me laugh and I bounced up onto my feet and took his hand and lead him into the kitchen. Use your eyes, I said. Just cos it's not RIGHT in front of you doesn't mean it isn't THERE. I pulled open the freezer door and took out two ready-meals, ripped off the box, pierced the plastic with a fork and then banged them in the microwave for like ten minutes or something.

Markus seemed happy now, for a bit.

It was dark outside and I watched the night and the moon and some of the stars from the back door. Babe was dead-calm and nice and it was like EVEN he was a different person since mum had died. He wandered around the backyard and I watched his black, liquid eyes shine in the dark.

Just then Markus ran through and took my arm, GET IN, he said without moving his mouth. Then he grabbed Babe by the collar and pulled him inside, shutting the door behind us. All the time he had a finger to his lips and his eyes were all large and weird and stuff.

Aunt Tars is back, he whispered.

We was under the covers as footsteps and knocks and coughs sounded around the house. We lay flat, holding hands. Holding breaths. Next there was the clap of the letterbox again only this time there was a voice. Tara's thin voice sliding through the gap in the door, filling the room.

Hello. Hello? Anybody in? Anybody here? Anybody there? Erica?

A pause.

The letterbox closed and opened again.

Erica? Mel? Markus are you in there?

Pause.

Adele?

Hearing my sister's name made me feel funny. Out of ALL the names hers got to me the most. It's like I was only just realising what we had done. Having someone else here, another voice, was, a kind of Reality Check kind of a thing.

Soon the voice went away and Markus let out a big sigh. We could hear her car start up and pull away.

Bitch is determined, Markus said.

Don't call your OWN aunt a bitch, I said.

Markus laughed and pulled a face, looked at the ceiling/my mum's bedroom floor above us.

You serious? He said.

About 45 minutes later another visitor came, another intruder. Another adult. More footsteps. Another knock. Another cough only not a female one this time, not an Aunty Tars one. There were more knocks at the door this time, louder, more forceful ones, more confident. Again Markus had to turn down the volume on the telly and Babe began to bark.

Police, he said.

How do you know?

I can tell by the knuckles.

What?

By the knocks on the door.

Oh.

Police always bang like that.

Oh.

HUSH.

It could have been true cos the footsteps were different too, slower, more thoughtful. We heard him walk around the back and all of a sudden I panicked cos like, I'm sure I left the backdoor unlocked. I didn't want to tell Markus this cos I know he would have gone flippin mental. Instead I kept it to myself and prayed that he wouldn't climb the gate and let himself in and catch us red-handed. I got paranoid about the blood too. The death smell. Cos, what if like, if we had got used to it by now? What if we had been laying with it for so long that our noses didn't smell it anymore? What if The Death Smell had left through the walls and filled the avenue, the town?

We kept our heads down and our mouths shut and at last the policeman footsteps went away, back into the policeman car.

We had a bit more time.

We had maybe one more night.

It was getting late now but I still wasn't tired. Maybe that siesta earlier had put some energy back into my body. The room was dark, and The Suicide Table with The Suicide Bucket on made everything look creepy. We watched a film that Markus really liked but I didn't. It was about a family who hired a cop to kill the mother. They were doing this to get money. Only they ended up not getting the money for some reason so now the killer was going to kill them, the family. The last scene was absolutely gross. The killer cop beat this woman up into a bloody pulp and then made her suck on a chicken leg, pretending it was his penis. It was so gross and disturbing I had to put my hands over my ears and look the other way.

Why did you even make me watch that? I said when the film finished.

Markus didn't even answer me so I asked him again. When he blanked me a second time I got kind of freaked out. Markus? I touched him but he didn't move. Markus!

When I looked over I could see his eyes were closed. My first thought was that he was dead. Maybe he had taken some of tablets without telling me?? His face was warm and his chest slowly rose and fell so he couldn't be dead!!

I had never seen My Big Bear sleep. I had NEVER seen him asleep. Like I didn't OFFICIALLY know what it looked like and stuff.

Most people sleep ugly, I think. I know I do. Like they make loads of noise or pull weirdo faces and that. Not Big Bear, not Markus. His expression didn't change. It was all still and serene and stuff. I watched him. I watched him for ages. I watched him for maybe like an hour or more. I began to space-out and trance, almost like a daydream, night-dream. For some reason I was suddenly drawn to his neck, and the gentle pulse of blood that moved under the layer of creamy white skin. I imagined going back upstairs and getting that knife. The knife that was still in my room, on my desk, the one with the grey and white handle. The one that had done the deed. I imagined bringing it down and turning it onto the killer, the murderer, HIM. My Markus. I pictured it all so vividly. Pushing it into to his skin, breaking flesh, his voice box, his life. I thought about making death.

Then I thought not of killing myself but of turning myself in. Blaming him. Saying he killed my family so I HAD to do him, like a self-defence kind of a thing...

... my imagination got broken as Markus stirred and rolled over in his sleep ... almost like he was dreaming what I was thinking. Almost like his mind was in my mind.

I put the knife down in my head and lay next to my BF. My hand resting on his beating heart, although I couldn't feel it. I couldn't feel anything. I couldn't hear anything either. There was no movement or sound anywhere. And I didn't like this cos it meant I was alone. Alone for the first time. Alone for the last. Alone in this room, this house. Alone with the dead. Markus was asleep. Babe too. Mum was. Del was. You was. The world is. Everyone was. Everyone apart from

me.

Friday

Markus

Tara had to take the day off. Nephew and his darling had been missing for nearly thirty-five hours. They had obviously gone on the run again.

Little bastard runs my life. Little bastard ruins my life. Well, no more. No more. It ends now, today, this minute. When he gets back from his attention-seeking little adventure he's out. I'm kicking him out and I don't care where. I've done my bit. Done my part. I've done my years, the crucial years, the hard years. I did my best. I did what she asked but now it's over. Done. I'm taking my life back.

Tara was taking her life back for good this time.

She switched on the kettle for her eleven's. Popped a teabag into a mug and took three biscuits from the tin.

Little shit even has me smoking again.

She jumped up onto the worktop, threw open a window and sparked up. Taking in a deep drag while her mind went into overdrive.

Where can he be? Where can he be this time? How come his bike is still here? Maybe they've jumped a train or caught a bus? Little fucker might have even stolen a car for all I know. How come her mum isn't in? Maybe she's taken them away and he just hasn't bothered to tell me? No. No. That's not it. He's not even allowed in the house so she definitely wouldn't take him away on holiday. It has to be something else. I need to contact her. I need to reach her. Why doesn't she answer her phone? How come it was ringing yesterday but now it's dead? Makes no sense??

Her mind went round and round, over and over, lost in thought while her eyes drifted around the kitchen.

Just then something stopped them, stopped her eyes and caught her breath. *The wooden knife block.* The wooden knife block with *only* one handle sticking out. Only one while the other three were missing? All of a sudden the sounds around her came alive, the probing tick of the clock, the angry boil of the kettle, the vicious scream of her neighbour's hedge-trimmer. The wooden block became the centre of her world. She stared at it and stared at it; her eyes drawn to the patch of heat swimming on the light brown wood.

"Markus."

"My nerves are shot," he turned and looked at his GF.

It was unusual to see this look of anxiety on his face. It must have been contagious because a knot suddenly tightened in Mel's stomach. "Why?" she said.

"Only a month to go and Leicester have done it," he said. "If they can *just* hold onto this five-point lead then history will be made!"

Markus looked back at the telly, where a team of blue players were running around a bright green pitch like ants.

"Football?" she said.

Markus nodded.

The knot in her tummy unravelled and she sighed. "For a moment I thought something bad had happened."

After the news Markus turned and faced his girlfriend. "Hey you got changed?"

She nodded. Her yellow PJ's were gone, replaced by some black leggings and a black t-shirt. "Showered too," she said.

Markus grabbed her legs and pulled her in. "Wish you'd have told me. I could have joined you."

"You were watching football."

"I'm not watching football now." He dropped his head into her neck and tried to kiss her.

"Don't," she said.

"What?" He leaned back and looked at her.

"I don't want to."

His hands slid up towards her crotch area.

"No," she said, stopping him. "Your hands smell of blood."

"What?" he said with a screw-face.

"They do."

"Bullshit. I showered this morning while you were asleep."

Mel was looking around the room. "It's not that," she said. "I don't want to while *they're* up there."

"Well I can't move them," he said with a crazy smile.

He tried again and again she backed away.

"Fuck's sake!" he said, temper flashing in his eye.

He threw the remote against the couch and it bounced off.

"Well we did Wednesday night," he said. "Just hours after so why is *now* so different?"

She dropped her head and flipped her shoulders.

"Fine," he said, pointing the remote back at the telly, changing channel.

"Don't be like that," she said.

He didn't answer her.

They sat quiet for a bit, watching a documentary on sharks. They watched a scene where it showed how sharks cleaned their teeth. They swam upright with their mouths open while smaller fish ate off their teeth.

"How come the shark doesn't just eat the little bastards?"

"Cos then their teeth won't get cleaned," Mel said.

"So?"

"And then they will rot and fall out and then they won't be able to eat *anything*."

Markus said nothing, just kept on staring at the screen. When the show ended Markus got back on his feet and fixed the curtain, sealing off the tiniest crack of light.

"You know you weren't the first don't ya?" he said from nowhere.

"What?" Mel said.

There was a long pause and Mel could tell he was focussing on the words before he turned them loose. "You weren't *the first*," he said.

"You mean like sex, virginity and stuff?"

Markus nodded solemnly and sat down opposite her, almost in a lotus position.

"Oh," she said.

Markus was shocked that it didn't make more of an impact.

"Like, what was her name?"

Markus breathed in, and out. Raised his eyebrows. "I don't remember."

"Oh."

"She lived in the estate, I think."

"Was she pretty?"

Markus slowly shook his head. "No. She was kind of fat."

"Doesn't mean she can't be pretty."

"She wasn't pretty," Markus said.

His lips were wet and his eyes looked wide and serious.

"Why are you like, only telling me about this now?" she said. "It is like, cos I won't have sex with you and stuff? Like a revenge kind of a thing?"

Markus picked some fluff off his sock that wasn't there and flicked it. "No," he mumbled. "Just thought you should know. I mean, you're always going on about *the truth* and that."

Mel nodded her head without saying anything for a bit. Then, "fanks."

"Thanks?"

"Well yeah thanks for telling me the truth in the end."

"Aren't you bothered?"

"Bit," she said. Babe had woken up and was wagging his tail against the kitchen door. "But like, suppose it doesn't really matter now."

Markus nodded. Then he sighed and fell back on the bed, putting his eyes on the ceiling. "I hope they catch us today. I'm bored as fuck."

PC Tromans watched his colleague step out of the station and head towards the car. He walked around to the passenger side and slid in next to him.

"Where we off?"

"McDonald's."

Tromans smiled and pulled his jacket down. "After that?"

"Top end of town."

"Anything exciting?"

"Runaway teens."

"Oh?"

"Pair did one last October. Made the papers, remember?"

"I don't read the papers," Tromans said, getting ready to start the motor.

"Pair of fourteen-year-olds, boy and a girl, a couple. Think they've done one again. Boy's aunt's been making a fuss. Says she's been round to the girl's house but no one's there. One of *our lot* popped over about ten last night. Nothing. So here *we* are. Sarge says no one answers this time we've got to break in."

Tromans hit the ignition. "Bit much in it?"

His colleague shrugged.

"We got bust-in quip?"

"In the boot."

"Better get on it then, no coffee for us."

"Nah. It's just around the corner from Maccy's. Two birds with ... "

Mia Massey held an audience in the canteen. She sat in the middle of them like she was telling a story around the campfire.

"Mel, Del and her mum have left Kimble for a few days to get away from Markus Venner. I mean, it's the only explanation. They just need to take time-out and become a family again."

A boy who was sat behind her coughed and cleared his throat. "But to not tell anyone. To not *even* ring school. It's weird."

Mia put a finger in the air. "No I believe Erica called school on the Thursday morning."

The boy was shaking his head. "She didn't dude. I should know. My mum's the secretary."

The bell rang and kids began to stand and break away. "No," Mia said. "Mel's my bestie and ... "

A girl shot her a look on the way out. "Mia admit it, you know about as much as the rest of us ... "

Mia went to say something but by now there was no one to say it to. The canteen was practically empty.

Tromans pulled onto Lawson Avenue around noon. The two officers, both over six-feet, stepped out of the car and looked around.

"Quiet street," Tromans said.

"They always are," his colleague replied, holding a rueful smile before heading towards the number five door.

Tromans joined his side and the other man knocked, a loud knock which echoed around the small cul-de-sac. "Fucking hell Graham," he said from the side of his mouth. "Hope none of these neighbours are working nightshift."

The officers waited for a few moments before Graham wrapped on the door again.

"Looks like nobody's home."

"Or if they are they're not very sociable."

Tromans stepped back and gave the house a once over with his eyes. "Curtains closed, all of them."

"Looks like we're going in then."

"Let me just take a look around the back first," Tromans said.

He edged along the fence and stepped back onto the road, closing one eye off to the sun, gazing up at the bathroom window. "Yeah, there's something not right here."

His colleague didn't hear him.

"That dog bark from this house or the neighbour?" Tromans said, his hands cupping the top of the fence.

"Here, I think."

"I'm going over."

Tromans did. It didn't take much to get his tall, athletic frame over to the other side.

"Owt there?" his colleague said.

Tromans surveyed the yard. He saw an empty J20 bottle lit up by the sun, next to a rusty bench. "Junk," he said. "And a big fucking dog scratching at the back door."

Tromans saw shards of police uniform move about in the cracks of the fence.

"C'mon then," his colleague said. "Let's get in."

"They're taking out the top window," the girl said.

Boy showed no reaction, just kept on watching TV. Girl sat cross-legged on the bed, looking up like she was waiting for the teacher to walk into class. "Shall I like, just open the front door?"

"No!" he said.

"They're gonna get in anyway."

"So?"

The sounds were loud, an electric sawing noise. Soon the curtain began to move and light blazed in and hurt her eyes. She had to put a hand up. The boy never moved, barely blinked. Dust particles floated in a cone of sun which cut diagonally through the room. Babe was going flipping mental.

"Whoa," she said, as she watched a thick, black-sleeved arm reach into the room.

"Is anybody there?" a voice said.

The girl went to speak but the boy glared at her not to. She could smell burning and sawdust. In the next few minutes the window began to open up and there was a hole in the house. Two tall police officers were climbing through it.

"I heard a dog in there. Is there a dog?"

"Yeah," the girl said.

"Is that thing chained up? Are we safe to enter?"

"No," the boy said.

"Yeah," the girl said.

"Which is it?" the officer said.

"Like, he's locked in the kitchen and stuff."

The two officers were now in the room, standing over the teens. They looked at the bed, the television, the pots, and the pillows and cushions and DVD cases.

"We were gonna take them," the girl said unprompted, nodding at the blue bucket on a fold-up table.

Tromans stepped forward and peered into the bucket. "Where's your mum?" he said with something in his voice.

Now the boy's face had an expression in it at last. "Why don't you go upstairs and find out."

Tromans was surprised to see his colleague so remarkably calm. It's like he had no idea.

"You wait with them," Tromans said.

Graham did. He turned the TV off and stood looking at the pair, slight amusement on his face as his partner took to the stairs. "What have you kids been up to?" he said.

The girl put her head down while the boy kept on looking at him.

The dog had stopped barking. The house went silent for a few moments.

Graham looked up at the ceiling, where Tromans' slow footsteps could be heard. They then moved onto the next room. Graham's radio began to spit with noise.

"Aren't you gonna answer that?" the boy said.

Graham didn't like the boy's attitude, his cockiness. He didn't like his eyes.

An impatience was beginning to grind on him while he waited for his partner, who was now, at last, starting to make his way downstairs, one slow step at a time.

"Cuff-em."

"What?"

"Cuff these bastards."

Graham was surprised to hear himself call Tromans by his first name. "Phil?"

The boy was already on his feet, turning around in slow motion, placing his hands coolly behind his back. "Fuck life," he said. The girl watched on with an open-mouth, a cold blankness on her face, like she didn't have a clue what was going on.

More police came. More cars. Uniforms. Suits. There was tape everywhere, tying up the street, webbed from post to post. Shiny signs were put up, a red one and a blue one and a gold one. Neighbours were kept inside, serious faces stuck on the windows. All eyes were on them, the girl and the boy who were now being led into separate cars, hand on their heads, putting them into the back. After about ten minutes the cars began to move. At the bottom of Lawson Avenue one car turned left and the other turned right. Two people moving in opposite directions. From the rear windows they looked at each other, held eye-contact for as long as they could, until one car made another turn, and broke it.

After The End

All is Wild, All is Silent

Mel

13.4.2017.

Dear Diary,

First off, You're like this boring blue, A4 notepad with a shiny band running down the edge. You're big and heavy, much heavier and chunkier than You were last time. It's like You've put on weight, ha! But seriously, It doesn't feel much like a Personal Diary at all, but more like something formal, something you'd have in an Office or School or Somewhere. I put in a request at the end of March and You arrived like probably a week ago. It's kind of weird having You back. Strange having you around again and part of me wanted to dive-in and write like Straight Away. But, The Truth is I needed to wait, wait until Today. Cos as You see from the date above it is Officially a year ago since The Night.

Now You're here in my hands and The Truth is I FEEL a little awkward and unnatural about it all, shy and self-conscious, weird and edgy, and it's like I don't really know what to say or how to begin.

Well Officially, technically, I already HAVE begun but You know what I mean ...

See,
So ...

I guess what I'm trying to say is that EVEN though we used to speak like Every Day, and for years and years and years ... it may take a few pages to find My Voice again...to fall into my stride and rhythm and flow ...

So ...

Patience, yeah?

Kay.

Anyway.
Either way.

I'm sitting on the bed with my back to the cold of a white wall. My head is next to a small solid window with bars across. There's music through the walls, some kind of rap. There are always voices, footsteps. The sound of keys, doors opening and closing. Sometimes laughter. Sometimes crying. Occasionally a scream. Mostly there is peace, some kind of peace anyway. Right Now I have the room to myself cos My Bestie and Roomy Ragan is out doing an activity. And tbh I actually waited until she was gone so I could have You All to Myself, like a privacy kind of a thing.
    So ...

Hello. How you been? What's been going on for You in the last 12 months?
    Time is tricky, don't ya think? Cos like, it feels WAY longer than A Year. It feels absolutely ages since we spoke, a lifetime ago.
    Does it to you, too? Feel like ages ago??
    I guess this is because Life just has a life of its own.
    I guess this is because we blinked and missed it all.
    I guess this is because So Much has happened, SO, SO much You wouldn't EVEN believe it. We might not get through it all today, Diary, but as always, I'll do my best.
    The ink flows, the page turns.

First off, after The Arrest, things began to get big. Like I had no idea just how BIG they would get. All this mad-attention, all these faces and adults and noise. All these rooms. All these chairs to sit on and ceilings to look at. All this swirling, spinning chaos. Craziness. Just wild. It was totally insane and I had no idea how to deal with it. It was like living in a dark room all your life and then suddenly being pushed out into the sun. Everything was bright and blinding, blazing and intense. I remember That Friday afternoon, after He was gone, after He was taken away, after He was taken out of My Life for good. I remember how tremendously scary that was, like falling with no safety net at the bottom. They took us to different police stations, I think? Me out of town, on a long, longish drive. I think it was Lincoln or Grantham or Somewhere. I don't remember. I don't quite remember. Wherever it was the atmosphere was dead-strong, like police were dead-quiet and were looking at me like I was some kind of alien, a freak. They were looking at me SO serious like they couldn't work me out. Like I was some kind of mystery to them. But it was confusing because they were quite nice too, like they made sure I had loads of drinks and food and that. After a while we started the Interview Bit. Like they asked me what happened and I told them. I told them The Truth. I told them The Truth the best I could. The Truth as I remembered it. I was kind of amazed by how much They wanted to know. I mean They didn't just want to know about The Murder but They wanted to know EVERYTHING. Like every little detail that lead up to The Murder. Even down to the colour of my pyjamas?? I've got to say it was pretty tiring and draining and a lot of it made my head hurt cos I seemed to be repeating myself again and again, like going round in loads of circles for hours and hours. It was odd too cos even though I had done something Kind of Bad they were giving me all these compliments, about like how Honest and Clear I was. They said I had a good memory and was being a really good help. Then on the Second Day They told me that He was keeping quiet, not saying a word, well only two words in fact: No Comment.

No Comment. No Comment. No Comment.

They asked me why I thought He was doing this and I shrugged.

It's just what he's like, I said. He doesn't like adults.

They asked me if He had bullied me into it and I said, No.

No he didn't, I said. In fact it could have ALL been my idea in The First Place.

Was it? The Police Interview Lady said.

I think so, I said.

I'm struggling to believe that you're capable of this Mel. She said. Oh.

Do you realise how serious this is Mel?

I nodded my head.

For the record the suspect has just nodded her head in the affirmative.

Do you realise how serious this is Mel, she said again. And could you answer verbally this time?

Like, yeah. I said. I know it's like dead-serious and stuff.

At the end of that interview there was another, and another. Another day and another interview. Days and interviews piling on top of each other. Some of them were for Police People and some were for Psychology People and some were for Solicitor/Barristery/Law People. One man I saw a lot. His name was Mr Cavendish and he said that my case could go to trial. If we're lucky.

It could go to trial, he said, because I believe that you were not 100% responsible for what took place that night.

It was funny cos I thought Mr Cavendish spoke like he was on TV.

But I did it, I said.

Yes but you didn't ACTUALLY physically do it. He said.

No but like, I was there and I planned it and stuff.

Yes but I believe, and my professional colleague also believes, that you were not mentally responsible. It is our belief, that there is a chance that you were not of sound mind, at the time of the crimes. And that's why we believe that this deserves to be tried in a court of law.

Oh. So like, I might be able to go home then?

This made him laugh for some reason.

No Melanie, not quite.

He had a pale face with little mole-eyes and a head full of brown curls. At the time I remember thinking how he would make a good dad.

The days went on and I talked and talked and told my story more and more.

I didn't mind the Talking Bit too much cos I got to be around people but what really freaked me out were the nights, especially the first few nights where I was in this dead-scary police cell. It was cold and ugly and it made me have The Worst Nightmares Ever.

I don't want to go to prison, I told Mr Cavendish. I don't want to live in a police cell for the rest of my life.

Well, he said. We're going to do the best we can. What I can tell you Melanie is that you won't be going to a prison right away, and it won't be for the rest of your life. Right now though we need to concentrate on the case, and take each day at a time. Okay?

Kay.

You're being wonderfully brave and commendably honest. All this will work in our favour.

Mr Cavendish was a clever man. He was clever at talking. He was a bit like the teachers at school only a million times cleverer.

Now Markus is quite a strong boy isn't he? He said.

The strongest. I said.

I don't just mean physically but psychologically, emotionally?

What do you mean?

Would you say Mel ... that it is fair to say, that Markus had quite a lot of control over you, in the relationship?

Erm ... yeah ... I mean ... in ways ... but then suppose I kind of had control over him, too.

Cavendish always put lots of pauses between words. He also pulled lots of faces while he was talking and thinking.

I'll put this in a nutshell, he said. Do you think it was possible that Markus Venner persuaded you to go along with it, taking into consideration ALL the trauma and stress you were under at home?

What do you mean?

Mr Cavendish pulled another face, like an impatient kind of a thing.

Did he make you do it?

I shook my head straight away. I wanted to do it. I said.

But ...

The Truth is I wanted them dead, I said. Maybe not my sister at first, but def mum.

Cavendish pulled yet another face. I'm going to give you some more hours with Dr Chavda.

Who?

I met with this Brown Doctor Guy loads of times and tbh I couldn't tell a word he was saying. His accent was thick and he changed the subject a lot. Like one minute he was talking about The Past and the next he was talking about The Future. He was confusing. Anyway at the end of it all Mr Cavendish told me that Dr Chavda had given me the diagnosis of ... Attachment Adjustment Disorder.

Oh no, I said. Does this mean I'm like some kind of freak?

At first I couldn't understand why Mr Cavendish was so happy about this.

This is good news Melanie. It means we have enough to take to a court of law.

What?

We're going to trial.

Oh.

We're going to try and get a manslaughter charge instead of a murder charge, he said.

Does this mean I might be able to go home?

No Melanie, but it does give us a chance of a lesser sentence and ... well ... like I said let's not think about the outcome yet but concentrate on each day at a time.

I liked Mr Cavendish. I liked this woman called Caroline too. She was called An Advocate and she was going to be with me at All Times throughout the trial and all through My Life while I'm in custody. Tbh all the adults were dead-nice and in time I actually started to like them and All This wasn't that scary anymore.

October came around and it was time for My Trial.

I'm dead-nervous, I said.

You're going to be fine, Mr Cavendish said.

Is it going to be on TV?

No Melanie, it isn't going to be on television.

Oh.

But you need to get your hair cut.

What?

Cut it short, shorter. Cut it to your ears.

What??!!

Just do it. We need to give ourselves the best possible chance.

???

Anyway I did what he told me. Mr Cavendish reassured me that everything was going to be okay and I believed him.

All Okay apart from one thing ...

... it meant I was going to HAVE to see Him again.

He smiled and I smiled back. We were in that Glassy Thing at the back of the court and I'm not EVEN gonna Lie but it was quite amazing and powerful and head-fucky to see Him again. There in flesh. It was like I kind of missed Him again, almost like some of that Old Love Feeling came back.

Caroline Advocate took me to one side and whispered in my ear.

Remember what I said Mel, try not to look at him. Try not to look at anybody. It will be hard but you need to keep your eyes on the judge, or whoever it talking to you and concentrate. There will be people in the public gallery who you might recognise too but you must keep your head forward. Understand?

I nodded that I did.

But above all, she said with serious eyes, you really must not look at HIM, pretend he's not even there ...

Kay.

The court was big and bright and unreal. Just like all those Telly Programmes mum used to watch. Only I was confused cos the judge and the barristers and that didn't wear them Wig-Things. Later I found out that in kid-cases they don't wear them cos it's like, supposed to be intimidating.

Anyway on the First Day there wasn't much to do except make The Plea.

Guilty or Not Guilty?

I did my best not to look at him but it was hard. We had loads of adults around us but it was still tough. He's always been like that. He has this way that makes you want to look at him all the time. I could feel his presence press against the corner of my eye. So much that it hurt.

First The Judge asked Him and he took ages to answer. He had loads of big police guards around him and one of them must have nudged Him to answer.

Guilty, he said.

I was surprised to hear how deep his voice was. Like it had gotten LOADS deeper since I last saw Him six months ago. He said Guilty loud and clear and cocky, almost like he was proud of it.

He sat down and I stood.

Caroline Advocate told me to stop pulling the sleeves of my grey cardigan over my hands.

How do you plead?

I looked down at Mr Cavendish and he nodded and mouthed the words, Not Guilty.

Not Guilty, I said.

It was weird cos I felt my voice laugh at the end, like a nervous kind of a thing. But for some reason this made people gasp in the court.

Straight Away I felt Him on me, all his force and rage. It's almost like his anger yanked my head and made me look at him. I could see my own betrayal glare back from the hate in his eyes. If the guards and the Court People weren't there then I think he would have killed me.

574

There was this death-stare.
His face blank and white, his eyes black.
It was then that I knew we were Officially Over.
Not BF and GF no more.
Mel and Markus were done; through, fin.

It's okay, Caroline Advocate said. You won't have to see him now
till Sentencing.
Oh.

The Second Day the Jury were sworn in. I was told that I shouldn't
really look at them either. Best to keep my head forwards, They said.
The Prosecution Man was called Mr Denson and he had a scary
voice and a big purple nose. He wore glasses too and he was kind of
old. He had to introduce the case, he said, by reading an A to Z
chronological account of the events, starting on the Saturday at
McDonald's and ending on the Friday, at the time of the arrest. It's
weird cos most of the Stuff I didn't EVEN remember and I
ACTUALLY wondered if they were making some of it up. When they
got to the Bath Bit, just after the killings someone shouted out from
the public gallery, Sick Bastards.
I didn't get why they shouted that cos we was only washing The
Blood off like any normal person would??
The day was long and boring and I couldn't believe I had to keep
my head forward The Whole Time.
Next They showed The Court the layout of my house. They
showed it through this like computer, digital kind of a thing, almost
like a cartoon of my house which was kind of trippy. It showed where
the rooms were, and where my sis and mum lay. I've got to say it kind
of made me feel a bit sad looking at that. They also showed where the
knife was left, on my blue desk, next to my white watch and polka-dot
soap bag.
Then They did something really insane. They ACTUALLY brought
the ACTUAL weapon out into court. There in the flesh. It was in a
long plastic tubey thing and they passed it around all the jury. I could
hear little gasps and heavy breathing and I felt all this horror and
hard eyes burn into me. I had my hair cut like Mr Cavendish had
told me and luckily it was like a curtain I could hide behind. Didn't
want Them to see my face.
Next Day they showed a video of me being booked in at the police

station on that Friday Afternoon. It's weird cos I kind of don't remember any of that either. I was standing there with my head down. I couldn't believe how small I looked and I wondered if I was really that small in Real Life.

The WHOLE court was looking at the telly, then at me. People were looking at me all the time. For five days I had people looking at me. Eyes. Eyes. Eyes. Eyes. One time I did look up at the public gallery and a man was looking at me but I didn't look back. Didn't look at his eyes. Didn't look at him. But more, through him.

That tall police man was first on the Witness Stand, talking about the morning he found us. I could tell he was upset when he got to The Bit about going upstairs cos all of a sudden his face went pale and his voice changed. It will stay with me forever, he said at the end.

On the 17th The Judge said the court will pay their respects to My Sister Adele. It was her birthday. She would have been 14 years old today. I closed my eyes and thought about her, remembered her. An image of That Night suddenly came flying back into my mind and I had to fight to keep it out. Her Hair and the Pillow. I also remembered her bday last year cos it was the day the police brought us back from Skegness. From the time we went on the run.

The Last Day was the Psychology Bit, The Bit that really mattered, The Bit that was a matter of murder or manslaughter. The Part which decided whether I had this Diminished Responsibility Thing or not.

Dr Chavda took to the stand and I'm not even gonna Lie but The Prosecution Man just like TOTALLY battered him and stuff. Like I have to say it was kind of cringe to watch, like a painful kind of a thing. It made me think of zebras being ripped apart by tigers. Just like the talks I had with him no one could tell a word he was saying. Like he was all whispery and foreign and stuttery and The Judge must have told him to Speak Up and Speak Clear like a thousand times. The Prosecution Man was so clever and ruthless that he ended up making Dr Chavda sweat like mad. He made him panic and babble and forget things. He tied him up with details and timelines and stuff.

Mr Denson stepped forward and pointed at me while he was talking to Dr Chavda.

You say that Melanie has a … an attachment what?

An Adjustment Attachment Disorder.

Speak up Dr Chavda I can't hear you. The jury and the court can't hear you … again.

An Attachment Adjustment Disorder. He repeated, mixing the words up, and only a bit louder.

And how does this ... "Attachment Adjustment Disorder" ... come into being?

It is triggered by a traumatic event.

Could you speak up doctor?

I felt so sorry for the doctor, like part of me just wanted to get up and give him a hug. Although his shirt was kind of gross cos it was covered in like, massive dark disks of sweat and stuff.

It is triggered by a traumatic event.

And what was the event? The Prosecution Man said.

Pardon?

Stop stalling Dr Chadva you heard me clear enough. The jury can hear me so I'm sure you can. What was the event?

Erm, well ...

You say that this Attachment Adjustment Disorder was brought on by a traumatic event ... so ... what was the event?

The event was ... the event was ...

Mr Denson looked at the jury in disbelief, before cutting Dr Chavda off again.

Typical! He shouted. Typical. So she has this mysterious disorder that makes her kill her own mother and sister, that you say takes ALL the responsibility away from killing her own mother and sister yet you can't say how or when this disorder was triggered??

Dr Chavda took out a handkerchief and wiped his face for the millionth time.

I would say, he stammered. I would say that seeing her belongings tied up in a bag ... her mum ... when her mum put all her belonging in a bag ...

On the Sunday? The Prosecution Man said, interrupting.

Yes.

But Melanie, he said, pointing at me. Had already thought about murder on the Saturday, the day before this ... "traumatic event" ... in McDonald's when her friend suggested it. The notion had already crossed her mind.

Well yes ... but thinking about it is different to ...

Now The Prosecution Man was smiling a big smile at the jury ... I don't think I need to say anymore your honour ... I think the jury understand.

Next the other Dr Guy came to the Witness Stand, only he was on

The Other Side, the side of the prosecution. His name was Dr Moore and he was not like Dr Chavda at all, but the opposite. He was cool and confident, almost too casual on the Witness Stand, not like he was in court but more like he was stood in the queue at Starbucks or Somewhere. He looked arrogant and talked arrogant.

I have had hours upon hours with the suspect Melanie Ellis and I can categorically say that I could not pick up any diagnostic psychiatric disorder. Even if Mel was suffering from what Dr Chavda proposes, an Adjustment Attachment Disorder is very low on the psychiatric spectrum in terms of its severity, and would not be responsible for a crime like this.

A crime like what? Mr Cavendish fired back.

The Defence Man could not disrupt his rhythm.

A crime of this nature.

And what is the nature of this crime?

Mr Moore was smiling smugly. Well a crime with prolonged planning, of strategic foresight and perseverance. A crime, a murder, if there ever was one resulting from this disorder it would be at best, a lashing out, something impulsive. Mel and her accomplice planned this over five days. It was cold and calculating, above all it was rational, which only someone of a sound mind could do.

Mr Cavendish was stuck, he tried a different angle.

Are you implying that the defendant is suffering from some kind of psychopathy? Because if you are doctor that is a very serious title to be knocking around a courtroom about a fifteen year old girl.

No. Dr Moore coughed into his fist with that same smug smile. I am not implying that at all. First the defendant is too young to even be considered for that particular diagnosis, and even if she wasn't, I would still have reservations. I have seen no traits of childhood behaviour that is indicative of psychopathy; fire-setting, cruelty to animals, lying. If anything Mel has a pathological need to tell the truth.

The Judge coughed and spoke up. I think we are getting a little side-tracked here.

Dr Moore carried on talking anyway.

As misguided and detached as Melanie was, and maybe is, about these crimes she does display empathy. In my professional opinion grief and remorse may feature later on in her life, with maturity, and the realisation of her misdeeds.

Okay, The Judge said, I think that will be all.

*

The Verdict was obvs, and really I could have predicted it from The Start. Mostly cos it made sense. It was, The Truth.

Guilty came back and there wasn't even any real noise in the court. No surprise. The Media People was looking at me for a reaction, something on my face that They could write in the papers only I didn't give them one. Overall I was just glad it was over cos all that sitting around and staring forwards kind of drove me mad. I say Over but it wasn't quite. I still had The Sentencing and that wasn't for another month. And The Truth is That Part I was actually nervous about. Nervous to find out how long I was going to be locked up for but also nervous about seeing Him, again.

Mr Cavendish gave his Professional Predictions. Best 12, worst 20, expect 15.

He said it in a sing-song way and it's like he didn't care anymore. Now he'd lost The Case it's like his mind had already moved onto something else.

Oh well.

The Sentencing was scary and the courtroom was absolutely packed tight. They even had to set-up extra chairs and throw some people out. It was so busy it all got delayed by about ten minutes. I didn't look at the people but I knew they were all there, Aunt Tars, Mia, Ryan, even My Dad and some of his family and friends, mum's friends, people from church, Kitts. For some reason I felt that Mr Dukes was there, my old teacher and First Love. I felt like he was sitting somewhere at the back, and that like, he was The Only Person in the World who didn't hate me.

He was already sat there when I entered the dock, in cuffs, surrounded by guards. I could see the brown of his big hair and the blur of his foot-tapping in the corner of my eye. It reminded me of school days because this is how he sat, restless, distracted, like he had somewhere else to be. Again the world was looking at me, only more people than ever. This was the nearest to fame I'd ever get and I didn't like it. Not one bit. Not like he did.

His barrister then asked The Judge if the cuffs could be removed because it was ... excessive and unnecessary and humiliating.

Judge took this into consideration. It was then mentioned that He had already been moved from one Young Offender's Institute to another and that his behaviour had been a constant cause of concern. Again his barrister argued, mentioned some adult murderer who had not had to wear cuffs, again stating that it was unnecessary and *humiliating. The Judge nodded and agreed and then someone came over to the dock to speak to Him. He had to stand and put his ear to the glass and that's when I saw him In Full for The Very Last time.*

Markus Venner had his handcuffs removed.

He stood tall and looked slowly around the court.

I seemed to be sat there for ages, way longer than any part of the trial. At last there was silence and I had to listen to the WHOLE crime again, from top to bottom. After The Judge gave the Mitigating Circumstances and Aggravating Facts, then he did the Summing Up.

I don't remember all of what he said but I remember some of it.

This case is, in some respects, without parallel ... unprecedented ... stranger than fiction ... there was remarkable premeditation and planning ... cold ... callous ... both victims were vulnerable and at home in their beds ... they were stabbed in their throats while they slept ... and then smothered ... executions ... grotesque ... it was entirely a joint offense ... both of you could have backed out at any time, but you didn't ... you were fourteen at the time, now fifteen ... the youngest couple to commit double-murder in British criminal history ... I sentence you as children ...

The 20 years took my breath away cos Mr Cavendish said that he doubted that very much. He lied to me. But, at this point in time I suppose there was no difference 10, 15, 20, 50. It's all the same. It's what I deserve.

I was going away for a Long Time and I knew this as I was taken out of court ...

So.
See.

Baker Hill Safe Centre. This is where I live now. This is the place I call Home and have done for the last four months, or so. I don't actually know where it is so don't ask. Not too far, I don't think. Sometimes from my window the sky looks like That Kind of Blue. The kind of blue which could be near the sea, so somewhere near the coast, I guess. It's not how I expected it to be. There's no high-wire fences keeping us in, or armed guards standing in towers. The Screws don't wear uniforms or carry bats. If anything it's like school, only you don't get to go home at the end of the day. There's three main blocks, one for 11 to 13 year old's, one for 14 to 15 year old's and one for 16 to 17 year old's. I'm in the middle one. A lot of the classrooms and activity rooms look like little chalets, like what you'd see in Skegness or Ingoldmells or Somewhere. And then there's a big field around the back where we do sports or go on walks and look at nature and stuff. There's a garden too, only a small one but it's where people go if they get stressed-up so they can look at the flowers and the pond with fishes in. Most of The Staff are dead-cool, cooler than teachers, they swear and tell jokes but are stricter than teachers too. Like some of them can be quite scary if you cross them. My favourite is Paulina. She's Swedish, she's also covered in tattoos and got a bald head. At First I was dead-scared of her but now I flippin ADORE her and she's definitely The Nearest Thing I've Ever Had to a Mum. She has all these wise sayings about life and she gets you to look at things differently, like she teaches you stuff about emotions and thinking and that. Her favourite saying is: It's Not What You Did but What You Do. She has this kind of Tough Love thing going on, like if you start to go into yourself she tells you to Get Tough and Get a Grip. No one said it was gonna be easy, she says. Only the strong stand tall at the end. Some of the other girls really intimidated me At First, too. There's a gang of black girls from Nottingham who scared me to death, mostly cos they spoke in this language I didn't understand, like a street kind of a thing. They seemed like way older too. Too old to be living in the same block. Some of them had heard what I did and I could tell they didn't like that. Like one of them pushed me in the back and made this weird sound with her teeth. After a while though they liked me and I liked them. One of them plaits my hair and tells me about her life in the city. All these crazy-mad adventures that kind of blows my mind. I would tell her about life in Kimble Wells only it'd be way too boring. My Bestie is my Roomy Ragan. We clicked like Straight Away and have become Besties For Life ever since. Like I couldn't imagine life In Here without her and she says the same. I'd say I've never been as close to anyone in my ENTIRE life before. Ragan is in for the same crime as me, Murder. Only hers is different cos hers was an accident whereas mine, as you know, was on purpose. She killed her baby brother by smothering him with her hand only she swears she didn't mean it. I believe her even though no one else does. I believe her cos she's always In Absolute Bits whenever she talks about it. Sobs her heart out. Sometimes I climb into her bed and hold her until she stops. Then when I'm Down she'll climb into mine and hold me. Having her here means Everything and I'm already dreading the day she leaves. It's confusing cos even though we committed the same crime I've got 20 years whereas she only got 8.

Probably cos you killed two people, she said.

Oh. Yeah.

Ragan is a big girl with hairy arms. Her face is covered with acne. Some of the other girls call her for the way she looks but I don't care. To me she's The Most Beautiful Person I've Ever Met. She's also a genius drawer. Some of her paintings and stuff have even made it into a published book. She drew a picture of me once and I have it up on my wall.

I can't Lie, I'm actually happy here. I'm not saying it's the Happiest I've been cos it's not. I miss Total Freedom like anyone would. I miss not going into town or walking The Clementine. I miss school and my friends. I miss McDonald's and cinema and taking the bus. Silly little things. I'm not my happiest but I AM my calmest. Calmer than ever. There's people, routine, support, attention, and, equality. People get treated the same and looked after. No one is favoured, no one is left out. It's what you'd call, A Tight Ship. It's like a massive wheel that I am a part of. Time passes, as one day ends another begins. And one day is pretty much the same as the day before. A safe structure. For me the pattern is perfect, it works, it keeps you tucked in. Paulina My Favourite also does a class called Mindfulness. She gets you to meditate and watch your own mind. She gets you to leave your mind and float upwards, over Your Self and over the world. It's pretty trippy. She gets you to stay in the moment so that each moment matters. Even boring everyday things like washing the pots or cleaning your teeth can be turned into a magical experience. Ha! Mad!

As for the Outside World Paulina says it's best to not even think about the Outside World. It doesn't exist, she says. Right Now you're Right Here. Let your mind wander and be free but don't WISH you were out there. Don't beat yourself up. Don't torture your mind with what you COULD be doing.

My only contact to The Outside World was Mia.

She wrote letters. She sent loads of letters, at first. One a day sometimes. In the beginning they were just normal Mia letters, full of drama and stories about herself. But then they got weird. She kept apologising for what she said at McDonald's on that Saturday. About me killing mum and Sis. She kept saying that it was ALL her fault. No matter how many times I told her that it wasn't, that we would probably have killed them anyway, she wouldn't stop. Then the letters started to get all religious, like a churchy kind of a thing. You know, about Jesus and that. She kept quoting The Bible and went on about Forgiveness and Redemption and Salvation. The letters got weirder and more intense and in the end I didn't have a clue what she was on about. So much so that I had to stop replying because there was no point. There was no conversation. It was all just warped and one-sided. She's quit too now and I guess our friendship is Officially Over.

Then there's Him.

Tbh today, writing This, is probably like the First Time I've thought about Him in months. At first, like in the first few weeks it was horrible. Part of me missed him and part of me was terrified of him. I thought about Him all the time and no kind of meditation or mindfulness would make Him leave my mind. He was stuck here. Even in sleep he would visit, nightmares, awful graphic nightmares that would wake me up screaming. One in particular that kept coming back and coming back, like a reoccurring kind of a thing. I would be in this horrible room. It was like a dungeon with no windows. Just these slimy bricks. I could hear a tap dripping. In front of me was this big iron door. Next to that was a table with an envelope on. I would get up and open the envelope and inside was a single word written in his handwriting, written in blood. It was messy and hard to read but in the end I could make out that the word was, TRAITOR. At that moment the iron door would slide open and he would be standing there with that cold look of his. He was wearing a white apron and in his hand was That Knife, the very same blade that was used on The Night. Then he would slowly step forward and the fear would be incredible. By then I knew I was dreaming and would try to wake up but couldn't. Trapped in a nightmare. Trapped in Hell. He would walk around me, no expression on his face, the knife huge and lethal, shining in that dark, dark dungeon.

Then I'd wake up, or Ragan would wake me up, then she'd hold me until I knew Real Life was back and all the fear had gone.

It was awful and I used to dread falling asleep.

I saw him in the daytime too, outside in the field, crouched in the long white grass. It spooked me and made me jump. There he was, looking up at me. His soul was inside the body of a black cat. It was

Him. I swear it was Him. I know it was Him. Those eyes, His eyes. It was that momentary look he does, a flash. It was the same look as the first time I saw him, same look when he took my virginity, same look on The Night and the same look in the courtroom. I felt a cold scream shake my spine, and when I looked back the cat was gone. He, was gone.

Other Times I imagined him escaping from wherever he was, hiding out for a while, changing his appearance, before coming to find me, find whatever way he could to get inside Baker Hill Safe Centre.

I know he could do that. I know he's just about capable of anything.

Diary, diary, I know what You're thinking!! I know You must be thinking that I'm trying to make out that he's The Big Bad Wolf while I'm this Frightened Little Lamb well I don't think that at all. I know I was wrong. I know I was bad. I know I was half to blame. 50/50. Straight down the line, straight down middle. Like The Judge says, It Was Entirely a Joint Offence. I know my mum was right too when she said Ticking Time-Bomb. WE was, and were, and that bomb went off on the night of April 13, EXACTLY a year ago.

Sometimes I manage to read articles about what happened although that is strictly forbidden In Here. Somebody once wrote that this was a case of what French People would call ... Folie a' deux. Which apparently means Madness in Two People. Then they go on to ask who was the maddest? Who was mad first? Whose madness influenced the other?

I often think about That One and think that maybe we used each other, in a way. I used him as a kind of weapon whereas he used me as an excuse, an excuse to do what he was always going to do, what he was destined to do. In another article someone said that ... 'without him she would have been just another angry, depressed teen, hating her mother like so many of millions around the world, whereas without her he would have killed anyway, eventually.

I dunno. I don't know about that. I couldn't possibly comment.

What I DO know is that I've been free of Him lately so I'm gonna stop talking about Him NOW cos I don't want Him coming back.

And.

And You more than anyone should know, that The Mind is a funny thing and not to be messed about with!!

So,
See,
Anyway,
Either way.

Most of the time I'm good, better. Maybe You can tell? Maybe You can hear it in my voice or read it in the words I use??

But what about Them, You're probably thinking, the people who This Whole Thing is really about? The poor people. The real victims. What about my mum and sis, Erica and Adele Ellis?

Well, the dead don't make noise. The dead don't really get a say.

And I wish I could tell You that I am plagued with guilt and remorse and torment every day. But, The Truth is, I'm not, but that doesn't mean I'm totally free of it either. It's coming. It's coming bit by bit, day by day. The more I talk about it and explore, as They make me do at Baker Hill Safe Centre the more it takes shape, like dead fish in the sea, they're starting to surface. At first I wanted this guilt, craved this guilt; almost forced myself to feel it only it wouldn't come. Then I'd pretend, fake it, act like I was In Bits, hoping that this would make it come for real only it didn't. Mostly I think this is because it felt like it wasn't me who was there that night, who committed those horrible crimes. It felt like someone else, another girl in another world. It's like I had forgot, had forgotten. Only now it is starting to take form; images, flashbacks appearing at the most random times.

I'm sixteen in a couple of months and I'm feeling my mind start to creep towards some kind of adulthood. I'm beginning to see that we are responsible for the things we do, and that everything we do, good or bad, has consequences. Like a stone plopped into a pond the ripples go on ...

Sometimes this is all a bit too much to take and it throws my head into a spin.

When this happens I go see Paulina, and she'll either talk me through it or get me to do that Mindfulness thing. Failing that she'll give me some music to listen to. There's an album which always seems to work. It's by this band called Balmorhea. It's not like singing or anything but more like instrumental music, like the kind you'd hear in a film. It's calming but powerful too. On it is like my Official Favourite Song of All Time. It's called Truth. As soon as that song comes on I feel my body begin to sink and my mind lift. It's like I'm in this glass elevator going up and up, floor after floor until I'm through *the clouds and into the blue. Towards the end of the track there's this real fast Piano Bit and that's when my mind bursts and covers Earth and it's like I'm apart of everything and everyone.*

Wait. Hold that thought. Gotta go pee …

Right. Back.
   Back and just counted 12 pages! Wow. Lol. Not bad for a First Entry, first entry of a new book of a new life. Guess you could say we have our flow back.
   Yes. Yes. This is the first of many.
   I'm going to write inside You every day now, just like before, just like the last time.
   Promise!
   You are going to be with me for the next twenty years and I guess that's something, at least.
   You'll see me grow and change, break down and build back up, whereas I know YOU will remain exactly the same. Just like you always are, and always have been.
   And who knows maybe one day we'll get to meet? Like, in flesh, in Real Life and stuff. You can meet me at the gates when all this is over. When my time is done. We can go for a walk or a coffee some place. Sit me down and tell me everything you know. I'll listen carefully and take it all in. Hang on every word.

   Cos deep down, I know I could learn a lot from you.

Acknowledgements

Shout-Out to

My Inner Circle & To Those Who Supported This Particular Piece

Me Mam, Stiltz, Heba Rashed, Sista Keira, Swanflower, Rusal Bostan, Master Roo, Minley, Mad Dad Mick n' Archers, Wayne Walker n' The OWLS boys, The Don n' Fam, Abi n' The Sherwood Crew, Devonshire Mob, Emilee, Pammie, Dargatz, All Those at Choir Press, Selina & My Beautiful Boys – Prince Pablo, King Simeon

to the memory of EE & KE

www.ingramcontent.com/pod-product-compliance
Lightning Source LLC
Chambersburg PA
CBHW032252020726
47495CB00001B/79